CONTRAPASSO

a novel

NATHAN JORGENSON

CONTRAPASSO
a novel

NATHAN JORGENSON

Flat Rock
Publishing

NathanJorgenson.com

First paperback edition 2019

Cover and interior design by TLC Book Design
TLCBookDesign.com
Cover: Tamara Dever, Interior: Erin Stark

ISBN: 978-0-9746370-7-5
ISBN: 978-0-9746370-8-2 (E-book)

FLAT ROCK PUBLISHING
NathanJorgenson.com

CHAPTER ONE

——◆——

Matt Kingston's footsteps echoed softly as he crossed the empty narthex. Only a moment earlier, the gathering area of Our Savior's Lutheran church in Sverdrup, Minnesota, had been full of mourners. Now the funeral was about to begin, and everyone had moved into the sanctuary. He'd arrived a few minutes late because curiosity had taken him on a short tour of his hometown and some of the places where he'd played a generation earlier.

He tried to hurry to join the crowd in the sanctuary, but a nagging hip injury caused him to wince every time he swung his right leg too quickly. He slowed his gait just enough to avoid limping, and he took a look around as he crossed the room.

Not much had changed at his old church. All the same black-and-white portraits of retired ministers, with a few additions since his last visit, hung in the same place as they had forty years earlier. The ornate wooden carvings, and even the coatracks, were the same. And he could smell coffee, too, just like back in the day; the church ladies who always volunteered to serve meals at funerals were downstairs getting things ready. But other people lived their lives here now. Not him.

He'd spent so much of his childhood here. He wanted it to feel like home, but it didn't. The place was familiar, but it wasn't *his* anymore. He'd felt the same way forty-some years earlier, when he'd come home from college for the first time. When he took that first step inside the house where he'd grown up, he knew that it was wasn't his home anymore, and never would be again.

He stood with an ear close to the oak doors of the sanctuary and listened for a second. Then he opened one door as slowly and quietly as he could, and peeked inside. The immediate family had been seated already, way up in front, and the organist was playing a somber prelude while a reverent silence settled over the church. When he pivoted slightly to slip between the heavy doors, a familiar pain stung his hip and a tiny whimper escaped his lips.

As he looked about for a place to sit, he was relieved to find an empty seat in the back row. He eased the heavy door shut behind him, holding it until it closed without a loud clunk, and then slipped into the last row. But he realized all too late that he was sitting next to Oskar Lund, a memorable character from his childhood. Even all those years ago, Oskar had smelled like he started every day by pissing on his clothes and then placing a couple of mothballs in the pockets to cover the stink. It was one of Matt's most powerful memories of church. Oskar always seemed to sit near Matt and his parents, but Matt didn't remember ever speaking to him. He wasn't about to strike up a new friendship today, either, but he was pretty impressed that Oskar appeared to be wearing the same brown double-knit suit he'd worn decades ago. He turned away from Oskar, who was probably there just for the free meal the church ladies were preparing, and looked around.

Matt tried to ignore the aura of piss and mothballs, but it took him back in time. He had other memories of this place. Plenty of them. Church had been an ordeal for a little boy like Matt; so many endless, boring hours sitting there in his stiff and scratchy Sunday clothes, waiting for church to be over so he could go home and play. His mother had made church a punishment, and he'd last set foot in this church twenty-five years ago, on the day of his mother's funeral. He hadn't thought of the place since.

But today he'd returned to the headwaters of his life. He was a grown man now, maybe an old man, and he thought about this place and all the roads he'd traveled on his journey away from it, and back to it.

Alvie Glasnapp, a teacher and coach from Matt's high school days, had passed away at the ripe old age of ninety-three, and along with a couple hundred others, Matt had come to pay his final respects. The sanctuary of the little church was full, and even from his seat in the back row, Matt recognized a few schoolmates, family friends, and childhood buddies; even some teachers.

Matt began to recognize others, and memories rushed back. There were boys and girls he'd sat beside in elementary school, church, junior high, and high school. They'd played schoolyard games. They'd whispered about which of the girls they had crushes on. They'd played varsity sports together for good old Sverdrup High. And then he'd lost touch with all of them. They'd been allowed to just drift away and live on only in memories that grew cloudier with each passing year. A sense of rediscovery came to Matt like a warm summer breeze. He'd expected to reconnect with a few old friends today, but he never thought the lost friends could rekindle so many forgotten moments. The only similar experience he could recall was opening an unmarked box in his attic, and discovering toys that he'd once loved and then forgotten.

Matt looked about the room and wished that Jane, his wife, could have been here. She'd grown up in an affluent suburb and attended a high school many times larger than his entire hometown. Matt's young life and school days were far different from hers. He'd told her stories about many of these people, but she'd never met any of them. If she were here now, she just might catch a peek at who he once was. He'd never thought about that before, but now that he'd returned to this familiar place, he wished that his Jane could see him as a boy.

Jane, however, was in the Twin Cities visiting her sister, who was going through a painful divorce. Her trip to the Twin Cities had been planned for weeks and there was never any discussion of canceling to attend the funeral of someone she'd never met, and whom her husband hadn't seen in forty years. It was the right thing for her to go and see her sister, no doubt about it. This was something for Matt to do alone. Nonetheless, he wished she was here.

The minister began to talk about God's love, and salvation, and the forgiveness of sin, and Alvie's long life. Matt allowed his thoughts to wander away from the eulogy and all the usual things that a young clergyman would say about an old-timer that he never really knew.

Alvie was a good enough teacher, and Matt supposed that he was a nice man—the father of several of his best friends, and someone he'd known for his entire life. But Matt never liked Alvie Glasnapp, not really. He'd been difficult to play for. He was always confrontational with his boys, always barking instructions and pointing out incorrect technique or lack of effort. There had never been one word of praise or encouragement, for anyone. Matt never got very close to Alvie, and he always felt that Alvie didn't care much for him, either. But over the years, Alvie had gradually morphed into an icon in this little town. He was a lifetime coach, the proverbial guy with the gray sweatshirt and the whistle around his neck. There had been a few head knockings with stubborn baseball players, and some memorable antics, both on the ball field and in the classroom. But he'd been a part of so many lives through the years that his irascible behavior became his trademark, and he gradually became a living legend. Former players and other members of the community told and retold stories from Alvie's colorful past.

Alvie had only coached one boy who had the talent to play ball for a living, and John Velde had thrown it all away—the baseball, anyway. Maybe life in general. Sverdrup was just another little town out there in the vastness of middle America. And like every other little town, Sverdrup produced a savior every few years: a kid who looked really good in his uniform and got some headlines in the local press, and then flopped in college. John Velde was that boy, in spades. But it should never have happened that way; John Velde actually had a gift. He *was* the boy who came along once in a coach's lifetime; he woulda, coulda, shoulda, but just like all the pretenders, he never did. Just the mention of his name made Alvie Glasnapp gnash his teeth, right up to the end of his life. But John Velde wasn't there today, and Matt was content not to think about all that just now.

In the background, the minister was still speaking about Alvie Glasnapp, but Matt found it difficult to listen. This minister was new in town and hadn't known Alvie back when he was really Alvie Glasnapp. His message today was based on secondhand information about Alvie's life, and he had no passion for the moment. Matt's ears let go of the minister's sermon and he let his eyes move about the room. He stretched his neck in search of one special person, and then he found her.

Maureen Glasnapp was the youngest of Alvie's three children, and his only daughter. Matt had dismissed Maureen from his life forty-some years ago, too. He'd thought of Maureen from time to time . . . less and less as the years went by. But now something called to him from all those years ago. An enduring tenderness still remained in his heart, and he liked the feeling. He wanted to look at her and talk to her again. He wondered how she'd greet him later. He hoped she'd smile, and be glad to see him, but . . .?

Maureen was sitting in the front of the church with the rest of her immediate family. Some guy, Matt assumed it was her husband, gave her a tissue when she needed to wipe some tears away. Donnie and David, her two brothers, and their families all sat together close to Maureen and her family. Even though Matt could see only the back of her head, he recognized her immediately. Matt stared at her until she turned to say something to her husband, and then he saw that pretty face again. The long auburn hair was streaked with ample gray now, but just a passing glance at the side of her face triggered a comfortable rush. Matt allowed himself a wistful grin, and he remembered.

Matt had some history with Maureen—Mo—Glasnapp. They'd been schoolmates, and she was the first girl to make his heart go pitter-pat. She was the girl who'd starred in his daydreams and fantasies back in high school. She'd held his hand when they walked together. She'd stood on her father's front steps and whispered to him after their dates. With her cheek touching his, she'd made lame attempts to resist when he tried to steal a kiss. But she'd liked the kisses, too. Matt still remembered the starry look in her eyes when he kissed her goodnight. They had shared so much joy and so many tender memories. But he'd severed their relationship just before he went off to college. He'd just let go of the line that tethered his life to hers, and then let her vanish into the mist of his early life. There had been no painful breakup, and no sad goodbye. He'd just stopped calling her and then gone away forever. He knew why he'd stopped calling her, but he'd never told her. He let himself think of it all now, for the first time in years.

Matt looked away from Maureen, feeling that by staring at her he was intruding on a private moment that should be left to her and her family. He searched the sanctuary for other familiar faces, but he thought of Maureen.

Someone sang a solo, the mourners all sang a hymn, and the funeral director walked to the front of the church and instructed six young men to stand up.

The pallbearers, all grandsons, carried Alvie Glasnapp out to his final resting place in the rural cemetery, about two hundred feet from the door of the church, and the mourners followed Alvie's immediate family on a short walk through the other tombstones. A cold front had come through the day before, an inch of new snow covered the ground, and all the mourners hunched their shoulders and shivered while they walked. Matt cast a glance to the other side of the cemetery, where his parents were buried, and he remembered other funerals at this place.

Eventually, when the mourners assembled around them, the family stood together under a tarp, and the minister said a prayer. From his vantage point, Matt could see the minister's warm breath condense in the cold air, and he could hear gentle sobbing from the family as they said a final goodbye. The color guard from the local American Legion fired a salute, and people turned away slowly to return to the church.

As was the custom in every Lutheran church in Minnesota, the church ladies had prepared a meal of ham sandwiches in the church basement. Dozens of mourners were already seated at various tables in the dining area when Matt found himself carrying a plate with Jell-O salad and a ham sandwich, looking for a place to sit down. He found an empty seat at a table of some seriously old folks, and he introduced himself to some friends of his parents that he hadn't seen or thought of since high school. Each handshake and small reunion triggered a series of questions. All around him, at his table and every other within earshot, people were asking each other about parents, and siblings, and classmates. "What ever happened to . . .?" seemed to be part of every conversation in the church basement.

Familiar faces were beginning to mill about, and Matt wished that he'd chosen a different table. He stood up and excused himself from what he thought was the geriatric table, to seek out some other friends. He pushed his chair back under the table and took several steps toward a small group of people on the far side of the room when he felt a hand on his shoulder.

"Nice to see you, Matt," came a voice from the past, and Matt recognized it immediately. Donny Glasnapp, Alvie's second son, had his arm around Matt's neck, and was soon shaking him playfully. Donny and Matt had been classmates from kindergarten through grade twelve.

"Nice to see you too, Donny," Matt said as he returned the hug. "My deepest sympathies at your loss. Alvie was one of a kind." It felt odd to smile so openly and feel such joy in this reunion, and then express his sympathy in the next breath. But before Matt could say another word, someone slugged his arm and pulled him away from Donny. David, the oldest Glasnapp brother, had an arm around Matt, too.

"Glad you could make it," David said.

"Me too," Matt replied. "I'm sorry for your loss, David."

"Don't be. He had a great life," David said. "How've *you* been?"

"Really good, David. I wish we could get together once in a while, and—" Matt halted his reply when he saw two more familiar faces approaching from behind David. "Jeez, they'll let anybody in here," he said, while his face lit up with a smile.

Joe Fogal and Steve Saathe, also K-through-twelve classmates of Matt and Donny, crossed the room together and shared enthusiastic handshakes with Matt and the Glasnapp brothers. Saathe and Fogal had been inseparable friends back in school, and they still seemed to be.

"So, did you guys ever get married . . . to each other?" Matt asked.

Joe cupped his hands as if he was about to shout something, and then leaned close and mouthed the words "Fuck you." Matt's spirits rose; *this* was what he'd hoped for today, not a ham sandwich at the geriatric table.

After a few minutes for the five of them to catch up on careers and children, and grandchildren, Donny looked right and left, leaned forward, and asked Matt if he remembered the time they'd pooled their resources and bought a six-pack of beer, then driven out to a deserted farm and had their first taste. Matt smiled and reminded Donny that it was actually Colt 45 malt liquor, and that only one can had made his face go numb.

A smile was still fixed on Matt's face when he turned and saw someone else approaching. He'd been glancing over his shoulder since the moment he'd arrived, wondering how these next few seconds would go. Maureen had finally spotted him and she was walking directly toward him. Matt had known her as Maureen Glasnapp all those years ago, and now he realized that he didn't know her married name. Her eyes were puffy from crying, but as she drew near those red eyes began to show a smile.

She raised her arms, asking for a hug, and Matt felt something he hadn't expected. As she closed the distance between them, she brought with her all the sweetness of their high school friendship. Neither of them had any idea of the heartaches, or sadness, or failure, or love, or triumph that the other may have experienced since the last time they'd seen each other. And none of that concerned either of them just now. All they could see was a special friend emerging from a lost world; returning safely from, well, neither of them knew where from. But they were back.

Mo stepped into his embrace and squeezed him as if she was afraid he'd run away. This was the greeting he'd hoped for, and it was wonderful.

Saathe, Fogal, and Mo's brothers all knew of this special friendship, and they turned away to talk among themselves in order to give Mo and Matt a minute.

"Ah, Mo . . ." Matt sighed when he put his arms around her. "You have my deepest sympathy, and it's so nice to see you again."

"Thanks," Maureen sniffled. She was just about cried out after an hour of greeting friends and family, but new tears were welling in her eyes now. "It's been such a long time," she whispered in his ear. "I didn't know if I'd ever see you again."

"Yeah," Matt said softly, "I couldn't miss this. I'll bet it's been forty years since we've spoken."

"Forty-three," she corrected.

"So, fill me in on those missing four decades," Matt said. He listened to her and studied her face while she squeezed forty-three years into a ninety-second story. She'd married a nice guy who had a successful law practice in Rochester, Minnesota. She'd earned a PhD in pharmacology and was now the clinical pharmacy director at St. Mary's Hospital, in Rochester. She had four daughters and three grandchildren, and she pointed them out as they played with other children in the church basement.

The last time he'd spoken to her she was a sophomore in high school, and now here she was, describing a successful career and showing him photos of her grandchildren. He couldn't make himself not smile as he listened to her. He marveled at the passing of so much time, and while she told her story his eyes searched her face. The softness was gone from the skin on her neck, she had some wrinkles at the corners of her eyes, and her hands were no longer as elegant as they'd once been. Some other parts had shifted a bit too, but there was no doubt about it: Maureen was still an attractive woman.

Then she laughed, just a bit, and Matt saw what he'd been hoping for. The long auburn hair had some gray in it, but the gray hair and the other changes could not hide what he wanted to see. Pretty young Mo Glasnapp was still there! A voice he hadn't heard, and green eyes he hadn't seen in forty-three years, stirred the happiest of memories. She was peeking through a veil woven from a lifetime of experiences that he knew nothing about. But Mo Glasnapp, his girl, was still there, and it was thrilling to see her again. For one fine moment he was eighteen years old, and there could be no melancholy attached to that.

Now, suddenly, he was glad that Jane wasn't there. He wanted this moment with Mo Glasnapp just for himself. He wanted to let Mo look into his eyes and see that the boy with square shoulders and hair bleached from a summer of work on the farm, the boy who once had a serious crush on her, was still there, too. He could never have talked to Mo, and held her, and looked at her like this if Jane had been there. He felt a bit of guilt about that, too; he was hiding something from Jane. But the guilt was slight, and it was fleeting—he merely wanted to have this reunion all by himself.

Eventually Mo said that she'd heard through the grapevine that Matt had married a beautiful girl. Then she asked about Matt's family. Matt kept his answers simple; he agreed that Jane was beautiful. He said that she was from Minnetonka, and was now the director of nursing at the regional health care center in Pine Rapids. Then he added that they had two grown sons who lived on the West Coast.

"Hey, Matt," Donny said, stepping close to him again, "where's Velde? Isn't he here?"

Matt pursed his lips and shook his head. "Nope."

"He shoulda been here," Donny said. "I know he and my dad locked horns a few times, but . . ."

"I know it, Donny. I told him he needed to be here, but . . ." Matt shook his head.

"Do you still see John?" Mo asked.

Matt nodded yes.

"Why?" Saathe and Fogal asked in unison.

"He's my friend." Matt shrugged.

"Why?" Everyone asked in unison, and then laughed at the tone of their question.

"Whatever *has* become of Velde?" David asked.

"I thought he was an idiot, and a bully, when we got a bit older," Saathe interjected. "He quit hangin' around with us, and went with a bunch of older guys. He turned into a real prick there, at the end. I never understood why you ran with him."

Matt smiled and nodded his understanding. "Yeah, I suppose you're right," he agreed, "he could be pretty unlikable when he chose to. But he's my friend . . ." Matt shrugged. ". . . always has been. I can't remember a time when he wasn't my friend." He thought for a moment, then added, "I guess you love your friends right where they are, in spite of the crazy things they do. If you didn't, well, then none of us would have any friends."

"I thought he ran away to California," Mo said.

"He did," Matt replied, "and I think he had couple lost years out there. You know, drugs and bad behavior. Anyway, he lives in Pine Rapids now, and he has a taxidermy business on the edge of town. He lives about two miles away from me. I still see him all the time."

"You guys remember the time he blew New Ulm away?" Donny asked gleefully, and the conversation shifted.

Matt stepped up, shoulder to shoulder, into the little circle of his old friends and said, "Oh yeah! We were up against New Ulm when we were seniors," Matt started, "and Velde was pitching . . ." Everyone in the small audience knew John Velde, and his reputation as a great talent but a wild card, and they all drew a step closer, ". . . and he was throwing *smoke* that day. New Ulm was always better than us, so the only chance we ever had against them was if Velde pitched. He was an evil genius that day." His friends had all heard the story before, but now they were grinning with anticipation. "He had a shutout, a no-hitter going, and he was striking everybody out. That's the only way we'd ever beat New Ulm, or anyone else; if the other team ever put the ball in play we just kicked it around and gave them the game, but on that day, John was *dealin'*, and the New Ulm bench started to ride him. Hard.

"So, in typical Velde fashion, late in the game, after he struck out their cleanup hitter he made his right hand into a pistol and raised his index finger to his lips so he could blow the smoke away. You know, sort of a 'screw you' for the New Ulm boys."

Mo stood close to Matt, and as she watched and listened to him tell an old story she remembered the way Matt had made her laugh when they were young.

"Well, naturally the boys on the New Ulm bench went crazy, which only drove John to a higher level. Pretty soon he was pointing that index finger at all the batters after he struck them out, and then blowing the smoke away again."

"Dad *hated* that kind of stuff. He musta been getting pretty upset with Velde," David said.

"Oh yeah, but Alvie didn't beat New Ulm very often; in fact, I don't think he *ever* did, so he *really* wanted this one. Besides that, he knew there were college and pro scouts at the game just to see Velde, so he let it go. It was really bothering him, though. He was definitely conflicted; he didn't like that showboat stuff, but he sure liked to win. Between innings he told Velde to knock it off, but that was just pissing in the wind; there was no stopping Velde that day," Matt said. "So anyway, it was scoreless in the top of the ninth when Velde came up to bat, and he hit a bomb, a homer that landed in the river, with nobody on base. As he rounded the bases he was taunting their pitcher." Matt shook his head and continued, "So when he took the mound in the bottom of the ninth we had a one-run lead and every kid in the New Ulm dugout was standing up and yelling at Velde. He blew the first guy away on three pitches; good morning good afternoon, good night. The ball sounded like bacon sizzling; the kid had no chance. And then he hollered to the kid to go sit down after he shot him with his index finger." Matt was grinning, as was everyone else in the small crowd, when he continued. "Well, the New Ulm bench went wild and started screaming. And that's when Velde did it. He was standing on the pitcher's mound and he turned toward the New Ulm dugout, real cocky and arrogant, and he *challenged* them to a fight! He gestured for them to come out to the mound if they had something to say, and then he called them out: 'Anybody who wants a piece of me, c'mon right now . . . one at a time or all at once . . . I'll kick all'a yer asses. C'mon.' Then he gestured for them to come for him."

The group listening to the story was silent with anticipation. "Well, New Ulm runs a pretty classy program and their coaches would never allow a fight to break out," Matt said. "So the New Ulm boys just swallowed hard and stood there, and then Velde says, 'That's what I thought, you pussies,' when no one came out to fight him."

"So, what happened?" someone asked.

"Velde struck out the side, six more pitches, then looked at their bench and laughed. Alvie tried to give the appearance that he was disappointed with Velde for acting like a dick, but he loved winning one, and I'm pretty sure Sverdrup has never beaten New Ulm in the ensuing forty-some years."

It was a good story on its own, but all of them knew Alvie, and that incident only served to remind them of a few other Alvie anecdotes. "Remember the time Dad got pissed at that huge fat umpire up in Marshall?" Donny asked.

Matt took Mo by the hand and gently pulled her away from the others while Donny started a new John Velde story. "Are you all right?" Matt asked. "I know you were pretty close to your dad. Are you doing OK?"

"Oh . . ." Mo sighed, and tried to sound as though she'd found some closure with her father, ". . . I think so. Donny and David and I have been in town for a few days, going through the house, and Dad's things. You remember how that felt, don't you?"

Matt nodded that he understood the agony, and all the poignant moments involved in the process of disposing of a parent's private things. "It's hard, Mo. It can break your heart."

"Yeah, the other day I opened Dad's closet door," Mo started, ". . . and there were his Sunday shoes, all polished up and ready for church." Tears were welling up in her eyes again.

Matt put his arms around her but said nothing.

"And then I found his Sunday suit, the new one he *just* bought at J.C. Penney in Mankato . . . about thirty years ago," Mo laughed and cried at the same time. "He was such a snappy dresser." She laughed softly once more and then had to choke her feelings back when she said, "I just stood there and stared into the closet, and I realized that Dad wouldn't be need-ing his clothes, his things, anymore." Then she asked, "How do you deal with moments like that?"

"I don't know, Mo," Matt answered softly. He held his old friend for a while and let her cry while he struggled to hold back his own tears. He knew exactly what she was feeling.

Then she stepped back from Matt. She'd just remembered something else that she wanted to share. "I took a few minutes yesterday and drove out past your parents' farm," she said, her eyes asking him if he knew what she was getting at.

He looked at the floor and nodded. He knew what she was asking. "Yeah, I've seen it," Matt said. "I heard about it, but I hadn't been out there to look until this morning. That's why I was a bit late for the funeral." He shook his head with sad resignation.

The Kingston family farm, the place where Matt, and his father, had grown up, had been sold when Matt's parents passed away a few years earlier. Recently the farm had changed hands again, and the new owner had promptly bulldozed all the old buildings and then, in the spring, planted corn on the spot where three generations of the Kingston family had lived. Only a small pasture remained. There was no sign that the family farm had ever been there.

"It was spooky," Matt said. "I turned onto that old gravel road where I'd been a million times, and when I looked up, the place was gone, just gone." He stopped and shook his head in disbelief. "When I was young; when you and I were . . ." Matt paused while he searched for the right word, ". . . friends," he said finally, "I guess I thought things would always . . ."

"I know, Matt," Mo said in a rich, low voice. She knew that he was reaching back, hoping to grasp something from the life he'd left behind. "I know."

"I just never thought . . ." Matt let his words trail off. "I remember . . . that was a great place to be a kid." The words stuck in his throat.

"Mo pulled him close once more and whispered, "Where did the years go? Where did everything go? We were best friends."

Matt squeezed her tightly, as if he was trying to savor one last taste of a fine wine. They both knew they could never go where this moment was taking them.

"Uh-oh," Mo said with chuckle, "I'm gonna have some explaining to do. My daughters are pointing at us and giggling."

"Oh, sorry," Matt said, and he tried to step back. But Mo held on.

"It's OK, I pointed you out to them before I came over here. They're just teasing me."

"Well, what about your husband? Where's he?"

"He's sitting with a few of Dad's contemporaries, over there," Mo said, as she pointed across the room.

Matt turned to look at the table where Mo was pointing, and his eyes fell on a group of vaguely familiar faces. The only person Matt didn't recognize looked up at Mo and waved. "That's your husband?" Matt asked.

"Yup. That's John. He's sitting right next to Burt Shinder. Do you recognize Mr. Shinder; senior English?"

"Wow. Clown Hair is still alive." Matt sighed.

"Shame on you," Mo said, but she made no effort to hide a giggle. Then she slugged Matt in the arm.

"It was a *bad* rug, Mo," Matt chuckled. "Really bad, and even though he was your dad's assistant coach, Alvie never liked him either, and you know it. He was a terrible teacher, too."

"Yeah, I know," she agreed. "Mrs. Fjelstad is over there too."

"Oh, you mean Monkey Lips?" Matt said.

"Shame on you!" Mo blurted with an even bigger giggle, and another slug to Matt's arm, but her protest was weak; she remembered the faculty nicknames too.

"And is that . . ." Matt squinted and leaned toward the table where Monkey Lips and Clown Hair were seated, trying to identify the man sitting beside Mo's husband.

"Yup, it's Pigeon Tits!" Mo said, then she covered her mouth. "Shame on *me*!" she said through her laughter, and she asked Matt, "How did our *basketball* coach get the nickname Pigeon Tits?"

"Velde!" Matt replied. "Velde gave them all a lasting moniker!"

"He was terrible!" Mo said.

"He still is."

As she was smiling about John Velde's mean-spirited nicknames, Mo signaled for her husband to come and join them. A moment later he rose from his seat next to Clown Hair Shinder and made his way toward them. As all men do in such situations, Matt quickly sized up his old girlfriend's husband and formed an opinion in about five seconds. He was maybe an inch shorter than Matt, a bit soft around the middle, and his hair was thinning. He seemed like a nice man, but not at all what Matt had expected for Mo; she could have done better. Matt knew how childish it was to compare himself to Mo's husband, but damn, he did feel a devious sense of satisfaction in the notion that maybe he was better, and would have been a better catch for Mo. He smiled openly at his own crazy idea, glad that no one knew just what he was smiling about.

When Mo's husband arrived, she let go of Matt's hand. She stood close to her husband and put her arm around his waist. "John, this is Matt Kingston, my first boyfriend."

As John extended his hand to Matt, she said, "Matt, this is my husband, John."

"It's nice to finally meet you. I've been hearing about you for forty years," John Lawson said with a smile.

"All good, I'm sure," Matt said, and the conversation rolled along on a pretty predictable course for a few minutes. John explained that he'd met Maureen in college and they'd married during their junior year at the

University of Wisconsin. John had majored in business, gone on to law school, and was now a partner in a large law firm in Rochester.

While Matt and Mo and John chatted, a line began to form behind Matt; other old friends wanted to visit with Mo, too. When Matt realized that he was monopolizing Mo, he stepped back and tried to dismiss himself, but Mo grabbed his hand. She turned to the woman standing behind John and said, "I'll be right back." She led Matt several paces away from the others.

"Is this goodbye? It is, isn't it?" Mo asked.

Matt nodded. "It's time for me to go."

Mo stepped close to Matt and took both of his hands in hers. Her lips were almost touching his ear when she said, "My dad always told me that people come into our lives for a season, a reason, or a lifetime."

Matt sighed, then he put his arms around her waist and pulled her close.

"I wish we'd had more than just a season," Mo whispered. "I always wanted to tell you that."

"Ah, but it was a pretty good season." Matt smiled.

"Sure was." She gave a sad smile.

This was it; Mo Glasnapp, like Alvie and the Kingston farm, would be gone soon. They'd probably never see each other again. Matt kissed her cheek and said, "You're still my girl, Mo. You always will be, and you'll always have a special place in my heart."

"Me too," she said, and then she stepped back. Her eyes were filling with tears again while she watched Matt say goodbye to the others standing nearby, and then he turned to leave.

He glanced back, just as he put a shoulder into a heavy oak door, and he saw that Mo was still watching him. He smiled. She smiled. Neither of them understood what they were feeling.

When he walked across the parking lot toward his car, he braced himself against a chilly breeze and thought that he never wanted to come back to this place again. But he knew he could never leave, either.

CHAPTER TWO

——•——

Matt sat high in a gnarly old white oak deep in the woods, waiting for a deer to walk by down below on the forest floor. After the things he'd seen the day before, he needed to think. He needed to be alone. He did his best thinking on the little trout stream about three miles to the north, but French Creek was frozen up for the winter. This big old tree, deep in the silent woods around his home—this was a pretty good place too.

He'd attended Alvie's funeral not much more than twenty-four hours earlier, and he'd been able to think of little else since he came home.

Visual images and short verbal exchanges from the funeral kept on playing over and over in his mind while he struggled against the bitter cold in the woods and waited for darkness to descend. With his compound bow across his lap, an arrow nocked, and looking down at a well-prepared ambush sight with several fine shooting lanes cut through the brush, Matt was ready. His right hip was beginning to ache, as usual. It always did now when he sat still for long stretches. His toes were uncomfortable from the cold and he wiggled them to stimulate some blood flow. His fingers were cold, too, so cold that he wondered if he'd have enough feeling to handle the delicate arrow release and make an accurate shot if a buck should happen to wander past. But a lifetime in the woods had taught him that the sudden appearance of a whitetail buck would get his blood pumping. For sure.

This was the magic hour: the last hour of daylight, when deer begin to move about in search of a meal. Whitetail deer lived at the edges; the edges of the day, the edges of the forest, and the edges of his dreams. They appeared mostly at dawn and dusk, and they came silently, like ghosts, to those places where food and cover shared the twilight. He was waiting in ambush and he needed to remain vigilant, keeping an eye peeled for any subtle movement in the woods. But after an hour perched in the oak tree, the cold was beginning to bite his toes and fingers, and it pressed at his back. He couldn't take it much longer. He had to move his hands and feet every so often in order to stave off the chill. He hoped his fidgeting wouldn't reveal his position to an approaching whitetail.

He lowered his chin, searching for the warmth inside his sweater, and he pumped his right hand inside his coat pocket as he scanned the motionless forest below.

The cold, however, was not a powerful enough distraction to keep his mind off the things he'd seen the day before. While the frigid twilight of Minnesota's silent woods gnawed at his fingers and toes, a little movie projector in his head played and then replayed vignettes of the previous morning's experience. He stared ahead, seeing, but not seeing, and let himself drift back to the little church. For the past twenty-four hours he'd thought of little else besides Alvie's funeral.

Damn, the cold was getting worse, Matt thought, when a frigid message from his toes jolted him away from his thoughts. He'd spent this day stacking wood and getting his home ready for a long winter, and he'd looked forward to ending the day in this deer stand, but now he questioned whether he could stay in this tree and endure the cold until dark.

Ah, he'd make it. Hell, he was Matt Kingston, and he was stronger than the cold. He'd done this many times before. He was sitting in his best deer stand, at prime time. He'd make it a little while longer. He always made it. He wiggled his toes and fingers and sneaked a look at his watch: forty minutes of daylight left. Jane would be home late tonight; she'd have dinner with her sister and then make the four-hour drive home from the Cities. The thought of Jane warmed him a bit; she'd been his best friend for nearly forty years. This quiet time in the bitter cold, the hunt, was just what he needed to keep him busy until his Jane came home.

And if he happened to kill a deer? He'd be busy tracking and field dressing it until she got home. If he didn't, well, he'd have a hot shower and a tall scotch and then get the bed warm for when she got home. Matt was OK, just fine. But damn, it *was* cold.

It was early December, and the rut was over. Most of the does had been bred already, and most of the bucks were exhausted from the effort. But maybe, just maybe, there would be a nice buck out here still searching for a doe, or more likely, for something to eat. The odds were slim, but nonetheless, he needed to be out here just now; this was the place he came when he needed to be alone.

He stared blankly into the woods once again and let some of yesterday's pleasant memories of childhood, and school days, and his first love, mingle with his gentle despair at the passing of so much time. It had been fun to reconnect with the Glasnapp boys and other childhood friends, but while he'd been with them the conversation had often turned to stories of illness and surgery and retirement and Medicare and grandchildren. Yesterday he'd been confronted by a fact he could no longer ignore: His life was in the seventh inning too, maybe later. His first love, the girl he once thought he'd love forever, had three grandchildren now. His family farm was gone, just gone. His life story was being erased so that a new story, someone else's story, could be written over it. He'd returned to the headwaters of his life and warmed his hands by the fire of his youth. It was nice to revisit happy times and happy places, but much had happened since then, and it was hard to make sense of it all just now.

His brain slipped into neutral, and he began to retrace the long journey that had led him from Sverdrup to this tree. Matt could still see his father waving as he drove away and left him standing in front of Pioneer Hall, at the University of Minnesota. Other scared and excited eighteen-year-old college freshmen were milling around and carrying luggage into the dorm, too. That was when his first roommate, a kid from Hibbing who didn't really want to be in college, and didn't last there very long, walked over, put his arm around Matt's shoulder, and said, "Wanna go get some beer?" Matt knew right then that college was going to be OK.

Dorm life that freshman year was a great adventure. Most nights began with a bit of studying, but the call to close his books and go party with his new friends had been powerful, and Matt found himself in bars and beer joints several nights a week. The nights that he stayed around the dorm and gave his studies a better effort usually ended with several boys huddled over a pizza and embellishing glorious stories about their stardom in high school sports.

The freshman roommate from Hibbing had a couple of older buddies who lived in an apartment off campus. That was where Matt was introduced to some music that he'd never heard before, and pot, and girls that were far different than any he'd known in Sverdrup.

A fog that he'd allowed to settle over those college memories lifted, and Matt saw himself sitting in a circle, cross-legged, on the floor of that apartment. There were several guys and several girls passing a joint around and pretending to have deep insight into the ways of the world. The faces of the other guys were all gone now, but he remembered the girls. He remembered long legs, long hair, tight jeans that been worn real thin in places. Several of the girls wore shirts and blouses that seemed to have been chosen specifically to reveal the fact that they weren't wearing bras.

Sometimes, deep in the night, when the college kids sitting in that little circle had said every profound thing they could think of, they all went out for breakfast at some all-night restaurant and talked about how much smarter they were than everyone else.

Those days and nights, talking about life and all the things he planned, had helped him understand who he really was. He'd said some stupid things during those late-night gatherings. Probably a lot of stupid things; he'd been trying to impress the girls with insight and wisdom that he didn't have. But eventually he began to recognize the foolishness and bullshit coming out of his own mouth. Then he heard the bullshit and foolishness coming from the others, too. Maybe his real education, the one that would put his life on track and keep it there, had its beginnings on the floor of that apartment?

Matt shivered, and memories of faded jeans and late nights were bumped back into the fog of long ago. He adjusted his collar and his hat and settled back against his tree. The woods were quiet. Nothing was moving. He tried to stay vigilant, but a dreamy apparition of Jane soon took shape and he was lost in time once more. That's the way it often worked while he sat in this tree and watched the world go by. Incongruous thoughts would begin to stream in front of his mind's eye, and unconnected daydreams often drifted by as if he were dozing in a soft bed, waiting for sleep to come, instead of shivering in a tree, deep in the forest. He didn't mind; he had no control over it anyway.

The image of his Jane gently transposed itself over the woods below him. Matt was lost in his daydreams once more. He was looking at her on the day they met.

In the spring of his freshman year in dental school, Matt had gotten a call from Andy Hedstrom, a classmate, a good guy from Cannon Falls. Andy said he'd just met this nice girl, and he was sure that Matt would like her too. She was tall and pretty and the two of them were going to go to some formal sorority function, with nice clothes and a nice meal and a dance . . . and would Matt like to take this pretty girl's roommate? They'd all go together, and it would be a great opportunity for them to meet other girls, too.

"What's wrong with her? The roommate, I mean?" Matt had asked, and now a faint smile creased his lips with that memory. "If she's so great why doesn't she already have a date?"

Andy chuckled, but he knew exactly what Matt was asking. He tried to reassure Matt that the roommate was all right. But just to be safe, he suggested a preliminary double date so that Matt could see for himself.

They all met at a bar called the Improper Fraction, just down the street from the dental school. Both girls were indeed pretty, and smart. But that double date hadn't worked out the way anyone intended. The four of them found a small table and Andy introduced the two girls. "Matt Kingston," Andy began, "this is Linda Nathan, your date; and this is Jane Monahan, my date." Linda, Jane's roomie, sat at Matt's left, Andy sat facing him, and Jane was on his right, and they all ordered burgers. Matt said hi to Linda, then turned to his right to look at Jane. It seemed to Matt that they'd all said something about school, and then Matt said something that he thought was pretty clever. Jane smiled, sort of, and then fired something back at Matt. He couldn't recall precisely what he'd said, but he remembered thinking that it was pretty clever; he'd started right off with his best material. He couldn't recall her exact reply, either. But he remembered a skeptical challenge in her eyes. She was pretty, and smart, and her eyes told him that she was leery. She must have heard all the best pickup lines from a hundred other college boys, and she had a hair trigger on her bullshit detector, which Matt appreciated.

The bar had been crowded that night, full of college kids and grad students, and the service was slow, so Matt offered to go to the bar for the first pitcher of beer. Jane said she'd go along and scoop up a dish full of peanuts. Some memories of the bar that night had faded, but one vision that would always remain was that short trip to the bar. Jane was standing beside Matt, waiting for the bartender to fill a pitcher, when another college guy noticed her standing there. The guy stepped right up on the other side of Jane, probably unaware that she was with Matt, and was about to say something to her. Matt hadn't seen the guy and was just reaching to take the full pitcher of beer from the bartender when he heard Jane bark, "Fuck off!"

When Matt's head spun to see what was going on, Jane was still scowling. "Oh, not you," she said without a smile, "him." She tossed a thumb at the shell-shocked guy next to her. Matt had only known Jane for a few minutes, but nonetheless, her response struck him as a bit harsh. But since he wasn't on the receiving end of it, it was actually funny.

Matt grinned as he carried the beer back to their table, and Jane followed him with a paper dish full of peanuts. When he'd poured a glass of beer for everyone, he squeezed a peanut shell, flipped a peanut into his mouth, and tossed the shell onto the floor. "You should learn to stop candy-coating things," Matt teased. "Just say what you really think. You didn't have to let that guy down so easy."

Jane held onto her scowl for a second; she was still irritated by the other guy's obvious intentions.

"You scared *me*," Matt said. Then he feigned a frightened face, put his hand in his lap, and added, "I think I peed, too . . . just a little bit."

That did it for Jane. Her eyes softened first, then the corners of her mouth curled until her teeth showed.

Talk soon turned to hometowns and school, and Matt tried to look to his left, at the girl he'd been brought there to meet. But he was drawn to Jane's sense of humor. Well, maybe her pretty face, too. By and by her eyes began to sparkle when she spoke to him, and she lowered her guard.

The hour or so that he spent at that bar was a singular moment in Matt's life; he would never forget the way Jane smiled at him that night. Her eyes were so hard and skeptical at first, then a bit softer and friendlier, and finally they narrowed when she leaned back in her chair and shook with laughter. He saw the change even in the short time they talked and laughed over a burger. On that evening, nearly forty years earlier, Matt and Jane both sensed that something new, and special, was happening. Matt and Jane laughed and joked with each other for the entire evening. They weren't rude, or totally detached from the others, but they edged away from them, into a zone all by themselves. At times it was awkward for Andy and Linda because Matt and Jane were having a *fine* time together . . . alone, and just across the table from them.

Even now, shivering in this tree, decades after the fact, an involuntary smile spread across Matt's face as he tried to move his chin closer to the warmth of his collar.

After their date at the Improper Fraction that night, when the laughter and the French fries and the burgers and a couple of beers were done, Matt went straight home and called Andy. "Hey, buddy," Matt started, "thanks for setting me up." He paused. "Linda is really nice, but I'm sorry, here . . ." Matt took a moment to find a better way to put it, then blurted, "There's no way I'm taking Linda to any party. I mean, she *is* pretty, and . . . but, I'll take *your* date."

"That's not gonna happen," Andy had replied. "We'll find somebody else to go with Linda." Click!

As far as Matt knew, they'd found a date for Linda. He didn't care. He just waited until about a week after the sorority party that he'd begged out of, and then he called Jane Monahan and asked her out. He knew that Andy was dating a couple of other girls and had no real interest in Jane. Matt found another burger place, a nice bar in downtown Minneapolis called Ike's, and chose a quiet booth.

"Why didn't you take Linda to the party?" Jane asked as they were still settling into their booth.

"'Cuz I didn't want to be at a party where you were with some other guy," Matt answered, without hesitation. "It had nothing to do with Linda." Then he added, "Why did you agree to go out with me tonight? I mean, what about Andy?"

Jane leaned back and measured her answer. Her guard was up, just as it had been on that night at the Fraction, but her eyes revealed some playfulness. "There's nothing between Andy and me. He just likes it that I have a nice car, and he thinks I'm rich. You knew that. Why did *you* call *me?*"

"Well, you knew that we had that little get-together at the Fraction just so I could see what was wrong with Linda? I mean, since she needed a date I figured she must have been a troll or something."

"And . . .?" Jane tried not to smile. "Keep going."

"I told you, she's fine." Matt shrugged. "And I'm sure she's nice. But I didn't want to go out with her."

"I sorta knew that."

"I liked *you*. And tonight, well, I guess I wanted to talk to *you*, and find out what's wrong with *you*."

"Pardon me?"

"The whole time we were talking that night at the Fraction I just kept wondering how someone like *you* could still be . . . unattached." The spark that had passed between them at their first meeting was still there, and growing. Matt could see it in her eyes, even more than the caution she hid behind. "I started to wonder if you had some disgusting personal habits, like maybe eat your earwax, or live with twenty-three cats and do your laundry in the sink."

A giant smile spread over Jane's face, but she stifled a laugh. "It's way worse than that," she said. "I go out with dental students."

"Ooh," Matt groaned, and he pulled an imaginary arrow from his heart. When he looked across the table, he couldn't miss the spark in Jane's laughing eyes. "I knew you'd find me *fascinating* if I could just get you alone," he said. "I *was* pretty clever that night we went to the Fraction, but you haven't seen anything yet." Matt nodded in agreement with himself.

Jane's eyes narrowed, and when she laughed, her eyes showed him something he'd never seen: She just might be the one. He could see that she was wondering about him, too.

There was no need to explain or apologize about roommates or other guys any longer. Everyone else had just been dismissed from both of their lives.

Matt had no memory of anything else that night at Ike's, but he'd never forget the feeling of their conversation. They sat in that little booth and talked for hours. It was their first date, and he was already talking to his best friend.

A sudden breeze whooshed through the pine boughs around him and Matt glanced to his right, as if he might actually see it go by. It was as if God had tapped him on the shoulder to remind him to pay attention to his hunt.

While the western half of the sky still held the light blue of afternoon, a huge yellow moon was sneaking into a deeper blue of the night sky on the eastern horizon, just barely above the spires of the lofty pines and balsams on the far side of Scotch Lake. The tree he was sitting in was only twenty yards or so from Scotch Lake, and now as he looked out across an expanse of sparkling new snow on the surface of the frozen lake, that big ol' moon was framed by pine boughs and a sheet of white. He stared at the awesome sight and whispered, "Wow."

Suddenly there was movement on the other side of a brush pile, about thirty yards away. It was a mature doe and it had just appeared, like a ghost. Damn, how could a deer get this close to him before he noticed it? He was waiting in ambush. He should have seen it coming, but he'd been daydreaming.

Thoughts of Jane Monahan vanished, and Matt was on red alert.

He waited, motionless, for a few seconds, and the doe moved again. His hands weren't so cold anymore, for an ancient game had begun. The deer took several steps and then looked from side to side. The doe was thirty yards away and Matt was well hidden in his tree; he knew that if he didn't move, the deer would never see him. He sat stone still and watched.

A second mature doe appeared right behind the first one. He wasn't interested in harvesting a doe. He'd wait for a buck, a buck with trophy antlers, and if such a buck did not appear, then he'd go home empty-handed. But it was always a thrill to see big game this close up, and the appearance of these two deer was a good sign; maybe a buck with lust in his heart was following behind.

The first doe took several steps toward Matt and stopped to look around again. Her ears twitched and then she became rigid as she scanned the woods for the sound of a twig snapping or the crunch of snow under the foot of a predator. When she heard and saw nothing, she seemed to relax, and she walked for almost thirty feet before she stopped again. The other doe followed, but this time when they stopped, they both looked back where they'd come from. This was another good sign; there might be a buck following them. Sometimes bucks follow does because they think they're on a date, other times they follow because they're allowing some-one else to check for danger before they come any farther. Matt hoped there was an amorous buck following close behind; love made everyone ignore their own safety, and it always made the hunt easier if a buck was looking for love, not dentists hiding in trees.

The body language of the two does, frequent glances back at where they'd come from, indicated that a buck was probably following them. But the afternoon light was fading fast. If there was buck nearby he'd have to show himself soon or it would be too late. The sun had dipped below the skyline a few minutes earlier and there were only a few more ticks on the clock before it would be too dark to shoot. This had happened more times than he could remember: A buck showed up late, too late, as nothing more than a gray blur, twenty minutes after dark, and he'd had to walk home knowing he'd come close, but not close enough.

Then there was more movement, back on the trail where the other deer had come from, and Matt saw what he'd hoped for: a shooter buck, as big as he'd ever seen in these woods. The buck took a few more steps and . . . Jesus! It was Mr. Whitehorns! Matt's heart was in his throat now, and thumping so hard he feared that the sound in his chest would frighten all the deer away, or that his heart would explode. He moved his fingers inside the chopper mitten on his right hand and positioned his arrow release in his hand. If Mr. Whitehorns kept coming, Matt would have to withdraw his right hand from his warm pocket and then attach his release to the bow string without being noticed.

The buck seemed pretty interested in one or both of the does, and the does kept looking back at him. They were all less wary than they should have been, and Matt cautiously began to shift his weight to get ready to draw his bow, if the opportunity presented itself. But his heart was beating wildly. If he couldn't get that under control, and soon, he wouldn't have the strength to draw his bow. This had happened to him twice before, many years earlier. Both times his screaming heart had sapped all the strength from his arms. He'd been unable to handle the sixty-pound draw weight of his compound bow, and trophy bucks had just walked on by, unaware they'd cheated death.

Mr. Whitehorns was approaching; he was now twenty-five yards away and standing broadside, close enough for an easy kill shot. Matt was confident of that, but the massive buck was still partially obscured by a thicket of tangled brush. When, or if, he stepped into an open shooting lane, Matt would kill him.

Both does were close to Matt, almost directly under his tree stand, maybe too close. But this was working out about as well as he could have hoped. Matt was ready, and when the does looked away he took a deep breath and moved his right hand to the bow string. Then he arched his back, extended his left arm, which held the bow, and leaned into it. It was a struggle, but when the wheels on each end of his bow rolled over and the draw weight let off he was in control. His breathing was steady and although his heart was beating quickly, he was ready. He put his nose on the bow string and centered the bow sight just behind Mr. Whitehorns' front shoulder. If the old buck took three more steps, maybe two, Matt would release his arrow.

Matt waited. Several seconds slipped by.

And then it happened. Mr. Whitehorns raised his tail: the universal warning sign that something was wrong. From the corner of his eye, Matt noticed that both does were on full alert too.

One of the does snorted a loud whistling sneeze that always told other deer to run for it because danger was close. The two does bolted and were gone in an instant, with Mr. Whitehorns at their heels. Matt could hear them busting through heavy brush as they raced away.

"Well, shit!" Matt said, easing his bow back from full draw. What could have gone wrong? He had done everything properly, and he'd do everything the same way if he had the chance to do it all over again. Had one of the does winded him, picked up his scent? Had he made a noise when he drew the bow, or had one of them seen some movement? Maybe they'd picked up the scent of a coyote or timber wolf? It didn't matter now.

"Shit! Fuck!" he said again, as he tied his bow to a rope and lowered it to the ground. His day was over. With the same caution he always used, he climbed slowly down the ladder of his tree stand and then untied his bow from the lift line. Everything had been perfect, and then everything went to shit.

It was almost full dark now, and he had a twenty-minute walk ahead of him. He stood at the base of the oak tree he'd been sitting in and took a minute to get his feet under him. His hip hurt, and his knee hurt, and his back was stiff. At least he didn't have to track a wounded, dying deer in the dark, and then field dress it, and then drag *it* home too. So maybe this was OK?

But damn, that was Mr. Whitehorns, a big buck that other hunters had seen and talked about over campfires, and Matt's heart was still thumping. He looked up at the stars and the moon, and then he looked across the lake and saw that the new snow and the full moon had combined to light up the landscape.

Ah, maybe that was enough, *more* than enough for today? He'd had a dandy thrill, and after all, wasn't that why he did this stuff? There would be other days, other deer, maybe another shot at Mr. Whitehorns. He decided to walk down to the lake and then follow the lakeshore back to his home instead of walking through the woods. There was no need for a flashlight out there; the light of the moon would show him the way home.

As he set off across Scotch Lake, the trees around him all cast giant moon shadows on the sparkling new snow, and off to his left the moon had changed from yellow to white as it rose in the sky. The new snow out on the lake sparkled all around him, as if he were walking ankle deep in a field of tiny diamonds. His boots made the only sound in the world: muffled crunches in the soft snow.

Then he heard the distant groan. It surprised him, scared him a bit, at first. But when he recognized what it was, he turned to face the broad, flat expanse of sparkling snow in the middle of the lake and said, "OK, let's hear that again." He waited. Several seconds later another low-pitched groan rumbled over, and under, the lake. Then another, followed by a huge gurgle, as if there were a giant just beneath the ice he was standing on, and the giant had a bellyache.

Matt smiled, and sighed, and stared again at the brilliant moon shining down on the lake. This was good, all good. Scotch Lake was making ice. The sound was mystical, enchanting, and Matt stopped to savor it. When he stood still there were no other sounds—no trucks rolling along on a distant highway, no dogs barking or birds chirping—just the rumble of a big lake making ice.

The sudden arrival of colder temperatures had sent the winter freeze-up into hyperdrive on the area lakes. When water freezes it expands, and now there were great sheets of ice out there, like tectonic plates, grinding into and over each other as they grew. When the noise from these collisions rose from the lake and into the surrounding woods it sometimes had the strange feel of malevolent, brooding spirits wandering through the North Country and crying out.

Although there was already an eight-inch crust of ice, Scotch Lake would make another two feet or so in the next couple of weeks. It was plenty safe to walk out here on this area of the lake, maybe even to drive his truck. Matt stopped and turned in a slow circle.

Up on the north end, by French Canyon, where the spring-fed French Creek emptied into the lake, there would still be large patches of open water. And that thought triggered in him a thousand memories of trout fishing in the summer. Ah, French Creek, which drained the cedar swamp in French Canyon—that was his favorite place. It held a healthy population of native brook trout, and because it was relatively inaccessible, Matt could usually count on having the place pretty much to himself. Maybe when he got home tonight he'd tie some flies, listen to the lake making ice, and think about summer.

Matt Kingston loved this place. He always would. His home, an older cabin that he and Jane had remodeled and added on to several times, was the only home on this side of the lake, and it was just up the shore, maybe half a mile. After several more groans from Scotch Lake, he started off toward home again.

He was plenty warm by the time he stepped into the clearing around his home. Today's hunt was over, and it was time to go inside. But he stood still for a moment and looked back at the moonlit winter landscape around him. These moments, like the one he'd shared on that first date with Jane, needed to be pressed into a man's soul. At some point, later on in life, he'd need to cling to these things, these little treasures, to remind himself who he was. He *knew* that he had a connection to something here . . . but what was it? God? His place in the cosmos? He didn't really have a handle on the connection yet, even after all the years of searching; he'd have to think about that some more. He stared out over the lake and tried to drink in all the colors, and shadows, and shapes.

CHAPTER THREE

—◆—

His hands ached and he was tired as he stepped out of his clothes and into the shower. It was OK that he wasn't still out there dragging a deer back home across the lake or beginning the arduous task of butchering it. After a long, hot shower he dressed in a gray sweatshirt with "Gopher Hockey" printed across the front, boxer shorts, and heavy wool socks. Maybe he'd sit at his desk and tie a few caddis flies; that was always a good thing to do on a winter night.

He glanced over at the fire he had started in the fireplace before he'd stepped into the shower. It was crackling now, and he'd soon have coals to stare at. "Ah, screw the flies," he muttered to himself, as he pumped his stiff hands into fists and shuffled off toward the kitchen. He was about to get *real* comfortable.

He found a cocktail glass with a duck engraved on the side, opened the freezer, scooped out a handful of ice cubes, and plopped them into the glass. He liked the way the ice cubes sounded as they plinked about. Then he opened the cupboard above the fridge and sorted through several bottles of scotch, searching for the one he wanted tonight. Sometimes he drank Cutty Sark, ever since he'd read a book called *The Mulligan*, about a dentist who chucked it all and moved to Montana. The guy in that story drank Cutty, and Matt liked the story, so he kept some on hand now, too. But tonight he reached for his favorite: a bottle of twelve-year-old Aberlour.

Matt poured about three fingers into the glass, thought about it for a second, then splashed in a bit more. What the hell? He was home alone and he had the rest of the night to sit by this warm fire and think. He flicked off the overhead lights and plugged in a string of colored Christmas lights that he'd strung around the mantle on the fireplace. The little greens and reds and blues from the lights mixed with the yellow firelight dancing all across the logs and the cedar planks on the walls of the old cabin. He dropped heavily into the couch and listened to the worn leather settle around him. The coffee table in front of the couch was actually a split-log cribbage board, about four feet long, made from a giant Norway pine that had once stood nearby. He'd made it himself, many years before, but never managed to play a game of cribbage after Jane had converted it into their coffee table. He raised his feet onto the coffee table/cribbage board and sighed.

If he had a long stick in his hand he'd have poked it in the fire. Every boy, even sixty-two-year-old boys, he reasoned, loved to poke a stick into a fire. Orange coals, blue flames, the scent of wood smoke; there was something in a fire that drew a man's eyes in, as if he might see something on the other side of this life, if only he looked carefully. Perhaps somewhere in the glowing coals or flickering flames a man might see that message from God.

A long, low rumble, fast on the heels of a higher-pitched moan, rose from the lake outside. A second later the lake sent out a loud bang, like a shotgun blast, into the night; a crack, maybe a quarter mile long, had exploded through the middle of the growing ice sheets. "Ooh, nice one," he said, as he tossed two more pieces of split birch onto the fire.

He wondered just where Alvie Glasnapp was at that moment. Maybe up in Heaven, taking his first look back at Earth? He wondered about the old friends he'd seen yesterday, and when he'd hear of *their* passing. He thought of his own father and mother, and his friends who'd died and left him here—were they up there in the night sky, looking down at him, too?

A bed of coals under the burning birch log crumbled and changed shape. Matt got up again and walked over to the fireplace. He stirred the coals with a poker and thought about the path that had brought him here. He'd led a charmed life, compared to just about everyone he knew. He'd never been sick or injured, he'd been in love with a woman who loved him back for nearly forty years, and his two grown sons were healthy. He had a good job and was living in his dream home. Why had he been so fortunate?

He couldn't help but think of a couple of classmates from dental school. Grant Thorson, a good person, but not a particularly close friend, practiced over in Walker and the guy had suffered huge, painful losses: He and his wife had lost a son while they were still in school, and then his wife had died young. Grant and another classmate, Will Campbell, had been inseparable best friends until Will was killed in a horrific hunting accident. One of them was dead, the other scarred for life. Why them, and not him?

Matt had come to so many forks in the road, and always chosen the right path. Why? Maybe his will was strong enough to shape his own future? How many more forks in the road would he come to? And what about all those forks that he *hadn't* taken? What fortune had awaited him if he'd taken a different path here and there along the way? And when would *his* number be called? What stories would old friends tell at *his* funeral? The answers didn't seem to be there in the embers of a fire tonight. But the scotch was pretty good.

Jane would be home in few hours, and that thought made him happy. He wanted to tell her about the close encounter with Mr. Whitehorns. He wanted to tell her how he'd felt yesterday when he saw that his family farm was gone, and when he'd seen his old friends. Jane would smile when he told her about visiting with an old girlfriend. But she'd never understand his feelings about his childhood home. How could she? She'd grown up in an affluent home in an affluent suburb; she'd never been a part of that life, never known the people and places of his early life. He'd tell her about it all, and she'd nod her head and ask a few questions, but she'd never understand.

But it felt good to think about her; they'd wake up in each other's arms, under the warm covers. He let himself imagine how they'd spoon; he'd reach around and hold her breasts while he pulled her close. He leaned back, way back, on the couch, and thought about the way her hair would tickle his lips, and the feel of the soft skin on her bare legs. She'd purr and ease herself back into his embrace. Later, they'd talk and share a few laughs.

He swirled the glass and listened to the ice cubes clink against the sides for a moment. Then he raised the glass and let a tiny bit of the amber fluid slide into his mouth. He held it under his tongue and savored the aroma, and the taste, for a few seconds before he swallowed it. The scotch was *so* warm and *so* cold at the same instant . . . and *so* smooth. He let another sip glide past the ice cubes and then roll over his tongue. He could taste the smoke from the fire that had roasted the barley, along with the oak barrel it had been aged in for years.

Just above the pleasant crackling of the fire, even though he was inside the house, he could still hear Scotch Lake groaning from time to time. He swirled the drink in his hand and once again savored the happy music made by ice cubes clinking softly against his glass. He looked about the room and considered this moment, this evening, this day, his life. He *was* a lucky man.

He and Jane had dreamed of a home like this since their earliest times together, and they stumbled onto their happy place while Matt was still in school. The place had been built around 1950 by an old German carpenter who'd wanted a fishing and hunting retreat deep in the woods and far from the rest of the world. The man had found this prime lot on Scotch Lake, and according to courthouse records he'd paid the princely sum of five hundred dollars for twenty acres. Although Matt had never met the man, he'd come to admire him. The guy had used oak two-by-fours in the construction, and the bones of this home would probably withstand a nuclear strike. Cedar siding on the outside had been restained a dozen times and looked as if it would last another fifty years. All the inside walls featured the cheapest material available at the time of construction: ten-inch bullnose cedar planks. But now, the paneling on every inside wall had acquired a rich, red patina, and it would have cost a fortune to duplicate today. The original footprint consisted only of a great room with a kitchen and a bedroom. After Matt and Jane bought the place they'd added bedrooms on both ends of the house, preserving the feel of the original home as much as possible. The great room still featured a long bank of windows with ten-inch panes, and a stone fireplace. The floors in most of the house were a bit uneven and revealed its age. It was plain to see which parts of the house had been added on, even though Matt had done the best he could to make the new parts merge with the old.

He took another small sip of the scotch and thought some more about the passage of time. He was a sixty-two-year-old man who'd eased past his prime a few years ago. He understood that much, at least on an intellectual level, and he'd been OK with it, until yesterday. The years had piled up behind him without much notice, and now, after what he'd seen at Alvie's funeral, he understood that his life's journey was much closer to the end than the beginning. He needed his glasses to read the newspaper, and he found himself asking others to repeat themselves more and more all the time; people seemed to mumble more these days. His hands and feet and knees were stiff in the morning, and his hip ached a little more all the time. Those changes had pretty much snuck up on him, and he'd been able to convince himself that they were just the everyday aches and pains that everyone joked about. They were nothing that a pair of bifocals and some exercise couldn't fix, or so he'd reasoned. What he'd seen yesterday was forcing him to rethink that.

Someday, before too long, his physical skills would begin to diminish. Ah, shit, he thought, who was he kidding, they already had. Trudging back through the woods and the snow tonight had been difficult. Several years ago, he could have done it without breaking a sweat. Now his hip was barking at him and the muscles in his legs were sore.

But for the moment he was satisfied that he could still do the difficult things. And he still had passion for the things that he'd always loved. There was plenty left for him to do. Wasn't there?

His cell phone rang as he raised the glass to his lips once more. It was Jane, and he suddenly realized that he'd forgotten to call her. He answered the call and blurted, "Hi, honey. I'm sorry I forgot to call. I just forgot."

"Matt! You're supposed to call me before *and* after you go hunting!" Her tone was stern. "Did you go hunting by yourself again?"

"Yes."

"Matt . . ."

"I'm sorry, honey. I should have called you, I know."

"I worry about you, climbing up a tree all by yourself. What if you fell?" Jane sounded like a mother scolding a disobedient child. "Really, Matt, what would happen if you fell out of your tree?"

"Ah, you know I wear a safety harness, so I guess I'd just hang around until somebody came and—"

"Matt! I'm not kidding, and you're too old for that," Jane interrupted.

"Ah, don't go there, honey! I'm not too old for anything. I had a close encounter with a big buck tonight. I'm still like Jeremiah Johnson: 'a great hunter and a fine figure of a man.'" He chuckled, quoting from his favorite movie.

"And you've been drinking, haven't you?" she said.

"No," he lied.

Jane questioned him with silence, and he could feel her eyes on him, even over the phone.

"A little bit," he admitted, as if he was giving up a secret.

"Drinking by yourself; that's not OK."

"Lighten up a bit, honey. I'm just fine, and I'm not too old, so you can let that go. I'm sorry I forgot to check in with you when I came in from the woods. I won't do that again. I *am* sorry for that." Matt's tone was calm and reassuring, and there was a hint of laughter in his voice when he added, "And it's OK for me to sit on the couch by myself and have a drink at the end of a long day; I'm a grown-ass man. And nothing bad's gonna happen to me because I'm harder than fuckin' blue twisted steel."

Jane laughed out loud at that. It was the kind of outrageous thing Matt might say after a bit of scotch had loosened his tongue. She loved how he could still make her laugh. "Yeah, I guess so. But you're safe now and sitting by the fire, right?" she asked before she moved on: "So how was the funeral? Did you have a chance to visit with some old friends, like you'd hoped?"

"Sure did! A bunch of old friends. I'll tell you all about it tomorrow."

"Was it a sad funeral?"

"Not really. It was a celebration, actually, like they're supposed to be."

"That's good, I guess, how's everything else?"

"Good." Then he asked, "When will you be home?"

"I left the Cities about an hour ago, so I'll be home in about three hours. Are you gonna wait up for me?"

"Sure, I'll be busy warming up the bed for you. I might look like I'm sleeping, but I'll be wide awake."

"What are you doing tomorrow?" she asked, as the conversation was about to end. She knew he'd be sound asleep later when she slid under the covers with him.

"Well, I'm guessing that you'll want to sleep in, so I'm gonna get up early and go have coffee with John Velde," he replied.

Matt could actually hear Jane smiling. She liked John Velde, she always had. How could she not like him; every time he said hello to her he seemed to be wearing a smile, actually a "shit-eatin' grin," as Matt always referred to it, which oozed mischief. But Jane had never really trusted John Velde. She was certain that he would never steal from Matt, or come up with some illegal scheme and drag Matt into it. But she could never shake a vague and shapeless fear that John would talk Matt into ice fishing with him before the ice was strong enough, and then they'd break through the ice and drown, or that John would do some thoughtless and dangerous thing in a boat when they were fishing in the summer, or that John would bring a bottle of scotch or a case of beer along and start drinking while the two of them were in a truck, driving to or from a fishing hole or a hunting cabin. John Velde had just never proven to Jane that it was safe to leave her husband in his company. He still seemed more than likely to reengage in the senseless behavior of a high school boy and drag Matt Kingston along with him. Jane even wondered if some people in town thought poorly of Matt because of his friendship with John Velde.

People around Pine Rapids either liked John or disliked him immediately, because he said and did whatever he wanted. Some of the locals who knew him smiled at the mention of his name, others turned away and groaned. Jane had known John long enough to recognize and appreciate that the bullshit and outrageous behavior was all part of the person John Velde *wanted* to be; maybe not who he really was. "Well, honey, don't let John be a bad influence on you," Jane said.

"My mother used to say that very same thing to me fifty years ago."

"Well, I mean it!" Jane teased. "I worry about you when you're with him."

"Don't worry, darlin'," Matt said. "I love you, and I'll see you in a couple hours, maybe. Drive careful."

"Always do. See you soon. I love you, too." She hung up the phone and then said to herself, "a grown-ass man . . . fuckin' blue twisted steel." Jane Kingston still had a crush on Matt, even after all the years. She smiled as she drove home through the darkness. She still thought he was indestructible, too.

Matt put his phone down on the arm of the couch and took a sip of the scotch he'd been holding. He'd had a thrill with a fine buck tonight, he was sipping scotch in front of a crackling fire, and a pretty girl still loved him. Sometime later, in the middle of the night, that beautiful woman would get naked and crawl into his bed. Maybe he wasn't *that* far past his prime?

He turned his eyes toward the fire once more and tried to think about Jane, and the full moon over the lake, and childhood friends, while he stared at the glowing embers.

Soon enough, the long day, and the scotch, and the warm fire, pulled his eyelids closed.

CHAPTER FOUR

———•———

Jane was beside him, breathing softly, when Matt let his eyes ease themselves open. Just beyond Jane's form, which was covered by a quilt, Matt could see out the bedroom window where the eastern sky was growing pale as a prelude to sunrise. A thousand small, leafless oak limbs—black varicose veins in the winter forest—slowly came into focus, backlit by the slate gray morning sky.

Matt turned onto his side and pulled her close. Her back was firm against his chest and he caressed her breasts, just as he'd dreamed. "I love you," he whispered into her ear. Then he kissed her neck.

"Mmm," she sighed.

"What time did you get home?" he asked.

"'Bout one thirty," she said, still half asleep. Then, from the same sleepy fog, she added, "You were out like a light when I came to bed." He pulled her a bit closer and pressed his hips against her backside. "Mmmm," she purred. She knew what Matt was thinking about. "Later . . ." she murmured.

Matt grinned and squeezed her gently. "Later" was fine with him, whenever later happened. He ran his hand down her stomach and then along her hip and over her thigh. She was still long and lean, and so soft and inviting. She was athletic, and she moved with an air of assurance and confidence. John Velde had told her once that she "walked like a dude." He'd meant it as a compliment, and that was how Jane took it. Her hair was light brown, almost blonde, and her eyes were the color of sand on a summer beach.

He kissed her neck once more and then got out of bed. "Are you still planning to go fishing with me today? Maybe we'll get into the crappies and save a few for dinner tonight," he said as he stepped into his blue jeans. "Might be a little chilly out there, but we'll be fine."

"Uh-huh." Jane pulled the quilt up to her chin, then she rolled over and faced the other way.

Matt pulled his Gopher Hockey sweatshirt over his head.

"Where are you going?" she asked through a sleepy haze, her words muffled by the quilt.

"I told you, gonna meet John for coffee. You go ahead and sleep in. I'll see you later."

"Behave yourself. Don't let John get you into trouble," she said, and before she drifted off again she added, "And remember, the days are pretty short now, so get home early. I don't want to miss the afternoon bite."

"Wouldn't miss it for anything," Matt said as he slipped away.

The morning had dawned cloudy and cold and everything was as it should be. As he drove his truck down the tree-lined trail that led out to the highway he felt the simple happiness he always felt at times like this. While Jane lay in her warm bed, enjoying a chance to sleep in, he was off to have coffee and tell a few stories with an old friend. Life was good.

When he rolled into in Pine Rapids, Matt turned onto Shorewood Avenue and decided to make a quick stop and say hello to John Velde's brothers before he picked John up for coffee.

The Velde boys—John, Tileen, and Darrell—were a unique bunch. They hadn't exactly grown up poor; their father, Odin, was an over-the-road trucker, and their mother had taught third grade at Riverside Elementary School for thirty-eight years. The Veldes made some money, but they never seemed to have anything to show for it. What Matt mainly remembered about the Velde home was that the boys had never had much parental supervision. Childhood had been pretty much of a rough-and-tumble experience for the Veldes.

Tileen's school days had come to an abrupt end one day in wood shop when he was a sophomore in high school. The story was that Mr. Wodnick, the shop teacher, disliked Tileen and they'd had a stormy relationship for most of the school year. Then, one pleasant morning in the spring, Mr. Wodnick said something that irritated Tileen, who was a tall and usually unflappable kid. They exchanged a few heated words and Tileen snapped. After a brief scuffle, he put Mr. Wodnick's head in a vise on one of the wood shop benches and then cranked it so tight that Mr. Wodnick began to cry. Tileen bent down, his lips close to Mr. Wodnick and hissed, "Fuck you." Then he kicked Mr. Wodnick in the ass, hard, and walked out the door. No one in Sverdrup saw Tileen Velde for more than ten years after that, but it was common knowledge that he'd driven directly from Sverdrup High School wood shop class to San Diego and joined the Navy. After years of wandering, he'd returned to live in Minnesota fifteen years ago, when he and his brother Darrell opened a fur business in Pine Rapids.

Then there was Tileen's nickname. One day when he was about ten years old, Tileen had appeared at the playground with a large booger dangling in one nostril. The thing moved in and out when he breathed and talked, but it never broke free, and Matt remembered the way the other boys who'd been at the playground that day stared and then tried to impart body English to the booger in order to help it break free. Tileen's personal appearance was pretty disheveled in every other way, too. He always seemed to show up with his zipper open, or his shirt buttoned wrong, or two different socks on. But the booger, well, that was an altogether different and more spectacular fashion statement. John, who was two years older than Tileen, and a typical big brother, took special pleasure in telling Tileen about that big ol' snag in his nose. After a bit of bantering, John grabbed Tileen and put him in a headlock. While Tileen thrashed and screamed and laughed, and all the other boys, including Matt, watched and cheered, John took Tileen's hand in his and then used Tileen's index finger to pick the booger from his own nose, and then wipe it on his shirt. John, and all the others, began calling him Snag on that day, and the name just stuck. All through his school days no one ever called him Tileen again. When he got his letterman's jacket for varsity football he had Snag embroidered on it, not Tileen.

Darrell Velde, the youngest of the boys, was a different breed of cat, too. From the earliest days, he'd fancied himself as an artist, or intellectual. Sometime around ninth grade he'd purchased a cheap guitar, and then taken to walking the streets and country roads around Sverdrup and strumming the guitar and singing, like a wandering minstrel. He walked, and strummed, and sang, and made sure that people saw him. He had some limitations, however; he was only willing, or able, to learn about three chords, but that was enough as long as he had "the look" working for him. He was also tone deaf, and a horrific poet. But he liked the wandering-minstrel look, so he worked it. Hard.

Everyone in Sverdrup pretty much assumed that immediately after high school the Darrell Velde Wandering Minstrel Show would pack up, hit the road, and go where it belonged: California. And they were right; Darrell was gone soon after graduation.

John Velde somehow found a way to circle Earth in a much tighter orbit than his brothers. All through childhood he'd been "one of the guys." He played school-yard games with Matt and the other boys. They built forts with scrap lumber from their fathers' garages. They went to movies and to the swimming pool by the fairgrounds together. They did everything together. But then one day John Velde hit puberty. He'd always been the best athlete in his age group, but suddenly he was bigger and stronger and he had sideburns and a deep voice and he was a better athlete than all the upperclassmen, too. He started hanging out with older boys, which led to riding around in cars, and cigarettes, and older girls. When he was in ninth grade he was a three-sport varsity athlete. He was the best athlete in the area, and he was sexually active. By the time his contemporaries caught up with him he'd changed, and the only one of them who remained his friend was Matt Kingston.

In spite his behavior issues, the University of Minnesota offered John a full athletic scholarship for baseball, and during the early spring practices in his freshman year he was clearly the best player on the team. He was a pro prospect, what the scouts were calling a "five-tool guy"; he could run, throw, hit for average, hit with power, and play defense.

But the wheels came off the wagon for John Velde just after the snow melted that spring. He decided to buy a motorcycle, so he talked a banker into loaning him a thousand dollars. He said he intended to buy a new Kawasaki with a 750cc engine. The next day he stopped by a Kawasaki dealer, and while he was looking at a shiny new black 750 he noticed that the dealer also had a *used* 750; a much flashier purple one with really loud pipes and only a few miles on it.

John bought the used one because it was screaming fast, and it was sparkly and called everyone's attention to it, and that's what John wanted during those years. But then he had a *real* problem, the kind that vexes young men; he had a hot new bike that begged to be ridden, and $300 in his pocket. So he did the only logical thing: He quit school, took a road trip, and walked away from baseball and a free college education. He rode his bike to California and stayed there for twenty-five years.

Matt was stunned at the time. He loved sports; he'd been a three-sport guy in high school, too. But Matt, unlike John, had only enough talent to make the high school team. Nothing more. He was the kid who gave it everything he had every day in practice and worked his tail off just to stay on the team. Matt would have given anything to be as good as his friend John.

But John Velde was the kid who loafed in practice or skipped practice altogether. And at precisely the moment when some important doors were swinging open for him, John had thrown baseball, and college, away. It made no sense. But now, given the advantage of hindsight, Matt knew it was just the kind of thing that John did. At every turn.

———

The small parking lot in front of Darrell and Snag's fur business was choked with muddy pickup trucks. The sign on the front of the building read "The Shorewood Furist." It was obviously Darrell's doing, a play on Robin Hood's Sherwood Forest, and it made Matt smile every time he saw it. Darrell Velde said, and did, a lot of stupid shit, but every now and then he made Matt laugh, and Matt decided to pull in and say hello before he picked up John.

Matt had spent countless hours with the Velde boys, and he had a treasure trove of crazy stories about them. Today, as his truck rolled to a stop, Matt thought of the way John always introduced his brothers to strangers: "This is my brother, Snag, and my other brother, Darrell." It was a ripoff from the Bob Newhart TV show character who always said, "This is my brother, Darrell, and this is my other brother, Darrell." Every time John Velde said the line he held eye contact with the person he was introducing to his brothers and raised his eyebrows as if to say, "get it?" Matt always got it, and always laughed. Every time. Even now he couldn't help but smile.

The inside of the Shorewood Furist building looked like the landscape of Hell. There was a large pile of skinned beaver carcasses in the middle of the floor, and there were blood splatters about four feet up on the walls over on the far side of the place where the skinners were working. But the smell was the thing that could take a strong man down. The inside of any animal smelled pretty bad to begin with, but dozens, or perhaps hundreds of small critters, broken and in various early states of decomposition, could leave a powerful stench in a thirty-by-thirty-foot room. In addition to that, several hundred beaver and coyote hides had been stretched on frames and were hanging in a large room adjoining the skinning area.

Through a smeared glass window in the dingy little business office that overlooked all the action in the main work area, Matt made eye contact with Darrell, who was on the phone. Darrell waved and smiled. It was a stark little room with gray walls and the stink of a gas station men's room. It featured an avocado-colored rotary-dial phone, a desk, and a small bookshelf, both piled high with papers and ashtrays, and it was where Darrell entertained his clients. Matt waved back and then stepped over a couple of carcasses as he made his way toward Snag.

Snag was busy, holding a wet beaver skin against a lathe that was designed to beat and strip the flesh from the inside of the pelt. His hands were covered with a greasy moosh when he stopped what he was doing and extended his hand for a handshake. Matt shook his hand, smiled, and then wiped his hand on a dirty rag hanging from a hook on the wall. "How's it going, Snag?" Matt asked. He had to raise his voice in order to be heard over the noise of the lathe. Just as he'd hoped, Snag flipped a switch and turned the lathe off so that he could visit with Matt for a moment. Snag Velde had morphed into a "character" even by the standards of Pine Rapids, Minnesota, where you had to be unique indeed to be regarded as a "character."

Snag lived at the Shorewood Furist. Well, he had a single-wide trailer, back in the woods north of town, too, but he slept at the shop quite often during the busy season. Adjoining the business office where Darrell was still talking on the phone was another dingy little chamber, also with gray walls, and Snag had furnished it with a single bed and a nightstand. This bedroom also had a glass window, like the business office, which allowed Snag to sit on the side of his bed and look out over the little slaughterhouse while he began and ended each day with a cigarette. Matt had wandered in there once, just to look around, and discovered that Snag's bed linens looked like the Shroud of Turin: Imprinted on the pale gray sheets was the even grayer outline of a man. Apparently Snag had no great need for clean linens.

Naturally, he carried a full aromatic "bouquet" around wherever he went. But the most memorable thing about him, and there many memorable things about him, was the first impression he made visually. Snag was about six foot three and weighed maybe 190 pounds. His hair was not quite shoulder length and he appeared to keep about a half pound of Crisco in it. Sometimes he wore a filthy green stocking cap, but most of the time he let his grayish, shiny hair go wherever the wind blew it. He always had about a five-day growth of scraggly whiskers, and his shoulders were slumped inside a grubby plaid shirt that seemed to ride four inches north of his grubby blue jeans, which was unfortunate because the twine he used to hold his pants up didn't do the job very well, and about three inches of his ass crack was always visible.

Matt had always liked all the Velde boys. To be sure, he had a different relationship with each of them. Snag? Well, Snag was without question the grubbiest person Matt knew, and second place was way back there. But Snag was a good guy, a true friend who would do anything for Matt.

"Didja get your buck yet?" Snag said to Matt as he lit a cigarette.

"Had a close look at Mr. Whitehorns," Matt said, "but I never got a shot. You get one yet?"

"Nope, but I seen Mr. Whitehorns a couple days ago," Snag said. "So I'm still in the hunt." The lit end of the cigarette in Snag's mouth bobbed up and down as he talked. He raised his eyebrows and smiled at Matt with the cigarette still wedged in the corner of his mouth, while with his hands he was using a rusty can opener to open a can of tuna. "Somebody's gonna get that big boy wunna these days," he said. The cigarette was still bobbing between his lips, and his eyes were squinting to fend off the cigarette smoke. Then he lifted the top off the tuna can.

Matt knew what was about to happen; he'd seen it a hundred times. Snag picked up a fork that was lying beside an overflowing ashtray. A hammer, a vice grip, several nails, and a couple of empty tuna cans lay nearby. There was still beaver flesh and fat and blood wadded between Snag's fingers, and a half-smoked Camel was still dangling from his mouth when he used the dirty fork to lift a piece of tuna from the can, and then bring it to his mouth. "Wanna bite?" he asked Matt, then smiled to display a row of stained brown teeth.

"No, thanks," Matt said. "Gonna take your brother out for breakfast." The first time Snag had made such an offer he'd actually made Matt a bit queasy. Now that Matt had grown accustomed to all of this, he reveled in these visits and enjoyed stopping by to see just what level of grossness Snag had descended to.

"So, you're keepin' busy then?" Matt asked.

"Oh, shit yes," Snag said, while he chewed the tuna with what was left of his teeth. "If we was any busier there'd hafta be two of me."

"Scary thought," Matt joked, then added, "How's Darrell doing?"

"I think he's on the phone," Snag said without looking.

Matt glanced at the office and saw that Darrell was indeed on the phone and probably would be for a while longer. Darrell had spent his whole life trying on a different persona every so often, hoping to find one that fit. Shakespeare said that all the world was but a stage, and all the men and women merely players. Darrell Velde showed up ready to play a new and different role whenever he tired of the old one. The wandering minstrel had given way to the tormented poet/artist, which was followed by misunderstood genius/intellectual, and now Darrell Velde seemed to envision himself as the eccentric wheeler-dealer, an entrepreneur who was about to corner the market, or strike it rich, or kill the fat hog, by finding a deal that no one else could see. He always had some big deal in the works, but none of them ever amounted to anything.

"OK then," Matt said, "I won't take any more of your time. Say g'bye to Darrell for me, will ya? He looks like he's got another big deal cookin'. And good luck with Mr. Whitehorns."

As Matt turned to leave, Snag asked, "Hey, how's Jane?"

With a shrug of his shoulders, Matt replied, "She's doing OK."

Snag Velde was fond of Jane Kingston. He and Jane had been friends since their first meeting when the Velde boys had moved to town fifteen years earlier. It was sort of a crazy-uncle thing. She'd always smiled and giggled when he did goofy magic tricks, and told bizarre stories about the feathers or rocks or bottle caps or whatever odd things he might pull out of his pockets. Snag seemed to open up and talk to Jane in a way that he couldn't, or wouldn't, with anyone else. He began to make little gifts for her from scraps of rabbit, or fox, or beaver hides, and the gifts gradually evolved into things like exquisite fur mittens and hats.

At first Jane was bothered, really bothered, by the stink and gore at the Shorewood Furist. But because she was fond of Snag she made an effort to get around the awfulness of the place and stop by from time to time and say hello. She'd stroll right past all the grisly messes and ask Snag if he had anything new for her. She saw something kind and gentle in him. The usual crowd in and around the Shorewood Furist was almost exclusively a collection of very scruffy men, so it was strange to see a well-dressed, attractive woman step through the front door of the place. She made a point to openly display her friendship because she knew it meant so much to Snag: Jane Kingston would come to a place like *that* and seek out someone like *him*. But Snag's appearance and personal hygiene issues were impossible to ignore completely. Every so often she was able to make herself give Snag a hug. She felt bad that she couldn't greet him with a hug every time, but sometimes he had small pieces of animals clinging to his forearms and hands. On those days she clung to Matt's arm and made Snag settle for a wave and a smile. Snag loved it either way.

"Well, you say hi for me, and tell her I'm working on something for her," Snag commanded, and he let a grin crease his face.

"Sure thing, Snag," Matt said, as he turned away once more. It was literally a breath of fresh air to step outside after that gray, stinky hell hole. He started his truck and drove half a block to Velde's Taxidermy.

The contrast between the Shorewood Furist and Velde's Taxidermy could not have been more pronounced. When Matt opened the door and let himself into John Velde's place of business he was greeted by the fresh smell of pine boards. The cement floor was immaculate, and the walls were covered with beautiful hunting and fishing trophies: muskie, trout, walleye, pike, and a dozen or so pan fish, along with ducks and grouse and other birds that looked as if they might get up and fly away. One entire wall was covered with magnificent trophy whitetail deer. "Wow," Matt couldn't help thinking to himself. The place seemed empty, and Matt called out, "John! Where are you?"

"Back here. C'mon back!" came a muffled response from the back room. Matt opened a door that connected the showroom to the workroom. That was when the smell of formaldehyde greeted him, though it was not overpowering. The floor in John's work area was, as always, spotless, and the tools of his trade were neatly organized on a long pegboard wall above a long workbench. In the middle of the large work area were three heavy tables, each about eight feet in diameter, and on each table several partially restored taxidermy projects lay waiting for John's skilled hands to finish them.

Back in the far corner, an aging avocado-colored refrigerator and a small yellow oven, both from the 1970s, were at the center of a small kitchenette, the only kitchenette Matt had ever seen in a taxidermy shop.

Two old-fashioned wooden chairs flanked a well-used kitchen table, placed beside a barrel-shaped woodstove.

Next to the yellow oven, on a shelf above a laundry tub that also served as a kitchen sink, John kept several small drinking glasses that had once contained Welch's grape jelly. All the jars featured characters from *The Flintstones* TV show. Next to his Flintstone collection, John kept a visible bottle of J&B scotch, but the J&B was only a decoy for casual visitors. Underneath one of the heavy workbenches, John kept a bottle of Aberlour for medicinal purposes, and for the occasional long philosophical discussions with Matt.

"I'm back here," John said again. He was digging through the contents of a shelf on the back wall of a cluttered closet, and all that Matt could see was his back. "What did you bring me?" he asked.

"A good story," Matt said.

John turned and smiled. "That means you fucked up again, huh? Missed an easy shot . . . fell asleep?" He was handsome, with a square chin, a row of white teeth, and a bit of gray hair showing beneath the felt hat he always wore. John was six feet four inches tall, still broad in the shoulders and narrow in the hips, and his cowboy boots and hat made him look like a giant. As he'd aged he'd grown a bit more bowlegged. When he walked, his movements made it clear that he'd once been a fine athlete.

"Pretty much," Matt replied.

"Was it Mr. Whitehorns?"

"Yup."

"Well, hang in there; you'll get a nice deer with your truck soon enough," John said, as he turned and finished arranging a stack of paint cans. Then he stood up and carefully avoided the cans as he backed out of the closet. "You pissed over the side of your stand again, didn't you?" John asked when he was facing Matt.

"No, but I've told you a million times, that doesn't matter. Deer are curious animals; they're not afraid of some piss in the woods. All the other creatures of the forest piss in the woods."

"Deer have spectacular noses, and they can pick up your scent from a hundred yards away," John groaned. "How many times do I have to tell you about this?"

"Mr. Whitehorns was twenty yards away, and broadside. He didn't care about any piss."

"Well, he's *miles* away now, so you musta fucked something up," John scoffed.

"Yeah, well, if I'd been wearing aftershave, or just washed my clothes in scented laundry detergent, or . . ." Matt gave up. "Why do I argue with you? You don't know shit."

"That's right; what would I know about this stuff? If I wanted to know more about deer hunting I'd naturally ask a fuckin' dentist." John chuckled. He closed the closet door behind him and asked, "Are you ready for coffee, or do you have more stupid shit to say?"

Matt shook his head and turned toward the door. As they walked back through the showroom, heading for their trucks, Matt asked, "How come you don't share a building with Darrell and Snag?" John was locking the front door, and he ignored the question. He knew that Matt was poking at him, searching for a chuckle with the sarcastic comment on the difference between his place and theirs. John never cracked a smile.

"So you stopped by for a chat with my brothers, eh?" John said. "How'd the place look today?"

"Oh . . . 'cept for the pile of dead, skinless beaver carcasses there in the middle of the front room . . . shipshape, like any other business in town!"

John ignored the sarcasm. "Darrell was on the phone, I'll bet, lining up the next big deal?"

"Yeah, looked like a teleconference with a few other movers and shakers in the beaver pelt business," Matt said. He was ready to move the conversation along to something else. "So, what've you been up to these last few days?"

"I was at a sportsman's show in Duluth. Had a booth set up with some of my stuff on display. Trying to drum up some business," John said. "Jeez, I'm getting too old for that dog and pony show. Every Jack Pine Savage that walks past a booth like mine has to stop and tell me a bullshit story about the big deer they killed, or the fish they—"

John stopped in his tracks and pointed a finger at Matt. "Hey!" Wide-eyed, he'd obviously remembered something important or unusual. "Do you remember a woman named Linda . . . Linda . . ." John lowered his eyes and began to search his memory; he'd forgotten the woman's last name. "Linda . . . Linda . . ." he said a few more times, as if he was actually trying to recall the last name she'd given him. "Ah, shit!"

"What did she look like? Was she pretty? Blonde hair?" Matt asked.

"Oh, yeah!" John nodded, suddenly with a very clear memory, at least regarding the way she looked. "She was about this tall . . ." John held his hand at his chin. "Tall, nearly six feet, with blue eyes and blonde hair, real cute. Linda . . . Linda . . . shit!"

"Linda Pike?" Matt asked. He already had a pretty good idea who John was describing.

"No! Maybe? Shit, I don't know. Cute, though," John answered.

"I knew a girl named Linda Pike, back in college. But I don't know her married name."

"Ah, shit. Dammit! She told me her last name, too. Shit!" John groaned.

"So, anyway, get on with it. Why do you ask?" Matt said.

"Well, she walked past my booth with some guy—I s'pose it was her husband—and they took one of my business cards. Then about ten minutes later she came walking by again, this time by herself. And she looked at the card I gave her, and she said she noticed that my card said I was from Pine Rapids. She took a step closer and asked if I actually lived in Pine Rapids. I said yes, and then she asked me if I knew Matt Kingston. And I said 'Hell, yes! He's my best friend, and we grew up together.' So, I asked her how she knew you."

"What did she say?"

"Well, she looked away and she sorta smiled, but not really. Then she said, 'He broke my heart.' Then we talked for a couple minutes and she walked away. She looked kinda sad. So, what's the story there, buddy? You never mentioned her to me."

"Ah, we went out for a short time back at the U, and we broke up," Matt answered. "I hurt her feelings." John's story made him feel bad, and he didn't want to talk or think about Linda Pike. He let John see that much in his eyes.

"You heartbreaker," John teased.

"Let's go get breakfast."

John drew a breath as if he was about to pry for more information about an old girlfriend, but then he then exhaled and shook his head. He knew that Matt would say no more, so he turned and walked toward his truck. "Jump in with me and we'll head over to the Blue Line."

CHAPTER FIVE

The Blue Line Café was actually long gone, having closed down a few years back, after the owner, a crusty old guy named Hans Rhonhovde, died. The building had been purchased by someone from the Twin Cities, so the story around town went, and then remodeled and reopened as an upscale coffee shop. "Damn, I miss Hans," John said when he stepped inside. "This just isn't right."

Hans's Blue Line Café had been a landmark in Pine Rapids for nearly fifty years. It was the iconic small-town café that featured hot black coffee and bacon and eggs in the morning, roast beef with mashed potatoes and brown gravy at lunch, and it catered to a blue-collar crowd. A haze of cigarette smoke and burning bacon grease always hung halfway down from the twelve-foot ceiling. Hans had been a hockey fanatic and every wall had been decorated with black-and-white photos of old hockey players with missing teeth, hockey jerseys, hockey gear, and old newspapers with headlines about long-forgotten hockey games. The booths and tables were made of ancient oak, and the dark-stained wood had acquired a patina along with scars: Names or initials had been carved into the furniture over the years, and a few of the initials had hearts whittled around them. There had been spittoons on the floor, between each booth, until just a few years before Hans died, when the Minnesota Department of Health had forced Hans to remove them. In the front of the café, by the door that opened onto Main Street, had been a glass counter that displayed shotgun shells and fishing reels. Behind that counter was a tank full of live bait: minnows, leeches, and wax worms, and a refrigerator full of night crawlers during the summer months. Every little town had at least one restaurant like Hans's, back in the day.

Both men paused to look around at all the changes when the door had swung shut behind them. The old booths and tables were gone, along with the hockey stuff, the lunch counter, and the grill behind it, where Hans had smoked cigarettes and cooked for two generations.

The Blue Line Café had been gutted and then remodeled with cedar paneling and log tables. The new owner had tried to give it the look of an original, authentic old north woods building. It was nice, but it was an imitation. Hans's Blue Line was the real deal. Now the place just looked like every other coffee shop in northern Minnesota designed to lure tourists. It just wasn't the Blue Line. Its new name was the Human Bean.

"Well, all good things gotta come to an end," Matt commented. "The coffee's pretty good, so they say, and I heard that the woman who bought the place is really nice."

"Yeah, right," John scoffed. "Shit, look at all the fruitcakes in here. Really! Look around. It's a bunch of yuppies staring at their cell phones and iPads, and nobody's talking to anybody. Remember when we used to step in here and the place smelled of bacon, and Copenhagen, and cigarettes, and dishes were clankin', and you could hear the old farts shakin' dice to see who was gonna pay for coffee?" John shook his head and looked around. "Jesus, look at this place. Instead of live bait, which would be useful, now we can come in here and buy a coffee mug with Barbara Streisand on it for chrissakes, or a CD by Yanni, or a tiny little four-dollar bag of chocolate-covered goat turds." He shook his head in disgust and seemed to grow surlier as he stood there.

"Yeah, well," Matt said, "we all knew that when Hans died this place would never be the same. Lighten up. Things change."

They took their places at the end of the line by the coffee brewing area and waited their turn to order, but not very patiently. Matt knew that John had already made up his mind to be unhappy, and that was not likely to change. The muscles in John's face began to twitch when the woman at the front of the line stared up at the menu on the wall behind the counter and struggled with uncertainty for nearly a minute over what she wanted to order. Then she turned and asked her four-year-old daughter what she'd like. The little girl stared at the menu, even though she couldn't read, and changed her mind several times while she stumbled through the process of ordering something. Nearly five minutes passed before the little girl and her mother were finally served.

John was staring a hole into the server working behind the counter when a nicely dressed woman just in front of Matt, who looked like a tourist, which irritated John even more, stepped up and took her turn to order. She knew exactly what she wanted, but it took her thirty seconds to rattle off her detailed instructions for additions and subtractions and variations.

John leaned forward, close to Matt's ear, and said, just loud enough so even the woman on the other side of the counter could hear, "Jesus Christ, NFL quarterbacks are told to keep it simpler that." The woman stiffened but never turned around.

When Matt finally took his place at the front of the line, John stepped around him and said sarcastically, "We'd both like coffee. Just coffee. Do you have *that?*"

The woman who had waited on the other customers, and who was now waiting on them, looked to be about forty-five, maybe younger, and when she turned to look at Matt he was surprised to see a long, jagged scar on her face. He'd noticed something on her face from the back of the line, as they'd been approaching her, and he'd thought maybe it was a lock of hair that she'd allowed to hang down over one eye. But now, up close, he saw it was a scar. A nasty one. Two raised, rosy, parallel lines began on her forehead, maybe an inch above her left eye, though it was hard to tell because her dark hair covered its beginning. Then it ran down over the center of her eye, and extended about three inches below the eye, onto her cheek. She had eye makeup on, but Matt could see that whatever had made that scar had traveled over the eyelid, too. She blinked once, and then once more, and Matt could tell that she had normal vision in the eye, but somewhere along the line she'd had a *very* close call. Her face was pretty, very pretty, but that scar was like a grease stain on a clean shirt: it called your attention away from everything else.

"What size?" the lady said to John. She'd clearly picked up on the angst in John's voice but chosen not to acknowledge it.

Matt stared at her face while she locked eyes with John. She must be the new owner, Matt thought. There was a hardness about her; she was a woman who knew how to *work*, how to survive. The scar? It had to be from a chain saw. What a horrific accident that must have been, Matt thought.

"Large," John answered, as if it was dare.

"Anything else?" the woman asked.

"Yeah, two eggs, hash browns, bacon, and some pancakes," John said in the form of a challenge. He knew he couldn't get a traditional breakfast here, and he was just trying in his own twisted way to confront the changes he didn't like.

"We don't have that," the woman replied calmly, staring back at John with no smile.

"OK then, I'll just have one of these dried-up, crusty little dough balls that stick in your throat," John said.

"A blueberry scone?" she said calmly, showing impressive restraint at John's sarcastic commentary as she reached into the bakery counter. "And you, sir?" she said to Matt.

"I'll have a scone, too," Matt said. While they waited for their coffee, John noticed a pudgy kid behind the counter and picked up on the boy's look immediately. The kid was wearing tight black pants and a black T-shirt. His hair was cut close to the scalp in several places, and several other places featured five-inch tufts of black hair that had been spiked into horn-like projections with hair spray. He wore two different-colored canvas tennis shoes and had a handful of studs and rings piercing his face.

"Hey, Hardware Hank! Nice look you got going there. Do you ever have refrigerator magnets fly over and stick to that?" John slapped the palm of his hand against the side of his own face and stared at the boy.

"Not yet," the kid replied, also with impressive restraint.

Matt cringed, as he'd done for most of his life when John Velde chose to do things like this. "I'm sorry, Miss," he said to the woman who was making their coffee, "but my friend here is just an asshole." He paid her for the coffee and scones, then added, "I don't think he has any control over the stupid things he says. Hell, he's my best friend and I don't even like him." Then he shrugged and grimaced at John, and added, "What's wrong with you?"

"It's all right," said the woman behind the counter. "I spit in his coffee—this one." She marked one of the coffees with an X, then walked away.

John stared at Matt for a second. Then a smile spread over his face, a bizarre look of approval. He reached into his pocket, pulled out a twenty-dollar bill, and waited until the woman with the scar looked back at him before he winked at her and put the twenty in her tip jar.

"Do you have to be a prick to everyone?" Matt said when they'd found an empty table.

"Well, it's what I do." Then John added softly, "Did you notice that scar?"

"Hard to miss, wasn't it?" Matt said without looking away from their coffees, then he took the lid off his cup and squinted at John. The stupidity of his question went unspoken.

"I wonder how that happened," John said with a bite of scone in his mouth.

"Had to be a chain saw, by the look of it. Lucky girl, though, I bet it coulda been much worse."

"Yeah, but it's kinda hard to look at that scar and say 'Lucky Girl,' isn't it?"

"Hmph." Matt nodded. "She's actually pretty, too."

"I thought so too," John said. He glanced over his shoulder at the woman once more. "When she turned around to get our coffee I noticed that she had a nice caboose, too."

Matt changed the subject. "I went to Alvie's funeral yesterday."

John took a sip of his coffee but said nothing.

"And you should have been there, John."

"He was a dick. He kicked me off the team. Twice!" John blew on his coffee.

"He caught you smoking in the locker room. Twice! You moron. What was he supposed to do?" Matt squinted as if he was looking at a bright light.

John smiled. He knew Matt was right; he just said things like that to see how Matt would respond. He knew he'd done some stupid things, plenty of them, and he knew that Alvie had only done what integrity required of him: suspend his best player. John Velde had always done stupid, senseless things, things that would derail other men. But at every turn John just found another set of tracks and went on his way again.

"See anybody else?" John asked.

"Fogal and Saathe." At this, both Matt and John broke into huge smiles. The memory of one particular stunt by John always brought a laugh, even now, more than fifty years later. As fourth-graders, marching down the hall of Riverside Elementary School on the way to a scheduled bathroom break, John had announced that he could piss farther than Fogal, or Saathe, or Matt, or anyone else, for that matter. Shortly, the four boys were all lined up, shoulder to shoulder, at a set of little urinals when John said, "GO!" and they all started pissing and backing up. All four streams of piss were quite impressive, and the boys were backing up and giggling loudly while the other boys in class cheered . . . right up until a dark and malevolent presence appeared in the doorway to the boys' room. Miss Bureson, the principal of Riverside Elementary School, had been drawn there by the commotion, and now she stood there glaring, with her arms crossed. Their matronly, softhearted teacher, Mrs. Helegas, had always just stood in the doorway and scolded them from the hallway, but had never rushed in when they'd misbehaved in the past. But Miss Bureson had no problem with bursting into the boys' bathroom.

"Remember her? Miss Bureson, I mean," Matt asked, as his grin widened.

"Sure, she was just under seven feet tall, with those great big snow-cone tits, the kind that might poke someone's eye out if they bumped into her in the hallway," John said. Clearly, he still held on to some hard feelings for Miss Bureson. "Her back was ramrod straight and she walked liked a Nazi storm trooper. That's how she always looked at us, too; peering down at us, over those gargantuan knockers, and scowling. She was just trying to scare us. Frau Bureson."

"Worked for me! I had nightmares about her for years after our days at Riverside," Matt laughed.

Both men sipped their coffee and remembered the incident. The other boys in the pissing contest saw her glaring at them immediately after she burst in, and while they recoiled in horror they worked frantically to stop peeing and zip up, lest a girl, albeit their ninety-year-old principal/storm trooper Miss Bureson, see their peckers. But John had not noticed Frau Bureson. He was still backing up and smiling at the others and nodding his head in approval of his own magnificent stream of piss when she grabbed him by his ear and began to twist. Miss Bureson was angry, and out to make a point. She had John Velde, Riverside Elementary's king of bravado, in a compromised position. He was careening around trying to free himself from her grasp, but his stream of piss was out of control and he was spraying urine on Fogal and Saathe and Matt while he struggled to stop the stream and zip his pecker back in his pants just like the others. Every mortified little boy in the bathroom that day was weighing one horrible reality against the other: Was it worse that Miss Bureson had seen their peckers, or that John Velde had just sprayed piss on them?

Now, John and Matt both leaned back in their chairs and laughed out loud. "Miss Bureson never trusted us again after that," John said through his own laughter.

"Imagine that?" Matt sighed. "Remember how she always came in the bathroom with us after that and stood there with her arms crossed and scowled while we peed?"

"She just wanted another look at my dong," John said.

"Yeah, right." Matt wiped one last tear of laughter from the corner of his eye.

"Did you see anybody else yesterday?" John asked.

"Pigeon Tits . . . Monkey Lips . . . Clown Hair Shinder." Matt shrugged, then began to grin. "No one asked about you, though."

John returned the grin. He sipped at his coffee and asked, "Jeez, Clown Hair was a shitty coach. I used to do things just to piss him off at practice. How 'bout Mo? Did you see Mo?"

Matt leaned back and nodded, still smiling. "Yup."

"How'd she look? Is she still as pretty as she once was?"

"Prettier. She married a nice guy and it looked like they've had a great life."

John knew all about Matt's high school romance with Mo Glasnapp, and he saw in Matt's eyes that he was savoring some good memories of her. "So, when we were in high school . . ." John made a circle with his left thumb and index finger, then moved his right index finger through the circle as he asked, "did you two, you know . . ."

"Sorry to disappoint you." Matt grinned and shook his head. "I sure liked her, though." He swirled his empty coffee cup and added, "I guess I'll never see her again, now."

He was about to tell John that his family farm was now gone, wiped from the face of the earth, when John turned away and studied the woman with the scar on her face. "I really don't think that chick spit in my coffee," he said when he turned back toward Matt. Then he changed directions again. "So you saw Mr. Whitehorns. Really?"

"Yeah, that bruiser shows up every so often." Matt was looking down at his coffee cup. He wasn't thinking about Mr. Whitehorns anymore. His hip ached and he shifted his weight in his chair. John picked up on it.

"What's bothering you, buddy?"

"Hip's kinda sore. This muscle I pulled just won't heal. Getting old is the shits."

"Prob'ly no lead in your pencil either, huh?"

"Not what I was getting at, but thanks for your concern," Matt said, and he couldn't help but smile at John. Times like this were a big part of the friendship that held them so close. John was sitting there smirking while he spoke outrageous bullshit. And he knew full well that everything he said was bullshit, and that Matt knew it was bullshit, too. It was Alvie's fault that John decided to smoke a cigarette in the locker room, and Miss Bureson just wanted a look at his dong. Really? There was always an avalanche of bullshit poised to break loose and come rushing down the mountain.

"Just asking," John replied. "And I am sorry about your sexual dysfunction."

Matt ignored the sexual dysfunction thing. "What I was *trying* to say, is that things seem to be getting more difficult, and I always thought that by this point in life things would be getting easier."

"That was fuckin' stupid," John said.

Matt nodded. "Thank you for pointing that out."

"Well, we *are* getting a bit older," John began, "and sure, you look a bit worse than I do, but you're still not so bad. You're married to a smokin' hot woman who thinks the sun rises and sets in your pants. Go on home and give her a ride on the baloney pony!" He turned his palms up and passed an incredulous scowl at Matt.

Matt shook his head.

"Jane doesn't like me, does she," John said, taking the conversation off in yet another new direction.

Matt shrugged. "Nobody likes you. You're a dick."

"No, I'm serious. You're my best friend, and I'm around Jane quite a bit. I can tell she doesn't like me. How come?"

"She likes you just fine, but think about it . . ." Matt considered his words. "My Jane is sort of a straight arrow, and she came from a home where her parents dressed her and her sister up in dresses and white gloves and took 'em to church every Sunday. She has no idea what to make of you. She's never completely certain when you're bullshitting and when you're being sincere. You love to crush her crackers. And she's heard *almost* all of my stories about our school days . . ." Matt stopped and raised his eyebrows. John met his gaze and then nodded, agreeing that those stories might give her reason to worry. "And then there is the issue of your women friends. I mean, if you were Jane, would you want me to hang around with someone like you?" Matt paused, then added, "And she thinks you can be a real dick sometimes."

"I think that hangin' around with me is your only chance for an education," John said. Then he pointed his thumbs at himself and asked, "She thinks I'm a dick?"

"*Everyone* thinks you're a dick. *I* think you're a dick." Matt shrugged. "All my *friends* were busy this morning or I'd be with somebody else right now."

"I'm gonna go get us a couple refills on the coffee," John said. He was smiling as he stood. He'd heard it all before. He knew that Jane liked him. He knew that Matt was a solid friend who loved their ongoing banter. He carried both cups over to the woman at the counter and then returned. When he placed the cups back on the table he pointed to Matt's and said, "I think *that's* the one she spit in."

Matt ignored him, then asked, "So how's *your* love life? I haven't talked to you in a while; maybe that special girl you've been waiting for has finally been released from prison, or maybe she's graduated from junior high school? Is there someone new in your life since I saw you last? Maybe you're ready to settle down and get married?"

"Nah." John sighed. It was his turn again, and he was about to explain one of the cornerstones of his credo. As usual, Matt had made it easy for John; he'd set a concept on the edge of a mountain, and John was about to give it a shove. John leaned back in his chair and shrugged. "Women are like buses . . ." The avalanche of bullshit was about to come rolling down the mountain.

"How's that?" Matt knew that John was about to pontificate on the nature of love in the same way that a college professor might solve a difficult calculus problem in front of his class.

"Well, if you miss the one you want, just wait about five minutes and there'll be another one coming, just like it," John replied.

"Oh? You don't think you'll ever find someone you want to be with forever?"

"I have lady friends, lots of them. Got one in Fargo, got one in Detroit Lakes, got one in Duluth, got a couple of 'em right around Pine Rapids. Why would I want to have just one?" John asked. "Why would I want to limit myself to one woman? Why would I want to be saddled with the expectations and baggage of *one* woman when I could enjoy the affections of *many*?"

"Yeah, I guess you do have a point there," Matt said. He hadn't seen it coming, but John's words had triggered a moment of introspection. He looked at his coffee and thought for a moment before he replied. "You know, there was a time, back in college, when I thought that was true. Well, I never really *thought* about it; I just assumed it was true, and I suppose I thought that's the way my life would be; you know, many women, like you just said. But then I met Jane, and I was never interested in anyone else. Ever. There was just this great connection. I wasn't looking for it, it just appeared. I think that connection is what people have been writing songs about for a thousand years."

"Ah, OK, I know what you mean about you and Jane; she's special. I'll give you that. But men, real men, don't have women friends. That's what we have men for," John said with absolute certainty. He furrowed his brow to mock Matt for asking such a stupid question.

"I have women friends," Matt objected.

"No you don't."

"Sure I do. I have Donna, my office manager, and Tammy, my assistant, and the hygienists, and—"

"They're not your friends," John interrupted.

"Sure they are."

"Ever go fishin' with 'em?" John asked.

"No."

"Ever get drunk with 'em?"

"No."

"Ever think to yourself, 'Jeez, I think I'll go over to Donna's house or Tammy's house and talk about shit that's bothering me, or borrow some tools, or a gun?'"

"No."

"They're not your friends. They're just people you know. It's not the same."

"OK, let's leave normal people, like me, out of this conversation," Matt conceded. "Don't you think maybe someday one of these princesses might emerge from the primordial ooze of your love life, and you'll love her and want to be with her all the time?" Matt was pushing, giving John another chance to expound.

"That's just stupid." John shook his head in disgust. "Lemme explain something to you."

"Please do. Should I be taking notes?"

"No one wants to be with the same woman forever. It's not normal."

Matt squinted, as if John had just thrown sand in his eyes. "I do. I love my Jane so much . . ." Matt put his hand over his heart and raised his eyebrows.

"I told you, you and Jane are different, and I'm actually *not* tryin' to be a dick here—"

"I think you're trying to be a dick," Matt interrupted.

"No, I'm explaining a cosmic truth," John said, still clinging to a scholarly facade. "You're just the exception that proves the rule."

"Like someone would turn to *you* for cosmic truth and relationship counseling?" Matt chuckled.

"Damn right!" John shot back. "I've been married once, and I've had *dozens*, no *hundreds*, of *other* successful relationships, too! I know about this shit."

"Good one. Continue."

"OK, when I was young I mighta made a few shaky moves, I'll give you that." John was enjoying the delivery of his own verbal manifesto. "But I figured something out a long time ago, and I decided I was gonna suck the marrow out of this life."

"Well, can you tell me where to find the marrow, in case I'd like to do some sucking myself?"

"I sure as hell can, but I don't know if you're ready to hear it." John said, working hard to hide the shit-eating grin.

"Try me."

"All right, but don't talk, just listen. I know you. I've known you my whole life. You've always been my friend; you've always been there for me. When no one else was there, you were. And when we were young I thought you knew everything. I thought you had all the answers. But you don't." John paused and for emphasis he nodded approval of what he'd just said. "You listened to that romantic bullshit everyone pushed on us. You know, that shit about how people in fairy tales all live 'Happily Ever After,' and the shit about old couples being in love for fifty and sixty years, until one of them croaks. That shit *never* happens."

John folded his hands and leaned forward so that only Matt could hear him. "The marrow of life is a *time*, not a place, and it's found in that moment between when a woman looks at you—you know the look; their eyes are asking you to come a bit closer and maybe talk—and the time she moves in with you. The period between those two moments; *that's* the marrow of life." He spoke as if he were explaining a complex math problem again.

"Oh, really?" Matt let sarcasm ooze out with each word.

"Really!" John replied with conviction. Then he seemed to remember something important and quickly amended his affirmation. "Well, except for fishing and hunting, but that's a whole 'nother story." He took a sip of coffee and nodded at the obvious truth in his own words, then he continued. "OK now, think about it. That's when every little conversation carries the hint that another will follow, and you start to have that little twitch in your belly when you see her. That's the time when she first touches your hand and lets you feel the suggestion that she'd like more. That's the time for the first kiss, and a lot of other firsts. You can't keep your hands off each other. The things you talk about are exciting and clever. The sex is fantastic." John paused.

"And then she moves in . . ." John's voice lowered and he slumped his shoulders. ". . . and starts trying to fix you. Now she's got a headache every night, and she's got a list of shit for you to do, and she wants you to knock shit off—like fishing and hunting and softball and all kinds of other shit that didn't seem to bother her before she moved in. She needs to run the vacuum while you're watching football, and there always seems be a bag of garbage that really needs to be taken out, right now." John paused. "Voila! The marrow has been sucked out! It's time to hop on another bus. Sorry for mixing my metaphors there."

"You mean you really don't think anybody stays in love forever?" Matt asked.

"Hell no! You mean that bullshit they hand us about old people having a loving friendship and taking care of each other until death does them part, or some such nonsense?"

"Yeah, that's what I mean," Matt said.

"Ah, that's just fear, fear of being alone. And it gets twisted around into something that sounds better: love and enduring commitment? What a crock of shit! Hell, we all know people, lots of people, who spent their whole life living with someone they didn't even like, just because they were afraid to be alone. It's like walking past a cemetery late at night; if you're all alone it's kinda scary, but if you have somebody, anybody, with you it's not so scary anymore. It's not love, buddy. It's fear."

Matt stared at him.

"Hey, I know it's a lot to get your head around all at once, but don't worry; I'm here for you," John said.

"That's truly comforting." Matt pushed his chair back and stood up to leave. "And I'll think about—" He dropped back almost to his seat and winced in pain.

"Whatsamatter?" John said as he lurched to catch Matt.

"Ah, shit, my hip. It never gets any better. I just can't sit here any longer. Let's go. I promised Jane I'd take her ice fishing today. I gotta go."

"She *is* the exception that proves the rule," John said as he straightened up. "And she has that one special quality that I know you were looking for in a woman."

"What's that?"

"Low standards."

"Well, you'd know about *that*," Matt fired back.

"She *is* amazing," John said. "I mean, she's so pretty, and smart. And then I picture her pulling crappies through a hole in the ice, and drinking brandy from a flask?" He said this as if he'd asked himself a riddle.

Matt nodded. "Yeah, who'd a thunk it? She's a fisherman. She loves it."

CHAPTER SIX

Low-hanging gray clouds had preceded the cold wave that swept across the north, and now every tree for miles was coated with hoarfrost. A half inch of white frost covered every tree and bush in the forest. This afternoon, under the gloomy canopy of winter clouds, the only colors in the world were white and gray.

The frozen surface of Scotch Lake was calm and windless as Matt's ATV rolled along toward their favorite fishing hole. Jane rode behind him with her arms around his waist, as if they were crossing the Great Plains on a Harley, and behind them they pulled a sled bearing a collapsible shelter and fishing gear.

When they arrived at their destination, Matt would extend a couple of aluminum tent poles and pull the insulated tent over the top of the sled. He'd use a small, gas-powered auger to punch two holes through the ice, move the sled and tent over the two holes, and they'd each have a place to fish that was cozy and protected from the wind.

While they crossed a large expanse of ice, Jane put her mouth close to his ear and asked, "How thick is the ice?"

Matt had to raise his voice to be heard over the motor noise of the ATV. "'Bout ten inches, but getting thicker by the hour!"

"Good!" she shouted back. "But it still makes me nervous to drive out here like this! I don't think I'll ever get used to it!" Then she asked, "Where are we headed?"

"The Flemish Cap!" Matt replied. He didn't need to look; he knew that Jane would be smiling at that reference. Several years earlier they'd discovered a productive winter fishing hole that was as far away from their home as any place on Scotch Lake could be, and she'd borrowed "The Flemish Cap" from the movie *The Perfect Storm* precisely because it was so far from home. Unlike most women that Matt had known, Jane could refer to and quote from "guy movies."

Two years earlier she'd been fishing with Matt one frigid winter morning. After she'd pulled a fine walleye through the ice, she'd turned to him and said, in the most gravelly voice she could muster, "God help me, I do love it so . . ." When Matt had turned to her for clarification she'd explained, "George C. Scott. *Patton*."

"OK, let's try right here," Matt said when the ATV rolled to a stop. Jane's face was bundled with a red scarf and she wore a baby blue bomber hat with white rabbit fur on the ear flaps and brim. She wore a bulky black snowmobile suit and heavy pack boots that made her movements clumsy. Matt was dressed in camouflage hunting pants and a camouflage parka as he dismounted the ATV and reached for the ice auger in the sled.

After two quick pulls on the rope start, the auger barked to life and Matt drilled several small holes, each about thirty feet apart, as quickly as he could. As soon as he'd lifted the auger from the first hole Jane used a large ladle to clear away the crushed ice remaining in the hole, and then placed the transducer from a sonar depth flasher into the hole.

"Nice work, honey! We got fish right here!" she called out.

A moment later Matt had moved the sled beside the hole Jane had cleaned, then he used the auger to punch a second hole about three feet away from it. While Jane cleared the ice chips away from that hole, Matt raised the insulated tent over them and extended the tent poles.

Ten minutes later they both were sitting comfortably, elbows resting on their knees, on seats that were fixed to the sled, and they'd lowered their fishing lines into the holes.

"I put a minnow on mine, but I used a wax worm on yours," Matt said. He didn't need to explain any more than that to her. Over the years, Jane had learned that the plan was always for each of them to try a different bait when they first arrived, and if one them started catching fish, they'd both switch to whatever bait was working.

They both stared at the depth flasher now, which told them that the water was fifteen feet deep, there were fish moving about on the bottom, and that their bait was suspended at about ten feet. "OK, we have some movement already," Matt said, and they both watched a red, flashing mark on the screen, which they knew was a fish, begin to rise from the bottom, toward the green flashing mark, which they knew was Matt's bait. "He's gonna take it . . . right . . . now!" Matt said, as he lifted the short fishing rod, which bent in half at the weight of the crappie on the other end of the line.

"Nice one," Jane said, when Matt lifted the crappie through the hole. "Jeez, it's huge." Matt tossed the crappie into a five-gallon bucket, then he quickly re-rigged with a new minnow and dropped his line back down the hole. They both knew that crappies moved in schools, and when they moved through, under your hole, you needed to get your bait in front of them as quickly as you could, before they moved on. Sometimes they stayed close to you for an hour, sometimes five minutes, and you never knew when they'd move away or return.

When Matt looked to his left he saw that Jane was hurriedly changing bait. She pulled the tiny wax worm off her hook and then plunged a bare hand into the icy water of the minnow bucket in search of a minnow. Seconds later she'd run the hook through the flapping minnow and then lowered it through the ice.

Jane hadn't noticed that Matt was watching her, and while he witnessed the stone-cold look of a killer in her eyes, he couldn't help but smile at the memory of her transformation from a city girl to a hard-core fisherman.

Shortly after they'd married, Jane had made a conscious effort to immerse herself into the culture of the north, and one of the corner-stones of the culture was fishing. On a spring morning, several decades earlier, Jane had asked Matt if he'd take her fishing, and of course he was happy to oblige. He told her to get a hat and some polarized sunglasses and meet him by the boat dock in ten minutes. He was sitting in his little green duck boat, waiting for her, when she strode onto the dock, and he'd never forget the way she looked. She wore a long blonde ponytail through the back of her baseball cap, an old plaid shirt of his, and blue jeans. He marveled then, and quite often since then, how a woman wear-ing a ball cap and an oversized shirt could look so sexy. But the thing he noticed more than anything else that day was that she was also wearing two leather gloves, the kind of heavy cowhide gloves he'd wear to handle rough lumber, or do yard work.

"Are your hands cold?" he'd asked.

"No."

"So why the gloves?"

"For touching fish," she explained, as if he'd asked a stupid question.

"OK," Matt had said, "jump in and we'll go see if we can find 'em."

They fished together for several hours, and had a delightful day on the water. While they fished they also discovered what all fishing buddies do:

that it was a great place to just talk. They talked about her job at the clinic and his dental practice. They talked about life in Pine Rapids. They talked about life in general—all the things friends talk about when they're fishing. Jane discovered that she loved to be on the water; the clean air, the greens and blues of the forest and the sky and the lake made her happy. Matt loved what he saw in Jane's eyes, too, and he was pleased to share a lifetime of glorified fishing stories and anecdotes, some of them outright fabrications, with her.

Gradually, as that day wore on, Jane began to touch the fish she caught. At least she tried. When she caught a fish, and she caught plenty, she held her fishing line with one hand, the fish dangling there and waiting to have a hook removed from its mouth, and stared at the fish while she summoned the courage to actually grab the fish with her other hand. Each time she reached for a fish, it would naturally flop a bit when she touched it, which frightened her, and her gloved hand would flinch away as if she'd just grabbed a live wire, throbbing with electricity. Eventually, after dozens of aborted attempts, she was able to hold the crappies and sunfish and walleyes in her gloved hands and remove the hooks.

Several days later she asked to go again. This time she arrived at the dock wearing a glove on only one hand.

"A tribute to Michael Jackson?" Matt asked.

"Shut up and take me fishing."

Several days later she walked onto the dock wearing a pair of latex gloves—still protecting herself from the fish, but with less armor. Matt smiled, but said nothing; she seemed to be easing herself away from her queasiness about touching fish. Also, on that third day, she'd asked about the minnows, and put one on a hook all by herself, aided, of course, by the security of the latex gloves. She'd also asked Matt about the wax worms, which he explained were simply grubs, or maggots, which fish liked to eat. No wax worms were handled that day, but she studied them, and watched to see that they did not attack Matt when he handled them.

One week later she'd weaned herself down to one latex glove. A week after that she handled her own bait, removed hooks from fish she'd caught, and did it all with bare hands. Matt knew that her metamorphosis to a fisherman was complete on a day shortly after that, when, as she kissed him goodbye on his way to work, she asked, "So, are we using minnows or wax worms tonight?" as if the answer mattered to her.

Now, on this dark winter day she sat beside him on a foot of ice and watched an electronic flasher for signs of fish. The inside of the little shelter was dark and smelled like the mice that made their home in it during the summer months in storage had used it for a urinal. A five-gallon bucket sat near Matt's right foot. It contained a couple of spare fishing rods, each about eighteen inches long, several small tackle boxes, pliers, a flashlight, and something else that Matt had packed along just before they left home. "Would you like a little shot of something to warm you up?" he asked.

Without looking over at him, Jane replied, "Don't you ever think about anything but sex?"

"I was thinking of my flask, it's full of brandy. *You're* the pervert. Sheesh!"

"Oh, sorry." Jane smiled. "Sure, I'd have a snort, but the question still stands." She took a swig from the flask and handed it back.

Just then the lake underneath them gurgled several times, then moaned. A second later, a far-off rumble began and then roared toward them. The ice under their feet shuddered and heaved and sent what felt like a cannon blast up through their boots. Jane flinched at the sound of Scotch Lake making more ice, then snatched the flask from Matt once more. "I need another shot," she said, and then she returned it to him again. "That scares me every time."

"It's awesome," Matt said.

"Still scares me. It feels like the ice is gonna open up and swallow me."

While he was screwing the cap back on the flask, Jane put her arm around Matt's shoulder and pulled him close for a kiss. Their winter clothing carried the faint scent of mothballs, which blended nicely with the mouse piss and dead minnows to yield a unique bouquet. But the softness of Jane's lips, and the warm sweet taste of brandy on them, and the fact that she loved to be here like this, and the way she reached over and pulled *him* close when she wanted a kiss . . . only Jane Monahan could make a moment like this feel sexy.

"You taste good," Matt whispered. "I love you."

"I'd never heard of a lake making noise until I met you and came here," she said while her lips were still close to his. "It's awesome, though, almost as good as seeing the White Horses run." She kissed him again and then made sure he looked into her eyes before she added, "I love you, too."

White Horses had become an insider thing for them, a reference to a phenomenon whose meaning was known only to a few people. Many years earlier Matt's classmate in dental school, Grant Thorson, had given the label of "White Horses" to the morning fog that sometimes appeared on northern lakes—the white clouds caused when warm vapors from the lake rose into the cool morning air and condensed into fog. When the fog tumbled off the lake, driven by a morning breeze, the White Horses were running. Matt and Jane had always felt that the appearance of White Horses held a mystical promise of happiness.

"I love you more," Matt said. Then he leaned closer, requesting another kiss, and when she'd brought her lips close again he said, "I've been think-ing that maybe all that noise coming from down below, in the lake, is just that big ol' herd of White Horses rumbling around beneath the ice, trying to get out. You know, like all the good times of summer are locked away for a while.

"Ooh, good one!" Jane said. "I like that! We're gonna go with that." She nodded with satisfaction and softly repeated, "White Horses . . . that's good."

"Would you say that it turned you on?" Matt asked with twisted grin.

"Well, actually, it did. You're sort of a renaissance man, aren't you?" She thought for a minute, then added, "Ever do it in a fish house?"

"With who? John Velde?" Matt frowned.

"Well, it was more of a rhetorical question," Jane said, "maybe even a proposition." She flicked her eyebrows and grinned. Jane had been raised in a conservative home and was pretty innocent when she'd met Matt back in college. But an extraordinarily playful sense of humor had been lying dormant until her romance with Matt had allowed it to blossom.

Matt pursed his lips and looked at her. He let her see his eyes move about the little shelter and made it clear to her that was calculating the possibilities of a sexual experience. "Well, you know your feet might get cold if—"

"Ooh! Fish on!" Jane reacted to the sudden strike of a crappie. Her fishing rod bent in half and Matt saw her excitement as she reeled the fish up through the hole in the ice.

A school of crappies had moved in and was parked under them. The action was steady for the next few minutes, and by the time the school meandered away they'd caught enough fish for several meals. Ten keepers, all about twelve inches long, lay in a five-gallon bucket at their feet.

The frenzy ended just as suddenly as it had begun. The crappies had just swum away slowly, to some other place. Matt and Jane sat together, side by side, and watched their electronic depth flashers for several minutes. The screens on their sonar flashers were blank now, and the sudden inactivity told them the bite was over, at least until another school came along.

"You still wanna fool around?" Matt asked, his elbows resting on his knees while he leaned forward and watched for signs of returning crappies on his depth flasher. "We seem to have some time."

"No." Jane leaned back, hurriedly unzipped her snowmobile suit, threw off her hat, and began fanning herself. "I'm having a hot flash now."

Matt made no reply. He reached down to the ice, picked up the flask of brandy, and took a swig. When Jane's hot flash had passed and she'd zipped her suit closed and replaced her hat, Matt held the flask out to her.

"Thanks," she said when she twisted the top onto the flask. She gave the flask back to Matt and stared at the ice under her feet for a second. "Hey," she said with surprise, "my hole is frozen shut."

Matt said nothing, but he turned slowly toward her and let her see the grin creasing his face. "Maybe I can help you?" he suggested.

"Well . . . I didn't mean . . ." Jane giggled. "Shut up."

CHAPTER SEVEN

Matt spent an hour cleaning the bucketful of big crappies on a plywood plank in the garage. His hands were cold and stiff and sore when he stepped into the shower afterward, but after several minutes in there, he felt much better. He stood with his head under the nozzle, leaning against the wall of the shower stall, and let a torrent of hot water break over his head and back. While a cloud of steam filled the bathroom, he let himself luxuriate in the steamy vapors and think about what lay ahead of him tonight.

A few minutes earlier, while he'd been washing the crappie fillets in the kitchen sink, he'd seen Jane twist a corkscrew into a twenty-dollar bottle of Merlot, and then heard the little pop when she pulled the cork. He knew she'd be sitting on the couch, bare feet resting on the coffee table, wearing her softest pink fleece outfit, and sipping wine when he stepped out of the shower. After dinner they'd drink some wine, sit by the fire and talk for a couple of hours, and they'd make love.

He dried himself with a towel and used his bare hand to wipe some steam off the bathroom mirror so he could see to brush his teeth. While he was squeezing toothpaste onto his toothbrush he began to daydream about how she'd look later tonight when she was holding him in a lover's embrace. The little movie projector in his head was busy again, just as it had been the night before, but for now there were only X-rated videos. He brushed his teeth and put on some blue jeans and a gray sweatshirt.

When he reached for the knob on the bathroom door, he heard her talking on the phone. He listened for a moment, trying to figure out who was on the other end of the call. Matt opened the door and walked quietly into the great room. Jane's voice was soft and familiar; she was talking to her sister, and she *was* sitting on the leather couch nearest to the fireplace, with her feet up on the cribbage board/coffee table, with a glass of wine in her hand. When she noticed that Matt was watching her she raised the nearly empty glass and raised her eyebrows, asking him to get the bottle and pour some more for her.

He nodded that he understood. After he'd poured a refill he put on a pair of slippers and went outside to start a fire and get the oil hot so he could cook the crappie fillets when she was ready to eat. Then he set the table and dimmed the kitchen lights. It would be a nice little private dinner for two. And then . . .

When he came back inside he warmed his hands by rubbing them together for a few seconds. Then he poured himself a glass of wine and sat down at the kitchen table. What he could hear of the conversation indicated that she was trying to buoy her sister's spirits.

He sipped at his wine and flipped through a hunting magazine while he waited for the call to end. She was far enough away that he could only make out a few words now and then.

Finally, he heard her say goodbye. A second later she called out, "Matt, c'mere! And bring the wine, will you?"

He rose quickly, grabbed the wine bottle, walked to the great room, and plopped down on the couch, next to her. "It's nice to be home," she said as her eyes moved over him. "I missed you." Then she kissed him.

"Who was on the phone?" he asked.

"Nancy."

"Sounded kinda serious. Weren't you just with her, for two days?" He tried to show the irritation he felt: How could she spend the previous two days with her sister and come home and talk to her for another hour?

"Yeah, she's going through a hard time. You know her divorce has been really ugly."

"That's too bad," Matt allowed, "but I thought you just spent most of last week talking about her bad marriage, didn't you?"

"Yeah, that and other things," Jane said. "What's for supper?"

"Crappie fillets! Sort of a shore lunch, but without the mosquitos and wood smoke," he said with a smile.

"What else are we gonna have with the fillets?"

"Well, for dessert, I'm gonna have you," he replied.

Her phone rang as Matt spoke, and when she reached to pick it up Matt saw that the call was coming from Meghan, her sister Nancy's best friend.

"Maybe . . ." Jane said, and with that she turned away and pretty much dismissed Matt for the time being. She was obviously more concerned with Meghan's call than with what he wanted for dessert. They'd been married for a long time, and he sensed that this might be another long phone call.

"I'll go check on the oil, see if it's hot yet. But I won't put the fish on until you're off the phone. It'll only take about four minutes, so lemme know when you're done," Matt said with a sigh.

Jane nodded, but she was listening to Meghan, and not him. Uh-oh, Matt thought. He'd been down this road many other times. Here they were, home alone with a bottle of wine, and she'd been in such a good mood, but a depressing conversation with her friend just might ruin that.

Matt shook his head and walked away. Men were always in the mood, but women were a bit more unpredictable.

He sat by himself at the kitchen table for twenty minutes and listened to her talk to Meghan. There was a bit of laughter, but most of the time she spoke softly, seriously. Finally, he heard her say, "OK, goodbye." And when she'd been silent for a while he was pretty sure that the evening phone calls were through, and she was ready to eat with him.

He cracked an egg, placed it in a shallow bowl, and whipped it with a fork. Then he placed the crappie fillets, one at a time, into the egg and swirled them about. He dropped each fillet into a plastic bag containing his mother's secret recipe for fish batter, then lowered the fillets individually into a vat of very hot oil. The fillets crackled and the oil bubbled and the kitchen smelled like so many shore lunches from his past. For a fisherman, there was no treat like this: fresh crappie fillets coated in his secret batter, and deep fried in oil.

But when he lifted the wire basket containing the golden fillets from the gurgling cauldron of boiling oil, the cooking noise subsided and he could hear her talking on the phone again. Someone *else* had called.

"Crappies are done!" he called to her from the kitchen. Surely she'd tell whoever was on the phone that she had to go. He looked at the fillets, still sizzling on a plate, and stole a taste. They would never taste better than in the next few minutes, and the sweet flesh, along with his mother's crisp batter, was superb.

"Crappies are done! And they're really good!" he called again.

He picked at the fillet he'd already sampled, and poured himself some wine while he waited. But Jane continued to laugh and chat with whoever was on the phone.

His disappointment deepened; she was making him eat alone so she could talk on the phone. She had no idea how much this little meal, this evening, meant to him. This delicacy, this prize he planned to share with her, would grow cold on the kitchen table while Jane talked on the phone with . . . who? Her sister who she'd just spent a few days talking to, or her sister's friend, or some other asshole who should be told to call back some other time?

He took another bite and let the rich flavor roll over his tongue before he swallowed, and his appetite began to wane. An empty feeling rose inside him while waited, and he hoped she'd come soon.

Twenty minutes later the insult was complete. He stepped away from the table and opened the freezer, then the liquor cabinet. The clinking of the ice cubes made an angry sound inside the highball glass, and he covered them with Cutty Sark before he carried the cold plate of crappies into the great room.

Jane was still talking to Meghan, or Nancy, or whoever it was now, when he set the plate of crappies on the couch beside her and walked away. He went directly to the small den which he used as his private office when he was at home. A red plaid couch and brown plaid recliner had been stuffed into the cozy little room. When he raised the footrest on the recliner his feet were so close to the TV on the opposite wall that he had to move them apart so he could see the screen. "Jesus, didn't you just spend a week out there talking to these same women about this same shit?" he grumbled to himself.

He found the station that carried Gopher hockey and pretended to watch the game while he fumed. By the end of the second period, Matt had thought of nothing but his anger toward Jane. He'd been watching a team dressed in maroon and gold and a team dressed in red and white dash around a hockey rink for almost forty minutes, but he didn't know the score when he stood up and walked back out to the great room.

Jane was *still* on the phone with somebody! Unbelievable, Matt thought. He briefly considered some sort of nonverbal communication, like stomping his feet or breaking something in order to show her how angry he was. Even after a tall scotch, that seemed a bit too adolescent, so he tried to let the feeling go. But when he passed by the couch and the fireplace he saw that the fish had gone untouched since he'd left the room. The fillets were stone cold now. That did it.

He walked to the coffee table in front of Jane and picked up the plate with the cold fish. Then he walked to the kitchen and scraped it into the garbage. The sight of that beautiful fish now sitting on top of coffee grounds and a banana peel made him even angrier. Since he was already in the kitchen he decided to make himself another scotch, a *really* tall one, and then finish the evening in his man cave. With the door shut.

He'd wanted, expected, Jane to share this night with him, not some blubbering bitches. He wanted it to be special, but Jane had given it to someone else; someone less important, well, someone who *should* be less important than he. He'd wanted her to be just as excited about being with him. When he returned to his man room he glared at the little TV but saw only colored uniforms dashing about on a sheet of ice.

Midway through the third period of the hockey game Jane opened the door of his office and stood there for a second. "You threw the fish in the garbage?" she asked, searching for an explanation.

"Well, you pretty much made your point. You let me know where I rank," Matt said from his recliner, without looking up.

"Oh, c'mon, stop your pouting."

She'd made a bad choice of words, thrown a little more gas on the fire, and she knew it immediately.

"Pouting? Are you shitting me?" Matt barked. "I planned to share something special with you tonight. We could have had a *moment*, you know, a fine meal and a glass of wine beside a flickering fire? But you threw it away! And for what?

Jane stood in the narrow doorway and stared.

"Hungry?" he taunted. "Go out and make one of those cardboard pizzas from the gas station. And if you need someone to talk to, well then call one or two of those dented cans you were just talking to. Tell them all about our dinner tonight. They'll be glad to hear about something shitty from your life, too." He paused for a second, but refused to look at her. "You're my best friend, but you made me feel like shit on your shoe tonight."

He turned his face toward the hockey game on TV. "*I'm* the one who loves you," he said. He turned away to look at the TV and added, "Shut the door. I'm busy now."

The door closed while he was looking at the TV, and Jane was gone. Great. Now she was probably more pissed off than he was, he thought.

Maybe he shouldn't have said all those things? But he'd needed to hurt her the way she'd hurt him. Now he felt worse than ever.

Goddammit, why did life have to be like this? Young people who were just finding their way in life should have fights like this, not someone who'd been married for forty years. He wanted to go out there and talk it out with Jane. But if he did that now he was sure to walk right into one of those pissing contests where he got to see the veins in her face stand out while she reminded him of stupid and selfish things he'd done in the past. Shit! He'd just sit here and fume; that would show her a thing or two.

There was a time, not that long ago, when this evening would have gone just as he'd hoped. Jane would have laughed, and flirted, and sought his company. Now, sometimes, actually more and more all the time, he felt as though he came in second, or third, or much lower, on Jane's list of priorities.

Two hours later he lowered the footrest on his recliner and stood up. He had a real fine buzz from all that scotch, and he needed to steady himself a bit. He didn't remember, or care, who'd won the hockey game, and he'd tried, unsuccessfully, to get interested in a couple of old movies. But the incident with Jane had bothered him all evening. He wanted to make peace, but he supposed he was ready to drop the gloves and argue if that's what she wanted. No, he just wanted his best friend back. "Aw, shit," he mumbled when he stood straight, "I didn't want this to happen."

It had been quiet in the great room ever since Jane had closed door, and Matt wondered what he'd find when he opened the door and stepped out of his office. He turned the doorknob slowly and peeked around the edge of the door. Jane was still sitting by the fire, but she was reading now, still wearing the pink fleece. When Matt came to the foot of the couch he stood still for a minute, and Jane put her book down.

"You were right," she said softly.

"I was?" Matt muttered, and tried to blink himself out of a drunken fog.

"Yes, and I'm sorry." She patted the palm of her hand on the cushion next to her in an invitation for Matt to come and sit beside her.

"Really?" Matt was incredulous. This never happened; the argument was over and she wasn't angry. She'd said *he* was right, too. Hmph, *that* was a new one. But he was too tired and fuzzy to think about all that had been said anymore. Instead of sitting beside her, he lay down with his head in her lap. It was his way of surrendering too.

She began to pass the tips of her fingers ever so softly around his ear and his face, then she said, "I never should have taken any of those calls."

With his eyes closed, Matt drew in a deep breath, then expelled it. He was so tired, and the couch was so comfy. He reached a hand inside her bathrobe and softly stroked her bare leg. The sigh, the things he *didn't* say, and his easy touch told her all she needed to know: the fight was over, they were good. After so many years, she could feel all of that in her lover's touch.

He whispered, "I love you. I'm sorry too." After a long pause he added, "The fire is still warm. Lay with me?"

In a moment Jane lay with her back pressed against his chest and he put his arms around her. He held her breasts and kissed her neck while both began to surrender to the fatigue of a late night. Each of them, even through closed eyelids, could see firelight bouncing off the log walls that surrounded them. "You wanna fool around?" Jane whispered.

Matt pulled her closer.

———

When daylight began to peek into the bank of windows across the great room, Matt was awakened by a stabbing pain in his hip. Then he felt Jane stir next to him. His right arm was numb and he was unable to move it; her head was resting on it. He raised his head slightly and realized that he'd been drooling on Jane's head for quite some time. A patch of hair behind her left ear, about the size of his hand, was wet from his saliva, and the wet patch extended all the way to the back of her head.

"Ugh," Matt groaned, as he tried to sit up.

Jane reached back to feel her sopping wet head and uttered, "What the . . .? Were you drooling on me?"

"Yeah, it looks that way. Sorry, darlin'," Matt said. He shook his right hand, trying to get some circulation back into it, and watched as Jane felt the huge wet spot on her head.

At first a bit of anger, maybe it was disgust, registered in her eyes when she touched her wet hair. Then the laughter began, slowly, as a small rain shower might, one drop at a time. Then it steadily grew into a deluge. Her shoulders were bobbing, and through her laughter she said, "It feels like I slept with my head in a pool hall spittoon."

At first Matt was embarrassed about his drooling, but her laughter, as always, proved to be infectious. He used his left arm to throw his still numb right arm over her shoulders, then pulled her close and kissed her. All the while he made sure Jane noticed the way he avoided the wet hair on the back of her head.

There had been no sex. They'd both fallen fast asleep and then awakened in a puddle of drool, cramped and sore. "The last thing I remember was talking about having sex," Jane said.

"Yeah, me too," Matt sighed. "Did I miss it? Was it good?"

"You chose sleep over sex," Jane said, while she touched several probing fingers against the side of her head to assess the perimeter of the drool spot in her hair.

"Well, I wouldn't say that I *chose* it," Matt started, "it just sorta happened, and . . ."

"It never would have happened a few years ago." Jane chuckled.

Matt could only smile back at her and nod in agreement.

"I guess this is a 'moment' too, huh?" Jane squinted and dabbed her fingers in the tangle of her wet hair. "Jesus, you must be dehydrated."

"Sorry, darlin'," Matt said through his own laughter. "I guess you just can't plan a 'moment,' huh?"

CHAPTER EIGHT

With his left thumb pressing gently against the ramus of John's mandible, just a bit superior and distal to the twelve-year molar on John's lower left, Matt guided the tip of a 29-gauge needle parallel to the plane of occlusion and then introduced it into the oral mucosa. John had broken a tooth the day before and was about to have a ceramic crown made.

As Matt moved the needle deeper into the soft tissue in John's jaw, he felt his patient's eyes on him. Matt knew that John had something to say, and it would be a very inappropriate attempt at humor. "Shut up," Matt whispered, his face only inches from John's.

John made no sound, and his lips never moved, but without even looking, Matt could sense a smile in his friend's eyes. When the tip of the needle was about an inch and a half into the soft tissue, Matt began to depress the plunger on the injection syringe. He pulled back on the syringe to be sure that he was not about to inject the lidocaine into a blood vessel, and when no blood flowed back into the glass carpule of local anesthetic, he slowly pressed on the plunger again until all of the 1.8 cc's of clear liquid had been injected.

Matt withdrew the needle and placed the syringe on the countertop behind John.

"Hey, I got a little lightning bolt on my lip and tongue that time, Matt. What was that all about?" John asked.

Matt removed his vinyl gloves but remained seated in his chair. "Well, you know I'm trying to block the inferior alveolar nerve, which innervates the left side of your lower jaw. If I put that anesthetic nice and close to the nerve, then your lip and tongue and gums, everything on the lower left, will get numb for a couple hours." Matt paused and put his hands on his thighs. "But sometimes I hit right on the nerve, or very close to it, and you get sort of a short circuit there. Feels like I hit your crazy bone, right?"

John nodded.

"Well, that's actually a good aim. I'll bet you're getting numb already. Right?"

"You got that right." John raised his left hand and felt his jaw.

"All right, then," Matt said, "I'm gonna give this a few minutes to soak into your hard head. When I come back we'll prepare your tooth for a crown." Matt stood up, rolled his chair back about six inches, and before leaving the room he leaned forward and in a quiet voice added, "You did good, John. Usually you act like such a pussy."

John cocked his head to the side and shrugged as he replied, "Well, I guess I'd say the same thing that Jane always says to you: I didn't feel a thing."

Matt's dental assistant, Tammy Leiding, rolled her eyes as she assembled the rest of the instruments and materials that Matt would need to prepare John's tooth for a crown. She'd heard them banter many times.

John could hear Matt's footsteps as he walked away, down the hallway outside the little room where he now sat waiting, with Tammy. "So how are *you* today, Tammy?" John asked. John knew Tammy Leiding very well, too. She was about forty years old, her husband was a nice guy, her children were good kids, and she loved cats. She wore a pin on her lab coat that featured a perky little tabby cat, and the wallpaper on her cell phone was a picture of her and her four cats. But she was *so* gullible; John loved to crush her crackers.

"Pretty good," Tammy replied, as she arranged some dental instruments on the tray in front of John.

"I had something really sad happen this morning," John said, while Tammy kept busy.

"Oh?" Tammy replied without looking up.

"Yeah, a cat ran right in front of my truck on the way here."

"Ohhh . . ." she moaned. The tinkling noise of steel instruments stopped for a moment, and Tammy's voice was filled with a cat lover's pain. "Did you—"

"Yeah, it was really sad." John shook his head with regret. "I missed it."

"You're terrible, John. That's not funny."

"He's an asshole," Matt said as he stepped back into the room and rescued John from the lecture about cats that he was about to receive.

"You ready to go?" Matt asked John.

"Yup, I'm pretty numb," John said.

"OK then, Tammy, let's go, and you can stab him some if you want," Matt said. Then he turned to John. "OK, buddy, I'm gonna use this . . ." and he held his dental drill up for John to see, ". . . to remove the enamel from tooth number nineteen, your lower left six-year molar, so that I can make a crown, which is just a filling that fits down over the top of the whole tooth. With me?"

John nodded that he was ready, and both Matt and Tammy leaned close. Tammy held a high-speed vacuum beside John's tooth while Matt used a drill that sprayed air and water and produced a high-pitched whine. About ten seconds into the procedure, Matt asked John, "Are you doing OK?" and John gave him a thumbs-up.

After a few minutes, Matt stopped, put his drill down, and announced that he was done with the preparation. Tammy then handed Matt what looked like ET's finger: a wand with a long hose connected to it.

"Are you done already?" John asked, then he turned to Tammy and said, "I bet Jane says *that* all the time, too."

Matt ignored John's joke and went on explaining the procedure for making the crown. He held the wand up for John to see, and said, "I'm done preparing your tooth, and now I'm gonna use this camera and take a series of photographs. Then I'm gonna feed those images into this computer over here." Matt pointed to a computer on wheels, with a keyboard and a computer screen, which was sitting at his right elbow. "This computer is sort of a 3-D, CAD/CAM thing with software that will allow me to design a crown for your tooth. It's called a CEREC unit. CEREC stands for Chairside Economical Restoration of Esthetic Ceramics, I think. Anyway, when I'm done designing your crown I'm gonna email the design info I put in there to the little robot that's sitting in my lab, just down the hall, and that robot will make your crown."

"So I'll get my crown today?" John asked.

"In about an hour."

"Hmph," John said, and then he opened his mouth so Matt could continue.

An hour later, Matt was sitting in his chair, next to John, and polishing the new crown in his hand. "You wanna come over and watch the Gopher hockey game tonight?" he asked John, without looking away from the crown. "Jane is going back to the Cities to be with her sister, so it'll be just you and me."

"Sure. Will I be able to eat?"

"Absolutely," Matt replied. "But unfortunately, you'll be able to talk, too."

"Should I bring a pizza?"

"Yeah, that sounds good. Come on out about sevenish. I wanna sit in my deer stand for the last hour of sunlight, and sunset will be around four-thirtyish. That'll give me time to clean up before you get there." Matt returned to the business at hand. "OK, I gotta try this in and see how it fits. Open up." Matt tried the crown in place, then removed it a moment later and began polishing it again. "Looks nice, but I need to adjust a couple things."

"That'll be perfect; the game tonight, I mean. I've got some things to finish up at my shop, too." Then, while he was watching Matt, he asked, "Why did my tooth break? I was having *oatmeal* for breakfast."

"Normal aging," Matt answered. "Shit wears out, shit breaks."

"Well, my mother had soft teeth, and—"

"Hold it." Matt interrupted and pointed the drill at John for emphasis. "*Nobody* has soft teeth. *Nobody*! Tooth enamel is the second hardest thing that occurs in nature; only diamonds are harder." Matt shook his head in disgust. "I've listened to that one my whole life. It's an excuse that gets used by people who live on Ding Dongs and Mountain Dew, and who never find the time to brush their teeth." He pointed the drill at John once more and added, "*Never* tell me you have soft teeth. Your tooth broke because it's had a lifetime of use, and it broke. That's all."

"OK, just don't hit me." John smiled.

Matt returned his attention to polishing the crown. As he did so he mumbled, just loud enough so John could hear him, "soft teeth . . . that's just stupid . . ."

As Matt was mumbling, Tammy walked back into the treatment room and said, "Doctor, I have a couple things for you."

"Shoot," Matt replied.

"OK, the patient whose wisdom teeth you removed yesterday?" Tammy held up a sheet of paper with a name written on it so that only Matt could read it.

"Yes, I remember," Matt said.

"He's having some postoperative pain and would like a prescription for some pain medication," Tammy said.

"Sure, that was nasty one," Matt said. "Write a script for Percocet, the usual dose, with no refills, and I'll sign it."

"I thought you would say that, so I wrote a prescription already. Will you sign it now?"

Matt signed the small piece of paper and Tammy went on to the next thing. "And some bad news: Tom Black passed away this morning."

Matt looked up. "Aw, that's too bad. He was such a nice guy. What did he die of?"

"Well, he was ninety, and he's had cancer for a while. I thought you knew that?" Tammy replied. Matt shook his head and frowned. "Also," Tammy continued, "Hal Peck's son called today. They moved Hal to a nursing home in Duluth. He has Alzheimer's and doesn't recognize anyone anymore, not even his son or his wife."

Matt shook his head once more and sighed.

"I know," Tammy said, "everybody likes Hal, but—" She stopped herself, then added, "Anyway, both of them were due to come for dental checkups after the first of the year, but I guess we won't be seeing either of them again. It's kind of sad, isn't it?"

"Let's send a sympathy card to Tom's family, and a . . ." Matt hesitated. "I guess we don't send a card to Hal, do we?"

"I'll get a sympathy card ready and we'll all sign it," Tammy said, as she turned away.

John saw the sadness on Matt's face, and watched for a moment while Matt made final adjustments to his crown. He knew that Matt was thinking, and that something was bothering him. "You know," Matt said while he studied the ceramic crown, which he turned one way and then the other while he pondered something, "that might be the saddest thing there could be; worse than death."

"What's that?" John asked.

"Having all your memories erased . . . I can't imagine that. And think about how terrible it would be if the *other* person lost all their memories of you." Matt's eyebrows tightened; he was clearly bothered by his own words. "All of those loving memories of your lifetime would be gone. You'd lose the connection to your wife . . . if I lost that connection with my Jane . . ." That was more than Matt wanted to think about, and he went silent for a moment before he changed the tiny polishing bur in his dental handpiece and redirected the conversation.

"So, what do you think your memories are, John? I mean, they can't be chemicals, or your brain would be the size of a truck by the time you were ten years old, and if you ever had a head injury, some of your memories might drip out and be gone. So, what *are* memories? Are they just tiny messages written in some elaborate code, and stored in your brain? And how can a memory be stored in color, along with some emotion, like love, or hate? And what is an emotion, really? Think about it, what do you think love is—"

"I'm getting a headache here," John interrupted. "Where do you get this shit? You're the only person I ever met who thinks about shit like that."

"Sorry." Matt chuckled, still polishing the crown. "I was just rambling."

"You know, Matt, this *place*, all this *stuff* you have here; this is pretty impressive. I always knew you were pretty smart; well, smarter than me, and smarter than the other guys we hung around with when we were kids. Some of the guys didn't like you because of that, did you know that?"

"Yeah, I figured that out after a while," Matt said, without looking up.

"You never got very good grades, though, if I remember correctly?" John said, inviting a reply.

"I thought high school was boring, but I liked the sports," Matt replied.

"You were better at school than sports. Way better," John teased.

"Turns out I was way better at sports than dentistry, too. Open wider, will you, I can't see for all that blood," Matt said, as he looked back into John's mouth. High school classes *had* been boring for him; he'd graduated in the bottom half of his class, from a less than outstanding high school. But his SAT and ACT scores had been off-the-charts high and he'd been accepted to the University of Minnesota. John was right about sports, too. Although Matt loved football and basketball and baseball, he was never more than a smiling face in a team photo. He was the kid who loved every drill in practice; the kid who hustled, and had whatever minimal success he had because he had desire. Matt Kingston lacked real talent, but the coaches all wished they could put Matt's heart into John Velde's chest.

Matt knew his limitations and his strengths, too. As he polished John's crown, a flurry of high school memories flashed through his mind. Then his college days went streaming by on that old movie projector in his brain, too. He'd been bored with his first couple of years in college, just like high school. After fall quarter of his junior year he'd compiled a not very impressive GPA of 2.22, which he realized, almost too late, would severely limit his career options. And he realized that his grades were so poor not just because he wasn't challenged in school, but because he traded his love of sports for a serious interest in beer and girls. Somewhere in the middle of his junior year in college, Matt had righted his own ship, both academically and personally. He had a 4.0 GPA from that point until he graduated, and his Dental Admission Test scores were high, much higher than he'd expected. For lack of anything else that interested him, Matt applied to dental school at the University of Minnesota and was accepted—selected from a thousand other qualified applicants. As he finished polishing John's crown he thought of the crazy and random paths he'd chosen in life, and how they'd led him to a pretty good place: here.

When John's new crown was cemented in place, Matt removed the excess cement. "Looks good!" Matt announced. "Get outta here. I'll see you tonight. You're bringing the pizza, and remember: It isn't pizza if it doesn't have pepperoni on it."

"Just be sure you have plenty of beer," John said. "See you at sevenish."

CHAPTER NINE

———•———

The woods around Scotch Lake were covered with animal tracks as Matt limped out to his deer stand. It wasn't quite as cold as the last time he'd been hunting, so that was good, but he had fairly low expectations for a successful hunt. It was maybe twenty degrees, and the sun was beginning to cast longer shadows when he reached the ladder that he'd have to climb to reach his hiding position. He just wasn't feeling it today. The hunt had the feel of an exercise in futility, but he loved the woods and he knew that if he didn't pay the price by sitting there and waiting, he'd never harvest a buck. That thought brought another, similar thought to mind, and he smiled when he remembered the words of his basketball coach, "Pigeon Tits," way back in high school, during a game. The opponent and the outcome were long forgotten, but Matt remembered that it was a close game. He'd taken a shot and missed, and Pigeon Tits had leapt from the bench and called a time-out. As the boys were walking toward the bench to form a huddle, Pigeon Tits put his arm around Matt's shoulders and said, "Look, we can't score if we don't shoot—we gotta shoot it up there—but next time throw the ball to John!" At that moment, Matt raised his eyes and looked across the small circle of players, all standing shoulder to shoulder, and met John's gaze. John was grinning fiendishly, and nodding his agreement with their coach. Matt and John were only eighteen years old, but a familiarity that only exists between the best of friends was already in place. John was aware that this game meant nothing, and he was teasing Matt, who always took these things far too seriously. Matt could still see the smile on John's face almost five decades later, as if there were a little cloud above John's head, and his thoughts were written there: "Yeah, stupid, throw the ball to *me*."

Matt felt the smile on his own face now. Damn, those were good times, he thought. A silly memory from long ago had taken his mind off it for a while, but his hip was sore from walking in snow when he reached his deer stand, and he was thankful that there had been no new snow since last weekend. After a short rest to calm his breathing, he attached his bow to the rope that hung from the seat at the top of the ladder; when he was safely in his seat he'd hoist the bow up. Then he attached the strap on his safety vest to the climbing harness, which was connected to a heavy rope that was secured to the tree. With each step up the ladder he slid the climbing harness along just ahead of himself. That way, if he should fall, he'd only fall a foot or two. The safety harness worked the same for both his ascent and descent.

When he reached the top of the twenty-foot ladder, he turned around and sat down on what was actually a pretty comfortable seat. Then he reached for the lift line and raised his compound bow hand over hand. Once his bow was in his lap, he strapped his arrow release onto his right wrist, adjusted his hat and face mask and gloves, and then nocked an arrow. He looked around his field of fire and tried to imagine any shot he might have to take, then he found a comfortable posture and started the wait.

He always made an effort to be stealthy on the walk out to his deer stand, but as always, he'd made some noise on the way out here. Any deer in the vicinity would have heard him coming and run away, at least for a while. If he stayed still and silent, they'd all wander back.

All he had to do now was wait. The hard part, as usual, would be to stay alert—actually, to stay awake. Earlier in the season, when it was relatively warm, he often struggled to stave off sleep. He knew that many hunters had been seriously injured, or killed, by falling asleep and then falling from their trees. With that thought Matt checked his safety harness once more.

But it would be relatively easy to stay awake today, he thought; the cold would take care of that. He was warm now, but in a few minutes he'd begin to feel the bite. The first concession he'd make would be to adjust his face mask to keep his breath from condensing into icicles on his nose and eyelashes. Then his fingers and toes would go numb. He could sit here today for ninety minutes, maybe two hours. No more.

Random thoughts and memories began to stream through his brain, and as always there seemed to be no obvious reason why one thought triggered another. Small vignettes, scenes from school days or other hunts played out in full color, like the ball game when Pigeon Tits told him to throw the ball to John. They seemed to play in their completeness, in real time, too, but in reality, they couldn't. They showed themselves to Matt in flashes, and then gave way to the next scene. Then Linda Pike's face appeared and stopped the show. Matt heard John's voice repeating what Linda had told him: "He broke my heart." He hadn't thought of Linda since college, but now he remembered her beautiful face, and the way he'd charmed her clothes off, had his way with her, and then thrown her away. He had no idea what to do with that memory, and no others followed after for a while.

Below him, on the forest floor, a red squirrel scampered onto a fallen log, and another followed soon after. The squirrels began chasing and scolding each other as they raced up and down one nearby balsam tree and then another. Several years earlier, while two other red squirrels were playing just like this, he'd dozed off, only to be jolted from his slumber when one of the squirrels raced up the tree he was sleeping in, and then ran up his leg. He'd been terrified. He'd flinched violently and actually cried out in fear. Now the memory made him smile.

Over the years he'd seen fishers, foxes, ruffed grouse, and all the other creatures of the forest wander by. He'd always been fascinated as he watched them search for food and try to coexist. Several times he'd seen them try to attract a mate. But he'd been part of one special incident that unfolded while he sat in this very tree and watched, and he let himself relive it.

Years ago, on a cold evening much like this one, a trophy buck much like Mr. Whitehorns had wandered by just in front of him. It had been a silent hunt. The sun had already set in the west, and a full moon was beginning to peek over the tall balsam firs on the east side of a frozen Scotch Lake. Only a few minutes of the gray twilight remained when the buck stopped and turned broadside to Matt. It was an easy shot and Matt took it. He heard the arrow hit its mark with a loud slapping noise, and he watched the buck leap with a classic mule kick. The buck had been stung, and it dashed into some nearby brush. It crashed through brush and cattails and emerged at a full sprint onto the frozen and snow-covered surface of Scotch Lake. With its head held high, the old buck raced across a sheet of white that sparkled in the moonlight, framed on all sides by the spires of lofty pines and balsams. The strength and speed and grace of the buck made Matt begin to wonder if he'd missed his shot. The buck seemed strong as it raced in a wide arc out on the lake and then turned back toward the safety of the woods. But the buck began to slow as it drew near to the trees, and when it left the lake and reentered the woods about a hundred yards from Matt, he wasn't so sure of the buck's fate.

Matt waited for a few minutes and climbed down from his tree. He turned on a flashlight and began to search for the spot where the deer had been standing when he loosed his arrow. When he found the arrow he knew it had passed through the deer's heart, and he simply turned to follow a wide blood trail out onto the ice. That walk across the lake had been glorious. And ugly. He was a hunter and he'd just made a kill. But the sight of that buck racing across the frozen lake, trying to outrun death, had never left him.

A chilly breeze brought Matt back into the moment. The squirrels were still playing grab-ass over in the balsam tree next door. But there were no deer anywhere to be seen, and he quickly returned to his daydreams.

One consciousness drifted into the other, and a young Jane Monahan was soon smiling at him, her eyes filled with love, and lust. He remembered their first time. They'd been dating for a few weeks, and neither of them wanted to be away from the other. There'd been a lot of touching, but no sex. Then one Friday afternoon they'd gone to a shopping mall and walked around holding hands and talking. She'd bought a Fleetwood Mac album; he bought one by James Taylor. They went back to Matt's apartment to get something to eat before going to a movie, and while Matt was staring at the inside of his refrigerator he noticed that Jane was nowhere to be seen. When he peeked into his tiny bedroom he saw Jane's clothes in a pile beside the bed. Jane was in his bed, smiling, with the covers pulled up to her chin. When he walked over and tried to lift the covers back, Jane had clutched at them and kept herself covered. She was still smiling, but her eyes were hungry, and she watched while Matt undressed. There was no movie that night.

The sex became white-hot. They'd been unable to keep their hands off each other. And he remembered the little burger joint in downtown Minneapolis where there they sometimes went to talk, and an all-night breakfast place out on Interstate 494 where they went when everyplace else was closed. They usually went out simply because they had to take time off from sex every so often, and while they were having coffee or a burger, or an omelet, they laughed and flirted and began to talk about their future; their future *together*. The two of them were all-in from the beginning, and they knew it.

All thoughts of trophies and squirrels and young love stopped suddenly when Matt realized that darkness had settled over the woods, and there would be no close encounters with deer today. He began to gather his things and prepare to head for home. He'd seen only the two squirrels, but that was all right; he'd had some time to think.

When Matt reached his house his hip was killing him. No matter what he did, nothing ever seemed get that muscle to heal. Even as he'd crossed the flat easy surface of the lake, he'd had to walk in half steps, basically dragging his right leg home.

He stood still by the back door of his home for a second and tried to forget about the sore hip. He wished Jane was still here. The place just felt better when she was home. Most days when she was home there was a fire in the fireplace all day long and a wave of warm air would rush out to greet him when he swung the door open. Sometimes she'd be sitting at the desk in her small office, and she'd stay in there until he came and sat with her and asked about her day. Other days she'd be in the kitchen, waiting for him. But there would always be a kiss, and an "I love you," and a long hug. Maybe she'd rub the back of his neck and listen to whatever it was that had frustrated him that day at work. Maybe she'd be the one who needed the knots rubbed out of a tired neck, or a back rub, or just a good friend to complain to. But there was always a sense that she wanted to hold him as much as he wanted her.

There would be none of that on this Friday night, however. He and John would watch the Gophers play North Dakota tonight and then again Saturday in an important two-game series. Most weekends John was busy with one or more of his lady friends. But he told Matt that he'd given all his girls the weekend off so he could have a sleepover with his buddy. They'd have a good time tonight. Matt looked up into the dark sky and shivered against a sudden chill before he started up the back steps.

John rolled into the driveway a few minutes later. As always, he let himself in the back door. He was carrying a jumbo Carnivore Special with extra green olives from Dan and Mary's Pizza in Pine Rapids. Matt was seated in front of the TV, waiting for John. A flickering fire jumped around inside the fireplace in the great room, and the TV announcers were introducing the Gopher hockey players.

"Got beer?" John called from the kitchen.

"In the fridge. Grab one for each of us," Matt replied. "I didn't wanna start without you."

A moment later John placed the pizza and two cans of Leinenkugel's beer on a coffee table in front of them, and he unzipped his heavy winter coat.

"Just throw your coat on that chair over there by my computer," Matt said, and before John plopped onto the couch next to him, Matt flipped open the pizza box to help himself, then he groaned, "Ah, shit. North Dakota just scored . . . put a slap shot right through the goalie's legs, right in the five-hole." They ate and drank and laughed and watched hockey for the entire first period, unencumbered by the weight of the world. They were just boys again, for a while.

"I gotta toss a wiz," John announced, as he stood up and walked to a bathroom in the hallway. He peed with the bathroom door open, leaning back, looking over his shoulder, and trying catch a glimpse of the hockey action on TV.

"One twenty-seven," John said when he returned from the bathroom and sat back down on the couch.

"Huh?"

"One minute and twenty-seven seconds," John said, as if that was enough explanation.

"What are you talking about?" Matt asked. "It's the middle of the first period, and there's no power play on."

"I just peed for a minute and twenty-seven seconds."

"Well, that's fascinating." Matt turned back to the game.

When it came to potty talk, John always had something to say, and like all grown men who were still little boys at heart, Matt and John had always found their humor to be hilarious. In spite of all the lectures from his mother, and then Jane, Matt still laughed at John's fart stories and bathroom jokes. He assumed that every right-thinking boy, of any age, did the same. And most of the time he joined right in.

John got up again to get two more beers from the kitchen. As he passed by, Matt opined, "Sounded like a three-year-old girl when you were peeing, by the way; sort of a pathetic dribble."

"Yeah, it gets more like that all the time," John said. He stopped and put his hands on his hips. "I think it must be sort of an old man thing, huh? I mean, it used to sound like somebody left the garden hose running. Now I gotta hold my thumb over the end in order to get that much pressure. You noticing that when you pee too?"

"Maybe. Let's have a little hustle on the beer run, OK?"

When John reappeared from the kitchen thirty seconds later, he had more to say. "And have you had that thing start to happen now that we're a little older . . . you know, where you're standing there, and you think you're done peein', so you tuck your dong back in your barn door, but then it turns out you still weren't quite done, and you piss on your nuts, just a little bit?"

Matt turned a sideways glance at John, then ignored the question.

"I'll take that for a yes," John said. He handed a can of beer to Matt, then he walked over to the small writing desk where Matt and Jane kept a computer. "Hey, can I use your computer? I gotta check something." He turned the computer on.

"No amateur porn websites," Matt said. "Remember, you gave your girls the night off, so don't be stalking them." He was still seated, watching the Gophers, when John began tapping at the computer keyboard.

"Good one," John said, "and that reminds me: Did I ever tell you about the time I—" John interrupted himself, suddenly quiet. "Hey, what's Mo Glasnapp's married name?"

"Lawson," Matt said. "Why?"

"She sent you an email." John raised his eyebrows as if he'd stumbled on to a secret. "See? She still wants a ride on your baloney pony!"

"Really?" Matt said, showing surprise, and interest, at the arrival of Mo's email while at the same time ignoring John's reference to sex. "Get away from there." He stood and crossed the room.

Naturally, John ignored him. Hurriedly, before Matt could get over to the computer table, he pretended to read the note. "I'll just read the verbs. Let's see . . . lick, pound, hammer—ooh! That could also be a noun as she's used it here."

"Get outta here," Matt said as he pushed John away from the computer. He sat down in front of the screen, put some reading glasses on, and began to read the note silently while John returned to the Gophers and the pizza.

Dear Matt,

I wasn't sure if I should write, I hope it's OK. I'm listening to an old- ies radio station at the moment and I just heard a couple songs that reminded me of you, and then I couldn't help thinking about the wind-ing roads we've all taken in life. Anyway, I got your email address from Donny and I just wanted to tell you that it was so nice to see you again at Dad's funeral. I would have preferred a happier setting, but none-theless, it made me feel so good to talk to you again. After the funeral Donny and David and I, and our families, all got together and had something of a party. The boys told stories and your name came up quite a few times. I know you always thought Dad didn't like you, but he did. He told me that many times. He wasn't always the best at sharing his true feelings. It was great to see you again, old friend.

—Mo

With a broad and somewhat bewildered smile plastered across his face, Matt turned and stared at John until John returned his gaze.

"What'd she say?" John asked with a mouthful of pizza, and then with-out pause he added, "Gophers just scored again."

Matt turned back to the computer screen and started reading Mo's note out loud for John to hear. Then he added his own ending: "P.S.— My dad always wondered why you ran around with that low-life shitbag John Velde."

It was John's turn to smile. "That was a nice note," he said. He paused, then added, "But you gotta read between the lines here, buddy. She wants to tune your meat whistle." He gave a nod and turned his attention back to the hockey game. "Trust me."

"Ah, she was my best friend for a while there. I'd like to think she's still a good friend," Matt said. "We just came to a fork in the road and each of us chose a different path."

"Men don't have women friends," John said without looking away from the game. "I told you, it doesn't work that way."

"OK, enlighten me on that point again," Matt said, reaching for another piece of pizza.

"Don't believe me? Think back to the last time some woman broke up with you."

"That's absurd, why would any woman ever break up with *me?*" Matt said.

"Oh, I forgot about your wonderfulness." A familiar mischievous smile settled over John's face. "Let me tell you how it works. When a woman is done with you, she'll always say that she thinks you both should 'see others' for a while, but she wants to still 'be friends.' Hell, they don't want to be your friend, they just want you to go away." He shrugged and added, "Even women understand that men can't have women friends."

"Oh?" Matt raised his eyebrows with a request for a more thorough explanation.

"Think about it for Chrissakes; what *guy* would have a *woman* for a friend?" John turned away from the hockey game. "They can't and don't like to do the things we do: huntin' and fishin' and sports 'n stuff. I mean, would you ever wanna play golf, or go fishin' with a woman? Hell no!"

"I do it all the time," Matt said.

"You're married! Married to the same woman for nearly forty years! You don't know shit about this!"

"You know how stupid that was, what you just said?" Matt sipped at his beer and shook his head.

"Well, I was on the spot there. I had to think of something fast," John replied, unable to hide the bullshit improvisation he was attempting, then he got back on track. "OK, we'll leave *you* out of this discussion and talk about normal men, OK? Can we do that?"

Matt closed his eyes and waited for the inevitable.

"The only time *any* guy would *ever* do something like that—you know, fishing or hiking or museums—" John rolled his eyes, "with a girl, would be when he's just starting to get to know the girl, and he thinks maybe something like that will help to get her in the sack. Period! That's like sitting around and talking about your feelings with a woman." John rolled his eyes again. "Now, *you* might actually do something like that because you might be having a gender identification crisis or some other shit. You'll snap out of it one day soon. There's more to all this, but I think it's over your head."

"OK, try me." Matt shrugged.

"All right, then, the other thing you hafta remember is that being friends with a woman always winds up leading to other things." John flicked his eyebrows.

"No it doesn't."

John rolled his eyes. "Sure it does. Are you stupid? Well, OK, there is one exception; women can have *men* friends, but the men must be gay. That works because they have two things in common: They both like to have sex with men, and they both like to talk about their feelings 'n shit. And nothing ever happens between the sheets to change their relationship. Simple."

Matt shook his head, trying to clear something away, before John continued.

"C'mon, *think* about it! Why would any guy, any *straight* guy, strike up a friendship with a woman, unless he was trying to get her in the sack?"

"That's crazy."

"No, it's not. Men just can't have women friends; it simply doesn't work that way. They'll always wind up hating each other. You gotta trust me on this one; I know what I'm talking about. When I was young I had dozens of women friends, or tried to, and it just never worked."

"Why? What happened?"

"Well, we always stayed up late and talked about our feelings 'n shit . . ." John started.

"Yeah?" Matt said. "Then what?"

"I fucked 'em and ruined it all."

Matt coughed beer through his nose and bolted forward.

"Hey, it happened every time. And that was all I really wanted anyway, so it worked out all right, I guess. But from that point on they all seemed to think I'd given them permission to start fixing all the shit that was wrong with me." John shrugged and crinkled his face at the same time; a strange gesture which revealed the simplicity and the complexity of it all. "You just can't have women friends."

Matt could only smile. He turned his attention back to the hockey game. There was no way to refute a man's entire life experience, and somewhere way back in his mind, Matt could hear a tiny echo of truth in John's ramblings.

Four hours later the game was over, and so was the movie that came on after it. The TV was off, the pizza was gone, and both men were inching close to a beer-induced coma. They were side by side, slumped on the couch with their feet crossed on the coffee table, and both of them were nursing one final beer. Empty beer cans and a pizza box covered with crumbs and grease spots lay on the coffee table by their feet.

"I'm not driving home tonight," John groaned. "Gonna flop right here on your couch."

"Sure . . . figured that." A minute passed, then another.

John raised one leg from the coffee table, held it there for a moment, and then farted.

"Nice tone," Matt said. He raised his shirt up over his nose. "Be careful not to push too hard on a moist one like that; you could wind up with duck butter on your five-hole."

"Ah, I could tell it was just was just a blank; not enough heat to do any damage," John replied without looking at Matt.

Matt lowered his shirt, took a sip of beer, and then brought his shirt back up over his nose.

"Ever do premarital farting?" John asked, still staring at the ceiling. It was the opening salvo in a game of very gross one-upmanship that had dated back to high school days. Matt recognized it immediately and fired back.

"You mean cut the cheese in front of a girlfriend? No, I saved farting for the sanctity of marriage," Matt said, as if that was an indicator of character and fidelity.

"I farted lotsa girls," John replied, with a sense of pride. It was a great sentence, and he'd returned the volley.

Matt stared at the ceiling and stifled a grin. He considered his response carefully, then sighed. "Well, farting without commitment is empty. Besides that, I wouldn't want to marry some girl that every guy in town had already farted."

John pondered Matt's words as if there was actually a trace of wisdom in them, then he offered, "Well, it's one way to take your relationship to the next level," still without a smile.

Now the ball was back in Matt's court, and the little game had to continue until somebody broke down and laughed. Still staring at the ceiling as if this bizarre conversation carried some profound meaning, he finally replied, "Yeah, well, maybe for you and me, but if you're a girl it's a risky move."

"You got a point there." The first hint of a grin curled John's lip. "But girls don't fart, right?" he added. The grin blossomed.

Matt gave a devious smirk, then he laughed. "Yeah, right." He raised his beer can and clinked it against John's. The game had ended in a draw.

A silent moment passed while each man opened a private vault of memories and sorted through it.

"Remember the time that Knutson kid coughed up a chicken in study hall?" Matt asked.

"Huh?" John said, with a wrinkled brow.

Matt was recalling the story. "He'd been shoveling chicken shit all weekend, at his grandpa's farm. You know how that can be so dusty and dirty? So on Monday afternoon, sixth-hour study hall, he's leaning back in his chair, sleeping, and he starts to cough—"

"He was humping that Johnson girl, right?" John interrupted, momentarily derailed by a different memory of the Knutson kid.

"Yeah, well, he *said* he was. So anyway, he starts to cough—he was sitting right next to me—and suddenly a big ol' green snag about the size of a fried egg shot out of his mouth and stuck on his desk." Matt had to stop and laugh at the memory, and John turned to look at him. "Jeez, the thing just sorta laid on his desk and quivered for a while, like green Jell-O; it was a huge lunger. But the most amazing thing was that it had three little tiny chicken feathers stuck in it, and those little feathers were just fluttering in the breeze. I thought I might puke, but I couldn't look away." Matt laughed again.

"I beat the shit outta him once," John said. The story of Steve Knutson coughing up a big green snag *was* interesting, but John had even more to add. "We were at basketball practice, down at the old armory. Remember how you could flush a toilet and then scald the shit outta everybody who was takin' a shower at the time?"

"Sure do."

"Well, he did it one too many times," John said.

"You always thought it was funny when I was in the shower and *you* flushed a toilet," Matt said.

"That was different."

A long silence settled over them before Matt broke it again. "Remember that Ford LTD you had when we were back in high school?"

"The silver one or the black one?" John asked.

"The silver one. Hell, I forgot all about the black one."

"Sure do! It was nicer than the black one; it had those plush red seats," John said.

"Yeah, that's what I was gettin' at; you know what I remember about that car?" Matt stared at the tops of his feet as he spoke.

"What?"

"You used to hurry over to my place and show me every time you had new 'stains' on those seats." Matt grimaced.

"Pecker tracks . . ." John sighed, then a new memory popped into his head. "I liked that car. Remember what happened to it?"

"It's on display in the Museum of Infectious Diseases?"

"I was driving home from some girl's farm about two in the morning." John ignored Matt. "I was cruisin' along pretty good; that thing had a big ol' V-8 and I was *movin'*! Anyway, the hood latch opened up while I was goin' about eighty. That big ol' hood flipped back over and smashed the livin' shit outta the windshield; stove in the roof, too." He thought for a second. "Man, it got dark real fast, too. I didn't know what happened; it was so loud. I thought I was dead for minute there; scared the shit outta me."

"So what did you do with the car?"

"Junked it and bought that black Chevy from Jim Jorgenson."

"That was a good car, too."

"Yeah, that was one that the Porisch boys put a live pigeon in one night when I left it unlocked at the ball park. I had no idea that *one* pigeon could shit so much in one night."

"I remember." Matt yawned.

Finally, there was no conversation left for the old friends. It was getting to be too much work. Even with the memories and the chuckles, they were both fighting a losing battle with heavy eyelids. They stared up into the night, and the past, and thoughts of pigeon shit and pecker tracks carried them off to sleep.

Jane, and quite a few others over the years, had wondered about the bond of friendship between John and Matt. If they could only have been a mouse in the corner just now, and listened to the chat that had just ended, maybe, just maybe, they'd understand. Good, bad, crazy; it would never matter. Matt shared a colorful past with John, and they had laughed together, something like soldiers who'd bled together.

An hour later Matt woke up with a sore neck. He rose, threw a blanket over John, and with the usual stabbing pain in his hip, hobbled off to his bedroom.

The first thing John saw when he rolled over and opened his eyes the next morning was Matt, wearing a T-shirt and boxers, hunched over in front of the TV. A steaming cup of black coffee had been halted on the way to his lips, and now it lingered there, motionless, while Matt stared at the screen.

"Coffee on?" John groaned as he rolled over a bit. Then he scratched his nuts and farted. He sat up slowly, making the effort appear to be a physically demanding athletic task. He rubbed his face and got his feet under him before he stood. Sometime during the night he'd taken his pants off, and now his bowed and hairy legs extended from his black-and-white checked boxer shorts. He shuffled his stocking feet across the floor toward the bathroom in an agonizingly slow gait.

Matt plugged his nose and said, "You better hurry up," with his eyes still on the TV screen.

Ten minutes later Matt was still watching the news when John returned to the great room with a cup of coffee and settled back into the couch. "Yikes, who's that frumpy little mutt?" John asked.

"That would be Congresswoman Marlene Douglas, from Ohio," Matt replied. "She's the speaker of the House. You know, the United States government House of Representatives? In Washington?"

"Oh, I've heard of that," John deadpanned. Then he leaned forward on the couch and made a point to focus on the TV screen. "Congress *woman*? If we were playing golf with *Marlene*," John emphasized her name in order to question her gender, "I believe I'd need to see some DNA before I let *her* hit from the ladies' tees."

"OK, so Marlene's not so cute—"

"No shit," John interrupted, "I'll bet her parents had to tie pork chops to her ears so the dogs would play with her."

"Yeah, but don't you think it might be a bit hurtful to always point that out? I mean, somewhere out there, she's got to have a boyfriend, or a mother who loves her."

"All right, a mother maybe, I'll give you that one. But if there's a boy-friend out there I'll eat the peanuts outta your shit." John sipped at his coffee and reached for a day-old newspaper.

It was gross, and it was sexist. Matt knew he shouldn't do it, and he tried to hide it, but he allowed himself a grin as he walked to the kitchen for a refill of coffee.

"So what do you have planned for the day?" Matt asked when he returned with his coffee.

"I got some work to do at the shop. It's a busy time of year for me; the deer season is almost over, so I still get customers walkin' in every day with heads to mount. On a Saturday morning like today I'll bet several guys show up with bucks they wanna hang on the wall. The only bad part is that I hafta listen to the whole story of how they bagged the big one. But I'll be back tonight for game two. Maybe the Gophers'll win again? Let's burn some hamburger on the grill tonight. I'll stop at the beer store and pick up a case of Leinies. I'll get some fixin's for supper, too."

"Sounds good," Matt said. He got up from the couch and carried the pizza box stacked with empty beer cans to the kitchen.

"You walk sorta like you have a bowling trophy stuck in your ass," John said.

"I think that would be an improvement. This muscle in my hip just won't heal."

CHAPTER TEN

———— ·•· ————

Maintaining a dental practice in a little town was the perfect job for Matt at this stage of his life. Most of his patients had been part of his practice for a generation. He knew them, he liked them, and there was comfort in the gentle routines that had been established over the years. Patients brought him pictures of their children, and their grandchildren, and the deer they'd taken last season, and just about everything else that a friend might share. Some of the older ladies made cookies for him. Once, several years earlier, a patient had even given him a handmade hunting knife. He liked the pace of his office to be busy, but not hectic, and he took time for lunch with John Velde several times a week.

As this morning wound down he repaired a broken denture, extracted a couple of wisdom teeth, and cemented a porcelain bridge in place for the principal at Pine Rapids High School.

"OK," Matt said to his last patient of the morning, "We're gonna draw some blood before I extract that broken tooth. I explained that all the other day, right?"

The man nodded yes, and Matt wrapped a rubber hose around his biceps in order to make the veins in his forearm stand out. "Then we're gonna spin this little vial of blood in a machine over in my lab, across the hall, so all that's left is some plasma, and then we'll mix that with some stuff that'll help you grow bone in this extraction site, so we can place a dental implant back in there later. You remember the procedure?" As Matt talked, he introduced a short needle into the man's vein and watched the glass vial fill up with red blood.

"Sure, Doc, I remember," the man said. "But ol' Doc Anderson never did stuff like this up there above the drug store. I remember he used to use a little hammer and pounded gold fillings into my teeth! How 'bout that?"

Matt chuckled. "Yeah, that was called a gold foil. I haven't done one of those since . . . well, I've never done one since I took the state board exam." He placed a cotton ball over the needle hole in the man's vein and bent his arm to prevent any bleeding.

"Dentistry sure has changed," the patient said.

"Sure has. OK, let's get that tooth outta there."

Ten minutes later, after the simple surgical procedure, the man sat on the side of the chair and rubbed his numb cheek. "Didn't hurt a bit."

"Well, good, that's the way it's s'posed to work!" Matt said, as the man stood up to leave. "Call me if you have any problems."

"Sure thing." The man shook hands with Matt and walked out to the front desk.

When Matt turned to walk in the other direction, he nearly collided with his receptionist. Donna Dilly had been working in Matt's office for nearly thirty years, and she knew everybody in Pine Rapids. She was beyond competent; she pretty much ran Matt's practice for him, and she'd been standing in the hallway, waiting for him to finish up with his last patient of the morning so she could talk to him.

"Jeez, Donna, you wanna dance?" Matt joked at their collision.

But there was only the hint of a smile on Donna's face. She was ten years older than Matt, and she was barely five feet tall. She was seventy-two years old, and she could have retired years ago, but she liked her job, she liked the other employees, and she liked the fact that she was indispensable at the office. Donna was more than a longtime employee. She was Matt's friend, and she looked out for him. She'd worked there so long that Matt jokingly referred to her as "Mother" or "The Boss." Now she stared at him for a moment and then raised her eyebrows. "You're off this afternoon," she said firmly.

"Whaddya mean? Everybody canceled their appointments? Or what?" Matt furrowed his brow. Two hygienists and Tammy, his assistant, scurried about behind Matt, careful to keep their heads down, trying to go unnoticed.

"I canceled them," Donna said.

"Why?"

"We're all pretty tired of watching you hobble around and wince. You whimper when you stand, or sit, or move in any way. It's obvious that something is wrong with your back or your leg, or *something*," Donna said. She put her index finger on his chest and added, "I made an appointment for you over at the clinic at one o'clock today. You're gonna have some X-rays and then visit with the doctor." Her facial expression was firm and she was clearly ready to argue if Matt chose to.

"Really?" Matt asked.

"Really! It's time, and you know it."

Matt began to smile, quizzing her with his eyes.

"Which doctor?" he asked.

"The new guy. Everyone likes him, but he's really busy," Donna replied.

"How'd you get me in so quick?"

"I made the appointment a month ago."

Matt stared at her while he considered this.

"I know you keep talking about this pulled muscle thing, and you've tried all the holistic cures and all the alternative medicines"—Donna paused for a second—"potions and homeopathic drops and herbal diet supplements. Next you'll be carrying crystals in your pocket and sleeping under a pyramid." One of the hygienists over by the sterilization sink overheard the part about sleeping under a pyramid and giggled. "But none of that's working. You're getting worse. You limp around here like a Walmart shopper." The hygienist behind them kept her eyes down but giggled again. "We're getting worried about you. What if this is cancer, or some other dreadful thing, and what if you wait too long to check it out?"

He stared at her and then acquiesced. He nodded gently, in agreement. "OK, thanks, Mother."

"The nurse said for you to be there a little early and bring some urine with you," Donna added. "And one more thing. You are *off* this afternoon. So take it easy."

Two hours later, Matt sat with crowd of coughing, obese chain smokers and several crying babies in the clinic waiting room. He'd had a couple of X-rays taken earlier and then been told to take a seat to wait. Several ashen-colored old men, and one pale old woman, sat and coughed without covering their mouths while they waited their turns to see a doctor. Matt could hear things, unhealthy things, moving around in their chests and he tried not to smile when he remembered the vision of the feathered, green, lifelike mass quivering on the Knutson kid's desk all those years ago. The clinic waiting room smelled like a bad tennis shoe that had been used as an ashtray, and Matt was getting impatient to get on with things.

Finally, a young nurse called his name and then ushered him down a long hallway until they came to a T intersection. Matt was familiar with the clinic, and he knew that all the doctors' offices were on the hall that went to the left. He was surprised when the nurse turned right and led him the other way. Maybe there's been some remodeling, Matt thought, as he followed the nurse. The hallway on this end of the building had newer carpet and rich walnut trim on the doors and windows. The light fixtures were elegant, too, and this end of the building had a much more subdued, calm feel about it.

At the end of the hall they came to a door with "Dr. Ronald Hested" painted on it. Ron Hested was a longtime friend of Matt's, but he was also a psychiatrist.

"Whoa, wait a minute," Matt said. "I'm supposed to see the new guy, not Dr. Hested. I'm not crazy; my hip hurts."

"I'm sorry about that, but Dr. Curtis, the new family-practice doctor, was called away on an emergency. We were just about to reschedule you when Dr. Hested told me to have you take a seat in his private office. Is that all right with you? I just saw him a minute ago, and I know he's on the way right now." The nurse turned her palms up in the universal gesture for "I'm just doing what I was told."

"OK, I s'pose I can see Ron, but I'm not crazy."

Matt thought he'd made a joke, but the nurse didn't smile. She simply turned and led him a few feet farther down the hall to a door with nothing written on it. "This is Dr. Hested's private office," she said. "He told me that his office hours were over for the day, and no one would be here, but this door would be open." She seemed relieved that it was actually unlocked, and when it swung open she and Matt stepped inside. "He said he'd be right behind me." She then stepped out and pulled the door closed behind her.

This must be where Ron talks to crazy folks, Matt thought. Soft lights had been left on, and the window blinds were half closed, leaving the office with a warm, comfortable feel. Bookshelves covered two of the walls, and Ron had a large, ornate desk. But it looked like he didn't sit behind the desk when he talked to patients; there were several overstuffed chairs arranged in a group, a few feet from the desk. On the desktop was a black-and-white photograph of a young Dr. Hested holding up a huge muskie for the photographer, a stack of mail, a computer, a telephone, and a conspicuous box of tissues . . . for crying patients, Matt assumed. He took a seat in one of the overstuffed chairs and sat with his hands folded on his lap while he looked around the office.

Less than a minute had passed when the door opened and Dr. Hested stepped in. "Hi, Matt," he said as he closed the door behind him. Then, in one fluid motion he shook hands with Matt, loosened his tie, plopped into his desk chair, opened the window on the other side of his desk, and lit a cigarette. After drawing in deeply, he expelled a cloud of smoke and asked, "Did you get a buck this year?"

Matt had known and liked Ron for many years, and he knew all about the doctor's colorful past. He was seventy-four years old and appeared to be in great physical shape, in spite of the fact he'd smoked a pack or two of Chesterfields every day of his life since about the tenth grade. He had some deep crevices in his weathered face, but he was still trim and agile. Maybe "weathered" was a better term for him.

He was a serious outdoorsman, too—a man's man. But he had a few demons, mainly women and alcohol. Matt had known Ron's first three wives. Wife number one and wife number two had been unable to tolerate Ron's bad behavior and dalliances with other women. Matt thought the first wife had been a nice woman who just happened to marry the wrong guy. The second wife was a hasty choice by a lonely man, a mean-spirited bitch, and Matt was glad to see her go. The third wife, well, Matt had never gotten to know her very well. She didn't seem to have much passion for anything and she was soon gone too. But Ron's fourth wife, Elaine, seemed to make him happy, at last. Elaine was much younger than Ron. She brought some of her own baggage into their marriage: She'd been married a couple of times too, and in her younger days she was known to party. A lot. She was pleasant—no, outgoing. Everybody liked Elaine Hested, but every time Matt thought of her he remembered something John Velde had said: "Yeah, Elaine has a lot of hard miles on her . . . about six inches at a time."

Matt was now sitting with a psychiatrist, talking about deer hunting, after having his urine examined and an X-ray of his right hip. Something wasn't right. "No, I haven't got my deer yet this year," Matt responded, then he leaned forward and asked, "What the hell am I doing in *your* office, Ron? Did they find a personality disorder in my urine?"

"No," the doctor said without a smile, "but we didn't run *that* test." He took another long drag on his cigarette and then exhaled in the general direction of his open window.

"Isn't this a nonsmoking facility?" Matt asked.

"Well, yes, it is, as a matter of fact, but I own the whole goddamn building, so I'll just have a cigarette if I want to." The doctor leaned forward and turned on his computer. While he was waiting for the monitor to light up, he said, "You're in my office because Dr. Curtis, the new guy, just got called away to the emergency room—a car accident or something. Anyway, I was in his office, chatting with him while he was looking at your X-ray when he got the call from the ER."

"Is *he* crazy?" Matt asked.

"A little bit . . . drinks a lot, too. Makes his hands shake real bad in surgery," Ron joked. He took another drag on his cigarette. "Anyway, while we were talking I noticed your name on the X-ray, and I told him that we were friends. Then Dr. Curtis said, 'Well, your friend needs a new hip.'" Ron stubbed out his cigarette and lit another.

"No," Matt sighed.

"Yup. He said he didn't even need to do the exam." Ron turned the computer screen so that Matt could see his X-ray. "He was about to run off to the ER when I offered to see you in his place."

"So I'm gonna have a shrink tell me that I need a new hip?"

"Dr. Curtis was in a hurry to get to the ER, but he told his nurse to get you in to see him next week." Ron exhaled another cloud of smoke. "But he thought it would be fine for me to go over this with you, for now." He shrugged and gestured with the burning cigarette in his right hand. "Hey, this is rural America, Matt. He said this surgery should be done soon, and he wants you to see a colleague of his in Rochester, at the Mayo Clinic."

"I'm too *young*," Matt said indignantly. The implication that such a diagnosis was impossible filled the room. "It's gotta be some sorta lower back thing, or a sprained groin muscle."

Ron pointed to the computer monitor, which displayed Matt's pelvis, lower spinal column, and long bones in the legs. Then he took a pen and pointed it at the right hip in the X-ray. "He said this is the classic pathology. Your femur has changed shape into the textbook pistol grip, and you have no joint space between the femur and the socket on your pelvis. These are arthritic changes. You're bone-on-bone in that right hip—"

"Yeah, but I'm too young," Matt interrupted.

Ron folded his arms. "You're sixty-two, for Chrissakes. What is the minimum age for hip replacement?"

Matt slumped. He stared at the doctor with questioning eyes.

"Do I question you when you tell me that I need a root canal, or a crown on my tooth?" Ron asked, looking over the top of his glasses.

"Yes, as a matter of fact, you do."

"Well, that's different." He brushed Matt's words away before continuing. "He said you might not believe it, and that you might think he was mistaken. He told me to ask you this: You can't put your shoes and socks on your right foot by yourself, can you? Hurts in your groin when you try to cross your legs, and then it hurts all over your ass when you walk very far, doesn't it? Hurts when you bend over, doesn't it? And this pain in your hip is why you quit playing golf on men's day, isn't it? Feels like somebody is stabbing you in the groin when you rotate your hips, doesn't it?"

Matt nodded yes, and Ron added, "Can't move that right leg very far to the right before it starts to ache, and you can't cross your right foot over your left knee, can you?"

Matt sighed and relinquished his objection, but immediately asked for an explanation. "Well, why me? What's going on here? I mean, I am kinda young for this."

"This happens in people a lot younger than you," Ron said. "And you're actually not that young, as far as that goes."

"Thanks, Ron," Matt said sarcastically.

"Well, it's the truth, so get over all that 'I'm too young' stuff. Who knows why you've got this thing. You know you've led a pretty active life; you spent a lot of your life standing in ice water up to your ass trout fishing and duck hunting; your lifestyle may be a factor here."

"I know, Ron, but listening to you lecture about a healthy lifestyle is like asking Ted Kennedy for advice on ethics."

"Yeah, maybe so," Ron said as he dropped his cigarette butt into an empty Coke can. "But this one is a no-doubter. Dr. Curtis said that if he were to grade hips on a scale of zero to ten, with ten being the worst, yours is a nine. The only thing worse would be if the condyle just broke off. You need a new hip."

"How soon? Did he say?"

"No rules on that, but he said sooner is better than later. You take some time and get your mind around this. Then see Dr. Curtis next week so you can hear it all from him, too, and he'll set you up with a surgeon.

But understand that without the surgery, your pain will never get any better than it is today. You can continue to fart around with natural remedies, the stuff you've been trying—eye of newt, six earthworms baked on a shovel, shit like that. But it won't help."

"So, I just had a shrink tell me I need a new hip. I never saw that coming when I woke up this morning," Matt said.

Ron took a long drag on another cigarette. "Well, would you rather have Dr. Zoch, the proctologist on the other end of the building, stick his finger in your ass and then tell you you're crazy?"

Matt could only smile. "Well, Ron, I'd rather have him tell me I was crazy than handsome, at that point."

"Get outta here," Ron chuckled.

When Matt left Dr. Hested's office he walked slowly, trying to hide his limp as he moved through the corridors of the medical clinic. If he walked slowly enough, no one could notice the limp, but when he dialed it back that far he was only a bit more mobile than a glacier. He wanted to hide his condition from everyone, so he had to move as though he was just taking a leisurely stroll. He brought his cell phone up to his ear and acted like he was listening, even though no one was calling him. This way, if someone was watching him, they'd think he was concentrating on talking, not walking. He'd try to look like a busy man who was on a business phone call, not an old man with a bad hip.

When he reached his truck, he needed to use his hand to lift his right leg into the seat. When he turned the key and his truck roared to life, he realized he had nowhere to go. He sat in the parking lot and heard Dr. Hested's words several times: "You need a new hip."

"Well, shit," Matt sighed. He stared out over his steering wheel and watched the cars moving, several blocks away.

This stuff was for old people, not him. Now he really was no different than his aging friends and classmates at Alvie's funeral. Damn, he'd had himself convinced that he was somehow different from everyone else. Now this. The diagnosis was a real kick in the nuts. His old friend Ron had just delivered him to the other side of some line that he'd thought he wouldn't cross until he was much farther along in life's journey. He shook his head and lowered his eyes. "Fuck."

He took his phone from his pocket and decided to call Jane. He wanted, needed, to talk to her now. Her office wasn't that far down the hall from Dr. Hested's. He should have walked down there and told her, but he'd actually been embarrassed. He was about to press the call button when he hesitated.

Wait, he thought, I'm about to tell this beautiful woman, my lover, that I need a new hip. Maybe after that I should ask her to pick up some denture cream and a few adult diapers and drop 'em off at the nursing home for me. He couldn't tell Jane, not now. Not yet.

Maybe he'd go to Gray's Outfitters, in downtown Pine Rapids, and wander around? Gray's was his favorite store. The place was jammed with fishing tackle and guns and outdoor clothing. He always felt good when he went there. Maybe he'd treat himself to a new pair of hunting boots while he was thinking about all of this. Yeah, new boots might make him feel better. Besides that, he had nothing else to do.

When he got there, he had to circle the block several times to find a parking place. Finally, he found an empty space close to the front door. He got out of the truck and with his first step came the familiar stabbing pain in his hip. With no hesitation, he drew his phone from his pocket and faked another phone call in order to deceive anyone who might recognize him and wonder why he was walking so slowly.

He pushed through the front door, still on an imaginary phone call, and wandered back to the shoe display. He actually considered saying a few words to the fictitious caller on the other end in order to help sell this lie, but he made it to a rack of boots before that was necessary, and he put his phone away.

A young woman wearing a hat like Santa Claus's stepped up to him and said, "Merry Christmas! Can I help you?" The girl was beautiful, with shoulder-length brown hair and the face of an angel. Her skin was smooth, and her khaki pants and shirt strained perfectly against the tautness of her athletic physique. Her little red-and-white Christmas hat gave her an air of innocence.

"Well, you sure can," Matt replied in an overly friendly voice. He explained that he was looking for the warmest pair of boots he could find, and she turned away go find a size 11½ for him to try on. When she returned a minute later, carrying two large boot boxes, Matt was prepared to charm her with his clever wit. When she handed him a boot he said something that was sure to get a smile. But she didn't laugh, and when he looked up at her she was staring at someone about fifteen feet behind him. He thought nothing of it and then stood up when the boot was laced. After a couple of steps to his right, and then back, he said something else that he thought was clever.

The girl still wore a vacant stare. Oh, she was aware that he'd spoken, sort of, but she hadn't heard a word of his witty retort. She was still focused on something behind him. So, when he sat down to try on the other boot he stole a glance over his right shoulder and saw two college-aged men looking at the boot display on the wall. He laced up the other boot and made a point to stand up so that he was directly in between the pretty girl and the college boys, blocking her view of them.

Things got worse; he thought maybe he was invisible now. The girl was looking right through him and she could muster only the weakest effort to acknowledge his presence. He made yet another witty comment about staying warm, and the girl made no response at all.

Damn, this was his best material, too. A few years earlier this girl would have been giggling and smiling. A few years before that she'd have given him her phone number, but today, she couldn't even see him. She could not have been more disinterested. He was just some old fart looking for boots and blocking her view.

"I'll take these," Matt said as he put the boots back in their box.

The girl nodded but didn't look at him again. He stood up, and with the boots under one arm, he limped over to a display of fleece coats that had been designed for archery hunters. As he tried on one of the coats he looked back and watched while the young lady who'd found him to be quite forgettable laughed and flirted with the college boys.

He wandered on, to the back of the store, ostensibly in search of new broad heads for his arrows, or new gloves, or something, anything that might make him forget about his hip, and this thing that just happened with the young girl. He drifted through some displays of fishing tackle, and then some duck decoys. Eventually he came to a display for ice fishermen: a little sled with a pop-up tent and a couple of stools to sit on. It was much nicer than the one he already had—the one that stunk of mouse piss and mothballs—and it was a good place to rest. Matt plopped down on one of the stools and texted Jane:

<I need a new hip.>

His phone rang before he could put it back in his pocket.

"A new hip?" Jane asked with no other greeting.

"Yup."

"Well, good! Now we know what's wrong. Get it fixed and you'll feel better right away. Everyone who gets a new hip says they wish they'd done it much sooner."

Matt was taken aback by her enthusiasm, and that she had made no protest about his being too young. "Yeah, but don't you think I'm too young?" he asked.

"Apparently not."

Matt didn't respond right away and Jane picked up on his dark mood.

"It'll be fine! Lots of men your age do this," she said.

The words "men your age" rang in Matt's ears, and he was slow to respond again.

"Bo Jackson had a hip replaced when he was a lot younger than you are, and he came back to play in the big leagues. And he's still a hunter, like you." Jane made a point to put some cheer in her voice.

"Yeah, I suppose so."

"Hey, I gotta go! I've got a call on the other line. I love you, honey, and I'll see you when you get home. This is a good thing. Bye." She was gone before Matt could goodbye.

Matt sighed. "Shit."

It was almost ten o'clock that night when Matt sat on the side of his bed and began to undress. He stripped down to his T-shirt and boxer shorts, but groaned when he tried to raise his right foot to take the sock off. He used his hands to lift his foot closer and felt an even more intense stabbing pain in his groin. The pain caused him to release his foot and let it thump onto the floor. He shook his head in despair and then began to use the toes on his left foot to pull the sock off his right. "Ouch." He made an effort to stand straight but had to hesitate when the pain in his hip grabbed at him again.

He made his way toward the kitchen, with each step an adventure: no pain with his left side; then a jolting, grinding ache in his right hip; then a smooth step; then a protective hobble on the right. Damn, this was getting hard to bear.

He reached up to the liquor cabinet above the refrigerator and brought down the bottle of Aberlour and poured a couple of fingers' worth into a glass. The walk over to the leather couch by the fireplace seemed longer tonight, as he took every step slowly to minimize the pain. At least he didn't need to fake a phone call in his own home. When he reached the chair in front of his computer he stopped for a moment. There was no particular reason to stop at the computer desk, but the office chair looked pretty comfortable, so he sat down and leaned back.

Maybe he'd try to talk to Jane again? Nah, she was already asleep. Besides that, Matt couldn't shake his expectation that she'd be embarrassed about her husband needing an old man's surgery. She'd been so upbeat about just going ahead and replacing his hip; she just didn't understand the implications here. But maybe that was good—why rock the boat?

And John Velde? Hell, he'd laughed out loud when Matt told him about this earlier in the day. "Too much pelvic thrusting, eh? Or not enough?" John had said. John had actually ended their conversation with, "Do they have to shave your balls for that operation?" That did get Matt to laugh a little bit. But John wasn't the one to talk to right now either.

He'd just take the Aberlour over to the couch and think about life by himself, instead of talking to anyone. But first, since he was sitting here, he'd turn the computer on and check his email.

As usual, there was nothing new except a few stupid jokes from a couple of buddies. He scrolled down through the in-box and was about to shut off the computer when he came across the note Mo Glasnapp had sent a while back. He read through it several times, and he found himself thinking about how happy he'd been back when she was his best friend. The image of Mo and him standing on Alvie's front porch while he kissed her goodnight lingered in his mind. Life was pretty simple then.

He set the glass of scotch on the table and wondered about Mo. Then he hit Reply and started typing.

Hey Mo,

I'm sorry it's taken so long to get back to you. I just kept waiting for the right time. I guess this is it. It was nice to see you again, too, after so many years. And it was nice to meet your family. I knew they'd all be handsome and smart.

You are correct, I never seemed to be able to please your dad, but he sure did create some colorful memories for all of us who played for him.

Those were good times, happy times. And the times with Donny and David were always good, too.

But my friendship with you was the best. And you're there in all of my best memories of that time in my life. Can't tell you how nice it was to see you (and steal another smooch). I miss the way we were.

All my best,

Matt

He hit Send and leaned back in the chair. Recalling pleasant vignettes from high school, he felt good for the first time all day. And an odd thought came to him: He wondered, just for a second, if Mo still had feelings for him.

He stood up and waited for his hip not to hurt before he walked to the couch and plopped down. No matter how he eased himself into any chair, his hip ached. After a sip of scotch, he considered the unavoidable surgery that awaited him. He already understood the surgical procedure, but the mental picture of some doctor doing that to *him* caused an involuntary grimace. He closed his eyes and rubbed his forehead while he admitted to himself that he was afraid of the surgery.

But more than the thoughts of what would be done to him, there was the reality that this was, in fact, a problem that old people dealt with. He wasn't simply easing past his prime, he was getting old. This had all come so quickly, especially on the heels of Alvie's funeral and reconnecting with Mo and the others.

From this day forward, he'd never know that thrill of rounding second base and digging for third—that weightless feeling, and the knowledge that he could do anything he wanted. OK, maybe that door had actually closed behind him a while ago; he knew that much, intellectually. But this hip thing, this surgery, this was such an emphatic demarcation into old age. He'd never fly around second base again, for sure. But what else would be lost?

The conversation with the cute young salesgirl in Gray's earlier—that had been a real kick in the nuts too. Always, or until today, it seemed, he'd been able to make the girls smile. He had absolutely no interest in taking that girl home; that wasn't what hurt. It was the cold, absolute indifference of a beautiful woman, which he'd never experienced before, and the undeniable implication that maybe he was in rapid decline as a man. Several doors, the ones that separated youth—OK, middle age—from old age, were slamming shut behind him. Damn, he hadn't seen this coming.

CHAPTER ELEVEN

—•—

Matt opened the door of his truck and stepped out, making a point to stand still before slowly straightening himself to his full height. The stabbing pain in his groin, as usual, nearly took his breath away. He stood still for a moment after the pain went away and considered his next movement; that was going to hurt too. So he took very short steps and tried not to limp as he made his way across the street toward the coffee shop where he planned to meet John in a few minutes.

He'd talked things over with Jane, and since neither of their sons would be coming home for Christmas this year, he'd made an appointment to have his right hip replaced on December 26 at the Mayo Clinic in Rochester. Until that day he'd try to continue with all of his normal activities.

"You look like shit," came a voice from behind him. He didn't need to turn and look, to know it was John. "God, you walk like you're ninety years old."

"It gets worse every day," Matt said, when John caught up with him. "I'm gonna have my hip replaced the day after Christmas."

"Oh, bummer." John reconsidered. "Well, maybe that's a good thing."

When they reached the glass door of the Human Bean, John pulled it open and held it for Matt. "Hey, I drove down Shorewood Avenue today on the way over here," Matt said as he stepped inside. "What's up with that eighteen-wheeler parked over at Darrell 'n Snag's place?"

"Aw, Jesus! You won't believe it," John said. He stomped the snow off his boots before he stepped through the doorway. "Darrell bought sixteen thousand dead skunks. That whole damn trailer is fulla *skunks*! You believe that shit?"

Even to Matt's ears, sixteen thousand dead skunks came as a surprise. He'd seen a few dozen of Darrell Velde's other moneymaking schemes come and go over the years, but this one seemed inspired. His face lit up with a smile before he asked, "So what's he gonna do with dead skunks?"

"Well, it's a refrigerator trailer, so the skunks are frozen," John began. "His plan is to take out a couple hundred every day and let 'em thaw, then skin 'em the next day."

"'N'en what?"

"The ultimate plan is to use the pelts to make skunk blankets, like the beaver blankets we're experimenting with, and then eventually some other skunk apparel and accessories," John said.

"Skunks? Really?"

"You can buy a shitload of skunks for not much money, and they are kind of a unique-looking pelt," John said. "He hopes to corner the market on skunk wear along with the beaver and coyote blankets."

"So, what does one pay for a frozen dead skunk?"

"Not much; 'bout fifty cents apiece."

Matt wondered if there actually might be a chance to make a buck in the whole process.

"Aw, shit, you won't believe it," John said, shaking his head. "At the end of every day now they have a pickup load full of skunk carcasses, which smells about like you think it would, so when they have a nice big ol' pile o' skunks, they either need to call the rendering plant down by St. Cloud, or make a clandestine run out into the woods and dump the critters, which I don't think is legal. Then there's the skunk pelts, which also carry a pretty pungent bouquet until after the hides are cured. And then a' course there's Snag. How do you think *he* smells at the end of the day, after cleaning a couple hundred skunks?" John sighed. "His truck, his trailer, the fur shop, that whole end of town smells like dead skunk. They're already dealing with complaints from the residents over there about the smell. I don't know if Snag can get all those critters skinned before the city makes 'em get outta town."

"Where does one go in order to purchase a truckload of frozen skunks?" Matt said, unzipping his coat.

"I never even asked." John took off his gloves and hat and changed the subject. "So how was your visit to the Mayo Clinic?"

"Good, really good. I had a nice visit with a surgeon and he explained everything, and then I scheduled the appointment." When Matt finished his sentence, he looked at John and saw that John wasn't listening to him.

They were standing at the end of a line of people waiting to order coffee, and John had gone into a slow burn. He hated to wait in line anyway, and just in front of them stood four women. All of them looked to be about forty years old, and they were all talking and looking up at the menu on the wall behind the counter. "Just watch," John whispered. "Every one of these women is gonna get to the front of the line and not know what they want. Then they're gonna look up at the menu behind the counter and ask a few stupid questions. Then they're gonna need to talk about their feelings toward a mocha versus a latte. Then they'll order some goddamn complicated thing, and then they'll change their order . . . twice." His face hardened and Matt saw the storm building on the horizon.

The woman with the scar, the one who'd threatened to spit in John's coffee a few days earlier, waited patiently while the customers in front of her studied the menu. She looked toward the end of the line, made eye contact with John, and looked away.

Matt knew what was about to happen but could think of no way to prevent it. "Relax," he said softly into John's ear, "we're in no hurry."

John's head seemed to expand when he looked at the women in front of him; the pressure was already building. A minute went by, and still none of the women could make a decision about what to order. The muscles in John's face began to twitch.

"OK . . ." began the woman in the front of the line. She was still looking up at the menu and she paused again.

Matt glanced at John and felt as if he was watching a stovetop with a pot about to boil over. He made an effort to defuse the escalating tension by distracting John with conversation about something else. "Yeah, they sure do a nice job down there at the Mayo Clinic; I mean, getting so many people through that place in such an efficient manner."

John's steely glare never changed, even when the woman ordered some sort of mocha. He'd heard what Matt said about the Mayo Clinic, but it was now impossible for him to think about anything except the woman in the front of the line and how long it was taking her to order coffee.

The woman behind the counter asked the woman who'd ordered the mocha if she wanted white or dark chocolate. There was a pause, a moment to consider what kind of chocolate she wanted, and John's aura went dark.

The woman thought for a second, then asked how many grams of fat were in the white chocolate. At that point, the woman with the scar admitted that she didn't know, and the woman who'd ordered the mocha seemed to think she really needed to know about the fat content of the white chocolate before she could safely order. So, the woman behind the counter walked a few steps away in order to check the label on a bottle behind the counter. When she returned, and told the other woman how much fat was in the white chocolate, John had smoke coming out his ears.

"Well, how much fat is in the *dark* chocolate?" the woman asked, and that did it for John.

"Jesus Christ!" he exploded. "I got moss growing on the north side of my head back here! Maybe you coulda done your research on fat before you got to the front of the line. In fact, it looks like you shoulda checked into it some time ago! Chrissakes, do you know there are other people—"

"All right! That's it!" barked the woman behind the counter. She snapped her fingers and pointed at John and Matt. "You two! Over here!" She pointed to a small table in the corner as she scurried out from behind the counter.

John went silent but wore an amused smirk when he stole a glance at Matt. Matt was so embarrassed he wanted to run away, but he dutifully followed the woman's instructions and followed John over to the corner table. The woman met them by the table, and she was staring daggers. "Sit!" she hissed. The scar that ran down from her forehead on to her cheek was now red, even more red than usual, because her face was flushed with stifled rage.

When the men, who were both a foot taller than her, had seated themselves, she poked John with her index finger and said, "Just shut the fuck up and I'll bring you some coffee in a minute." After the briefest pause she added, "Can you do that? Can you try not to be such an *asshole*? Can you just behave yourselves till I come back?"

John nodded yes, but he still hadn't let go of the smirk. The woman hurried back to her position behind the counter, where she listened carefully as the others made their orders. Matt watched her from the corner of his eye, and he was impressed by the way she could hide the anger from a moment earlier with a suddenly happy smile as she waited on the women back at the counter.

Matt leaned forward and said to John, "Great! Just great! You asswipe! How old are you gonna be when you finally grow up? I can't believe the shit you say and do. You know, I've been kicked outta more than a few bars because I was with you. I've been kicked outta several private beer parties because I was with you. I got my ass beat once because I was with you." Matt's frustration grew, and the intensity of his narrative mounted, but he kept his voice low. "I even got kicked outta school, elementary *and* high school, because I was with you." He leaned a bit farther forward and crinkled his face before he added, "And now we're sixty years old and I get kicked out of a coffee shop fulla old ladies, because of you?"

"Relax," John replied. Even now, after the stern rebuke from the woman behind the counter, he showed no sign of contrition. "We didn't get kicked out of anything." He flicked his eyebrows once and showed Matt the devilish countenance he'd been flashing for nearly sixty years. His eyes sparkled with the assurance that a tsunami of mischievous behavior was about to roll out of him at any moment. "I think the lady with the scar is kinda cute."

"What? She wants to stab you in the throat! I don't think she's flirting. Aw, Jesus, John, here we are huddled in this little corner, waitin' to get our asses chewed again. It's just like fourth grade, when Miss Bureson stood there and watched us pee so she could be sure you weren't inciting some new round of bad behavior." Matt covered his face and added, "When does this end?"

"Well, *never*, if we do it right," John said, grinning. "You're such a rule follower."

Several minutes passed, and when all the ladies in front of them had been served, the woman from behind the counter brought two coffees to the table where she'd banished John and Matt. She was pretty, really pretty, even prettier than the last time he'd been here, Matt thought. She was petite, with short dark hair, full breasts, and an athletic figure. When she placed the coffee on their table, she crossed her arms and stood close, so her thighs were almost touching their table.

"Listen," she started, lowering her voice, "those women drive me crazy too. But they're nice people, and they spend a lot of money in here. I worked hard, really hard, to buy this place and I won't have you coming in here and insulting my customers. So, the next time you do that I'm gonna throw your asses outta here. Forever. Got it?"

Matt was embarrassed, humiliated, and he nodded his understanding. John nodded too, but there wasn't a hint of remorse in his eyes, only the remnant of the same old shit-eating grin. The woman turned to leave them, and Matt stopped her. "Hey, Miss . . ." he said, "just so you know, I didn't do anything. My associate here is the one who—"

"I know that, and I know who you are, Dr. Kingston, and that's the only reason I didn't give both of you the boot," she said.

"Well . . . I . . ." Matt stammered, then he recovered. He tilted his head to the side and said, "Really?"

The woman pulled a chair from a nearby table and sat down with them. "Well, Dr. Kingston, if you run with a bad crowd . . ." She glanced at John, then back at Matt, ". . . you get yelled at by the lady at the coffee shop. That's the way it is." She turned her gaze to John and held it there. "Look, this is a small town. That's why I came here. I also know that this place is no longer Hans's Blue Line Café. It can never be that again. I miss the way things were, too. But Hans is dead and gone; times change. I can't bring back the past. But maybe someday, if you give it a try, you might like this place as much as Hans's." She stood up and prepared to go back to work, then added, "But if you don't, just shut up and go somewhere else. OK?"

As she turned to leave Matt stopped her again. "Hey, what's your name?"

The woman seemed to relax a bit. "Sally Durham. I just bought this place last summer."

"Matt Kingston," he said, extending his hand. "Welcome to Pine Rapids. It's nice to meet you, and I'm sorry for the way this asshole behaves. The only reason he's with me today is because all my friends were busy."

Sally Durham almost smiled.

"John Velde," John said, also extending his hand. And after he'd shaken her hand he gave her the check for the coffee, along with two twenty-dollar bills. "I'm sorry, too," he said, doing a pretty good imitation of someone who was actually sorry for something. He quickly added, "But just so you know, Dr. Kingston here isn't a real doctor—he's just a dentist, and he's an asshole, too." Then he flashed the old shit-eating grin.

Sally looked at the bills, softened even more, and let a smile come to her lips. "Look, you guys, let's make deal here, OK?" She looked back and forth between them. "In the future, when you children come in here together and I'm busy at the counter, just come and sit down over here at this table. I'll see you, and I'll bring you your coffee as soon as I can. That way you won't have to grow any more moss on the north side of your head." She raised her eyebrows and asked, "Is that all right with you?"

Matt nodded, then Sally tightened her eyes and turned to John. He nodded his agreement too, rather unconvincingly.

She held up the twenties for John to see and reminded him, "Remember, next time this won't be enough: You're gone. History. Pfft. Outta here!" She topped her sentence by gesturing "you're out!" with her thumb.

John made a point to stare at Sally's behind while she walked away. When she was barely out of earshot he whipped his head around to face Matt. "I'm in love!"

"Really?" Matt said, incredulous.

"She just kept getting hotter and hotter as she talked," John said. "And that scar on her cheek is kinda cute."

"You just don't get it, John. She was really pissed at you, and all she did was commute our sentence. Instead of kicking us outta here, she says we have to sit here, in the dunce corner, so she can keep an eye on us. This is no different than Miss Bureson standing in the boy's room watching us pee."

"Uh-huh," John halfheartedly agreed, before he slurped at his coffee. He was still watching Sally and thinking more about the moving parts under her dress than what Matt was saying. "I'm thinking Sally Durham wants to see my dong, too, just like Frau Bureson."

Matt gave up, took the sports section from a nearby table, and started scanning the headlines. There was no point in trying to talk to John just now.

John disengaged from the Sally Durham fantasy and rejoined Matt back in the real world. As they sipped their coffee they talked about sports, politics, and sports again, and then all the skunks in the trailer at the Shorewood Furist.

"Hey, I heard the crappies are really bitin' on your lake. You wanna go fishin' when we're done with coffee?" Even as John was asking about going fishing later in the day, he was watching something behind Matt, so Matt turned around to see what it was.

A young boy, perhaps eight years old, was bussing dirty dishes back to the kitchen. The kid was wearing heavy Sorel boots and clomping them loudly with each step. He was a cute kid. Matt and John both watched him work for a few minutes, and then the boy walked over to Sally and said something. Sally nodded yes and the kid carried a garbage bag from behind the front counter and out the back door.

"Think the kid *works* here?" John said.

"Too young. Must be one of the waitress's kids."

"You want some more coffee?" John got up to get himself a refill.

"Sure."

When John returned a moment later with their refills he said, "It's Sally's grandson." He put Matt's coffee down on the table and added, "I bought us each a scone, too, and Sally, my new girlfriend, said she'd bring it over in a minute."

"OK, thanks," Matt replied. Then he added, "I think I'm done deer hunting for this season, and I won't be doing much ice fishing for a couple months after my hip surgery, so yeah, let's go fishing later; might be my last time out for a while."

The little kid arrived at their table carrying a paper plate with two blueberry scones on it.

"These are for you," the kid said.

"Well, thank you, young man!" John said. He handed him a five-dollar bill. "Here. This is a tip. It's for good service."

The kid looked at the five-spot for a moment and then turned around and walked right back to Sally. Matt and John watched the boy point to John and tell his grandmother what had just happened, and he held the money up with both hands. Sally said something and nodded her head, and the kid walked back to their table.

"Thank you very much," the kid said to John.

"You're welcome. You keep up the good work."

Sally watched her grandson thank them, and when John and Matt looked over at her she smiled, put her hand over her heart and mouthed, "Thank you."

John nodded and turned back to Matt before he started off in another direction: "So, during this hip replacement surgery; when you're asleep—I bet the nurses are gonna peek at your weeny and laugh."

It was full dark, and Jane was beginning to wonder if she should worry about Matt and John, when she saw the headlights from the ATV. The men were finally returning from an afternoon of ice fishing, probably Matt's last time out on a frozen lake until next winter, when he'd be healed from his hip surgery.

She heard the motor noise from the ATV go silent, and a moment later she heard the commotion, as if Matt and John were having a fistfight in the garage. Then the door to the back entryway, by the kitchen, flew open, and it sounded like ten men had burst in instead of two.

Jane ran to the kitchen and found both men talking and laughing at full volume while they unzipped heavy coats and bib overalls, and took off stocking caps and mittens and threw everything in a pile by the back door. Both of them had rosy cheeks from the extreme cold outside, and their hair was matted down from sweating under their warm hats.

"Oh, God, you shoulda been there, honey!" Matt bellowed when he saw Jane. John was laughing uncontrollably and holding himself up by resting his hands on his knees.

"What? What happened?" Jane asked. She was laughing along with them now, and had no idea what was so funny.

"Gimme a beer," Matt said to John, as he kicked his coveralls toward the door and plopped into a kitchen chair.

John opened the fridge and took out two beers before he sat next to Matt.

"So, what happened?" Jane asked again.

"OK . . ." Matt said, and he took a deep breath to collect his thoughts, ". . . so we're sittin' there, out on the Flemish Cap, and we're catching some nice crappies—nothing special, but the bite was on. We had two holes drilled and we had about a dozen keepers in the bucket—"

John began to laugh and then covered his eyes. "Unbelievable, never seen anything like it," he interrupted. Then he tipped his can of Leinenkugel's back and drank heavily.

"So we've got some nice ones in the bucket," Matt began again, "and we're talking about fishin' and huntin' and we're passing the flask of brandy back and forth—" He stopped and looked at John and they started laughing all over again.

"What? What happened?" Jane pleaded.

"So all of a sudden I see this faint shadow under the ice, and then . . ." Matt paused for emphasis, "a *muskrat*, a really pissed-off, nasty-faced little bastard, came flyin' up outta my hole! Scared the livin' shit outta me!"

"Me too!" John chimed in.

"So now we have this hateful little fucker, who's obviously taken a wrong turn on his way home from work, in our fish house," Matt said, "and he's *really pissed off!*" Matt dissolved into laughter again, and John picked up the narrative.

"So this *rat*, who goes about a pound and a half, is clearly after a shot at the heavyweight title! He's jumping up on my boot and biting at it and I'm screaming and kicking and covering my nuts—I was terrified!" John was unable to continue.

"So I picked up the ladle that we use to scoop ice shavings outta the holes, and I started swinging at him," Matt said. "So the little monster turns on me and starts bitin' at my boots and coveralls, too. 'N then John's got the thermos in his hand and he's tryin' to bash the rat's brains out—"

Both of them had to stop and laugh again.

"So after about one minute of pandemonium," Matt continued, "we have four broken fishing rods, the flask of brandy is gone—down one of the holes, along with two tackle boxes and a flashlight—and the muskrat dives back down the hole he came through, and the sneak attack is over."

John threw his empty beer can into a wastebasket and took two more out of the fridge. He plopped back into his chair, took a deep breath and asked, "Jeez, what a gong show it was. Do you guys have anything to eat?"

"Just some leftovers," Jane replied, surprised at the sudden change of conversation. "What happened then?"

"We came home." John shrugged.

As if he sensed that Jane needed a better ending to the story, Matt added, "I bet that rat is sitting at his kitchen table right now, telling his wife and kids about how he scared the shit outta those two white boys on the Flemish Cap."

The chuckles faded away as Matt and John raised a glass and toasted each other from across the kitchen.

"OK then," John said, as he stood up and opened the fridge. "Let's see here . . ." he mumbled to himself as he looked inside the refrigerator, "eggs . . . coupla leftover hamburger patties . . . two leftover baked potatoes . . . some sweet peppers . . . nothing green growing on anything, that's good." He turned to Jane and asked, "Do you have an onion?"

"Downstairs, in the cellar," Matt replied.

"OK then, we're good," John pronounced. "I'll make my specialty: Trailblazer Medley! But you gotta go get me that onion, Matt." He'd just invited himself for dinner and then decided to prepare it, also.

"OK." Matt rose from his seat and limped toward the basement stairway.

"And see if you can find a little hot sauce down there in the pantry too, eh?" John commanded.

When Matt was just out of earshot, John took another Leinenkugel's from the fridge, opened it, and gave it to Jane. As he extended his hand toward her he said quietly, "We have good times."

"I've noticed." She smiled.

John lowered his voice and added, "I did a lotta stupid shit when I was young, and—"

"You still do," Jane interjected.

"Ooh, good one." John groaned and pulled an imaginary arrow from his heart. Then he leaned close and clinked his long-neck beer bottle against hers. "But that's not my point just now." He paused. "I'm sixty-two years old, and today, for just a while there, I was a little boy again. My friend Matt and I were little boys, fishin', and talkin', and laughin'. And that's powerful stuff." John pointed a spatula at Jane and added, "So, thanks for letting that happen. I know you don't always think I'm a very good influence on him."

"Well, I guess that's what *I'm* here for, to be a good influence on him," Jane said.

Neither of them spoke for a moment, and the only sound they heard was Matt rummaging around in the basement.

"So, what is it that you're after, John? What will finally make you happy?" Jane said softly.

"You don't think I'm happy?"

Jane shook her head.

"Hmm, what am I looking for?" John sighed, and in repeating her question he'd confessed to the search for something. "I dunno." He shrugged. "But I think I'll know it when I find it."

There was a small crash in the basement, and they heard Matt mutter, "Shit!"

"How 'bout you, Jane? Are you searching for something?" John asked.

"Nope. I already found it, but I'm not sure if I could ever explain it," she said. "Do you ever talk with Matt about stuff like this?"

"Yeah, and sometimes lately I think Matt seems a bit depressed. Maybe it's just the thing with his hip." John lowered his voice and added, "Even today, before the muskrat attack, he seemed depressed, in a dark place.

While we were sitting there on the ice, he stared straight ahead and talked about getting old, and things he regrets. I've never seen him do that. You *know* this thing with his hip is bothering him. The long-term chronic pain can mess up your head some, and then having a hip replaced does sorta hint at getting old."

Jane held the beer bottle in her lap and considered John's words. "Depressed? You really think so?"

"Yeah, when I was in his office a while back his assistant came and told him about a couple longtime patients in his practice; I think one of them had died and the other had been moved to a nursing home. I could see that really bothered him. And he talked about both of those two patients today. He's struggling with something—maybe he's thinking about getting old, or dying?"

"Yeah, maybe." Jane nodded. Then she added, "Did he actually mention that; dying, I mean?"

"No, but he sorta talked around it. You know, how a person does that sometimes when they just don't wanna say what's really on their mind. Do you ever talk to him about stuff like this?"

"Sure, we talk, but Matt can go Norwegian on you pretty fast."

John understood exactly what Jane was saying. A stoic hardness, a stiff upper lip, and a refusal to recognize or discuss failure or fear would always be Matt's first response.

Footsteps coming up the stairs told them that Matt was about to rejoin them. John smiled, closed his eyes, and nodded. There wasn't much more to say just now. When Matt reached the top of the stairs he was unaware of the conversation between his wife and his friend.

CHAPTER TWELVE

———◆———

Supper, or "Gourmet Club," as John had named it, was long over. John's Trailblazer Medley had simply been scrambled eggs with an onion and some leftovers tossed in. The three of them had talked about everything and nothing, and then revisited the attack of the vicious muskrat while they did the dishes. After John went home, Matt and Jane spent a quiet evening reading in front of a fire.

Matt was wearing baggy wool socks, boxer shorts, and a gray T-shirt as he stood in front of the bathroom mirror and brushed his teeth before bed. His hair was more salt than pepper now, and he tried to turn his head in all directions, looking for a bald spot in the back. He hoped others didn't see it yet, but the muscles in his shoulders and arms and chest were getting smaller, or, at least, there was not as much definition as there once had been. When he put nice clothes on he thought he still looked young enough. But now, like this, he could see the changes that age was making on his body. "Jeez, we need to use candles in here, or a five-watt bulb," he mumbled to the man staring back at him in the mirror. "Who *are* you?"

"What did you say?" Jane said from her closet. She was getting ready for bed, too, wearing only panties and a maroon T-shirt that said Pine Rapids Baseball across the front when she joined him in the bathroom. "Ooh, hold still," she said.

"What?"

"Just hold still." She fumbled through a small drawer and produced the razor she normally used to shave her legs.

"What are you doing?" he asked.

"You have a bunch of scraggly hairs here, on your ear." She stood on her tiptoes and used one hand to turn his head and catch some better light. Then she drew the razor along the outside curve of his right ear.

"You're shaving my ear?"

"A little bit. Now turn the other way." When she was done with his left ear, she brushed it with her hand to make sure she'd done a thorough job, then said again, "Don't move." She fumbled through the drawer again.

"What? What now?"

"You have a bunch of hairs growing out of your ears, too." A few seconds later she reached up, pulled his head down to her eye level, and began using a tiny scissors to snip at the hairs she'd noticed. When she was finished with both ears she said, "OK, let's have a look at your eyebrows."

"Jesus." He gave a heavy sigh.

"Well, you look like that general on *Hogan's Heroes*. You know, the one with the bushy eyebrows," she said while she snipped at his eyebrows.

"General Burkhalter?"

"I knew you'd know his name." Jane giggled.

"You know, a few years ago you if you'd come in here wearing a T-shirt and panties and looking like that, we'd have been *real* busy by now; I'd be wearing *you*."

Jane ignored him and put the tiny scissors back in the drawer.

"But tonight, you're shaving my ears." He closed his eyes and shook his head, then picked up his toothbrush and got to work. "Sheesh," he mumbled, with toothpaste foam building around his lips.

From the corner of her eye, as Matt leaned over the sink and brushed, Jane stole a peek at him. "You're shaving my ears" was a pretty good line, and it brought half a grin to one corner of her mouth. He was funny. He always had been, and she couldn't help but remember the boy who'd swept her away at the Improper Fraction all those years ago. His comment about "wearing her" a few years ago? She didn't see an old man in his boxer shorts brushing his teeth; she saw her lover, just as handsome as he'd ever been.

"How did you get to be such good friends with John?" she asked, trying to imagine the two of them as high school friends.

"We were *always* friends," Matt said. "We were little boys together. We'll be friends forever." He spat into the sink, put his toothbrush away, and turned toward Jane. "Wow, you're still a pretty girl," he said. He grabbed her quickly and kissed her as he ran his hands under her T-shirt to her breasts.

"Ooh, your hands are cold," she protested. She brushed his hands away but stood close, inviting a warm embrace. "Don't touch me with your hands."

"Well, what would you like me to touch you with?" He wrapped his arms around her and rubbed his hands together behind her back until they were warm enough to pass them over the curves of her panties and pull her hips closer.

"You think you're gonna have your way with me tonight, don't you?" she asked.

"Yeah, but I'm kinda tired, so not more than three—OK, four times, all right?"

She laughed and pushed him away, "Go warm up the bed while I brush my teeth."

Matt was sitting up in bed a minute later, wearing reading glasses and skimming through a fishing magazine, while Jane leaned toward the bathroom mirror and began taking off her makeup. "Really, how did you get to be such good friends with John Velde?" she called out.

"Well, we did little-boy stuff together. You know, fishin' in the creek, and sports. Damn, that guy was always fun to be around." He threw the fishing magazine onto the nightstand beside their bed and started a story. "One time, I think we were about ten years old, there were four of us: John and me and Steve Saathe and Joe Fogal. We were sitting at a picnic table out in front of a little neighborhood grocery store back home. It was a tiny little store with mostly candy, and a few convenience items; we used to go there on hot summer afternoons and buy baseball cards and drink Dr. Pepper and talk about sports and girls. So one day John was drinking his Dr. Pepper and he reached into his pocket and pulled out a couple of those little smoke bombs. You remember those? They were little colored balls that gave off bright colored smoke—purple or green or red, whatever. Anyway, John lit the fuse on a green one and threw it in the street and a cloud of green smoke billowed out of it, and we thought it was pretty cool. So John holds up a purple one and says, 'Hey, I'll bet it would look really cool if I threw this into that garbage can. There'd be purple smoke comin' out all over!'

"We all agreed that would be pretty cool, so John lit the fuse and threw it in the garbage can. The idea that maybe all that paper in the big ol' garbage can might catch fire just never crossed our minds. Not much crosses a ten-year-old boy's mind, I guess. So pretty soon there's a cloud of purple smoke, and then black smoke, *and* flames, roaring outta that garbage can. And then Delbert—that was the name of the old guy who owned the little store—came running out of the store swearing to beat hell, and he sprayed a garden hose on that garbage can. Jesus, it was a mess: burnt papers fluttering everywhere and Delbert stomping on flaming garbage. We were scared, and Delbert was pissed, really pissed. I guess he thought we'd set a fire deliberately. How could he know we were just stupid?

"So Delbert takes us inside and makes us each call our father and confess to our malicious crime. He made a point to sit there and watch while we all dialed home and told our fathers about the fire."

"What did your father say?" Jane asked from the bathroom.

"Oh, Dad could tell I was scared and upset, and he knew I wouldn't set a fire on purpose, so he just told me to come home and we'd talk about it all."

"And the other boys?" Jane asked.

Matt folded his arms, and a faraway smile came to his face as he remembered. "Well, after we'd all called our fathers, Delbert let us go. He also told us not to come back for the rest of the summer. So we're all walkin' along real slow, feeling bad, and Fogal says, 'What did *your* dad say, Matt?' So I told him. And then Saathe told us what *his* dad had said. And then I asked John what *his* dad had said."

Matt shook his head and chuckled. "So John looks up and says, "I didn't call my *dad*. Are you *stupid*?" And he crinkled up his face as if I'd just asked the dumbest question he'd ever heard. "My dad woulda beat my ass. You think I wanna call him and ask for it?"

"Saathe and Fogal and I stopped walking and just stared at him. Even at that age, the guy had balls. He was like a master criminal in our eyes." Matt tipped his head back and laughed before he continued. "So I said, 'Well, John, Who *did* you call? I saw you dial the phone.'"

And John said, "I just dialed any old number. I wound up talking to some telephone operator. Jesus, was she confused! But I sure as shit wasn't gonna call my *dad*."

"'So you never talked to your dad?' I asked him again, and John answered me with a face like he was getting tired of all the stupid questions. 'Hell no,' he said." Matt closed his eyes and shook his head at the memory. "It's been fifty years since that day and I laugh every time I remember that conversation. *That's* why I liked to hang with John. It was like hanging around with a movie star, a gangster, a guy who could, and would, do things I'd never dream of. But that's why I got in trouble sometimes, too."

"So what ten-year-old has the presence of mind, or the balls, to do something like that?" Jane asked.

"I dunno, but I never knew another one like him."

"Well, I think I understand him a little bit better as time goes by," Jane said. John was outrageous, and he did make life interesting. But Matt was clever, and smart. On John's best day, he could never be Matt Kingston. She brushed her blonde hair back with one hand, looked at herself in the mirror, and picked up a roll of dental floss.

"So how was *your* day?" Matt asked. "Did you spend the whole day in your office, on the phone?"

"Yeah, pretty much, and had a couple of pretty boring meetings," Jane said, as she pulled a length of dental floss from a small white spool.

Matt was not interested in details about meetings with someone from OSHA, or the hospital administrators. He picked up the fishing magazine once more.

As she was flossing her teeth, she walked to the side of the bed and looked at Matt. "You wanna floss me, don't you?" she teased.

"Wanna floss your brains out," Matt replied without looking up from his magazine. She knew he was struggling to keep a straight face, so she began moving her hips seductively, in sync with her flossing.

Matt turned a page and kept his eyes glued to his magazine.

Jane walked to the bathroom, threw her floss away and picked up a tube of toothpaste. "Ooh," she sighed passionately, until Matt simply had to raise his eyes.

She began, ever so slowly, to twist the cap off the toothpaste tube, each twist drawing an exaggerated sigh of erotic pleasure from her, and a thrust of her hips.

Matt bit his lip, but looked on.

She held the toothpaste tube upright, close to her face, and gazed at it seductively, clearly implying that it was an erect penis, and that she was infatuated with it. She touched it against her cheek, and then moaned softly.

For the moment, Matt kept a relatively straight face.

Slowly, deliberately, she moved one hand along the length of the tube. She stopped twice to make eye contact with him. After a few seconds of stroking the tube she began to squeeze, slowly moving her hand along the tube. As a bit of toothpaste rose from the opening she began to breathe heavily and whimper, as if she was about to have an orgasm.

Matt brought a hand up to cover his face.

Jane shuddered several times, then spread the toothpaste over the bristles on her brush and began to brush her teeth. She brushed and moaned and ground her hips for a while as she brushed, and let Matt watch. "Ooh! Yes! Yes! *Yes*!!" she said as her mouth filled with white foam, until she had to tip her chin up in order to keep the foam from spilling out. But the final "*Yes!*" drove a large slurp of foam over her lower lip and onto her chin.

That was it. She burst out laughing at her own behavior, ran back into the bathroom, and spat the rest of the foam into the sink. Then she used a hand towel to wipe the foam off her chin. "I hope it's warm under the covers," she said, as she turned and ran toward the bed.

But she stopped in her tracks about halfway to the bed, while a look of horror crossed her face. "Shit! A spider!" she gasped.

Suspended in front of her at about eye level, in the middle of the bedroom, was a spider on a single strand of spider web. "It's the middle of winter. What the hell is *he* doing here?" she asked Matt as she pointed at the spider.

"I dunno." Matt started to get out of bed, intending to kill the spider.

"No," Jane said. "Stay put." She began to walk backward. It was still showtime, and she wasn't done entertaining him yet. Raising her knees as if to soften her footfalls so she could retreat in silence, she backed into the bathroom, grabbed the hand towel she'd just used to wipe away the toothpaste, and then started creeping forward, toward the spider.

"Be veh-we veh-we quiet!" she said, in a horrible attempt to imitate Elmer Fudd as she twirled the hand towel. She was preparing to snap the tiny spider with a towel, just as an eighth-grade boy would snap a buddy in the locker room.

When she was at arm's length, the proper towel-snapping distance, she turned sideways and prepared to strike. She bobbed and weaved a bit like a prize fighter about to throw a punch, then made an attempt at the Ali shuffle.

This was the Jane that only he knew. For him, Jane would lower all the fences; this little show was just for him, and he was loving it. Dressed in panties and a T-shirt, the firmness of her legs and rear end were on display, and everything under the T-shirt was moving just right, too. Even the Elmer Fudd thing was sexy, and funny; it made no sense, but it was.

When the moment was right she sprung at the spider, but it was a bad miss. The towel shot to the left of the spider, and then on the back swing it knocked the spider onto Jane's right forearm, the arm that held the towel.

"Shit! Dammit! Fuck!" Jane gasped and began to dance around in panic, waving her arm and swinging the towel, as if she'd been attacked by a poisonous snake. She was actually afraid of spiders and now she was terrified to have thing crawling up her arm. She was growing more desperate with each passing nanosecond, as if the spider might strike back and kill her. Suddenly, she made a violent motion with her right arm, trying to use the towel in her right hand to snap the spider off her own right arm. It was a seriously bad martial arts blunder.

The tip of the towel made a crisp, loud *snap*.

She'd snapped herself perfectly, and hard, right in the middle of her own forehead, right between the eyes.

"Ow! Shit!" She winced, just before she crumpled to the floor. She was curled in the fetal position, holding her forehead when Matt got out of bed.

"Down goes Frazier!" Matt called as he stood over her. "You OK?" He knew she was all right—definitely embarrassed, though, and trying not to laugh at herself.

"It's not funny, dammit!" Jane whimpered, still coiled up and holding her face.

But it was.

"You looked like you got into some bad mushrooms there for a second," Matt laughed. He found the spider on the floor, a few feet from Jane, and crushed it with his fingers. He walked over to the bathroom, laughing all way, and dropped the spider into the toilet before he washed the spider guts off his fingers. He was laughing even harder when he returned and bent over Jane once more. "And then you looked like a sniper took you down."

Jane was laughing now too. She rolled, pulled her hands away from her face, and looked up at Matt. "Is there a mark?" she asked.

"No, not at all," he lied. A large red welt was growing on her forehead, and Matt collapsed on the floor beside her and took her in his arms. In an instant they were both laughing, convulsing, each of them feeding off the other. Matt tried to speak, but the only word he could utter was "unicorn." Several times he stopped laughing long enough to look at her forehead, then he'd start laughing again.

Eventually, Jane got up and walked to the bathroom so she could examine the knob growing on her head.

Matt was back in bed, waiting for her, when at last she turned out the lights and came to bed. Just before she lifted the covers she stepped out of her panties and pulled the T-shirt over her head. She slipped under the covers and eased herself backward, into Matt's waiting arms. He cupped her breasts, pulled her close, and let his heat warm her.

As she settled into his embrace he let his lips rest behind her ear, and as soon as he did so he smiled once more. He couldn't help it; what she'd done to herself a moment earlier was pretty funny. Jane felt the smile come to his face, as she knew it would, and she protested just a bit: "Shut up. It's not funny."

"I'm not really laughing," he replied, but she could still feel the smile on his face.

He held her for a while and said no more until the humor faded. He made slow, tiny circles around her nipples, and then ran his hands over her flat stomach. He kissed her behind her ear and whispered, "I love you."

"Mmm, I love you, too."

He squeezed her breasts softly, kissed her neck again, and held her so she could feel what was rising behind her. Each of them knew the other's desires, and each of them sensed a lover's growing hunger. Jane slowly arched her back and raised both arms above her head. It was a request, a familiar one; it was the way she asked for more of his tender touch.

Several minutes later, when he was inside her and moving with a powerful rhythm, she opened her eyes and saw that he was looking at her, too. This, this connection that she shared with Matt, was what she'd been unable to describe to John. Her body, and her soul, were one with Matt. She closed her eyes, clutched at him, and let the depth of their connection reveal itself once again.

CHAPTER THIRTEEN

Matt sat on the corner of a queen-size bed in the hotel room, brushing his teeth, while Jane stood at the bathroom sink, doing the same thing. Neither of them had spoken for a while. Tonight they would share this room at the Ramada Inn in Rochester, and tomorrow at 5 a.m. they'd both rise and go to Methodist Hospital, where Jane would wait and worry while he had his right hip replaced. They'd gone out for an early dinner, and now all they could do was wait for morning.

Jane spit in the sink, rinsed her toothbrush, and said, "Are you afraid, Matt?" She already knew he was afraid, but she walked over and sat in one of the overstuffed chairs beside their bed and hoped that talking about it would help.

"Yeah, sure. Who wouldn't be?" Matt mumbled, with a mouthful of toothpaste. He rose and walked to the sink, and spat his toothpaste just as Jane had done a moment earlier. "I *know* what they're gonna do to me tomorrow, so sure, I'm afraid." He shrugged when he sat in the other chair, across the room from her, and put his feet up on the bed.

But Jane saw that something more was troubling her husband. Sometimes lately he'd sit and stare, and not speak for long stretches. Tonight at dinner he'd made some small talk, but had been unwilling to open up at all. "C'mon, honey; what's wrong?" she probed. "I can see that something is bothering you."

"Well," Matt started, "I guess this hip thing sorta feels like a harbinger of old age. You understand, don't you?"

"You can't think like—"

Matt held his hand up to stop. "Tell me you didn't think that very same thing when I told you I needed a new hip. You know, that your husband is now an old man."

Jane smiled sheepishly. "No. Well, maybe a little, but—"

"I rest my case," Matt cut in.

"But honey, you're still young in so many ways. You'll feel so much better when this is done. You'll be able to do all, well, *most* of the things you've always done, and—"

"I know that, and that's all good," Matt cut in again. "But here's the deal, the part that's bothering me. From the earliest times I can remember, way back when I was a kid, and all the way up until about three months ago, I pretty much understood that I was way back at the end of the line."

Jane had no idea what he was talking about.

"I was at the end of the line. You know, I couldn't even *see* the front of the line. I was just waiting to get on with my life, and I thought I just might live forever. But *now*, from where I'm at right now, I can see the front of the line." He smiled at her. "Get it?"

Jane understood, now, that he was talking about his own mortality. "Oh, Matt, you're still young. You're the youngest sixty-two-year-old man I know. You're gonna live a long life. And the doctor says that after your new hip is healed you'll be able to play golf, and walk, and get into your boat just like before. You're gonna live a long life!"

"Well, that's actually what I'm afraid of," he replied.

Jane understood the part about dealing with death, but her husband was getting at something more.

"Jane," Matt said in a very deliberate tone, "you're a beautiful woman. You're tall, and sexy."

She crinkled her face, wondering where he was going with this.

"Do you know how men look at you sometimes, in that way?" he asked. She nodded.

"And do you like it when they look at you that way?" Matt asked.

"Well, sure, if it's a man who . . . well, you know." She was getting embarrassed. "Why are asking me this?"

"A while back I went into Gray's to buy some new boots, and there was a pretty young lady who was waiting on me. She was *with* me, but she was focused on some young studs about twenty feet away from me. Hell, I thought I'd become invisible. She just lost track of me. She couldn't see me or even hear me talking. Get the picture?"

Jane smiled and nodded.

"It happened on the same day Doc Hested told me I needed a new hip, so maybe it was just bad timing all around." Matt stood up and paced at the foot of their bed, growing more animated as he spoke. "I was once a fine figure of a man. Girls used to flirt with me, and I liked it. Then suddenly I'm just some geezer with size eleven shoes who needs a new hip. Am I supposed to take comfort in the fact that women can't see me anymore, and all I have to look forward to is waddling around a golf course with a bunch of other old farts, or sitting in my boat and drowning worms?"

Jane had never heard this kind of talk from Matt before, and she had no idea what to make of it.

"I wasn't done being *me* yet," he said.

"Well, I still think you're indestructible. You're a grown-ass man, fuckin' blue twisted steel!" Jane blurted. "You're gonna be fine . . . for a long time." The words "fuckin' blue twisted steel" had just flown from her lips, and they had the desired effect. Matt's smile reappeared.

Matt and Jane had forged a friendship in a campus bar nearly forty years earlier because they made each other laugh. They shared a connection, and it was still strong. They got under the covers and lay in bed and held each other and talked about things. And then each of them drifted off into silence, pretending to sleep, and allowing the other to have a shot at the real thing.

When their alarm went off at 5 a.m. they'd already been holding hands under the covers and coasting for half an hour. "You gonna shower first, or me?" Jane asked.

At five minutes to six they were seated in a large room filled with other people who were also waiting to be called for one sort of surgery or another. "I wish I could have a sip of your coffee," Matt said as he leaned close for a sniff of Jane's brew.

"Nothing to eat or drink for twelve hours before surgery," she reminded him. "But I'll be waiting for you after it's done, and I'll sneak a burger in here so you don't have to eat hospital food."

Before Jane had finished her sentence, a nurse who seemed far too young entered the waiting room and called out, "Matt Kingston."

When Matt and Jane stood up the nurse asked, "Are you Mrs. Kingston?" Jane replied that she was indeed Mrs. Kingston, and the nurse said, "You can come too."

The nurse led them to a little room with a hospital bed and a bathroom and a chair for Jane to sit in, then she directed Matt to step into the bathroom and change into the hospital gown she was holding for him. When he returned and sat on the hospital bed, she asked him for about the third time what his name and birthdate were, and what he was there for. Then she asked if he'd had anything to eat or drink in the past twelve hours. Eventually, while she was starting an IV line in his left arm, she asked him if he was wearing underwear.

"Do you have any idea how long it's been since a young lady asked me if I was wearing underwear?" Matt said with a straight face.

The girl giggled and then turned to look at Jane.

"Yeah, he's a real stitch," Jane said, rolling her eyes.

Several minutes later, when Matt was ready for surgery, the nurse had him sit in a wheelchair and told him to say goodbye to Jane. It all seemed so uneventful. He kissed Jane goodbye and the nurse wheeled him off.

The whole surgical experience went about as he'd expected. He'd been wheeled down a long hall and then into a surgical suite that was so cold it felt like a meat locker, where another nurse had asked him to sit up on the side of his bed and then she'd rested her forehead against his. Or did she? Then she'd wrapped her arms around his neck and told him to be sure and stay still while the anesthetist on the other side of the bed injected a spinal-block anesthetic. When he lay on his back once more he asked the anesthetist how long it would take for the drugs to go to work, and then he wiggled his toes and said, "Nothing yet."

"Won't be long, Dr. Kingston," the anesthetist replied. "I'm going to give you a little intravenous cocktail that will make your arm feel cold right now, too."

"Everything's cold! Turn the heat up in here!" Matt joked, and those were the last words he spoke for several hours. The IV cocktail sent him off to a sleepy, carefree place.

His world was gray, or maybe black. His eyelids were closed. Maybe they were just too heavy to open, or maybe he was somewhere between asleep and awake. He didn't know and didn't care. But off and on, from his darkened world, he heard noises and felt people tugging on his leg. At one point during his surgery he *did* hear the Sawzall that was being used to cut the top of his femur off. There had been no pain and no sense of anxiety, just a detached knowledge of what was going on. And once again he felt that his right leg was being tugged and pulled, and not very gently. Still no pain. Then he heard a steel hammer ringing as it struck something else that was steel. That noise was loud, and he felt himself move a bit each time the hammer struck. He knew, on some level, that the doctor was pounding some titanium parts into his femur. It sounded like someone was driving railroad spikes, but his world remained pretty dark and carefree.

He remembered being rolled into the recovery room and looking about, too. It looked like the Jonestown massacre in there, he thought; there were dozens of bodies strewn about. A pleasant nurse had tended to him in the recovery room. She'd spoken to him softly, and asked how he was feeling, but all the while she'd been busy looking at medical instruments and making notes. He remembered that he'd spoken to her several times, but he couldn't recall anything she'd said. The fog hadn't cleared yet.

Jane was waiting for him when he was rolled back into his hospital room. He remembered that, too. "How do you feel, honey?" she'd asked.

"Pretty good," he'd mumbled, but talking was hard work. After being somewhat awake through the surgery, he now fell asleep, but only briefly. The bed felt like a pile of cinder blocks, and then every time he felt himself dozing, really dropping off to a nice, deep sleep, another nurse would burst into the room and stick a needle in his arm, or take his blood pressure, or give him a pill to swallow.

After an evening meal of chicken soup, Jane supervised a groggy phone call between Matt and each of their sons. Then she went back to the hotel room while Matt tried to get some rest.

But the parade of nurses went on all night, and he slept very little. It didn't help that he had a catheter in his bladder, and a blood-filled plastic tube extending from the surgical incision on his hip all the way to the foot of his bed, where the tube emptied into a container about the size of a large peanut butter jar, which gradually kept filling with red blood from his incision. Apparently, the jar and tube were designed to draw blood away from the surgical wound and aid in healing.

The next morning, before Jane returned, a woman who was dressed differently than the nurses strolled into his room and said, "Good morning, Matt! I'm your physical therapist. Would you like to go for a walk?"

"Not really."

"Sure, you do," she shot back. "Let's give it a try."

"I'm afraid it's gonna hurt," Matt said.

"I think you'll be surprised," the woman said. With quite a bit of assistance, he swung both legs over the side of his bed. The woman placed a walker in front of him, then attached his catheter bag full of urine, and the peanut butter jar full of blood, to the walker, and off they went.

"It's amazing," Matt said after a couple of wobbly steps. "There's no pain."

"Well, they put some morphine in your spinal block yesterday, and I'm pretty sure that's helping with the pain. And I'm sure they used some Marcaine, a very long-lasting local anesthetic, so that's helping, too."

One trip down the hall outside his room was about all he could tolerate before he got tired, however. When they returned to his room, the woman took a few minutes to go over instructions for physical therapy with him. By the time she finished the detailed instructions, Matt was exhausted.

He closed his eyes and began to drift away just as another nurse came through his door and announced that she was going to remove the plastic tube that had been draining blood from his hip. That procedure was surprisingly painless and easy: she just pulled the smooth plastic out of the wound channel. "There," she said. "You have almost no swelling." She smiled and left.

Matt readjusted the bed, prepared for a nap, and sure enough, another nurse stepped into his room. "Good morning, Matt. Would you like that catheter removed?" she asked.

The answer to that one was a definite yes. It would be great to have that uncomfortable thing gone. But then all of his enthusiasm vanished as quickly as it had arrived when Matt realized what was going to happen next. This nurse was young and cute, and bore a strong resemblance to the salesgirl at Gray's. The modesty, actually the vanity, of an old man rushed over him when understood that this young lady was about to "handle" things. Oh, he didn't want *that* on several levels. This procedure would most certainly hurt. It had to! But just as important, the little man who lived in his pants was looking a bit overwhelmed by the catheter experience. Cold water wasn't the only thing that caused shrinkage, and Matt just didn't want a woman to see or handle anything.

While the nurse rolled a cart that seemed to be covered with torture devices next to his bed, Matt wished that somehow this nurse would get called away and replaced by an ugly old one who'd never seen shrinkage before.

"Are you ready?" she asked.

"OK," he said in a timid voice. He'd have to man up and do this. "Let's get that thing outta there."

Before he had the chance to prepare his psyche for any further damage, the young nurse lifted his hospital gown and studied things briefly. Matt looked away and began to grit his teeth. The nurse made sure she had a good grip on the little man with the Nazi helmet with her left hand, and then with her other hand she deflated the catheter's little balloon that was inside his bladder. She paused for just a second, then withdrew the catheter with her other hand. A new and unusual pain stung him in all the wrong places.

Matt whimpered once, and the nurse used a towel to blot away some urine that splashed over him. "There! That wasn't so bad, was it?" she said cheerfully.

"Huh-uh," he lied. He'd expected it to feel like she'd jerked about fourteen inches of rusty barbed wire out the end of his pecker. But it wasn't that bad. The burning began to ebb, very slowly, and Matt's eyes revealed his relief. Finally, when he understood that all modesty was long gone, he said, "Maybe next time you could use a smaller catheter; you know, like the one you use for an eight-year-old boy?"

The nurse was busy collecting his catheter and his bag of urine, and a few other things, so she never looked at Matt. But she did smile just a little, and then in an effort to justify the large diameter of the catheter, she said, "Well, I like a tight fit."

She recognized her poor choice of words instantly, and she began to blush, and reflexively her head spun to look at Matt and see if he'd picked up on it. She hadn't meant to toss out that impressive sexual innuendo, but there it was, and she was mortified.

Matt did not have the willpower or the good judgment to let that pass. "Yeah, well . . ." He started chuckling. He held both hands over his package, and while the pain was still fresh he tipped his head back and laughed out loud. The young nurse closed her eyes and turned away from Matt in order to hide her blush. But she knew he could see her shoulders convulse as she laughed along with him. She was perhaps more embarrassed than any person he'd ever seen.

They both tried to regain their composure twice, and they almost had it, but then the uncontrollable laughter returned. The nurse finally took off her latex gloves, got herself a Kleenex, and sat down on the visitor's chair beside Matt's bed while she wiped away her tears. There was nothing more either of them could say, and they simply let the incident ease to a close.

Finally, the nurse drew in a deep breath, stood up, and finished gathering the things she'd originally intended to remove from his room before all the laughter had begun. He watched her place the tubes and bags inside a bigger bag. She was looking at the items in front of her, but she was still grinning.

She finished her work and turned toward the door with an armload of used medical supplies. When she got to the door she looked back at him and said, "Hey, Matt?"

"Yeah?"

"It was good for me, too." she said. This time she flashed a grin that was designed to acknowledge yet another one of those singular moments that sometimes happen between strangers. And then she was gone.

The girl from Gray's had no idea what she'd missed out on, Matt thought.

Jane entered his room immediately after the nurse departed, as if she'd been standing in the hall and waiting her turn. She was carrying two large cups of coffee from a nearby Starbucks. "Hi, honey! How do you feel today? Have you had breakfast yet? And why was that nurse laughing when she left your room?" Jane placed one coffee on the tray beside his bed and kissed him. "Did you just wake up?" She sat in the visitors chair next to his bed.

"Well, honey," Matt started as he reached for the coffee Jane had brought him, "I've already been up walking, I took a stroll down the hall and it didn't hurt. Actually, the little spin I just took down the hallway felt better than yesterday morning when I hobbled in here, so that was pretty amazing. Then I did some physical therapy exercises with a nice therapist." He took a swig of coffee. "Then a nurse came and removed that plastic tube that was drawing blood out of my hip."

"Did that hurt?" Jane asked.

"Not at all. And then that nurse you just met came in here and removed my catheter."

"So why was she laughing?" Jane asked again.

"Well, that's sort of a personal question, honey," Matt said, "but let me just say that she held me in a special way and—"

Jane hurriedly put her index fingers in her ears and began to hum, "mmmmm . . . I don't need to know any more . . . mmmmm."

"OK, I won't share any more details," Matt said. "But did that nurse look exhausted, and was she smoking a cigarette?"

Jane ignored the question.

While they sipped their coffees, Matt told Jane about things he thought he experienced during his surgery, and all the things he'd been told about postoperative pain, the medications he'd need to take for the next few weeks, his physical therapy, and when he could go home. He said he understood that he was clear to go home on Wednesday if there were no further complications. By and by he got drowsy, in spite of the large coffee he'd just finished, and he told Jane that he'd like to close his eyes for a while.

Two hours later he stirred and glanced over to see Jane reading a paperback. He didn't think he'd been given two consecutive hours of peace and quiet since he'd been in the hospital, and he was thankful for the chance to sleep.

The door to his room was open a crack and there had been the constant noise of human traffic all morning. That noise had actually been comforting, and now as he lay there and listened to bits and pieces of other people's conversations he began to doze off again.

A man wearing a white coat startled Matt. He was just standing beside Matt's bed, reading his chart, when Matt noticed him. Apparently, he'd drifted off to sleep and then his surgeon had stopped in for a visit. "How ya doing, Matt?" the doctor asked, when Matt's eyes fluttered open.

"Well, I feel like somebody gave me some bad mushrooms, cut my femur off, and stuck a hose up my weeny."

"You went for a walk today?" The doctor showed no sign of a smile, ignoring Matt's comments. Matt figured he'd heard the same thing from hundreds of others.

"Yup."

"How'd that go?" the doctor asked.

"Purdy good."

"Have you had a bowel movement yet?"

"Yup, a dandy."

Still no smile from the doctor; Matt figured there was no point in trying anymore.

"Are you Jane Kingston, the nurse from Pine Rapids?" the doctor asked, looking over Matt's bed at Jane for the first time.

"Yes," Jane replied with an inquisitive smile.

Matt squinted and said, "You figured that out from my bowel movement?"

This time the doctor smiled. "Good one." He made a few computer entries on the machine next to Matt's bed. He then lifted the sheet covering Matt's incision and examined the surgical site as he said, "My mother was a physical therapist in Bemidji and she used to talk about her friend, Jane Kingston, who was a nurse in Pine Rapids. Then just now I noticed your wife's name in your chart. That's why I asked."

"OK, good," Matt said.

"What is your mother's name?" Jane asked.

"Debbie, Debbie Marlton," the doctor replied.

"Oh sure, Debbie! I haven't seen her for a while," Jane said.

"She retired last year," the doctor said.

"Oh, well please greet her for me?"

"Sure thing. Small world, eh?" The doctor turned back to Matt and said, "The surgery went very well, Matt. Everything below the equator is working again?" The doctor pointed low, clearly asking for reassurance that Matt's insides were functioning. "And you were able to walk with crutches, correct?"

"Yes," Matt replied.

"Well, then, you should be free to go home tomorrow. Is that all right with you?"

"Yes, and thank you, Doctor," Matt said. When the doctor left the room, he turned to Jane and said, "How 'bout that. Home tomorrow?"

A moment later there was yet another knock on his door, and Matt was annoyed. Why wouldn't they leave him alone? The knock was tiny, like all nurses knock just before they came stealing in to draw some blood, or give him a pill, or take his blood pressure. As he turned to look at the door, which was creeping open, he hoped it would be the catheter nurse, back for another chuckle.

But the woman creeping into his room caught him totally off guard: It was Mo Glasnapp. She peeked around the door and said a delicate, "Hello, Matt." Then she noticed Jane, and froze in her tracks, as if she was considering whether to back out and go away. "Have I come at a bad time?" she asked apologetically.

Matt read in her eyes that she didn't know who Jane was, and was suddenly uncomfortable about coming any farther into his room.

"Ah, Mo, what a nice surprise, c'mon in and meet my wife," Matt said. Jane stood up and extended her hand as Mo approached her. "Jane, I'd like you to meet Maureen Glasnapp, well, she's still Maureen Glasnapp to me, I guess, but her married name is Lawson. And Mo, this is my wife, Jane."

The women exchanged greetings and then Mo stood awkwardly beside Matt's bed for a moment.

"Well, what about me?" Matt said as he held his arms out demanding a hug. Mo bent over and hugged him, while Matt kissed her cheek.

Jane returned to her seat on the far side of his bed and waited for her husband to get a conversation going, and Mo sat in a chair on the other side of Matt's bed.

"Honey, you've heard me talking about Mo and her brothers and her dad for all these years . . ." Matt finally offered. "Her father was my coach and teacher, and her brothers were playmates and teammates. I guess we've known each other our whole lives."

"We reconnected at my father's funeral a few weeks ago," Mo said. "And Matt told me all about you. Well, actually, I'd heard about you through the grapevine back home over the years. You know, small-town stuff. Anyway, I was hoping to meet you today." Then Mo reached over and took Matt's hand in hers and smiled. She nodded and said, "It's so nice to see you again."

"So how did you know I was here?" Matt asked.

"Well, I work here, and most days over coffee I sneak a look at the daily admissions list. I suppose that amounts to breaking some HIPAA laws, but who cares? So, when I saw your name on the list yesterday, I just figured I'd stop by and say hello," Mo said with a shrug. "So how do you feel?"

Jane watched while a strange woman held Matt's hand and spoke to him with genuine affection. This was something new, and she had no idea how to process it.

Before Matt could answer Mo's question Jane stood up and said, "I'm just gonna let you two visit for a minute. I need to make a couple phone calls and check in at work. I'll be right back."

When Jane left the room, Matt turned to Mo and said, "I think she was sizing you up."

"Oh?" Mo grimaced.

"You know; she was trying to decide how you compared to her." Matt grinned.

"That's crazy."

Matt pursed his lips and raised his eyebrows, asking her for the truth.

"OK, you're right, I was sizing her up, too. You did real good there, old friend."

"Damn right I did, Mo. I love her so much it hurts." Matt made a point not to let go of Mo's hand, and they began to chat about old friends and current events, and he wondered if she was making a point not to let go of his hand, too. Each of them asked the other about friends from their hometown, and then a few more questions about all that had happened in their lives during the forty years they'd lost contact with each other.

Mo eventually got teary-eyed when she tried to tell Matt how much she still missed her father, and she had to let go of his hand in order to dry her eyes with a tissue. Then her cell phone rang and she apologized before she answered. She paced about in his room and then stepped out into the hallway for a while, always talking in a low voice.

"Just a problem back at my office," she said when she returned. "It's OK now."

"Maybe you need to get back to work?" Matt asked.

"No, I can stay for a few more minutes."

"Good." Matt reached over and held her hand again. "Remember when we used to sit together alone, on your parents' porch, and talk about our future? We held hands, just like this"—he squeezed her hand—"and we each told the other about all of our dreams and all the things we planned to do in life."

Mo nodded.

"Did your dreams come true?" Matt asked.

"Yes. Did yours?"

"No." Matt smiled. "But I got some new dreams when I went away to college." He thought for a moment. "And most of 'em came true."

"We sure went our separate ways," Mo said, and there was a clumsy silence. A secret was buried deep in their past, and he wondered if Mo wanted to ask about it. They both hung their heads and waited for the other to talk. But there probably never would be a time to ask about that. Not now, not after so many years, and the moment passed.

"Have you had a good life, Mo? Are you happy? Tell the truth," Matt finally asked.

"Yes. I have a great family, my girls all live right here in town and I see my grandchildren all the time, and John's had a successful career. How about *you*? Are you happy, old friend?"

Matt swallowed hard and thought for a moment. "Yeah, I'm happy, really happy. I've been lucky, really lucky, to meet the people I did."

Neither of them spoke for a long moment while they considered whether to ask the other what they were thinking. Mo wanted to hear him say that he included her in that statement, and he wanted to spell it out for her, but both of them let the words hang in the air for a while. "Matt," Mo finally said cautiously, "in all those years, did you ever think about—"

The door whooshed open and Jane walked in, unaware that she'd interrupted something. "I just talked to John. He's in town and he's coming over here in a while. Said he's bringing beer and pizza," she announced. Both Matt and Mo turned to look at her.

"John Velde?" Mo asked.

"Yeah," Jane said. Then she remembered. "Oh, sure, you know John from your school days."

"Yes, I do." Mo grinned. "And on that note, I think I'll head back to my office."

"He's a good guy, Mo," Matt said.

"OK, but he's your friend, not mine. And I really need to get back." She walked over and shook Jane's hand and said, "It was nice to meet you. Take good care of this old man." Then she leaned over and hugged Matt once more, "Goodbye, old friend. I don't know when I'll see you again," she said softly.

"Yeah, take care, Mo. You're still my girl," Matt whispered. He held her close for a second longer, then kissed her cheek.

Mo said goodbye to both of them once more and then walked out the door.

When she was safely out of earshot, Jane raised her eyebrows and turned both palms up, requesting more information about Mo.

"I told you. She was my first girlfriend. I've known her my whole life," Matt said.

"She's really pretty, Matt." Jane raised her eyebrows a bit further, asking the obvious question.

"She's happily married. Her husband is a nice guy and they live in town here. They have four daughters and three grandchildren. And yes, I think she's pretty, too. She was my first girlfriend, my best friend for a while there in high school when I needed a good friend to keep me away from . . ." His words trailed off.

"John Velde?"

"And other things." Matt smiled.

Jane had barely settled back into her chair when the door to the room whooshed open again. This time there was no timid knock. "Hey! How's it hangin'?" John Velde said in a voice too loud for a hospital. In one hand he carried a large cardboard pizza box, and the rich aroma followed him into the room. In his other hand was a brown paper bag. "You hungry?" He placed the pizza on the table beside Matt's bed. Then he took his coat off and threw it on the floor by the window and said, "Really, how're ya doing? Can I see your scar? Did they shave your nuts?"

John was admiring Matt's scar and listening to his stories about the surgery when yet another nurse walked in to take Matt's blood pressure yet again, and to give him his medication. As she was pumping up the blood pressure cuff she looked over at John and watched him lift a six-pack of Leinenkugel's from the paper bag. Then her face hardened, and she resembled Miss Bureson, fifty years earlier in the boys' room at Riverside Elementary. "What are you doing?"

"Brought a pizza for my friend," John replied with an angelic tone and an innocent look. He was already aware of what the nurse was about to say, and he was trying to steal her thunder.

"Your friend is taking several painkillers and that beer would be . . ." she started, as if she were about to scold him and then maybe throw him out.

"Don't worry; the beer is for me," John reassured her, his voice dripping with butter, "and for Jane here, the good doctor's wife." John went on, "Matt is a doctor himself. Well, he's not really a doctor, he's just a dentist, but he knows enough not to mix drugs and alcohol."

The nurse turned her gaze to Jane, hoping for some validation, or reassurance.

"It's OK," Jane assured her. "I'm a nurse." She pointed at Matt and said, "I can make sure this one behaves." Then she tossed a thumb at John and added, "But I have no control over that one."

The nurse looked at John.

"If you'd like to come by the room when your shift is over there'll be one for you, too," John added. This time he was smiling.

The nurse, who was about fortyish, turned her attention back to Matt's blood pressure cuff, and when she'd made her entry in his chart she looked over at John. "I'll shut this door so no one else sees what's going on." Then she pointed at Matt. "And no beer for him. Got it?"

John nodded and winked at her.

"OK, so keep it quiet, and if you're still here at ten o'clock when my shift ends I might stop back," the nurse said as she left the room. She'd recognized the steady flow of bullshit from John, and she was smiling when she left. She was actually thinking about coming back for the small party, and Matt thought he saw the woman wink at John, too.

"How do you do that?" Jane said to John.

He smirked. "It's a gift. I can't explain it."

CHAPTER FOURTEEN

—◦—

Matt returned home three days after his surgery, using only a walker to get around. For the first few nights he slept in his recliner because he was unable to comfortably get in and out of bed, and Jane slept on the couch next to him in case he needed anything during the night. When he did make trips around the house, behind his walker, Jane hovered over him, always fearful that he might fall. But his recovery progressed speedily.

"What are you *doing*?" Jane had snapped early one morning, seven days after surgery, when she awoke on the couch only to find Matt standing beside the coffee pot on the kitchen counter. "Did you walk over there by yourself? Where's your walker?"

"Don't think I need help walking anymore," he said. "There's no pain, and I can walk normally, if I go slow." He stood on one foot, then the other, to show her. "I think maybe this thing with a new hip wasn't such a big deal. Maybe I'm not gonna be an old man just yet."

Matt did his physical therapy religiously, and he walked around the house for hours each day, trying to reestablish a normal gait. He'd been dragging one leg, hobbling and wincing for nearly two years before the surgery, and he knew that a big part of a complete recovery would be to unlearn the limp that had characterized his stride for so long. He wanted to go outside and take longer walks, but Ron Hested had called Jane on Matt's first day home from Rochester and been very clear about not letting Matt "go outside and fall on his ass" until there had been more healing.

Three weeks into his recovery, Matt was going stir-crazy. He needed to get out of the house and he was driving Jane crazy, too, with requests and demands for field trips into town for groceries, or coffee, or anything that might get him out.

The sun was still far below the eastern horizon on a Saturday morning in February when Matt awoke, ready to get up for the day. He could hear

Jane's soft, regular breathing beside him and he slid one hand toward her, under the covers, until he found her hand. "You awake?" he whispered when she squeezed his hand.

"Yeah."

"You wanna coast for a while?" Matt asked.

"No, I'm ready to get up. I was wondering if *you* were awake yet."

He was lying on his back, looking into the darkness above him, when he said, "Honey, I gotta get out and take my new hip for a maiden voyage. I'm ready to try things out. I'm going back to work next week, you know. I'm ready."

"I think so, too."

"Really?" Matt perked up.

"Yes, really. I already set it up with John. I'm gonna drop you off at the Shorewood Furist, and while we're there I'm gonna invite the Velde boys out to our house for Snag's birthday next week. Then you're on your own with John for a while. How does that sound?" Jane asked.

Matt was already out of bed and walking slowly toward the shower when he replied, "Good, real good. Thanks, honey."

The forests and lakes around Pine Rapids were covered with snow and ice and would remain locked up for another two months, maybe more. The air was fresh, and filled with the clean smell of pine forest, except in the area just downwind of the Shorewood Furist.

Snag Velde had been busy skinning skunks all winter, but he still had some work to do. A pervasive odor of skunk still rode the wind through town every day, and the locals were getting angry. Snag had promised the city fathers he'd have things cleaned up by the first of March, but he still had a week, maybe two, and a thousand skunks to go. Most of the skunk pelts had already been sent off to a tannery, so that wasn't the problem. And Snag had found a place, deep in the woods, far north of town, where he'd been dumping the carcasses, so that wasn't the problem either. It seemed that the nearly empty, still-functioning refrigerator semi-trailer, *and* the Shorewood Furist building, *and* Snag himself, had all taken on the permanent smell of skunk.

Matt and Jane made their way to the front of the scruffy Shorewood Furist building and Matt put his hand on the door handle. "Brace yourself," he said to Jane, and they both drew in what they knew would be their last breath of fresh air for a few minutes. When Matt swung the door open they both winced at the smell that rushed out to assault them.

"Ugh," Jane said.

"Yup," Matt agreed.

But both of them smiled and waved happily when Snag turned toward the door and noticed them.

"How's it going, Snag?" Matt asked.

"Really good," Snag replied. When he noticed the look of distress on Jane's face he apologized, "Kinda stinks even worse than normal, don't it? But I'm just about done with them skunks, so it'll get better after that."

Jane walked over and put her arms around Snag. "What's new?" she asked.

"I can't show you just yet, 'cuz I'm not finished, but it won't be long, and you're gonna like it," Snag said, and he showed Jane and Matt a row of yellow teeth.

"Well, that's OK, we just came by to invite you to a party—your party. We're having a birthday party for you next Saturday, our house. So be there!" Jane said, and she poked Snag in the ribs.

"Sure. I'll be there," Snag said, with an even bigger smile.

"And be sure to tell Darrell," Jane reminded him. "We'll have a meal and cake and candles."

As Jane was speaking, Snag turned toward Darrell, who was talking on the phone in his dingy little office, sitting at his dingy little desk, and bellowed, "Hey Darrell! Party at their place next Saturday!"

Darrell nodded, smiled, and gave a thumbs-up. That was about all that Matt or Jane wanted of the Shorewood Furist, and they retreated out to their truck much faster than they'd come in. They were thankful to see John standing beside his truck and waiting to take possession of Matt so they all could try to escape the stink surrounding them.

"Ready for coffee?" John asked.

"Jesus, get me outta here," Matt chuckled, and then he waved to Jane as she sped away.

Five minutes later they walked through the front door of the Human Bean coffee shop and stopped in their tracks. The smell of fresh coffee and pastry was heavenly, in comparison to the place they'd just left, but there were a dozen people standing in line, *and* two rotund women were already sitting at their predesignated "dunce table." John put his hands on his hips and tilted his head in disgust. When he raised his eyes, he found that Sally Durham was staring at him from her position behind the counter. He turned his palms up and grimaced like he'd just come across a Band-Aid in the drinking fountain. He pointed at the women seated at what he'd been told was *his* table, and raised his eyebrows to ask the question, "Do you want to handle this, or should I?"

The woman in the front of the line, about to place her order with Sally, was still looking at the menu, and Sally took advantage of the pause. She straightened her back, raised her chin, and pointed her finger at John. The unspoken message was "Improvise," and her eyebrows knit as if she was giving him the answer to a question he shouldn't need to ask.

John stole another quick glance toward the two ladies seated at *his* table, then he brought his eyes back to Sally. The unmistakable message in *his* eyes was, "OK, if you're not gonna make these people move, then I will." He let her see him shrug his shoulders and then he walked straight to the table where the two large women were seated.

Sally saw the message in John's eyes, and she knew immediately that he was planning to order the women to move to another table. Her eyes tightened into BBs, and it looked as though she was about to leap around the counter and throw John Velde out, once and for all.

"C'mon, John, there's a table open by the fireplace," Matt said. He'd been unaware of the nonverbal exchange between John and Sally, and he gave John a little shove in the direction of the fireplace. But John turned and walked directly toward *his* table, the dunce table. At the last instant, he swiveled his head back over his shoulder, and just as he'd expected, Sally's angry glare was still fixed on him. She jabbed her finger at him and let her face reveal that the gates of Hell were about to open.

He met her restrained fury with a fiendish grin. Then he turned and sat at the table Matt had chosen. He pursed his lips, opened his eyes wide, and shrugged—the universal gesture for "*Gotcha.*" He'd known all along that she was watching and waiting for him to insult someone, and he'd played her like a fiddle.

After he sat down and made himself comfortable at the little table Matt had selected, he looked back at Sally one more time. She was still watching him but now her face was blank, as the unused anger drained away.

While she was still looking his way, he held up two fingers with all the feigned innocence he could muster. He pointed down, to the little table in front of him, to be sure Sally understood the order for two coffees. He nodded the unspoken and unnecessary question, "Did you get that?" The joy he felt in teasing her was unmistakable. Then he snapped his fingers, requesting a little hustle, and flicked his eyebrows.

With no hint of acknowledgement, she turned her eyes back to the woman standing at the counter, just in front of her. John watched, and waited, and waited, while Sally listened to the woman at the counter, until a she could hold it off no longer and a smile came to her face. She knew John was looking at her, too.

"How old do you think she is?" John asked Matt, when Sally finally showed him her smile.

"Who?" Matt asked, still unaware of the exchange between John and Sally.

"Sally. You know, Sally. Over there." John gestured toward the counter with the back of his head.

"I dunno, forty-five-ish? Why?"

"I'd drink her bathwater for week, just for a chance to listen to her fart over the telephone."

"Aww, I had no idea that your tender feelings ran so deep," Matt said. "Only Shakespeare could have found a more poignant way to express them."

John leaned forward and rested both elbows on the table and said, "Do you think I smell like skunk?"

"Wow, that was a treacherous segue, my friend, but you pulled it off; you went from drinking her bathwater to smelling like skunk," Matt said. "And once again, I believe that only you, and the Bard, could have done it so elegantly." Then he crinkled his face and added, "OK, one bit of craziness at a time here. First of all, you feel a budding attraction, deep in your loins, to Sally, correct?"

John nodded his agreement.

"Second, you wonder if you stink of skunk?" Matt lowered his chin and peered over imaginary spectacles, waiting for confirmation.

"Do I, or do I not? I stopped over there to help Snag move a couple boxes and now I can't get the smell out of my nose."

"Well, it's hard to say." Matt sighed, appearing to agonize over the complexity of the aroma, and unwilling to confirm or deny any skunkiness on his friend, just yet. He wanted to tease for a while.

"Do I *stink*, or not?" John blurted. "Don't be a prick."

"I dunno." Matt shrugged honestly. "I just took a direct nose hit from a couple thousand dead skunks myself. I'm wondering if the skunk I smell is just stuck in my nose for a while, or if it's you."

"Man, Snag's gotta get that mess cleaned up," John said, as he sniffed at the sleeve of his jacket. "That stink just won't go away. Snag smells so damned awful after cleaning so many skunks. He can't get the stink off himself, and we're afraid that somehow, just handling those expensive beaver pelts after handling the skunks, that he's gonna get that nasty stench on them. So we decided to have him take some time off from the rest of the business until he's done with the skunks and . . ."

"Here's your coffee, gents. Sorry it took me so long," Sally said. She'd surprised them and caught John in mid-sentence. "Thanks for being so patient."

John shifted gears immediately. He leaned back in his chair and sighed, "Well, patience is a virtue . . . you know me."

"You just had a near-death experience," Sally said, in reference to the large women seated at their dunce table.

"You were just about to climb on your broom and sic the flying monkeys on me a few minutes ago, weren't you?" John asked.

She put both hands around John's neck and pretended to choke him. "What am I gonna do with you?" she chuckled.

"Well . . ." John started, his eyes barely masking some sort of improper innuendo.

"Shut up. I can still sic the flying monkeys on you." Sally dismissed his wisecrack as she pulled a chair out and sat down at their table. "May I join you, just for a minute?" she asked, looking at Matt.

"Sure," John answered.

"I heard you had some surgery," she said to Matt.

"It was a penis enhancement! But don't tell anyone, OK? He's a bit self-conscious." John held up his index finger and thumb, about two inches apart.

Matt allowed himself a grin as he took the lid off one of the coffees and made eye contact with Sally.

"I know it was your hip. How do you feel? You look great and it's nice to see you again," Sally said. Then she added, "Why do you hang around with him?"

"I feel great. Thanks, and it's nice to see *you* again," Matt said.

A group of eight women, all of them talking and laughing, burst into the room, and Sally stood up to leave. "Gotta go back to work," she said.

"Glad you're back, Dr. Kingston." A second later she made a point to bump into John, and added, "You too, but not so much as him."

"That girl is warm for my form," John said softly to Matt.

The words were barely out of his mouth when Sally reappeared and leaned over their table as if she had a secret to share. "Do you guys think it smells like skunk in here?"

Both men acted surprised at the question and shook their heads no.

"Oh, well . . ." Sally sniffed at the air. "Maybe it's just me?" and she was gone.

"Well, there's your answer about the skunks," said Matt. "Maybe we should get out of here."

"Nah, tell me about your surgery. It had to hurt, didn't it?" John asked, while he sniffed his sleeve once more.

"Not a bit. Absolutely painless. Well, except for some soreness during recovery. Wanna know what the worst part was? It was having my catheter removed."

"Really?" John grimaced at the thought.

"Yeah. There was a lot of unspoken angst going on at that point. I found that you don't need cold water to get some serious shrinkage."

A fiendish grin twisted John's face and he leaned forward. "Oh?"

"Well, the day after surgery I was doing just fine, but I really wanted that catheter outta there, and suddenly this nice-looking young nurse came into my room and said she was gonna remove it."

John's eyes lit up.

"When she lifted the sheet, and my hospital gown, she sorta gasped, and stepped back in awe. 'Oh my God!' she said. 'Do you use that thing on humans?'"

"Right." John grinned.

"Can you blame her? I think she was terrified."

"Yeah, OK, keep going," John said.

"But then the harsh reality of the moment struck me. What was about to be done to my weenie was gonna be embarrassing, and cause even more shrinkage, for sure. And what had already been done to my pecker had caused it to resemble a timid puppy, not a snarling beast. But then I suddenly realized that she had no other expectations. She thought of my binky, and this whole thing that was going on between us, as just another day at work! Let me tell you, it was really strange, far from the rest of my life experiences, to have a totally disinterested woman handling my weenie."

John's face went blank for a moment; such a thought had never crossed his mind before, either.

"Then she pulled that thing outta me and it felt like a hemp rope that had been soaked in gasoline. My pecker nearly changed from an outie to an innie."

John stared at his coffee while he imagined the scene in Matt's hospital room, and he could not find a way to hide the devious pleasure he felt. His best friend's discomfort was palpable. John grimaced, but there was glee in his eyes, too. Other people's problems, especially this one, were funny to him. He reached a hand under the table and covered his own crotch as if he wanted to protect it from a similar attack.

"OK . . ." John said. Then he shook his head, as if that gesture might clear away the image of the catheter removal. "You just said something else that I can't get out of my head."

"Oh?"

"Yeah, you said, 'a totally disinterested woman handling my weenie,'" John blurted, and the same gleeful grimace from a moment earlier returned to his face. "I never thought . . . I can't imagine . . . I mean, that's . . ." He had no words to finish the thought. He leaned forward and displayed body language that begged for more.

Sixty-two-year-old Matt and John were now transported back in time; they were ten-year-old boys once again, giggling in the lunchroom, as it were, and all the rules of little-boy behavior compelled Matt to press on with another story.

Sally watched them from the counter, unable to hear any of the dialogue, but certain of its nature. Matt was leaning forward, trying to be emphatic in his words and gestures, but keeping his voice low enough that no one else could hear him, while John laughed steadily. Matt was telling a dirty story, that much was obvious, but the contrast between the two animated men at one table and the other stone-still zombies scattered around them at surrounding tables and staring at their cell phones made the scene a bit more memorable.

"Had something worse happen once," Matt offered.

"Oh?"

"A wood tick—" Matt paused and pointed to his lap, "down there."

"Your weenie?" John beamed.

Matt shook his head slowly.

"Your nut sack?" John was glowing; he had a pretty good idea where the answer would carry them.

Matt nodded, then said, "The *left* one." He hitched his eyebrows. "And he was *on* there!" Matt made both hands into claws and showed his teeth for emphasis.

John rocked back and laughed. Then he rocked forward and asked, "How'd you get him off?"

Matt bent over and looked at his lap, and made a point to squint when he looked up. "The little shit was in a *bad* place, in a couple ways. First of all, that's pretty tender area. Second, he was kinda small, and I needed some magnification if I was gonna grab him with tweezers. I decided to use my loupes; you know, the telescopes I use at the office, in order to get a good look. With me?"

John was nodding, grinning, and waiting for more

"So, I'm naked, except for the loupes and some heavy socks; my feet were cold."

"Awesome." John rolled his eyes. "Keep going."

"So anyway, the focal distance for those loupes is about here." Matt held his palm in front of his face. "But no matter how far I bent over . . ." Matt pushed his chair back and bent forward to illustrate the problem, "I couldn't get close enough to focus properly." He was making fun of himself now, and John was laughing out loud.

"So Jane had to do it."

John slapped the table and laughed like a fiend.

"So I lay on our bed with my knees up in the air. She put my loupes on and got a tweezers." Matt paused to let John stare at that word for a moment. "Well, she *said* it was a tweezers; I think it was an ice pick and a six-iron. But she finally got it." Matt grimaced. "She took a couple divots on the first few swings; it was not a precise surgical procedure. When she held it up to show me it looked like a tiny little toupee." Matt made a face and held his crotch.

That did it for John. He slapped at the table and barked when he laughed, so loudly that a few other patrons looked over and couldn't help but laugh along with him, even though they had no idea what he was laughing at. He was rocking in his chair and wiping tears from his eyes.

Soon enough, the irresistible force of his buddy's laughter had drawn Matt in; even as he'd finished the story he'd begun to lose control and laugh right along with John, and now he was out of control, too. No one can watch a buddy laugh like that and not join in.

Once their howls had subsided, Sally approached their table. "Was it something in the coffee?" she asked.

"Ah, I wish you could sell us a laugh like that every day," John said.

"Me too. Would you like a refill?" Sally asked.

"Please," Matt said. When she'd taken their cups back to the counter he added, as if talking to himself, "She *is* pretty. She gets prettier every time I talk to her."

She returned with their refills. "Thanks, Sally," Matt said. "You look sharp today, by the way, really nice."

"Well, thank you!" Sally said when she turned to walk away.

"Whoa, nice work!" John said.

"What? I just paid her a compliment. Everyone likes a compliment now and then, and she's been pretty good to us."

"True," John said. "But remember, I called dibbies on her first."

"You know people sometimes say nice things just to spread a little sunshine? Ever heard of that? Maybe you could try it sometime."

"Yeah, whatever." John was about to ask another question when the front door opened and Jane walked in.

"Hey, honey, come over and sit with us," Matt said. When he noticed that Sally was looking at Jane, he pointed at the counter and said, "Jane, this is my friend Sally—"

"We've met," both women said at the same instant, and Sally gave a wave.

"Coffee?" Sally asked from behind the counter.

"Well, I just came in here to pick this guy up." Jane pointed at Matt. "But sure, coffee sounds good."

"How do you know each other?" Matt asked when Jane sat down with them.

"I came in here over lunch one day about a week ago and the place was pretty quiet, so I introduced myself and then welcomed her to Pine Rapids," Jane said.

"We did that too. She even set aside a special table for us," John offered.

"Yeah, that's what she said," Jane replied. "She also asked me if there was something wrong with you."

"She has a strong physical attraction for me," John said with a nod.

"Hmm . . . she didn't mention that," Jane said. "But she did tell me that she's raising her grandson because the boy's mother is in rehab and not likely to rejoin society for some time, if ever. Pretty sad story."

"We met him. Cute kid," Matt said.

Sally came to their table and placed a coffee in front of Jane.

"How's Timmy? It *is* Timmy, right? Your grandson?" Jane asked.

"Yes, his name is Timmy Clements, and his birthday is next Thursday," Sally said.

"Oh, well that's wonderful! We have another friend whose birthday is the same day, and we're having a party for him at our home on Saturday. Please come and we'll all celebrate together—cake and candles—you know."

"Well . . ." Sally hesitated.

"I'll be there," John said, as if that information would be enough draw celebrities, too.

Sally smiled. "OK then. But I'll need directions to your home. I don't know my way around here very well yet."

Matt was grinning as he walked to the door with Jane, and the grin only widened when Jane leaned close to him and said, "Do you smell skunk?"

CHAPTER FIFTEEN

———

Jane was looking out the kitchen window at noon on Saturday, searching for a sign that the party guests she'd invited for Snag Velde and Timmy Clements's shared birthday party were on the way. She leaned one way and then the other, trying to see down the snow-covered driveway that led from the Kingstons' home in the woods to the county road a half mile away. "Do you think they got lost? Maybe they forgot? I gave Sally the directions on Monday," she said, with her back to Matt.

Matt opened a bag of potato chips and took the lid off a container of French onion dip. "I think it's barely noon. They'll be here. Did you put any beer in the upstairs fridge?" he said, munching on a potato chip. "And the Veldes, well, who knows about those guys? I told 'em noon, but that means any time between eleven and four to them."

"Here they are." Jane saw Sally's blue Toyota ease into the clearing by the garage. "Did you get the boys' old video game thingamajig hooked up?"

"Yup," Matt said, as he dipped another chip, "but this kid is gonna think it's an antique."

"It is!" Jane said. "It was our boys' video game controller twenty years ago, but it's what we have, and Timmy might like it. We needed to have *something* for him to play with." Then she swung the back door open and welcomed Sally and Timmy to their home.

"What a beautiful place you have here!" Sally exclaimed, as she took her coat off and then helped her grandson with his. "Your driveway winds through all those trees—it's like a tunnel, and the trees are all covered with snow! Here, Timmy, take your boots off, too. And your *home*! It's just what a home in the woods should look like; all this beautiful timber . . . it's just what I would have pictured for you, Dr. Kingston."

"It's Matt, and c'mon in," Matt said. Then he added, "How ya doing, Timmy?"

"Good," Timmy replied, with his head down, as any little boy would do in a new place with unfamiliar people looking at him.

"Well happy birthday, young man!" Jane said. "How old are you now?"

"Eight."

"Do you like video games?" Matt asked.

"He loves video games," Sally replied.

"Well, if you follow me I'll show you some of the games my boys played when they were your age," Matt offered.

Timmy looked up at Sally, and she gave him a nudge. "Go ahead, Timmy. I'll be here in the kitchen, helping Jane for a while. You can see what kind of games Matt has to show you."

The two women watched Matt and Timmy walk into the great room and turn on the TV. Then, surprisingly, both Timmy and Matt sat down on the floor in front of the TV and started handling the game controls.

"I didn't think your husband could do that so soon after surgery," Sally said.

Jane smiled. "Yeah, he always sat on the floor with our boys when they played those games. Now I guess the real question is, will he be able to stand up again without help." She looked out the window and said, "The three Velde boys are supposed to be here any minute, too. They are a unique bunch, to say the least."

"Well, I know John, but not the other two . . ." Sally said.

"Each of those boys is one of a kind," Jane said, as she took some dishes from a cupboard. "I couldn't begin to describe them. You can see for yourself in a few minutes."

"I think John could be a lot of fun," Sally said.

"Hmph." Jane smiled. "That would be one way to put it." She opened the refrigerator and as she looked around inside it she explained, "This is a birthday party for two little boys: one is eight, and the other is sixty. The other day you said that Timmy likes baseball, so I thought I'd stay with a baseball theme and have hot dogs and brats, just like at the ballpark. And it'll maybe remind us that spring is only a few weeks away. I hope that will work for Timmy?"

"That's perfect! You must have read my mind—I bought him a new baseball glove," Sally said. "Now, can I help you with anything?"

"I think everything is just about ready," Jane replied. "Sit down and relax, and tell me how you're liking Pine Rapids. Are you meeting people? How's business? How's your first winter in the north?"

"Everything is good. We like this place and we're both making friends. But I worry. I feel so bad for my daughter, Timmy's mother. I don't think she'll ever be free from drugs. She's been in and out of rehab so many times. And I worry about Timmy making friends in a new school and a new place, but he seems to be doing all right."

Jane was surprised by the lack of emotion in the woman's voice, but she assumed that life had hardened Sally Durham.

"Yeah . . ." Sally started again, "I never dreamed I'd be living here and raising a child, by myself, when I was fifty. Life can be kinda strange, huh?" She gave a faint smile.

In the great room, Timmy was holding a video game control in both hands and staring intently at the TV screen while he guided an airplane in a dogfight. His head and shoulders jerked one way and then the other as he tried to impart extra movement to his aircraft. Flaming missiles streaked past his plane while he guided it through a hail of gunfire. Then a giant explosion stopped the game.

"How'd you get so good at this?" Matt asked Timmy.

"This is a really easy game. I think it's pretty old, and we've got it set at beginner level. These planes are going real slow," Timmy said.

"OK, kid, let's try it again. But before we do, tell me one more time: How do I fire my missiles?"

Timmy was explaining the fundamentals of video game aerial combat when Matt heard the Velde boys approach the house. He looked back over his shoulder and then elected to let Jane handle the introductions.

"I brought the birthday boy," John said, as he led his brothers up the back steps and into the kitchen.

"Hi, John, hi, Darrell, and happy birthday, Snag!" Jane said, as she stood on her tiptoes and gave Snag a hug and kiss on the cheek. "C'mon," she teased, "you can do better than that." Snag struggled with moments like this. For a sixty-year-old man who basically lived in a slaughterhouse, he had pretty good social skills, and he was no dummy, but he always seemed a bit unclear about how to respond to a hug, or any kindness, from Jane Kingston. His fondness for her was always evident in the way he stole a glance, or threw in a clever comment, but the affection she lavished on him was just not a part of his everyday world, and sometimes when she did things like this he seemed to freeze.

But this time, he smiled broadly and he wrapped his arms around her. Then he stood straight, and when Jane's feet were dangling a foot off the kitchen floor he asked, "Howzat?"

"Much better!" Jane said, as if she was correcting her child's poor behavior. When he lowered her back to the floor she added, "That's the way you do it."

By anyone's standards, Snag looked like a million bucks today. He'd showered, shaved, and run a comb through his shaggy gray hair. He wore clean khaki pants, a golf shirt, and a sweater. His clothes, however, fit him as though he'd failed to try them on before he bought them; everything was too big. Snag had one of those bodies that was guaranteed to make even expensive clothing look like it came from a Salvation Army store.

Jane turned to Darrell gave him a warm hug, too. Then she extended her arms toward John, and as he bent low and reached for her he said, "No tongues, OK?"

"No problem," Jane said with her arms around his shoulders.

When Jane stepped back from John, it was time for him to introduce his brothers to Sally. He placed a hand on Snag's shoulder. "Sally, this is my brother, Snag," and then before anyone could speak, he put a hand on Darrell's shoulder and said, "and this my other brother, Darrell."

As always when John reached for a laugh with this punch line from the old Bob Newhart show, Snag and Darrell were unmoved and Jane rolled her eyes.

But Sally had never heard it before and she laughed as she greeted the Velde boys.

"So, where's the doctor?" John asked.

"In the great room, playing video games with Timmy," Jane said. "Why don't you boys go on in there and meet young Timmy Clements, the other birthday boy, while Sally and I get things ready in here. We'll open presents after lunch . . . and cake 'n candles."

Sally and Jane watched from the kitchen as the Veldes walked into the great room and introduced themselves to Timmy before they all sat down around the TV. "They all grew up together?" Sally asked.

"Well, I don't think it would be accurate to say that anyone in that room has ever grown up," Jane replied. She then pointed at the developing scuffle between John and Matt, who were already wrestling over whose turn it should be to use the video game control in Matt's hands. Matt was laughing and rolling on the floor on his side as he clutched the control close to his chest with both hands. John was lying on top of him and trying to pry the control out of Matt's grasp.

"Lunch in ten minutes!" Jane called out. As she closed the pocket door that separated the kitchen from the great room she added, "And don't make me come in there!"

———

All of the partygoers were seated around the table in the kitchen wearing small, cone-shaped party hats an hour later. Snag was pushing the last inch of his third hot dog and bun through the remaining puddle of ketchup on his paper plate when Jane asked, "Who's ready for cake and ice cream?"

"I am!" Timmy blurted.

"Me too," Darrell added.

"I might have another hot dog," Snag said, his words muffled by the one still in his mouth.

"Oh, sorry, Snag," Jane chuckled, as she stood and walked to the oven, where several more brats and wieners were kept warm in a covered pan. "You want a brat this time?"

"Yeah, sure," Snag answered.

The birthday party and lunch, thus far, had been like a door swinging open for Sally. These people had invited her to have a look into their little world, and maybe ease herself into it if she wanted. She'd watched the men play video games with her grandson as if the eight-year-old had always been part of this group. Jane had spoken to her with sincere concern about her move to this new place. And now when she watched Jane deliver yet another brat to Snag, she witnessed something unexpected.

After Jane placed the brat on Snag's plate, but before she returned to her own chair, Jane bent over and put her hand on Matt's cheek. She waited for him to turn toward her, and she kissed him softly on the lips. Before she could straighten up, Matt ran a hand up and down her thigh. And while their lips were still inches apart, Jane said, "I love you." She said it softly, but she had no intention of hiding this display of affection from anyone. And, Sally judged by the reaction of the Veldes, this type of thing was pretty common because none of them seemed to notice.

"So, does anyone else want more before we get out the cake and ice cream?" Jane asked as she sat down in her chair beside Matt. "I didn't mean to hurry anyone."

Matt raised a hand up and softly stroked Jane's neck for a second and then said, "Why don't we give our lunch a chance to rest before we have cake? Let's open presents first." Sally studied the way his hand caressed his lover, even while he spoke of birthday cake. The affection these two still felt for each other was undeniable.

"Ooh, then I gotta go get—" Snag said, quickly pushing his chair back to get up from the table.

"Stay put, Snag. I'll go get it," Darrell said. When everyone at the table cast a questioning look his way, Darrell explained, "Snag brought something too." And with that, Darrell was out the back door. A truck door slammed, and Darrell reappeared with a very large cardboard box. "I don't know what's in here, either," he added.

"OK, Snag," John said, "don't let it bother you that poor Timmy over there is waiting to open his presents. Just take your time . . ."

With a very loud snap of her fingers, Sally caught everyone's attention. She turned an icy glare at John and pointed her finger as if she was looking down the barrel of a gun. "I can throw your ass outta here, too!" she hissed. "Now behave yourself and let your brother finish his brat."

Timmy wasn't sure what to think of Sally's outburst, but the others were all laughing at his grandma before she was finished speaking, so he joined in too.

"OK," Snag said a moment later. "I'm done eating."

Timmy proceeded to open his gifts, and before Sally could finish stuffing the used wrapping paper into a bag, he was wearing a new Twins hat and a new baseball glove on his left hand and pounding his right fist into the pocket.

"Nice glove!" John said.

Snag held up a new fleece jacket and a gift certificate from the Human Bean and said, "Thanks."

While Snag was holding the jacket up for everyone to see, John extended a hand, and when Snag accepted what was in it, John said, "Here's twenty bucks. I forgot to wrap it." Then he added, "So what's in the box? Did you bring a present for yourself?"

When Snag reached over and slid the box close, everyone stopped what they were doing and watched. He fished around in the box for a moment and then lifted out two black-and-white pelts, which everyone immediately identified as skunks. But it took only seconds to realize that the skunk pelts had been transformed into something exotic, even though no one at the table could tell what it was.

"Whaddya got there, Snag?" Darrell asked.

"Well, they're not really slippers." Snag hesitated as he displayed them. "You wouldn't want to wear 'em around much. They're for those cold winter nights when you're sittin' on the couch, reading or watching TV. I sewed in another layer of insulation." He handed the skunk socks to Sally.

"I . . . I don't . . . well . . . thank you!" she stammered.

John snatched one from Sally's hand and sniffed it. "It doesn't stink! What'd you do?" he asked.

"Well, you know that one lady that you hang around with sometimes?" Snag said. John returned a blank stare. "The one who sells essential oils," Snag tried to explain.

"Jenifer?" John asked.

"Yeah, that's her. She showed me how to get that last bit of stink out with some combination of those oils. You put three different oils—I forget which ones—into a candle and then—"

"Jenifer?" Matt piped in. He knew plenty about Jenifer the essential oils girl, and was teasing John. "Is she the one who—"

John closed his eyes and shook his head. It was clear he had no intention of talking about Jenifer in this company.

"So, try them on," Jane said to Sally, and Jenifer was banished from the conversation.

"Perfect!" Sally said a moment later, as she raised one foot above the table. "But it's not my birthday."

"I didn't have time to make you anything more," Snag apologized.

"Well, thank you so much, Snag. I'll wear them every night. They're beautiful, and so warm," Sally said.

"What else is in that box?" Darrell asked.

Snag reached in and started to withdraw a queen-sized blanket made of beaver pelts, and the room fell silent. He'd taken about fifty supple pelts and sewn them together with Teflon thread and then sewn in a fleece liner on the hide side. As he lifted the blanket he raised his eyes and looked at Jane. "It's for you."

Jane stood slowly and walked over to the box. She ran a hand over the fur, then lifted the blanket to her face and gasped, "Oh my God," before she held the luxurious fur against her cheek. "I never . . . it's . . . I don't believe you, Snag! This is the most beautiful thing I've ever seen!" Then she sat on his lap and kissed his cheek a dozen times.

It may have been the finest moment in Snag's life. He was thrilled to have pleased Jane so completely.

Matt cleared the paper plates from the table and brought more paper plates over for the cake and ice cream. Jane had made chocolate cake with chocolate frosting for Snag, and a white sheet cake with white frosting, decorated like a baseball diamond, for Timmy.

The "Happy Birthday" song and the smoke from the candles were both still hanging in the air as conversation at the table migrated from a problem at Jane's office to some gossip that Sally had picked up at the coffee shop, and from there to Timmy's previous day at school. Timmy was busy staring at the green frosting and the writing on his cake when he thought of something that had made everyone on the bus laugh. "Hey, what's white and lies at the bottom of the ocean?" he asked during a brief lull in the conversation.

Matt and John had heard this one many times and they knew what was about to happen. They looked at each other while they waited for the moment to ripen.

"What?" Jane said.

"Moby's dick!" Timmy blurted the punch line to an old joke, then he looked around to see who would laugh first.

But there was only stunned silence. Timmy smiled expectantly, still waiting for the laughter to begin. But it never came.

Matt and John froze. Matt covered his mouth and John smiled openly.

Sally and Jane stared first at Timmy, then at each other, then at John.

"What are you lookin' at *me* for?" John said. Then he leaned back in his chair and covered his smile with his hand.

"Where did you hear that one?" Sally asked Timmy, trying to betray her extreme interest, so as not to make the incident, and the joke, too memorable for Timmy.

"On the bus." His face was completely innocent. He still expected them all to burst out in laughter, like the older boys on the bus. He had no idea what he'd said, only that some older kid had told a joke that made some other older kids laugh, and he'd repeated it.

"Well, you probably shouldn't tell that joke anymore, all right?" Sally said.

"Do you sit with the older kids?" Matt asked, trying to ease the conversation on down the tracks and away from Moby's dick.

"Sometimes I do," Timmy said. "They protect me."

"From what?" John asked, his curiosity piqued.

"Ah, there's a kid named Jason who pushes me down sometimes," Timmy said, with his eyes lowered.

"What do you mean, 'pushes me down'?" John asked, with an edge to his voice.

"He pushes me and I fall down."

Both Matt and John sat straight now, ready to offer assistance. John appeared ready to go over to Jason's house, wherever that was, and deal with Jason.

Sally cautioned them with her eyes, and then spoke up. "The principal at Timmy's school called and told me about this Jason the other day. Timmy's teacher and bus driver have spoken to the other boy, and the situation is being dealt with. Don't get upset, you guys."

"How long has this been going on?" John asked, unable to hide the anger rising in his chest.

"Since the beginning of school, in September," Sally said.

John straightened a bit more in his chair. "Really," he said very slowly. "Does he hit you?" John asked through lips drawn tight.

"Sometimes, and he pushes me down and stands over me so I can't get up," Timmy said.

John simmered for a moment and then began, "OK then, Timmy, this is what you do—"

"John," Jane interrupted, "he'll get in trouble for fighting, and nothing is ever solved by violence."

"That's just not true, Jane," John countered. Both of his elbows were resting on the table, and he was getting animated. "Many things are solved by violence, and this will be one of them." John pointed an index finger at Jane. He turned back to Timmy and continued, "The next time this Jason is picking on you, you just wait until he gets close to you.

Then, while he's talking, and he *will* be talking, because bullies love to talk, you wind up and punch him right here on the end of his nose. Don't threaten him first, and don't tell him what you're gonna do. Just *hit* him, as hard as you possibly can, but make sure you put that first one right on the end of his nose—"

"John!" Jane interrupted, growing embarrassed that John was parenting Sally's grandson.

John held up one hand to silence her. "Then you hit him again, right away, as many times and as hard as you can swing. If you land that first one on his nose he'll be crying and backing up. Then you go after him; hit him again and again, as many times, and as hard as you can. Pound his ass. If he falls down you get on top of him and keep on punching until somebody pulls you off."

"John! That's terrible! Don't tell him that," Jane said.

Timmy was grinning gleefully and glancing around the table.

"Yes, you can, boy. And if you ever want to be free from that little son of a bitch you'd better do it the next time he starts in on you!" John said, with real anger in his voice.

"Timmy, you just tell the bus driver if Jason bothers you again," Sally corrected.

John waited until Timmy looked back at him. "I'm sorry, Sally . . ." John started, without looking away from Timmy. Holding the boy's attention, he slowly raised his index finger up and touched the tip of his nose with it. "Right here, boy, right *here*. He'll drop like shit from a tall cow, and he'll *never* bother you again."

Timmy's smile was so wide they could see every tooth in his head.

"John!" Jane scolded once more. "He can't—" She stopped herself when she saw the look that Timmy was sharing with John. Timmy's mouth still hung open a bit, and the fiendish nature of John's advice had drawn his eyes into reptilian slits. He loved the tough talk from this old man.

John ignored Jane, held an index finger on the tip of his nose and nodded at Timmy. "Right here, buddy."

"Sounds like the voice of experience," Sally said. "Were you the bully, or the one who stood up to the bully?"

"Let's just say that I know what I'm talking about here," John replied.

"All right, who wants some more ice cream?" Jane interrupted, in an effort to change the subject.

Timmy's hand shot up in the air. "I do!"

"Me too," John said.

When all talk of bullies was done and the table was cleared, everyone migrated into the great room for coffee before the party broke up. Matt and Timmy went back to their aerial combat game, and Snag was waiting for a chance to go up against the winner, when the women joined them in the great room. But Darrell and John held back in the kitchen, examining the beaver blanket Snag had made. They were both wondering the same thing.

"How much do you think we could get for one of these?" John asked.

"A lot," Darrell replied. "A *lot!*"

CHAPTER SIXTEEN

Fluffy white snowflakes drifted through the black night and softly settled onto the pine boughs, the oak limbs, and the forest floor. Nearly eleven inches had fallen since noon. There would be no travel, no commerce, and school had already been canceled all across northern Minnesota for tomorrow. This storm had begun as a Hollywood snowfall, but the northwest winds were supposed to pick up any time and whip the snow around until visibility was zero and remote roads were drifted shut. Some of the roads would remain impassable until the spring thaw.

Matt loved these moments. He stood close to a window that looked out over Scotch Lake, so close that his face could feel the icy chill coming from the windowpane. "Wish we could put the snowshoes on and go for a walk on the lake before the wind picks up," he said.

Jane was bent over, using a poker to stir the ashes in the fireplace. "Me too. Next year . . ." She sighed as she placed another log on the fire. Her face was getting warm from the glowing embers. She still hadn't looked back at Matt when she added, "when your hip is strong again."

The change that Matt had expected, or feared, after his hip replacement, had never come. He didn't morph into a frail, bent-over little old man. Rather, his health and his swagger quickly returned in the absence of the chronic pain in his hip. He was walking confidently once again, free of pain, and looking forward to resuming his life as it had been. His doctor had told him to avoid strenuous workouts, but normal day-to-day activities were fine.

"OK, it's showtime," Jane said, when the logs on the fire were arranged properly. She moved over to the leather couch, put her feet up on the old cribbage-board coffee table, and lifted a Hudson Bay Company blanket over herself. A moment later, when everything was just as she wanted it, she patted her left hand on the couch, inviting Matt to sit next to her. "Put the movie in, will you?"

Matt walked over to the TV and put the DVD into the player. "Did you talk to the boys?" he asked.

"Yup, just a couple minutes ago," Jane said. "Both of them are just fine."

Matt couldn't help smiling. All was well in his world just now; both of their grown sons were doing well. If only the boys lived closer, and would get married and start having children. But that would come in its own good time. Tonight he was alone, by a crackling fire, with the girl he'd been in love with for forty years. Life couldn't get much better than this.

The TV lit up and a moment later, the opening credits for *The Searchers* burst across the screen.

Matt slid under Jane's blanket and snuggled next to her, taking her hand in his. "Great story," he sighed, "and maybe John Wayne's best role, and best acting, although I think I prefer him as Sean Thornton in *The Quiet Man*."

Jane smiled but didn't let Matt see it.

"Anyway," he continued, "John Wayne is the hero who rides in on the big horse and overcomes all kindsa shit, and saves the girl."

Jane leaned over and kissed Matt.

"I still wanna be John Wayne," he said.

"I thought you wanted to be Mickey Mantle. You know, the Oklahoma Kid, number 7, the best there ever was?" She was teasing Matt now. She loved his enthusiasm, the way he could reach back and roll around in the joy of childhood.

"Well, yeah, he was in there in my dreams, too," he allowed. Jane's teasing had derailed his manifesto. "I guess we should just be quiet and watch the movie, huh? But if you have any other questions, please ask."

Jane lifted her hand, the one that was holding his, and kissed the back of his hand. "I love you," she said, and she moved closer and rested her head on his shoulder. As they began to watch the film, each of them had to clear their crowded minds of distractions.

Reclining on the couch, with her feet on the coffee table, Jane had to look beyond the wool blanket that covered her, and beyond own feet, in order to see the TV. The glowing hearth, only a few feet away, the amber light dancing over the cedar plank walls, the faint smell of wood smoke, and the gentle touch of her lover—it had all come together, the fruition of her dreams, and Matt's. Every day when she left work and started for home she felt as if she was leaving on vacation. What a great way to feel about your home, she thought. They'd bought the place for a song, and then raised their boys here. How had she been so fortunate?

"OK, this is a good part right here," Matt said, bringing her back to the moment.

John Wayne was racing around on his horse when Jane snuggled closer to Matt. She was aware that some buildings had been burned by bad Indians, and John Wayne was angry and about to get some revenge, but she found herself thinking of the way she'd met Matt. She'd never had a boyfriend. She'd been popular in her sorority, and she'd dated some but had never even taken a boy home to meet her parents. Until Matt.

Matt was an original, a one-of-a-kind in her life experience. He was handsome, she noticed that right off, though there were plenty of handsome guys at the University of Minnesota. But Matt had two qualities that made him irresistible to Jane: his sense of humor and his confidence. The more he talked with her on that first night she'd met him at the Fraction, the handsomer he got. But he made her laugh, too. It wasn't that he was a comedian; he just had something clever or some little twist on a phrase at every turn in the conversation that night. Jane often thought of Marilyn Monroe's great quote: "If you can make a woman laugh, you can make her do anything."

He was brimming with confidence, too. She knew on that first night that Matt Kingston could overcome anything at work, or in school, or in life. He stepped into her life that night and dismissed any other men she might have been interested in. She wouldn't be needing them anymore; she was swept away by Matt.

John Wayne was riding his horse and talking to another man on a horse, and Jane sat up with her legs underneath her and her back flush against the back of the couch, so that she was several inches taller than Matt, then she put one arm around his shoulder. "John Wayne should wish he was you," she whispered.

Matt reached a hand under the blanket and softly stroked her leg. He sensed an unspoken message in the way she'd moved closer to him, and his thoughts drifted away from *The Searchers*. Jane had nursed him back from the surgery and supervised every step of his rehab. In those first days home from the hospital he'd been unable to get into and out of bed, so she'd made it easy for him to sleep in an old recliner. She'd slept on the couch, beside his recliner, in case he might need her during the night. She'd changed his bandages, helped him shower, prepared his favorite meals, and urged him through some difficult postoperative physical therapy.

The TV screen was now just muted colors and figures moving, talking, and riding horses, and Matt found himself remembering the way Jane had laughed when she snapped herself with that towel. Damn, they had good times together, Matt thought. He moved his hand over the softness of her bare leg, and then turned to kiss her. All he intended was a peck on the cheek and another "I love you." But when he turned his head her pajama top opened just enough to expose one breast, and the sight triggered a wonderful little twitch way down in his belly. He got his kiss, then pulled her so close that her breast was pressing against his cheek.

An Indian chief was riding his horse across the screen, but the movie had suddenly devolved into a distraction, and Jane reached under the blanket until she found what she was searching for, and then felt it begin to swell. "Would you like to bury the hatchet, so to speak?"

"Over and over again," Matt said. He used the remote to turn the movie off.

Jane slipped out of her panties and then lay across Matt's lap and looked up at him. "I love you, Matt."

He moved one hand under her pajama top, then over her thighs and between her legs while she arched her back. "Are you sure this is OK? What if I break your hip?" she asked.

"Well, I'm gonna try to break yours," he whispered as he pulled the blanket up, over them both, and their house was all quiet, except for the growing howl of the winter wind, and the giggling.

—— · ——

There would be no sunrise when they awoke the next morning, only the gradual spread of gray dawn until there was enough light to see wind-driven snow moving past the windows, and the harsh swaying of naked oak limbs in the winter wind.

Jane's eyes opened when the bedroom was just light enough to make out her surroundings. She raised the quilt and the beaver blanket that covered her and Matt, and tucked it under her chin to keep out the chill of the frigid winter storm. The fire in the downstairs fireplace was long dead. Matt would stoke the coals when he woke, and the house would warm quickly. Maybe she'd snuggle closer to Matt, too.

The walls and ceilings of their home were planks of old cedar and white pine. Jane liked to lie in bed and let her eyes wander about the bedroom. The walls all had a story to tell and she often wondered about the knots and the grain. Sometimes in the half light of morning or evening the planks revealed shapes—animals, sometimes faces, sometimes a hint that other secrets were there, waiting to show themselves to her. No one else she'd ever known had a home like this, and she often wondered about the history, the things that had happened in this rustic place.

She moved her eyes to a chest of drawers that had been in this house for a century. The reddish-brown patina of the wood spoke of a long life, but the piece also was marked in a dozen places, scarred from a lifetime of use. It had no real value—it was not an antique, made by a long-dead master craftsman—it was just a solid old friend.

The bedroom windows had sixteen separate panes, and from where Jane lay, they framed the north country perfectly. The world outside them was still wild, the forest was still home to bear and fox and beaver and other critters that men still trapped and hunted. The woods and the lake just beyond it were places for her to go and think about her place in the world.

She turned to look at Matt. The room was light enough that she could see the whisker stubble on his face, and he looked so peaceful. He was breathing softly, and Jane studied his face. There were several small scars, and she knew the history of them all. The one on his eyebrow was from an elbow in a high school basketball game, and the one on his chin came from a fall on the ice. A boyhood playmate had thrown a wooden block at him during a childhood scuffle and left a nice little scar in the middle of his forehead. He had some wrinkles at the corners of his eyes now, too, and a few more on his neck. He still had power, though; he exuded a reassurance, that everything would always be OK if he was around. The years were beginning to pile up, but he was still her champion. She reached over and touched his face, and his eyes blinked open.

"Good morning," she whispered when Matt's eyes focused on her. "I love you."

"Mmm. I love you, too," Matt said. "Wanna make breakfast?" He then pulled the beaver blanket up to cover most of his head.

"Ahh, let's just coast for a while," Jane said. She scooted closer until she was pressed against his side, and she reached an arm under the fur blanket and draped it across his chest. They listened to the whisper of the wind in the trees outside and made a point to be touching each other while they waited to wake up a bit more.

"What are you thinking about?" Matt asked, after a few minutes.

"Coffee. You?"

Matt pulled her closer. The gray light of dawn, the security of their warm bed, and the softness of her skin carried him back to other mornings, long ago. That first winter when their love was new and sleepovers were an adventure that no one else knew about; that was a fine time. They'd sleep in, either at his place or hers, and then make breakfast in their underwear.

Jane slid her bare legs out from under the blanket and sat on the side of the bed to get her balance before she pulled a T-shirt over her head, and then a bathrobe.

So many years had gone by, Matt thought, as he watched her stretch and then walk to the kitchen. Sometimes, at moments like this, he used to wonder if he was her first lover. He didn't know why he thought about it, but he did. He'd asked her several times, and she always smiled and said it was him. Matt knew that he was her first real boyfriend, and he knew that she was fairly ignorant about sex when they started dating. He'd tried, every so often, to tease or trick her into blurting a different truth.

But he wanted coffee now, so he pushed the warm blanket away and let the morning chill overpower a warm bed and ancient curiosity. He sat up on his side of the bed and got his balance while he listened to Jane's footsteps moving into the kitchen to start the coffee brewing.

The smells of bacon, coffee, and biscuits soon filled the old house. The north wind had blown itself out just after dawn, and in the woods just outside their windows everything was motionless. The only color outside was the dark green of pine boughs, half covered with snow and bent toward the earth; the sky was gray, and everything else was white.

With a coffee cup in one hand, Matt poked a fork at a cast-iron frying pan filled with sizzling bacon. His hair was mussed, and he wore a gray sweatshirt that said Muskie Days in faded green letters, tattered gray sweatpants, and red wool hunting socks.

As Matt started breakfast while the coffee perked, Jane had dressed for the day and now returned to the kitchen. "Nice look ya got going there," she said, as she poured herself a cup of coffee. She went to the kitchen window and peered out at the sheet of white that was Scotch Lake. Her back was turned to Matt, and she was surveying the landscape, taking in the beauty of the morning. He couldn't help but notice the way the worn spots on her blue jeans accented all the best curves. She wore a red fleece pullover and her blonde hair was pulled back in a ponytail.

He put his coffee down and went to her. He cupped her breasts with both hands and held her close. His lips were touching her ear when he said, "You made some *noise* last night . . ." He let the words linger in the air for a moment; he knew they'd draw a response.

With his cheek pressed against hers, Matt could feel the smile spreading over her face. Mischief was rising in her, and she was sure to tease him with her reply. "I don't remember. I blacked out for a minute there." She turned to face him, and added, "You animal."

With his arms around Jane, and the kitchen full of the smell of coffee and bacon, Matt said softly, "I love you more than words can say. The greatest thing I'll ever do in this life is to be the boy that Jane Monahan chose."

"Hey, let's put some music on," she suggested, and Matt stepped back to tend the frying bacon. "How 'bout some Gordon Lightfoot—"

Matt's phone rang and interrupted Jane. "Huh," he said with surprise, "it's John." When he raised the phone to his ear he joked, "I'm *busy*; what do *you* want?"

"I broke another tooth," John replied.

"Bummer." Matt poked a fork at the bacon in the frying pan. "How'd that happen?"

"Well, when I left your place I stopped at Lefty's for a bump. You know, just one beer on the way home."

"And you got in a fight?" Matt said.

"No," John corrected. "But I did run into Jenifer."

"Who?"

"Jenifer, the essential-oils girl who fixed our skunks," John said.

"Oh, OK, *that* Jenifer . . . and she broke your tooth?"

"Not exactly, but I did go home with her. And this morning when I was trying to push my truck out of the snowdrift in her driveway I was clenching my teeth and another tooth broke."

"Where?"

"In her fuckin' driveway. I just told you."

"Where in your *mouth*? What *tooth*?" Matt cringed.

"Lower molar, right next door to one you just fixed. Am I gonna have a toothache?"

"Does it hurt now, right this minute?" Matt asked.

"It only hurts if I put something cold or sweet on it, but it's really sharp on my tongue."

"Then you're not gonna have a toothache. You just have some exposed dentin, which is pretty sensitive to cold and sweets, so that's normal. And the jagged edge of your broken tooth is irritating your tongue. That's all." Matt used the fork to lift a bacon strip out of the frying pan. "Obviously I can't see you today, but if our road is open and I can get in to the office tomorrow I'll have Donna work you into the schedule."

"Great. Thanks, buddy."

"So how's Jenifer?" Matt asked, inviting whatever repartee John might want to toss back at him before they hung up.

"Well, you know she's kind of a shaman, the way she can use those essential oils to heal things," John replied.

"She's a warmed-over hippie shaman. Have her fix your tooth," Matt suggested.

"Nah, she's got her hands full with other things," John said. There was fullness to that thought, an unspoken sentence filled with the usual sexual innuendo. Matt could picture the grin plastered on John's face at that moment.

"OK then, as long as you're in good hands until tomorrow," Matt said as he hung up the phone.

"He's at Jenifer's place?" Jane asked, while she scanned a magazine.

"Yup."

"Do you ever wonder if John is happy?"

"Yeah, I *do* wonder about that. He keeps things right on the surface most of the time, like he's afraid to look a little deeper. I know he's a smart guy, but . . ." Matt shrugged and dismissed John from his thoughts. "I wonder about other things, too."

"Like what?" Jane asked.

"Oh, I dunno . . ." Matt set a plate of bacon in front of Jane and heaved a sigh.

"What does *that* mean?" Jane leaned back and squinted at Matt. "Are *you* happy?"

"Oh, I regret some things I did, or didn't, do. There were a few people I could have treated better. And what we have, you and me—I worry sometimes that I won't be able to hold it together."

"That's not the boy I fell in love with talking. My Matt was fearless." She leaned over and kissed him. "C'mon, let's hear from my Matt."

"As long as you think of me as *yours*, I'm happy." Matt smiled. He picked up a broken piece of bacon and bit it in half, and after he swallowed he said, "I think happiness is something that we carry around inside us, but it's nurtured by the love of others."

Jane turned a quizzical look at him.

"John thinks that happiness is something you come across one moment, one thing, and one woman at a time," Matt said. He stared at his plate of bacon, then he added, "I sorta wish it was that simple."

CHAPTER SEVENTEEN

"What's the deal here?" John asked, as he plopped into the overstuffed chair in Matt's private office. He was rubbing his chin, checking to see if the local anesthetic was wearing off yet. His new crown was minutes old. "Why are all my teeth breaking?"

"I told you, John, it's just normal wear and tear. These two teeth that broke recently both had large fillings in them, fillings that old Doctor Anderson probably placed when we were kids, up above the Rexall drug store down on Main Street? Right?"

John nodded yes.

"And then they were replaced when you were about thirty?"

John nodded.

"And now they've worn out again. But this time there's not enough tooth left to make a filling, so I had to make a crown. You'll probably have a couple more crowns, too, in the next decade. And if that's the worst thing that happens to you, you're having a pretty great life."

"Yeah, I guess you're right," John said, still rubbing his chin.

"That'll wear off in the next hour," Matt reminded him. "I've got a little bit of paperwork to do, but I took this afternoon off. If you can stick around for a few minutes, I'll buy you lunch?"

"Sure, I can wait," John said. He reached for a fishing magazine and began flipping through the pages. "Hey, instead of sitting in a restaurant, let's go over to the Ashley Hotel and pick up a burger to go; their burgers are the best. Then let's take the burgers back to my shop and sit by the wood stove and bullshit, like we used to do all the time. We haven't done that for a year or more."

"Sure," Matt said, reading his mail. "I love that burger they make with avocado and bacon and the special horseradish sauce of theirs. And of course, the ambiance of your workroom adds something special—animal heads scattered around and staring at us, with one eye, or one horn."

After glancing at magazine photos for only a minute or so, John stood up and looked out the door of Matt's office. He looked right, then left, then closed the door and sat back down in his chair. "Got a question," he said in a subdued tone.

"Shoot," Matt replied, without looking up from his desk.

"The last time I was in here you prescribed some antibiotics," John began.

"Yes, so?"

"And you prescribed some painkillers for me about two years ago when you took out that infected tooth—that really hurt, by the way."

"You waited too long to call me . . ." Matt looked up and added, "stupid," before he went back to his paperwork.

"Yeah, I'll give you that one," John said.

"So what's the question?"

"Well," John hesitated, "can you prescribe Viagra, too?"

Matt looked up and shrugged. "Sure. Well, according to my DEA license I can, but nobody else ever asked me before."

"So, can you?" John flicked his eyebrows.

"Sure, I'll call it in right now." Matt picked up his phone and then asked John, "The pharmacy at Walmart OK?"

"You bet!" John replied. While Matt made the call and waited for someone to answer, John added, "Don't you want to give me some shit about this?"

"Well, I'd love to, but I just don't want to talk about the lead in *your* pencil." Matt grinned, then he looked back at his desk top and recited the prescription into the doctors' automated prescription line at the Walmart pharmacy. "You can pick it up in an hour," he said when he hung up the phone. "Did you wanna tell me something, about the Viagra?"

"Hey, I'm OK," John said quickly. "But I *am* curious, I guess." After a short pause he added, "And, well, sometimes the little guy who lives down there . . ." John pointed to the place, "well, he just loses interest. He never used to do that."

"So, what do you do?" Matt asked.

"I beat him like he owes me money," John replied. "Have *you* ever tried it? Tell me the truth."

"Viagra? Or beatin' my dick like it owes me money?" Matt smiled and leaned back in his chair.

"Viagra, smartass."

"For guys our age that stuff can be a recreational drug, too. Or maybe sort of an insurance policy," Matt said.

"Yeah, yeah, that's what I'm talking about. So, *have* you?" John pried.

"Not yet." There was a tiny knock on the door. "C'mon in," Matt said.

Tammy, the dental assistant, poked her face through a small opening in the doorway. "I'm sorry to bother you, Doctor, but Roger Senesac is on the phone and would like to talk to you. Do you want to take the call, or should I tell him you'll call him back?"

"I'll take it," Matt replied, and Tammy left them alone. "She hates you," he said to John, as he reached for the land-line phone on his desk and pushed a blinking button. "Hi, Roger. What's up?" Roger Senesac was the baseball coach at Pine Rapids High School and also head of the town's baseball association, and a longtime friend.

"Hi, Matt. I'm in the liquor store and I just bumped into your wife. She said she had to make a run because Velde drank all your beer again."

"Some things never change," Matt said.

"Yeah, well, anyway, as you know, I'm always trying to find coaches for the younger kids—"

"Let me guess," Matt interrupted, "Jane volunteered me to coach a team this summer, right?" John heard this and made a point to let Matt see him cover his mouth and point and laugh at him.

"Yup, she said something about the woman that owns the new coffee shop. Her grandson wants to play ball. Will you do it? Will you coach his team?" Roger asked. When Matt hesitated, Roger turned up the heat. "It's only two nights a week for seven weeks. You can't take that pretty girl fishing every night, and it's basically a social thing. Not much coaching required, mainly babysitting and a bit of basic instruction." Roger waited a second and then added, "C'mon Matt, you're really good at this stuff. I remember when you coached your boys, and—"

"Sure, I'll do it, Roger," Matt said.

John was making a display from his chair, holding his side, miming laughter and pointing at Matt.

"I'm looking forward to it, and Velde will be my assistant coach," Matt said, with his eyes locked on John, and John began to shake his head in protest immediately. "He's sitting here with me right now, and he'll be happy to help."

"Well, that's great. I'll put you guys down for one of the eight-year-old teams. That's the age group that Jane said you'd want."

"Perfect!" Matt said. John scowled and shook his head.

"OK then, I'll be in touch with more information in a few weeks, and say hi to Velde," Roger said.

Matt replaced the receiver, and John folded his arms. "No way!" John scoffed. "I'm just not a coach, and I'm pretty busy in the summer, and—"

"John." It was Matt's turn to interrupt. "You're *not* too busy; that dog won't hunt. You're gonna do this with me and we're gonna have some fun."

"No . . . Fucking . . . Way," John insisted defiantly.

The office door opened a little bit, once again, and Tammy peered through the opening, just as she'd done a few minutes before. "I'm so sorry to bother you again, Doctor, but the pharmacist from Walmart is on the phone."

"Yes?" Matt said.

"Well, did you write a prescription for *him*?" She pointed at John, with disdain. "A prescription for Viagra?"

Instead of blushing and sinking back into his chair, John turned to Tammy and took on the air of a teacher who was about to chastise a student for a breach of proper behavior. "He can't answer that. It would be a HIPAA violation," John scoffed. "That stands for Health Insurance Portability and Accountability Act, and it's designed to protect the privacy of all patients' medical information. Sheesh, you should know about that, Tammy."

Tammy rolled her eyes, then looked at Matt and waited for him to answer.

"Yes." Matt smiled.

"Well, he says he won't fill it because it's outside the scope of your practice," Tammy explained. She was trying to appear embarrassed to bring her boss this message, but she clearly enjoyed delivering it in front of John.

"Tell him it's for *oral* sex!" John blurted. "That's within your scope of practice, isn't it?" His grin was more devious than ever.

Tammy closed her eyes as if that might protect her from the sight of some disgusting thing that had been coughed up right in front of her. "I hate you," she added.

"Well OK then, Tammy, just tell him that I'll find somebody who *will* fill it," Matt said. When Tammy was gone a second later, Matt reached into the top drawer of his desk and withdrew a prescription pad. He wrote on the top sheet, tore it off, and then extended his arm toward John. "I have a buddy, a pharmacist in Bemidji, who'll fill this for you."

"Thanks." John reached for the small piece of paper in Matt's hand.

"No problem," Matt said. Then, at the last instant, just as John was about to take the paper, Matt pulled his hand back. "But it's for baseball coaches only."

John slumped. "You rat bastard."

"Yeah, I guess so." Matt grinned.

John cringed. "Really? You're gonna withhold my boner pills unless I help you with this? Really?"

"Look, you know I'm only doing this to help little Timmy Clements have a good summer and make some friends. It's only two nights a week, Tuesdays and Thursdays, and I'll bet you know most of the kids who'll be playing, or at least you know the families."

"Who? Name a few of the players," John said, skeptically.

"Well there's the Senesac twins, Roger's boys, and the Willet kid, and the Schultz kid, and the Pavelkos . . ." Matt tipped his head back and started reciting as many family names as he could remember, counting them on his fingers, "Rozinka, Babich, Neuman . . ." Matt looked at John and turned his palms up.

"How 'bout that Hested kid?" John asked. "Doc Hested's grandson?"

"Yeah, him too."

"And that Larson kid, the one who looks like a rat? I think his old man is in the slammer someplace?" John asked.

"Him too."

"And the Katzenmeyer kid, the one who looks like he's lost most of the time?"

"Uh-huh."

"Tuesdays and Thursdays?" John asked, just to be sure one more time. "That's all, right?"

"Yup."

John was still considering the bargain Matt was proposing when Matt showed him the prescription for Viagra once again. He extended his arm a second time and said, "*Or*, you can beat your dick like it owes you money."

John snatched the paper from Matt's hand and sealed the deal, then he groaned, "You rat bastard."

"That was quite a bit easier than I thought," Matt teased. "Why did you ask about the players?"

John folded his prescription and put it in his wallet before he looked up and played his trump card, as though he'd withheld it during the negotiations all along and chosen to play it now, after he'd won. "It's a *fine* crop of single mothers. Now let's go get some lunch."

———

The air was bitter cold just after noon, and as Matt and John approached the front door of the Ashley Hotel they could look to their left and see thin whiffs of snow being blown violently across the frozen surface of Wiigwaas Lake. "Yipes! That wind is cold," John said, as he raised his left hand to protect his face from the north wind. When the heavy door closed behind them, they both stomped snow off their boots and unzipped their coats.

Tink Ashley had been a wealthy man back at the turn of the last century, and he'd built the Ashley Hotel on the shore of Lake Wiigwaas in 1910. In its day, the Ashley Hotel had been grand, but time had taken a toll on the three-story brick building. It was about to be demolished a decade earlier when some real estate investors from Milwaukee had purchased it and spent a fortune restoring it. It was now a luxurious boutique hotel with a first-rate restaurant overlooking Wiigwaas Lake—a bona fide tourist attraction and popular nightspot for locals and summer people.

"Hi, Dr. Kingston," called a pretty young girl from behind a huge old front desk across the lobby. "Are you here for lunch?"

"Hi, Angela, and yes, we're here to pick up a burger," Matt replied.

"Well, you know the way to the restaurant." The girl gestured toward a long hallway decorated with dark-stained oak and floral carpet.

When Matt and John walked around a corner in the hallway they were greeted with the sounds of clinking dishes, the rich smells from the kitchen, and an expansive view of Wiigwaas Lake. They took a seat at the bar and ordered burgers to go. Above the bar, and on every wall, were posters advertising the annual ice-fishing contest held on the lake.

"Hard to believe that whole area out there is gonna be covered with fish houses in a few days, isn't it?" John said, as he looked out at the current desolation.

"Yup. Some serious bad behavior after dark, too," Matt agreed.

Every year since the 1960s, the Pine Rapids Chamber of Commerce had held an ice-fishing contest. Initially, it had been an attempt to draw tourists to return to the north and spend a few dollars in the winter months. The boom in popularity of snowmobiles at about the same time had fueled an event that grew every year. This year, and for the past dozen or so years, there would be a forty-foot stage on a semi-trailer flatbed so that "fishermen" could be entertained by live music every night. The surface of the lake would become a small city for a few days, with fish houses arranged like city blocks. Beer distributors would set up circus tents and invariably someone would set up a tent with a couple of stripper poles.

John stood and walked over to read one of the posters. "Hey, look," he said, "they're gonna have *five* "Ten Thousand Dollar Fish" this year."

Some years earlier, the Chamber of Commerce had made a big deal out of planting a walleye with a tag attached to one fin. If anyone caught that fish during the contest it carried a prize of $10,000. No one caught the fish for the first eight years, and each year another was introduced. Finally, an old man from Bemidji caught the tagged walleye, and from that moment on the quest for the tagged walleye became something like the quest for the Holy Grail. The people on the Chamber of Commerce liked to point out that the popularity of the ice-fishing contest paralleled the prize walleye, but just about everyone knew it was the beer and the music, and the bad behavior, that drove the contest to new levels each year.

When their burgers were ready, wrapped in a couple of layers of paper to keep them warm, Matt and John hurried back out to Matt's truck. Heading back to Velde Taxidermy, they noticed several trucks parked in front of the Shorewood Furist. Darrell was standing by the curb, talking to two other men Matt didn't know. Over by the semi-trailer that had arrived full of dead skunks a couple of months earlier, he noticed Snag pushing a wheelbarrow full of dead skunks toward the back entrance to the fur shop. Not far from the fur shop, several carpenters were putting the finishing touches on a new pole barn that looked to be about seventy feet wide by one hundred feet long.

Matt parked his truck on the street, and he and John walked toward Darrell and the other two men. As they drew near, the two men hurriedly finished their conversation with Darrell and then walked over to join the carpenters working on the pole barn.

"What's going on? Looks like some new construction here," Matt said. When he came within a few paces of Darrell he pulled his shirt up to cover his nose and added, "Still stinks around here. You must still have a few skunks to skin?"

"You are correct on both counts, Sherlock," John said.

Darrell began to explain all that was happening around the Shorewood Furist. "Man, things are getting crazy around here. After John and I took a close look at the beaver blanket Snag made for Jane, we did a little market research and decided to test the waters. We've already got orders for several dozen blankets at $4,500 each! We just bought a sewing machine and some other equipment, too, and as soon as Snag gets those skunks cleaned and outta here we're gonna get busy makin' blankets. We've also got orders for coyote and raccoon blankets."

"What are you gonna do with the 16,000 skunk pelts?" Matt asked.

"Skunk blankets! You believe that? We've got orders for skunk blankets, too, and for a lot of money, although skunk blankets go a bit cheaper than beaver or coyote," Darrell said.

"Naturally," Matt said. "But do you need a building that size in order to make blankets?"

"Hell, no," Darrell replied. "The rest of that space is for our freezer, and grinder, and some room to grow."

"Your what?" Matt asked.

"That's the other thing I stumbled across," Darrell said. "You know how we always had all those beaver carcasses to dispose of?"

"Yeah," Matt said.

"And you know that there are hundreds of sled dog mushers around here; actually, all across Minnesota and Wisconsin and Michigan, hell, all over the north, all the way to Alaska?" Darrell said.

"Yeah," Matt said.

"Well, I found out that sled dogs really like to eat beaver," Darrell blurted.

Matt cast a sideways glance at John, daring him to ignore the sexual innuendo and not say something sophomoric. For once, John obliged, but his eyes revealed the temptation he was struggling with, and Darrell finished his explanation.

"So, I bought this old grinder from a commercial meat packer. The thing is huge! I can stuff fifty beavers into the opening, and now when we get a pile of carcasses, we grind 'em all up, guts, bones, and everything.

The result is dog food that's rich in fat and protein, and the dogs love it! We're freezing the stuff and sending it everywhere. Mushers all over the north country are buying it."

Matt looked at John for confirmation.

"Yup, he's not kidding, we're busy, and we're making some money," John said with a nod.

One of the men working on the pole barn gestured to Darrell, as if he had an important question regarding the construction, and Darrell immediately moved toward the nearly finished building. "I gotta go. See you later, Matt."

"See ya, Darrell. Say hi to Snag," Matt called after him.

Matt turned to John once Darrell was out of earshot. "Really? Darrell's finally on to something good?"

"Really," John reassured him. "And I guess it's about time for Darrell. He's had so many crazy schemes. Remember a couple years ago when he bought the equipment to make acrylic deer antlers, then he started saving rabbit skins so we could start mass-producing jackalopes and corner the jackalope market?"

"I thought you actually *did* corner the jackalope market, only to find out it was an extraordinarily small market," Matt said.

"Yup," John laughed. "But I think he's got a couple good things going now." Then he added, "Let's get over to my shop and sit down. The burgers are getting cold, and it stinks around here."

The faint smell of wood smoke was heavier than the smell of preservative chemicals as Matt and John let themselves in through the back door of Velde Taxidermy and made their way across John's spotless work area. Matt was always impressed by the way John kept his business so immaculate. The long workbench along the far wall was swept clean of dirt and crud every night, and washed with disinfectant. All of John's tools were cleaned and left in the same place at the end of every workday. Much like the wood shop at good old Sverdrup High, there were two large butcher-block work tables in the center of the room, and they were both cleaned daily.

John set the brown paper bag containing their burgers on a small table in a corner of the work area and then stoked the dying fire in the woodstove. "We'll have 'er good and warm in here in a couple minutes," he said. He carried an armload of split oak and birch to the woodstove and carefully fed the wood into the belly of the stove. A moment after he closed the heavy door of the stove they began to hear the whoosh and rumble of air being drawn into the fire, and the crackle of dry wood popping.

Matt set their places at the rickety table, putting paper towels down as place mats and then setting a Styrofoam box containing a burger and some fries at each place. "You got any ketchup?" Matt asked.

"Sure, in the fridge."

Matt swung open the avocado refrigerator door. The inside of the fridge was sparkling clean and stocked with every sort of condiment, along with eggs, hot sauce, cheese, and a case of Leinenkugel's beer. "Wow, you always keep so much food in here?" Matt asked, as he bent over to survey inside the fridge.

"Yeah, more all the time, actually," John answered. "I like to make myself breakfast here. Sometimes lunch, too. Saves a lot of time. I can just put stuff down on the workbench, and walk over there and make my own lunch."

"Charming ambiance, too, with all of the undead surrounding you," Matt said, with his head inside the fridge.

"Grab a couple Leinies while you're in there," John called out.

"It's noon! Kinda early, isn't it?"

"We're sixty years old . . . there are no rules anymore. Besides, you're not going back to work anyway."

"OK then," Matt said a moment later, when he produced the ketchup and two cans of Leinenkugel's. "Beer and burgers at noon. What does *that* make you think of?"

John chuckled as he lifted the top of the bun off his burger and inspected it. "Now *that* one was a close call," he said, and they both let an old memory roll over them.

In the spring of their senior year at Sverdrup High, Matt had finally stockpiled enough bravado to match John, at least for a short time. John had accepted a baseball scholarship at the University of Minnesota, and Matt had scored so well on his entrance exams that the admissions committee at "The U" had overlooked his lackluster academic performance in high school and accepted him, too. So, on a warm Friday in May, two weeks before their high school graduation, John and Matt had skipped school. They'd picked up a bag full of hamburgers and fries at the A&W and John had purchased a six-pack of beer from one of the hoods he ran with sometimes. After third-hour classes that morning they'd simply walked out to the parking lot on the north side of Sverdrup High and driven away in John's '65 Chevy, the one he bought from Jim Jorgenson. They drove to Clear Lake, a little pond about five miles west of town, where they planned to sit on the bank and treat themselves to a grown-up lunch, do some fishing, and talk about the great things they were about to do when they got out of this little place. The sun was warm on their broad shoulders that morning, and life couldn't get much better.

Matt was thinking about the end of the day, after baseball practice was over, when the sun would be setting and the dew would be gathering on the thick grass at the ballpark. He'd go home, shower, and then pick up Mo Glasnapp for a date. Maybe tonight would be the night, he kept thinking. His relationship with Mo was getting serious even though she was two years younger than he. They'd had their hands on each other more and more as his senior year had gone along, and he was aching to try sex. Everybody else seemed to be doing it, but not him. A fine daydream was taking place when John frightened him back to reality on that May day all those years ago.

"Oh shit! We are gonna *die*!" John had gasped.

"Huh?" Matt said, startled back into the moment.

"Look!" John pointed to the road, where a brown Ford pickup with a brown-and-white topper on the truck box was rolling along toward the pretty little picnic area where they were sitting. "It's your dad! We gotta get outta here!"

Ten seconds later, John's Chevy was bouncing over some very rough, freshly plowed black dirt on the edge of Jim Lilliberg's farm field, using a grove of elm trees to shield his car from view. The ride was so rough that French fries and beer and hamburgers seemed to be suspended in the air, as if weightless in a spacecraft. They sped across Mr. Lilliberg's pasture, then they crossed a ditch and rolled up onto a winding county road. "What's wrong with your dad?" John said, "He's supposed to be at *home*, working!" At that moment the boys were pretty certain they'd pulled off the great escape, and they began to laugh. The laughter hadn't really stopped in forty-three years.

Now they each pulled a chair up to the rickety little table by the barrel stove and prepared for yet another lunch of beer and burgers.

"Oh God," Matt said, as he dipped a French fry into a slurry of ketchup and then brought it up to his mouth. "My dad would have stood on his head and shit rubber nickels if he'd rolled in there and found me with beer, on a school day." He dipped a second French fry and asked, "I wonder if he ever found out?"

"Doubt it," John said, and with that he changed the subject. He leaned forward and asked, "Tell me again how you wound up living here, in Pine Rapids? I forget. It's a long way from Sverdrup."

"Ah, well," Matt said. "I was all done back home; I knew I could never go back. I had no real plans, but always liked the north. I was a freshman in dental school and a buddy of mine, a kid named Will Campbell, took me up to his family place over by Walker, and I loved it. I knew at that moment that I'd find a place, a small town up here, somewhere, and live my life. When I was about to graduate, I bought a practice here in Pine Rapids from an old dentist who'd just found out he had cancer. I moved here a week after I graduated and it's been great. How 'bout you? Why did you move back here, from California?"

"You," John said with a shrug.

"Really?"

"Do you remember when we were little boys and we were always playing at each other's houses?" John started.

"Sure. Summa the best days of my life."

"Me too," John said. "But there was something I never told you. Hell, I guess I didn't think about it, or understand it myself, until this very minute."

"What are you talking about?" Matt asked.

"I wanted something that you had. I really didn't know what it was, either. But I just knew you had something I wanted."

"I don't understand," Matt said.

"When I came to your house your mother used to bake cookies for us. She was good to me, even though she knew she had to keep an eye on me so I didn't screw something up. She'd let me stay at your house for sleepovers, too. Remember staying up and watching *Gunsmoke* before your folks sent us up to your room, where we'd lie there in the dark and talk about sports and girls?"

"Yeah. Good times." Matt smiled.

"*My* mother used to send me off to school with a can of Coke and couple Twinkies for lunch," John continued. "That's why I always sat with you and ate outta your bag lunch. I knew your mother sent extra stuff to school with you, for me. And your dad acted like he actually liked you, *and* me. I felt good at your house. I felt safe."

Matt waited now, while John organized something in his mind.

"'N'en, when we got a bit older, and I was bigger and better than you in sports, I started hangin' around with all the fuckin' delinquents and troublemakers that kids like me seem to find. I sorta fell away from all the other good kids, but I made a point to keep that connection with you. Or maybe it was you who made a point to keep it with me? Anyway, I knew, or maybe I just sorta understood, that if I let go of you I was likely to fly off into a world of bad shit. You were smart and followed the rules, pretty much. I needed to stay close to you. I mean, you were my *buddy*, but I *needed* you. You were the only thing that kept me tethered to a better life, and I knew it."

"So why did you just walk away when we were in college?"

"Well, there's a couple things I never told you either, Matt," John answered slowly. "You wanna know about the last time I saw my dad?"

"Sure."

"My dad . . ." John shook his head. "I don't know why he got married or had kids. I think he was just too lazy or belligerent to step out of the way, and life just ran over him." John stared at his hands for nearly a minute, apparently trying to decide if he wanted to finish the story he'd started.

"So, one summer night when we were in college, I came home from some amateur ball game and I caught my dad trying to fuck my sister." Now John glanced over, looked into Matt's eyes, and nodded that it was true. "So I beat him, beat him bloody. My mother was screaming and crying. My sister was screaming and crying. I left my father lying in his own blood right there on the kitchen floor. He was crying too. I twisted his arm so hard I dislocated his shoulder. I stood over him and told him, no, I *promised* him, that I'd kill him if it ever happened again. Next day I got on 'nat new bike and headed west. I was done, here."

"I'm sorry, John. I never knew any of that."

"Well, I wasn't very proud of it, so I kept it all a secret, till now."

"And you're telling me now because . . .?"

"I dunno, I've wanted to tell you for a while now. Maybe I needed to tell you . . . tell *somebody*." John shrugged. "We had a great time; our school days, our childhood . . . it shoulda never ended that way."

"So why did you come back here?"

"Well, I knew you were here. I guess I figured if you were here, and I came here, then things might be like they always were. It was a great childhood, you know."

"Jane says our childhood never ended," Matt said.

John sat quietly for a few seconds. "She's amazing. You know, sometimes I see her touch you—I mean, just put her hand on your shoulder, or around your waist—and then I see something I *never* see anywhere else. About a year ago you walked up to her at a high school hockey game and kissed her." John glanced at Matt. "She kissed you back and I saw something pass between you. Something I've never felt."

This conversation had taken on weight that Matt had never known while talking to John Velde.

"Well, I—"

"Don't try to explain anything, you'll just say something I wouldn't understand anyway," John said.

"Yeah, prob'ly," Matt said. "I love my Jane."

"Yeah, watching you guys together can be like old-people porn." John reached in front of Matt and picked up the salt shaker. "Damn, these are good fries." Matt stared at the slurry of ketchup on his plate as if it were the glowing embers of a campfire. John took a swig of beer and then belched. "Keep going."

Matt smiled and blinked his eyes as if to clear some cobwebs. "I remember the first time I kissed her goodnight, too," Matt said. "It was on her porch—"

"Did she drop some tongue down your throat?" John interrupted. "She did, didn't she?" He took a bite of his burger.

Matt grimaced, and then went on. "I slid my hand under her shirt, onto the small of her back." His gaze was still fixed on his fries. "She gasped, like we were having sex."

John looked up, finally aware that Matt was sharing something special with him.

"I guess we saw each other about every night for the next couple weeks," Matt went on, "and things kept escalating."

"I'm getting a boner here," John said.

"We just couldn't keep our hands off each other. At first it was wild. I mean four and five times a day."

"Wait a minute," John said. He stood up and adjusted the front of his pants. "OK, go on; the pressure down there was making it difficult to swallow. Five times a day?"

"That was our personal record. We've backed off that pace considerably." Matt chuckled. "That was the greatest time in my life. Our courtship, I mean. The laughter, and the good times with friends, and the sex, and planning our future together."

"But, the same woman, for all these years?" John asked with his palms turned up. "I mean, even Jane . . ."

Matt tapped his hand on his heart and said, "We have a *connection*. You know that little twitch you get way down low in your belly when—"

"Yeah."

"It's never changed. Ever. Well, it's actually better, richer now. The connection feels eternal."

"You lost me," John said.

"I guess that's just over your head."

"No shit. Way over."

Matt picked up his burger and changed the subject. "OK, it's my turn. All those years ago, when you left school . . . you never said goodbye to me. You just didn't show up at baseball practice one day. You left your stereo and most of your stuff in your dorm room and disappeared, and I didn't see you for twenty years. What was going on in your head? And didn't you at least miss the baseball?"

"I was sick of baseball. Well, I was sick of coaches yelling, and getting up early to go to practice." John shrugged. "It wasn't so much fun in college. Even worse, I hated getting up early to go to class; *that* was raising hell with my social life, and a young man has to keep his priorities in line. Besides, I already knew everything, so what did I need with any more school?" He thought for a moment, then added, "But that shit with my dad . . . I had to get outta there. So I left. Or, as you would say, I took a different fork in the road. How was I to know that fork was gonna come way back around and lead me here again?"

"Glad it did, buddy."

"The baseball?" John said. "You asked about the baseball?"

"Yeah."

"I knew I was pretty good. And I knew I was gonna get drafted by somebody, but I knew I'd never be a big leaguer. It was just out of my reach. I knew I wasn't in love with baseball enough to do the things I had to do in order to make it. And I knew I was gonna come up short, anyway. There were just too many guys who were better than me."

"But, you were so close. Maybe—"

"I just didn't care anymore," John said.

Matt shook his head as if to dismiss John's words. "I don't get it, John."

"Ah, well, it's a done deal now. Wasn't meant to be."

Matt wiped his lips with a paper napkin and then said, "Yup, and it worked out pretty good for you." He looked right and left at all the tools and benches and half-done critters lying about the room.

John nodded his agreement and Matt crumpled up all the papers from their lunches and threw them in the woodstove. Then stood up to leave. "OK, John, we'll see you for dinner tomorrow night at my place? Jane's making venison stroganoff."

"Sure thing; strokin' off is one of my favorite things." It was an old joke, one that guys like John could never pass up. He grinned, and then he offered Matt his hand.

"No handshakes today, buddy. Gimme a hug."

"OK, but I don't want our packages to touch," John said.

CHAPTER EIGHTEEN

—•—

Matt eased open Jane's office door at the clinic and saw her sitting at her desk. "You ready to go?" It was mid-afternoon on the Friday of the Wiigwaas Lake fishing contest.

"Yup." Jane pushed her chair away from her desk. "I'm kinda hungry." She reached into her pocket and pulled out a yellow plastic bag. "But all I've got is a bag of peanut M&Ms. You s'pose we can pick up a late lunch out on the ice? There must some food tents out there by now."

"Sure, there'll be all sorts of health food available out there," Matt replied. Jane had her coat and hat on a moment later, and the two of them headed for the party out on the lake.

The community of fish houses was spread across the ice in front of the Ashley Hotel in fairly neat rows, with trucks and snowmobiles parked all around them. The semi-trailer/outdoor stage equipped with amplifiers and lights for a midnight light show was parked about two hundred yards out on the ice, and several large white circus tents, each owned by a different brewing company, were set up nearby.

"Not much of a crowd yet," Matt said, as they walked hand in hand down Main Street toward the boat landing, which, now that the lake was frozen, gave pedestrians and vehicles access to the festivities on the ice. Contestants lumbered about in heavy pack boots, parkas, mittens, and gaiters. Some wore camo, some blaze orange, some wore gear that displayed the logos of their favorite brand of ice auger or fishing tackle.

"Not much going on over there, either," Jane said when they came upon what looked like a swimming pool. An opening about ten feet wide and twenty feet long had been cut through the ice with a chain saw. It was done every year as part of an event called the Polar Plunge. Anyone brave or drunk enough could strip down to their undies, or the costume they'd made just for the event, and jump into the thirty-three-degree water. The reward for this literally breathtaking leap was a hearty cheer from the bystanders. "I don't know how anyone can do that," Jane opined. Then she added, "Where is everybody?"

"I guess it's still early, and judging by some of these zombies milling around I'd say there are quite a few fishermen with hangovers from last night's partying," Matt said. About fifty feet in front of them were two young men who looked to be in their early twenties, walking ever so slowly. One of them was dressed in camouflage bib overalls and a camouflage hunting coat. The other man wore black-and-yellow coveralls, the kind snowmobile racers wore, with decals everywhere on the chest and back. As Matt and Jane drew nearer, the bigger of the two men stopped, bent over with his hands on his knees, and threw up.

Jane groaned and covered her eyes, but Matt couldn't help laughing. When the young man with the black-and-yellow coveralls saw Matt laugh he returned a broad smile, patted his friend on the back and said to Matt, "He's a first-time drinker."

"Good times!" Matt replied with plenty of sarcasm. Then he turned to Jane and said, "Still hungry?"

"Not really. Let's go look around for a while, and maybe I'll forget what I just saw."

"Hey! Nice work, huh?" John called out to Jane and Matt. He was walking out from behind a tent and pointed to the guy who was still bent over and dry heaving. "Looks like he got an early start." Then he gave the puker's friend a thumbs-up.

There were rows and rows of fish houses, some as small as eight by eight feet while others were twenty feet long and ten feet wide—castles in the ice-fishing world. All of the houses were arranged like city blocks, in a residential area. Most of the fishing shelter houses had chimneys that were sending wood smoke into the air, and a vehicle parked close by. And the fishermen had only a short walk to the nearby temporary "business district" on the lake.

Several of the beer tents had stages for live music performances, and musicians were setting up their instruments while crowds began to gather. Local restaurants had set up tents too, and all were doing a steady business selling sandwiches and anything that fishermen could carry away. Sally Durham, in a nice stroke of marketing, had purchased a vendor's license and set up a coffee shop/pharmacy to treat hangovers and headaches, and maybe warm up a few frozen fishermen.

"Hey, there's Sally's coffee tent right there. Let's go say hi," said Jane.

As they crossed the "street" in front of Sally's tent and wound their way through the wandering zombies and creepers, some of whom now seemed to have nursed themselves back to the edge of humanity, Matt said to John, "Jane and I were guessing that you would have asked Sally out for a date by now."

"I get a funny vibe from her," John said.

"Whaddya mean?" Matt asked.

"Well, like she's kinda interested . . . but I think she has a boyfriend."

"Really?" Matt looked puzzled. "Jane told me that Sally seemed to be eyeballing you at the coffee shop a while back, and she asked a few questions, too. I'm surprised."

"Me too," John said.

The smell of fresh coffee greeted them when Jane pushed the tent flap aside and walked into Sally's tent. It was about thirty by thirty feet with a coffee bar in one corner and picnic tables spread about. Six young men sat, leaning forward with their faces over steaming coffee cups. None of the men moved, or seemed capable of movement.

Sally waved when she saw John and Matt and Jane enter. As they made their way toward the counter, Jane pointed to the young men and said, "We figured you'd be busy treating these wounded men. I can hear *that* guy's head pounding clear over here."

"Yup, I've been handing out aspirin as a gesture of mercy." Sally automatically began pouring coffee for them, and then turned a warm smile and big hi to John.

"Looks like we missed the rush?" John said.

"Yeah, earlier in the morning we actually had quite a few customers in here looking for hot coffee—the ones who really fish, or maybe the ones who only got kinda drunk last night. Then, from about ten a.m. until two p.m. the walking dead started limping in here." Sally closed her eyes and shook her head. "It looked like a crowded emergency room in here, but the crowd is thinning out pretty good now."

"Well, we're gonna go check out the beer tent across the street. Would you like to join us?" John asked.

"Yeah, I would!" Sally replied. "Just give me a few minutes to close up for the day, and I'll come over there and find you." She immediately began to straighten things behind the makeshift counter in front of her. "I'll be there as soon as I can."

"Well, that was borderline encouraging," Jane said to John, when they were walking through the growing crowd on the way to the beer tent. "Why didn't you stay and talk for a while; help her close up?"

"I told you, I think she has a boyfriend. What's the point?"

"Oh, it's probably some guy who's just a friend," Jane said.

"Men don't have women friends," John said.

Jane slugged John in the arm. "Don't be stupid." She sipped at her coffee, took a few more steps and said, "Maybe she wants you to keep trying. Maybe you just read something else into it? Maybe you just don't understand women?"

"Yeah, right," John scoffed.

"Forget it, honey," Matt chimed in. "It's about to start raining bull-shit."

"Let me explain something," John said to Jane, without turning to face her.

"Hold it!" Jane stopped in her tracks and raised her hands. "They're selling walleye sandwiches right there." She pointed to a food truck with about ten people standing by a small window and waiting for their orders. She pointed at Matt, then at the food truck, and said, "I'm not gonna have M&Ms for dinner. Get me a sandwich and some of those cheese balls, too, and whatever you want for yourself, and whatever this guy wants, too," she said, pointing a thumb at John.

John looked at Matt. "Get me walleye sammich, too, and I'll share her cheese balls."

"No way!" Jane said. "Get him his own cheese balls, honey."

Matt took his place in line at the food truck while Jane and John stood together a few feet behind him and waited. John's voice was a bit muffled by the surrounding crowd, but Matt could hear bits and pieces of John's manifesto about the nature of man-woman friendship while he waited for the kid inside the food truck to put three walleye sandwiches and three orders of deep-fried cheese balls in a paper bag.

John was talking and making hand gestures, and Jane was laughing with her mouth open when Matt rejoined them and opened the bag containing their evening meal.

"It's no use, is it?" Matt said to Jane.

"Yeah, she just doesn't get it," John said, as though Jane was the one who didn't understand things.

"Just gimme my sandwich," Jane said as she reached into the bag. "Have you heard this crazy shit before?" she added as she gestured toward John.

"Many times," Matt said. Darkness had settled over the frozen surface of Wiigwaas Lake before the threesome had finished eating and chuckling at John's worldview. While they stood on the frozen lake and talked, the volume of the music coming from the beer tents increased steadily.

"I need a beer to wash that sammich down," John said. "Let's go check out the Big Top and I'll buy the first round. Maybe a beer will help you to understand the social complexities I was expounding on during dinner."

"Yeah, beer makes everyone smarter," Jane said, as they set off for a huge tent with Big Top written on the front and colored spotlights streaming around on its white roof. A band was playing oldies from the '60s and '70s and two lovely and very young-looking ladies, one on either side of the stage, were dancing. The girls were wearing fur earmuffs, fur mittens, fur bikinis, and snowmobile boots. They were showing plenty of skin, and the place was about half filled with male patrons, all of them drinking their way into party mode. A handful of young women were scattered about, but ninety-eight percent of the crowd was men, and every one of them had a plastic cup filled with beer in one hand. Many of the men were wearing outrageous fur hats, as if there was an unspoken contest going on to see who could turn the most heads. Matt thought the hats looked more like taxidermy, made especially for events like this, than headwear purchased in a store.

"Look at that," Matt said to Jane, as a fairly drunk young man wobbled by them. The kid was grinning and winding through the crowd with a beer in each hand. His "hat" had been made from the skin of a large northern pike, which seemed to coil around the man's head after rising up from his back. The pike's skin was hardened like an old leather football helmet, and the pike's huge head sat directly on top of the man's head. Its mouth was open wide. Nasty, threatening teeth were exposed, and the fish looked as if it was about to strike anyone who looked at it.

"It's a custom fit. I made it," John volunteered. "He's got a fleece stocking hat underneath it to keep his head warm, too."

"Nice," Matt said.

"Yeah, I had fun with that one," John said. "See that guy over there, the one with the badger hat that's snarling, and the guy next to him in the coyote hat? I made those, too." The man wearing the badger hat recognized John and then raised his beer in greeting from across the room. As John was waving back at the man in the badger hat he said to Jane, "That was the only time I ever asked anybody how many teeth they wanted in their hat." Then he added, "This place is gonna get crazy in a couple hours. You see those stripper poles over there? They're not just for show."

"Really?" Jane asked.

"Yeah, last year they had an amateur night, sorta like karaoke for drunk fishermen and fisherwomen. Wasn't too bad! But the main event, the pros from Minneapolis, doesn't start for hours. Stay right here and I'll go get us all a beer. We may as well join the party." John turned to walk away and then stopped in his tracks, reversed himself, and leaned close to Jane. "You're the prettiest girl here, Jane, and if you're inclined to take a shot during amateur hour I'll get you a large beer," he teased, and then flicked his eyebrows.

"Just *go*," Jane groaned, and she gave him a shove.

Several more dancers took the stage, all of them wearing very small fur bikinis and heavy winter boots. When Matt saw the lingering grin on Jane's face he remembered a very different response that she'd given to Will Campbell, Matt's classmate from school, on their first visit to the Pine Rapids fishing contest many years earlier. Will had brought them to Pine Rapids to look around for a home after dental school and they'd made a point to check out the party on the ice since they were in town. Will had made a flippant remark, much like the one John Velde had just made, but Jane had interpreted it as a proposition and snapped at Will. It took only a few seconds to clarify the misunderstanding that night, and afterward they'd joked about it for years. Thinking of the incident now, Matt remembered the way she'd barked at the guy to "Fuck off" way back on their first date, too.

A new DJ took the stage and the familiar opening notes of "Boots" by Nancy Sinatra filled the big tent. The atmosphere in the tent intensified immediately when the young dancers began to strut with the music. John was bobbing his head with the music and carrying three beers when he returned.

It was impossible for Matt not to smile, and when leaned close to Jane's ear he sang, "*DING* dadda ding dadda *DING* dadda ding dadda . . ." along with the guitar. He put his arm around Jane's shoulders and added, "You *should* get up there and show those girls how to do that."

"Yeah, right," she scoffed.

John was standing only a few feet away from Matt and Jane after he'd given them each a beer. The music was too loud for him to hear what they were saying to each other, but he knew them well enough to know that they'd drifted away to a world of their own. Matt stood with his arm around her and they were alone together, in the middle of a crowd.

There was a tap on John's shoulder, and when he turned around he saw Sally standing there. "Hey!" Sally said with a big smile. "Where'd you get the beer?"

"Over there." John nodded toward a long line of people. "I just made a run. I'll go get you one in a minute, when that line's little shorter." Then he offered her a sip from the beer he was holding and said, "Party's just getting started; you only have a little bit of catching up to do."

"Don't mind if I do," Sally said, and she took the beer from his hand. She drank half the beer in a couple of gulps and then handed it back to John.

John made a point to examine the half-empty cup and said, "Nice work."

"Just trying to catch up," Sally said with a shrug. She moved closer to John and locked her left arm around his right arm. It was a warm, friendly move, but there was an unmistakable message attached to it: She was interested.

John liked her touch, and he liked the little tingle that came with it. "So, did you have to tell anyone to shut the fuck up today?" he asked.

"No, it was pretty boring. You're still the worst person I know," Sally said, as she bobbed her head along with Nancy Sinatra and squeezed his arm.

John grinned. He liked Sally. He drank the rest of his beer and then turned to her. "Still thirsty?"

Sally nodded yes.

"OK, I'll go get us both another beer, but it's gonna cost you."

"Oh?"

John bent forward and pointed at his lips, requesting a kiss.

Sally kissed him once, then a second time. "Make it a *large* beer."

"No problem," John said. "Wait right here." He paused for a moment and then said, "I have to check something before I leave. It might not be safe here." Then he bent way down and looked at Sally's feet. "I guess it's OK, for now."

"What?" Sally asked, puzzled.

"You're gettin' hotter by the second. I just wanted to see if the ice was melting around you."

"Oh! Now *that* was a good line. You *are* good!" Sally said. She looked over imaginary bifocals and pointed at him for emphasis.

"I thought so too. I'll be right back."

The guitar refrain from Johnny Rivers's "Secret Agent Man" moved the excitement level up another notch as John disappeared into the crowd, and Sally noticed that Matt and Jane had been standing only few feet in front of her. She was about to step forward and say hello when she noticed that there was something going on between them, and she didn't want to interrupt.

Matt held his hand on the small of Jane's back, and then slid his hand down, onto the smooth curves of her behind. He began to pat her butt in time with the beat, and then sing along with Johnny Rivers. Sally could see that he was having fun, making fun of himself and his parody of Johnny Rivers as he serenaded Jane.

When the instrumental break in the middle of the song came, it looked to Sally as if Matt was about to unleash his best dance moves from back in the day. "Don't do it," Jane hollered, raising her voice above Johnny Rivers and flashing a grin. "You'll hurt your hip!"

Matt didn't break out and bust a move, but he continued to sing along until the song was over. In the short break before the next song, Sally couldn't help but notice the way they looked at each other, a couple of sixty-year-olds still in love.

"Here's your beer!" said John.

"Look at those two," Sally said, as John handed her a large cup full of beer.

"Huh?"

"Look at them. They look like kids."

Immediately on the heels of "Secret Agent" came "Shout" by the Isley Brothers, and the Big Top became electric. Matt took Jane's left hand in his right and they both held a half-full plastic cup of beer in their other hand. "Wellll, wait a minute . . ." the lead singer began, and everyone under the Big Top got ready to sing along. "You know you make me wanna SHOUT . . . Throw my hands up and SHOUT . . ."

A thousand hands, most of them holding beer cups, shot up. Matt and Jane began to weave and bob from side to side in time with the music, along with everyone else in the place. They raised a beer over their heads and lifted their own "shout" into the cool air whenever the Isley Brothers called for it.

Sally and John sang along, too. Sally was having a fine time on her own, forging a new bond with John, but with every SHOUT she looked at Jane and wondered about her. Jane was so pretty, and smart, you couldn't help but like her. What had her life been like? How did she wind up here, and did she have any idea how fortunate she was to own the love of a man like Matt? Sally had heard that Jane came from some money. She'd had an expensive education at a fine university, and she'd had a great career. Every time she hoisted that cup of beer into the air and hollered SHOUT she looked at Matt, and passed him a look of love that Sally had only seen on the faces of the very young.

As the Isley Brothers were finishing, the DJ started "Jump" by the Pointer Sisters, and the beat went on. When the scantily clad dancers raised their arms and jumped along with the Pointer Sisters, every guy in the place cheered.

During the previous half hour, while the DJ had been ramping up the energy in the Big Top, the beat from inside the huge tent had rolled across Wiigwaas Lake and hundreds of fishermen had come to join the party.

The noise level inside the tent made it hard to hear, and when the DJ played "Louie Louie" by the Kingsmen, Sally finally reached forward and tapped Jane on the shoulder.

"Oh, hi!" Jane hollered. "HAVING A GOOD TIME?"

Sally could only nod, and then watch, as Jane reached into her pocket and withdrew the bag of peanut M&Ms and put one in her mouth.

"Gimme one?" Matt asked.

Jane shook her head no, teasing him and daring him to do something about it.

"C'mon," Matt demanded playfully.

"Huh-uh." Jane teased as she put another M&M in her mouth.

Matt suddenly grabbed Jane and pulled her close, as if for a kiss. She shrieked with delight but struggled to pull back, away from Matt, and he pulled her even closer. When his lips were touching hers, he tried to use his tongue to pry her lips apart and search for the M&M. Jane howled with laughter and when she couldn't help but open her mouth Matt's tongue swept over hers.

Jane was still laughing and slugging Matt's arm when she realized that Sally and John had been watching them. Matt simply opened his mouth and showed them the red M&M that he'd just stolen from Jane, then he chewed it up and swallowed.

Sally gawked and wondered about them a bit more. When she looked at John, he answered her unspoken question, "Yeah, they do that sort of thing all the time."

With that, Jane put another M&M on her tongue and then held it out to tease Matt again. When he leaned close she quickly swallowed it and laughed. Then she placed a green M&M on her tongue and displayed it for Matt again. This time when he came close she held still and let him lick it from her tongue. Then she turned to the others and said, "Sometimes I just like to suck the chocolate off his nuts." Her hand shot up to cover her mouth and she doubled over in laughter.

John turned to Sally and deadpanned, "Do you have any M&Ms?"

CHAPTER NINETEEN

———•———

Spring was in the air during the first week of May. Most of the winter's snow had melted away, but a few of the bigger lakes around Pine Rapids were still covered with ice and would remain frozen for another week, maybe two. Midday breezes were warm, and the craziness of the Chamber of Commerce fishing contest was long forgotten. People were getting their boats ready for summer, and there was cheerful talk of how a spring rain would surely wash winter away now, and turn the forest and countryside green once more.

Tomorrow Jane would accompany Matt to Rochester for a road trip. They'd check into a nice hotel, and the next day he'd have an X-ray taken of his new hip and his final postoperative visit with the orthopedic surgeon who'd placed it. And the surgeon would tell him what he already knew, that everything was fine.

While he was meeting his surgeon, Jane would have her yearly physical and a mammogram. That evening they had tickets for an orchestra concert at the Rochester Civic Center. After a nice weekend together they'd be back at work on Monday morning, getting ready for another summer on Scotch Lake.

But today Matt had a busy day scheduled at the office. The morning had passed quickly. Matt had restored several dental implants, seated two long-span ceramic bridges, and seen six patients for routine operative dentistry. It was 11:45, and he was finished with his morning schedule fifteen minutes early when he carried a cup of coffee into his private office and sat at his desk.

He was reading through the Post-it notes that had been left on his desk phone when Tammy Leiding entered the room. When Matt looked up to see what she wanted, Tammy rolled her eyes and said, "John Velde is on the phone. Line one."

Matt was well aware of Tammy's disdain for John. "He's not so bad," Matt said. "He just likes to crush your crackers."

"Whatever," Tammy muttered, and she left the room.

"Hello," Matt said into the phone.

"I'm over at the coffee shop, sitting at our dunce table. Get your ass over here for lunch."

Matt glanced at his watch. "I've got a big afternoon scheduled, and—"

"Get your sorry ass over here. Sally started making sammiches last week, here at the Human Bean, and they're really good. I just ordered one for each of us," John interrupted.

"I can't come back late from lunch today, I have patients right after lunch."

"Then get your ass here now. You're literally two minutes away, if you walk real slow. It isn't even noon yet. We're way ahead of the noon rush. And we need to talk about this summer baseball thing."

"Ah, OK. I'll be right over."

"You want wheat bread or toasted sourdough for your sammich?"

"Sourdough."

"I ordered wheat. Tough shit," John said.

Matt hung up the phone and went to the reception desk where Tammy was seated, by the waiting room. "Gonna meet John for lunch," he told her.

"But, you have a big afternoon," Tammy blurted, and then she leaned forward as if she was trying to grab him and keep him from leaving.

"I know," Matt said, a bit annoyed. "I'll be back on time." Then, when he registered the distress on Tammy's face, he stopped. There was something troubling his assistant. "What? What's wrong?" he asked.

"Well, um, do you have your cell phone, just in case?"

She was nagging, Matt thought, but he said nothing. He showed her his cell phone and then put it back in his jacket pocket as he walked out the front door of the office.

John was waiting at their table with an extra cup of coffee when Matt arrived. "Big day at the office?"

"Yeah, well, it's a good, not a big, day." Matt made a show of sniffing the air around their table and said, "You'd don't stink like skunk today."

"Skunks are gone. The truck is gone. The pelts are all at a tannery in Wisconsin, and we cleaned the place with some stuff that the guy at the tannery told us about. We're back to the usual bad smell." John smiled. "And Snag and Darrell are busy makin' blankets, and money."

At that moment Sally Durham arrived carrying a plate in each hand. "Hi, Matt," she said as she placed a sandwich in front of him.

"Hi, Sally. You've expanded the menu," Matt said.

"Yeah, we're getting busier all the time, so I decided to serve lunches, too. Let me know what you think."

"Sure thing." When Sally was out of earshot Matt took a bite. Before he could swallow, he raised his eyebrows at John and said a muffled, "Wow, this is good."

"Mine too," John agreed. "But, tell me more about this player draft for Timmy's summer baseball. It's in a few days, right? Do I have to be there?"

Matt waited until he swallowed his next bite, then said, "The draft is in Roger Senesac's classroom over at the high school, on Monday night at seven. And you should be there." Matt's cell phone began to vibrate and he put his sandwich on his plate so he could answer.

John was already complaining about his involvement with summer baseball. "Aw, shit, why do I have to be there?"

"Hello," Matt said into his phone. His caller ID told him that Jane was on the line.

"Where are you?" Jane asked. Matt knew instantly that she had something important to tell him.

"At the coffee shop, having lunch with John. Why? What's up?"

"You left the office early?" Jane sounded agitated, but also relieved to have made contact with him.

"Well, yeah. What's wrong?"

"I was afraid I'd missed you. I thought—"

"What's wrong?"

"Nothing . . . nothing at all. But there would be something wrong if I'd missed you."

"Huh?" Matt squinted.

"I'm at the Ashley Hotel, room 206." Jane said, and let those words linger in the air for a few seconds. "I'm wearing those black panties you gave me last year. Well, I *was . . .* until a minute ago . . ." She paused again. "I'm getting pretty lonely . . ."

"I'll be right there," Matt said. Now he understood! Jane had a special surprise for him.

"Hurry," Jane said. She was trying to sound seductive, but Matt could hear the muted laughter in her voice.

"What's up?" John asked, as Matt put the phone back in his pocket and pushed his chair away from the table.

Matt knew he couldn't tell John about this, but he also knew that if he smiled he'd never be able to sell the lie he was about to tell. "Emergency, back at the office. I gotta go." He was doing a good job keeping a straight face, but he knew that the longer he lingered at the table, the more likely he was to give away this secret.

"Well, shit!" John said. "You coming back?"

"Nope. Put my sandwich a box?"

"Sure, but—"

"Gotta go, maybe we can get together for Gourmet Club tonight?" Matt said, trying to act flustered as he left.

"OK, but—" John was still trying to say something as Matt walked away.

———

Matt hurried down the long, dark hallway in the Ashley Hotel. When he found room 206, the door was open just enough for him to let himself in without help from someone inside the room. He pushed it open and slowly stepped inside.

The room smelled like scented candles, and the curtains were drawn. He closed the door behind him and then peeked into the suite until he saw Jane. She was sitting on the bed with her legs crossed, wearing a black lace chemise.

Matt was squinting, still trying to get his eyes to acclimate to the low light. "The door was open. What if—"

"I saw you walking across the street," Jane explained. Then she stood up and Matt saw that she had indeed removed her black lace panties. "Close the door and lock it."

Matt did as he was told, and walked toward Jane. When he put his hands on her hips and pulled her close she said, "Slow down."

"I only have about forty-five minutes now."

"That's not exactly true. I had Tammy make up a bunch of things to fill up your schedule, but there's really no one coming. You're off this afternoon," she purred. "We have *hours.*"

"Oh, well . . ." Matt started. He smiled and gently kissed her lips. Although this Ashley Hotel plot was a first for Jane, she did this type of thing often, because she knew Matt loved it. Once, while they were on a long walk in the woods, she'd begun to tease him seductively, and they'd had sex by a little meadow overlooking Scotch Lake. Several other times, she'd assumed provocative postures while they were in their fishing boat, fishing on warm summer afternoons, and they'd had sex in an open boat. Once while she was standing at the kitchen sink, and once while raking leaves in the yard, she'd bent over, ostensibly to pick something up off the ground or kitchen floor, only to reveal the fact that she wasn't wearing anything below her waist, and Matt had always responded with vigor. But this was whole new level of erotic temptation.

"Do you remember what happened when we did it in the meadow that time?" Matt whispered into her ear.

"Uh-huh . . ." Jane whispered back. "No chance of that today." Her cheek was pressed against his and he could feel her face bend into a smile.

On that day in the meadow, many years earlier, the sex had become so urgent after only a moment of holding each other that they'd dropped to the ground in a fever of lust. When they stood up twenty minutes later they discovered that they'd been lying on a long-forgotten roll of barbed wire fence, left there by someone many years before. Matt did a quick exam and found that Jane's back had several small puncture marks. "I never felt a thing!" Jane had said, then quickly corrected herself to say, "No, not that way . . . I meant the *barbed wire!*" They'd laughed about that memory for years.

Today, this rendezvous at the Ashley Hotel would be a special moment, a one-of-a-kind experience. Matt leaned back and looked her in the eye, and smiled. Jane was about to lead them both on a fantasy.

Her eyes were drunk with lust, and she began to unbutton his shirt and then in great detail she explained all the things she was about to do to him, and all the things she expected him to do.

Jane was still long and lean, and her blonde hair flowed down over her shoulders as she undid his belt and let his pants drop to the floor. Matt put a finger under her chin and raised her face until he could see the sandy color of her eyes. "I love you," he whispered.

Jane stepped back, lifted her chemise over her head, and gave Matt a minute to look at her, then she took him by the hand and led him to the king-size bed without saying a word.

"You have Redi-Whip and some strawberries over there on the table," Matt said.

Jane straddled him, with her face a few inches above his, and she breathed, "Yup." While her hair hung down over his face and shoulders,

Matt moved his fingertips slowly up her sides and onto her breasts. "I love *you*," she whispered.

———

It was still light when John Velde's truck rolled into the Kingstons' driveway at about 5:30. Jane had arrived home at 4:30, after the flesh feast at the Ashley Hotel with Matt, and she was sitting on the couch, looking at the lake and wondering what to make for supper. John let himself into the kitchen, with a brown paper bag under one arm, and called out, "Anybody home?"

Matt had returned to the office after their private party in room 206 in order to finish a couple of small projects on his laboratory bench before he came home for supper. While he was there, trying to get caught up with work, John had called and asked if they were still on for Gourmet Club and Matt had said yes. John had then called Sally Durham and Timmy and invited them, but no one had thought to call Jane and let her in on the plans.

"C'mon in, John, I'm out here!" Jane called.

When John walked into the great room and saw the look on Jane's face he knew exactly what had happened, and he knew this was another great opportunity to jerk someone around.

"Hi, John," Jane said with a pleasant smile. "What's up?"

"What are you *doing*?" John said, trying to muster all the disappointment and frustration he could into one short sentence. He'd quickly recognized that Jane was unaware of the dinner plans everyone else had made for her house. He knew she'd be a bit upset about that, and he decided to see how far he could push, just for the fun of it.

"What?" Jane mumbled.

"Well for Chrissakes! You have company coming for dinner and you're sitting here on your ass!" John scoffed, and as luck would have it at that moment Matt's truck, followed by Sally's car, turned into the driveway. John made a big display of his contempt, and disappointment, as he pointed at the cars that were now slowing down by the kitchen door.

Jane was confused and taken aback. "Well, I . . ."

"You've got people coming for dinner and you haven't done jack shit, have you?"

"Um . . . I . . ." She continued to stammer, and then her confusion flashed into anger as if he'd thrown gas on a fire. "Goddammit, John!" she exploded. Her eyes were hateful slits. She was tapping his chest with her finger and he was in full retreat by the time she saw the grin on his face.

"Careful now! You might say something you'll regret later." His face lit up, as if a bright sun was bursting through dark clouds. He was backpedaling, and both of his hands were raised in the universal gesture for "don't shoot." Then Jane understood that it had all been an act.

"*Goddammit!*" she said again, as the tsunami of anger lingered at high tide for a second and then quickly drained away. "I *hate* it when you do that." Even as she said the words she began to smile too. "Damn you." She slugged his chest. "*Why* do you do that shit?"

"Got any beer?" John smirked, unable to hide his satisfaction with the response he'd drawn from Jane.

She pointed at the refrigerator, then slugged his arm again.

"It *is* Gourmet Club, though," John said, as he popped the top of a can of Leinenkugel's. "So you really *do* need to get off your ass and get to work."

Seconds later, when Matt stepped into the kitchen, he reached behind Jane's waist, pulled her close, and kissed her. Then he said, "It's Gourmet Club, honey. Sorry I forgot to call you. What are we having?"

"Watch out," John said. He took a swig of beer and added, "I just asked her the same thing and I thought we were gonna hafta call a priest: her head started spinning around and green vomit—"

"Shut up, John." Jane laughed, then she turned to Matt and said, "He came in here and started scolding me for not having supper ready."

"I thought the Alien was gonna burst out of her chest," John said.

Matt ignored them both. He'd seen John do things like that for years, and he thought it was pretty funny, but now he had Gourmet Club on his mind. "What's in that bag you have there?"

"Ah, some cheese, and a loaf of French bread that's been in my kitchen for a couple months," John said, "and your sammich from lunch today."

Jane took the bag from him and peeked inside. She slugged his arm again and gave the bag to Matt. "The bread is fresh. I'll get some olive oil and Parmesan cheese and we'll open a bottle of wine while we discuss the menu."

Sally and Timmy let themselves into the kitchen while Jane was rifling through the liquor cabinet in search of a corkscrew. "Hi, Timmy, what are *you* thinkin' for dinner tonight?" Matt asked. "And hi, Sally."

"Mac and cheese," Timmy replied, while he took his shoes off.

"Ah yes, orange death, as we called it back in college," Matt said.

"And I brought some bread and cold cuts and cheese from the coffee shop," Sally offered.

"Looks like sammiches and orange death, then," Jane said. "I'll start boiling some water for the macaroni."

Half an hour later the kitchen table was strewn with sandwich ingredients, a cutting board, some knives, empty wine bottles, and a couple of empty beer cans.

"So, you're both going to the Mayo Clinic tomorrow?" Sally asked Matt and Jane.

"Yup, routine physicals for both of us, and a post-op check for Matt," Jane replied. She held out a wineglass and nudged John, requesting him to open a new one. "And we have tickets for an orchestra concert, too."

"What do you do with your office, Matt? Just close it down for a couple days?" Sally asked.

"Not much else I can do," Matt said.

"Hey, that reminds me!" John blurted. "How did your emergency at the office turn out today? Did somebody have a stroke, or what?"

Jane put her hand on Matt's thigh and squeezed it.

"Nah, nothing that serious; just a cavity I needed to fill," Matt said, and he felt Jane squeeze his thigh a bit harder. Then he couldn't resist the temptation to add, "But it took me a couple tries to get it just right."

Jane kept her eyes down.

"Does that happen very often?" Sally asked. "That it takes several tries?"

"It happened a lot more when I was younger," Matt said, then he leaned close to Jane and gave her a kiss on the cheek while she dug her nails into his thigh.

"Hey, not to change the subject too much," John said, "but does that kid still bother you on the bus, Timmy? Did you ever deal with that kid?"

Timmy shoveled a couple of bites of orange death into his mouth without answering, until his grandmother said, "Timmy, John asked you a question. Did you ever have any more confrontations with Jason, on the bus?"

"Yeah," Timmy admitted, as if it was old news.

"You never told me about it," Sally said, with surprise in her voice. "What happened?"

Everyone at the table stopped what they were doing and waited for the answer.

"He pushed me down one day after school," Timmy said.

"So did you punch him in the nose, like I told you?" John asked, trying not to give the incident, or Timmy's response, any more weight than necessary.

Timmy scooped up another spoonful of orange death, and then stopped it on the way to his mouth. "No. I kicked him right in the *wiener*. That worked."

Timmy thought nothing of his answer, other than the simple fact that kicking a bully in the nuts had solved a problem. The laughter that rose from the adults at the table made no real impression on him. He just kept shoveling mac and cheese into his face.

CHAPTER TWENTY

---◆---

Driving to Rochester a day before their appointments had been a good idea. After a night at the Ramada Inn, they'd both have their checkups at eight o'clock, and then after a leisurely lunch together, they'd attend an orchestra concert, and go home the next morning.

The spring morning was sunny and mild, and hundreds of people were moving about on the sidewalks. As they crept through the traffic for several blocks around the great medical complex, it was impossible not to stare out the car windows and look at all the people. Some rolled along in wheelchairs or on crutches. Many of them seemed to be on their way to work in the clinic. It was impossible to read the faces and determine who was sick, and who wasn't. Some of them had to be dealing with dreadful, terminal health issues. But which ones were they? There were hundreds of stories out there, and it was hard not to wonder who was walking around with a heavy heart.

The sixth level of the parking garage was dark and cool when they stepped out of their car and gathered the papers that would guide them through the Mayo complex for the next couple of hours. They went through a short checklist before they locked the car, and both tried to ignore the little cloud of fear that hovered over them. Sure, they were both here for routine tests and exams, and they both had every reason to expect satisfactory results and then have a nice day together. Nonetheless, all they had to do was look around if they needed something to worry about.

As they joined a number of other people making their way to the parking ramp elevators, the sense of morbid curiosity deepened. Other people, other stories, were now only an arm's length away, and Matt and Jane both stole glances at the people who boarded an elevator with them. No one spoke. Most of them carried a folder with some papers. One passenger, an older man, sat in a wheelchair and had an oxygen mask covering his face while a young woman pushed the chair. None of the others had any obvious injuries or illnesses, but they all seemed to have plenty on their minds.

The elevator ride was silent, and it carried them from the parking ramp to the basement level of the Gonda Building. The doors opened to an elegant lobby where dozens of people were moving about. A silver-haired white woman was playing a grand piano, and young black kid was singing into a microphone while patients wandered by or sat down and listened for a while.

A smartly dressed older man with a gray mustache made eye contact with Matt and asked if he could help. The man wore a blue vest and was obviously an employee of the Mayo Clinic, or a volunteer, whose job was to help people find their way around the huge complex. Matt showed him the paper they'd been given with the time and location for Jane's appointment. The man glanced at the letter in Matt's hand and then pointed and directed, "Take those elevators to the second floor. Take a left when you get off. It's right there." Then Matt showed him the letter with the time and location for his appointment and the man pointed the other way. "Follow that hallway until you see the sign for radiology; it'll be on your left."

Matt thanked the man, then said to Jane, "Let's get you to where you're supposed to be, and then I'll go have my X-ray taken and see my orthopedic guy. We can meet back here in the lobby, by the piano, when we're done. Then we'll go have lunch."

Matt escorted Jane to the Breast Clinic, on the second floor, where a large, comfortable waiting area opened up in front of them. On the far side of the waiting area was a long counter, where patients stood in line to report for their appointments. "Want me to stick around till you're checked in?" Matt asked.

"Nah, you go ahead to your appointment. I'll be fine." She kissed him goodbye, and after a short wait in line she gave her papers to a woman behind the counter and took a seat in the waiting area. Ten minutes later Jane was peeking around at the other people who were also waiting. One old man was talking way too loud to another old man; probably waiting for their wives, Jane thought. Most of the women who were waiting nearby were reading or looking at their phones, trying to be distracted.

Ten more minutes passed in the waiting area before a young woman called Jane's name. She was taken to another room, this one with small lockers, and the woman who'd escorted her there gave her some instructions about what to do next. When Jane had removed her clothes from the waist up, put on the hospital gown she'd been given, and locked her clothing in a small locker, she took a seat along with more than a dozen other women who were there to have mammograms. Most of the women in the little room sat in silence, staring at the floor in front of their feet. A couple of others tried to read whatever they could find nearby, still searching for something to distract them from the thing at hand. Jane guessed, no, she was pretty sure, that each of these women already thought that something was wrong and were about to have their worst fears confirmed.

"Jane, would you like to come with me?" asked a radiology technician, and Jane followed her down a short hallway, then into a dimly lit, noticeably cool room filled with medical equipment. "What's your complete name and date of birth?" the tech asked.

Jane answered her, and then said, "I've been asked that about a dozen times already today."

"Well, we just want to be sure we have the right patient in the right place, and we're doing the right thing." The technician smiled.

"I know. I'm a nurse," Jane said.

"OK then, you know how it works." Jane looked around the room and recognized the mammography equipment. Yes, she knew what was about to be done. "You can take your gown off now, and hang it right there," the technician added.

A small motor inside the mammography machine was humming, and although the room was clean and uncluttered, Jane found the place intimidating. The technician asked Jane to raise her arm, and was polite and gentle as she placed Jane's left breast between two layers of clear plastic. Jane gasped when her breast touched the cold plastic, and the technician said, "Oh, honey, I know it's cold. Sorry."

"It's OK," Jane said, trying to hide her discomfort.

Then the technician placed another piece of plastic over Jane's breast, and compressed the breast between the two pieces of plastic it until it was uncomfortable, and Jane flinched again.

"I'm so sorry, but I have to do that in order to get a good image." She hurried over to the control panel and the thing made a clicking noise when it fired. Then the technician hurried back to Jane and tilted the mammography machine on its axis. This time when the breast was compressed between the layers of plastic, the mammography machine would record a vertical image of the breast.

"OK, honey, now let's do the right side." The technician repositioned the equipment, and Jane turned her right side toward the machine.

A few minutes later she stepped out into the waiting room where she'd said goodbye to Matt. She stood still for a moment and scanned the room. She'd had blood drawn earlier in the morning, and now she needed to get to her next and last appointment. Her doctor would review her blood panels and her mammogram, do a breast exam, and send her on her way. Then she'd meet Matt in the lobby downstairs. They'd have lunch, and then tonight they'd see a concert at the Civic Center.

Matt was sitting by the piano in the main lobby, waiting for her, when the visit with her doctor was finished. Jane spotted him from the top of the stairway she was descending. He was sleeping with his chin nearly resting on his chest when she sat in the chair next to his.

"How'd it go?" Matt asked. He leaned forward and stretched his back.

"Good. Healthy as a horse! You?"

"Good! It looks like I have a hardware store in my hip, though. You could see everything on the X-ray, and it's healing just fine. They wanna see me in a year. Are you ready for lunch?"

"Yes! I'm really hungry, let's go!" Jane stood up. As an afterthought, she added, "They didn't have the results back from my mammogram yet, but she said they'd call me."

"OK. I'm hungry too." Matt stood and took Jane's hand in his and then looked around the lobby.

"What's the matter?" Jane asked.

"I'm just looking for somebody to ask where we can find a good burger."

"Well, there's the guy who gave us directions before." Jane pointed at the man in the blue vest.

"He's too old," Matt said, scanning the lobby for someone else to ask. "Let's ask somebody younger. Let's find a place like the Fraction."

"Best burger in town is a place called Nate's," came a woman's voice from behind Jane. When they looked around to see who'd spoken, they saw a woman smiling at them. It was the woman who'd been playing the piano earlier. "I heard you talking," she added, "and it's full of college kids, like you two." Now the woman was teasing them. "I remember the Fraction." The woman touched Jane's arm and laughed. "I used to hang out there too, back in the day. Nate's is about three blocks thataway."

"Well, thanks," Matt said.

"You'll love it," the woman reassured them. Then she sat down at the bench in front of the grand piano and began to play with no sheet music. "Have a nice day," she added over her shoulder, as Jane and Matt turned away.

"That was pretty cool," Matt said. When they stepped out onto the street to head toward Nate's, the air felt clean and a mild breeze swirled through the buildings of the Mayo complex. Cars, trucks, and a sea of milling clinic employees and visiting patients sent a cloud of noise into the noon bustle on the street.

A block away from the Gonda Building, the pedestrian traffic around them was beginning to thin when Matt said, "You know, I thought John had a little thing for Sally Durham."

"Oh, I can't see that," Jane said with a frown. "She's not his type. Not at all."

"What do you mean?"

"John likes big hair and big boobs, and he likes 'em kinda slutty," Jane declared. "And Sally is none of that. I think she's really plain." She tilted her head and said, "John is attracted to *her*? Really? You *do* mean Sally from the coffee shop with the scar on her face?"

"Yeah, I think he is. Well, I know he is," Matt said.

They were crossing the street when Jane said, "Now I feel bad. I just said she was plain and made that sound bad. I didn't mean it that way. She has a nice figure, her skin is so fine, and her eyes and cheekbones . . . I wonder if she has some native blood in her. She's pretty. But she dresses plain. You know, like a businesswoman, not a hooker. She doesn't wear much makeup, she wears her hair short and it's dark, not blonde, and she doesn't act like a bimbo. I just don't see John with her."

"Well, I think she's the only woman who ever called "bullshit" on him," Matt said.

"What? Really? You think he likes that?"

"Well, you know, when he does stuff that only John does, she gets right up in his face and puts a stop to it. I guess you might say she gives him some boundaries, and I think he likes it."

"Hmm. How did she get that scar? Did you ever find out?" Jane asked.

"I don't know about that. I try not to stare, and I'm afraid to ask, but it looks to me like it was made by a chain saw."

Jane cringed. "Ooh. Can you imagine?"

Still walking, Matt was looking around for Nate's when he noticed Jane staring at her cell phone. "I just missed a call, and it was from my doctor," she said.

She stepped away from the street and called her voicemail, then put the phone close to her ear and covered the other ear while she listened. A moment later she turned a frightened face to Matt and said, "She wants to see me back in her office at one o'clock."

Matt shrugged. "Probably standard procedure."

"Doctors don't leave messages like that for standard procedure. There's something wrong."

"C'mon, honey, don't get all crazy—"

"Something is wrong with the mammogram," she said, with a suddenly quivering voice.

"Well, OK, let's go eat and—"

"I'm not hungry."

Matt stood on the busy sidewalk and looked into his wife's eyes. He saw fear, and he knew Jane well enough to understand that she would not breathe easy until the doctor told her that everything was OK. "So, we'll go back to the doctor's office and wait until one o'clock?" Matt asked. Jane nodded yes, and they walked back across the street, the way they'd just come. "OK," Matt said. "We'll just go eat after she tells you everything is all right."

Precisely at one, a nurse stepped into the waiting room of the Breast Clinic, where Matt and Jane had been sitting in silence for an hour, and called out, "Jane Kingston."

Jane stood up and looked at Matt. Her face was drawn, and there was fear in her eyes. "Do you want me to come with you?" Matt asked.

Jane grabbed his hand and pulled him to his feet. She *knew* something was wrong, the next few minutes were going to be bad, and the one thing she needed was for Matt to be there with her for this visit with her doctor.

The nurse led them down a long hall and into a small exam room with the standard-issue doctor's examination table, a desk, and a sink. "The doctor will be with you in a few minutes," the nurse said, and she closed the door and left them alone.

The room grew silent and Jane reached for Matt's hand.

"*Relax*, honey, it's gonna be OK," Matt said.

"Something is wrong," she repeated, and she used a tissue to blot some tears away.

A moment later there came a gentle knock, and the door to the little room swung open. "Hello again, Jane," said the doctor. She thrust a hand toward Matt and introduced herself. "I'm Dr. Palmer."

Matt guessed her to be about forty. She had straight brown hair and wore no makeup. She was skinny, like an athlete with an eating disorder. Her clothes fit her poorly, like she didn't care about them, or didn't want to take the time to shop anywhere but J. C. Penney. But Matt liked the look. He sized her up as the college girl with no social life because she studied all the time in order to maintain a 4.0 GPA and then get into medical school. He also assumed that she finished med school at the top of her class and in her free time now she read textbooks and ran marathons because she was compulsive about accomplishment. She was the one he'd pick for his doctor, too. Matt stood up and shook her hand. "I'm Matt. I'm with her."

Dr. Palmer sat down on a chair with wheels and rolled it close to the computer monitor on her desk and turned the computer on. "The radiologist saw something on your mammogram," she said, as she tapped on the keyboard and brought up the images from Jane's mammogram.

Jane's chest rose and fell several times, and she squeezed Matt's hand.

"What? What is it?" Matt asked. He knew Jane would be struggling to remain calm now. He could feel her fear growing.

"Well, here it is." Dr. Palmer turned the computer monitor so everyone could see. She took a ballpoint pen and pointed to a tiny white speck on one image, and then another. In each breast. "There's something going on here. Both places."

"Is it cancer?" Jane choked, then dabbed the tissue at her eyes again.

"I don't know. That's why we need to schedule a biopsy. The only way to know is to put it under a microscope and have a look."

"I knew it," Jane sniffed.

"When? When do we have the biopsy, Doctor?" Matt asked.

"Tomorrow. Can you be here at eight o'clock?"

Jane nodded yes, and then began to sob. Matt felt something new and terrible. Something that was meant for other people, not him. His throat tightened and each breath came with a clutch. His eyes welled up with tears. He put his arm around Jane and summoned every ounce of his strength to maintain his composure. "It's just a biopsy, honey. It'll be all right." He wasn't sure he believed his own words, and it didn't seem as though his wife had even heard him.

———

After a sleepless night in the Ramada Inn, Matt and Jane were seated, once again, in the second-floor waiting room of the Gonda Building at eight o'clock the following morning. They'd skipped the orchestra concert and spent the evening walking around town and pretending not to be afraid.

"You gotta remember, darlin', this is a biopsy, that's all. Odds are they'll be telling us to go on home in a couple hours because it's just some benign lump. It's gonna be OK," Matt said. He squeezed her hand, brought his lips close to her ear, and whispered, "It's gonna be OK."

"I have something suspicious in both breasts," she reminded him, unable to mask her fear. "This can't be all right."

"You can't think like that," he said.

"Jane Kingston?" It was the same woman who'd escorted Jane into the clinic the previous day. Jane and Matt both stood up. Matt kissed her and whispered, "I love you." Jane followed the woman through a heavy door, and the door slammed shut behind them.

Before she'd taken the first step, the woman who'd called Jane's name said, "What's your full name and date of birth?" Jane answered, and the woman said, "Follow me." She followed the woman down a hallway and into a plain white examination room equipped with a large reclining chair. There was also a tiny bathroom behind the door. Jane was already apprehensive and afraid on several levels, but these sterile little rooms always raised her level of anxiety. Maybe if they used muted colors and kept them a bit warmer? No, the twist in her belly would still be there; how could it *not* be? She was told to remove her clothes and put on another hospital gown, then sit down in the recliner and wait for a nurse to come and start an intravenous line for sedation.

When the door closed she looked down at the little anti-skid stockings she'd been given. She looked around the bare walls. This was bad. She was all alone now, waiting for . . . what? What was going to happen to her in the next hour? Would it change her life? She felt overwhelmed. Things were out of control, and weakness and fear had her on the verge of tears. Oh, somebody please come in here and be with me, she thought.

Footsteps and a mumbled conversation just outside the door were quickly followed by the entrance of nurse who was almost Jane's age. "Hi, can you tell your full name and your date of birth?" the nurse said.

Jane told her.

"And we're going to have a breast biopsy today, correct?"

"Yes."

"Which breast?"

"Both."

"All right, then." The woman rubbed a cotton swab on the back of Jane's left hand. "This will be just fine. You have Dr. Palmer today and she's very good. Now I'm going to start a line and we'll give you a little sedative in just a while. This will pinch." When she'd placed the line in Jane's vein she taped a clear plastic tube to her arm and smiled. "OK, Jane, if you want to use the bathroom before your biopsy, this would be a good time. I think they're about ready to come and get you."

Someone did come to get her almost immediately, and she was soon lying on her back in a surgical suite, with both arms extended to the side while several more nurses and the doctor placed a surgical drape over her right breast.

"Are you doing all right?" asked one of the nurses, while others scurried around behind her.

"Yes, but I'm kind of afraid," Jane said.

"That's pretty normal," the doctor said, as she looked over the top of the telescopic lenses in her eyeglasses. "But we'll be good to you. You know you're going to be awake the whole time, so you can tell me if anything is uncomfortable. OK?"

"OK."

"Now, I'm going to give you some local anesthetic, like the dentist, and it will pinch a little, but that won't last for long," the doctor said.

Jane saw the syringe and closed her eyes. "My husband is a dentist," she said.

"Really? Where do you live?" the doctor asked.

"Pine Rapids."

"No kidding. My husband and I have a cabin over by Longville," said the doctor.

"Hey!" One of the nurses piped in. "My parents have a place up there on Ten Mile Lake. We love it up there."

"Yeah, we sure love it, too." Jane felt a pinch just above her breast, and she squeezed her eyes shut a bit harder.

"Did I pinch you? I'm sorry," the doctor said. "That should be about the end of that." Jane could feel that the doctor was doing something to her now, but only because she could feel herself move in response to someone else's touch. She knew the doctor was adding more anesthetic in several other places around her breast, but there was no pain. The small talk about lake country was a convenient way for the surgical staff to make an upbeat connection with her, and perhaps distract her to make the procedure a bit less scary. She knew that much. But talk of home seemed so at odds with this moment. She was completely exposed and vulnerable, and everyone in the room knew that this biopsy was being performed in order to validate something that they already suspected.

"All right," the doctor said, "I'm going to make a small incision and remove the entire lump."

Jane made no reply. She kept her eyes closed and tried to stay strong.

— ·—

Matt was sitting in the second-floor waiting room when the clinic door swung open and Jane emerged. She was walking toward him, but something wasn't right. Her arms were not moving, her shoulders were raised a bit, and she was leaning forward. The upper half of her body seemed frozen.

"You OK? How'd it go?" Matt said when he stood to greet her.

"It hurts. Let's go." Jane was uncomfortable and she wanted, needed, a place to rest. Her gait was rigid, as though she was trying not to jostle her breasts or disturb the bandages.

"So what's next?" Matt asked as they walked to the elevators.

"We come back at 2:30 and go over the results of the biopsy," she said flatly, and she kept walking.

"Did it hurt?" Matt turned to follow her.

"Starting to hurt now."

"Do you want eat something?" Matt asked, as they waited for an elevator.

"No, but you should."

They found an Italian restaurant they'd seen earlier in the day, and they stared at each other while they waited for their waitress.

"What if it's cancer?" Jane whispered.

"What if it isn't?" Matt reached across the table and took her hand. He knew what she was thinking. All the possible dark scenarios were playing out in her head, and she was trying to deny them. "C'mon, let's have some positive vibes here. It's more than likely some benign tumor, or lump."

"Do you really think that?" Jane asked. "Really?"

"Yeah, I do. I think most of these biopsies turn out that way. And I think later this afternoon you're gonna be laughing at the way you kept expecting the worst. Jeez, honey, think of all our friends who've had lumps removed and been just fine."

Jane turned away, took her cell phone from her purse, and began to check for text messages, voicemail, and email. Anything to distract her. "I hope so," she said, without looking up.

The late lunch was only an excuse to help pass some time. They each picked at a salad and tried not to think about the things they were thinking about. When they'd spent what seemed like an appropriate amount of time in the restaurant they returned to the second-floor waiting room and sat down beside each other.

Finally, just after 2:30 a nurse stepped into the waiting room and called out, "Jane Kingston." Jane and Matt stood up and walked to her. This time he didn't need to be told that she needed him. "What's your full name and date of birth?" she asked.

Jane told her, and the woman said, "OK, follow me." It was a familiar experience, following a nurse into a doctor's exam room, but this time there was a sense of dread. A few steps down the hallway the woman turned and pointed into a small office where a computer screen sat on a small desk beside a narrow vinyl-covered bench. "Have a seat. Dr. Palmer will be here in a minute." And she closed the door.

"I love you," Matt whispered, while the silence of the tiny room settled over them.

Jane took his hand in hers and closed her eyes. Her grip was iron, and Matt knew that she was afraid. The last time she'd held him in that manner was when they'd stood together on the altar of the church on their wedding day, and then turned to face everyone after they'd been pronounced husband and wife.

"It's gonna be OK," Matt said softly.

As usual, footsteps and a muted conversation just outside the door heralded the doctor's arrival. Then the door swung open. Dr. Palmer stepped into the room and said hello to them. Dr. Palmer sat at the little desk and turned on the computer. She studied the screen for a minute, then said, "How are you feeling, Jane?"

"OK," Jane said.

The doctor leaned forward in her chair and took a deep breath before she said, "You have hormone-positive stage two invasive breast cancer. In both breasts."

The little room went silent again. The doctor's words struck them both like a hammer, and sucked all life from the room. Jane's lower lip began to quiver, her face twisted, and tears welled up in her eyes. Matt felt his throat tighten, and he reached an arm over her shoulder. When their cheeks touched, both of them began to sniffle in small, gasping breaths. There was no sobbing, no wailing. They held each other and let the tears come while the doctor watched.

For the moment, Jane needed no specific explanation about the nature of her cancer. Her deepest fears had been confirmed. She had cancer. Her number had been called. It was now her time to deal with things that had always been reserved for others. A demon had stalked her and then taken possession of her. People died of this; they suffered and then died a hideous death. Everything she ever was, and everything she ever had, could be taken from her. God, she couldn't think about that. Her brain could not allow her to proceed any further in that direction.

As Matt held his best friend, and their tears mingled, the pain and fear that made her chest heave was his, too. For the first time, he actually *felt* the pain of another person. The look on her face would be etched in his memory forever. She was lost and terrified.

As Matt kissed her cheek and softly stroked her hair, he came to understand something about love. Jane was a part of *him*; they were one. Her soft cries and sobs twisted in *his* chest. He squeezed her and tried to comfort her for several minutes, until her crying abated.

"It's all right to cry," Dr. Palmer said, as she extended a box of tissues to Jane, then Matt, and waited for them to cry it out.

Eventually Jane wiped her tears away, and in a weak and halting voice asked, "So what does that *mean*, invasive stage two hormone-positive breast cancer? What are we going to do?" She squeezed Matt's hand as she asked the question, but now her greatest fear was that she already knew the answer.

"Well, let's back up a little bit," the doctor said. "There are five stages of breast cancer; stage zero through stage four, and there's a treatment protocol for each stage, pretty much. In stage two, which is what you have, the tumor is about two centimeters in diameter, and the cancer cells have come through the walls of the ducts in your breast tissue. We won't know if the cancer has spread to the lymph nodes until after your surgery."

Jane wiped tears from both eyes and then asked, "The surgery?"

"Well," Dr. Palmer began, "there are basically two options for you. One is for the surgeon to perform a lumpectomy. In that procedure, only the cancer, or the lump, is removed from your breast. After the surgery, you'll be treated with radiation and probably some sort of chemotherapy, and you'll take a drug called a hormone blocker for at least five years. The hormone blocker will stop your body from making estrogen. Your breasts are a target organ for the estrogen, and many studies have shown a significant drop in the reoccurrence of breast cancer in women who take the hormone blocker."

"Why the radiation and chemotherapy and hormone blocker if the lump is removed?" Jane asked.

"Good question. We treat lumpectomies with radiation and chemo because in that procedure we leave some, or most, of your breast tissue behind, and there will always be a chance that we could also leave some cancer cells behind. So we want to be certain that we've been thorough in removing the cancer."

"What's the other option?" Jane asked.

"Mastectomy, both breasts; and then chemotherapy, depending on what we find in the lymph nodes," the doctor said, without a flicker of emotion.

Jane's head fell toward her lap, and a small cry of anguish escaped. This was devastating, more than she could bear, and she reached for Matt once more.

"It's a much more invasive procedure, the mastectomy, you know that. But if the lymph nodes are clear there may be no need for radiation or chemotherapy, and the cancer will be gone.

Dr. Palmer waited and watched respectfully as Jane and Matt broke down again. Matt whispered from time to time while they held each other, and after a minute or two Jane dried her eyes once more. The doctor went on to explain, in detail, the surgery she was recommending, and the postoperative treatment that she anticipated. She understood the enormity of the issue and was willing to sit with them for as long as they needed to get their minds around everything.

"So what do we do now?" Matt said when it seemed as if all their questions had been asked and answered several times.

"Well, first, you need to decide between a lumpectomy and a mastectomy," Dr. Palmer said.

"I want 'em off." Jane sniffled and used a tissue to wipe her nose, then added, "I don't need breasts anymore."

Matt was taken aback by Jane's swift answer and the certainty in her voice. But he knew Jane very well, and he heard fear in her voice, too. He looked at Jane and then turned to the doctor. "Would you advise her to do one of these procedures over the other?"

"No, but I think the mastectomy is a good choice," Dr. Palmer replied, and when she read the need for something more in Matt's eyes, she went on. "Look, Jane has a bomb on her chest, and she wants it off." She turned to look at Jane and added, "I can see it in your eyes; you know what I'm talking about, don't you, Jane?"

Jane nodded.

"You understand that too, don't you, Matt?" the doctor said.

"Sure, but—" Matt replied.

"It's all been so sudden, and it's so much to think about," Jane said, as she blotted a tear from the corner of her eye.

"I know, and I'm so sorry," Dr. Palmer said.

"I think we should do the mastectomy," Jane said. "If that's the thing that's most likely to get rid of the cancer."

"Like I said, I think that's a good decision," Dr. Palmer replied.

"So what's next?" Jane asked.

"I'd like you to meet with a surgeon," Dr. Palmer said.

"When?" asked Matt.

"The surgeon I want you to see has office hours this afternoon. Would you like me to ask if he can see you today?"

"Today?" Jane said.

The doctor nodded yes.

"OK. Thank you, I just didn't think I'd be able to see someone, a surgeon, so quickly," Jane said. "But then, if I meet with him today, when would the surgery happen?"

"Well, as soon as possible, I suppose?" Dr. Palmer made her answer into a question.

"That sounds OK," Jane replied.

When Jane and Matt left Dr. Palmer's office and passed by the front desk, they were told that Jane had an appointment with a surgeon named Dr. Kwon at 4:30 p.m.

"Wow," Matt said as he looked at his watch. "This is happening so fast."

"Get me some water, will you?" Jane croaked. "My mouth is so dry."

They walked, zombie-like, across the second-floor lobby and toward the elevators that would take them to the main lobby in the Gonda Building, the lobby with the grand piano. Once in the elevator, they stared at the doors and ignored the eight other people who rode with them. Other people's problems weren't so interesting anymore.

When the elevator doors opened they stepped out and continued their zombie walk into the midst of a sparse afternoon crowd. Matt took her hand in his and stopped walking. Now what? Where should they go? How were they supposed to talk about this? Matt drew in a deep breath and tried to think of something to say, but when his eye met Jane's they both began to weep again.

Now *they* were the ones everyone in the lobby noticed and tried to look away from. They had a terrible secret, and everyone who sneaked a glance at them wondered if it was Matt, or Jane, or someone they loved, who'd just been handed an uncertain, terrible fate, or a death sentence. Matt took Jane in his arms and they both let the tears come once again. It didn't matter who saw their struggle now. Their insides were empty; there was no joy left in the world.

"I don't want to have cancer," Jane sobbed as Matt held her. She'd just been told that she had a deadly disease. And now, not two hours later, she had to make a decision like this.

"Maybe this is all happening too fast. Maybe we should slow down, get a second opinion," Matt suggested.

"No, we're at the Mayo Clinic, Matt. If you must have cancer, this the place you want to be. And I'm thankful that this is happening so fast.

Can you imagine if we had to go home and wait to find out about . . . and to wait for a long time for surgery?" Jane put her arms around Matt's shoulders and whispered, "I want you to come with me later, when I meet with the surgeon."

"Sure."

"I need you to listen to what he says. There's so much whizzing through my head, I'm not sure if I'm hearing and understanding everything," she explained.

"Absolutely." Matt held his wife and tried to imagine the fear in her heart. This was happening so fast, and all he could do was hold her close.

They made their way to Dr. Kwon's office and before they could seat themselves in the waiting area, a nurse called Jane's name and then led them to yet another small exam room.

Dr. Kwon followed immediately and he was instantly likable. He wore a happy smile, treated Matt and Jane like old friends, and spoke of the mastectomy as if it was a routine procedure. He oozed confidence, which was a timely gift for both Matt and Jane.

After his pleasant introduction and brief conversation, Dr. Kwon asked Jane to remove her blouse and her bra, and then he began to examine her while Matt looked on. It was a bit surreal to watch the man examine her breasts. He lifted and measured them. He made a couple of marks on her chest with a felt pen. He looked at her from one side, then the other. All the while he explained everything in a very confident but matter-of-fact way, as if what he intended to do was no more difficult than fixing a broken screen door. He said it would work out just fine, too; he was going to save the nipples, if he could, but he'd have to sort of "melon ball" her breast tissue away after making an incision underneath the breast and . . .

That was the point at which Matt felt the pain in his own heart. He'd been in the operating room before and he had a pretty good idea what the procedure would look like. It was more than he wanted to envision for the woman he loved, and he tried to shut out any more thought of it.

Dr. Kwon went on to say that it would be great if he could save the nipples and the skin on her breasts because then he could place a "tissue expander" in each breast that would allow the skin to heal nicely so that a few months later Jane could return and have breast implants placed. He said she'd look as good as new. Matt liked Dr. Kwon immediately, but he wondered what Jane was thinking.

"Well, what if I just want 'em gone?" she asked with more than a little bit of defiance.

At that point the surgeon took his hands off her and stepped back. "Well, Jane, you *can* do that. And it will work out. But your clothes won't fit right, and—"

"I think I just want them *off*," Jane said again.

The surgeon looked at her and waited for more.

"I just want the cancer off me," Jane said. "It's like Dr. Palmer said, there's a bomb on my chest and I want it off." Jane was unwilling, or unable, to look anyone in the eye, but she was still defiant.

"Can I have a minute with Jane?" Matt asked the doctor. "Just a minute by ourselves, please?"

"Sure. Take your time." Dr. Kwon rose to leave and said, "Just open the door a crack when it's OK for me to come back."

Jane was sniffling again when Matt wrapped his arms around her, and then the dam busted. "Why? Why did this have to happen?" she sobbed. "I don't want him to do what I know he needs to do. Oh God, I'm so afraid." Her tears came freely now, and her chest heaved, and her sobs were loud and mournful.

Matt held her and cried along with her until all the tears had cleansed something away. "I just want them off," she said after she blew her nose. "I want the cancer *gone*. I just wanna live."

"I know, honey, and this surgery will fix you, but the implants are for after all this, when—"

"Breast implants are for porn stars and vain, insecure women," she said.

"Aw, Jane, you know that isn't true. OK, maybe it is sorta true, but think about it for a minute. You're a beautiful woman, and you like to look good. I know you do. You know that our culture places value—granted, maybe too much value—on how we look. But that's the way it is. All the doctor is talking about is placing the spacers so that if you want to place implants after the cancer is gone and the surgery is healed, you'll have that option."

"I can get a bra with boobs already in there, and not fool with all this other stuff."

"Yes, you can, and I'm OK with that, too, if that's really what you want. But the doctors told us that ninety-five percent of women in your situation choose the implants, and they're glad they did." Matt stopped and made a point get Jane to look him in the eyes. "You've had so much shit dumped on you today. I don't think you're thinking clearly. I know this is more than you can get your mind around. But let him put these spacers in there? All that will do is allow healing to progress in such a way that you can place the implants later, if you choose. If you don't want to get implants at that time, then don't, but I think you'll be glad you left that option open in a few months."

Jane reached for him once more and held him close. "Yeah . . . maybe you're right," she whispered.

When Matt opened the door, Dr. Kwon returned and finished his exam. His tone was even more gentle than before when he asked, "Do you want me to place the tissue spacers?"

"Yes," Jane replied.

"Good, Jane," Dr. Kwon said. "You can get dressed again, too."

As Jane dressed herself, Dr. Kwon sat down on a hard chair between Jane and Matt, and then turned to Jane. "You will be beautiful again, Jane."

Jane nodded and tried to smile. "Thank you. I'm sure you'll take good care of me."

"Of course I will. And when I see you for your follow-up visits during the time you're healing, we'll be able add a bit more fluid to those tissue expanders and shape your breast however we want to."

"How do you do that?" Jane asked.

"We just use a needle and inject some saline into them."

"Won't that hurt?" Jane asked.

"No, the skin on your breasts will be numb," Dr. Kwon explained.

"For how long?" Jane asked.

"Forever." Dr. Kwon shrugged.

Jane let that unwelcome bit of information pass, then she asked, "So you're ready to do this surgery?"

"Yes." Dr. Kwon nodded.

"When?" Jane asked.

"Tomorrow. I'll do it tomorrow if you'd like, and if I can find time in the schedule."

—·—

The door to their room at the Ramada Inn thumped itself shut behind them and put an exclamation point at the end of an unforgettable day. "C'mere, honey," Matt said as he took Jane by the arm and then hugged her. There weren't many tears left for them to cry, and they simply stood there in each other's embrace.

"You OK with all this? You OK with tomorrow?" Matt asked.

"Yes. I just want 'em off. I want to live." She seemed resolute when she turned to look at Matt. "Like I said, I don't need breasts anymore."

"Are you sure?" Matt asked. The day had been scary and surreal for him, too, and Jane had just uttered a sentence that was so far away from anything he ever thought he'd hear.

"I want to see my boys get married. I want to see my grandchildren. I want to *live*, and I want to do whatever gives me the best chance to do that."

"Well, then that's what we'll do." He knew his wife. He'd watched her over the past few hours, and he knew she'd condensed everything down to what was most important. And he knew she was right.

Jane walked to an overstuffed chair and slumped into it. Matt followed, and when she leaned back he kneeled on the floor in front of her chair, and leaned forward until his head was resting on her chest. She reached a hand up and softly stroked the back of his head. Neither of them needed to speak now. An enormous thing had happened to them, and it was time to own it.

"You should call Donna," Jane finally said, as their room began to grow dark. "I know it's late, but she should be at home. You need to call her and tell her what's happened so she can rearrange your schedule at the office."

"What about you?" As the director of nursing at a large clinic, Jane would be missed at work, and the clinic administrator would need to find a short-term replacement for her.

"I don't want to talk to anyone tonight. Can you call…"

"I'll call Ron Hested. He can let the administrators know about this tonight, and everyone at your office at the clinic can find out in the morning. I'll call right now and tell them we won't be home for a few days."

"Call the boys, too."

"Do you want to talk to them?" Matt asked.

"I can't . . . not tonight."

When Matt stood up and began to make the phone calls that had to be made, it all became a bit more real. Jane rose, went into the bathroom, and closed the door behind her so she wouldn't have to listen to Matt say the things she didn't want to hear again.

When all the phone calls had been made, and they'd brushed their teeth, and there was nothing more to do or say, they turned out the lights and got into bed. Matt put his arms around his Jane and tried to think about what had happened, and what might happen next, and what terrible thoughts might be racing through her mind.

Several strands of her hair tickled his lips when he pulled her back close to his chest, and he kissed her ear when he snuggled as close as he could. She wasn't asleep, and she wasn't about to doze off any time soon. While he listened to her rhythmic breathing, Matt allowed his own questions to come. It was stage two cancer, and that was good, well, better than it could have been. But the numbers said that the cancer returned and eventually killed one in five women with stage two breast cancer. Would his precious Jane survive? How could he ever live without her? And what of the surgery? How disfigured, body and soul, would she be without her breasts? And how would this affect their relationship, their sex lives? Sex had always been a powerful glue that brought them together and restored their connection. Now what? Would there, could there, ever be another adventure like the one they'd had at the Ashley Hotel? Was that door about to slam shut behind them? Then he felt bad, and selfish, for thinking about sex at a time like this.

His mind's eye began to play images of his lovely Jane, just as it did when he sat in his tree and waited for a deer to walk by. He saw her beautiful smile in old, familiar photos, and he remembered birthdays and Christmases, and camping trips. In every little vignette he saw his Jane, and he felt the connection that made him whole.

His life had always seemed to be a huge vessel, filled with good times, and he could just keep on pouring out the good times forever. But now, for the first time, he began to understand that there were only so many good times to be poured out, and he wondered how many remained. God, how many opportunities to be kind, to love this woman, and tell her how much he loved her, had he let slip away?

It was too much to think about in this dark hotel room.

While his lips were touching her ear, he whispered, "I'll try not to drool on your head."

He didn't have to see her face; he could feel her response. He could hear a little sigh and feel a tiny smile crease her face, then she reached back and patted his leg, just a bit.

At least he'd given her *something*, just a little something to make her smile, even at a time like this. It was a tiny reminder that he was there, right behind her, and that he'd never leave her. He would be her strength through all of this; his will would bend and form the future. He kissed Jane's ear and said, "I love you. I have from the beginning and I always will. I know you're afraid, but I'll be with you, and we have miles and miles yet to travel together."

While they lay together in the darkness, Jane wondered if she'd live to see her grandchildren. She wondered about the surgery, and how different the rest of her life was going to be.

While Matt lay there and stared at the darkened curtains, and listened to trucks out on the highway, he thought about death, too, and the dreadful surgery. He was about to sail off into uncharted waters, and he already longed for the safety of a time and a place he'd never see again.

———

After a mostly sleepless night, they rose at 5 a.m. and got ready for the short trip to Methodist Hospital. Everything that needed to be said had already been spoken. There was no pep talk or verbal reassurance for times like this.

An hour later they found themselves in yet another waiting area. Once again a nurse appeared across the room and called Jane's name; she'd come to take her and get her prepared for surgery. "What's your full name and date of birth?" she asked, and Jane told her. "Have you had anything to eat or drink since midnight?" she asked next, and Jane replied that she had not. Then she reminded Jane to be sure and give all valuables—wallet, cell phone, whatever—to Matt. Jane said she had already done that.

Jane, Matt, and the nurse stood in a small huddle as the nurse explained to Matt that he would have to say goodbye now, but he could watch a TV monitor in the family waiting area and keep track of Jane's progress. Her status—pre-surgery, on deck, in surgery, and recovery room—would be posted there. She said it would be a long day, and she would call Matt from time to time and let him know how things were going, specifically whether or not any cancer cells were found in Jane's lymph nodes, which would prolong the surgery.

Matt said that he understood, and then it was time to let the nurse take Jane away. The goodbye was nearly impossible for both of them. Matt broke the silence first, and said, "You know I love you, and you know I'll be waiting for you later." Then he kissed her one last time and watched her follow the nurse around a corner. This was all a bad dream. A terrible nightmare. But Matt knew he wouldn't wake up in his bed with Jane beside him; he'd sit around in this bleak place and wait for more bad news. This nightmare was real.

Jane was gone, out of sight now, and the fear in her eyes was torturing him. He wished he could stay with her. He wished he could take her place, but Jane had to make that walk to surgery all by herself. He saw the horrible fear in her eyes once again as he turned away and went looking for a place to sit.

Then, for a reason that he'd never understand, the movie projector in his head clicked on and began showing him images from a book he'd been forced to read in college, Dante's *Inferno*. Dante had told the story of a man's trip through Hell. At first, all Matt could think of were the dreadful illustrations. Some artist had made black-and-white drawings and done a powerful job of portraying the agony of existence in Hell. Maybe it was the look in Jane's eyes that triggered the memory. What he saw on Jane's face resembled the anguish and fear on the faces of the people in those illustrations. Then, immediately on the heels of those dreadful images, came another far more disturbing thought: his *contrapasso*.

Dante had described all the levels of Hell. The lower levels provided more suffering and were reserved for the worst sinners, as far as Matt could remember. But Dante had also introduced the concept of a contrapasso, the idea that all sinners would be punished in equal measure to the sins that had landed them in Hell.

This cancer, this awful twist in his life, this might be his contrapasso, his punishment for the things he'd done. He found an empty chair in a quiet waiting room and tried to think about something else.

Forty minutes later, when Jane was prepped for surgery with an IV drip in each arm, she was allowed to rest in a hospital bed in a quiet room until she was placed in a wheelchair and rolled into the operating room. Several people, all wearing scrubs and masks, were busy arranging equipment as she was placed on the operating table.

"How are doing, Jane?" asked a man who looked too young to be there.

"I'm good. It's cold in here."

"Yes it is," the man agreed, and immediately someone was tucking a warm blanket around her. "I'll be starting your anesthetic pretty soon," the man said. She could feel that someone was doing something to her left arm, and then . . .

CHAPTER TWENTY-ONE

Several scruffy-looking young men were moving wooden crates filled with beaver pelts that had just returned from the tannery. Two other men, both of them older, and obviously lacking the physical strength to carry such heavy crates, were washing the walls and floor of the Shorewood Furist. The trapping season was long over, and the place was getting a thorough spring cleaning. Darrell's office and Snag's private chambers had both been given a fresh coat of white paint. The cluttered desk and the bed that looked like the Shroud of Turin still remained, however.

John and Darrell sat on folding chairs and Snag sat on his cot while John explained all that had happened and was about to happen to Jane.

"Is she gonna die?" Snag finally asked.

"Probably not. Well, no, not today, anyway," John replied. "But they never know how far the cancer may have spread until after the surgery." The little room fell silent.

"What does 'mastectomy' mean?" Snag asked, still trying to comprehend everything.

John drew in a deep breath and let it out slowly. He didn't want to say the words he was about to. "They're gonna cut her breasts off, Snag. It's the best way to make sure they get rid of all the cancer."

Snag thought for a long moment, and then said, "She'll still be beautiful." It was a statement, not a question.

"Yup, she will. No doubt about it, little brother." John smiled. Snag's words, and the simple implication about just where beauty came from, restored some of John's confidence, too.

"When? When is the surgery?" Darrell asked.

"Today, right now." John looked at his watch and added, "Matt said that surgery was planned for 8 a.m."

"She'll still be beautiful," Snag said once more.

"Yes, she sure will," John agreed. He went over to sit down beside Snag, and he placed a hand on the back of Snag's neck. "I talked to Matt last night, and he told me that Jane wanted to say a special hello to you, and to tell you that she'd be home soon, so don't worry." John squeezed Snag's neck and pulled him a bit closer. "Do you still say your prayers every night, brother?"

"Not so much as I used to."

"Well, tonight might be a good time to shoot one up for Jane," John said. Then he stood up and said that he was going to the coffee shop to tell Sally Durham about Jane's cancer.

"How come?" Darrell asked. "I mean, why do *you* need to tell *her*?"

"I dunno, Darrell," John said with a shrug, "I guess I just want to be the one to tell her." All the while he was driving across town on his way to the coffee shop, he thought about Darrell's question. Why *did* he want to be the one to tell Sally?

Sally was alone behind the counter when John walked in the front door of the coffee shop. She gave him a wave and a smile, but when she picked up on the look in his eyes she knew something was troubling him. "What's wrong?" she asked when he reached the counter.

John asked her to sit with him at the dunce table, and he told her everything he knew.

"When is the surgery?" Sally asked.

"Today." John looked at his watch. "Matt said he'd call me when she came out."

"What kind of surgery are we talking about? They'll remove a lump and send her home, I'm guessing?" Sally asked.

John shook his head. "Not so easy. She's gonna have a mastectomy, both breasts."

"Matt is there by *himself*? He's all *alone*? Today, of all days?" Sally was incredulous. "Why aren't you there with him? You're his best friend!"

"I offered! I told him I was coming right away. But you know him. Well, maybe you don't. He's pretty much a stiff-upper-lip kind of guy. We actually argued for a while, but he kept on telling me he'd be just fine. He said all he's gonna do is sit in the waiting room all day and he doesn't need any help to do that."

"Oh, he's gonna need a friend today. He'll need someone to talk to. You're his best friend, John. He turns to you for guidance and enlightenment." Sally smiled. "OK, maybe it's better that you're *here*." She reached over and touched John's hand. "But really, he needs someone to be with him."

"He was pretty clear on that, Sally. I'd like to be there, but—"

"OK, maybe he'll be all right today, but he *will* need some help with a few things when they come home."

John remembered something and groaned. "Hey, you know, the Little League draft is Monday night. What if Matt isn't here?"

"That's kid stuff, and you'd better plan on taking care of that all by yourself," Sally said.

"But—"

"You can do it. You *have* to do it. When he calls you later today, to tell you that everything has turned out all right with Jane, and everything *will* be all right, *you* be sure to tell him not to worry about summer baseball because you're all over that one."

"Yeah, I can do that, prob'ly," John sighed.

"Yes, you can, and you will. And you'd better know that Matt will need his friend"—she pointed at John—"for things you never expected."

———

The surgery would take hours, Matt had been told, so he made a plan to head for a coffee shop instead of sitting in the hospital waiting area all day. He thought he remembered seeing a Caribou, or maybe it was a Starbucks, on Third Avenue, kitty-corner from the Gonda Building, so he decided to take a walk.

The coffee shop was busy with the usual morning rush, a mix of patients and nurses, and people dressed in business suits—probably administrative types from the clinic, Matt thought. The line waiting for service extended out the front door and onto the sidewalk, and Matt took his place at the end and shuffled slowly forward as those in front of him were served.

His mind was blank while he stood in line, but the smell of fresh coffee was nice. He noticed a pleasant breeze on his back, and then the green color of the scrubs that one of the clinic employees in the line in front of him was wearing, and the distracted looks on people's faces, and the smell of fresh coffee. When at last he was close to the front of the line, he had to smile as he watched a middle-aged woman stare at the menu behind the counter and then stumble through the complicated process of ordering a mocha. He could almost hear the anger and impatience in John Velde's voice. Maybe he should have asked John to come and be with him today? He was all alone, and feeling lost.

When he had his coffee, he sat down at a little table and said a prayer for Jane. He tried to look at the sports page of the Minneapolis *Star Tribune*, but it all seemed so trivial now. He looked through the text messages and emails on his phone but soon found that nothing could hold his attention or distract him from thoughts of Jane. Everything in their lives could be, probably would be, different from this moment on. Even if things went well in the next few hours, the surgery and then the chemotherapy and all that came afterward would certainly change Jane, and him, in ways that he couldn't imagine. If things didn't go well, or if there were surprises, there was a chance that she would die in the next few months. Matt lowered his head, and with his elbow resting on the little table by the window he rubbed his forehead and tried to think this through. If Jane's health did return, just what changes *would* there be in her life after this? He felt selfish for wondering, but would sex ever be the same again? Would Jane still have the same joy for life?

Matt watched out the window as an elderly man and woman walked slowly past. They were walking side by side, each of them seeming to be holding the other one up. Just as he had while he sat in the lobby in the Gonda Building for the past two days, he wondered which one of them was sick, and how *their* lives were about to change.

A young man, perhaps thirty-five, followed behind the older couple. He was pushing someone in a wheelchair. As the man drew near, Matt could see that the person sitting in the chair was just a girl, maybe twelve years old, almost certainly his daughter. The girl was thin, way too thin, and she wore a cotton sweatshirt, a hoodie that was pulled over her bald head to keep her warm. The story that those two were living was pretty plain to see, but the extent of their agony and the outcome would never be revealed to Matt; they were just two more people on their life's journey, passing by Matt on the street.

Other people's broken lives and dreams were walking by him out there, and when he finished this coffee he'd go out and join them. Then someone else would watch him walk by and wonder about his life, but never really know. He wished that Jane was here to talk with him; she was always the one who said the right things to him, the things that brought some order and comfort in the midst of chaos. Again, he regretted not asking John to come and be with him; this was going to be a long day. With his mind in neutral, Matt stared into the crowd passing by, a few feet away.

A nicely dressed woman turned from the milling crowd outside and swung the coffee shop door open. To Matt, she was just another traveler until he noticed her enter the coffee shop and draw in a deep breath to smell the aroma. She looked to her left, and when her gaze found Matt she froze.

It was Mo! She stared at him as if she couldn't believe her eyes. She came toward him and asked, "What are *you* doing here?"

Matt stood and opened his arms for a hug. An old friend had stumbled into this place and found him. His sense of relief that came with Mo's sudden appearance surprised him. The only other moments he could recall that felt similar were the times as a boy when he'd been lost or in trouble and one of his parents had come along to rescue him.

Mo stepped into his embrace and while he held his cheek next to hers he said, "Jane has cancer, she's in surgery now." When the words had been spoken he felt Mo's grip tighten.

"Oh, I'm sorry," she whispered, and she squeezed him a bit harder. She rocked from side to side for a second and then said, "So you're sitting here *alone?*"

Matt nodded.

"You look like you're lost in the woods. Why didn't you call me?" She stepped back and looked him in the eyes.

"Well, I didn't want to bother anyone and I thought I could—"

"So you *are* here alone? You have *no one* to be with you today?"

Matt shook his head. "I just thought . . ."

"Sit down," Mo said. "I'll be right back." She turned on her heels and walked to the back of the line at the coffee counter. She was texting someone, and then talking to someone on her phone while she edged closer to the front of the line. Once she'd gotten her coffee she walked to Matt's table and sat down. "So, tell me everything. What's going on?"

"You look like you're on the way to work. Don't you need to—" Matt began to ask.

"I just called in and took the day off."

"Aw, Mo, you didn't need to . . ."

"Hey, old friend, today, more than you know, you need somebody to be with you. So here I am. Besides, it'll give us time to talk and fill in some blanks."

Matt leaned back and shook his head, telling her once more that she didn't need to sacrifice an entire day for him.

"I'm not going anywhere," Mo said firmly.

This was about what he would have expected from the Mo he knew all those years ago. There was a reason he'd liked her so much back then: She had a good heart. He looked across the table and saw a friend looking back and waiting. What an odd twist of fate, Matt thought, to have sixty-year-old Mo Lawson walk in here at this moment. Or was it sixteen-year-old Mo Glasnapp? He couldn't say for sure who was with him now, but he sure was glad she was there.

Matt spent the next several minutes relating the events of the past couple of days: mammograms, biopsies, gut-wrenching visits with doctors, everything, right up to his tearful goodbye just before surgery.

"You said hormone-positive invasive stage two cancer, right?" she asked.

"Yeah, I'm pretty sure that's what the doctor told us."

"How big was it?"

"I think they said two centimeters."

"Well, if you have to have breast cancer, that's a good one to have, I guess. You know that stage two means the cancer has spread from its original location to other parts of the breast, but maybe not to the lymph nodes or other parts of the body. Any word yet on the lymph nodes?"

"No, she just went into surgery. I think that will take hours, but the nurse said she'd call me when they got that far. I guess if the lymph nodes are clear, then that makes the surgery a bit shorter. If they find cancer there, then that changes the treatment after surgery . . ." His words trailed off.

"It'll be fine," Mo said.

Matt nodded. "I think so too, but this thing has been a real dose of reality. You always think this stuff happens to others, not you." Then he sat up straighter and put the conversation on a different track. "OK, tell me something about *your* life. How did you meet your husband? Tell me about your kids."

They talked and laughed a bit, and asked questions about when their parents had passed away, how old their children were, and shared a few stories about the frustrations of parenting.

"Would you like a little more coffee?" Matt asked when their cups were empty.

"Sure. 'Bout half a cup."

When Matt returned with their refills he was smiling. "We have a nice, upscale coffee shop like this in Pine Rapids now," he said. "I go there with John Velde all the time."

Mo stared, said nothing, and quizzed him with a stern look.

"Yeah, he's still a dick most of the time, but he's my friend."

"He drove my dad crazy," Mo said.

"I know. I was there. We both know John has some demons. I know him better than anyone, and I still can't figure him out. But I was thinking of him because he seems to have a thing for the lady who owns the coffee shop."

"Lucky girl," Mo deadpanned.

Matt arched his back and grimaced. "Hey, can we go for a little walk? My hip is sore from sitting so long."

"Sure."

Matt stood straight and stretched for a moment, and when they left the coffee shop a warm spring breeze rushed by them. "Ah, that feels good," he said.

"Hey," Mo said, "you know they have a TV monitor in the family waiting room at the hospital so you can follow along and see where she's at with her surgery, right? Let's walk over there and see. It's only a couple blocks."

As they walked along the sidewalk, Mo pointed to the building where she worked, and small talk came easily for them. When they arrived at the family waiting room where Matt had started the morning, the TV screen said that Jane had only been in surgery for twenty minutes.

"Wow, there must have been a problem with one of the surgeries before hers. They're way behind schedule," Matt guessed.

"Yeah, that happens," Mo said. "What would you like to do now?"

"I don't want to just sit here and stare at that monitor." Matt lowered his voice and spoke softly into Mo's ear. "And I'd love to talk to you with a bit more privacy than this . . ." He looked around the family lounge, which was packed with silent and anxious strangers, all of them waiting for news from surgery. "And I haven't eaten for a couple days. Can we go someplace for lunch? My treat?"

"Sure," Mo said. "Ever heard of a bar called Nate's?"

"Yeah, the lady who plays the piano in the lobby told us to go there too."

"It's a great spot. My husband and I go there all the time. Let's get going so we can beat the noon rush." When they stepped onto the street once again, Matt could feel a change in his heart. Things didn't seem quite so bleak and scary as they had a couple of hours earlier. He wondered if maybe things had shifted because it was such a bright spring day. But then as Mo was talking about her husband's job, Matt stole a glance at her and realized that Mo had come to his rescue, and he let himself be thankful for her appearance at precisely the right moment.

The bartender at Nate's called out, "Hi, Mo!" when they walked through the door. "Go ahead and take that table in the corner."

"So, you're a regular here?" Matt asked.

"I told you, we come here all the time," Mo said, as she led Matt to a table.

When they were seated and the waitress had taken their orders, Mo leaned close to Matt and said, "I have to ask you something. Will you tell me how you met Jane? The word in Sverdrup all those years ago was that you brought a different girl home from college every few weeks, and then all of a sudden you were married."

Matt laughed. "That's about right. Well actually, when I started dental school I was still dating . . ." Suddenly Matt didn't want to finish his sentence. ". . . several others."

"Oh?"

"Yeah, well, I had a girlfriend, but a classmate from dental school called me, said he had a date for some sorority party and he needed to find a date for his date's roommate. You still with me?"

"Yes."

"Well, *his* date was Jane," Matt explained, "and all through the evening I never stopped talking and laughing with her, and by the end of that first meeting I was smitten. I told my buddy I'd take *his* date, but not the other girl. So I waited a couple weeks and asked her out. Jane was special, I knew right away."

"What happened to the other girl; the one you were dating?"

"I don't know. I never called her again after that first night with Jane."

"Hmm . . . you just stopped calling your girlfriend." Mo drew out the sentence out as if it were an accusation. "You did a lot of that in those days," she teased.

"Mo, I know, and I'm . . ." Matt stammered.

"It was a long time ago, forget it. We both moved on. It just wasn't meant to be." Mo was laughing while she spoke, but she'd embarrassed Matt with an old memory.

"Yeah, but, I always meant to . . ." Matt stumbled some more.

"I said that's the end of it. I just had to get *one* shot in there." Mo smiled, and then went on. "So you got married and lived happily ever after?"

Matt's face still registered some discomfort, and Mo sensed that it had to do with their past. She reached across the little table and took his hand in hers. She needed to make a connection, perhaps to apologize for the shot she'd just taken, perhaps to forgive him, or maybe just to touch him again.

"Your dad called me one night just after you went away to college," Mo said. "He asked me to come out to your farm and see him after school one day."

"Really?"

"Yeah, we talked about you, and he told me he knew how much you cared for me, and he told me something else."

"What?"

"He made me promise not to tell you that!" Mo shrugged and grinned. "Sorry."

"So, you're not gonna tell me?"

"Nope, sorry." She shook her head. "Your dad was a nice guy. I knew he always liked me, and—"

"Tell me!" Matt begged.

"No." Mo shook her head and teased. "I made a promise." She changed the subject. "So how are *you* holding up?"

"OK, I guess," he said, as he played with his fork.

"You're wanting to tell me something, aren't you?"

"Have you ever read Dante's *Inferno*?" Matt asked.

"Ah, well, no. I've heard others refer to it for my whole life, but I never read it. It's a classic, and you know what Mark Twain said about classics: They're books that everyone talks about, but no one's ever read." She was puzzled by his question about Dante's *Inferno*. "Why would you ask about that?"

"Do you know what a contrapasso is?" Matt asked.

"No."

"Well, it comes from Dante, and his trip through Hell. The idea of a contrapasso is that sinners should be punished in a way that mirrors their sin."

"And your point?"

"I wonder if Jane's cancer is my contrapasso."

"Really?" Mo grimaced. "What sin did you commit that would make God punish you by giving Jane cancer?"

"I hurt someone." Matt saw Linda Pike's face and remembered what he'd done.

"Who?"

"A girl."

"And that would be the girl you were dating when you met Jane?"

"Someone else, too. I treated her poorly," Matt said. "There were a couple others, too."

"Couples break up, Matt. It happens all the time."

"Yeah, I know that, but . . . I hurt people."

"Wow. That's the Matt Kingston I remember. You *think* too much. Life isn't like that. And even though people seem to read *Inferno* as though it's another chapter from the Bible, it's just a novel. Dante made that stuff up. It didn't come from God. God doesn't punish one person for someone else's sins. Next, I suppose you'll be telling me that Scotch Lake symbolizes the River Acheron, which must be crossed on the way to Hell."

"You said you'd never read *Inferno*."

"I lied. I just wanted to see where you were going with it." Mo smiled. "But you just can't think like that, Matt."

"I can't help it," Matt said. The anguish was back in his eyes.

Mo squeezed his hands in hers and said, "I'd say you met the girl of your dreams and lived happily ever after."

"Hmph," Matt scoffed. "All I ever wanted, from the moment we met, was to be with her. And I guess the greatest thing I'll ever do in this life is to be the boy who Jane Monahan chose." He nodded. "And we *have* had a great life. Nothing but good times, until now."

Matt squeezed Mo's hands and said, "OK, now tell me about *your* life, and how you met your husband."

Mo thought for long moment, and she took her hands away from his and leaned back in her chair. Then her smile returned and she said, "Life has been pretty good to us, too. I met John at a beer party in college and he called me the next day. We dated for two years and got married. Happily ever after for us, too." Mo considered something for a moment before she added, "It took me a while to get over . . ."

Matt knew what she was about to say. He felt good to think that his girlfriend, the prettiest girl from his long ago, still had some feelings. "Me too," he said.

Both of them felt a clumsy silence and decided not to go where the conversation was taking them. Thankfully, their waitress brought their burgers and they let all thoughts of their high school romance drift away as they slid dishes around to make room for their lunch. Matt's mood turned a bit brighter when he squeezed a large puddle of ketchup onto the plate, next to his burger. He asked, "What do you hear from your brothers?"

Mo talked about Donny's life, and job, and family for a while, then David's. She mentioned several other long-forgotten friends from their school days, and then told him that Pigeon Tits, their basketball coach, had died a week earlier.

Matt smiled and said, "I'm sorry, but I can't help it."

"Shame on you," Mo teased, but she was smiling, too. "He was a nice man."

"I know, I liked him too, but every time I hear that name, Pigeon Tits, I think of Velde, and your brother Donny, and the day Pigeon Tits took his shirt off at basketball practice. You shoulda seen it. When he ran down the court, everything was moving in a different direction. Then Velde hollered, 'Throw it to Pigeon Tits!' And the name stuck forever."

Matt's phone buzzed, and he was still grinning at the memory of that high school basketball practice when he glanced at the incoming number. He knew it was the surgical nurse, calling with a status report, and his countenance changed completely. "Hello," he answered with his left hand. His brow tightened as he listened closely. Then he put his right hand over his mouth, in order to block out all the background noise from the bar. "Uh-huh . . . uh-huh . . . OK . . . thank you." He said. He turned the phone off, placed it on the table next to his plate, and stared at the table top for a second. Fracture lines began to form around his eyes and they spread, slowly at first, then with great speed. His lips began to quiver and he began to weep. He lowered his face and covered it with both hands. He wept as quietly as he could while Mo watched.

The last time she'd sat at a table with Matt Kingston she was sixteen years old, he was eighteen, and she'd had a serious crush on him. He had thick brown hair and shoulders, and his eyes were bright. He was lean and tan, from working in the sun, and his world was full of promise. He was *her* hero then.

At first, when he began to weep, she looked at him with no idea what to do or say. His head was bowed and his elbows rested on the little table, inches from her. His hair was turning gray now. The skin on his face was weathered, and his hands were wrinkled and scarred from a lifetime of work. Each of the little white scars on his hands had a story, and she knew none of them. It had been forty years since they'd had a moment together, and now they were sharing *this*. She was helping this old boyfriend deal with this dreadful thing that had happened. A few months ago, this man lived only in her most distant memories. But after all these years, and the changes that life had brought, she could still see that eighteen-year-old boy again.

Mo scooted her chair over, next to his, and put her arm around him. She huddled close and rested her head against his while she stroked the back of his head and said softly, "I'm so sorry, Matt." She whispered in his ear. Do you want to tell me what the nurse said?"

He looked at Mo, drew in a breath, and tried to speak once, but he failed; words would not come. After several more tries he croaked, "Lymph nodes are all clear, no cancer," and then he wiped his eyes.

"So, it's *good* news?" Mo said, her voice rising in surprise, and relief. She hugged him and held him close for a second.

Matt nodded and sobbed again, overwhelmed with relief. There was a chance now, a good chance, that Jane's cancer had not spread and that she would make a full recovery. He put his face down and tried not to let the people sitting nearby see him crying. Mo rocked gently with her face close to his, and whispered, "See, it's gonna be OK, Matt. No contrapasso, just a long, happy life. I *knew* it was going to be all right."

Eventually Matt sat straight, blew his nose, and wiped his eyes dry. Mo slid her chair back to where she'd been sitting earlier and smiled at him.

"I'm sorry I cried like that, Mo. But I was so afraid. And when that nurse said . . ." He wiped his eyes again. ". . . it was like a piano had been lifted off my back. But you thought it was bad news, didn't you?"

Mo nodded.

"I'm sorry, sorry I did that to you."

"I understand," she said. "What a load off your shoulders. Now you can push some of the fear and confusion away and go on with the rest of your lives."

The waitress brought coffee for each of them as they both wondered how to move away from the past couple of minutes.

"Nice lunch, huh?" Matt sighed and let her hear the sarcasm.

"Never had one quite like it," Mo agreed. "So, do you get to take her home in a couple days?"

"The day after tomorrow. At least, that's what they hinted at, before today's surgery." He swirled a French fry around in ketchup, then added, "We'll get through this. Things will get back to normal."

"Sure they will." Mo wasn't so sure if Matt was certain about getting back to normal, or if he really understood all that had happened to Jane.

Both of them looked at their unfinished hamburgers for a second, uncertain about what to do or say next. "Lunch is getting cold," Matt said, and then he ate the French fry he'd been holding.

"How's your burger?" Mo asked, as she reached to have another bite of hers.

"Good, really good." They ate for a bit while their conversation died out like an old campfire. "I'm glad you wandered into that coffee shop today, Mo. And I'm glad you stayed with me. I needed a friend, so thank you." Matt said this with both elbows resting on the table and a half-eaten hamburger in his hand.

"Me too." Mo dabbed the corner of her mouth with a napkin and then asked, "Do you remember the first time *we* met? You and me?"

He thought for second and said, "No, you were just always there."

"Me neither, or should I say, me too?" Mo said. "Isn't that strange?"

"But I remember you and your family always rolling into church, late, so you had to sit in the front row."

Mo laughed. "That used to make my dad crazy. And I remember you and your parents sitting there in the same pew over on the other side of the aisle every Sunday."

"That place, over by where the organist sat, that was chosen for us, by God. He wanted us right there, and we got there early every Sunday, just to be sure we were pleasing God." Matt was relaxing now; Mo's presence had lifted the burden of Jane's cancer, just a bit, and he wanted to enjoy this time with a special friend before he went back to the hospital to wait for Jane's return from surgery. He pointed a French fry at Mo and said, "But I do remember the first time I *noticed* you." He flashed a warm grin.

"Me too," she said, as she allowed the joy of a happy memory to show in her eyes, too.

"It was *cold* that night, after the basketball game."

"I was thankful for a ride home."

"Zat why you sat so close to me?"

"Yeah, I just wanted to be warm," Mo said. As a smile brightened her entire face, she gave up the silly lie and told him what he already knew: "I had such a crush on you."

"We just drove around for a while and talked. But I got the message. After that, I guess everything changed."

When their eyes met, both of them knew that enough had been said. It was indeed a pleasant memory; each of them knew that the other one felt it, too. But this wasn't the time to speak of it. Maybe that time would never come. Matt wanted to explain something else, too, but after so many years, it probably needed no explanation. And Mo wanted to share something that she'd never told anyone. Some things, unspoken things, had passed between them, however, during the past several hours. An incidental touch, or a smile, or the long-forgotten but now familiar turn of a phrase, had told each of them all they really wanted to know: An old friend, a best friend, was still there.

"I'd better get back to the hospital so I can be there in Jane's room, waiting for her, when she gets there," Matt said.

They left the restaurant and walked together for a block. When they reached a street corner Mo said, "This is where I leave you."

"Yeah, probably not such a good day for you to come up and say hello to Jane?" Matt said.

"I'm pretty sure she's not gonna be up for visitors. Some other time, maybe?"

Matt reached out and held her, then said, "Thanks, Mo. Thanks for spending this day with me. And . . . I . . . you're . . ." he stammered.

"I feel the same way," Mo teased. "Now go take care of your wife. I'll greet her another day," and she waved and walked away.

Mo hadn't really changed much; she was still his friend. As he crossed the street he thought of the way she'd slid her chair close to him at lunch and tried to comfort him. He hadn't seen her in forty years and she did *that*. "Hmph," he said to himself.

Matt had been waiting in Jane's room for two hours when a couple of nurses brought her up from the recovery room and rolled her in on a hospital bed. Jane was unconscious when the nurses transferred her onto the bed in her room.

"She's having a hard time waking up," one of the nurses said. "She was under general anesthesia for a long time. The surgery took much longer than the doctor expected, and she's really groggy."

Jane's eyes were closed and her mouth hung open, and she looked so pale and bad that Matt actually wondered if she was alive. His eyes fixed on her gaunt face and followed her as the nurses rolled her bed into place. Her ghastly image seared its way into his memory. His Jane, his beautiful lover, looked like a ninety-year-old cadaver. Matt covered his mouth and stared. Jane looked like she was gone.

Matt moved close to her bed and bent over so that his face was close to hers. He kissed her cheek, and then kissed it again when she failed to respond. "I love you, honey," Matt said, with his lips almost touching her ear. Her eyes flickered and threatened to open when Matt repeated, "I love you, honey. Did they tell there was no cancer in your lymph nodes? That they got it all?"

Jane blinked her eyes and gave a weak nod. "Thirsty," she croaked. It looked like her eyelids were made of lead, and she made no further attempt to open them. Matt found a cup filled with ice water and a straw, and when he touched the straw to her lips she was able to draw a swallow into her mouth.

"Do you want to sleep for a while longer?" he asked, after she'd had a tiny drink.

Jane blinked and nodded once again, then seemed to drift away. Matt sat next to her bed and studied her while she slept. She was still connected to several IV lines. Her mouth hung open again, and she looked pretty rough. He wanted to reach through the rails on the side of her bed and hold her hand, but he decided that might keep her from sleeping.

The sight of his wife, lying there in such terrible shape, created one more unpleasant visual image that would not fade away anytime soon. He had a vague idea of the physical pain she would feel in a couple of hours when the lights came back on for her. He couldn't imagine what she must have been thinking about while she'd been waiting, alone, before her surgery.

He felt ashamed that he'd whined about a hip replacement only a short time ago. Compared to this, a hip replacement was about like getting a new pair of glasses. He'd complained and fretted about the implications of getting old, while Jane had faced this, a potential death sentence, with so much courage. Just around the corner were issues like chemotherapy and radiation, or both. And from that day on she would wonder, for the rest of her life, if there was still a killer hiding somewhere else in her body.

He felt bad, guilty, to be thinking about the loss or disfiguration of her beautiful breasts. He knew how she looked at herself. She liked the way she looked. She liked him to notice the way she dressed, and the way she teased him, and more than that, the way he touched her. How would all that change? This disease, this surgery, would somehow result in the end of innocence, for both of them. The end of innocence . . . Matt thought that had happened more than a generation ago, but apparently there was still plenty to lose.

CHAPTER TWENTY-TWO

———•———

"How was the ride home? How is Jane doing?" John said. He was emptying a canvas bag full of short aluminum baseball bats in front of a plain wooden bench along the first base line of a small baseball diamond at the Pine Rapids Elementary School. The occasional sweep of summer breeze carried a scent of fresh-cut grass.

"OK, I guess," Matt said. "She's in a fair amount of pain, and she walks real slow and hunched over, like she doesn't want to jar anything loose."

"Do you think I can come out and see her in a couple days?" John asked.

Matt emptied another canvas bag, this one filled with plastic batting helmets and catcher's gear, beside all the bats. "Yeah, in a couple days. She's been pretty quiet so far, having a hard time with her feelings. It's hard for me to watch her be like this."

"Well, I can understand that, I think," John said.

It was Tuesday evening, and the first baseball practice of the summer was about to begin. There would only be two practices, then the games would commence. Matt and John had come to the baseball field a little early to get things ready. The evening was warm, and the sun was still high in the sky.

John used a truck key to cut open a cardboard box, then he looked inside. The box had been given to him on the night of the player draft. The woman who'd given it to him had explained that inside the box were fourteen new jerseys for the team, and sixteen new hats; the coaches were expected to wear hats that matched their players'.

"Jesus, look at this," John moaned when he opened the box. "We're *Orange*. I mean, that's our team name: Orange, for Chrissakes. Wouldn't you think they could choose names like Twins or Yankees or Red Sox? Real baseball teams? Who in the shit wants to be on the *Orange*?"

"I think we're supposed to cut back on the swearing," Matt said, while he arranged and inspected the team's modest assortment of gear.

John ignored him. "Yeah, right. Fuckin' *Orange.*" John muttered while he looked through the team jerseys.

"Here comes our first player," Matt said, when he noticed Timmy Clements walking across the outfield grass in their direction. Sally was right behind him, but Timmy was in a hurry to see who was on his team and what their uniforms looked like.

"Hey Timmy, c'mere and get your hat and shirt. What number would you like to be?" John asked, as he tossed him a too-big orange ball cap.

"Thanks," Timmy said, then he stood there struggling with anticipation while John rummaged through the box of orange jerseys.

"Here's number seven," John said, and he handed the boy a clean, new jersey. "Every kid wants to wear Mickey Mantle's number, right?"

"Who's Murphy Mantle?" Timmy asked, as he pulled the orange jersey with a white number 7 over his head.

John sighed. "We have some work to do on the lore and legend of the game."

Timmy bent the brim on his new orange hat until it was just right. Then he pounded his fist into his glove. He was waiting for John to give his approval.

"You look handsomer than shit!" John said.

It was all Timmy needed to hear, and he turned and raced toward Sally. "Wanna play catch, Gramma?"

"Now there's a sentence you don't hear much in the big leagues," John said. He looked out across at the three other primitive little baseball diamonds. Cars were slowing down and parking along the road by the complex, and kids were getting out. Someone was passing out red, and blue, and green caps and jerseys at the other diamonds, and parents and children were milling about looking for their team. "S'pose everybody will show up tonight?" John asked, as he watched for the players he'd drafted the previous week.

"They should be rolling in here any minute," Matt said. "Can't wait to see the team you put together."

Twenty minutes later Matt and John had rounded up the Orange players and assembled them at home plate. They passed out the shirts and hats and gave a printed schedule to each of them. Then, while the parents lounged on the grass behind the bench and visited among themselves, they took the players to the outfield and told them to pair up with a teammate and start playing catch. That was when the coaches first began to understand the extreme limitations of the team John had drafted.

Matt decided to bend the brim of his own hat and watch John supervise the first few minutes of practice before he took over.

Timmy had paired up with a kid named David, and the two of them could actually catch and throw without much supervision. The rest of the team was a gong show. No one knew where to stand, or how to throw or catch a ball.

"OK, OK," John said, waving his arms, "stop throwing, or whatever it is you're doing, and gather around me." Then, while the entire team watched, John took one particularly unathletic little boy by the arm and pointed him toward a girl about thirty feet away. "OK, we play catch with our teammates before games and before practice in order to develop our catching and throwing skills. You throw the ball to her. She catches it, and then she throws it back to you. Got it?" The kid stared blankly, and John went on. "Let's give it a try. What's your name, kid?"

"Mike Katzenmeyer."

"Mike, you throw the ball to . . . what's your name, little girl?"

"Brexley Babich," the girl said cheerfully.

"OK, Mike, you throw the ball to Brexley." John stepped back, and Mike stepped forward with his right foot and threw the ball about twelve feet with his right hand. It only had enough momentum to roll a few inches, and Mike's throwing motion looked as though he was trying to push a lead ball through a mud puddle.

"Jesus Christ, Mike, do you have a bad back? Were you in a car accident?" John gasped.

Matt bolted over to the group of orange shirts and hats before John could say another word. "John, why don't you take Timmy and his partner and work with them for a few minutes? I'll take the others to begin with," Matt suggested, and he pushed John in the direction of Timmy Clements and his new friend David.

A few minutes later, fourteen ball players were sort of playing catch in the outfield. Timmy and his partner were the only pair who actually caught the ball and successfully returned it to their partner. Matt had been forced to separate the ball players farther apart than he wanted, strictly for their own safety. Playing catch was proving to be dangerous. Several of the boys could throw the ball hard, and far, but no one had any idea where it might go or who might take an errant throw in the noggin. All of the girls, and Mike Katzenmeyer, made throwing a baseball look like the most complicated athletic skill imaginable. With each throw they twisted their upper bodies into knots just before their knees buckled and they collapsed.

Most of the players had at least some idea how to track a baseball in flight and then attempt to catch it. Sort of. They did wear their baseball glove on one hand, then extend the gloved hand as close to the moving baseball as they dared. But then, at the last second, when the ball was about to glance off their glove, they either flinched and made a stabbing, twisting motion with the glove, or they jerked their gloved hand out of the ball's flight path to avoid a collision. One boy, and one girl, decided it was safer to just stick their gloved hand out into the cosmos, and then cover their eyes with other hand. No one, except David and Timmy, caught a thrown ball that evening. But then, most of the throws were so wild or so weak that no one could have caught them.

Matt glanced at John several times and saw him standing, stunned and staring, open-mouthed, at the lack of baseball talent he'd assembled.

Batting was worse. Way worse. Matt pitched twenty or so pitches to each member of his team, and he soon noticed that most of the players were even *more* afraid of the ball when they were being pitched to. Matt lofted the ball underhand and tried to let it float by in the perfect place for each player to hit it, but only a few of them could make contact. One little girl would only swing the bat until it stopped directly above home plate, where she'd hold it, hoping for a collision with the ball. One of the boys could actually hit the ball hard, but with the completion of every swing, he threw the bat so that everyone near the chain-link backstop was in danger. Timmy and David put the ball in play with every pitch, but neither of them could hit it out of the infield.

By the time practice was over, Matt thought he knew everyone's name, and he felt that was quite an accomplishment, given the names on the roster. He was standing at home plate, putting the bats and balls back into the canvas bags as the Orange team, and their parents, wandered away from the little diamond toward their cars. John was slumped over on the bench, putting batting helmets back into a canvas bag, and Sally was playing catch with Timmy.

"Bye, Timmy," hollered David, the kid he'd been playing with all during practice.

"Bye, David," Timmy hollered back.

David was walking away all by himself and Sally asked Timmy, "Where are his parents?"

"He just lives over there, in the yellow house," Timmy said, as he pointed out across the baseball complex at a row of newer homes.

Matt looked up to see David trudging home in the lengthening shadows of the outfield, and a couple of the others walking in different directions.

Sally and Timmy were sitting beside John on the team bench when Matt walked over to join them. Two little girls, Heather and Whitney Compton, were waiting patiently, just behind the team bench, for their father to pick them up and take them home. Identical twins, the Compton girls both had blonde hair and blue eyes and they were adorable. While they waited, they smiled at Timmy, but never spoke.

"This could be an interesting summer," Sally said. She'd witnessed the fiasco that was their first practice, and she could see that the cupboards were pretty bare, talent-wise.

"Ah, we'll be just fine," John said, as if he actually believed it. Matt and Sally, however, knew the truth was that John really didn't care how bad the team was.

"Well, I think we'll have some fun, anyway," Sally said. She looked at Timmy, who was slamming his fist into the pocket of his new baseball glove, and then she turned to Matt and added, "Thank you. Thank you for coaching these kids." Then she looked at John. "And *you* . . ." She put her arm around John's shoulder and chided him. "You behave yourself around my grandson, and those gorgeous little girls. No bad language! Don't make me kick your ass outta *here*, too." She spoke softly enough so Whitney and Heather couldn't hear. Then she said to Timmy, "OK, let's go home."

Before Sally could stand up to leave, the Compton girls' father pulled up by the curb and the girls both said in unison, "Goodbye, Mr. Velde," before they sprinted to their father's car.

"Goodbye, girls," John said.

Matt looked at John, under the bill of his cap. "Who was the last person to address you as Mr. Velde?"

Before John could reply, Sally blurted, "Probably a police officer, or a judge." Then she set off after Timmy over the outfield grass. She turned back and waved. "See you boys Thursday."

Both coaches waved, and John shouted, "You did good, number seven!"

The outfield grass was all shadows when the last car drove away from the street by the baseball complex. But Matt and John still sat together on a bench made for children.

"Nice draft," Matt said, suggesting that an explanation was in order.

"We're OK," John replied.

"Are you kidding? We suck. We're terrible. And we're . . . *Orange.*" Matt grimaced.

"Yeah, well, I didn't have any control over that," John said.

"Oh, I guess you were so busy evaluating talent."

"Well, that wasn't entirely my fault either," John said.

"Oh? How's that?"

"Well, you know that coaches have to draft their own kids first, so we drafted Timmy on our first round. You with me?"

Matt scraped his shoe on the dirt in front of him. "Continue."

"OK, so every other guy who's coaching one of those other teams is the father of a kid who can *play*, and then they've all asked the fathers of several other kids, who can play, to be their assistant coaches."

"Yeah, I know how that works," Matt said.

"One of those pricks had three assistant coaches, and every one of those assistants had a boy who is a good player, and, aw shit, you know."

"Yup."

"So by the time I had a chance to pick, there were no players left."

"So, you picked Mike?" Matt said, questioning John's sanity, "Michelangelo Katzenmeyer?"

"Well, I had to do *that*. That was a no-brainer; did you see his *mother*? She is *nasty*; I mean *smokin'* hot. And she showed up at the draft with bare feet, and a pit bull on a leash!"

Matt blinked and tried to shake some cobwebs in his head loose. "First of all, did you really just say that? Did you really just tell me that you drafted the worst player in the world because his mother showed up with a pit bull on a leash?"

The implications of a smokin' hot single mother with a pit bull on a leash seemed self-evident to John, and he made no attempt explain them. "No shit! Her name is DeeDee. She has these really narrow hips, and wide shoulders, and she's long and lean, and her blue jeans were just about perfect, and she had lotsa eye makeup on, and blonde hair with dark roots, you know, sort of a 1980s mullet, and she had bare feet! Need I explain any further? The deal was *done*; I had to take Mike!" John shrugged.

"And the *others*?" Matt asked. He needed no further description of DeeDee Katzenmeyer.

"Well, the talent pool was pretty shallow for the rest of the draft. Did you happen to look over at the other teams tonight? Everybody has about seven right fielders, for Chrissakes."

"OK, I'll give you that. But where did David come from? You know, the kid who looks to be Timmy's new best friend? He might be a ballplayer."

"I dunno. He wasn't at the tryout night. I didn't even know he was on our team until tonight. I think he just moved here and the secretary at the city office stuck him on our team because . . . I s'pose she figured he was a little spaz, so he belonged on the Orange team."

"Well, I'm glad to have him. This summer could be brutal," Matt said.

"Yeah, we're not gonna win many games. But I think I have a plan," John said.

"Love to hear it."

"OK, here it is. Remember when we were kids and we never had enough players in those sandlot games, so we used a pile of scrap wood, or a wheelbarrow, or something like that to be the catcher; so all the foul balls and missed pitches didn't roll clear down to the river?"

"Sure."

"Well, we don't have a pile of scrap lumber, but we wound up with Doc Hested's grandson, the lard-ass, on our team? You know him, right?"

"Yes."

"Shit. The little toad, what's his name? He goes about a deuce and half and he's nine years old. Looks like he lives on Ding Dongs and Twinkies."

"He does," Matt said. "And his name is Bradley."

"Whatever," John continued. "He's our catcher. He won't stop as many pitches as a pile of lumber, but he can pick up loose balls and throw them back. He'll have thirteen teammates standing there facing him, so the little shit stain will almost certainly throw it back to *one* of them." John paused and considered the rest of team Orange. "Now, we only have two kids who can catch and throw, that would be Timmy and the new kid, David, so one of them will have to play first base, the other will be shortstop. Most balls will be hit to the shortstop, so we'll put our swingin' dick there, just like in real baseball. But after that, every other ball hit *anywhere* will be an adventure, not gonna lie to ya. Nobody, except Timmy or David, will catch a fly ball or scoop up a grounder all summer. Guaranteed! We'll just teach everybody to chase the ball, like a puppy chasing a toy, and then run it back in to the pitcher. I don't want any needless throwing; that will only lead to injuries and errant throws and baseballs rolling around. And with that in mind we have one real advantage: Those Compton girls can *run*! And I mean *run*! We'll put one in left center and one in right center and tell them to run, and I mean *show off* how fast they can run, to chase down balls in the outfield, and then run 'em back in; no throwing."

"You don't think we should begin to teach these kids about the rules of the game, proper throwing and batting mechanics, and outfield play and throwing to the cutoff man . . . stuff like that?" Matt asked.

"Hell no!" John groaned and then made a face like he was staring at a bright light. "Why don't you just get a hammer and pound on your head for a while? A couple of the girls didn't know where first base was! These little peckers all have vinyl baseball gloves that they just bought at Walmart on Monday. This isn't baseball. The only time these kids ever see their baseball gloves is Tuesday and Thursday night. Their dogs will be playing with 'em the rest of the week. And Mike, he's got a special technique; he uses his glove like a garbage-can lid." John mimicked the way Mike smashed his right hand down on the ball in order to make it stop rolling, then peeked underneath to see if he had anything trapped. "Baseball, real baseball, will happen to kids like Timmy and David, but not for a couple years, and by then almost all of these other kids will have moved on to other things. Hell, by the time they're sixteen they'll have families of their own."

Matt smiled and nodded at the undeniable truth in John's words.

"I think we concentrate on what kind of treats we're gonna bring for after the games," John added, "and the fact that I did draft at least *one* nasty-hot single mother."

"She's younger than your truck," Matt said.

"Yup, but I bet she'll give me a rougher ride."

"Hey, whatever happened to the little pitter-pat in your heart for Sally? I thought you and she were . . ."

"I asked her out a couple times," John said. "And I always got some lame excuse why she couldn't go. I think she has a boyfriend somewhere. So, I gave up. Her loss." John shrugged.

John Velde made life fun, that much was certain. "All right," Matt said. "On Thursday, we won't have to spend so much time passing out gear and talking to parents. We can do a little bit of coaching and maybe get to know the kids a little bit better. For now, let's go home."

But instead of walking to his truck, Matt sat down on the little bench and looked out at the deep green of the outfield grass and the way the spires of tall balsams in the east caught the last rays of golden sun. The afternoon warmth was fading into the cool of an early summer night. He slid his own baseball glove onto his left hand and slammed his right fist into the pocket a couple of times. He'd been taking care of Jane all day, and this was the first bit of time he'd set aside for himself.

"Remember how it used to be, John, on nights like this?" Matt sighed. "Spring winds were blowing. Maybe it was a Friday night? The grass was so green, and starting to get wet with dew? Man, we had no worries. Baseball practice was over for the day, and all we had to do was pick up our girls and drive around? Maybe steal a kiss?"

"A *kiss*?" John said this with a pinched face. "I always had a flesh feast in mind, and—"

"Once again," Matt interrupted, "you may have missed the point." He studied the tattered old baseball glove on his hand. Then he spread the fingers on his left hand and peered into the pocket of his "gamer" as if he might find something he'd lost. He brought the glove to his face, smelled the leather, and breathed his childhood into his lungs.

"You OK?" John asked. He'd noticed the melancholy in his friend, and he sat down beside Matt on the bench. "Or should I ask if Jane is OK?"

"I'm good," Matt said with little conviction. "And I think Jane is good. The cancer is gone; at least that's what everyone thinks. And the doctors said everything looks so good that there may be no need for radiation or chemo."

"That's great, right?"

"Yeah, it is, but when someone tells you that you have cancer, and then cuts away . . ." Matt stopped himself and shook his head. He stared into his glove. "She cries a lot." As he'd done a million times before, he refocused. Then he slugged his fist into the pocket of his baseball glove. "She'll be fine." Matt pounded his fist into his glove again. "I'll be fine too."

Somewhere, far off in the distance, they could hear the buzz of a chain saw, and a barking dog. The cool evening air held the familiar sounds of summer, and allowed the sounds to linger.

"You wanna catch a few?" John said. Then he tossed a scuffed-up, grass-stained baseball in the air toward Matt. "Just you and me, like we used to do?" He was offering his oldest friend something more than a catch.

"Yeah, sure." Matt nodded after he caught the ball. "I gotta get home and take care of my Jane . . . but yeah, sure." Both men stood up and John slid his glove onto his left hand also. As they backed away from each other they flipped the ball softly back and forth. Soon they were ninety feet apart, gingerly trying to recapture long-lost throwing motions, and throwing the ball a bit harder with each turn. They groaned, and rolled their throwing arms in big, slow circles, and stretched their arms between each throw.

For a moment, the simple joy of throwing a ball into the ether, and then having it return, was enough for Matt. The wonderful possibilities of his youth began to come back too, each time the ball returned to him. The quick "pop" of a baseball making a sudden stop in the well-worn pockets of their gloves joined the lingering noises of the chain saw and the barking dog in the evening air.

"OK," Matt said, "here comes the knuckler."

"Still sucks," John said, after it popped into his glove. "Here comes mine."

CHAPTER TWENTY-THREE

The day was fading fast in the twilight, and cool air from the deep woods carried the scent of pine pollen. Matt dropped an armload of firewood by the circle of charred stones in his backyard. The fire pit overlooked Scotch Lake and it had been there when they'd bought the place. Matt had spent countless hours sitting on the rough-hewn log benches that surrounded it. He'd told stories, sung a few songs, drunk too much, burned a few marshmallows, laughed a lot, and shed more than a few tears around that fire pit. It had taken on the feeling of sacred ground, and he hoped to find some comfort there that evening.

He balled up a few pieces of newspaper, then stacked some pine kindling over the paper and a few small pieces of poplar over the kindling, in the shape of a teepee. He put a match to the newspaper and let a little breeze fan the flame. A minute later the snap of burning pine and a narrow plume of wood smoke told him it was all right to add a few larger pieces of firewood. There would be a campfire tonight. There *needed* to be a campfire tonight. He hadn't warmed his hands by a campfire in a long time.

Baseball practice, and a few minutes with John, had been fun, had restored his confidence that life might return to normal. Whatever *that* was.

He sat down on one of the log benches to watch the fire grow. He stared into the tiny flames and let his elbows rest on his knees. Later, in the full darkness of night, he'd come back out and stir the coals with a stick. Maybe Jane would feel good enough to join him—she always liked that just as much as he did. Maybe if she could sit by a fire and tell a few stories she'd start to heal on the inside, too. And maybe if he stared into the coals of a campfire, he'd understand all of this a bit better.

This was Jane's third day home from her surgery. Any sudden movement of her arms seemed to hurt her, but she was slowly regaining some strength. She'd been spending most of her time in the recliner in the great room. She slept there at night because it hurt her chest to lie flat on her back in bed, and it was even more painful, actually impossible, for her to sit up from a prone position and then get out of bed. Matt had slept on the couch beside her recliner so he could help her get up for a drink or to use the bathroom. Except for this one evening at baseball practice he'd spent every minute with Jane. She hardly spoke to him, but Matt could see that she was doing her best to process all that had happened. He made it clear that he was willing to talk when she wanted to, but he made no effort to crowd her mind with small talk.

As part of his nursing duties, Matt had been busy making meals, assisting Jane with her medications, helping with sponge baths, and helping her empty the drains that were still inserted into the surgical incisions on her chest. Twice a day they'd go into the bathroom together and Matt would carefully expose the clear plastic tubes and the bulbs connected to them, which contained blood draining from her wounds. One tube exited each side of her chest, and the little bulbs were suspended by shoestrings pinned to the collar of her shirt. The bulbs were about the size of golf balls and they were usually filled with a fluid that resembled cranberry juice.

Tonight would be a special night in the healing process: Jane would take her first shower. She'd be able to remove the corset-like bandage that been applied to her chest in the hospital, and then replace it with a clean one. They'd been warned to be careful with this because it might be painful. In the end, Matt was hopeful that after a shower she'd feel good enough to come outside and take in some fresh air under the stars. Maybe he could tell her about the team John had put together? Maybe she'd smile as he told her about the team? He stirred the coals, piled a few logs on the fire, and looked at his watch. It was time for her shower.

Jane was waiting, her hands by her waist, and staring at herself in the bathroom mirror, when Matt found her.

"Ready?" he asked.

"Uh-huh." She was uneasy about what was to happen next.

Matt closed the bathroom door and turned on the shower. "Let's warm things up a bit," he said. When thin clouds of steam began to drift about, he reached for the zipper on her fleece sweater and opened the front. She moved her arms away from her sides as best she could, and Matt carefully removed the sweater so as not to bump her or tug on the plastic drain tubes. Then he pulled her cotton sweatpants to the floor and she stepped out of them one foot at a time. Next came her underwear, then her socks.

"OK, turn around so I can unbutton this little shirt," he said. When he'd carefully removed the lightweight cotton shirt, Matt tied a shoe-string around her shoulders, like a harness, and fastened it to the drains coming from her chest; he did *not* want to bump or dislodge them.

All that was covering Jane now was the corset-like compression bandage that fastened up the front with a Velcro strip. The purpose of the thing was to give some support to the tender tissue on her chest, and also help fluids to drain away from the surgical wounds.

"All right, honey, I'm gonna start to undo this Velcro strip on your corset. Tell me if it hurts, or, just tell me what you want me to do, OK?"

Jane nodded, and Matt could feel her anxiety. He reached for the Velcro strip and she raised her chin to give him better access. Ever so gently, he separated the hook and loop fasteners, and with each small scratching noise Jane blinked. When he had the fasteners separated about halfway down, between her breasts, he could see pain, or fear, or both, in her eyes.

"You OK?" he asked.

She nodded that she was, and he continued to loosen the Velcro, an inch at a time. Steam from the shower began to drift about and he asked her if she was warm enough. She nodded again.

He unfastened the entire corset and Jane winced. The support and pressure were released and she didn't seem to like the feeling.

"You OK, honey?" he asked again.

She nodded yes, and Matt slowly pulled the corset away. Jane's eyes were closed, and her face was turned away, but Matt looked at her breasts. He swallowed once, and stared. There was no bruising, only the clear plastic tubes exiting the incisions on the sides of her chest, where her breasts used to be. The drain tubes were half filled with the bloody, cran-berry-colored fluid.

Her breasts were ghastly. They were now loose flaps of skin draped over the tissue expanders that had been placed there by the surgeon to aid in healing and make room for breast implants in a few months. The tissue expanders appeared to be rectangular in shape, and they were the only things that gave shape to her breasts. Her nipples remained, but they were misshapen and appeared to have been squashed. Everything looked like it had taken a beating. She looked like a car that had been in a wreck and then had all the dented parts reassembled with duct tape.

Matt knew that Jane wanted, needed, to look at herself, and he knew she wasn't going to like what she saw. He raised his eyes and watched as Jane opened hers. She studied her reflection in the mirror, looking up and down for a long moment, and her face gave no hint of what she was feeling. Then she turned toward the shower. Her movements were slow and rigid, and she took Matt's hands in hers and squeezed. She looked back and stared, stone faced, for several seconds, and then turned her head away and stepped cautiously into the shower stall, still holding Matt's hands.

When she was safely inside the shower stall, and the warm water was running down her back, Matt glanced at her face. She was still looking at herself in the large mirror above the bathroom sink, and then, slowly, her face began to weaken. Her lips quivered, and in only an instant her beautiful face was shattered with anguish. "I look like Frankenstein," she cried. Then she lowered her face, as if to surrender, and began to sob. This awful thing had taken hold of her and would never let go. It twisted her face, like a demon trying to show itself.

It was the most painful thing Matt had ever seen. The best friend he'd ever know was being carried away with the agony and the loss. Jane's face was wracked with grief over the undeniable and irreversible thing that had been done to her. There was no way back home now. There were no words that could assuage her grief, or restore her loss, or comfort her fear. The hopelessness was in her eyes.

Matt had never felt so powerless. At times like this he'd always been able to say or do *something*. But there had never been a time like this. All he could do was hold her, and let her know that he was with her and willing to share the pain, for he certainly felt it now.

With his T-shirt and blue jeans still on, he stepped into the shower with her. He held her as tightly as he could, and he kissed her, and he told her, over and over again, that he loved her. Warm water ran over them both and they wept together. She wailed and sobbed, and let him hold her, for that was all she could do.

What was going through her mind? Matt wondered. He turned her so that the shower jets struck his back first, and the steam surrounded both of them. With his cheek pressed against hers and rivulets of water mixing with their tears, Matt held her, and stroked her back, and slowly rocked from side to side. He held her and tried to share whatever he could, or take some of the pain for himself.

His Jane, his beautiful Jane, was broken. Her awful, painful sobs came from a place deep inside her. He'd never heard anything like this before. He knew that she was pleading for him to save her. He felt her chest heave against his, and he felt the injured soul of his sweetheart reaching for his. He wanted to squeeze her and let her feel his strength, but she was so sore and brittle that any amount of pressure would hurt her. Minutes passed while he stood as close as he dared and let the water rush over them. It was a lover's embrace that neither of them could ever have imagined.

Eventually, because it was what had to be done, Matt kissed her cheek once more, and then stepped back. Wordlessly, he took a washcloth, rubbed a bar of soap over it, and began to bathe his broken Jane. He washed her back, and her arms, and her legs. His T-shirt and blue jeans were soaked and heavy, and still, neither of them spoke. Jane moved as he directed her, and then he washed her hair.

When the shower was finished, Matt stepped out of his wet clothes and left them in a pile in the shower stall. He was naked, too, when he covered Jane with a beach towel and began to gently blot her dry, so as not to bump or dislodge the drain tubes in her chest. All the while he tended to her, he wept softly. He sniffled, and sobbed as quietly as he could, and then wrapped her wet hair with a towel.

When he bent low and held clean, dry panties at her ankles, she steadied herself by leaning on him before stepping into them. The steamy bathroom was silent when he raised the panties to her waist and then put another corset on her. A couple of minutes later, as he buttoned the final button on her pajamas, Matt raised his eyes to meet Jane's.

"My best friend," Jane whispered.

"Mmm-hmm," Matt said, and he blinked a few tears away before he held her again.

The agony they'd shared began to ebb while they held each other. The shower was over, behind them. They hadn't expected it to unfold the way it had. But it did, and neither one of them would ever forget one second of it, no matter how long they lived.

"It hurts to raise my arms, or even use them for much. Will you brush my hair?" Jane asked.

"Sure." Matt found her brush and slowly brushed the tangles from her long blonde hair. "Ooh, sorry," he whispered every time he pulled the brush through a snarl. He kissed her cheek when he was finished and then said, "I made a campfire. Will you come out and sit with me? It might make you feel better to get some air. You've been sitting in that recliner for a couple days."

"No thanks, honey. I'm so tired. But you go. I just want to sit right here and rest." Her face was pale and blank.

"I don't want to sit out there without you."

"Maybe tomorrow."

When he'd wrapped a dry towel over her shoulders and got her comfortably seated in her recliner, Matt knelt beside her. The shower, and all that had passed between them a few minutes earlier, compelled him to kiss her again. He put his cheek against hers. "Darlin', you're still the prettiest girl I ever saw, and you're gonna be fine, just fine." He kissed her again. "We're gonna be just fine, you'll see."

"I know," Jane said, "I know we will." She kissed the back of his hand. "You can go sit by the fire. You don't have to stay here with me all the time. I'll feel strong enough to join you before long."

"OK," Matt said as he stood up. "I'm gonna have a drink by the fire. If you need me, just call out."

"Go. I'll be asleep before you're out the door."

The little birds of the forest had stopped chirping for the day, and the backyard was silent when Matt stepped outside. A plume of wood smoke was drifting skyward, directly toward a crescent moon, as Matt stirred the fire he'd started before Jane's shower. He placed his glass of scotch on the split-log bench and tossed a couple of oak logs on the fire. He picked up the scotch, and for the first time in what seemed like weeks, he put all his weight down and settled in by the flames. He'd never forget what he'd just seen. Never.

The agony on Jane's face just before she stepped into the shower would never leave him. Not tonight, or ever, no matter how long he lived or how much he drank. That shower was perhaps the worst moment of his life. It was right up there, anyway. Some moments a man could expect: death-bed goodbyes with loved ones, or horrific phone calls telling of sudden death. He'd had a couple of those. But this thing tonight—the sight he'd seen, and the look on Jane's face, and the shower—it seemed like a thing that he'd be handcuffed to forever.

And Jane; what was she feeling? There was no way for him to comprehend the things circling around in his love's mind.

The first sip of scotch washed over his tongue and he held it for a second before he swallowed. A loon, far across the lake, unleashed a haunting hail call, and Matt could feel the healing power of this place reach out to him.

Tonight, beside this fire, he'd let the beauty of a starlit northern sky and the smell of wood smoke soothe him. The beautiful girl that he'd given his whole life to was suffering something that he'd never imagined. He raised his eyes to the heavens, then lowered them to the shifting embers in the fire at his feet, but all he could see was the twisted wreckage of his lover, weeping in his arms.

He wiped away a few more tears and thought he might break down and cry out loud. But it would be bad if Jane, resting in her recliner, heard him crying. He needed to be strong. He took a deep breath and held off the dark emotions.

The wood smoke and the cool night air *did* begin to soothe him, and he tried to think of other good things while he sipped at the scotch. But the look on Jane's face would not leave him. What if he lost her?

CHAPTER 24

The front door of John Velde's taxidermy shop swung open easily, and even though Sally Durham was balancing two paper coffee cups, one on top of the other, she was able to catch the door with her foot and then push it closed. She stood by the door and looked about while she waited for John to come out from the back room and greet her. She could hear him back there working on something, but she could hardly take her eyes off the animals on display in the outer office.

Standing on all four legs in the far corner was a black bear, and it looked as if it might just walk on over and help her drink her coffee. The bear was not displayed in an intimidating pose, as Sally would have expected. It appeared to be strolling through the woods, and it seemed to looking at her. In fact, no matter where she stood, the bear seemed to be looking at her. The bear's fur was shiny and thick and its head and feet were enormous. She crept over for a closer look. This bear was the main attraction in the display room, and it took a few minutes for Sally to pry her attention away from it and examine the other animals.

A dozen or more deer heads hung on one wall, along with ducks and grouse and a few critters she didn't recognize. Then she turned her attention to the fish on the opposite wall. There were northern pike and muskellunge: huge fish, maybe five feet long, displayed in aggressive, predatory positions. There were walleyes and trout and crappies and, just as with the specimens on the other wall, several other fish she didn't recognize.

Still holding the two coffee cups, she inched closer to examine the fish more closely. They all looked like they might swim away if she frightened them. She wanted to touch them, but she thought that might be against the rules.

She heard more movement in the back room, what sounded like tools being placed on a workbench. A minute passed, and still John didn't come to see who was there, so Sally walked tentatively toward the door to John's work area, which had been left ajar. She peeked through a two-inch opening and saw John standing at his workbench with his back to her. Maybe he hadn't heard her come in?

She pushed the door open and intentionally dragged her foot on the floor so John might hear her. He did.

"Oh, hi," John said. "How long have you been standing there?"

"Not long. I brought you some coffee." She extended one of the cups to him.

"Well . . . thank you." John took the cup from her and placed it on his workbench. He pulled two old chairs over from the corner and invited Sally to sit down. He was startled, even a bit flustered, to have Sally surprise him like this. When she sat, he took a seat facing her and admitted, "I sure didn't expect *you* to come through that door."

"Well, I haven't seen you in the shop for a while so I thought I'd stop over and say hello. So, hello." Sally took a sip of coffee and asked, "Is this where it all happens?"

"Sure is," John said. "I hardly ever sit down here, though, like we are now; only when Matt and I sit around and bullshit. He likes to hang around with me because I tell him secrets about hunting, and fishing, and sex." John's eyes twinkled.

"So it's *all* bullshit then, right?" Now Sally's eyes twinkled.

John tipped his coffee cup and raised his eyebrows in a salute. "Pretty much. Would you like a little tour of the place?" He leaned forward as if he was eager to show her around, then reconsidered and leaned back again. "Or maybe you have no interest in this stuff? Is this just a social visit?"

"Well, I *did* want to say hello, so I brought you some coffee, and I *was* a little curious about this place, but I had another reason for stopping by. But before we get to that, I have to ask you about that bear in the other room. Tell me about that."

John smiled. "Oh, you mean BooBoo? Matt shot him."

"Really?" Sally asked. "Isn't that dangerous?"

"Not usually, but that one was."

"You're teasing me, right? There's a punch line coming, right?" Sally asked.

"Not teasing. Around here, hunters *bait* bear. They set out a pile of food they think will attract a bear, and then they sit in a nearby tree and shoot the bear when it comes around to investigate. Sometimes they put out some garbage—you know, dead fish, stuff that really stinks so a bear can smell it from a long ways away. But most hunters bait with sugar . . . candy bars, doughnuts, stuff like that." He sipped his coffee and then added, "It's not exactly a wilderness experience."

"So what did Matt do?" Sally asked.

"Nothing. That bear came to him."

"You mean it attacked him?"

"Well, sort of. Out by Scotch Lake, where Matt lives, it's still fairly remote, and not long ago there were a lot of bears out there. One summer when his boys were young, this bear," John said, gesturing toward the outer office, "kept coming by the Kingstons' house and eating the garbage, and wrecking their bird feeders, and digging up the garden, and in general vandalizing the place. Bears who do that are usually a little bit older and have lost their fear of man, or else they have some physical problem that hampers their ability to find food, so they come closer and closer to places where they can feed on our scraps. Anyway, as Matt tells the story, the boys were little, and toddling around in the yard, and Jane had just stepped into the house to do something in the kitchen when this bear walked out of the woods and slowly moved right toward the boys. Matt saw what was going on and chased the bear away, and then he and Jane brought the boys inside. They figured the bear was long gone, but nonetheless—"

"A bear would eat children?" Sally interrupted.

"Sure, if it was hungry enough. So, like I said, they thought the bear was gone, but about twenty minutes later they heard something on the back steps, by the kitchen. And when they looked out the screen door they saw the bear standing there, about to let himself in and treat himself to whatever Jane was baking. Matt didn't have much choice. He got his rifle as quickly as he could, and when the bear stood up on its hind legs he put a bullet in the bear's chest." John chuckled. "Jane said it sounded like a cannon went off in the kitchen."

"He shot the bear in his kitchen?" Sally gasped.

"Well, the bear was on the back steps, shaking the kitchen screen door, but *Matt* was in the kitchen!"

"Is that *true*? Really?"

"You know I have no trouble telling lies," John answered. "But that story I just told you is all true. Ask Jane."

"Wow."

"Yeah, sometimes you don't have any choice; you just have to *deal* with things like that. 'Zat answer your question?"

"Yup," Sally said. "And it ties in nicely with the other reason I stopped by today. I've been thinking, the outdoors, fishing in particular, is such a big deal around here. Maybe I should put some fish art on the walls of my coffee shop. S'pose you could help me? And yes, I would like a little tour."

"Well, sure," John said enthusiastically, then he quickly backed away in order to clarify Sally's request. "Do you mean paintings and sculptures of fish—that kind of fish art? 'Cuz I don't have anything like that. Or do you mean something like those graphite replicas I have on the wall in my display room?"

"Those are replicas? Not real, dead fish?"

"Yeah, they're graphite. Most of them, anyway. I painted them with an air brush. Pretty lifelike, huh?"

"Yeah, I like them, and I like the idea that they're not actually dead fish." Sally smiled. "You know, I watch people when they come in my shop. Many of them start looking around right away, and I always wonder if they're looking for something to tie in with the experience here at Wiigwaas Lake." She looked around the room, now searching for clues and a better understanding of how John created his art.

"OK, good! C'mere and I'll show you something," John said. He stood and walked toward a narrow door.

"I'll bet you say that to all the girls," Sally said as she followed behind.

Without turning back to look at her, John replied, "Yeah, but most of 'em aren't gullible enough to actually follow me in here." When he opened the door, they looked into a small room with a table in the middle and some masks and goggles hanging on the walls. A plain, ivory-colored fish that appeared to be a large plastic toy lay on the table. "This is a graphite walleye." He tapped a fingernail on it and it made a hollow noise. "Pick it up."

Sally lifted it gingerly, and put it down. "It's so light!"

"Yeah, it's made from a mold. I bought it from a supplier. Some guy up here on vacation last year caught a thirty-one-inch walleye and took a picture before he released it—"

"He put it back in the water?" Sally asked.

"Yeah, most fishermen do that nowadays. That way they can have a replica made, show it to their friends and brag about it, and then maybe catch the same fish again next year. Anyway, I'll use this air brush to paint that hollow fish, and if I do it right, which I always do, the fish looks like it's alive." John took Sally out to the display room and pointed to some fish on the wall.

Sally wandered about slowly and stood as close as she could to one of the fish. She reached into her purse and withdrew a pair of glasses so she could examine it more closely. "Can I touch this big one?" she asked.

"I'll bet you say that to all the boys," John replied.

Sally looked over the top of her glasses and said, "Good one, but I put it on a tee for you."

"Sorry, but I couldn't let that one go. And yes, you can touch the big one, but be gentle." His eyes twinkled and Sally still peered over her glasses. "You started it," John said.

Sally turned back to the fish and tapped it with the fingernail on her right index finger. The fish made a hollow noise, and she brought her nose within inches of the replica. "Wow, it's so lifelike, it looks like it might swim away."

"That's the idea," John said. "If you'd like to hang some of these in your shop for a while and see what kind of feedback you get, that would be fine. Might be some good advertising for me, too. I'll bring 'em over whenever you'd like. Or I'll make something just for you."

"Yeah, that would be good, but don't bother making something special yet. Just pick a few that you think will look good and bring 'em over any time. If they do the trick I'll buy some more. Is that OK with you?"

"Sure," John said. "Maybe I could leave a few of my business cards with you too, in case somebody who's looking for a taxidermist wanders in there."

"That would be fine." Sally smiled the biggest smile he'd seen yet, and she extended her hand for a handshake. "We can help each other." She liked the feel of his large hand, and she held on for a bit longer. "Nice doing business with you, John." As she turned to leave she added, "See you at the ball game tonight. Are you excited?"

"Excited? No, I wouldn't say that. But I am looking forward to seeing Jane at the game. I think this will be her first field trip outside the house since her surgery."

"Oh, good. How's she doing?"

"Matt says she's had a hard time finding her smile again."

"That's gotta be pretty normal," Sally said. "She'll feel better when she gets back to her routine and finds that things are still the same."

"Hope so," John said as Sally turned to leave. "See you tonight, and thanks for the coffee."

"You're welcome," she said, and then she remembered something, "Oh, John, would you like me to bring some treats for the kids for after the game?"

John was aware that post-game treats would probably be the only thing that Orange would enjoy tonight, but he hadn't given the idea much thought yet. "What did you have in mind?"

"Well, I recall that you're partial to blueberry scones. You know, those dried-up, crusty little dough balls that stick in your throat?" she said, serious as stone.

John made no attempt to hide his smile. Sally had fired back at him. "Well, yes, I do love those dried-up little peckers, but maybe tonight we should go with Popsicles or ice cream sandwiches?"

"You got it," Sally said, but she flashed a satisfied grin as she turned and walked out the door.

———

Two kids wearing Orange shirts and Orange caps were sitting on one of the team benches on a baseball diamond far across the athletic field, waiting for the rest of the team to arrive, when Matt and Jane pulled up to the sports complex about twenty minutes before game time.

"OK, honey, you just get your feet under you and wait until I get your lawn chair outta the trunk," Matt said. He watched Jane's tentative movements and guarded posture as she stepped out of the car and moved toward the curb. She held her arms close to her sides and seemed to be protecting her chest from any jostling. She was bent forward at the waist, just a bit, and her gait was slow and rigid.

Matt carried a folding chair under one arm and held onto Jane with the other as they slowly, cautiously, crossed the thick green outfield grass on their long walk to the diamond where Orange was about to play their first game. Matt's grip was steadfast, and he watched her with a close eye as she walked. Her movements were stiff, and she was clearly trying to guard against a misstep or a stumble.

He was glad she'd made the effort to come to the game. He knew it would be good for her to get out among friends again. But it was hard for him to watch the way she moved, and he knew that everyone in town who knew her would be talking about her.

He couldn't help but remember other times, other people, people he'd known for years, who showed up at a ball game, or church, or at his office, walking like Jane was walking now. The last time he'd seen them around town they were healthy and spry, and then suddenly they were frail and broken, and telling him about cancer or some other illness. Then, maybe a few months later he'd hear that they were dead. The thought of Jane dying came to him quickly, and then he banished it. He would not allow it.

Matt selected a spot for Jane to sit, about thirty feet behind the players' bench and along the first base line, and he unfolded her chair. "You should be safe from wild throws or foul balls out here, honey. I don't think anyone in the league can throw the ball this far," he said.

"Go on and get your team ready, coach." Jane settled tentatively into her chair. There was still some pain in her eyes. Matt knelt beside her for several seconds and stroked her arm softly, and he remembered the way she'd looked as she crossed the athletic field. "You're gonna be OK," he said. He kissed her lips and when he stood straight he said, "I love you."

"I love you, too." Jane smiled.

It was good to have her back to doing something of a normal activity again, but the smile she'd just given him lacked the sparkle he was used to. He turned and walked toward his team's bench, calling out, "OK, Orange, over here!"

From all over the baseball complex, little kids in orange, and green, and blue, and red jerseys and hats wandered to their assigned diamonds for the night's games. John had arranged the catcher's gear and balls and bats beside their bench, and he waited while their team straggled in. Matt was ready with a clipboard and a roster so he could take roll call when everyone was present.

Sally arrived by herself and set up her own lawn chair next to Jane's. "Hi, Jane, it's nice to see you again. How are you feeling?" Sally asked.

"Pretty good. Is Timmy ready to play some ball?"

"Oh yeah!" Sally said. "And I brought some treats for after the game." She pointed to the cooler she'd brought along.

The other parents of the Orange team gathered near Jane and Sally, and they sat on blankets and lawn chairs and socialized among themselves as game time drew near.

John was standing by the Orange bench, watching as the small crowd gathered. He noticed that DeeDee Katzenmeyer was sitting on the grass, without her pit bull, not far from Sally and Jane. John waved at DeeDee, who was once again barefoot and looking particularly slutty.

Orange would be playing Red tonight, and the coach of the Red team was already referring to his team as the Big Red Machine as he enthusiastically greeted each of his players. "I'm gonna puke," John whispered in Matt's ear.

"Lighten up, and try not to be yourself," Matt whispered back. He raised his voice and hollered, "OK! Orange team, over here!" and a scruffy collection of ballplayers slowly assembled around him. "All right, I'm gonna call your name, and I want you to remember the order I call you, because this will be our batting order. Are you ready?"

No one replied. Matt looked at the clipboard and began to call their names.

"Heather Compton."

Heather raised a hand and smiled.

"Whitney Compton."

Whitney raised a hand and smiled.

"David Norman."

Timmy's new friend raised a hand, then, because he was so excited, he started jumping up and down.

"Bradley Hested."

Bradley raised a hand.

"Where's your hat, Brad?" Matt asked him.

"I lost it," Brad replied. He was wearing a Yankees hat instead, and his tone was somewhere between defiant and ambivalent.

"I just gave it to you last Tuesday," Matt said.

"Oh, hell. The little shit stain didn't lose it," John hissed under his breath, just loud enough for Matt to hear. "He just wants to be different than his teammates."

Matt turned and passed a scowl to John, which John answered with a roll of his eyes.

Before Matt could say anything more, Bradley Hested shrugged as if he couldn't care less about losing his Orange hat, and he asked, "Do you have any bigger shirts?" His shirt was stretched to its limit. Bradley was more than twice as big as some of his teammates. His round belly hung over the waist of his polyester shorts, and he didn't seem to care about much of anything.

"That's the biggest one I've got, Brad. You'll have to wear it for tonight, but I'll see what I can do for next week," Matt said.

John whispered again into Matt's ear, "Jesus H. Christ, he looks like an orange wood tick, about to explode. And how did the little shit lose his hat in a week?"

In the most businesslike manner he could summon, Matt turned away from the team and into John's ear he breathed, very slowly, "Shut, the fuck, up?"

"I think we should check the kid for harpoon marks," John whispered in return, "then try to roll him back into the lake."

Matt was biting his lip when he turned back and finished the roll call/ batting order. After Timmy Clements there was Jaxon Zak, Nayson King, Bronson Wolff, Braydee Schultz, Brysen Johnson, Quevin Rozinka, and Brexley Babich. When he came to the last name on the list he hesitated and then called out, "Michelangelo Katzenmeyer." Mike raised his hand.

"Cool name," Matt said to Mike. Then he told the team to go out and play catch with a partner for a couple minutes, but try not to hurt each other. As he put the clipboard on the bench he looked at John and teased, "Your new girlfriend named her kid Michelangelo Katzenmeyer." Matt laughed, then repeated, "That's right, I actually *said* that: *Michelangelo*." He paused for effect, "*Katzenmeyer*. Michelangelo Katzenmeyer . . . has a nice ring to it, eh?"

"Maybe she's an art lover," John replied. "And maybe you didn't notice all the Brexleys and Brysens and Jaxons and Kevins with a Q, for shit sakes. We got a lotta X's and Y's running loose on that roster. A lotta dumb-ass white-person names there, old buddy. Not my fault."

"OK, I'll give you that one," Matt said. "But try not to say what you're thinking, fair enough? You don't need to piss *everyone* off."

John turned just in time to notice Bradley Hested, the belligerent Orange wood tick, pick up an aluminum bat. John recognized immediately that Bradley was about to take a mighty swing with the bat, and that he had no intention of looking around to see if anyone might be standing too close to him. Bradley moved his hands back toward his right shoulder and prepared to swing the bat, unaware that Whitney Compton was standing directly in the path of his follow-through.

John lurched through the scrum of little Orange people and all of them heard the palm of his hand slap against the barrel of Bradley Hested's bat just as Bradley started his swing. "Goddammit, Jumbo!" John barked, as he ripped the bat from Bradley's hands and saved Whitney from a fractured skull. "You coulda killed somebody! Watch what you're doing!"

Bradley scowled at John, gave up on practice swings, and waddled over to check out the catcher's gear.

"Lighten up," Matt said as he hustled over to John's side and took the bat from his hands. "He's just a kid."

"I hate him," John said through clenched teeth.

"Well, maybe now you know how Alvie Glasnapp felt," Matt snapped.

The words stopped John in his tracks. "Huh?"

"I bet you think you were a pleasure to coach?" Matt said, clearly angry at the way John had treated a kid, even a pretty unlikable kid. Before John could respond, he added, "OK, John, here's your assignment. You've got the summer to get something positive outta that nasty little shit. He's *yours*!" Matt poked a finger on John's chest. "That kid is your summer project! Don't fuck it up and don't piss me off again." He turned and walked away.

"Today?" John shouted at Matt's back.

"What? What are you talking about?" Matt pivoted and placed his hands on his hips.

"Did you mean don't piss you off again *today*, or for the rest of the summer?" John knew that Matt was actually angry with him, but that didn't matter. Matt could never stay mad at him. He'd break Matt down and get him to smile.

Matt stared at John for several seconds.

"Or did you mean *forever*? You know, like 'Don't piss me off again, *forever*.'" John was baiting Matt with an extra dose of false innocence, "'Cuz I don't think I can do *that*, forever; you know?"

Matt turned away, ignoring John again, and began to help Bradley Hested put the catcher's gear on.

"OK, we'll just shoot for today," John said to Matt's back. He smiled but decided not to push any harder.

Five minutes later the game was under way, and team Orange took the field. The umpire, a skinny high school student employed by the Pine Rapids Parks Department, stood by first base. Since there wasn't a player on any one of the four teams in the summer league who could throw a strike, the coaches from each team were expected to pitch to their own players when they were up to bat, and then when a ball was put in play they were to get out of the way and allow the team to play defense. There could be no strikeouts; a player would stay at the plate until he or she hit the ball and put it in play, and a player could only bat once per inning. Each half inning ended when three outs were recorded, or when everyone on the entire team had batted once, whichever came first.

When the Red coach trotted onto the field he gave Matt a thumbs-up and a big smile and then began exhorting his Big Red Machine to swing hard.

John made a point to get Matt's attention, then rolled his eyes. "Lighten up, John," Matt said. "He's just trying to be positive."

The Red coach checked behind him to be sure that all the Orange players were ready, then he lofted an underhand toss toward home plate. The batter let it float by, and when it plunked on the ground behind home plate it dropped just in front of the not very outstretched arm of Bradley Hested, who'd made a less than halfhearted attempt to catch the ball. Then it rolled all the way to the chain-link backstop. Bradley stood up and trudged toward the backstop, clearly pissed off that the Red coach had failed to put the ball in his glove. "A little hustle there, Bradley," John barked from his seat next to Matt. When Bradley finally got to the ball, he picked it up and threw it halfway back to the pitcher.

"Put a little more smoke on it there, Brad!" John barked again. He looked at Matt and groaned.

As the next pitch fluttered to the plate, the batter swung and hit a slow roller right back up the middle. A chorus of screeching mothers from the Red side of the diamond erupted with RUN, RUN, RUN!!!" and the kid took off for first base.

The ball rolled straight toward Brexley Babich, who actually *kicked* it. And when she deflected the ball, it took a path directly toward Mike Katzenmeyer. With his glove held high, about at his shoulders, Mike waited until the ball had almost stopped rolling. Then, like a Siberian snow fox, he pounced on it with his vinyl glove/garbage-can lid. He was on his knees when he lifted his glove, peeked under it as if he was checking to see if he'd captured a living thing, and then gleefully displayed the ball he'd played so masterfully.

"Jesus. H. Christ," John muttered to himself.

Nine batters later, several patterns had developed. The mothers of the Red team screamed "RUN!" with every ball put in play, and every player on the Orange team, except Timmy Clements and Dave Norman, seemed to be terrified of the ball.

"Good thing they can only bat around once per inning or we'd be here listening to those bitches holler 'Run! Run! Run!' all night," John said to Matt as yet another Red batter came to the plate. And sure enough, when the kid hit a roller to the left side, the screaming started up again. But this time the ball was hit to Dave Norman, and like the answer to a prayer, Dave scooped it up cleanly, planted his right foot, and threw the ball to first base, where Timmy caught it. One out!

John leaped from the bench. "YES!" he yelled. "Dave! Well done! And Timmy! Solid, man!" He turned to Matt, who was clapping and cheering too, and said, "We got somebody fuckin' *out*!"

Back behind first base, in their lawn chairs, Sally and Jane exchanged smiles.

Two batters, and seven fielding errors later, team Red had batted around and it was time for Orange to take their first turn at bat. As the teams changed places, Sally took advantage of a break in the action. She leaned close to Jane and said, "Matt is such a nice guy. He really likes this stuff, doesn't he."

"Yeah, he coached our boys when they were young. We had so much fun," Jane said.

"He still has a crush on you," Sally added. "I saw the way he looked at you in the beer tent last winter, and then again a few minutes ago."

Jane smiled for a moment and then her lower lip began to quiver.

"Oh, I'm sorry. I didn't mean to—" Sally began to apologize.

"It's OK," Jane said, as she blotted a tear from the corner of each eye. "It's been a tough coupla weeks, and I'm still pretty emotional."

Sally reached over and touched Jane's hand. "I know all about it. John shared it with me, and I'm so sorry for all you've been through." Without hesitating, she added, "Do you need anything? Do you need someone to drive you anywhere for your chemotherapy, or someone to help with household chores?"

"I don't know what the deal is yet, as far as chemo is concerned. I got a pretty good report, though, so maybe there will be no chemo."

"Well that's great. But if you ever do need anything, you can call me. Even if it's just to talk," Sally said. "I'm a good listener."

No one had called Jane to ask how she was feeling, and no one had offered to help with anything. In conversations with people from work, and even some longtime friends, everyone seemed to be afraid, or uncomfortable now, and Jane thought they seemed to be whistling past the cemetery when they spoke to her. But Sally Durham, someone she was just getting to know, had just offered to be there if she needed any help. "Thanks, Sally," Jane said. "Maybe we can have coffee?"

"I know a good place," Sally said. "Any time!"

The decision had been made for John to pitch to their team and for Matt to stay on the bench and coach from there while Orange was up to bat. All of the batting helmets were too large for the first batter, Heather Compton, and the smallest one Matt could find wobbled as she walked to the plate with a bat in her hand. John motioned for her to step up to the plate when the Red team was ready, and he gently flipped the ball toward her. Heather leaned forward and pushed the bat awkwardly through the strike zone as if it weighed a ton. She hadn't actually *seen* the ball; she missed it by two feet. John lofted another pitch her way, and she made another ugly miss. It was painfully obvious that she'd never swung a bat. The crowd at the diamond quickly grew silent out of surprise and courtesy to the cute little girl.

Sally leaned close to Jane and laughed. "Looks like she could use some practice."

"Hey, Heather," John called out from the pitcher's area. "Show me a practice swing. Just swing the bat hard once, as hard as you can." Heather swung the bat, much harder than before, and John said, "OK, do *that* every time." He threw two more floaters to her, hoping for the flight path of the ball to intersect with the swing path of the bat. Both were near misses. On the third pitch, she made contact and sent the ball dribbling back toward the pitcher.

Now the parents of the Orange team started screaming for Heather to "RUN!" John and Matt expected her to blaze her way to first and kick up a cloud of dust on the way, but when Heather started toward first base she held her arms out to the side and tiptoed slowly down the base path, while they watched in surprise. Luckily, the boy on the Red team who finally picked up the ball was only a bit better than Mike Katzenmeyer, and Heather made it safely to first base.

"Heather, c'mere," Matt said. Then he asked the umpire for a timeout and walked quickly over to first base, where Heather was smiling politely. "Is there something wrong?" he asked her.

"No," she said sweetly, still smiling.

"Well then, why did you run like that? So slowly?" he asked.

"My hat is really tippy," Heather explained.

"So?"

"I don't want to get in trouble if it falls off."

"Oh," Matt said, while he processed her words. "So you were just trying to balance that batting helmet on top of your head? Well, next time don't worry about that. If that ol' helmet falls off, you just keep on running as fast as you can. You won't get in trouble. I want you to show off a little. I want you to run down to first base like there's a dog chasing you. And don't stop at first base, just keep on running all the way around, no matter what. OK?"

"Sure." She smiled.

"And now when Whitney hits one in a couple minutes, you just take off for second base and don't stop till you get home. OK?"

"OK," Heather said, in what Matt thought might be the sweetest little-girl posture he'd ever seen.

"And remember, I want you to show off. Let everyone see just how fast you can run," he reiterated. When Heather walked back to first base her helmet wobbled as if it were resting on a pencil.

Matt walked away from Heather and had the same conversation with Whitney before he returned to the bench.

Then he turned to John and kept a straight face when he explained something that any experienced baseball man would know: "Her hat was tippy."

"OK. Makes sense." John smiled when he recognized the sarcasm.

When Matt returned to the team bench he signaled John to go ahead and pitch to Whitney. Whitney's swing was just as pathetic as Heather's, and it took John a few pitches to locate the place where Whitney's bat might happen to meet up with the ball. On the fourth pitch she tapped a slow roller toward first base and Matt hollered "GO!" to both of the girls.

Heather's batting helmet popped off immediately, and she was already rounding second base and kicking up a trail of dust when the kid playing first base picked up the ball and panicked. Whitney streaked by him and he threw the ball to second base, where no one was standing, and the ball rolled out toward left field. The left fielders for Red—there were two of them—were unprepared to take part in the action. One of them was watching a game on a different diamond and the other one was talking to his glove and picking his nose. By the time the nose picker figured out what to do, Whitney Compton streaked across home plate, and the Compton twins walked back to the Orange bench holding hands and smiling.

Timmy Clements and Dave Norman were jumping and cheering, and they made a point to slap the girls on the back when they reached their jubilant Orange teammates on the bench. Never mind that there had been six fielding errors committed by Red; in the hearts and minds of the Orange team, Whitney Compton had just belted a two-run homer.

John and Matt exchanged satisfied smiles. Sally Durham cheered along with the Orange parents.

Then Dave Norman strode to the plate. He, too, reached first base on another slow ground ball that proved to be unplayable for the Red infielders.

Two batters and two outs later it was Timmy's turn. His batting helmet, like all the players in this league except for Brad Hested, was also too big. He wore shorts and tennis shoes, and he carried a short aluminum bat to the plate.

"OK, number seven, get a good swing," Matt said to Timmy, then he clapped his hands and smiled at John.

When Timmy reached the batter's box and turned around, his face was grim. He was stone-cold serious. For him it was as if he was stepping to the plate in the seventh game of the World Series; this was his moment, his *first* moment, and he did what the situation demanded. He lowered his bat and tapped it against the side of his shoes to knock any caked dirt or mud off his cleats, just as he'd seen his heroes do on TV. Never mind that he didn't have cleats on, and that there was no caked mud for miles; this was what ballplayers did, and he was a ballplayer now, by God. He had a shirt just like his teammates and he wore number seven on his back.

John shot a glance at Matt, and both of them acknowledged that they had noticed Timmy's actions and intensity. Timmy took a mighty practice swing and raised the bat. He was ready.

Sally wanted to nudge Jane and remind her to look at Timmy and be sure to notice the stone-cold look on his face. This was the reason she'd changed the course of her life and come to this small town. Here she was, sitting beside a new friend on this dusty little ball field, watching her grandson living his dreams for the first time.

Timmy stood in the batter's box, such as it was, and waited for the pitch from John. When it came, Timmy hit a slow roller toward third base, which the other team's third baseman mishandled a couple of times before making a weak throw over to first base. Timmy Clements was safe at first, and that slow roller to third would now live on in his mind as a rocket to deep left field.

While Sally looked on, Timmy glanced over to see if she had actually been watching him and noticed the great thing he'd just done. Sally waved at him, but he ignored her. Ballplayers, *real* ballplayers, weren't supposed to wave to their grandmothers when they were running the bases. The moment was grand, and it was exactly what Sally had hoped to find in Pine Rapids.

Jaxon Zak hit a lazy pop fly that the shortstop caught, and the inning, and the moment, was over. As Orange took the field and Red came to bat, DeeDee Katzenmeyer, who'd been sitting on the grass a few feet in front of Jane and Sally, turned around and said, "Boy, that one girl can run like a cantaloupe!"

The absurdity did not escape Jane and Sally's notice. Was it possible the woman didn't know the difference between antelope and cantaloupe? Jane, always ready to smooth over an awkward moment, ignored DeeDee's misguided connection between antelopes and cantaloupes and added, "Yeah, her sister can run fast, too."

DeeDee nodded her agreement and then turned around to cheer for Orange again.

The fact that DeeDee had thought it over for a second and still not grasped it indicated that maybe she was not the sharpest tool in the shed. Sally looked at Jane and made a face that said, "Yikes! Did you hear that?" She leaned back in her chair and covered her mouth when she started to giggle, and soon both Jane and Sally's shoulders were bouncing. Jane's tears quickly morphed into tears of laughter, and the unexpected flip-flop from sadness to absurdity made it even more difficult not to laugh. They were doing the best they could to stifle their display, as if they were laughing in church and didn't want to be seen. Sally found a fresh tissue for both Jane and herself, and Jane put her hands on her breasts and giggled when she said softly, "Don't make me laugh so hard. It hurts my boobs."

The game ended forty minutes later, as the sun hovered just above a row of lofty balsams on the western horizon. Sally carried a cooler to the Orange team's bench and delivered their treats.

"Did we win?" Heather asked Matt, as he put the bats and balls into their canvas carrying bag.

"No, but it was pretty close, and you sure played well," he said. When Heather walked away, Matt whispered to John, "What was the final score, anyway?"

"I wasn't keeping track, but one of the mothers told me it was about 50 to 8," John said. "But nobody got hurt, even though Brexley, our kicker/assistant first baseman, cried a couple times."

"You're not supposed to yell at girls, you asshole," Matt said. He zipped the canvas bag shut and looked right and left before he smiled and added, "But after the third time she tried to kick a ground ball over to our other first baseman, I was getting a little surly too."

"Well, I apologized, and she's over there having a Popsicle and playing with the others, so I'm not gonna worry about it anymore. It's time to socialize." John turned and walked toward the crowd of parents and players milling around the bench. Sally had brought a cooler full of treats for the players, and now, chatting and laughing in the gloaming, most of the Orange team had ice cream or some sort of sticky goo smeared on their faces, along with some sweat and dirt from the infield.

Sally and Jane stood together during the post-game celebration, and Jane said, "I know Matt is going to make a campfire tonight when we get home. Would you and Timmy like to come out to our place and sit by the fire for a while? We can make s'mores. I bet Timmy would like that."

"Well, Timmy is going to stay overnight at Dave Norman's house, which leaves me all alone. Can I come by myself, and can I bring anything?" Sally asked.

"No need for you to bring anything, but I should warn you that ever since my surgery I seem to hit the wall fairly early. I may have to retire before you, so don't be offended if I leave the campfire and go to bed all of a sudden," Jane said.

"I won't stay late. I have to get up pretty early and open the coffee shop every day. But I haven't sat around a campfire for years," Sally said. She'd been talking to Jane, but her eyes had been following John as he stepped through the crowd of Orange parents and players until he found DeeDee Katzenmeyer.

From a distance, Matt also watched as John made his way over to DeeDee. He saw John deliver a clever greeting and then a few wittier, and probably suggestive, comments. Matt didn't need to hear them; he'd heard them all before. He looked over to where Jane was chatting with Sally, and he was glad to see her smiling. Her movements were rigid and slow, but at least she was here, and she seemed to be having fun.

From the crowd, Matt noticed Ron Hested walking his way. "That was interesting," Ron said as he lit a cigarette. Bradley Hested hadn't caught a single pitch throughout the whole game. He'd tried to crouch behind the plate as best he could, but his obese frame made any sort of athletic movement nearly impossible. He'd held his glove hand out as a target for the pitcher to pitch to. But he didn't understand that he had to move his glove sometimes in order to catch the ball. Perhaps moving his hand required more talent than he possessed. Almost all of the pitches missed his glove and then rolled to the chain-link backstop. The pitches that *did* happen to plop into his glove just fell out of it, and by the end of the game he'd grown angry and frustrated by the experience. Nobody else had caught many balls either, but he'd missed a couple *hundred*.

"Yeah," Matt agreed. "It *was* pretty interesting, and Bradley had a tough day. We'll put somebody else back there next time."

"Ah, don't worry about that. I don't think he's headed for the big leagues anytime soon," Ron said as he exhaled a cloud of smoke. Then he dismissed baseball. "How's Jane doing?"

Matt gave a sigh. "It's hard to tell, Ron. We've had a few heart-to-heart talks about all of this recently. That's been a little . . . heavy, as we used to say."

"I thought she got a pretty good report, though, all things considered," Ron said. "Is there something . . .?"

"No, the lymph nodes were all clear. It's just that when someone tells you that you have a cancer like that, and so many others have died from it, *you* know how the mind works. It's pretty normal to have a good long look at the dark side. And besides that, we don't meet with the oncologist for a couple weeks yet, so we still don't know about chemotherapy, or radiation, or what drugs they'll want her to take, or any of that stuff. There's just so much still unsettled."

Ron nodded his understanding and took another long drag on the cigarette. "How's your hip? Looks like you're doing pretty good?"

"Yeah, I haven't felt this good in two years. You were right, Ron. The hip was nothing, just a bit of unscheduled maintenance. I'll be ready to go after Mr. Whitehorns in the fall."

"Well, that's good to hear, but it all adds up and things change as we get older, and—" Ron stopped himself. Timmy was walking toward them, and Ron seemed to have something to say that he didn't want Timmy to hear, so he cut it short. "We'll talk another time."

Timmy's orange shirt had red drip stains from the cherry Popsicle that was still in his right hand. A stream of red syrup also ran down his arm and dripped off his elbow. "Hey Matt," Timmy said, "do you think our game highlights will be on ESPN when we get home?"

CHAPTER TWENTY-FIVE

———•———

Jane walked into the house, hunched over and with her arms curled in front of her, as if bracing herself against sudden movement. She looked fragile.

"You all right?" Matt asked, as he followed her into their bedroom.

"Uh-huh, I feel pretty good. I'm just afraid that any sudden movements will hurt, or jar something loose."

The ball game had been her first outing since returning home from her surgery, and it had been nice to see a few friends and get some fresh air. Tomorrow she would go to the clinic in Pine Rapids, where a nurse would remove the plastic tubes that were about done draining fluid from the surgical wounds on her chest. The tubes produced almost none of the cranberry-colored fluid anymore, and it would be good to be rid of them.

"Honey, why don't you help me with my shower now, before Sally gets here? That way, when I get tired I'll just come up to bed and leave you two by the fire," Jane said.

She still lacked the arm strength to undress and dress herself. When they both stepped into the bathroom, she turned to face Matt so that he could unbutton her shirt.

"It was nice to look over there and see you tonight," he said. "Our friends were impressed that you were there." He unzipped her fleece jacket and slipped it off her shoulders.

"I felt pretty good right up to the end. Then it started to hurt. It was time to go. I'm sorry I couldn't stay at the park and chat any longer."

"Ah, it was time to come home." Matt's face lit up when he changed the subject. "Did you see the look on Timmy's face when he came to bat that first time?"

"I did," she replied, and Matt could hear a bit of laughter in her voice. He was looking at the tiny buttons on her cotton shirt as he worked his way from top to bottom. Then Jane said, "I think Sally is curious about John. In a romantic way."

Matt stopped unbuttoning and looked at her. "Really?"

Jane nodded.

"I wonder about that sometimes, too. But he told me that he'd asked her out a couple times and got some bad vibes," Matt said. He gently put his arms around Jane and kissed her cheek. She pulled Matt even closer and held her cheek against his. There was a lot going on in her head, and while they held each other he stroked her back and rubbed her neck.

"C'mon, let's get this done," Matt said. He reached around her and turned on the shower. He pulled her cotton shirt off her shoulders, still careful not to dislodge the drain tubes, and then all that remained was the elastic corset that fastened in the front. Before he unfastened it, he asked, "Are you ready?" She nodded yes, and he gently separated the Velcro, starting at the top. Jane closed her eyes, as if she was anticipating pain. When he was nearly finished, Matt asked if he was hurting her.

"No," she replied softly. "But that thing, that corset, makes me feel safe, secure. It keeps things from moving around, and I'm afraid when you take it off, that things move. I'm afraid it will hurt." Then, with a stiff upper lip, she gave him permission to carry on. "OK, keep going."

With the final tearing sound of the Velcro she raised her arms, just an inch or so, to allow him to remove the corset and put it on the bathroom vanity. He watched her eyes as she looked at herself in the mirror again. Tonight there were no tears, and no mention of Frankenstein. There was no emotion, at least nothing that he could recognize. She was still looking at her scars, and drain tubes, and misshapen breasts when Matt unbuttoned her pants and slid them to her ankles. The bathroom was filling with warm clouds of steam when he slid her panties over her hips and to her ankles. When she was naked he held her once more and whispered, "I love you." It was all there was to say, but it never seemed like enough anymore.

Without another word, Jane cautiously stepped into the shower and pulled the curtain closed behind her. Matt stared at the shower curtain and tried to understand his own feelings. Then he reached into the shower stall, put some soap on a wash cloth, and bathed his wife. They'd showered together a few times, and those showers always had playful laughter and a passionate ending. The showers of late were only grim reminders of happy times that might never return.

Matt dried her with a towel, placed a new corset around her chest, dressed her in a soft fleece jacket and pants, and walked her out to the split-log benches surrounding the campfire.

"Ah, wood smoke," Matt said when he sat next to Jane. "It always takes me back to a thousand other fires and a thousand other nights." He reached over to a cooler filled with longneck bottles of Leinenkugel's beer, and opened one. "Do you ever wonder if each of us carries the DNA, the genetic memories of all of our ancestors, and when we sit by a fire and smell the smoke it stirs all those lost memories?" He looked out at the lake. "Look at that moon," he added, as if he'd never seen it before.

"You're the only person I ever met who says things like that," Jane said.

"Well, I think about stuff like that." He kissed Jane's hand and asked, "How are you doing, honey? You're pretty quiet these days."

"I'm glad to be home again."

A loon called from far across the lake. Then several more joined in, and the long hail calls morphed into a brief cacophony.

"They're glad you're back, too," Matt said.

The songbirds had all stopped peeping for the day, and now the only sounds in the woods around Scotch Lake were the loons calling to each other and the fire crackling at their feet. Dusk had brought a complete calm to lake, and it was a silent sheet of glass getting ready to reflect a rising moon. A three-quarter moon was beginning to show itself between the tall spires of several balsam fir trees on the far side of the lake, and a single line of wood smoke rose straight up into the cool evening air. The deep greens of the forest were changing in the low light. Everything would be a dark blue for a while, then there would only be silver moonlight, and moon shadows, and flickering firelight.

"Sally's here," Matt said, when he heard a car door close in the driveway.

A moment later Sally walked around the side of the house and joined them by the fire. "Wow, what a beautiful night for a fire," she said, as she found her way to the circle of stones and sat on the bench across from Matt and Jane.

"Would you like a beer?" Matt asked.

"Don't mind if I do," Sally replied.

A gentle breeze swirled over the yard and the fire as Matt reached into the cooler to get Sally a beer, and a small cloud of wood smoke wafted onto Jane. "Argh, I can't have that smoke get all over me. I just took a shower and I'll smell like smoke all night," she said, using her hand to fan away the smoke. When she tried to use her arms to lift herself out of her chair she grimaced in pain, and then sat back.

"Ooh, here, I'll help you up," Matt said, as he scrambled over to Jane's chair to assist her. He held her arm and then eased her onto the split log bench on the opposite side of the fire, next to Sally.

"This is better," she said when the breeze carried the smoke away from her.

"Nice fire, Matt," Sally said.

"Thanks. I love sitting around a campfire."

"Me too. I spent a lot of time sitting around fires when I was a kid." Sally set her beer bottle on the bench and stood up. "But we're missing something. To really enjoy a fire, you need to be poking a stick in it. Mind if I go find a good fire-pokin' stick?" She started toward the woods.

"Get me one too," Matt replied.

"Me too," Jane said. Then she cast an approving smile at Matt. She liked it that Sally was already comfortable enough to make herself at home with them.

Sally walked to the woods and they watched in the fading light while she found several oak branches lying on the ground and then broke them over her knee to bring them to the correct length.

"Here you go," she said when she handed the sticks to Matt and Jane.

"Looks like you've done this before," Matt said.

"What, sat by a fire? Yup." Sally began to stir the orange coals at her feet. "It's how I got my scar, too." She looked over her shoulder at them and smiled. "You probably never noticed that I have this little scar on my face?"

"No. What scar?" Matt joked.

"What happened?" Jane asked, surprised that Sally was willing to talk so freely about the hideous scar.

"I was born and raised in northern Wisconsin, over by Rhinelander, and my parents were poor. Well, we weren't starving or anything like that, but we didn't have much. Anyway, my father was an outdoorsman, and we lived in a cabin in the woods. Dad used to cut firewood and sell it to the people in town. One day when I was little, maybe four, my mother put my warm clothes on and sent me outside while she was putting her warm clothes on. We were gonna play on a big pile of snow. But my dad was cutting wood with a chain saw about a hundred feet from the house, and he had a little fire burning."

Jane covered her mouth. She knew where this story was going.

"Yeah, you guessed it." Sally nodded. "I saw the fire, and I saw my Dad, and I walked over to see what he was doing. He didn't hear me coming. I was just standing beside him when he turned and looked around. the chain was still running when he accidentally touched it against my face."

With her hand still over her mouth, Jane gasped.

"Coulda been a lot worse," Matt offered.

"Yeah, that's for sure," Sally said. "Actually, I was lucky. the chain cut about halfway through my eyelid, but no further. There was no damage to my eye." Now Sally closed both eyes and let Jane and Matt have a long look at the terrible scar that ran from the middle of her forehead to the middle of her cheek. "It's just a scar. We've all got scars."

"You're beautiful," Jane said. "And the scar just goes away when you talk, and smile."

"Thanks. That's a nice thought, but I see people staring at me sometimes," Sally said.

"Does it bother you to talk about this?" Jane asked.

"No, not at all. It's my story; it's all part of who I am." Sally shrugged.

"John and I talked about you, and your scar, on that first day when we came into the coffee shop," Matt said. "We pretty much guessed that it happened about the way you described things." He stopped and grinned.

"Really?" Sally said.

"Yeah. John said he thought it was sexy, and he thought you had a nice caboose," Matt replied.

Sally used her stick to stir some coals in the fire, then she flashed her own smile. "John . . ." She sighed. "I wanted to slug him that day. I was so angry."

"He has that effect on people," Jane said.

"He can be pretty charming, too," Sally said.

"OK, Sally, on that note, I have to ask you something," Matt began. "I can't help but notice, sometimes it looks like you're sizing John up, trying decide if you're interested."

"Matt! You can't ask her that!" Jane said.

"Oh, I like John," Sally laughed. "I did wanna beat him with a hammer there, that one time. No, several times. But he's a good guy, and you don't have to dig too deep before you come to the good. He's covering something up, though. He's hurting on the inside, and he does the things he does in order to protect himself." Sally paused for a second while she stared into the fire. "And I know about *that*." She looked at Matt and asked, "Do you know where his pain comes from?"

"Kind of, but not really. We grew up together, and we've been friends forever. He dropped out of the U, gave up a free education and went to California for a few years. I think he had some issues with his father before he went away, but he's never shared much about those lost years with me."

Jane leaned forward and surprised the others when she announced that she was done for the day. "I'm sorry, honey, and Sally, but I gotta hit the sack, or more accurately, I gotta hit the recliner. I'm still sleeping in a recliner until I'm strong enough to roll over and get outta bed."

"It's getting late, and I should go home too," Sally said.

"Stick around and talk to me. I'm not ready to call it a night yet," Matt said, as he stood up and brushed her words away with a stroke of his hand. "Stay here and stir those coals while I walk my girl up to the house. We have plenty more to talk about, and the moon is still climbing."

"OK, I guess I can stay for a while," Sally said. "But Jane, before you go inside, I wanted to ask you something."

"Sure, what?"

"I'm going to take a day off next week and go to Duluth to do some shopping. Well, mainly, just to get away. Would you like to join me? I'll drive. We can look around, see the sights, maybe go down to Canal Park and have lunch?" Sally asked.

Jane smiled. "Yeah, I'd like that. Thanks for thinking of me."

"I'll call you tomorrow and we'll work out the travel plans," Sally said.

"All right then, call me." Jane turned to walk toward the house. "You two enjoy the fire, and be careful you don't step in the bullshit when Matt starts to tell stories."

Several minutes later Matt returned to the fire circle and sat next to Sally. "Nice move on the day trip to Duluth. That's just what she needs. This was her first campfire since she came home, and she was really tired out just now when she plopped into her recliner."

Matt and Sally looked up at the bank of windows facing the lake and they could still see the soft amber glow from the reading lamp beside Jane's recliner. They were looking up at the house when the lights inside all went dark. "I'll bet she's asleep in . . . Hell, she's asleep now," Matt said.

"You still have a crush on her, don't you?" Sally said.

Matt stirred the coals in the campfire and ignored Sally's words.

"I see the way you look at her. I'm jealous. Nobody ever loved me like that."

Matt just smiled, and while he looked into the fire he tapped his right hand against his heart. He said, "Jane's parents had a love like that. They were solid."

"Not your parents?" Sally asked.

"Nope, not even close. My dad was in the second wave at Utah Beach on D-Day." He paused and listened to the silence of the summer night, and Sally knew that he was about to open up. "He survived that fighting without a scratch, and he survived the Hurtgen Forest, which was even worse fighting, without a scratch. Then about six weeks after D-Day he got a letter telling him that the girl he was engaged to had been killed in a car accident. How 'bout that for irony?" Matt reached into the cooler for another beer. "Hell, is that *irony*, or just what is it? Anyway, when he got home he met my mother and they got married. I think that would be what we call getting married on the rebound." Matt took a long swallow of beer. "She was a terrible person. She was always angry, and bitchy. I never saw them ever have a moment of affection. Once, when I was a kid, maybe fourth grade, I had a button pop off my shirt in school and I was so afraid of my mother I could hardly go home. When I finally did go home she absolutely went off. She ranted, screamed, and told me that I was nothing but a bother, and that she didn't know why she ever had a child."

"Wow," Sally said. "So how did *you* ever learn how to love someone?"

"Well, when I was in school I was a good-looking kid, you'd never know that now, but, anyway, I never had much trouble getting a date. I went out with some pretty nice girls, and based on what I knew from my early life, and what I felt, I thought I was in love a couple times." He took another swig of beer, and used his thumb to point at the house. "And then I met *her*. She showed me what love was, and taught me how to be a good man."

"Love at first sight?" Sally asked with a smile.

"Maybe, but I've learned a little bit about love over the years." He finished off his second beer and tossed the empty bottle onto the ground beside the cooler. "Would you like to know what I've learned?" he teased.

"By all means."

"Would you like another beer, before I tell you?"

"By all means!" Sally replied.

Matt opened another beer for each of them. He leaned back and crossed his legs. "OK then, I read something once, about that, about why we fall in love." He took a minute to get the words right. "We don't love someone because of the way they look; we fall in love because that person is singing a song that only we can hear." Sally could hear, *feel*, Matt try to swallow the lump in his throat when he finished.

"Pretty good," Sally said. "I think Leinenkugel's makes you into a poet." Matt needed a smile, and Sally gave it to him. She raised her beer and clinked the neck of the brown bottle against his in a toast to his poetry.

"Makes me a better dancer, too, but the dosage is critical on that." He clinked his longneck against hers and wiped his eyes dry.

"How is her recovery coming?" Sally asked.

"She's still tired quite a bit, and she's ready to get those drain tubes out, and she really hates those tissue expanders they put in her chest."

"Those *what*?"

"When they do this type of surgery they sort of melon-ball the breast and save the nipple and the skin; provided that they've already removed all the cancer. They place a rubber thing fulla water, a tissue expander, where the breast was, and then they sew the skin and nipple over it. The idea is to keep a space available for later on, after some healing, so the surgeon can come back and place breast implants. If they just let things heal without the tissue expander there's no room for implants later."

"I never heard of that."

"Me neither, until all of this. Jane says they're uncomfortable. She hates the way they feel. Sometimes she says she wishes she'd just had everything taken off. She says she could just get a bra with a couple falsies in there and it would be just fine."

"What do you think about that?" Sally asked. She hadn't expected Matt to open up and speak so candidly.

"I think it's still pretty early in the game to make some of those decisions. I wish she felt better about what she's done. Well, I guess *I* sorta talked her into having those tissue expanders placed. I hope I did the right thing." Matt tossed another empty bottle on the ground. "Ready for another?"

"No thanks, two is my limit, and I'm still working on this one. But you—"

"Don't mind if I do," Matt said, as he drew another beer from the icy water of the cooler and let the lid thump shut. "I think the thing I wonder about the most is whether or not life will ever be like it used to be. Not so long ago, I thought it would just go on like it always had been. But now I wonder . . . no, now, sometimes I'm afraid."

"Everybody's afraid," Sally sighed. "But nobody wants to say it out loud."

"Funny thing about that," Matt started, "saying something out loud, I mean. Sometimes when you hear yourself say something out loud it gives the thought illumination, and sorta lets that thought come alive. Other times it just sounds stupid, and then you can let it go."

"So what, exactly, are *you* afraid of?" Sally asked. "Let's go for some illumination."

"Loss. The losses that come with age, I think. What if Jane—?" Matt stopped. Sally thought he was trying to find the right words to finish his thought, then she heard his voice double clutch, and when she looked over at him his face was twisted and he was using the heel of his hand to wipe tears away. "Sorry," he said softly.

"She's gonna be fine."

"I watched her walking tonight, and I couldn't help but remember other people, some of them friends, who've died from this." Matt wiped at his eyes again.

"Oh, Matt, you have to be positive."

"That's what I *do*, Sally. I'm a rock. But I just can't do it all the time. Sometimes I'm so afraid. And I wish I could go back and live so much of my life over again. I'd love her better. I'd be a better man, a better husband." Matt kicked another log on the fire, sighed heavily to drive the tears away, and then added, "But I can't go back."

"We all wish we could go back," Sally offered. "But then we'd probably just find a way to get it all wrong the second time around, too."

Matt chuckled. "Good one. You know, people always say the things they regret most in life are things they *didn't* do. Well, I can think of a whole bunch of stupid shit I *did*, that I wish I hadn't."

"Like what?"

"Pissed on an electric fence one time," Matt said.

Sally covered her eyes and groaned.

"Too much information? Sorry."

Sally giggled. "Well, I've never known you to be so chatty. But I'm liking your stories. I think the beer has loosened your tongue."

"You are correct." Matt pointed a finger at her. "I do have a little buzz goin' here, and I like it. And you're easy to talk to."

"Yeah, I guess so." Sally shivered. The evening air had cooled quickly after sundown, and she crossed her arms over her chest to fight the chill.

Without a second thought, Matt moved over next to her, put his arm around her and pulled her close. Everything about his gesture spoke of friendship and not an improper advance, but nonetheless, Sally couldn't help but wonder if Matt had something more than staying warm in mind.

Matt extended his leg and kicked two small jack pine logs onto the coals. Then he crossed his legs and squeezed Sally a bit closer before he asked, "Better?"

"Uh-huh."

"Ah, we'll stoke the fire some, and finish our beer before we wrap it up for the night. OK?" Matt asked.

"Sure." Sally liked his embrace, and she was warm now, but nonetheless . . .

Not a leaf was moving, and the smoke from their fire rose in a single column until it cleared the tops of all the surrounding trees and then drifted out over the lake. Matt stared into the glowing embers at their feet. "I like the sound pine knots make when they burn, and the different colors they give off when the sap inside them catches fire," Matt said. "You ever burn apple wood in a campfire?"

"Sure, it pops and crackles more than pine. My dad used to burn apple wood in the fireplace at home, just to hear it snap and spark. I love that."

"Me too. Feels like it's talking to me, giving up some secrets maybe," Matt said. He leaned forward and stirred the coals with a crooked branch from a dead oak tree. When the coals collapsed and shifted a few minutes later, Sally took a turn, and stirred the coals with the same branch. Then she dropped the branch beside the fire and nuzzled close to Matt again. She was *pretty* sure this closeness they were sharing was the result of a very personal conversation, having let down some barriers a few minutes earlier. She liked sitting so close to this man, who felt like a friend. But still, in her experience, men just didn't do things like this without another motive. Way back in her mind, she began to wonder what she'd do if he tried to kiss her.

"Ever had a broken heart?" Matt said after a quiet spell.

"Coupla times. We all get a broken heart, sometime."

"Think so?"

Sally nodded. "Sure, and it healed every time." Sally shrugged. "But I don't think that's what's going on here, Matt."

Matt stirred the embers again, and waited for her to go on.

"I think maybe it's the loss of innocence," Sally said. "You know how historians like to write about how our country lost its innocence on the day JFK was assassinated?"

"Yeah."

"And then writers and romantics talk about how our loss of innocence is related to the first time we have sex?" Sally said.

"Sure."

Sally stole a sideways glance at Matt and saw only the shadow of a flickering campfire on his blank face. "But I think our innocence gets lost when some roadblock comes along—some *thing,* a thing that's just so big we can't get around it; one of those slings and arrows of outrageous fortune that Shakespeare talked about, and we're forced to realize that life just isn't going to be what we thought it was."

"Then what?" Matt asked.

"Then the lucky ones, or maybe the strong ones, realize that life doesn't have to be just what we thought it was, in order for us to be happy, and they get on with it."

Matt let Sally's words drift into the night sky, along with the single line of smoke from the campfire. "That was good, Sally, real good. Where did you find that wisdom?" he joked.

"Right down there, at the bottom," Sally said, pointing an index finger into the open mouth of her beer bottle.

"Well, we have a few more mysteries to solve, but thank goodness we have plenty of Leinies and firewood for the next campfire." Matt said, as he scattered the dying coals in the fire pit. This moment, this campfire, was over, and it was time for Sally to go home. Matt had no ulterior motives when he'd put an arm around her. He'd done it without thinking, just to offer her a bit of warmth. She understood that now, and the gesture had opened a door that would let her move a bit closer into the Kingstons' circle of friends. He was definitely one-of-a-kind in her experience, too.

"Hey Matt," Sally said, as Matt was about to stand up. She grabbed his hand in hers and held him on the bench for one last thing. "I have to tell you something. You did the right thing with Jane, and the breast implants." She was smiling a wicked smile, and it was plain to see that she had a story to tell before she left.

"Oh?"

"Yeah, I have a friend in Minneapolis who had the same surgery as Jane several years ago. Well, actually, she lost one breast, had it completely removed, and then got a bra with a falsie in the one side."

"Oh?" Matt grinned, wondering how this story would end.

"Yeah, and everything was just fine, until one day she was carrying groceries in from the car. It was an autumn day, and her son was playing football in the front yard with a few of his friends. She had a couple of clumsy packages to carry, and she was stumbling around lifting things out of the car, and she had to make several trips back and forth from the car to the kitchen. On her final trip out to the car she noticed that her falsie was gone." Sally stopped her story. "Are you with me?"

Matt nodded.

"OK, so at the same instant that she realized her boob was missing, she looked out in the yard and saw that her son was about to kick off to the other team . . . and the ball was resting on her falsie. Her son had found it in the driveway and was using it as a kicking tee!"

Sally allowed Matt to laugh along with her for a minute and then reassured him that someday his life would return to normal, or close to it.

"Well, if we'd had kicking tees like that back in the day, I'm sure John Velde would have come to practice more often," said Matt. "I wonder what he's doing at the moment."

CHAPTER TWENTY-SIX

Several young men stood outside Buster's bar, some of them leaning on a picnic table a few feet from the front entrance. John guessed that most of them were summer people, here to visit their cabins, and out tonight looking for a good time. This was a young crowd: more than half were men, no parents with small children. A couple of them were smoking cigarettes, and most of them were loud, talking about cars, or girls, or their friends. When DeeDee and John approached the front door, the conversation stopped. John watched the eyes of the men, moving up and down DeeDee's long, thin legs and the impressive cleavage that she dressed to display. Her cotton T-shirt stopped about five inches short of her waist and exposed a fair amount of smooth, tan skin there. She had high cheekbones and large round eyes, and her dull brown hair was streaked with some blonde accents. Her jeans rode low on her hips and featured lots of silver buttons around the pockets. She wore too much eye makeup, which made her eyes look dark and sunken. She looked young and slutty, and everyone noticed her.

John reached around for the door handle and when he swung it open he made eye contact with the guy standing closest to the door. John stared into the other man's eyes and sent the message that he was, in fact, *with* this girl. He'd been in this situation a million times, with other men sizing up his date, or him. He'd fought his way out of a few of these situations too. But tonight that seemed unlikely. These guys would say something after DeeDee and he had moved past them, for sure, but not until John and DeeDee were out of earshot and they could speak with no fear of insult or reproach.

A roar of loud music rushed past them as the door opened, and when it closed behind them John had to lean close to DeeDee's ear and then raise his voice to be heard. "Let's go sit outside on the deck, overlooking the lake, so we can talk," he said. He leaned so close to her ear that he could feel her hair tickling his lips when he spoke. He smelled her perfume, too, which he was fairly certain she'd bought at a dime store.

"OK!" she hollered back at him.

They walked through the bar and John continued to watch the eyes of other men move up and down DeeDee's sexy form. The bartender, a longtime friend of John's, greeted him with a nod and then a quick smile when he tossed a glance at DeeDee. John responded with a grin that said simply, "Yup."

As they reached the door that opened onto the deck and patio overlooking Wiigwaas Lake, a waitress brushed by John. Her name was Lori, she was in her early forties, and she knew John Velde quite well. She'd seen DeeDee first, and then John following behind her, and she'd sized up the situation accurately in about one second. When John looked at her, she closed her eyes and shook her head in sarcastic disdain. John had spent some lusty evenings with Lori a few years earlier, before she'd married a good man who owned a construction company east of town. They'd remained on friendly terms ever since. There had been no more romantic adventures between them, but she'd always seemed reluctant to completely let go of her "thing" with John. She liked to tease him when he brought friends to the bar now, especially his women friends. John returned her smile and led DeeDee to a quiet table by the cedar deck railing, as far from the music as he could get.

"Ever been here before?" John asked.

"No, I usually go to Spike's, or Lefty's, or the Tap In."

"Really," John said, with no further comment. The places she'd named were local shit holes, the kind of places where he'd already have been in a fight, had he taken her there. "Well, I think the food is better here. Would you like to get a burger, or a pizza?"

"Pizza." A few minutes later, Lori came to their table and stood with pen in hand, waiting to take their orders.

"What would you like?" John said to DeeDee.

"Let's get a Hawaiian Special. Isn't that the one with pineapple on it? That's my favorite," DeeDee said.

"Mmm, yes! You'll love it," Lori said, and she raised her eyes to pass a devious grin to John.

Lori the waitress knew that John hated, *hated*, the Hawaiian Special. She'd seen him go off on several beer-fueled tirades after softball games, right there on the deck overlooking the lake, when a teammate made the mistake of ordering a Hawaiian Special. "Jesus, what the shit is wrong with you?" he'd barked one night. "*Pineapple?* Snap out of it! If it doesn't have pepperoni on there it's not pizza, for Chrissakes." Lori looked at John gleefully, waiting for a similar outburst, but it never came. When John failed to make a fuss over this girl ordering a Hawaiian Special, Lori understood that John was behaving himself because he wanted something from the girl. Then Lori asked DeeDee what she wanted to drink.

"I'd like a shandy," DeeDee said.

"Oh, terrific!" Lori blurted. She nearly burst out laughing as she wrote DeeDee's drink order. "And you?" she said when she turned to John. She was enjoying the moment: DeeDee's drink order was the knockout punch. John always came unglued when someone in his party ordered a shandy. "Are you shittin' me?" he'd groan. "A beer with lemonade in it?" And then he'd go on to question the person's sanity, or gender.

Lori held her pen and order pad and leaned over in anticipation while she waited for John's order, and his response to DeeDee's order. She wanted to be sure that John could see how much she was enjoying this order.

"I'll have a Bud Heavy, a longneck," John said, and he stifled everything else he had to say about beer and pizza. He wore a look on his face as if his mother had just forced him to eat all the spinach on his plate. Lori made sure John could see she was absolutely giddy as she walked away with the order.

"So, where are you from, DeeDee? Where did you grow up?" John asked, once they were alone. He wanted to back up a bit, get away from Hawaiian Specials and shandies, and engage the girl in talking about something else.

"Jackson."

"Jackson, Minnesota?"

"Uh-huh."

"Here's your shandy!" the waitress interrupted cheerfully, a moment later. "And a Bud Heavy for you!"

John ignored the waitress and raised his beer. "Were your parents from the Jackson area? That's way down by the Iowa border."

"No, I was born in Ohio. My parents moved to Jackson because Minnesota has good welfare benefits," DeeDee said. "The first place the bus stopped in Minnesota was Jackson, so we got off there."

"Oh." John blinked away his surprise. "Well, what did your father do?"

"Nothing," DeeDee said, as if that was a pretty stupid question.

"How did you wind up *here*?" John asked, hoping to move the dialogue to a better place.

"My boyfriend and I moved here. He seen an advertisement for an electrician's job, so we moved here."

"So, what has become of your boyfriend?" John asked.

"He didn't like the electrician job, so he took a job out in the oil fields, out west."

"So, you don't see him anymore?"

"Not for two years. He got into meth and lost all his teeth when he was in prison. He has a different girlfriend now."

"I'll bet," John mumbled.

"Huh?" DeeDee asked.

"Ah, nothing," John said. Still, DeeDee Katzenmeyer was a spectacular woman. John tried not to let her see him staring at her chest, but the way her T-shirt and her suntan came together above her ample cleavage made it nearly impossible for him to look away. "So, the guy who lost his teeth in prison, is he Mike . . ." John hesitated, then clumsily decided to use her son's entire name, ". . . elangelo's father?" he stammered.

"No, Mike is from a previous relationship."

John decided to try a different topic. "OK, so what do *you* do?"

"I work at the hardware store. It's pretty boring, but them people are nice to me," she said. John was about out of questions, and very thankful when DeeDee asked, "What do *you* do?"

"I'm a taxidermist," John said.

"Oh! You mean like a doctor? You help kids with pimples? That's so cool!"

"No, not a doctor," John said. "I make the stuffed fish and birds you see all over." He pointed to a northern pike mounted above the front door and said, "I made that."

"OK, OK, now I get it," DeeDee said, and she leaned back in her chair, suddenly infused with new understanding.

"You were thinking dermatologist, right?" John asked, trying not to roll his eyes.

"Yeah. Did you make all them deer heads I seen on the wall in the Cabelas store?"

"No, I didn't do any of those particular ones, but that's what I do," John answered. DeeDee Katzenmeyer was getting less and less attractive every time she opened her mouth. Her use of the English language was terrible, and she was apparently quite stupid. John gazed at her face, which was less pretty than it had been a few minutes earlier. He let his eyes move to her breasts, which still looked fine, and the skin that showed below her shirt, and he tried not to hear the words "all them deer heads I seen . . ." playing over and over in his head.

"OK, here's your pizza!" Lori the waitress announced with gusto, and John looked up to see her mischievous grin as she placed the pizza on the table between them. "Enjoy." She then asked, "Would you like another shandy?"

"Sure," DeeDee replied.

"And you?" the waitress asked John. "Another longneck?" She understood the situation completely. John's plan to get this young thing in bed required him to *not* say what he was thinking, and that was torture for him. The waitress was savoring the struggle on John's face, and she was working the moment, baiting him.

"Oh, definitely," he said, "definitely another longneck. And hurry." Then he added, "And by the way, the Twins are playing in Seattle tonight, a late start. Do you suppose you could get that game on one of these TVs above the bar? There's a soccer game on now, and since this is a *sports* bar, you should have a real sporting event on the TV." Lori nodded and walked away, but she had no intention of changing the TV channel. She knew that John hated soccer, too.

DeeDee finished her first shandy a moment later. Then she brought a slice of pizza to her mouth and asked, "Where is Seattle from?"

"Pardon me?" John said.

"Where is Seattle from?"

"You mean, what state is Seattle located in?" He was surprised that anyone would phrase that question in such an awkward way.

"It's not a state?" DeeDee asked.

"You mean, is Seattle a city or a state?" He was growing incredulous.

"Yeah, well, where is it?" She asked as she chewed another bit of pizza. The city/state thing seemed to confuse her even further.

"Seattle is in the state of Washington," John said. "The Pacific Northwest, you know?"

DeeDee's face was blank. She didn't know. She shrugged, as if no one should be expected to possess such detailed information, then she added, "Oh well, I'm not very good at geometry."

John blinked his eyes, stunned, like a boxer who'd just taken a good shot and was trying to clear the cobwebs. Then he began to chuckle. He thought about correcting her, pointing out that it was *geography*, not geometry. But why would he do that? She didn't really care, or want to know the difference between geometry and geography, even if he explained it.

John raised his hand and signaled for the waitress to hurry with the longneck, and he started scraping pineapple chunks off a piece of pizza. He'd just do the best he could to enjoy this awful pizza, and then have a tumble with DeeDee.

"So, what do you want to do with your life? Don't you want to get a better job than working at the hardware store?" John asked.

"Yeah, I was thinking about being a cosmetologist."

John was about to quip that medical school would take at least eight years, so she'd better get to work, but then he realized that the joke was so far over her head she'd never get it. He looked across the table and watched her chewing her pizza and she smiled at him.

He wished Sally Durham was sitting over there. She'd get his jokes, and she'd return the volley. And as that thought moved through his mind, he lost interest in DeeDee completely. Soon he began to feel sorry for her, and then he felt bad about being here with her. He smiled when he thought about sitting at his dunce table at the coffee shop, and then he picked at a piece of pizza and tried to coax something intelligent out of DeeDee. But the longer she talked, the less attractive she grew. Eventually it got to the point where John was actually trying to help her understand some of the things they were talking about. Then it became clear that this evening and this relationship were not going to end as John had planned.

Thirty minutes later, when he followed DeeDee out of Buster's and out to his truck, he studied the curves of her jeans, and the skin of her back, and her long legs. But it was no use. He had no interest in DeeDee any longer.

John drove her directly home and let her out of his truck without even a goodnight kiss. "Do you want to come in?" she asked.

"No thanks, DeeDee. I have a really busy day tomorrow. But I had a nice time, though, and maybe we can do this again. We'll see you at baseball on Thursday, right?" He smiled and drove away.

John shook his head as he pulled away. These were uncharted waters. He couldn't remember *ever* turning down a sure thing with a woman like DeeDee. But tonight, he was happy to be going home alone. His smile grew wider as he drove through the darkness, then he laughed out loud. Tomorrow morning, first thing, over coffee, instead of telling Matt about his flesh feast with a much younger woman, he'd tell Matt about DeeDee's struggle with geometry, and the fact that he took her home early.

Definitely uncharted waters.

CHAPTER TWENTY-SEVEN

———

Clinking dishes and the dull thrum of voices surrounded Sally and Jane as they settled into their booth in a Thai restaurant in Duluth. "So, how do you feel?" Sally asked. "Better every day, I hope?"

"Yeah, I think so. It feels so good to be rid of those drain tubes and all the bandages," Jane replied. "But I started taking a drug called Arimidex. It's basically a female hormone blocker and it's already giving me some terrific hot flashes; sorta putting menopause into overdrive. Have you started having hot flashes yet?"

"Not yet," Sally said.

"Well, you have that to look forward to." Jane smiled and she began to tug on the front of her blouse in an effort to cool herself. "Ooh, here comes one now. I call it another personal summer." Jane fanned her face with one hand and tugged at her blouse with the other for a few seconds. "It sucks to get old. Anyway, thank you for taking me along on this little field trip. It's just what I needed. I love Duluth."

"Good! I'm glad we did this too." Sally looked out at an ore boat on Lake Superior. "I love this town. I always have a good time here." Sally raised her water glass and waited for Jane to raise hers so they could toast themselves, and the day.

"Hey, they have duck on the menu," Jane said, and a casual conversation began to evolve while they both scanned their menus. "I always think of my Matt when I think of ducks."

"He's a duck hunter?"

"Yeah, and he has a lot of crazy stories, which usually involve John. But more than that, I remember the first time I saw him kill a duck. He held the dead duck in his hand and stroked the feathers softly, straightened them and tried to make the duck look nice. I asked him what he was doing, and he told me that he was thanking the duck for dying so we could nourish ourselves. I never heard of such a thing, but I guess that's what the Indians did, too, like a prayer. He does that with deer and other animals, too."

"I guess I don't know Matt *real* well, but that doesn't surprise me," Sally said. "He's sorta spiritual about some things, isn't he?"

"You can see that in him?" Jane said, surprised at Sally's insight.

"I never noticed it until the other night at the campfire, after you went to bed. Excuse me, after you went to *recliner*," Sally said. "He had several beers and he shared some things about you."

"Really?"

"Yup. He really likes you." Sally tapped her hand on her heart.

"He likes you, too," Jane said.

"That's a nice thought," Sally said. "He's a real gentleman. It's so darn cute the way he refers to you as 'my Jane.' He got choked up when he spoke of you. No one ever loved me like that."

"He got choked up?"

"Yeah, and he got a little emotional there for a minute or two. He talked about how much he loves you, but then he swallowed it all back."

Jane smiled as if her little boy had just made her proud. "He doesn't usually open up like that."

"Musta been the beer, then," Sally joked. "Or maybe he was just desperate to talk to somebody, and you were already in your recliner for the night."

A waitress appeared at their table, and when she asked to take their orders, the campfire conversation was quickly forgotten.

"I'll have Tom Yum Goong," Jane said. She turned to Sally and giggled. "I don't know what it is, I just like to say it."

"And I'll have the duck, in honor of my new friend Matt." Sally then turned to the waitress and asked, "It's not *too* spicy, is it?"

"Nah, it's not bad," the waitress said.

"That wasn't exactly a resounding endorsement," Sally said to the waitress.

"Oh, it's *kinda* spicy, but you'll like it," the waitress replied.

"OK then, I'll try the duck. Stuff that's spicy hot doesn't usually agree with me, but what the heck. I'm feeling adventurous today."

As the waitress walked away, Jane turned to Sally and said, "Where were we?"

"I was about to tell you that I'm jealous," Sally said.

"Of what?"

"Matt."

"Mmm, yeah, he thinks he's . . ." Jane raised two fingers on each hand to provide quotation marks. ". . . fuckin' blue twisted steel." She leaned back in her chair and laughed. "He says that all the time, but he's got a pretty soft heart."

"Yeah, I see that now, and I see the way he looks at you," Sally said.

Jane smiled. "Yeah. My dad saw that right away too." She leaned forward and lowered her voice. "Can I tell you something?"

"Will it make me blush?" Sally asked.

"Probably."

"Good, then fire away," Sally said.

"Well, I never had a boyfriend, never brought a boy home to meet my parents, until I met Matt. And the first time I brought him to my parents' house, my dad noticed the way Matt looked at me right away. I mean, Matt opened doors for me, and was so polite to me. Like you said, he was a real gentleman, and Dad really liked that. We stayed overnight with my parents that night because we had some extended family in town for the weekend and everyone wanted to meet my boyfriend." The smile from a moment earlier disappeared when Jane spoke again. "My dad took me aside that night, after dinner, and we had a talk."

"Really? About what?" Sally asked.

"Well, I was sorta rough on boys, sorta down on men for a while there…"

"Why?" Sally interrupted.

"I dunno." Jane replied, but Sally noticed the way Jane lowered her eyes and seemed to be hiding something. "Anyway, my dad even noticed it. That night he took me aside and told me not to be so down on men, 'cuz there were some good ones around. Then he told me not to let Matt get away. How 'bout that?"

"I thought you were gonna tell me that your dad saw the way that Matt *looked* at you." Sally raised her eyebrows to convey the sexual innuendo.

"I wasn't going to tell you about *that*."

"Well, *now* you *have* to."

"OK." Jane leaned forward, grinned, and lowered her voice so that no one at a nearby table could hear. "So later on, when everyone was in bed, Matt and I found ourselves on the porch, in the dark, and we started to make out."

Sally leaned forward. "Yes . . .?"

"Well, my parents had assigned us different bedrooms, on opposite ends of the house, because that was just the proper thing to do." Jane paused.

"Yes . . .?"

"But, we were already, um, in love, if you know what I mean." Now Jane's eyes twinkled. "And while we were making out, things were getting sort of urgent." Jane stopped. "Jeez, I'm gonna *blush*."

"Keep going," Sally ordered.

"Well, we went for a walk. Looking for a place to, you know. We got as far as my green Chevy, parked out in the street, and it was a dark night, and the street was quiet, and there were overhanging tree branches everywhere, and my car was parked where no one could see us."

Sally leaned forward and gestured for more.

"So the next morning when we were ready to leave, everyone walked us out to my car." Jane put her hands on her cheeks and closed her eyes before she finished. "And there on the hood of my car were my hand prints, and my boob prints."

Sally covered her eyes and laughed.

"I don't know who noticed what. Maybe no one did, but Matt and I certainly did, and we sure said a hasty goodbye to my family."

"Anybody ever say anything to you?" Sally asked.

"What would they say? 'Looks like you got rear ended here last night, Jane'?" They both burst into laughter. "I can't believe I told you that," Jane said through her laughter. "You should be an interrogator."

When their food arrived a few minutes later they both were ready to eat. Sally placed a napkin in her lap and raised her fork. "That duck smells hot and spicy even from over here," Jane said. "Maybe we should pray for *that* duck right now."

They ate and talked, and the conversation moved from Jane's plans for future doctor visits in Rochester, to Timmy's summer baseball, to the weather, to ore boats out on Lake Superior, to problems at the coffee shop, and back to Jane. "I still sorta wish I'd had 'em both just taken off," Jane said while she picked at her lunch. "Then I'd be done with all this other business."

"You mean the breast implants?" Sally asked, surprised at Jane's negative vibe.

"Yeah. I just want to move on with life. I'm never going to look good again."

"That's not true," Sally said. "The plastic surgeons can do wonders! You're beautiful now, and you're gonna look great when you're healed up."

Jane sighed. "Ah, that's for porn stars and desperate women."

Sally pointed a fork at Jane. "Not at all. Boobs are a big part of our culture. Women want to look nice. It's normal, it's good, and we want our clothes to fit and we want men to—"

Jane interrupted and finished Sally's sentence: "—look at scars and flabby smashed-in boobs when we get naked?" She shook her head. "No, we don't."

"C'mon, Jane, you're just getting started with the healing. When the surgeons are done, no one will even know. I think you should go for that porn-star look! I bet Matt would approve." Sally giggled and then her hand shot up to cover her mouth. "Did I really say that out loud?"

When their lunch was finished, Sally said, "I have to go look for some clothes for Timmy. Then I want to browse around and look for some things just for me. Do you want to stay together, or wander around the mall by yourself for a while and then meet up later?"

"I'd like to look around in the book store and then maybe a few other shops. Why don't we go our separate ways for a while, and then meet in front of Macy's in two hours?" Jane suggested. "Then we can visit a few places together."

"See you then; two hours from now, in front of Macy's," Sally said.

Jane strolled through the mall, looking at windows for a while, and then she found her way to Barnes and Noble. She wandered through the aisles of the book store, picked up a couple of books for herself and one for Matt, and then walked back out into the mall. By and by she stopped at a coffee shop, bought a mocha, sat down in some mall furniture, and watched strangers stroll past her.

Today she had no schedule to keep and no rules to follow. This day was hers to enjoy. She couldn't remember the last time she'd relaxed like this. She'd enjoy this fine cup of coffee until she was done with it. Then she'd go and catch up with her life; it couldn't have gone too far while she was busy being sick.

When she resumed her window shopping, she found herself in front of a women's clothing store with some nice things displayed in the window. She looked at her watch and saw that she still had forty-five minutes to go until she was supposed to meet Sally. She looked at the mannequins in the window once more, glanced at her watch again, and decided to try a few things on.

She searched the racks for clothes that she could put on and take off without help from Matt or anyone else. She found a couple of sweaters and two nice dresses and asked a clerk to show her to a fitting room.

When the door closed behind her, she was facing three floor-length mirrors, arranged at angles that would allow her to examine herself closely. She stared at her reflection for a minute. The woman staring back at her looked curious and afraid. As Jane started to remove her blouse, she watched her own hand undo the buttons one at a time. The blouse opened and she began to study the white skin of her chest and shoulders. She took her blouse off and stared. There was no bra, as there had always been before. She was still wearing the corset with a Velcro fastener up the front that she'd been wearing since her surgery.

Her eyes were fixed on her torso, and she forgot about the things she'd brought to the fitting room. Tentatively, she raised both hands and began to loosen the fastener of her corset. She hadn't planned to do this, but now she had to see what was left of her. Slowly, an inch at a time, she unfastened it, and when she finished, she let the corset fall to the floor.

She kept her eyes on the floor, unwilling to look at herself yet. She slowly unbuttoned and unzipped her slacks, and let them fall to the floor too. She needed to raise her eyes and look. She needed to know if the woman she'd known for all these years was still there.

Jane raised her arms as far as she could until things began to hurt, and then she looked at herself.

The skin of her breasts drooped and hung loosely over the firm, rectangular tissue expanders that had been placed immediately after the surgery. Her chest still looked like it had been broken and poorly reassembled. She turned a bit, first to the right, then to the left, and her eyes took in her fresh scars, the misshapen nipples, the rectangular and uncomfortable tissue expanders that were poorly hidden by the flabby white skin of her breasts.

This wasn't how she wanted to look or feel. This wasn't the future she'd planned for. What did Matt feel when he looked at her now?

She held her arms to the side and tried to raise them above her head. Then everything in her chest began to hurt, and there was no way she could raise her arms any higher.

She bent her elbows and brought her hands up slowly and touched her breasts. They were numb, like her lips were after a visit with a dentist, and the sensation felt terrible. It would it always feel like this, she'd been told.

She moved the firm plastic things under the skin of her breasts and thought how wrong everything felt. And as she moved her arms she saw that the pectoral muscles in her chest no longer moved her breasts as they once had. Things just weren't connected as they should have been. The muscles in her chest contracted and showed themselves, but her breasts just hung there now, and didn't move along with her arms as they once had.

She didn't know how long she'd been staring at herself when a woman's voice startled her. "How're you doing in there, ma'am?" The sales clerk outside the fitting room door had a hint of concern in her voice.

"Pretty good, sorry I'm taking so long," Jane replied.

"No hurry, just checking, I didn't mean to hurry you. Did you see anything you like?" said the clerk.

"No," Jane said, and she quickly folded her arms across her chest as if the woman standing outside the door might see her. She put her own clothes back on without trying any of the clothes she brought in, and she returned the new sweaters and dresses to the displays where she'd found them. She drifted about the store and looked at handbags, and outerwear, and things that didn't make her think about the way she looked in that fitting-room mirror.

———

Sally had finished her shopping twenty minutes early, and she decided to look at some shoes before went to meet Jane in front of Macy's. She was holding a dress shoe, examining the heel and trying to decide if she wanted to try it on, or not, when she felt a tiny heat wave dash through her, somewhere below her waist. It was nothing, she told herself, and it was gone in only a second. She decided to try the shoes on. They were dressy, and the heels would make her taller. "Could I try on a pair of these?" Sally asked the clerk, who Sally thought was probably a college student.

When the clerk brought out the shoes, there was another warm tremor in Sally's belly, just below the equator. This one was a bit hotter, but it was also gone in only a second. Once again, Sally thought nothing more of it.

The shoes felt pretty good, so Sally walked a few paces until she found a mirror. She was studying the shoes, shifting her weight from one foot to the other, and feeling good about the way she'd look when she wore them, when another tremor, this one a bit hotter and more powerful than the others, shook the southern hemisphere. This time the tectonic plates growled when they moved, and a heat wave moved quickly toward the South Pole.

"I'll take 'em," Sally said to the clerk. She put the new shoes back in their box and walked straight to the checkout counter. Something was happening in her belly, and it was time to start looking for a ladies' room.

The checkout clerk, who was a different young girl, was scanning a small stack of sweaters for another shopper. A second woman waited in line behind the first one, and she had an armload of clothing to pay for, but the heat in Sally's lower unit had let up, sort of; there was still plenty of time.

"Sure is a nice day!" the checkout girl said to the woman in the front of the line, as she put the last of her new sweaters in a large bag. "You may swipe your credit card whenever you're ready," she added with a perky voice when the bag was full.

"It's beautiful weather we've been having," the customer agreed, as she swiped her card and waited for her receipt. The shopper said something else about the weather as she put her credit card back in her purse, and the young clerk said something about rain later in the day.

C'mon, hurry up, Sally thought as she watched the woman return her wallet to her purse at a leisurely pace, and then slowly pick up her shopping bag and move out into the mall.

The lady in front of Sally moved forward and put several things on the counter. Slowly.

"Did you find everything all right?" the checkout girl asked.

Hurry up, hurry up, hurry up, Sally thought. The lady was old. She was hunched over, and she wore a wig, and she moved *really* slow.

Sally's stomach rolled over again, hotter and lower, and she started thinking, planning, where she would find a toilet. She remembered that she'd passed a women's restroom just outside the entrance to this store, and now she peeked out into the mall and tried to locate the place.

"I think these slacks are on sale," the clerk said, and she turned away to look for a sales flyer in a newspaper by the register. "Oh, and this jacket is, too," the girl said, as she folded one garment and placed it on top of another. The transaction taking place just in front of Sally was moving at a snail's pace. *Jesus, please hurry*, Sally thought while she watched.

"Are you Marilyn?" the old lady asked the clerk.

Chrissakes, who cares? Sally thought. *Just hurry up.*

"No, Marilyn is off today," the clerk said.

The old lady and the clerk talked about Marilyn, and the weather, for another minute, and then the clerk told the old lady how much everything was going to cost. *Jesus, could you go any slower?* Sally thought. The fire down below was beginning to make her forehead sweat, and the girl at the cash register had no idea that there was a thermonuclear blast about to detonate in Sally's pants.

Finally, after the little old lady counted out the exact change from the coin pouch in her wallet, the girl behind the counter handed her a bag with her things in it and the lady tottered off into the mall.

The cashier seemed to drop into an even lower gear when Sally moved a step closer. Sally was clenching things tight, real tight. She inched forward, stiff-legged, while something angry and molten churned low in her belly.

"Did you find everything all right?" the girl asked.

"Yes," Sally said.

The girl opened the box with Sally's new shoes and checked to be sure that the shoes matched and were the same size.

Sally's brain was screaming, *JESUS CHRIST, HURRY UP!!!* She knew she should make a break for the toilet, now, but the spasm in her nether regions was so intense all she could do was fight on. When this last heat wave passed, she thought she'd be able to sprint, albeit stiff legged, and make it to the toilet. She'd had other close calls.

Mount St. Helens was beginning to smoke when, at last, the cashier gave Sally her receipt and her new shoes, and said, "Have a nice day."

Sally bolted, sort of. She attempted to run in such a way so as not to jostle things and lose her grip. She looked like she had two wooden legs, and her arms were fixed at her sides to help with her balance.

She was wobbling, like a train about to come off the tracks, when she reached a grouping of overstuffed furniture, a rest area where pissed-off old men could sit and wait for their wives to finish shopping. Another tsunami was roaring down there, all across the southern hemisphere. She squeezed her cheeks together with all her strength and plopped onto a leather couch next to a rotund and drowsy old man. The man smiled as if he'd just won the lottery: an attractive younger woman had chosen to sit right next to him while every other seat in the furniture grouping was open. Maybe women still saw him as handsome, and wanted . . .

Sally ignored the man's smile. All she could think about was keeping her sphincter closed for a few more seconds. That blazing duck she'd had for lunch was trying to peck its way out of her.

Beads of sweat were gathering on her forehead while she waited for this contraction to pass. When it let up, she hoped for one chance, just one more chance, to make it to the safety of a public restroom. "Oh Jesus, oh Jesus, oh Jesus," she whispered through clenched teeth. Then a terrible thought flashed through her mind: What if she made it to the ladies' room, only to find that all of the stalls were occupied and she had to wait even longer? Oh God, she couldn't let herself think that. All of her thought processes were required to hold back the molten tidal wave.

The pressure and heat abated ever so slightly, and Sally seized the opportunity. She stood and made a break for it. She made it almost to the sign with the diagram of a woman on it, just outside the restroom, and it was there, in the Duluth Mall, where she lost her grip. The dam cracked and something hot and foul began to gurgle. Down there. She felt the wet heat spreading quickly. She hurried and clenched things closed as best she could in order to hold back the rest of the mudslide, but there was no way to stem the tide now.

The handicapped stall in the women's restroom was available when she raced in. She burst into the stall and managed to unfasten her pants, but before she could sit down, the rest of the duck flew away in a powerful explosion.

Sally was mortified by the sight all around her. Sitting there with her pants at her ankles, she saw that her panties, her gray slacks, her socks, and her black shoes were covered with liquid shit, as was the floor, and both of her bare legs. The toilet seat she was sitting on, and the wall behind the toilet, had shit splattered everywhere, too. And the storm that had roared through her belly wasn't over yet. One final flaming hot contraction burned its way out of her with a wet explosion that was heard, and felt, throughout the ladies' room. The old guy out in the mall probably heard it too.

Then it was over.

Now what?

Still photos of the aftermath of residential neighborhoods that been destroyed by tornados came to her mind—twisted, mangled, unrecognizable wreckage of what had been beautiful homes only a moment earlier.

She found her purse, which was also sitting on the floor in a small puddle of shit, and removed her phone. She was overwhelmed by it all, nearly hysterical, when she called Jane. Her tears came faster when Jane failed to answer. "Oh God, come and help me! I'm in the public bathroom by the shoe shop on the west end of the mall!" she sobbed into Jane's voicemail.

Sally turned her phone off and then, still sobbing, she did the only thing she could do. She began to clean up the impossible mess around her.

Jane was hurrying, as best she could, when she finally drew near to the west end of the mall and spotted the sign for the women's restroom. Her chest hurt when she tried to run, and she had to hold her chest in order to keep things from bouncing. Based on the frantic plea for help, she'd assumed that Sally had been stricken by some catastrophic medical emergency. Or maybe she'd had been assaulted by a maniac. "Move! Move!" Jane called out, and frightened shoppers in the center of the mall scattered as she made the dash to help Sally.

Jane could hear a small commotion before she turned the corner and burst into the women's room, and she froze in her tracks when she saw her friend. Sally was standing, naked from the waist down, bent over and sobbing while she scrubbed her legs with wet paper towels. She began to weep hysterically when Jane finally arrived and they looked into each other's eyes.

But the scene in front of her made no sense to Jane. Sally's slender, athletic legs were bare, and her feet were bare. And her face was shattered. Jane could only stare and try to comprehend what she was seeing. Why was Sally half naked? Had she been raped, or assaulted? There was no blood anywhere. And the place smelled like an open sewer. This vision, this moment, was far from anything Jane had ever seen.

Two other women were huddled beside Sally. Both of the women were elderly, matronly. They seemed to be trying to comfort her. "Ohhh, honey, it's all right, it's OK," they both kept repeating in motherly voices. Each of them held a roll of toilet paper in one hand,

and in their other hand they held wet paper towels, which they kept dabbing on Sally.

What was happening? Jane wondered. Two old women were blotting her half-naked friend in a foul-smelling mall bathroom . . . this was *so* bizarre.

And then the pieces of the puzzle came together for Jane. There was no medical emergency. There had been no assault. Sally had simply lost control of a pretty impressive code brown and shit her pants. She was all right, she had not been harmed, and she was in no danger. She was, however, extraordinarily embarrassed, nearly distraught, over what had happened.

"Honey, it's OK," the old women kept repeating. One of them held a large plastic shopping bag in one hand, and the bag was quickly filling with the wads of toilet paper and paper towels that they were using to clean Sally, and Sally's shit-covered clothing.

The old ladies were simply innocent bystanders who happened to be good Samaritans, and their motherly instincts automatically kicked in during Sally's crisis. If this had happened in a men's bathroom, every guy in the place would have acted like they hadn't seen a thing and then walked away. But these two ladies were dabbing shit stains from wa total stranger and trying to make her feel better.

Jane found the moment to be bizarre by anyone's standards. The fear that had brought her racing through the mall had given way first to confusion, and then an immense feeling of relief. This moment cried out for laughter, not tears. It was *so* absurd. Jane covered her mouth and began to laugh. Her eyes met Sally's and passed the message that this moment of craziness was only that; crazy. And all they could do was laugh.

Sally was still sobbing, overcome with embarrassment, when she read the relief in Jane's eye's, and she saw Jane, her new best friend, bend over, put her palms on her knees, and surrender to the laughter.

Ever so slowly, because of Jane, Sally came to own the moment too. She understood that she was, after all, OK, and that she'd be home in a couple of hours in spite of the awful thing this duck had done to her. For a minute, she vacillated between crying and laughing; her spirit was still unsure just where to settle on this one. She sobbed, then laughed, then sobbed, and when she looked at Jane again, she allowed her friend's laughter to carry her away, too.

Neither Sally nor Jane was able to speak, or draw a breath. This was one for the ages. The attending two old ladies still didn't get it. They just kept dabbing shit off Sally's legs and repeating, "Honey, it's OK." Which made it all that much funnier.

As she laughed, and watched Sally laugh, Jane felt herself let go of something, and she surrendered to the insanity of it all. A few minutes earlier she'd been staring at herself in a fitting-room mirror and wondering about life. Now she was here, dealing with . . . this. She could still laugh. Her belly began to bounce and her chest heaved with laughter. Jane grabbed her chest and said, "Oh God, my boobs hurt from laughing."

Even the two little old ladies began to smile when they realized that the lady with the scar on her cheek was all right now, and the laughter was cleansing.

"I'll be right back," Jane said, after the long stretch of hysterics. She wiped the tears from her eyes and said, "I'll go over to Macy's and buy you some traveling clothes." Sally could still hear Jane laughing as she left the ladies' room, and just a few minutes later she returned with new panties, gray sweatpants, and some running shoes. They thanked the two wonderful old women profusely and then made their getaway.

No words were exchanged on their walk through the mall, or the parking lot, or for the first ten minutes of the ride back to Pine Rapids; there were only long quiet stretches separated by spontaneous and uncontrollable belly laughs. Each of them had been aware that the other was something of a kindred spirit, and they sensed that this incident in the ladies' room at the mall would cement their bond of friendship. After a long silent stretch while they rolled along on the road home, Sally barked, "Oh shit!"

"What? What is it?" Jane asked, afraid that some new gastronomic event was about to happen.

"You know those shoes I bought? The ones I decided to pay for instead of making a break for the bathroom? The ones that caused that nightmare?" Sally asked.

"Yeah?" Jane said.

"I forgot 'em, in the ladies' room, back at the mall!"

CHAPTER TWENTY-EIGHT

The afternoon lunch and coffee-break crowd had cleared out of the coffee shop when John's truck rolled up to the curb at about four o'clock. As he made his way through the front door, Sally waved to him from behind the counter. "Hey, I brought some fish for you," he called to her. "Do you have a minute to tell me where to put them?"

"Sure. Things usually slow down in here about this time of day," Sally said. She hurried out from behind the counter and followed John out to the street to peek into the box of his truck. "Wow," she cooed, "they're awesome. What's that big one? Let's hang that one first."

"That big boy is a muskie. Where would you like it?"

"Let's feature that one. Isn't that the fish that everyone is after around here? Let's put it where everyone can see it."

"Would you like that bear in my office? It's been standing in that corner for a long time; I'd be glad to give it a new home."

"No thanks on that one," Sally said. "I actually thought about that, but I think everyone would touch it and then it might also creep some people out. So many of my customers are women."

"That's what I figured, but just thought I'd ask. Yeah, you should stick with fish. I've got a pretty nice walleye, too. That's probably the other most sought-after fish around here. Let's find a good spot for that one, too," John said.

Several minutes later, John was ready to climb a stepladder and hang the fifty-two-inch-long graphite muskie on the wall, high enough where it could be seen by everyone and touched by no one. He had measured carefully, and he'd placed two wood screws in the exact places necessary to match the hardware on the fish.

John checked that the shop was empty, then asked, "Is that Vivaldi's *Four Seasons* you have playing?"

Sally blinked in surprise. "Yes."

"You didn't think I'd recognize Vivaldi, or any other long-haired composer, did you?" John grinned.

"Well, I wouldn't have picked you as a classical music kind of guy."

"I'm a fascinating man." John was staring at his hands while he bent a wire on the wall side of the big muskie.

"Who's your favorite composer?" Sally asked, holding back a smile.

"You testing me? You think I just pulled Vivaldi outta my ass . . . got lucky . . . don't you?"

"Maybe."

"Well, I go back and forth between Mozart and the Italians. The Germans and Russians have all those cymbals and cannons and shit going off. I don't like that, it's too busy. But I prefer the Italian composers, like Vivaldi. I like guys whose names end in vowels, to be more specific. Their stuff is more soothing. But day in and day out I like Mozart; he's just better than the others. I heard once that pregnant women who listen to Mozart have smarter babies." John thought for a moment, then added, "When I think I'm already smart enough, or I just wanna feel good, I go with John Fogarty."

Sally stared, openmouthed. "Wow."

"Told you I was fascinating." John began to climb the ladder, balancing the big muskie with one arm and keeping his balance with other.

Sally watched John move up the ladder, step by step, and said, "Albert Einstein said that Beethoven created great music, but he preferred Mozart because Mozart's music seemed to have always been there . . . part of the world, forever. Mozart just revealed it."

"Yeah." John stretched his arms far above his head and reached up to hang the tail end of the muskie to one of the wood screws he'd placed. He groaned as he extended his arms toward the wood screw in the wall. "DeeDee and I were just having that very same discussion the other night."

DeeDee's simpleminded comments had been floating around in his head for days, and now when Sally mentioned Einstein and Mozart in the same sentence, well, DeeDee naturally popped into John's head, and the unkind comment escaped from his lips.

It struck Sally as funny, and she began to chuckle. The absurdity of DeeDee and John discussing Mozart and Einstein loosened a rock slide of laughter inside Sally, which soon rolled over John, too. Soon his arms were shaking as his own laughter made him weak, and he was struggling to hold the big fish against the wall. "Dammit, don't make me laugh," John said, as the ladder he was standing on began to wobble too. Soon it was all he could do to stay on the ladder, but his hands were shaking so badly that he had to back down slowly or drop the fish. With a huge graphite muskie dangling from the wall by its tail, John stepped off the ladder and laughed, along with Sally, until the storm passed.

"A guy should be taking notes when DeeDee starts talking," John said, when the laughter subsided. "Now, don't make me laugh again while I'm working." He climbed the ladder once more.

"You're the one who started it."

An hour later, both of Sally's employees had closed the place up and gone home. John finished hanging the final fish, a crappie, and he stepped back to admire his work. "How's it look?" he asked.

"Looks like a coffee shop in Pine Rapids *should* look. Very nice!" Sally paused. "Thank you, John. Can I buy you dinner?"

"Sure, but we have a ball game in about ninety minutes. The kids, I mean. Maybe we could go out for dinner after that?"

Sally looked at John suspiciously. "DeeDee won't mind?"

John flinched and grabbed at his heart. "Ooh, you got me."

Sally waited for a better reply.

"OK, I'm a little embarrassed about that. I almost had to get the crayons out in order to keep our discussion going. What a fool I was to think—" John stopped himself. "And I ran into several old friends that night, and they all gave me serious grief for showing up with DeeDee, too."

"So, not that it's any of my business, but your date that night . . .?"

"Over before it started." John finished Sally's thought with a chuckle.

"So, you and her?"

"As DeeDee would say, 'That's water under the fridge.'" John turned to leave.

Sally smiled. "Go. I'll see you at the game . . ." Her words followed him out the door, and she pumped up the volume with each new phrase, "…and thanks for the fish . . . they look fantastic . . . you're an artist!"

"So, we're on for tonight, after the game, right?" John hollered from the curb. When Sally hesitated, John turned his palms up and asked, "It's just dinner. What could go wrong?"

"OK, dinner it is!" Sally hollered back. Then, as he drove away, she mumbled to herself, "Vivaldi and John Fogarty?"

—

Baseball and summer were in full swing that evening when the teams converged at the ball fields. Orange was about to face off against Blue, and John Velde could barely restrain himself. He was oozing contempt for the Blue team, especially their coach. The Blue coach was the one who'd asked several other dads to be his assistant coaches, and not coincidentally, all of his assistant coaches had big, strong sons who could play ball.

"Look at that clown," John groaned. With Matt at his side, he was lugging the canvas bag full of baseball gear across the outfield and ripping on the opposing coach for tonight's game. "Thinks he's over there coachin' the shit outta those kids because they can whup ass on these little geeks we have."

"He's a dandy," Matt agreed. The other coach was in full uniform: pants, jersey, stirrups and everything, and strutting about with his eight-year-olds. His uniform was from a local American Legion team for which he was an assistant coach. The Legion team had games on Tuesdays and Thursdays too, and he told everyone that he came to these games in full uniform simply because it was convenient for him not to change clothes on the way from those games at the varsity ball park each night. But everyone knew he just liked to be noticed. He was young, and judging by the things he said to his players on the Blue team, he was not exactly a repository of baseball knowledge, either.

"I'm guessing he was the third-team right fielder at Black Duck High School," John said.

"Yeah, or second base, where you put your weakest arm, and he was the number nine hitter, too, I'm guessing," Matt added. "Probably got beat up by his teammates fairly often, but thought it was a gesture of affection because they were so fond of him."

The Blue coach spotted Matt and John walking across the outfield and waved. "Bring your A game, coach?" he called out.

Matt waved and nodded.

John waved and muttered "Fuck you" under his breath.

The Compton twins were waiting at the bench when Matt and John arrived with the gear. "Hi girls," John said.

"Hi Mr. Velde," they both said in unison.

"Here's a ball. Go on out there and play catch for a while before the game," John said, and he tossed a ball to Heather. The ball bounced off her glove and rolled away. Both of the girls sprinted to pick it up, and when Whitney got there first, she raced to the outfield with her sister on her heels.

"Watch 'em," John said a minute later, when the twins were ready to warm up. "They both throw the ball like they just got into some bad mushrooms."

When the rest of the team straggled in, Brexley Babich and Nayson King had lost their Orange hats, and Bradley Hested had now lost his Orange shirt, too.

"That's OK, Bradley, you're the catcher, and that's an important part of this team, so you can wear whatever color shirt you want," John said. When John looked back at the bench, Matt was smiling at him. "Think the little dipshit fell for that one?" John asked.

Matt looked away and passed out a few more baseballs.

Jane and Sally were each carrying folding chairs and walking with Dr. Hested, who was also carrying a folding chair. When they reached their usual vantage point along the first base line, they set up the chairs and claimed their spots.

"Look at that," John said. He nudged Matt with his elbow and pointed at Jane and Sally. "They're sitting together, Jane and Sally. How 'bout that?"

Matt's telephone bleeped. He retrieved the phone from his pocket and saw he had a text message from Mo Lawson. He opened it right away.

<How's Jane doing?>

The simplicity of the message made him feel as if an old friend had just sidled up to him and asked the question. His reply was just as natural. He wrote the message and sent it without a second thought.

<She's good! A little sore yet, but better every day. We'll be back in Rochester for more surgery in a couple months, but I think that will just be for "cosmetic" stuff.

Thanks for being with me that day, Mo. Your words, and touch, and friendship were just what I needed. I still think about you, and our ride around town in my old red Ford; probably always will. Old friends are the best!>

Matt turned his phone off and put it back in his pocket.

"Who was that from?" John asked. "You were grinning like . . . it was *Mo*, wasn't it?"

"Shut up," Matt groaned.

"Men don't have women friends, buddy," John teased. "Just sayin'."

Matt turned his back and walked over to Jane and Sally. He took a knee beside Jane's chair and talked to her briefly, then kissed her and stood up again. As he was about to return to the bench and call his players in, he noticed Darrell and Snag walking across the green grass of the outfield toward the women. It was unusual to see the other Velde boys at a ball game. Actually, it was unusual to see them anywhere but at the Shorewood Furist. After exchanging brief greetings, Darrell and Snag sat on the grass beside Sally and Jane and the parents of the Orange players.

"Didn't think I'd see you boys here," Matt said.

"We had to come and see Timmy play," Darrell said.

"Yeah, but we really wanted to see if John was actually coaching," Snag added.

Everyone on both teams was gathered by their benches, ready to start the game, and Matt had to hustle over to be with his team. "You want to see if he's *behaving* himself, don't you?" Matt asked before he hurried off.

A moment later the Blue coach lofted the ball toward the plate and his leadoff hitter drilled a rocket over Heather Compton's head for a home run. Not even the Compton twins could run it down in time.

"Kid put a charge in 'nat one," John said to Matt.

The second pitch of the game was a little too high and the kid at the plate let it go. When the pitch miraculously dropped into Bradley Hested's glove and stayed there, both Matt and John applauded their catcher; it was the first pitch he'd ever stopped. "Merry Christmas," John whispered in Matt's ear, "I think Bradley's eyes were closed."

The third pitch, and every one after that, was scorched back up the middle and the Orange middle infielders scattered like bowling pins to get out of the way. Every time. The Blue team's twelfth batter hit one pretty hard, but right at Dave Norman, who scooped it up and threw it to Timmy at first base.

The kid would have been the last batter of the first inning anyway, since teams could only bat around once per inning, but Matt and John made a point to celebrate the one nice play the Orange had made. "Nice play out there, Dave. Nice catch at first base, too, Timmy," Matt said, in the most positive tone he could muster. "Now, we gave up eleven runs in that first inning so we're gonna hafta rally. Go on up there and take some good swings!"

Since John would be pitching to his own team, he gathered them and briefly explained that he'd try to pitch the ball right where they each could hit it, and that they didn't have to swing at pitches they didn't like. Heather tapped a slow roller to the first baseman and naturally beat him to the bag. Whitney did the same, but every other ball that Orange put in play was fielded perfectly and Orange was quickly retired and back in the field.

Blue scored eleven more runs in the second inning on twelve well-hit balls and several dozen fielding errors. When the Orange team came to the bench for their second turn at bat, John leaned close to Matt and whispered, "Jesus, this is gonna be a massacre."

"Sure is," Matt agreed. "I think the goal for you and I, tonight, is to emphasize the positive things. There's not much else we can do."

"Yeah, well, if something positive happens it should stand out. We'll notice it." John picked up a ball and headed for the pitcher's mound.

Bradley Hested walked to the plate with a bat on his shoulder, and John bit his lip to hide a smile. The kid was wearing a green T-shirt that was stretched tight around his belly. He was the only player on either team who was out of uniform. But he looked uncomfortable for a different reason: the largest batting helmet available was too small for him, and his fat cheeks were squished so badly that his lips were pushed apart. The same batting helmet that made the Compton twins look like bobblehead dolls was skintight on Bradley.

"Looking sharp there, Bradley," John said, when Bradley attempted to take an athletic batting stance. Truth be told, John thought Bradley looked like a plump turkey that had been stuffed into a small green shirt and a tiny batting helmet. When Bradley was ready, John rocked backward on his right foot and then lofted the ball toward the plate. The scuffed-up ball was floating on a cushion of air when it drifted lazily past home plate, but the flight path of the pitch had carried it a bit inside, a few inches from Bradley's left elbow, and Bradley jumped back from the plate as if John had buzzed a fastball under his chin. He was terrified of the baseball, even a baseball that could barely defy gravity long enough to reach home plate.

Matt was sitting on the bench, his arm around Brexley Babich's shoulder, trying to explain the complexities of base running, should she ever get on base, when Bradley jumped back from the pitch. When the ball was thrown back to John, Matt saw a devious, subtle glow come to his old friend's eyes. He'd seen the glow many times, and he knew what was about to happen: He planned to hit Bradley with the next pitch.

John rocked once and then lofted another pitch, this one even closer to Bradley. Before the ball could flutter into him, Bradley's front foot flinched away, toward third base and away from home plate, in order to get himself out of harm's way. Baseball coaches called it "stepping in the bucket," and it wasn't a good thing; it implied that the batter was afraid of inside pitches. Coaches and old ballplayers notice it immediately, and if a player at a higher level does it he is certain to see some pitches come a little closer.

John cast a quick, gleeful glance over to Matt.

"Don't do it," Matt whispered to himself, but he already knew what was going to happen.

John rocked once more, and in a slow underhand arc he brought the ball forward. When he released the ball, it was moving so slowly there was no spin on it, but it was headed straight for Bradley, just as John intended. Not exactly blessed with lightning reflexes, Bradley simply couldn't move his substantial bulk, even to avoid a pitch that needed a sundial to measure its flight time, and the ball hit Bradley just above his left elbow. The ball fell straight to the ground, but so did Bradley; the bat flew away and Bradley collapsed as if he'd been picked off by a sniper. It was a move he could only have seen Big Leaguers do on TV after being plunked by a sizzling fastball, and it was so over-the-top that parents on both teams chuckled under their breath.

"C'mon Bradley, man up," John called from the mound. "Should I get you a dress to wear? Get up." Then he stood and waited unsympathetically while Bradley brushed himself off and began to walk to first base.

"No no no . . . not so fast," John said. "You don't get to go to first base. There's no hit by pitch in this league. You get back in the box and take your swings."

Bradley looked at Matt, questioning him with his eyes.

"He's right, Bradley. Get back in there," Matt said.

Bradley glared at Matt, then John, and then picked up his bat.

John's next pitch floated over the heart of the plate and an angry, really angry, Bradley Hested took a good swing and hit a soft fly ball that was headed for right field. Both of the Blue right fielders stuck their gloves into the air and began to hope the ball would magically drop into it. But it plopped onto the grass in right field, and when it landed, both of the right fielders looked at it as if they'd never seen such a thing. The Bradley train coasted into first base while the Blue parents hollered, "THROW IT!" to the two confused right fielders.

Base hit. No problem. When he reached first base, Bradley stopped and smiled while he looked through the crowd to find his grandfather. His anger from a few seconds earlier was gone, replaced by the satisfaction of a small success. John turned toward first base and when Bradley looked back at him, John turned his palms up and said, "See, it was easy, wasn't it?"

The next batter, Nayson King, hit an incredibly weak ground ball, which the catcher picked up and threw to first base for one out. But in the instant that the kid playing first base caught the ball it was clear that he'd forgotten that the slowest runner in the world had just begun to rumble away toward second base. The first baseman began to celebrate the out he'd just recorded, and then his teammates began to holler, "THROW IT!" The first baseman was so happy to have caught the ball that he still hadn't noticed Bradley Hested plodding toward second base with no intention of stopping there. While parents and players from both sides hollered, the Blue first baseman took a few steps toward the middle of the infield. He was beginning to panic, uncertain where to throw the ball.

But Bradley solved the problem for him. Apparently, Bradley thought that since his dazzling speed had carried him to second base without a problem, he'd just go ahead and dash over to third base, too. However, as he rounded second base Bradley stumbled a bit, and he began waving his arms in a vain attempt to regain his balance. If he'd just fallen down immediately, things would have been all right, but he maintained his balance just well enough not to crash. For a while.

One, two, three, four steps he took, leaning a bit farther forward with each step, and windmilling both arms in a futile attempt to regain his balance. But it was no use; he was going down, and his descent to earth was agonizingly slow and painful to watch. Out there in the middle ground between second and third base, Bradley slammed into the infield dirt and sent up a plume of dust. He lay there for a second, like a turtle trying to roll off its shell, as the Blue team's first baseman ran over and tagged him out.

The dust hadn't yet settled when John raced from the mound over to Bradley, and looked down at him. "You OK, kid?" John asked. Bradley was too embarrassed and angry to answer, so John reached a hand to him and quietly said, "Good hustle, goddammit. Good for you! That's what I wanna see, Bradley!" He helped Bradley up off the ground and then gave him a high five, and made sure that everyone watching the game heard him say, "Good hustle!" as he ran back to the pitcher's mound. When Bradley made his way back to his team he was greeted by Dave Norman, who never seemed to stop jumping up and down, and Timmy. His teammates slapped his back as if he'd just hit one over the moon, and for the first time, Matt saw Bradley Hested puff out his chest and smile—his teammates liked him.

Several pitches and several ugly swings later, the Orange half of another inning was over and the massacre continued. When John plopped down on the bench next to Matt, he leaned close and said, "We may be getting a call from the seismograph people at Berkeley. That little fucker hit the ground *hard*, and there's an impact crater out there."

"What did you say to him?" Matt asked.

"Told him to keep that shit up. For once he was *workin'*."

A shrill chorus of "RUN!" exploded from the Blue team's mothers as their first batter of the next inning hit an easy ground ball to Dave Norman, and Dave made another nice play and threw the ball to Timmy at first base for one out.

The next batter hit a slow roller toward Michelangelo. He circled the ball fearfully, twice, and just before it actually stopped rolling he pounced on it, dropping his garbage-can lid/baseball glove like a hammer. It was far too late to throw the kid out, but nonetheless he'd covered the ball before it stopped rolling, and that was a success. By Orange standards it was a hell of a play, one for the highlight reel. "Nice catch, Mike!" Dave Norman yelled as he pounded the pocket of his glove and jumped up and down.

The situation was one out, with a runner on first base, when the next Blue hitter came to the plate. It was the same kid who'd driven one almost to the street earlier. John and Matt instructed their Orange players to back up, mostly as a means of self-defense. "Christ, I wanna holler 'Run for it!' or 'Cover your nuts!'" John whispered into Matt's ear.

"Back up will do," Matt said. Then he raised his voice and shouted, "FARTHER . . . FARTHER!" while he waved his arm.

The coach in full uniform rocked and pitched to the boy, and as everyone expected, he took a mighty swing. The ball shot up, way up, higher than any kid this age should ever be able to hit a ball, and every mother on the Blue side began to scream, "RUN!!!" The kid on first base took off like a shot, and the mothers screamed louder.

As the ball rose into the stratosphere, Matt knew about where it would come down and he grew apprehensive. He glanced at Timmy, standing a few feet from first base, and saw that Timmy was watching the ball, too. Timmy moved calmly, a bit to his right, as the ball was nearing its peak. None of these kids could catch a fly ball like this one, Matt thought. But Timmy was camped under it, staring straight up, calmly tracking the flight of the ball, and waiting. Little Timmy pounded his fist into the pocket of his glove and waited, and waited, as the ball began its return to earth. Timmy moved back to his left, opened his glove, and the ball popped solidly into it. Then Timmy looked to his right and saw that the runner who'd raced away from first base had rounded second base, but was turning to retrace his steps. While half of the mothers of the Blue team were still screaming "RUN!" and the other half were screaming at the runner to go back, Timmy trotted casually toward first base and stepped on the bag to complete an unassisted double play, ending Blue team's half inning. Emotionless, as if he did that sort of thing every day, Timmy flipped the ball to the teenaged umpire. "Nice play, kid," the ump said, as Timmy trotted past him as he left the field.

The Blue mothers were still screaming "RUN!" or "GO BACK!" as most of them had no idea what Timmy had just done. The ump looked over at the coach in full uniform and showed him his thumb. "That's a double play, coach." The ump grinned.

The only one of Timmy's teammates who understood what had happened was Dave Norman, and Dave was jumping up and down as if Orange had just won the World Series. He raced across the infield and leapt onto Timmy's back and pounded him while the rest of the Orange team wondered what was going on. It seemed like a good thing had happened, but no one knew for sure.

"Hey kid," the Blue coach called out, "nice play!"

Timmy mumbled "Thanks," and the Orange team got ready for another turn at bat.

Jane reached over and took Sally's hand. "Look!" Matt was on one knee, with his arms around Timmy.

"What? What happened?" Sally asked.

"Oh, it's just Matt," Jane sighed. "He's still a little boy too. And he was just like your Timmy. I can see it all now."

"What do you mean?" Sally asked.

"My Matt was never the one to hit the home run, like that big kid on the Blue team. He was the kid who knew the situations and had skills to make up for a lack of size or power. He'd have been the one to catch that ball, like Timmy just did." Jane squeezed Sally's hand and smiled. "I know he's choked up over what Timmy just did. I can read Matt like a book."

A moment later Matt stood up and looked over at Sally. He tapped his fist on his heart and nodded, then pointed at her as if to say, "Yeah, that was pretty good; what your boy just did."

"Told ya!" Jane said to Sally. Matt's response to Timmy's catch went unnoticed by everyone except Jane and Sally.

Then, while the teams were changing places in the field, Darrell commented, for anyone within earshot to hear, "That boy who the hit the ball just now: I think he's the one who hit the long home run earlier, and I think that's his dad out there, coaching the Blue team. I'll bet *he* was a pretty good player, too."

Darrell's words were still hanging in the air around the parents of the Orange team, and after a short silence DeeDee Katzenmeyer spoke up. "Yeah, like father, like son." Then she added, "It's a genital thing, I guess."

Sally, Jane, Darrell, and Snag all heard it and picked up on it, and incredibly, no one else even blinked. The tiny search engine in DeeDee's pretty head had passed by "hereditary" and "genetic" and then possibly skipped a bit when "congenital" sped by, and then it fixed on "genital" as the word she was looking for. It *did* sound a lot like congenital, so hell, it was close enough. DeeDee smiled and the others all nodded and agreed that the big kid must indeed have inherited his baseball skills from his father—it probably *was* a "genital thing."

Mercifully, the game ended earlier than usual because the Blue team scored their eleven or twelve runs quickly in every inning except one, and easily squelched every rally that Orange almost put together. Matt guessed that the final score had been 60 to 4.

When they were all gathered around, enjoying a Popsicle after the game, Ron Hested approached John privately and said, "A dress?"

"Well, Ron, I . . ." John tried to think of a way to dig himself out. He knew he shouldn't have implied that Bradley played ball like a girl, and that that was bad, but John Velde couldn't help himself, it was what he did. Now it looked like Ron Hested, a doctor, a man he really liked, was angry at him and he'd have to come up with an apology. This was precisely why he never did this sort of thing, coach youth sports. It was why his brothers had come to watch, too, because he always said and did the wrong thing. Damn, why did he let Matt talk him into this baseball thing? "I'm sorry, Ron."

"No, it was good. You challenged him, and it worked. Good!" Ron said. "He's got a pretty strong will, and he gets his way most of the time at home. My son and his wife haven't set many boundaries for him."

"Well, I actually *did* give him some positive feedback after he took his tumble, too," John said.

"He said you were swearing," Ron said. John closed his eyes as if he'd been caught swearing in school, again, and was about get a talking to from the principal. He'd thought he was off the hook for a second there for the thing about getting a dress for Bradley, and now he'd have to apologize for something else. He took a breath and was about to attempt to wriggle out from under this, too, when Ron spoke up. "No, he liked it. He thinks you're cool. He likes you."

"Really?" John said

"Really," Ron answered. "So whatever you're doing, keep it up."

"OK," John said, and when Ron walked away toward his car with Bradley at his side a minute later, John hollered, "Good hustle tonight, Bradley."

Bradley looked back over his shoulder and said, "Bye, coach."

"Hmph . . . *coach*," John said under his breath, as if it were a shirt he was trying on to see how it fit. No one, at least no little kid, had ever spoken or looked at him like that before. He walked to the cooler next to Sally's folding chair and helped himself to a Popsicle and was about to remind Sally that they had a dinner engagement when Heather ran up to him and asked, "Hey Mr. Velde, who won the game?"

"Well, it was pretty close, Heather, but I think we pulled it out, right there at the end," John said.

"I thought so," Heather said, and she spun around and ran to tell Whitney that they'd won, for sure.

Dave Norman was chasing Timmy, each of them with a Popsicle in one hand, and they were both laughing as they ran in circles. The pounding just handed them by the Blue team was already forgotten and they chased each other like puppies while they dripped Popsicle juice on themselves. As they swooped by in a close orbit, John held out one hand, requesting a handshake, and both boys gave him "five" with their empty, but nonetheless sticky, hands as they streaked by. He was grinning and using a towel to wipe the sticky red smear from his hand when he noticed that Sally was looking at him.

"Are you *smiling*?" Sally teased, as if she'd caught him breaking the rules.

"Yup," John admitted. A little kid had just called him "coach." Whitney Compton was adorable, and Timmy and Dave Norman triggered fifty-year-old memories of Matt and him playing together, back at the headwaters of their lives. This was all right, this coaching thing. He felt good, and while he was still wearing the same smile, he asked Sally, "Where would you like to take me for dinner?"

"Let's go to Buster's. I'd like to watch you aggravate a few of their waitresses. I think I'll enjoy the show a lot more if I don't have a dog in the fight. Do your best work and see if you can make some girl cry," Sally said.

John threw the towel into the canvas bag with the catcher's gear, then he said, "For you? The lid will come off."

CHAPTER TWENTY-NINE

The best part of a summer evening still remained, as players and parents wandered away from the ballpark toward their cars and homes. Shadows would lengthen, the air would cool, and a heavy dew would begin to form on the green grass. But not just yet.

Matt was stuffing bats and balls and batting helmets into their canvas bags as players said goodbye, or just straggled off with a buddy or two from one of the other teams.

"Hey John, you wanna c'mon out for a beer?" Matt asked.

"Ah, well, I sorta have a thing, tonight, with Sally. We're going to Buster's." John was gathering a handful of stray baseballs from the base of the chain-link backstop. He came over to Matt and dumped the baseballs into the bag that Matt held open for him

"You mean, like a date?" Matt spoke in a low voice so no one else could hear.

"Yeah, I think so," John whispered. Then, in a normal voice he said, "You need any help carrying that stuff?"

"Nah, see you tomorrow, or whenever." Matt bent over and zipped the canvas bag closed and added, "You kids behave yourselves."

"Yeah." John turned and walked to over to join Sally. Matt watched them walk slowly, side by side, across the outfield grass, until they reached John's truck.

Matt glanced around in search of any stray baseballs or equipment that might have been left behind. The ballpark was empty now, except for him, and Jane, who was still sitting in her folding chair. The grass was always a bit greener when the summer sun was about to drop behind the horizon, and Matt took a moment to let his eyes hold on to the deep green. He drew in a long breath and smelled the sweet evening air, too. Then he tossed one canvas bag on top of the other and walked over to Jane's chair.

Jane was looking out at the stillness of a ballpark that had been filled with laughter and the conversation of friends only a few minutes earlier. When Matt reached her chair, he took a knee beside it and reached into her lap and took her hand. "Remember when our boys were young, and we came to this park? I coached them, and after games on nights like this we'd go out for ice cream, or to somebody's backyard for a beer?"

"Mm-hmm," Jane replied.

"C'mon, let's go out someplace for a beer, or drop in and see some old friends, somebody we haven't seen for a while?"

"Not tonight, honey. I'm tired, and I just want to go home."

The lines on Jane's face were still pretty, still elegant. The angle of her jaw was firm. Her thin nose and lips were still delicate. The high cheekbones, as always, hinted at royalty. But tonight, well, most of the time now, her eyes were different; something was missing. The sandy-brown eyes that always sparkled had no light tonight. She spoke to him as if she couldn't see him.

"OK," Matt said, "maybe next week?"

"Maybe."

When they rolled into their driveway at Scotch Lake, Matt said, "Hey, there's still plenty of daylight left. You wanna take the boat out for a little cruise, just you and me?"

Jane answered by closing her eyes. "I just want to read for a while before I go to bed." She sighed. "I'm sorry. I know you're disappointed, but—"

"Ah, it's OK. Maybe I'll take the canoe up to French Creek and try to catch a trout. It should be a good evening for a caddis hatch, maybe brown drakes or hex . . . you know, those big yellow mayflies—"

"Yeah, you go and have fun," Jane said, as they entered the house. "I'm gonna take my makeup off." She gave Matt half a kiss. "I probably won't still be awake when you get back. G'night, honey." She then shuffled off toward their bathroom.

Matt watched her back as she left him. That was it. She was done with him for the day. He had the rest of the day to do whatever he wanted, and it felt all wrong. For years, no, forever, when Matt had taken the canoe and made a run to French Creek he'd felt that he was stealing away and ignoring Jane's expectations that he finish some domestic chore. But tonight she was happy to see him go.

He packed a few things into his fishing vest, grabbed his fly rod, and hurried down to the lakeshore. An old aluminum Grumman canoe lay waiting for him, bottom side up, with two paddles tucked underneath, about twenty feet from the calm waters of Scotch Lake. He flipped it over, made a quick check for spiders and garter snakes, and slid his old friend into the water.

He'd given himself the canoe as a wedding present. He knew it was heavier and noisier than the newer Kevlar canoes, but it was his friend, and it had been part of a thousand small adventures. John Velde had tried to give Matt an old wood-and-canvas canoe several years earlier because he said those boats had soul, and aluminum didn't. Matt understood what John was trying to say, and he agreed, at least on some level. But this old Grumman, by virtue of a lifetime of shared adventures, had soul, too, and Matt could never let it go.

The sun hadn't dipped to the horizon yet, and the surface of Scotch lake was smooth as glass. He sat in the middle of the canoe, put his back into each stroke, and made the short trip to the end of the lake in only a few minutes.

French Canyon, as locals called it, was a geological oddity for the tall pine country. The glaciers that scraped the entire area clean a few thousand years earlier seemed to have missed French Canyon, and had left behind a rugged series of tall hills, strewn with rocks and boulders. An area about ten miles square, bordered by steep wooded gullies, with a huge cedar swamp in the center, the canyon made French Creek virtually inaccessible from any direction except Scotch Lake. French Creek was merely a small, spring-fed stream that ran through the heart of the canyon for only about two miles, but it held a healthy population of native brook trout that very few fishermen knew about, or were willing to pay the price to pursue.

Matt paddled directly toward a riffle of gurgling white water that spilled out from a dense growth of tall cedar trees and over smooth rocks, which marked the place where French Creek emptied into Scotch Lake. He steered the canoe to a quiet eddy near the head of the riffle and then tied it to the same tree he'd used for years. The sound of the rushing water at his feet was all he could hear as he checked his gear and prepared to hike to his favorite fishing hole.

He smeared a layer of insect repellent over his hands and face and neck, then he checked all of his pockets to sure he had everything he'd need, especially the flashlight for the long walk out, after dark. He'd tied an army of flies, all designed to imitate various species of mayflies, in every stage of their life cycles. He was ready for just about any of the usual insect hatches he normally saw on the French, but he was fairly certain he'd see brown caddis flies tonight.

Conditions looked to be just right, and all the signs suggested that this would be a classic evening for trout fishing, but Matt had learned long ago that you never know for sure until it happens. He felt a bit of nervous anticipation in his chest when he stood straight. He double-checked the line holding his canoe to the tree, then he set off on the footpath that wound through the woods for a quarter mile to the pool he planned to fish. It took him twenty minutes to reach the spot, and when he peeked between two juniper trees, he saw snouts, decent-sized snouts, poking through the placid surface of the creek and plucking something from the film. This was good, real good, Matt thought. He crept along the shore until he reached the head of the pool. He stepped into the river and crept across it like a burglar, then sat down on a familiar boulder. He was in the perfect place. This water was so calm and clear that the only way he'd fool a brook trout into taking his imitation instead of a natural fly was to present it from upstream, and he was directly upstream from a few dozen fish that were already feeding sporadically. He dreamed of moments like this all winter long. He'd spent a lifetime learning the ways of trout, and it had been a labor of love. After thousands of failures he'd learned where to find them and what they'd be eating, and how not to spook them, and then how to release them back into the wild after he'd caught them. He'd spent countless winter nights tying flies, using bits of feathers and fur from ducks and deer and other animals that had nourished him and his family. He loved this place; sometimes it seemed like an open window that gave him a clear look at the cosmos.

The tall cedar trees that surrounded the pool would soon block the setting sun. If he could make short, accurate, delicate casts, he could catch trout on dry flies for the next hour, maybe longer. As he'd been paddling to this place, he'd wondered what insects, if any, might be hatching. He saw something flutter skyward, and he recognized it immediately. It was a brown caddis, a small aquatic insect that God had created simply to serve as trout food, Matt reckoned. Then he noticed another, and another. This was perfect. In a little while this insect hatch would be in full swing, and the surface of the placid stream would be covered with brown caddis flies, recently emerged from the bottom of the river, and trying to dry their wings before they flew away to make more caddis flies.

Far off, way out on Scotch Lake, a loon cut loose with the signature of the north: a long, haunting hail call, like a call to worship. Church would be starting soon, and Matt grinned at the thought. This was a far better place to seek God than the little church back in Sverdrup.

Then, another sound: a tiny, faint, malevolent drone began to rise from back in the forbidden, impenetrable swampy heart of this forest sanctuary. Mosquitos, squadrons of them, were humming, and lifting off from the backwaters all around him, and in a few minutes when they'd joined up into huge formations, they'd be strafing him. No sooner had that thought come to him than one of the nasty little sonsabitches buzzed its way into Matt's right ear. Reflexively, he swatted at his ear, and when he looked at his hand to check for a bloody carcass, he saw several more mosquitos walking on his forearm. He rolled his long sleeves down and then slathered another coat of bug repellent on the backs of his hands, and on his head and neck. The mosquitos were a hateful nuisance, but they were an omen, too. On evenings like this, when they were nearly unbearable, the trout fishing was often at its best.

The only thing to do now was wait. Matt tied a deer-hair caddis fly to his line so he'd be ready when the time was right. When he crossed his arms and took a deep breath, it happened: Visions of his Jane came to him. He'd been so intent on getting to this place, and getting ready for what was about to happen, that he'd thought only of trout, and mosquitos, and his canoe. But now that he had a moment to relax, it all came rushing back—the cancer, the surgery, the fear and the faraway look in Jane's eyes. And as thoughts of Jane swirled about, Mo made an appearance, too, and Matt remembered the look in *her* eyes when they'd greeted each other for the first time in forty years. What was it that he had seen there? He wished he could share this place, this moment, with Mo. It would be nice if Mo could see him now, and see the man he'd become.

Somewhere on the other side of the pool, on the other side of his dreams, a firefly sparked in the underbrush and brought him back to the river. He wondered how long he'd been away. Ten seconds? Ten minutes? It didn't matter; it was time to pay attention. The soft, cool evening air above the pool was full of caddis flies, and hungry brook trout had begun to rise. The silky surface of the water was broken by dozens of snouts, plucking caddis before they fluttered away. Game on.

Matt began to strip fly line from his fishing reel and plan his first cast. A fine trout, maybe thirteen inches long, was rising steadily about fifteen feet in front of him. He made two short false casts, then he tried to flip his deer-hair caddis fly onto the surface of French Creek, into the feeding lane of that brookie, so that the slow current would carry it directly to him. His leader unfurled just as he'd planned, and the caddis fly that he'd tied with deer hair from the buck he'd killed several years ago settled softly onto the glassy water about two feet upstream from the trout he'd been watching.

This was the little moment that lives in all trout fishermen's dreams. Matt was waiting, hoping for a trout to come to his fly. He'd spent *so* many winter nights tying flies and dreaming of moments like this. He'd paddled a canoe, stumbled through a swampy trail in the woods, and waded into a river strewn with slippery little boulders. He was dealing with the approach of darkness, uncertain footing, and a plague of biting insects, all in the hopes of fooling a trout into striking at his fly. If he did manage to catch a fish, he had no intention of killing and eating it. He'd just put it back in the river.

This wasn't about catching supper, or bragging to his friends. He was OK with both of those things, for sure. But moments like this were part of something much bigger. Matt was searching for something. Maybe it was only the reassurance that he had a place in all of this. Maybe it was more than that? Maybe if a wild trout came to his fly it was proof that he did have some knowledge of the workings of the cosmos?

He watched now, his eyes glued to the little caddis fly, as the gentle current carried it slowly toward the spot where he'd seen the trout feeding steadily for the past couple of minutes. Half the thrill was waiting for that fly to reach the fish. He knew he'd done the hard work and put himself in the right place. He was pretty sure he'd presented just the right fly, the one that the fish were all dining on. And he was pretty sure he'd made a perfect cast and put his fly precisely where it needed to be. But he just didn't know for certain. Yet.

The fly drifted slowly, inching its way along in what Matt thought was the right feeding lane. He bent over a bit, to reduce the glare from the water's surface, and stared at his fly.

And then it happened. The water beneath his fly boiled, a snout appeared, and his caddis fly was gone with a "pop" and a swirl. Matt raised the fishing rod, struck back at the fish, and felt the solid head shake of a nice trout as the quiet pool came alive. The connection he sought was there, in his hands, but also in his heart. The trout at the end of his line told him that maybe he'd someday understand his part in all this.

Once he'd landed the fish, he released it back into French Creek. He dried and dressed his fly so that it would float properly again, and he waited for other trout to begin rising. It took only a few seconds, and Matt was back in business. He caught a dozen more, perhaps two dozen. He was too busy to count, and the final tally was of no consequence anyway. What mattered was that he'd done a difficult thing well, and immersed himself in all of this. The mosquitos had buzzed in his ears continuously, but they'd found only a few patches of unprotected flesh. Just after sunset, the fireflies had begun to put on a light show that would continue well into the night. When the gathering darkness over the little pool made it nearly impossible for Matt to see his fly, or the rise forms of the trout, he decided to head for home. He was about to reel in and call it a day when a yellow moon slowly peeked over the trees on the far side of the pool. When the moon was high enough, just above the cedars, the black surface of the pool began to shimmer with reflected moonlight, and the pool became mercurial: blue and silver at the same time, with a yellow moon in the center, just like the sky above. The pool in front of him and the night sky overhead were mirror images of each other. Matt could see his fly on the water's surface again, along with rise forms of the trout; he was fishing in the sky.

He fished a little longer and caught several more, then he decided to call it a night when a nice brookie broke him off and swam away with his fly. It was way too dark to tie on another fly, but more than that, he knew he'd just had a moment that was not likely to repeat itself anytime soon. He reeled his line in and began to plan the journey home; he'd need to be careful walking through this pool with slippery rocks hidden just beneath the surface, and then on the muddy riverbank on the way back to his canoe.

When he was ready to start for home, he took a minute to look around. The air was filled with the scent of cedar trees. That far-off loon was still calling, and the silent pool was still shimmering. What he was beholding, and what he'd just done, were pretty far outside even *his* experience, and he'd been doing this sort of thing for a lifeime. He sensed, no, he understood, that God may have pulled a few strings with the natural order and extended this moment. "Thanks," Matt whispered, "for *all* of this. I know what you did."

He crept, one half-step at a time, across the pool, bumping into submerged obstacles every few feet, and then he stumbled over the dark path through the woods, until at last he emerged from French Canyon onto the banks of Scotch Lake and found his canoe. It was almost midnight when he started to paddle for home, and he wondered if Jane would be worried.

The moon was high in the sky and a soft breeze was blowing as he paddled across the large expanse of open water. Jane was probably sleeping, but he hoped she was awake, and sitting by the window, watching for his canoe to come gliding home across the shimmering lake. He wanted her to be there, waiting, and to be interested when he'd tell her about this little adventure.

Ah, but that probably wouldn't happen. She might still be awake, and if she was, she might listen to his stories, but she'd never understand. How could she? No, she'd just be glad he was home, and that he'd had fun. She'd kiss him and then she'd go to bed, and fall fast asleep while he was still sitting on the porch, and still had more to say. A day later, or maybe a week later, she'd smile at him over coffee, and tell him that she loved his enthusiasm for these little adventures. But they'd always be his. Not hers.

A jagged black horizon, made by the uneven silhouettes of balsams, white pines, Norways, and oaks, came slowly into focus as Matt worked his way home. The night sky behind the forest was peppered with a billion twinkling stars, and he began to search for the orange glow of a light from inside his house. He strained his eyes and his imagination, hoping to see a light still on as he drew near. But the house was dark, and he knew Jane was sleeping. She'd moved from the recliner back to their bed. When he let himself in, he showered and crept about as quietly as he could while he got ready for bed, so as not to wake her.

When he turned off the last of the lights and tiptoed across their bedroom, Jane was sleeping on her back and breathing softly. Matt raised the covers and then slid carefully into bed, as close to Jane as he could. He wanted to reach over and touch her. He wanted to put his arms around her and spoon. *That* was the connection he craved now, more than ever before. He wanted her to reach out to him as she once had. He wanted her to come to him for laughter, or strength, or just a gentle touch. He wanted to be her hero again, the guy who rode in on that big white horse.

But lately, since the cancer, all those little adventures, too, seemed to be his, not hers. She'd come loose from him, but how could that happen?

Ah, she'd be back to her old self soon enough now. Tonight, he'd be thankful to have his Jane sleeping beside him. While he lay on his back, he reached under the covers until he found her hand. It was soft. It was Jane. Tonight, that would be enough.

CHAPTER THIRTY

—•—

John and Sally stepped out of his truck in front of Buster's. "Have you been here before?" he asked her.

"This is my first time. I don't go out much at night. I need to be at the coffee shop so early, you know?"

There were no young men sitting outside by the front door tonight, and the crowd inside was considerably smaller and quieter than the night he'd brought DeeDee there. But loud music still blared from a dozen speakers in the rafters, and John asked Sally if it would be all right to sit outside, on the deck where they could talk.

"I was hoping you'd suggest that," she said.

Several tables were available on the deck, and they chose the one closest to the railing and farthest from the noise inside. But before she sat down Sally said, "I think I'll go use the ladies' room."

John waited alone and looked around to see if he knew anyone there, but he saw no familiar faces. After only a few seconds, Lori, the waitress he'd dated a few years before and who'd waited on him and DeeDee a week earlier, appeared on the far side of the deck, about twenty feet away. John smiled, waved, then gave an impatient shrug. Now *he* was teasing, telling her he was frustrated with the slow service. He turned one palm up and wiggled his index finger in the universal gesture for 'please come over here.' She acknowledged that she'd seen him, but her hands were full with an order for another table and she turned away with no further greeting.

John looked at the menu on the table, but he already knew it by heart and it held no interest for him, so he looked out over Wiigwaas Lake in search of boat lights. When he felt the table shift, he assumed that Sally had seated herself, so he turned to face her. But it was Lori who sat in Sally's chair, and she was smiling at John. She obviously thought he'd come in by himself.

"You know I don't usually come with just one finger . . . whaddya want?" she said with a devious grin.

John's mouth fell open in stunned surprise. He'd always liked Lori's sense of humor, but he hadn't had a private conversation with her in a couple of years. Now this. It was a pretty good line, and under normal circumstances he'd have laughed. But her timing was terrible: She didn't know that Sally had followed her to the table and was only a few feet behind her when she said it. John didn't think Sally had heard the waitress, but he wasn't sure, and when Lori saw the look on John's face, and then saw his eyes fixed on someone, or something, behind her, she knew immediately what to do. She stood quickly, and did not reveal a bit of embarrassment when she said, "Oh, I didn't know that someone was going to join you, sir." Then she pulled the chair out for Sally and asked both of them what they'd like to drink, as if she'd never met John before.

They both ordered a beer, and Lori was about to turn and leave when she stopped and said to Sally, "We're offering shandies tonight at half price." Then she grinned at John.

"Eww." Sally made a sour face. "No thanks, I don't like that stuff. I'll just have a regular beer."

Sally's answer was perfect, and John made sure to let the waitress see the satisfaction in his eyes when he turned to her and said, "Same goes for me, but thanks for asking."

As Lori walked away from their table, Sally smiled at John and said, "She sure is nice."

"Yeah," John agreed, then he moved the conversation away from the waitress. "So is Timmy having a good time with baseball, or whatever it is we're doing on Tuesdays and Thursdays?"

"Yes, he is. And he's making lots of new friends. Thanks for coaching him. He likes you. And it isn't so bad—the baseball, I mean. Is it?"

"Ah, it's just not the same as when Matt and I were boys. We were always playing ball. And we didn't have all these parents and coaches around to screw it up."

"What do you mean by that?"

"Well, we played ball during the *day*. You got up, put your glove on the handlebars of your bike, and rode off to find your buddies. There would always be a game somewhere. Our parents all worked during the day, so they couldn't hang around and bother us with all this organized happy horseshit. Anyway, you rode around on your bike until you found the game, and you just started playing. We played on vacant lots, or over on the ball field by the Catholic church; there was always a game somewhere. It was just a bunch of neighborhood kids. We never had two complete teams and we never had good equipment. We never had *any* equipment, and we usually only had one ball, so we took pretty good care of it. When the sun was going down, and the score was about two fifty to two fifty, and you'd been arguing about who was safe and who was out for about half the day, then you heard your mother calling and you went home for supper. After supper the same kids all got together for night games. See, it was better then."

"Night games?" Sally asked.

"Kick the can, usually," John said. "It was kind of like hide and seek, but—"

"I know kick the can," Sally interrupted. "But why was baseball better then?"

"Well, we learned the game—the rules, and the situations, and the skills—from experience, and from the older kids. There were always a few older kids around to pass along some tips. It was different, but better." John shrugged.

"Tips?" Sally asked.

"Yeah. An older kid named Mark Porisch showed me how to tag a runner out at home plate without getting run over. That came in pretty handy more than once. And then another older kid, Monte Beck, told me how to unfasten a girl's bra."

Sally closed her eyes and shook her head.

"The thing about tagging a runner at home plate had far more immediate value, since I was only ten years old. But I did file Monte Beck's tip away for later."

"Really? Do little boys really talk about things like that?" Sally asked.

"Well, sure." John let his face blossom with a huge smile. "But what you're really asking me is whether or not little Timmy is having thoughts about stuff like that, right?"

Sally pursed her lips, nodded, and waited for John's answer.

"Here's the way *that* plays out, pretty much for everybody," he began. "You're all sitting around at the ball field and some older kid tells a dirty joke and everybody laughs, but the younger boys have no idea what they're laughing at; they just wanna fit in. So they laugh anyway; no kid wants to be the one to confess that they don't get it. Then, maybe somebody shows up with a paperback with some sex in it and every boy reads the passage on page 226, and gets a boner."

Sally cringed.

"Then, later on, some kid shows up with a *Playboy*, and it's boner time again," John said.

"My little Timmy?"

"Sure, it's just life. Would you want it any other way?" John asked.

"I never had a brother, or a son, and my dad wasn't around much," Sally said. "And now I find myself as a single grandmother, raising a boy. There is no instruction manual for me on this one."

"Hey, you're doing fine. Timmy is a good kid. He'll be fine. But . . ." John stopped himself.

"But what?" Sally picked right up on John's aborted statement.

"Ah, what do I know, Sally? My father was predator, a piece of shit. And I'm just some guy . . . what do I know?"

"What were you going to say?" Sally asked.

"Well, all I was gonna say was that I think you need to let him be a little boy. To run and holler and get dirty and break some stuff, and know that no matter what, you still love him. That's all. I think you're already pretty good at the second part, the part about being sure that he knows you love him."

"But not the first part?"

"He's a good kid," John replied. "But he's wired pretty tight. He'll still be a good boy if you give him a little more space."

Sally nodded her head and thought for a moment. "You're a nice man, John. Why do you hide that part of yourself?"

John shrugged but had no reply. People didn't usually say things like that to him.

"You're afraid," Sally said with a raise of one eyebrow.

"Of what?" John scoffed.

"I don't know yet. Failure maybe? Or you might be one of those men who are afraid of success."

John stared, and crinkled his face as if there was a bad smell.

"And you secretly strive for Matt's approval. Don't you?" Her eyes twinkled; she knew she'd surprised John again. "Don't you?" she repeated.

"Well . . . I . . . he . . ." John stammered.

"It's OK. He thinks you're a stitch. You two have some sort of a bromance going, don't you?" She was teasing him and she could see by the look on his face that he liked it, but wasn't used to it.

"What are you, a psychiatrist, or what?" John asked while he squinted at her.

"No, I'm just fascinating, too, like you," Sally said.

"And you also like Mozart," John said.

"Well, naturally. There are no cymbals and cannons and shit," Sally teased, revisiting his comments about Mozart.

Damn, Sally Durham was clever! Every time she said something witty, or smiled at something he said, she got prettier. Those glowing eyes revealed an unmistakable attraction for him, too.

John was about to say something more about Mozart when the waitress arrived with their beers and to take orders for food. She held her order pad up and did her best to rattle John. "The special tonight is Hawaiian pizza. Would you be interested in that?" she offered, with extra sweetness.

Again, Sally made a face and said, "No thanks. I'd like a big ol' burger, and fries."

"I'll have the same," John said, dismissing the waitress with a look that said "nice try." While they waited for their burgers and fries, John and Sally talked about hometowns, and music they liked or disliked, and movies they liked or disliked. John told her about the taxidermy business and the fur shop, and a little bit about the ending of his baseball career, and even less about his days in California. Sally told John about her ex-husband and how they'd moved around the Midwest for a few years before he left her for someone else. Talk and laughter came easily for them, and when they were about half finished with their burgers John said, "OK, I have to ask you. What's the story with your scar?"

Sally looked up abruptly and furrowed her brow. "What scar?" She held a straight face for a few seconds and waited for him to explain the question. She stared into his eyes as if she didn't know there was a scar on her face.

John knew she was teasing, and he grinned at her until she gave up and smiled back. "I was just a little kid," she began. "My dad was cutting brush with a chain saw and I sorta toddled up behind him. Mom got distracted for a second and I walked over to see what Dad was doing. He turned around to look at something. He didn't know I was there because the chain saw was running. I was too close, and he bumped into me. I don't remember much about it, except that my parents each blamed each other. My dad felt terrible for his whole life."

"Wow," John said. "But you actually got kinda lucky. No damage to your eye, was there?"

"Nope. Amazing, huh? You can see the double track of the chain on my eyelid." She closed her eyes and kept them closed for a moment to give him a good look. "But it never cut through the eyelid." Then she added, "I told Matt all about it a while back. I thought he would have told you."

"No, he never said a word." John shrugged, then he surprised himself by blurting, "You're a pretty girl. And you keep getting prettier the more you talk."

"Honk! Gotta call bullshit on ya there, John. But it was a good line. Does it usually work for you?"

"Well, yes, it actually *was* a good line," John said. "Is it working for *you?*"

"I'm not sure yet. It all depends on how you follow up."

John reached across the table and said flatly, with no trace of a smile, "Well, I meant it, Sally."

John's unexpected sincerity surprised Sally, and a little grin settled on her face. But just then her phone buzzed, and when she glanced at it the grin vanished. "I gotta take this," she said. She stood up, excused herself, tapped the screen, and had her phone to her ear, with her other hand cupped over her mouth, as she walked away. She stood on the other end of the deck and talked into her phone for a few seconds, and then walked inside the restaurant with the phone still at her ear.

John waited, nibbling at his fries, for almost ten minutes, until Lori walked past his table and stopped. "Did your date leave you?" she asked, and then she looked back into the restaurant.

"She had a phone call," John said.

The waitress spun her head around once more and said, "Well, she's sitting at a table with some other guy right now, over there on the other side of the bar."

"Really?" John asked, surprised by the news.

"Really," Lori nodded. "Hey, John, she's the lady who owns the new coffee shop, isn't she?"

"Yeah."

"She's nice. What's she doing with you?"

"She finds me fascinating," John said.

The waitress smiled and nodded. "Right . . . What happened to your granddaughter, the brain surgeon you brought in here last week?"

John picked up a French fry, dipped it in ketchup, and put it in his mouth. "Good one, but don't you have a toilet to scrub in the men's room, or some vomit to clean up?"

The waitress laughed. "I gotta get back to work. But I'll let you know if she leaves with the guy. And by the way, did I mention that the guy is pretty handsome, and younger than you?" Lori was still chuckling as she walked away.

Ten more minutes passed, and John was about to get up and leave. He assumed that Sally had left for the evening, or was embroiled in some personal thing that was none of his business. As he was sliding his chair back, Sally stepped out onto the deck and hurried back to join him. "I'm so sorry. There was a problem with the freezer at the shop and I had to call an electrician."

"How convenient for you. Your electrician was sitting in the bar!" John said.

Sally looked across the table, sagged back into her chair, and frowned. "So, I'm busted, huh? I'm sorry, John. I lied so I wouldn't embarrass you."

"You need to be a better liar." But John *was* embarrassed, and he couldn't hide it.

"I just didn't want—" Sally stopped and then restarted. "I didn't think he'd come here looking for me. I'm really sorry, John."

"So, he's your boyfriend?"

"No . . ." Sally replied, but she sounded like she wasn't so sure that was true. "Boyfriend is way too strong of a label. We dated for a long time when I lived in the Twin Cities, and he thinks we're still a 'thing,' I guess. Well, maybe we kind of are, or were, I guess I never actually broke it off with him."

John played with a coaster on the table in front of him but said nothing. An unfamiliar feeling, something mean and heavy, was swelling inside his chest, and Sally could see it.

"John, this is *really* awkward for me, too. He's just something I left behind when I moved here. But he still calls me. I thought he'd figure it out and then move on. I should have been more honest with him. He drove all the way up here from Minneapolis to surprise me. He thought I'd be glad to see him."

"Well, is he bothering you?" John asked with a furrowed brow. "I mean, are you afraid of him? Is he stalking you? Do I need to go over there and—"?

"No, it's nothing like that." Sally sighed.

"So, what's wrong with him?" John asked.

"Nothing. He's a nice guy. I just don't have any feelings for him. I never did, really. But he was always nice to me. I didn't want to hurt his feelings, like I just did."

"You told *me* to shut the fuck up and go sit in the corner," John said, as a playful smile flickered in his eyes again.

"Oh, I *meant* to hurt *your* feelings."

"When I asked you out last winter and you brushed me off, was it because of him? Tell me the truth," John asked. His smile had vanished.

"No, that was because of *you*." Sally laughed, and she reached across the table for John's hand. He held her hand, but his smile did not return.

"I was all set to turn on the charm and be witty and insightful tonight. But now I feel bad, really bad. This just didn't work out right. Your boyfriend is sitting over there, and—"

"John, he's not my boyfriend. He never was," Sally said. Then they both watched her surprise visitor from Minneapolis walk to the bar, pay his bill, and leave Buster's without so much as a sideways glance. "He won't be back," she said.

"So, are you OK? Do you still wanna be here with me? Maybe I should just take you home and then I'll go back to insulting your customers, like before."

"No, I mean, *yes*. Well, yes to the first part, I'm OK, and no to the second part." Sally squeezed his hand. "I wanted to go out with you. I've been hoping you'd ask. And this, this *date* tonight, this is between you and me. That guy doesn't own me, he never did. And I'm so embarrassed about all of this. I'm so sorry for the way I left you, and that I lied, and that it was so uncomfortable for you. I didn't want it to be like this. So, can we just get back to whatever it was that we were talking about before all of this?"

"Let's cut the crap for just a minute," he said, and the darkness in his eyes from a moment before returned.

"OK . . . do you want to take me home?" Sally let go of his hand.

"I was *jealous* just now," John said, as if he didn't understand either, and the hurt, and surprise, in his voice surprised her. He seemed amazed by his own confession when he said, "I was *jealous*. You believe that?"

"Huh?" Sally said. It was as if John had slipped and fallen on a crowded public sidewalk, and then after a brief struggle with shame, or anger, he was able to dust himself off and laugh at his own uncomfortable feelings.

"I was *jealous* just now . . ." John repeated, "and I hated it. I felt *sick* for a minute there. Hell, I still do. I *never* felt like this before." He said this as if he was sharing a deep and profound secret.

"Well, good. That means—"

"I *never* felt that before," he interrupted.

Sally smiled and reached across the table again to take his hand. "Good."

"I hated it," John said.

"You already said that."

"I'm gonna need a kiss, to repair my hurt feelings," he said flatly.

"Oh?" Sally's eyes sparkled, and she still held his hand. She liked the man sitting across from her; he had her attention. He was getting more interesting with every little exchange. "That wasn't witty, or insightful, but I liked it."

"A good one, too. The kiss, I mean," John added, before Sally had much time to think. "Maybe some tongue."

Sally laughed out loud. She didn't address the tongue issue, but she teased him back. "Won't work. You're too tall."

"You can stand on the curb in front of your house," John said. He seemed about to say something more, but he stopped himself.

Sally nodded. "That'll work." She squeezed his hand. "What else were you going to say?"

"Nothing," John said, doing a deliberately poor job of hiding a smile.

"You were gonna suggest that if I lay down it might work better, weren't you?" Sally's eyes glowed with the question.

"Maybe."

"All right, you don't have to be witty, for a while, anyway, but keep talking and maybe it'll happen. The kiss, I mean. And standing up," Sally said.

They finished their burgers, at last unaware of the commotion around them. Sally asked more about John's life, and what had led him to Pine

Rapids. John asked about the coffee shop, and what had become of her parents, and the pleasant conversation of this first date began to form the basis of a friendship.

The Thursday-night crowd at Buster's was beginning to thin when John and Sally got up and made their way toward the door. By any standard it had been a memorable date. Lori the waitress nearly derailed it before it began. Then it actually did come off the tracks when Sally got up and left John for a while. But they'd eventually had a pleasant evening. Sally took John's hand in hers as they walked across the dark parking lot and got into John's truck, and she directed him as he made the short drive to her home.

"OK, this is my place, right here on the right," Sally said, as John's truck rolled to a stop. She stepped out of the truck, and as John got out the driver's side and walked around toward her, she found a place to stand on the curb.

"You're still too short," John said, before he'd come within ten feet of her. When he was at arm's length he paused, put his hands on her hips, and then stepped close, so that he could put his arms around her, and he was still a head taller.

"Let's try the front steps," Sally said. She took John's hand and led him to the concrete steps to the porch in front of her house. She stood on the first step, then the second, then she put her arms around John's neck and pulled him close for a kiss. The tip of her nose was touching John's nose when she whispered, "It worked."

"What worked?"

"When you said I was pretty, and then you said you meant it." Then she kissed him.

"That wasn't good enough," he said, and Sally leaned back to look at him.

"Oh? What wasn't good enough?"

John's lips were brushing against hers when he said, "The kiss. It was OK, but I think you can do better."

She kissed him again, and she held it for a long moment. She let her tongue linger on his for a while. "How was that?" she asked as she moved away.

"Oh, you nailed it that time," he said. He lowered his head, planted one more kiss, a much softer one, on her lips, and said, "I'm gonna call you again."

"You'd better."

CHAPTER THIRTY-ONE

A s John drove to work, he was thankful for his air-conditioned shop. The morning air was already hot. An outside job, or even a walk in the forest, would be nearly unbearable today. There would be swarms of black flies, and deer flies: those nasty little sonsabitches that liked to bite him right between his fingers, or toes, and then the bites always swelled up and felt numb. In the low, swampy areas there would be mosquitoes, hundreds of them, buzzing in his ears so his head looked like a uranium nucleus. Yeah, he was glad to be painting graphite fish with an airbrush, in a nice bug-free workshop today.

Before he went to work, he thought he'd stop at Sally's coffee shop, pick up some coffee, and flirt with her for a minute. As the baseball season had moved along, they'd made a point to go out for burgers and beers together after ball games on Tuesdays and Thursdays. They'd also dated on several Saturday evenings.

Unaware that he was smiling at the thought of another little visit with Sally, John let his truck roll to a stop in front of the Human Bean and got out with a spring in his step. It was Thursday, and Pine Rapids always drew in more summer tourists as weekends approached. Sally was sure to be busy this morning, but he'd have coffee and chat with her briefly before he went to his shop. He hadn't seen her since Saturday night, and he was looking forward to their post-game date and goodnight kiss.

As he approached the café, the sign in the window of the little tobacco shop next door caught his eye. He didn't know why—maybe he was just in a good mood—but he changed direction and entered the store. Ten minutes later he'd let the seventy-year-old leftover hippie who owned the place sell him an inexpensive pipe and some not-so-inexpensive tobacco. It seemed like a good idea at the time.

John proceeded to the coffee shop, where every table was occupied, except for the dunce table where he and Matt had been banished, so John quickly took his assigned seat and waited for Sally to appear.

Several minutes passed with no one behind the front counter, and John was beginning to worry when at last Sally emerged, carrying a large cardboard box. Her struggle with the awkward box caused her enough difficulty that she failed to notice him until she'd stashed whatever was in the box behind the front counter. When she finally noticed him, a warm smile instantly replaced her frustrated frown.

"Hey, it's nice to see you," Sally said a moment later, when she delivered a tall coffee to John. She sat down at his table and smiled as if she hadn't seen him for months.

"Tough day?" John guessed.

Sally closed her eyes and shook her head. "Ah . . . dealing with the public."

"What happened?" John grinned and waited for a story.

"Somebody did a bad thing in the men's room."

"And you were cleaning it up when I got here?" John was beginning to understand the situation.

"Yup. It was everywhere! How does that happen?" she said, and a smile crept over her face. She *knew* how it happened. But she could see that John had no idea why that question made her smile, and that's the way she planned to keep things.

It struck John as funny, envisioning Sally scrubbing the men's toilet, and cursing the guy who'd made the mess. "Bummer," he teased. "Did you wash your hands before you got my coffee?"

Sally met John's eyes, then slowly, deliberately, reached over and stirred his coffee with her index finger. "Oops, forgot." she said, then she dried her finger by flicking a few drops of coffee into his face. But she never stopped smiling.

"Well maybe I can do something to make your day better," John suggested. "Can I buy you dinner again, after baseball?"

"Sure." Sally put her finger in his coffee once more and continued to smile at him.

She and John had reached a point where she no longer saw him as some guy who came in for coffee from time to time. She thought he was special, and there was a youthful, romantic twinkle to her smile now. She was enjoying this little thing they were doing. She knew that John could see it, too, for his eyes were showing her the same thing.

"I gotta go to work," John said when he slid his chair back. As he stood straight, he brought his coffee cup to his mouth and took a sip before he put a travel lid on it. "Mmm . . . tastes kinda nutty," he said, then he added, "See you after the game."

Sally stood and made sure that John saw her examine her right hand, as if there was something under her fingernails. "Ew, I gotta go wash my hands," she teased. Then she flicked one more drop of coffee at him and said, "See you tonight."

John spent most of the morning painting two large graphite northern pike replicas, and he caught himself smiling several times as he remembered the brief morning visit with Sally. He saw her delicate finger stirring his coffee, and he felt the drops of coffee splat on his face. He saw the attraction in her eyes, too, and he liked the way it made him feel. Painting the fish today, with thoughts of Sally flirting with him, was a bit more fun than usual. Well, everything was a bit more fun than usual. Sally Durham was never far from his consciousness, and the morning flew by.

Just before lunch, as John was cleaning the airbrush he'd used to paint the fish, a stray thought fluttered through his mind and made him think of the waitress at Buster's. In the next second, he remembered how she'd told him that Sally was sitting with some other guy on the other side of the bar. And that was all it took to bring back the sick, angry feeling he'd felt that night with Sally.

But he'd seen that *look* in Sally's eyes when she joked with him. And he'd felt the little flutter in his chest when she smiled at him. There *was* something going on there, something that let him imagine . . . well, he didn't know what, exactly. Damn, he didn't want to think about her smiling like that at some other guy.

John checked his watch and saw it was 11:30, so he decided to take a break and clear his head. He'd drive to McDonald's and pick up lunch for Snag and Darrell.

The Shorewood Furist was bustling with activity when John let himself in, and he quickly crossed the concrete floor toward the dingy little office where Snag was seated. The pile of beaver carcasses was long gone, but the room still smelled horrible. The trapping season was long over, and the place had been cleaned up, sort of, at least cleaned up as well as any place like this could be cleaned up. John had grown accustomed to the stink, and he ignored it.

The beaver and coyote blanket business seemed to be pretty steady. Snag and another guy were both seated in front of large sewing machines, slowly feeding supple beaver hides into the machines to be joined together. A third guy was trimming the edges, wasting as little as possible, to make the blankets all approximately the same size. A fourth guy was using a different type of sewing machine to sew a fleece liner to each nearly finished blanket.

John carried a large white paper bag in one hand, and when he stepped into Snag's gray lair he set the bag on the desk and hollered, "Hey, Snag, boughtcha some lunch." Snag smiled when he noticed the McDonald's logo on the bag. "I thought you could use a healthy meal for a change," John said. He smiled, but the joke was lost on Snag.

"Thanks. What didja get?" Snag asked, while he rifled through the contents. "Ooh, coupla Big Macs . . . coupla Quarter Pounders . . . a ton of fries . . . nice work." Then he raised his voice and called, "Hey, Darrell, John brought us lunch!"

When Darrell appeared, he was dragging a metal chair over the concrete floor and the awful noise was similar to fingernails on a chalkboard. "Hi, John, what's in the bag?" He said this over the shrill metallic scraping of metal chair legs on the floor. Darrell swung the chair around and peeked into the McDonald's bag in one smooth motion, then he plucked out a Big Mac and sat in the chair.

"So are you makin' money, or are you just busy?" John asked, and he pointed to the new construction and new equipment.

"Makin' money," Darrell said. "Orders for these fur blanket-bedspreads keep coming, and the frozen beaver loaf continues to be a hit. We're shipping that stuff all over."

"Yeah, and we're gonna take the blankets and have a booth at a bunch of those house and garden shows next winter," Snag added. "That should get us some good exposure."

John took a Quarter Pounder from the bag for himself, placed it on Snag's desk, next to yesterday's empty can of tuna, and unwrapped it. In his mind's eye John envisioned the Minneapolis Home and Garden Show, where the Minneapolis Convention Center was filled with display booths and the aisles would be packed with people looking for things for their homes. Every aisle would be crowded with displays from businesses trying to sell patio awnings, hardwood floors, soapstone woodstoves, and fur blankets. The furs in the Shorewood Furist booth would stand out, though, and people would be drawn to them. And there would be Snag Velde, the face of the Shorewood Furist. John turned to look at his brother as he reached back into the bag and retrieved a handful of French fries. The long, greasy gray hair, the cigarette, the piece of rope holding his blue jeans up, the brown teeth, the too-small plaid shirt that didn't quite reach his waist; Snag was the total package for negative marketing. "So who's gonna work the shows? Who's gonna sit in those booths all day and talk to curious people?" John asked.

"I will," Darrell said. "I like that stuff."

"Yeah, I'll just stay here and do the real work," Snag added.

John nodded and breathed a sigh of relief. The kind of people who could afford a beaver blanket probably weren't the people who were likely to be impressed by Snag. But then, who *would* be impressed by Snag? If people didn't already know him they either turned away or just managed not to notice him at all when he went out in public. "Well, the blankets sure look great. It was a helluva good idea, Snag," John said, and he gave his brother a pat on the back.

"What's up with you?" Darrell asked John. "You look like shit."

"Thanks, Darrell," John deadpanned. "I've been keepin' busy with work, and baseball." He chose not to mention all the time he'd been spending with Sally.

"Hmm, you look like you could use a good night's sleep," Darrell said, as he unwrapped his Big Mac. Then he added, "How's baseball going, by the way? Did you get anything to drink?" Darrell asked two questions at once and peeked into the McDonald's bag.

"There's a coupla Cokes in the bottom of the bag," John said, answering the second question first, and first one second. "Kids don't play ball like we did. Remember how we always had a game going in some vacant lot, or over at the park?"

"Either that or we were spearing carp down at the river, or hauling Dad's spare lumber out to the woods so we could build a tree fort," Snag said.

"Yeah, kids don't do that stuff anymore. We played ball all day, every day. Now we have kids on this team who don't know *anything*. I mean, if they could actually pick up a ground ball, they still have no idea where to throw it. When they're on base they don't know when to run; they just rely on their mothers to holler "Run!" every time a ball is put in play.

Half of the kids look like they're gonna piss on their own leg when the bitches start screaming, too. Sorta makes me feel bad about all that's been lost in our culture."

"Yeah," Snag said. "How will the next generation ever hope to match our lofty accomplishments?" He used several French fries to point at the interior of the Shorewood Furist, and he chuckled.

John and Darrell joined in the laughter too, and for a brief moment they were just the young Velde boys again, sharing a laugh.

But the moment passed quickly, as such moments do for old men; it never had time to settle. It hovered briefly and was whisked away by the demands of real life: money and work. Such things had never interfered in the lives of little boys.

John was still chewing the last bite of his Quarter Pounder when he balled up a napkin and threw it in the bag. "I gotta go, boys."

"Whaddya got planned for this afternoon?" Darrell asked.

"Oh, got a couple deer heads to finish; gotta put the eyes in. That's the tricky part," John said. "Then I got a couple fish to paint. Then we have a ball game tonight, our last game of the season."

"Thanks for lunch, John!" Snag called as John walked away. "I feel healthier already!"

CHAPTER THIRTY-TWO

—•—

The final game of the season was almost over, and John was already looking around the Orange team's bench area, trying to locate all the balls and bats so he could stuff them in one of the canvas bags and make a run for it. The sun was low in the western sky and it was the bottom half of the last inning. The score was about 50 to 3, as far as John could tell, and as always, Orange was on the receiving end of a massacre. But the end was near. The kid at the plate would be the last batter of the season no matter what, because every other kid on the team had already taken their turn at bat in this inning.

The coach for the other team lofted a floater toward the plate, and John thought the ball seemed to hang there, frozen in time. The instant this game was over, John planned to rush out there and take the catcher's gear off Bradley Hested before the kid could lose it. He took a quick glance over beyond the first base line and saw Jane and Sally still sitting together and chatting. Hurry up, hurry up, let's get this over with, John thought to himself.

The kid at the plate took a mighty swing and sent a lazy pop fly into the summer evening. The ball was hit pretty high, and it was going to come down somewhere between Timmy Clements at first base and Michelangelo Katzenmeyer at second base. Closer to second base. Much closer.

Naturally, the mothers of the other team started shrieking for the batter and the two baserunners to RUN! As the ball rose into the sky, Timmy slowly began to drift over toward second base. He was looking up at the ball and tracking its path.

"Uh-oh," Matt said, and he nudged John. They both could see that the ball was clearly going to come to Mike Katzenmeyer, and they both knew that Mike had no chance. He was the worst player in the league; he had weaker skills than the Compton twins. His only hope was to get out of the way before the ball cracked his skull.

Everyone was looking up at the ball, except for Matt and John. Both of them were watching the terror grow in Mike's eyes. Sure, he could pounce on a dead ball with the best of 'em. But his baseball glove/garbage-can lid was only good for catching things that had stopped moving, and maybe for his mother's pit bull to chew on. Actually catching a fly ball with it—a fly ball hit by a big kid? That was out of the question.

Timmy was also watching the ball sail up and then begin its descent, and he understood that it would be better for his team, and better for his teammate, if he just drifted over there and caught the ball. As he shuffled slowly toward Mike, with his glove in the air and his eyes turned skyward, he said, "I got it." Mike was holding his glove in the air, mostly a defensive maneuver to protect his face, when Timmy stepped in front of him and caught the ball.

Mercifully, the game, and the season, were over. "Thanks, man," Mike said to Timmy, and they both ran to the cooler beside Sally's folding chair to see what kind of treats had been brought for tonight's celebration.

The players from the Orange team and most of their parents were soon working on Popsicles or some form of ice cream on a stick as they milled about and thanked each other for a fun season. John and Matt were standing together by the chain-link fence behind home plate, stowing all the baseball gear into the canvas bags one last time. Matt said, "We had a pretty good season, didn't we? Thanks for doing this."

"Yeah, it was OK," John said. He pulled the drawstring closed on the bag with all the bats in it, then he dismissed the baseball season and changed the tone of the conversation entirely. He lowered his voice and asked, "You ever been jealous?"

Matt cocked his head back and asked, "You mean, like, jealous over a woman?"

John nodded yes.

"Well, not really. I mean, Jane has never given me much reason to be jealous." Matt smiled, then squinted. "You in love?"

John did not reply, which was an admission of guilt, and it caught Matt off guard. He'd been teasing, and he'd expected a reply like "Fuck you" and then a fairly disgusting anecdote. But none came. Only silence. John was confessing something, some uncertainty. He was standing at the edge of a void.

"Sally, huh?" Matt asked.

John looked at him and nodded.

Matt stuffed a batting helmet into a canvas bag but didn't look up. "She mentioned some other guy, and made you feel sick, like you might puke?"

John didn't answer.

"Felt like you wanted to run away, or cry, or fight somebody, and then die?"

"A little bit." John shrugged.

"Well, welcome to the human race," Matt mumbled. "Took you long enough to get here." He shook the canvas bag with the batting helmets and catcher's gear in it so all the pads would settle to the bottom. He chuckled and added, "I like her, John. She's too good for you."

Before John could come up with anything to say to Matt, the Compton twins raced up and thanked their coaches for a fun time, and then they raced away with their parents.

"Cute kids," John sighed. "But I've got a date, and—"

"Hey, you two!" Another voice came from behind the chain-link fence. Ron Hested and Bradley were walking over to say goodbye. "Bradley had a good time this summer. Thanks!" Ron shook hands with John first, then Matt.

"It was a pleasure," John said, and he bent over and shook Bradley's chubby hand. "We didn't kick much ass, but we didn't take no shit from nobody, did we Bradley?"

Bradley's face lit up. "Are you gonna coach me again next year?" he asked.

"Well *Hell* yes!" John said. "Next year is payback time for those other sonsabitches!" He had established a rapport with Bradley. They'd come to like each other, and the cussing was something he shared only with his catcher. Bradley Hested loved it.

"But I gotta get going now. You have a good year in school, Bradley. See you, Ron," John said, and he walked off across the outfield grass, on his way to Buster's again, with Sally.

The crowd at the postgame party was dwindling rapidly, and Dr. Hested was about to turn and leave too. But while he was still alone at home plate with Matt he asked, "How's Jane doing? How's the healing?"

"Good! She's doing fine. I think we'll be back to normal soon," Matt said, while he stacked one canvas bag on top of another.

Ron made a point to let Matt listen to himself. He knew that Matt was doing what so many men would do in his situation: keeping a stiff upper lip. He was staying strong for the sake of his wife. Ron looked at Matt, and he let Matt see in his eyes that he was serious about what he was going to say next. "You have to grieve, Matt. You must grieve for the things you lose."

"We're fine, Ron. We're through the worst part, and we're good," Matt reassured him.

Ron lit a cigarette and nodded. There was no point pursuing this conversation just now. Matt Kingston didn't know what he didn't know.

———

Night sounds rode the cool air across Scotch Lake and through the woods into the screened porch. There was no moon, and the night outside the porch was as dark as a summer night could be when Matt opened the door of his liquor cabinet and withdrew a new bottle of Aberlour.

Jane was standing near him, at the kitchen sink, when he dropped a couple of ice cubes in his lowball glass and covered them with scotch. He left his drink on the countertop and moved close to her, so that his stomach was touching her back, and he brought his hands around her; his right hand came to her flat stomach, and his left hand gently brushed past her breast before it came to rest on her shoulder. Then he held her close and kissed her ear.

Jane went rigid, and in a flat tone, devoid of emotion, she said, "They're numb."

Matt kissed her ear again. "I just wanted to touch you. We never touch each other anymore."

"It feels creepy when you touch me there."

"I wasn't trying to turn you on. I just wanted to touch you," he said, as he moved his hands away from her.

Jane was still looking away from him, and she seemed frozen, unwilling to turn and face him. Matt stepped back and took his drink out into the darkness of the porch and sat in an old wicker rocking chair.

He wasn't angry. His feelings were hurt, and he was confused. Jane had just made him feel like a guy who'd made unwanted advances to a strange woman. She'd never done that before. She seemed upset with him. He wanted to go back and talk to her, but he had no idea what to say. A few minutes later she joined him on the porch and sat in the rocker next to his.

The easy, familiar groan of wicker chairs was the only noise for a while. The songbirds of the forest had roosted for the night, but every so often a loon called out. The ice in Matt's drink clinked with each sip of scotch. They rocked together on the porch as they had for nearly forty years, but now there was something between them that had never been there before.

"They're numb. What can I say," Jane finally offered.

"Are you numb *everywhere?*" Matt asked. "I just wanted to hold you. I still love you, you know. Don't you still have feelings for me?"

"I don't feel very sexy. I can't do it."

"I wasn't after sex. I just wanted to hold my girl. I miss you. We never touch anymore."

Jane said nothing, but Matt knew she was crying, and he saw her reach a hand up to her face and wipe away some tears.

"How can I ever touch you again? Will it ever be the same?" Matt said. "All I want is for you to know that I love you. I mean, will you tell me when it's OK for me to touch you?" He was stumbling on his words when he finished, just hoping to say the right thing. He stood up and then knelt beside Jane's chair. He kissed her once on the lips, then he put his head in her lap.

Jane slowly moved her hands over his shoulders and then ran her fingers through his hair. Neither of them understood where life had taken them, or where they'd go from here.

"Why?" Jane whispered. "Why did this happen to me?"

"Don't know," Matt said. "Who ever knows why?" But the *why* and the *what next* of it all were too much for this moment. Matt and Jane held each other and let the silence of the summer night close in on them.

"What was that?" Jane flinched, as if she'd just heard a burglar breaking into the house.

"I didn't hear anything,"

Jane flinched again. "Oh, shit!! It's a bat!" She shrieked and covered her head with her hands.

A second later Matt was trying to stand up and duck at the same time when a shadow whooshed past his ear.

"Shit!" Matt hissed. He was hunched over and clambering across the porch and then the great room on his way to a hall closet. He moved with the fear and passion of a soldier trying to dodge shrapnel during an artillery barrage. It had been a few years, perhaps ten, since he'd used it, but there was a racquetball racquet somewhere in that closet, and he needed to find it. Pronto.

He was on his hands and knees, digging through an assortment of old shoes that he hadn't seen in a few years either, when he found the racquet under a hunting boot with no laces in it. Jane had already run past him to the closet by the back door, and she returned wearing a fur hat and carrying a broom.

"Nice hat," Matt said, when he stood up and found himself nose to nose with his breathless wife.

"I hate bats," Jane said. "We gotta get him!"

"OK, here's the plan," Matt said. "You go stand in the great room and wave that broom around in the rafters. That'll drive him my way and I'll smash his ass."

The bat made two passes through the great room and Jane took a couple of weak swings and dropped the broom both times. "It hurts me to swing this thing!"

"Yeah, don't worry about it, I think the little shit has some sort of radar to help him avoid contact!" Matt said. "Just keep it up in the air and keep him flying. I'll get him when he comes this way."

Ten minutes later the bat was still in an erratic holding pattern above the dining room table and the couches in the great room. Jane's chest was sore from holding the broom up, and Matt had broken one lamp and knocked the oak trim off the kitchen door jamb with the racquet.

"Damn, he's a nimble little pecker," Matt groaned after yet another whiff, and Jane had had enough. Without a word of surrender she gave up her post in the great room and marched to the front door.

"What are you *doing?*" Matt cried.

"I think we need to just let it out! If we open the door I think it will go away on its own!" Jane shouted. She flinched as the bat strafed her again, and then she did a courageous thing: She opened the front door and held it open. At first she tried to look like the doorman at a luxury hotel, but a second later she flattened herself against the wall next to the door and squinted, bracing herself for whatever might happen.

"No, don't do that. We'll have a whole herd of bats in here!" Matt yelled from the dining room.

"No, I think we just need to—"

The bat flip flapped right past Jane, out the door and into the night, and the house was immediately peaceful again.

"Whoa, nice work," Matt said as Jane pushed the door shut. "You were right. We just had to let it go. How'd you know?"

"I didn't, but it seemed like you were gonna destroy our home if we didn't try to let it go," she said. After she'd put her broom and her fur hat back in the closet, Matt followed her into their bedroom and put his arms around her.

"You're a genius!" he joked. She kept her arms at her sides.

"I'm tired, I'm outta gas, and my chest hurts." Matt tried to kiss her and she turned away.

Every other time something this outrageous had happened there would have been laughter, and when they were younger there would have been sex, too, because the laughter usually led them to sex. But now Jane could think only of brushing her teeth and climbing into bed. She left Matt standing in the bedroom by himself, and she went into the master bathroom.

Matt went to the kitchen and made himself another scotch. Then he found his way out to the screened porch and let the darkness and the night sounds envelop him. From the porch, he could see the lights in his bedroom go out. Jane had plopped into bed without even a kiss goodnight.

He let a sip of scotch linger under his tongue for a second and waited for the next call of a loon. He wanted, needed, to share his feelings about all that had happened this evening with *someone*. He turned his phone on and sent a text message:

<Hey Mo, are you still up?>

<Yes. What's up? Everything OK?>

<Just a tough day.>

<You sound like you need a friend?>

<Yup. Just having a scotch before bed. Jane is tired and doesn't seem to want me very close.>

<Give her some room.>

<I wish you lived next door so we could sit by a campfire and talk.>

<Someday.>

<Glad you're back in my life, Mo. You're a good friend.>

<Me too…you too. Finish your scotch and go to bed, old friend. Things will be better in the morning.>

CHAPTER THIRTY-THREE

—•—

"Hey, you gotta stop over for a bump on the way home," John said into the phone, as he rummaged through the contents of the avocado refrigerator in his shop.

"Nah, I just left the office and I wanna get home," Matt said. "It's so good to be done with baseball, and—"

"Ah, c'mon, I'm all done with work, too. I'm in the break room, such as it is, making some hors d'oeuvres. I'm talkin' venison tips flash fried in butter in a cast-iron fryin' pan, and a cold Leinie's."

Matt looked at his watch and said, "I only have time for one." Five minutes later, he let himself in through the front door of John's shop. He went directly to the avocado refrigerator, next to the faded gold kitchen stove, where John was already cooking. John waved at Matt with the spatula in his hand and said, "Hi, buddy."

"Hey John." Matt opened the fridge and drew out a can of Leinenkugel's. "How's it going?" Matt popped his beer open and took a big swig before John could answer.

"Purdy good," John replied. "You?"

"OK, I guess." Matt shrugged. "So tell me about being jealous."

"It was odd, for sure," John answered. He used his spatula to cut a stick of butter in half, then he plopped one of the halves into the frying pan. "I never felt like that before."

"I guess that's a good thing," Matt said. "She's a big step up from your other lady friends."

"She's really smart." John was stirring the slumping hunk of butter with his spatula.

"You don't often talk about your lady friends in these terms. Usually you're more concerned with, what shall I say, describing the *action*."

"It's nothing like that at all," John said. He seemed happy, or satisfied, as if he'd discovered something he was unfamiliar with. He dropped a small package full of venison tips into the cast-iron pan and stirred the sizzling little pieces of lean venison with the spatula. "Sally's clever, and the more she talks, the prettier she gets."

Matt found a box of toothpicks and watched John stir the venison. "She's too good for you."

"How's Jane?" John asked. "Any pain, still? Is she healing OK? How's the chemotherapy going?"

"Still some pain. She's finding that all the surgery left her chest muscles weaker." Matt used a toothpick to select a nearly done piece of venison. "Mmm, really good!" He spoke with the venison still in his mouth.

John moved the hot frying pan to a cold burner and turned off the stove top. Then he used a toothpick to select a venison tip for himself. "Damn, this *is* good. I think this is the best way to fix ven. Roughed grouse, too."

"Yup, I concur." Matt tried several more tips, then added, "She's not really taking chemo. It's something else, some sort of hormone therapy."

"Well, she sure looks good, and she seems to be back to normal," John said. "I saw her the other day in the grocery store and we had a nice chat."

"Mmm. She's not there yet. Back to normal, I mean." Matt finished his beer and opened another. "I guess I have time for one more." He shook his head and said, "Everyone thinks she's back, but she's not. I'm starting to wonder if she ever will be." The sound of his own words made him pause, and while he was thinking about how he'd explain the changes in Jane, the door to John's shop opened. And a moment later, when Darrell and Snag stepped into John's work area, it was obvious that something was wrong. Really wrong.

"What now?" John asked. He braced himself for an answer involving money and all the additions over at the Shorewood Furist.

"Vicky's dead," Darrell said.

Matt hadn't heard any of the Velde boys speak of their sister for several years, and a pall settled over the shop.

John leaned back against one of the work tables and asked, "What happened?"

"Car accident," Darrell said.

"Jerry?" John asked. Matt knew that her husband's name was Jerry, but he'd never met him, and only heard the Velde boys speak of him from time to time.

"He was killed too," Snag answered.

"When's the funeral?" John asked.

"It was today, this morning," Darrell said.

Matt made a point to stay out of the conversation, but he opened the fridge and drew out a beer for Snag and Darrell, and they all sat down around the barrel stove.

"Where did it happen?" John asked.

"Kansas. Just outside the little town where they lived," Snag said.

"Why did nobody call us?" John asked, with a sigh.

"Well, you know she really shut us out a long time ago, when she moved away," Darrell said. "I haven't spoken to her, even on the phone, for ten years."

"Me neither," John said. "I think she was still angry with me."

"I talked to her every so often. Last time was about two years ago," Snag said. "I just wanted to talk to her. I guess we had nice talk, but she never called me again."

"But still," John said, "why would nobody call us?"

"Well, they never had any kids, and Jerry only had the one son, from an earlier marriage. He's the one who called me today. He said he had a hard time finding us," Darrell said.

"That's just bullshit," John said. He was upset but resigned to the sad fact that he could change nothing now.

Sitting in a circle of silence with his childhood buddies, Matt didn't know if he should get up and leave his friends or stay with them.

"I shoulda known," John said. "And I shoulda done something."

Matt knew very well that John was was referring the awful abuse that his sister had suffered from her father.

"None of us knew, John. Vicky hid it from us, too," Snag said.

"Mom knew," John said. "And she did nothing."

"I should leave you guys alone," Matt said, and he stood up to go. "I'm so sorry for your loss, and for all of what you guys are dealing with. I liked Vicky." The Velde boys needed some family time now, and Matt knew he was an intruder. If John had wanted him to know any more about their family's secret, he would have told him long ago.

"Hey, Matt," John said, "we'll talk tomorrow, you and me."

"OK." Matt let himself out the door. The taxidermy shop remained silent as the door slammed shut and Matt started his truck outside.

The brothers sat in what felt like an empty room for a moment until John said again, "I shoulda known. I never knew until the summer after my first year in college. And then I left. I just ran away and left her."

"I shoulda known, too. But I ran away and left before you did," Snag said.

"Yeah, I guess we all shoulda known, but we didn't," Darrell replied. "I stayed around for a while, after you guys left, and it was really bad. When Dad died, I was the only one at the funeral. You guys were both gone, and Vicky had met Jerry and moved away. She never came back when Mom died, either."

"Do you think she salvaged a happy life after that awful start?" John asked Snag. "You said she talked to you a couple times."

"Yeah, I think Jerry was good to her," Snag said. "I think she was OK . . . at least as OK as a girl could be after all that."

They talked throughout the evening about the signs, and what they should have done. And they talked about things they could or should do now, until they all understood that it was too late to do anything. Without verbalizing their need to move on, they eventually got up, said goodnight, and went their separate ways for the night. They each knew they'd have to do whatever they needed to do to find some closure with their sister, and with what had happened to their family.

———

It was after nine when the doorbell at Sally's house rang. "Hi" was all she could think to say when she opened the door and found John standing there.

His face was lit by a small light bulb just above the door, which had already drawn a moth, and the moth was fluttering around John's face. "Can I come in?" he asked.

"Sure, c'mon in. What's wrong?" Sally tried to shoo the moth away and hold her screen door open at the same time.

"I know you have to get up early, so I won't stay long," John said, once the tinny aluminum door had closed behind him.

"It's OK, I was just gonna sit on the couch and read for a while before bed. What's wrong, John? I can see—"

"My sister died," John blurted.

"Ohhh . . . I'm sorry, John. Come in and sit down. You never told me you had a sister. Why?"

"Oh, I guess I was ashamed of some things."

When John was settled in on the couch, Sally sat beside him, held his hand, and waited for him to start talking.

"Life is crazy," John began. He told Sally that Victoria Velde, his only sister, had been destroyed by her father while she was still a child. He told her about the monstrous things that her father did to her, at least the things he finally learned about when it was too late. It began while she was in elementary school and continued until John discovered her nightmare and then beat his own father senseless. Vicky had escaped from her father, as much as a thing like that is possible, when she married a nice man and moved to Kansas. Now she was dead.

"And you didn't know it was happening, at the time?" Sally asked.

"Oh, I could see that Vicky had changed, but I never thought . . . you know." John shrugged and let some anger show. "I never would have thought *that*. I didn't ever suspect it. I never would have imagined. And to tell the truth, I wasn't paying much attention to anyone else. I was pretty wrapped up in my own life. It was a full-time job being me. It was after I went off to college that I started to wonder what was going on at home. When I came home for Christmas that freshman year at the U, Vicky was really angry with me, for leaving her alone with Dad." John shrugged. "I thought he was an asshole, but I . . ."

"Weren't the others still home? Snag and Darrell, and your mother?" Sally asked.

"Well, in hindsight, my mother must have known. I mean, wouldn't a mother know about stuff like that? I think she just chose to ignore it, or deny the truth, because it must have been such a terrible thing to deal with."

"I dunno," Sally said. "What about Snag? Where was he?"

"Ah, Snag." John allowed a faint smile to come to his lips. "I told you that Snag had a bit of a problem in shop class; put the teacher's head in a vice and then quit school and joined the navy. I told you about that, right?"

"Uh-huh." Sally smiled too.

"That happened even before I went off to college. So Snag and I were both gone all of a sudden, and that left only Darrell. And Darrell . . ." John shook his head. "He was so far out there in his own fantasy world." John looked down and thought for a moment. "We all sorta left Vicky to fend for herself, with a monster. And then she ran away from all of us. Sometimes I wish I'd killed my father that night."

"Oh, John, you don't wish that. The damage was already done at that point."

"I know, Sally. I've been over this thing a million times, way before tonight. Life is just crazy. But I still wonder if I could have done something . . ."

"Would you like a drink?" Sally asked. John nodded yes, and she went into the kitchen and fixed him a tall scotch. When she returned, she gave him the drink and said, "All right, John, now tell me a happy story about Vicky."

John took a sip of his scotch. "That's easy. When we were little kids, and we went to my grampa's farm, Vicky and I always slept together in one of the upstairs bedrooms. Jeez, that old house was cold in the winter." John took another sip. "We used to put so many blankets on us that we couldn't hardly roll over. Then we'd snuggle up and talk about stuff. Vicky liked the Beatles, Paul more than John, and she talked about them a lot. Sometimes we'd just lay there in the dark and listen to the wind howl and tell silly stories."

Sally reached over and took a sip of his scotch. "Good one," she said. "Makes me smile to think of you like that. I wish I'd known you then."

"We used to tease Snag, too. We'd both stare at him while we were sitting at the dinner table. You know, we'd just stare across the table at him until he freaked out and started to cry, and then Mom and Dad would get pissed at him." John looked at Sally and flicked his eyebrows. "It was great, and then when Snag was crying, Vicky and I would look around like a couple innocent little angels." John leaned forward and placed his drink on the coffee table in front of him, but something had turned. He sat with his elbows on his knees and tried to enjoy the memory. "I haven't thought of that in forty years."

And then, slowly at first, the wall that had been holding everything back began to crumble. Sally watched as John started to rub his eyes. His shoulders began to move with each of his soft cries, and Sally reached over to stroke his back. "Let it go, John," she whispered, and she tried to imagine the things going through John's mind. "You're a good boy, John Velde," she said.

Sally went to the kitchen and returned with a box of tissues and a wastebasket, and she sat down beside John while he wept. There was nothing to say, and nothing that needed to be said. She understood that this was why John had come to her. She stroked his back from time to time but said nothing.

Then a tiny voice from the darkness on the far side of the room surprised them both. "Gramma, why is John crying?" Timmy asked. He was wearing Spider Man pajamas and his eyes were filled with fear, and surprise.

"Oh, Timmy, everything is OK, you go back up to your room, and we'll talk in the morning," Sally said.

"But why is he crying?" Timmy asked again.

Sally started to get up off the couch and lead him back to his room. "You go on back up to—"

"It's OK, Sally," John said. "C'mere, Timmy, and I'll tell you." John was still sitting on the couch, and Timmy crossed the room to stand eye to eye with John. "My sister died, Timmy, and I'm feelin' real bad. S'pose I could have a hug?"

John opened his arms, and Timmy stepped into them. Then he put his arms around John's neck and squeezed. "You can do better than that, kid. I need a *hug*!" John teased, and Timmy squeezed until John groaned, "OK, that was a good one."

Timmy released his grip and stepped back.

"I'll be OK, Timmy. I just feel real bad. Your gramma is about my best friend, so I wanted to come over and talk with her tonight. I'm sorry I woke you up."

Sally reached for a tissue and wiped her eyes, too. John had referred to her as his best friend.

"Did your sister go to Heaven?" Timmy asked.

John smiled and said, "Oh yeah, I'm sure she's there now."

"All right, Timmy, back to bed," Sally said, and she led Timmy toward the stairway.

"G'night, Timmy," John said.

"G'night, John."

"I'll be right back," Sally said to John from the bottom of the stairs.

When she returned from Timmy's bedroom she went straight to the kitchen and picked up the open bottle of scotch. With the bottle in her hand, she leaned against the kitchen sink and thought, *John Velde just referred to me as his best friend.*

John was waiting for her, about to get up and go home, when she sat down and poured him a second drink. Another tall one. "That was nice, what you just said. And it was good for my boy to see a strong man deal with grief like you did."

"I should go home, and you gotta get up for work, and if I drink *that*," he pointed to the drink in her hand, "I won't be driving anywhere."

"You came here to talk, John."

"But how'll I get home?"

"You've slept on a few couches in your day, I'm guessing."

"A few," he admitted.

"So talk to me."

"Thanks, Sally." He leaned back into the couch and put his feet up on the coffee table. After a long minute to think, he said, "I killed a gopher once, with my pellet gun, and Vicky and I were playing with it—"

"Wait a minute. You and your little sister were playing with a dead gopher?" Sally teased.

"Well, we didn't have many toys. So stop interrupting and I'll tell you the story. It's quite charming." John told stories, and laughed, and cried, and drank more scotch, until almost midnight, when his eyes went to half-mast, and his words began to slur.

"We should take your pants off," Sally said. She'd been laughing and crying right along with him, but now the evening was about over.

"That's what all the girls say to me."

"Yeah, I'm sure." Sally helped him wobble to his feet, and she steadied him for a moment. She loosened his belt and then lowered his blue jeans and helped him step out of them. "Nice boxers," she said as she helped lower him back onto the couch.

"I quit wearing tighty whities when I was fourteen."

"Yeah, well, that's probably all I need to know about that." Sally thought he was asleep when she covered him with a light blanket, but he surprised her by reaching up and touching her hand.

"Thanks, Sally," was all he could say before he finally slipped away.

———

The morning sun was obnoxious and unwanted, shining through the window and beating on his face when the throbbing of his skull finally woke him. John reached up, covered his face with the blanket, and hated the sun. He thought about returning to sleep, but a little voice, some-where near the couch, said, "Can I turn the TV on now? Gramma said to wait until you woke up. Are you awake, John?"

"Uh-huh," John said, then he coughed his lungs clear. "What time is it, Timmy?"

"It's nine."

"What time did your gramma leave the house?"

"I don't know for sure. She goes in to the coffee shop real early some days."

"And you sleep in?" John asked, his face still covered by his blanket.

"Yeah, most days. Then I walk to the shop and help with the noon dishes."

"Well, that's pretty impressive; a young lad with a job." John raised himself to sit up.

"Gramma said you took a sleeping pill."

"Yup." John wanted to grin but he thought it would require too much work.

"It kinda stinks in here. You farted a couple times while you were sleeping."

"Sorry, pal."

"It's OK, Gramma does it all the time too," Timmy said, while he selected a video to watch.

"Good to know," John replied.

"Gramma said for you to come to the coffee shop when your sleeping pill wears off," Timmy said. "She said she'll make breakfast for you."

"I think I'll just wake up a little bit more, and then take her up on breakfast."

"Hey, John?" Timmy said, as if he had a secret to share.

"Yeah, pal," John replied. He was watching TV while he stood to put his pants on.

"Next time when you come for a sleepover you can sleep upstairs, with me. OK?"

CHAPTER THIRTY-FOUR

John strode into the coffee shop by himself on a cool Friday morning in August. "Where's your friend?" Sally asked.

"You mean Matt? I dunno." John tilted his head as if he hadn't given Matt Kingston a thought. "Probably sticking a needle in somebody's head right about now, I suppose." The woman in line directly in front of John overheard him and made a face.

Sally picked up on the woman's discomfort right away, and explained, "His friend is a dentist." Instead of taking a seat at his dunce table, John stood calmly in line behind two young women and waited patiently while they ordered coffee. Then he stepped up to the counter when they moved off to a table by the fireplace.

"You OK?" Sally asked.

"Yeah, why?"

"Well, you seem distracted, and you weren't particularly rude to those women. I thought maybe something was wrong."

"Ooh, good one!" John pretended to pull an arrow out of his chest. "I'll turn it up a notch next time. But I wanted to ask you—"

Three more women burst into the coffee shop, all of them talking at once. In a second, they were standing next to him at the counter.

"C'mere." John motioned for Sally to move over a few feet, by the glass counter with the pastry and scones in it, so he could say what he had to say in private.

"What is it?" Sally leaned close to hear what he had to say.

"Will you go out with me tonight?"

Sally looked puzzled. "We've been going out several nights a week for a while now. Of course I will. I look forward our nights out. Why didn't you just call me like you usually do?"

John took her hand. "Well, I kinda want to do something special. You know, dress up a little bit, or something like that." He shrugged.

"Sounds great. Where are we going?"

"Mmm, that Italian restaurant over on the other side of Wiigwaas? Everyone says it's good," John said.

Sally smiled. "Sure. That'd be nice."

"I just want tonight to be a little special, that's all," John said.

"Pick me up at seven. I'll wear something new. But I gotta get back to work now," Sally said, and she hurried back to the women at the counter.

———

John's truck rolled to a stop in front of Sally's house at one minute before seven o'clock. When he walked around the back of the truck on his way to knock on her door, Sally was already standing on the front steps, waiting.

"Whoa, you look nice!" John said.

Sally opened her jacket to reveal a new sweater and a skirt. He'd never seen her in a skirt. She held the jacket open until John reached the steps. She was standing on the second step, looking at him eye to eye, when he slid his hands inside her jacket and pulled her close for a kiss.

"Mmm, that was nice," she whispered.

"You're a pretty girl, and you're teasing me. That outfit is really sexy."

"I'm trying," Sally said. "Maybe you wanna just stay *here* for dinner?"

"Well, I made reservations at the Italian place."

Sally kissed him once more, then held his lower lip between her teeth and tugged softly when the kiss ended. "You sure?" she whispered.

"Where's Timmy?" John asked.

"He's spending the night at Dave Norman's house."

"You know, I think I did hear something about mouse turds in the pasta out there," John said. "So I think maybe it would be better, safer, to just stay right here."

"Me too," Sally said. She took John by the hand and led him up the front steps and into her home. The little house was built into a steep hillside, about three hundred feet up from the lake, just like every other little house in her neighborhood. It was modest, built around 1950, and small, only about eight hundred square feet on the main level. It had a kitchen and a living room with a picture window looking out over Wiigwaas Lake, and two bedrooms upstairs. The neighborhood was quiet, and just a two-minute walk from Sally's coffee shop.

"It's pretty warm in here," Sally said, and when she opened a window on each side of the room, a gentle breeze off the lake moved the curtains. Instead of overhead lights, Sally switched on a lava lamp and opened the curtains on the picture window to reveal a view of boat lights moving about, far across the lake.

"How's that for ambiance?" she asked, and she kicked her shoes off.

"Just about right," John said. "What are you planning for dinner?" He kicked his shoes off, too.

"Well, I didn't really plan dinner, so it looks like Gourmet Club, or a frozen pizza. Can we discuss the menu over a drink or two?" Sally walked through the dim light into the kitchen. John heard dishes clanging, and Sally called out, "Would you like wine, or scotch?"

"Scotch." The small living room held the deepening blue-gray of twilight, while red, green, and white boat lights moved slowly across the calm surface of the lake. Then a glowing glob of lava shifted in the lamp and sent subtle shadows of orange light over the walls and ceiling.

"Good! I bought some of that Aberlour. Isn't that the stuff that Matt likes so much?" John could see the light from the inside of Sally's refrigerator, and then he heard ice cubes clinking into a glass, then more clinking in a second glass. "Sit down and take a load off," she said.

"Good plan. It's pretty comfy here," John said, then he raised his voice a bit to tease her. "But I think we should stay with the Italian format and have a frozen pizza. What kind have you prepared?"

"Oh, I found some Hawaiian pizza in the freezer at the gas station. Sounded real good so I bought a bunch of 'em," Sally shot back. She knew John hated Hawaiian pizza, and she heard him chuckling in the other room while she poured the scotch.

John was sitting on the couch when Sally entered the living room with a drink in each hand. "Do you like scotch, too?" John asked, as she handed him a glass. When she sat down next to him, she put a hand on his leg. The perfume she wore was wonderful.

"Yup," Sally said, "but I never buy this good stuff, except for special occasions."

"Like frozen pizza night at your place?"

"Mm-hmm." She tapped her glass against his. "Here's to . . ." She hesitated.

"Us?" John said. Her sense of humor was spot-on, and he loved the way she teased him. All the signs, everything she did, and the way she held herself caused an amorous twitch in his belly.

"That's what I was thinking." Sally smiled. She sipped her drink, held the scotch in her mouth for a second, and swallowed. "Wow, this stuff is good."

"Mm-hmm."

"Hey, before I forget, I have a favor to ask of you," Sally said.

"Shoot."

"At Timmy's school they have a thing called Dads and Doughnuts every so often. They open up the gym, and the art room, and a couple classrooms, and they put out some doughnuts. The idea is for fathers to come to school and then have the children show their fathers what they're learning about. S'pose you'd be willing to give it a try?"

"Really?" John asked, unable to hide his surprise. "Me? You sure?"

"Sure. Timmy asked me if you would come. He says the boys from baseball think you're pretty cool, too."

"Well, yeah, but . . ." John stumbled.

"You'll fit right in. It's a bunch of little boys."

"OK, sure." John shrugged.

"But you have to behave a little bit." Sally smiled.

"No problem. Not to change the subject too much, but you look really nice. That outfit, that sweater . . . it's just something I never thought I'd see you in."

"Only Minnesotans end sentences in prepositions," she teased.

John stopped as he was bringing his scotch toward his lips. "What are you, an English teacher?" he asked.

"I used to be."

"No . . ."

"Yup." Sally took another sip.

"Why did you quit? Why take such a big risk; move away and start your own business?"

"Seemed like I came to a fork in the road. I knew where one path would lead me, and I didn't want that. I wanted to see where the other path would lead." She shrugged.

"Did you make the right choice?"

"I think so, this time, anyway. But I sure made a couple of bad choices earlier in life."

"Didn't we all?" John said.

"OK, what about you? Tell me about one of your bad choices."

John shook his head. "Nah, some other time. For now, let's get back to the English teacher thing."

"OK, but I'm guessing that my bad choices weren't as interesting as yours," she said.

"Did any of your students ever have a crush on you?" John asked.

"I heard them refer to me as Scarface from time to time, when they thought I couldn't hear. So no, I don't think so."

John closed his eyes. "Little fuckers."

"They were in seventh grade." Sally shrugged.

John stared at the ice cubes in his glass for a moment, then he said, "Well, you're a teacher that I would've had a crush on."

"You just did it again."

"Did what?"

"Ended a sentence with a preposition."

"Oh, really. What would you give me for that?"

"Do you mean what letter grade would I give you?"

"Yes."

"It wouldn't be very good."

"Well, what grade would you give me if I could end a *proposition* with a preposition?" John challenged.

"I don't know. Let's hear the preposition proposition."

John tilted his head, thinking for a second, then he said, "OK, here's the proposition: I have something I'd like to see you sitting on top of." John flicked his eyebrows several times.

"Ooh," Sally said, "I guess I'd have to give you an F for the grammar, but a B-minus for the imagery. I would consider giving you some extra credit if you could expand your word usage. Because depending on the preposition that you choose, the imagery grows more and more vivid. For example, if you omit 'sitting on top of,' and then use a better verb and a different preposition, you have something like, 'thrashing underneath.' And, well, you can see a much more interesting word picture developing. I like the image created by that word picture. Do you understand?"

John nodded his understanding and said, "Mm-hmm." He took another sip of his scotch. When he swallowed, his throat made an audible noise and he acknowledged it by saying, "That always happens under stress." He was pretending to be embarrassed but biting his lip to stifle a smile.

Stress?" Sally asked, then she took a swallow of her scotch.

"It's the old English teacher fantasy thing." John shrugged.

"I see."

"You know, back in school, I would have been thrilled with a B-minus, but now I think I can do better. May I try another proposition preposition?" John asked.

"Sure."

"OK, how about 'arching against'?"

"Much better," Sally said. "Or you might try 'impaled on.'"

John's hand shot into the air, pretending to be a schoolboy who was begging for his teacher to call on him. Before Sally could give him permission to share his answer with the rest of the class, John blurted, "Bangin' like a screen door in a hurricane!"

"Not a preposition." Sally laughed and nearly spilled her drink.

"Oh, yeah, sorry, I got carried away there." John lowered his head and feigned shame.

"But again, I like the imagery," Sally added.

"How 'bout 'bent over in front of'?" John said with renewed enthusiasm.

"OK, OK, I think you've got it." Sally raised a hand to stop the barrage of sexual innuendo. "But I'm totally confused as to how I would grade you on the preposition proposition. The grammar was terrible, the imagery was quite descriptive, but the subject matter was inappropriate. So, how do I grade you? That's the ultimate English teacher conundrum."

"Well," John began, "I must admit that my lexicon is not as big as some men's. I don't know what a conundrum is." He had to bite his lip, and then compose himself with another sip of scotch. "So I have to humble myself, expose my tiny lexicon, and ask you a question." He hesitated.

"Yes? Ask the question."

"Well, just what article of your clothing would I need to remove in order to get a *real* good look at your conundrum?"

Sally burst out laughing, and John followed. She tipped her head back, finished her drink, and put her glass on the end table next to the lamp. After she'd lifted John's glass from his hand and put it on the end table next to hers, she moved into his arms and kissed him.

Soon, she was lying across his lap with her arms around his neck. Her bra was unfastened, and when she raised her knees her skirt fell to expose something more. John began to explore, and when the pleasure between her legs drove her hips into motion, she clutched at his hand to stop him and gasped, "We have to go upstairs, right now."

A while later, a soft breeze and the streetlight on the corner combined to toss fluttering shadows across Sally's bedroom walls when, at last, John rolled off her and onto his side. Both of them were spent and soaked with sweat, and John kicked the bed sheets away when he pulled Sally over to spoon with him.

She fanned herself for a moment and said, "Your lexicon is huge, and I think we used every preposition in the English language."

"You have a nice conundrum, too." John said, which triggered another belly laugh from Sally.

When her laughter died down, Sally inched herself backwards, further into his embrace, and whispered, "I hope we didn't ruin a good friendship, John."

CHAPTER THIRTY-FIVE

—•—

"OK, now, just think of me as a giant mosquito," Matt said. He was leaning close to the patient sitting in his dental chair. He'd placed a rubber strap around the man's bicep muscle and was waiting for a vein in his forearm to bulge.

"All right," Matt said when he was satisfied, "as I explained before, I'm gonna draw some blood, just like when you have a physical over at the clinic. Then we're gonna take the blood back to the lab and spin it in a centrifugal spinner in order to separate things. Then, when your broken tooth is gone, and the socket is ready, and we've spun your blood sample down, I'm gonna come back with a little plug of leucocyte platelet-rich fibrin and suture that back into the socket in order to stimulate your jawbone to heal nicely so we'll have a nice place to come back and place an implant in a few months."

"Yeah, but is this gonna hurt? That's really all I wanna know," the man asked, as Matt wiped an alcohol swab over the skin on the man's arm.

"Mmm, no. It's about as painless as things around here get," Matt replied.

"Well, that leaves a lotta room for error," the man replied with only a hint of humor.

"OK," Matt said with a smile. "Let me rephrase that. No. How 'bout just no? It's not gonna hurt at all."

"Much better answer," the man said, still with only the trace of a smile. He wanted to laugh and joke with Matt, but he couldn't do it.

Matt removed the plastic cover from the needle and then gently inserted the needle into a large blue vein on the man's forearm. Then Matt released the rubber strip that he'd tightened around the man's bicep and watched while a stream of blood began flow into the carpule he was holding. When the vial was full of blood, Matt removed the needle, placed a cotton ball over the needle hole, and bent the man's arm in order to stop any bleeding. "How'd I do?" Matt asked.

"You done already?" the man asked. He'd been looking away, but the sense of relief was heavy in his voice.

"Told ya!" Matt chuckled.

For the next half hour, as Matt extracted the man's tooth and then placed the gelatinous glob of leucocyte platelet-rich fibrin back into the extraction site and sutured things back together, a little vignette played over and over in his mind. He saw blood flowing steadily and painlessly from his patient's arm while the man simply looked away and waited for pain that never came.

———

Just before noon, Matt's morning patients were gone and he was sitting at his desk. The door to his private office opened several inches, very slowly, and Tammy's face appeared in the narrow gap. "Sorry to bother you, Doctor, but John Velde is here. Do you have time to see him?"

"Sure." Matt leaned back in his desk chair and grinned.

John stepped around Tammy as he eased into the small office. "You're looking particularly fetching today, Tammy," John said.

Tammy's eyes met Matt's, and she gave him the "yeah, whatever" look before she closed the door.

"She's kinda hot for me, isn't she?" John said, as he settled into an overstuffed chair opposite from Matt.

Matt ignored the ridiculous question. "What are you doing here? Winter is finally over. It's a sunny day. I thought you'd be fishing."

"Just came from the elementary school. They have a little get-together every so often called Dads and Doughnuts. Sally asked me to go and sorta step in as a father-like figure for Timmy." John paused. "I've been doing it about once a month, for most of the school year. Gimme some coffee, will ya?"

"Really?" Matt said, as he reached to the coffee pot beside his desk and poured a cup for John. "What's it like?"

"Scary, downright scary. Thanks," John said, when Matt gave him the coffee cup.

"Oh?"

"Jeez, I thought I was in the wrong place at first. I thought it was the lobotomy room in the asylum. Everybody was in the gym, right across the hall from the cafeteria and the art room, and there were about thirty dads there." John shook his head. "I mean, guys with a five-day growth of whiskers, wearing slippers and sweatpants and white T-shirts with food spilled on the front. I'm not shittin' you, Matt. These guys, the dads, made Snag look like a snappy dresser."

"What'd you do?" Matt asked.

"Well, I had a doughnut with Timmy . . . I think the majority of those slack-jawed zombies were only there for a free doughnut, by the way . . . and then we had a game of H-O-R-S-E in the gym."

"We?" Matt asked.

"Timmy and me, and Bradley Hested, and Mike Katzenmeyer, and David Norman. The boys from baseball, mostly."

"So, you had fun?" Matt asked.

"Actually, I had a blast. We laughed, ran around and played grab-ass, like little boys do. After it was done, I felt like maybe . . . I did some good. How 'bout that?"

"Now that's a scary thought. Did you swear at 'em?"

"No, but I kicked their asses at H-O-R-S-E!" John laughed. He slid forward in his chair, and as he was about to stand up he said, "I gotta go, but before I do, there's one more thing."

"What's that?"

"Can you write me another prescription for Viagra?"

"You're going through a lot of it," Matt said as he scribbled on a prescription pad.

"Really wasn't looking for any editorial comment."

"You must be sucking the marrow from life," Matt said as he wrote. "Are you in that part of the relationship where everything is great, but she's about to get her vacuum cleaner and move in with you? Try to change you and ruin it all?"

When Matt looked up there was no longer a smile on John's face. He seemed confused. "Huh?"

"I was just referring to your theory about relationships, based on the hundreds of successful ones you've had," Matt said. But then he realized he'd struck a nerve, and he raised his eyebrows. John looked as if Matt had hurt his feelings, and Matt poked him again. Harder this time. "Sooo, Sally might be special?" Matt teased, as he waved the prescription at John. "Did you step in your own bullshit? Whatsamatter, cat got your tongue?"

"Fuck you," John sighed under his breath, and he took the piece of paper from Matt's hand.

"Now that's a healthy doctor-patient relationship!" came a voice from just outside the office door, and Ron Hested let himself in. "Mind if I join you boys for a few minutes? Your hygienist just knocked some barnacles off my teeth, and I saw you two sitting in here as I was walking by."

"Hi, Ron," John said.

"C'mon in, Ron," Matt said. "How did your cleaning go?"

"Good. Your new hygienist is nice." Ron searched his pocket for something, then he added, "She told me to stop smoking." Then he found a pack of cigarettes and put one in his mouth.

"Don't smoke in here, Ron," Matt said.

In a slight gesture of contrition, Ron moved to a window and opened it. Then he lit the cigarette and held it by the open window. That was about as far as Ron Hested was willing to go in compliance with any no-smoking rules.

"It would be better if he smoked a pipe, right?" John said, and he held up the pipe he'd been carrying in his pocket for a while.

There was no use in arguing, and Matt simply placed his hand on his chin before he said, "I'm glad both of you could be here today and help us observe National Healthy Lifestyles Day."

"You wanna buy my boat?" Ron asked John. It was as if there had been no mention of his smoking.

"Which one?" John asked.

"The Ranger."

John sat straight in his chair. "The twenty-footer with the two-fifty Merc?"

Ron nodded.

"Fiberglass, with the metallic purple paint job? Looks like a Puerto Rican wedding?"

Ron nodded.

"How much?" John asked, the level of excitement rising with each question.

"Fifteen five."

"Why are you selling? What's wrong with it?" John asked.

"Gonna upgrade," Ron said.

"Jesus, how far up can you upgrade from that?" Matt asked.

Ron simply shrugged and admitted, "Ah, I just want a new boat."

"Hell yes, I'll take it!" John said. "I always liked that boat."

"I thought you would," Ron said.

John looked at his watch, and he stood up suddenly. "Well, hey, I gotta get to work, you guys. Got a guy coming over from Bemidji to pick up a couple deer heads in about half an hour." He turned to Ron and said, "You know, the ice just went off the lake yesterday. This is perfect timing. When can I pick up the boat?"

"I'll bring it by your shop today, after work," Ron said.

"Great, see you then. I'll write you a check." John edged out the door of Matt's office. "And Matt . . ." waving the prescription, "thanks for the Viagra."

He clicked the door shut behind him.

"Viagra, huh?" Ron asked, with only the hint of a smile. "You write that script for him?"

Matt nodded.

"Nice work. Great drug." As Ron often did, he changed the subject with no transition. "How's Jane? It's been what, a year since the cancer?"

"Yeah, 'bout a year. She's pretty good," Matt said, but his eyes told a different story, and he looked away.

When Matt did look up and make eye contact with Ron, he found that the old psychiatrist was staring back at him and restating the question with his eyes.

"She seems happy, and she's returning to normal, whatever that is. But it's not like before . . . between us."

"Matt, do you remember me telling you a couple times last summer that you need to *mourn* all the losses that come along with what you and Jane have been through?"

"Sure. And I do that. We'll get through this and we'll be back to normal before long."

It was clear to Ron that Matt just didn't get it, didn't want to get it, and was determined to cling to strength as a reason to deny all that happened.

"Talk to me, Matt," Ron said softly after a long silence. "As a friend, if you'd like, and not a doctor. I've been down this road before. This is the reason I stuck my head in here today, to talk to you about this."

Matt stared at his empty desk top, trying to decide if he wanted to open up with Ron.

"All right, Matt, but if you want to talk, you can call me any—"

"It's like she doesn't want me anymore," Matt interrupted. Then he stepped over and made certain that his office door was completely closed. "The past year has been tough on her. I get that. I was there when the doctor told her that she had cancer. I was there for the surgery, too. Both surgeries. The plastic surgeon's claim about making her look as good as new was somewhere between overly optimistic and unrealistic. I mean, she looks great with her clothes on, but I see the way she looks at herself in the bathroom mirror now. I feel so bad for her."

"Do you feel any different towards her?"

"I love her more than ever, Ron. And I tell her so. Every day. Her strength is returning, along with her sense of humor, and the sparkle in her eyes. But when I stand close to her, and touch her, I can feel her recoil." Matt stopped, frustrated at the difficulty in explaining. "When Jane and I were young, and new in love, I could come up to her; in the kitchen, in the front yard, it didn't matter. And I could touch her. Just put my arms around her waist, or kiss her cheek, or just hold her close. She liked it, and she came to me. She knew I wanted her, and she wanted me, too." Matt turned a hard stare at Ron. "And yeah, I'm talking about sex, I suppose. But the sex was just the way we opened up and found our connection." Matt shook his head and looked away. "Can you understand that, Ron?"

"Sure."

"Well, *now*, that connection is just not there like it once was, and I'm *not* a selfish alpha male who's only thinking of my own needs. Well, maybe I am." Matt sighed. "But I miss the way it was, and I want it back. But Jane . . ." Matt stopped again. "She still loves me, I know that. But it only goes so far. She's happy to just tell me loves me and then move right on to something else, like doing some laundry, or something, anything, that doesn't involve being with me. I don't know how to describe it, but *something* has changed, and I don't like it. I'm not ready to just be done being in love with her, like we used to be."

"Matt…"

"Let me finish, Ron. A while back we were having a nice talk, Jane and I, and I asked her if maybe we could go out for a nice dinner, over at the Ashley Hotel. As soon as I said the words, her face changed. It got sorta hard. And she said, 'I can't do it, Matt.' So I asked her what she meant, and why she never wanted to go out and start living again."

Matt closed his eyes and shook his head. The thing he was about to share was hurting him already. "She said, 'Because I know you, Matt. And I know how this works. If I said yes to dinner, you'd take it as a green light for something intimate after dinner, and I just can't handle those expectations.'" Matt paused and brought his eyes up to meet Ron's.

"What did you do?"

I was angry, and hurt. Really hurt. I could see that she was angry, too, and I didn't think I had that coming. I tried not to show my feelings, but like she said, she knows me pretty well, and she could see everything on my face. I asked her if my expectations were really that repugnant. If I was that repugnant."

"And . . .?"

"She said, 'I just can't do it. I can't manufacture those feelings on demand.'" Matt shook his head in despair. "I can't stand the rejection any longer, Ron. It stings a bit more every time. I said something I shouldn't have, but I was so angry and hurt. Then I got all pissed off and stomped away."

"What did you say?"

"I said, 'Oh yeah, I forgot, you're numb; clear to the bone! Sorry I tried to get close. Sorry I still love you!' Something like that, anyway."

"Not good, Matt."

"I know. We sorta made up a little bit that night after we both cooled off a bit, but things aren't right. I hate the way things are now."

"You should see me in my office."

"Ah, we'll get through this. We're good."

"You're *good,* but you hate the way things are?" Ron deadpanned. He stared, challenging Matt to pick up on the absurdity of what he'd just said.

The silence that followed was soon broken by a small knock on the door, and Tammy poked her head into the office. "I'm sorry to interrupt, Doctor, but everyone is waiting for you and we're behind schedule."

"I'll be there in a second," Matt said to Tammy. When she was gone, Matt turned to Ron and said, "So, the happy part of our lives is over? Is that what you're trying to say?"

"No, but I think you should come and talk to me at my office."

Matt looked away and let his body language tell Ron that he had to get back to work, and also that he probably wouldn't be making any appointments.

"OK, Matt." Ron conceded that no more would be said for now, and he stood up to leave. "I'll let you get back to work, but just remember, my door is always open."

CHAPTER THIRTY-SIX

—•—

Jane's car was on John's bumper when his truck rolled to a stop in front of Sally's house. "Good timing!" Jane called out from her car window, as he walked up the sidewalk. "And you behave yourself tonight," she added. Tonight, he'd be in charge of entertaining Timmy while Jane and Sally had a girls' night out together.

"What's Matt doing?" John asked. He was carrying a large brown paper bag with a section of white PVC pipe sticking out.

"I dunno. Tying flies or watching a ball game, I s'pose."

The front door opened and Sally stepped out before John was halfway up the walk. "Good timing!" she said, as she brushed by John. "You behave yourself. What's in the bag?"

"You don't wanna know."

"John..." Sally started.

"You girls have a nice time," John replied, and he hurried up the steps. Timmy was waiting, watching the street in front of his house when John walked up to the front door. When Timmy threw open the door, John said, "Hey, buddy, what's up?"

"What's in the bag?" was all Timmy could manage in the way of a greeting, while he tried to peek inside.

"Ever made a potato gun?" John asked.

"No."

"Well, since your gramma chooses to leave us alone, with no adults around, we're gonna have some fun tonight." They went directly to the kitchen table, where John dumped out the contents of the bag. They sat down and sorted through cans of aerosol hairspray, assorted pieces of PVC pipe, and a twenty-pound bag of potatoes.

"This stuff really stinks, doesn't it?" John asked a few minutes later, as he smeared a layer of PVC adhesive to a piece of the white pipe and then inserted that piece into another.

"How does it work?" Timmy asked, while he held his nose closed with one hand.

"Well, it's very complex. You have to be a genius to design and build one of these. Gimme that other piece of pipe, will ya? No, that one, right there," John said. "Now, Timmy, you use this drill to make a hole right here." John used a magic marker to show Timmy where he wanted the hole drilled, and then he helped Timmy with the drill. "Perfect, now let's glue this detonator switch into the propellant chamber, and we're done." John coated the striker button from a gas grill with PVC adhesive, then he helped Timmy fasten it into the PVC gun.

"There, we're done," John announced a minute later, when the adhesive was set.

"How does it work?" Timmy asked again.

"We'll shove a potato down the bore . . ." John took a potato out of the bag and gave it to Timmy. "Here, you do it."

Timmy took the potato and pushed it down the barrel as far as he could, then he looked at John for approval.

"Good. The potato is just a little bit bigger than the pipe. It's a snug fit. Now use that broom over there to shove it in a bit farther," John said, making certain that Timmy heard the expertise in his voice. "Now, unscrew this end of the gun, then we'll shoot some of this hairspray into the ammo chamber and then quickly screw the end back on the gun. Then you push that red button right there . . ." John turned to Timmy, opened his eyes wide, and said, "The hairspray will ignite, like gunpowder, and BOOM! The potato goes into orbit! But don't press that button till we're outside."

Timmy was stone serious as he carried the potato gun out to the backyard. He held it as if it were a nuclear weapon that might detonate if he dropped it.

They were surrounded by a plank fence, several oak trees, a small, single-stall garage, and the back wall of the house. Timmy turned a pair of questioning eyes to John.

"I'll hold the barrel," John said, when he read the uncertainty in Timmy's eyes. "But you wanna fire it, don't you?"

Timmy nodded eagerly.

"OK." John gripped the barrel. "Ten. Nine. Eight. Seven . . ." When he reached "Zero, FIRE!" Timmy pushed the red button. The potato gun went *foomp* and tried to jump from their grip. It also launched a potato into the pale blue sky of an spring evening.

Immediately after the potato returned to Earth and splattered into a dozen pieces, Timmy once again turned his eyes to John.

"Not bad!" John said. "But we need to add a bit more rocket fuel, don't you think?"

Timmy's entire face was a smile.

"All right, go get that bag of potatoes on the kitchen table and we'll just see what we can do with this thing," John said.

Forty minutes later, the backyard, and the oak trees surrounding it, and the side wall of the old garage, were covered with smashed potatoes.

"Only one potato left," John said. "Wanna see just how far we can shoot it?"

"Yes!" Timmy said.

"OK, we'll use the last of the hairspray, too." John held the button on top of the hairspray can and they both listened to the can make the usual *sssssssss* noise for several seconds longer than he'd done for any of the other potatoes.

"Maybe I'd better hold the gun for this one," John said, after he'd screwed the fuel chamber back in place. He had some second thoughts about the large amount of propellant he'd used and he was uncertain if the PVC he'd used would hold together when the fuel was detonated. "You go over there by the back steps," he told Timmy. "Just in case."

Timmy was thirty feet away and standing by the steps when John braced himself. He turned to Timmy. "Ready?" The yard was nearly dark now.

Timmy nodded.

"OK, start the countdown!" John said.

"Ten. Nine. Eight…" Timmy counted, and when it was time for liftoff, John pushed the button. *Fa-woomp!* barked the white cannon in John's arms, and a flash of fire about four feet long sent a sizzling potato into the stratosphere.

"Whoa!" John laughed. Then he decided to cover his head while he waited for the ballistic vegetable to return to Earth.

"Did you hear it land?" John finally asked Timmy, after nearly a minute's wait.

"Uh-uh."

"Did you hear any glass breaking, or tires squealing?" John asked.

"Uh-uh."

"We're probably OK, then." John shrugged. "I think it's time for supper. What would you like?"

"Pizza!"

"OK, sounds good," John said, ignoring Sally's instructions for a balanced meal. "Let's go get one, and we should get going before somebody shows up looking for us . . . with a baked potato on top of their head!"

John put the potato gun down by the kitchen steps and said, "You wanna drive my truck?"

Timmy grinned, but he said, "I'm too small."

"Well then, you sit on my lap. I'll run the pedals on the floor and you steer. Howzat sound?"

In John Velde's world, little boys were supposed to holler and run, and when they saw a mud puddle, they were supposed to stomp all the water out, because that's what boys do. Timmy had always been cautioned not to get his feet wet or his pants dirty or make too much noise. The thrill in his eyes was unmistakable whenever John made it clear that all that stuff was OK.

When they returned with pizza, they brought the truck to a stop in front of Sally's house. "You'll be able to reach the pedals in a couple years," John said. "Then you won't have to sit on my lap. I'll carry the pizza in."

"Can we watch a movie, and eat in the living room?" Timmy asked.

"Does a bear shit in the woods?" John quickly covered his mouth and said "Oops" while Timmy giggled. "What movie would you like to see?"

"*Star Wars*," Timmy said without hesitation.

"They blow a lotta stuff up in that one, right?" John asked.

"Yeah."

"Sounds good."

When they were finishing their pizza, and Han Solo was blasting imperial fighters from the sky, John slowly, deliberately, leaned over toward Timmy and scrunched his face into a wrinkled mass and waited for Timmy to look at him. When Timmy looked, John let loose a surprisingly loud fart, which actually startled Timmy.

"What was that?" John asked, pretending to be shocked at the noise that had just come from the couch beneath him. He whipped his head around to search for the source of the noise.

Timmy squealed with laughter and said, "You farted!"

"No way!" John said, overacting badly. "It was a barking squirrel, out in the yard!" He whipped his head around again, pretending to scan the yard outside.

"Huh-uh!" Timmy argued.

John ignored the accusation and turned his attention back to the movie in front of them.

"You farted," Timmy said again, a moment later.

"No way," John insisted. "I told you, it was a barking squirrel. They're sneaky little sonsabitches," he added, without looking at Timmy again.

Timmy returned to his paper plate with pizza on it and giggled while the words "sneaky little sonsabitches" played in his head.

They finished the movie, then a half-hour TV show about Bigfoot, then another one about ancient aliens. John was about ready to tell Timmy to go brush his teeth and get ready for bed when, without warning, an impressive ripping noise rose from Timmy's end of the couch.

John knew what had happened, and he chose to play along and resume the fart humor from before. He whipped his head to look outside again, and exclaimed, "Another barking squirrel! Did you hear it, Timmy?" When he did finally turn to see what the eight-year-old on the other end of the couch was doing, he saw a little boy wearing a smile that covered every inch of his face. Not only was Timmy proud of what he'd done, but he was just as proud of the comical response he'd drawn from a grown man. He was staring at John, waiting for any further reaction. John could see several oversized permanent teeth mixed in with several baby teeth, and there was white showing all the way around the blue of Timmy's eyes. John let himself laugh out loud too.

"Nice one, kid," John said, and he held his fist out toward Timmy. "Gimme some knuckles on that one!"

They were just two little boys now, laughing at farts. "OK," John said, "it's getting late, and it's time for you to get ready for bed. I'll clean up the dishes while you brush your teeth."

As Timmy headed upstairs to get ready for bed, John called, "You don't have to tell your gramma *everything* we did tonight, you know."

When the dishes were done, John turned on the TV and found an old cowboy movie, and he forgot all about putting Timmy to bed until the boy reappeared. "Are you going to listen to my prayers?" came a little voice. John turned his head and found Timmy standing beside the couch, wearing his Spider Man pajamas. John guessed that he'd been waiting upstairs for a while, and then come looking for him.

"Uh, sure," John said. He hadn't expected that one of his duties would be to listen to prayers. He followed Timmy up the flight of stairs to his bedroom and wondered how this listening-to-prayers thing would go.

The small bedroom was dark, and Timmy climbed into bed and snuggled in under the covers. A cardboard box, overflowing with toys, sat in one corner of the room. Timmy's Orange shirt and cap, from summer baseball, hung from a hook on the wall, like a shrine.

"OK, show me how you do this," John said when knelt beside the bed. Timmy closed his eyes, folded his hands, and thanked Jesus for all of his favorite things, listing most of them individually. Then he asked Jesus to watch out for his mother, so she could come home and live with him again someday. In the next breath he asked Jesus to make Jane's cancer go away and help her get well, too. He asked Jesus to especially make sure that his gramma would be OK. John thought he was almost done with his prayers when he asked Jesus to say hi to John's sister, up in Heaven.

"And God bless John Velde," Timmy added, just before he finished with, "In Jesus' name, I pray, Amen."

When Timmy was finished, he reached his arms out for a hug.

John hadn't hugged a little kid for, well, he'd *never* hugged a kid. Ever. But there was Timmy, waiting for one, so John leaned over and let Timmy put his arms around his neck. It all felt strange to John. This was a place he'd never been before.

And then Timmy kissed him! Just a goodnight kiss, the kind any kid would give a parent.

John tousled Timmy's hair and said "Goodnight, buddy" as he backed away. But his head was swimming. The innocence and the tenderness of a goodnight kiss from a little boy were things that lay outside the scope of his life experience. Far outside.

He was bewildered by what he felt as he walked back downstairs. He plopped onto the couch, turned the TV off, stared into space for a minute, and tried to digest what he'd just been a part of. Timmy had just asked Jesus to bless him.

The bartender smiled and waved when Jane and Sally stepped into Buster's and paused to look around. "Good, there's not such a big crowd tonight. The music won't be blaring, either, so we can hear ourselves talking," Sally said. She led Jane past the bar and most of the tables, until she found a table near a window that looked out over the lake. "How's this?"

"Perfect," Jane said, as she seated herself.

A waitress appeared at their table and placed menus in front of them as they were still settling in. When she asked if they wanted anything from the bar, Sally answered immediately, "I'll have a beer; one of those dark beers you have on tap."

"Me too," Jane said. "I haven't had a beer in a long time. There should be something we can celebrate."

"Duh!" Sally blurted. "Here you are, healthy and looking good! What better thing could we celebrate?"

When the waitress brought their beers, they each raised a glass, and Sally toasted, "To your health!"

"I'll drink to that!" Jane said, as she tapped her glass against Sally's. She took a sip and set the glass down on the table. "So, what do you think John and Timmy have planned for this evening?"

"I dunno, I guess I didn't ask. Maybe it's better if I don't know?" Sally smiled. "Timmy really likes John, and it kind of surprised me at first, but I can see that John enjoys hanging out with Timmy, too."

"Well, John behaves like an eight-year-old most of the time, so they should get along pretty well," Jane offered. "I never pictured you and John together . . . dating."

"He makes me laugh."

"John said he thought you were involved with someone else?"

"I was."

Jane said nothing but gestured for more information with a tilt of her head and a rise in her brow.

"He was a nice guy," Sally started, "and I really liked him, but there was nothing there, no connection. Know what I mean?"

Jane nodded her understanding. "So, he's outta the picture?"

"Yes. But he was still *in* the picture when I started to notice John, and I didn't tell either of them." Sally sipped her beer, smiled, and then closed her eyes as if she wanted to forget something. "But that didn't work out so good. I got busted. Right over there."

"Huh? What happened?"

Sally shook her head slowly, then she told Jane all about the night when her old lover surprised her and interrupted her date with John.

"Wow, that must have been a little embarrassing?" Jane asked.

"Yeah, it sure was, but it turned out OK. But I should have just told the other guy that . . ." Sally stopped herself and thought for a moment. "It had been a while since I'd seen him, and I thought he understood. I knew it was all over with the other guy. And I'd been aware of this 'thing' happening between John and me all along."

"How did John react that night?"

"He was good; a gentleman."

"Really?" Jane grinned.

"Yup, it was sorta strange for a minute there; I was embarrassed and he was jealous." Sally raised her eyebrows and then confessed, "But I *liked* it that he was jealous. You know, it isn't just that he makes me laugh, he's a good person."

"He sure can be, but I have to ask you something." Jane took another sip of beer, then she interrupted herself. "Ooh, that's pretty good." She put her beer on the table, leaned forward, and went back to her question. "Don't you just wanna stab him sometimes, right in the throat?"

Sally laughed. "I sure did the first few times I met him. I thought he was a complete jerk. But after I told him to shut the fuck up he did a complete one-eighty."

"I heard about that," Jane said.

"Ooh, I was really angry, and it didn't seem to faze him. I mean, he didn't get upset or anything. In fact, he sorta grinned at me." With that, Sally's face opened into a smile, and she pointed at Jane. "But your husband almost peed in his pants! He looked like a little dog that I'd just whacked with a rolled-up newspaper."

"Yup, that would be Matt," Jane said. "So how did you ever make friends with John after that?"

"Oh, he can be a charmer." Sally sipped her beer. "You know what I mean?"

"Yeah, but usually I just want to stab him."

The waitress returned and said, "Are you ready to order yet?"

"Ahhh, sure . . ." Jane said slowly, and took a small sip of beer in order to stall for a few more seconds to reexamine the menu.

"Do you have *duck?*" Sally asked flatly, while she scanned her menu one last time. "And does your ladies' room have a safety harness and a roll bar, like those dune buggies?"

Jane coughed, then choked, then some beer dribbled out her nose. Both women covered their faces and dissolved in a puddle of laughter.

"I'll come back in a few minutes," the waitress said, when she realized that neither Jane nor Sally had the composure to order anything. The waitress was chuckling too, even though she had no idea what was so funny, when she backed away from the table.

Sally, with eyes that were compressed into narrow slits, nodded yes, it would be all right for the waitress to go away and then come back. Jane couldn't manage even that much of a response. "Oh God," Sally sighed a moment later when she was able to speak, "I'll never forget that awful day." Her face twisted with the memory. "You know, there was a moment, just after I stood up and made a break for the bathroom, when I thought that maybe there was a little fart down there, and I thought that if I could just let one—not a big one, just a little freeper—well, maybe that would let some of the pressure off and I could make it to the bathroom." Jane was still laughing and covering her face, and she leaned forward to listen closer. "But I knew that if I trusted a fart at that point, well, it might not work out. What a terrible feeling!"

The strained look on Sally's face as she told the story, and then the word "freeper," sent Jane over the top again. Several minutes went by before either of them could breathe properly and begin to wipe away the tears of laughter.

"Good one," Jane said finally. When the waitress returned, they both ordered cheeseburgers, fries, and more beer. "Is that the most embarrassed you've ever been, more than your date with John?" Jane asked.

"Pretty hard to top the blowout in the mall. How 'bout you? What was your worst moment?"

"My first date with a boy, I think," Jane offered.

"Does the story involve a duck?" Sally teased.

"No, nothing that spectacular." Jane took another sip of beer. "I was sixteen and pretty awkward. I had braces on my teeth and this nice, older boy took me out for pizza. We were talking, I don't remember what about. I'm sure it was just the nonsense that kids babble about. Anyway, while I was talking to this boy, one of those little rubber bands snapped off my braces and flew out of my mouth and landed on the piece of pizza he was just about to take a bite from. I was *so* embarrassed! Top that."

"Hmm," Sally said. "I don't think I can pinpoint my first real date; I sorta eased into dating, you know, hanging around with older boys. I wish those early dates would have been about pizza, and rubber bands on my braces."

"Whaddya mean?" Jane asked.

"Well, I told you how I got my scar?"

"Yeah."

"Both of my parents blamed the other for the accident. They divorced when I was about twelve, and my father drank himself to death a few years later."

"Oh, I'm so sorry."

"Yeah, those were some tough years. I suppose a psychologist would tell you that I had abandonment issues because my father had dismissed himself from my life. Anyway, the scar, and my *issues*, sorta led me to some bad decisions. I think I was looking for the love of a man because my relationship with my father was so screwed up. Anyway, I got pregnant when I was sixteen."

Jane leaned back and let the surprise on her face show.

"Sorry. I didn't mean to be such a buzz kill. That's just my story. But it's worked out pretty well," Sally said.

"Sixteen?" Jane asked.

"Yup. Tough start in life, huh?"

"What'd you do? You must have been so scared."

"Got married." Sally shrugged. "Another bad move. That lasted about two years. Then I got a job and took classes at night until I got my college degree. I taught school for a while, and then decided to start my own business."

"I'm impressed!" Jane said.

"Well, I made some bad choices early on, and then I just did what I needed to do in order to fix things." Then, as if she was brushing away some bad memories, Sally said, "I'm guessing that you and I took different paths to get to this place in life. How did you meet Matt?"

"A blind date. Actually, a double date, and I was the other guy's date. My date knew Matt from school and volunteered him as a date for my roommate. 'Zat make any sense?"

"Sure. But that didn't work out so good, did it?"

"Oh, on the contrary, it worked out fine," Jane said. "Matt and I clicked right away. Matt just stole the show that night. Looking back, I should have been embarrassed. Matt sat there and talked to me all night, while he ignored my roommate." Jane took the coaster from under her glass of beer and flipped it from one side to the other while she remembered something and thought about how much of it she wanted to share. "I was pretty rough on guys back then," she continued. "Actually I was just plain mean to a few of them. I knew what they had in mind." Jane paused and looked at her beer glass.

"Yeah? That was bad?" Sally asked.

"I wasn't interested."

"You were a straight arrow?" Sally laughed.

"Mmm, I didn't trust men."

"Why?"

"I dunno." Jane stared ahead for a moment. It was clear that there was much more to that story, but she shrugged it away. "Anyway, that night, when Matt started talking, I gave him a hard time at first, but then I saw something so genuine in his eyes. I liked him. I wanted more of him." Jane smiled to herself, then raised the smile to Sally. "I just dropped the other guy, Matt's friend. I never liked him very much anyway." Jane made a show of fanning some heat away. "Matt and I were all-in pretty much right away."

"Every now and then you hear about a blind date working out like that, but not very often," Sally said.

"That's for sure. I only went on one other," Jane said. "That guy turned out to be *such* a geek. A physics major, Hushpuppies, pants pulled up over his womb . . ."

Sally coughed again and choked on a swallow of beer.

"Well," Jane said, "what do *you* call it when a guy pulls his pants up real high, and—"

"Smashes his package?" Sally blurted. "It's called Moose Knuckle. The male version of Camel Toe."

Jane was bewildered. "Moose Knuckle? Camel Toe?" she repeated. She'd never heard the terms.

"Think about it," Sally deadpanned.

When the words and visual images clicked into place, Jane's eyes opened wide, and then she ducked her head like a turtle while she covered her mouth. "Ooh, I get it!" She giggled. "Moose Knuckle, huh? I don't remember that, but he actually had a slide rule on his belt, and dandruff, and a couple zits that were oozing and bleeding. About twenty minutes into our date I made up some story about having to pick my parents up at the airport just so the guy would take me home early."

"Nice!" Sally laughed as the waitress approached their table. She looked at the food on the waitress's tray and grimaced. "Now I'm gonna try to forget the image you just painted for me of oozing zits and dandruff. It sorta took my appetite away." Then she leaned back in her chair and let the waitress put a plate covered with French fries and a huge cheeseburger in front of her, and Jane. They talked on, about books, and movies, and Pine Rapids, and life, until long after the waitress had cleared away their table scraps, and the crowd in Buster's began to thin out.

When Sally finally felt the moment was right, she asked, "So, how're you doing? Really. How do you feel after all you've been through?"

"Good, I guess," Jane said slowly. "But I don't think you ever see life the same again, after you've done something like I did."

"Whaddya mean?"

"Well, you always think stuff like this is for someone else, but when somebody tells you that it's *you* that has cancer, and they need to do what they did to me . . . you know . . ."

"Yeah, I think I can understand that part," Sally said.

"First, you start to think about your own death, and how much you don't want that to happen, because you're afraid of the pain and suffering that might come along with it, and also because there are so many things you haven't done yet." Jane's arms were folded, resting on the table, and her gaze reflected something in her soul. "And if you're a human being you wonder about the life you *have* lived, and your own redemption. You know, God and Heaven and eternity." She glanced up at Sally to see if she was making sense.

Sally nodded her understanding.

"And then, when you're at the point I'm at now, you wonder how much of your *life* was actually cut away, and what your life will be like without the parts you've lost, and just how much humanity was lost along with those parts. I remember when my father was getting old, bits and pieces of his life were going away. He told me that it was OK because he took the time to mourn all the gradual losses. Dr. Hested has talked to me about that, too. I thought that was pretty good, and I've tried to do it."

"You've got a long life ahead of you. Don't worry too much about the losses just yet." Then, worried that her unsolicited advice was inappropriate, Sally added, "I'm sorry, Jane, it's not my place to give advice."

Jane smiled. "It's OK. That's what friends are for."

"No, I think your real friends are the ones who listen, just listen. The value in your friendship comes when they let you talk and then hear *yourself* say the things that were in your heart. That's when you find some clarity. Your friends just allow it to happen."

"Good one. I think that's really true." Jane thought for a moment, then said, "But you did share something with Matt that was right on the money, and it makes me laugh, still."

"I did?" Sally asked

"Yeah, when I was getting ready to have my implants placed, I couldn't help thinking about your friend's little boy, the one who used her falsie as a kicking tee for his football." Jane chuckled. "That helped in the decision making, and now I feel good."

"No pain or discomfort anymore?" Sally asked.

"Nah, just little reminders, like when I try to lift something heavy. I've lost some strength. And they're numb. My boobs are numb."

Sally said nothing, but she turned her palms up and raised her eyebrows, making it clear that Jane could say more, if she wanted.

"It's OK," Jane said. "It's just a strange sensation."

"Well, is that the worst of it, after all you went through?"

"No. You change when this sort of thing happens. You can't help but change. Maybe it's just a reminder about your mortality." Jane paused for a moment. "I'm having some killer hot flashes, too." She considered how much more she should share with Sally, and then went on. "And I just can't ever get in the mood."

"Welcome to menopause, right?" Sally shrugged.

"It's more than that. I'm taking a hormone blocker, too. It's a good drug, so they say: one that reduces the risk of the cancer coming back. But it sorta puts menopause into hyperdrive. You can't believe the hot flashes. Sometimes, maybe five minutes after a shower, I'll have one. When they start to come on I get nauseous, and then, instantly it's like I just ran a marathon and I'm covered with sweat. God, my glasses even fog up when I get them at work, and I get several of 'em in the middle of the night, every night, too. There's no rhyme or reason to it. I call them my personal summers."

Again, Sally nodded her understanding.

Jane swallowed, then lowered her eyes, and added, "There's something else, too." She took a few seconds to choose her words. "When you take this hormone blocker you have no estrogen, no female hormone." Jane's face grew weak and she uttered, "I'm turning into an old woman. I thought I'd get old slowly, but it didn't happen that way. First it was the surprise of cancer, and then I was old." Jane wiped a tear away from her left eye. "I don't want it to be like this."

"What? That's not true! You're beautiful! You're the prettiest sixty-year-old woman I've ever seen!" Sally said.

"I barely feel like a woman anymore. My body is changing all of a sudden. I have some flab where I never used to have it, and my skin is changing, it's not soft anymore, and I have wrinkles in my face that make me look old, and . . ." Jane paused again, "I'm a dried-up old woman."

"Sex?" Sally asked.

Jane sighed and shook her head. "It's not like it used to be. It seems like a door has closed behind me, and it makes me feel bad. Really bad."

"You know there are things you can do," Sally began, then she realized that there was no need to explain the issues of postmenopausal sex to the local hospital's director of nursing. "But you already know all about that." She changed direction. "How has Matt been through all of this?"

"He's a rock. His strength has been unwavering, as always," Jane said without hesitation. "He's my best friend, and I never would have made it through without him. But now there's a layer of stress, or distance, between us that was never there before. He thinks things should be like they were before, and they just aren't like that anymore."

Their waitress passed behind Jane and Sally signaled to her. When the waitress looked over, Sally called out, "We'll have another round."

"Oh jeez, Sally, I could feel that first beer, and the second one made me . . . chatty." Jane grinned at the adjective she'd settled on.

"So, let's move right on from chatty to brilliant! This is our night out together," Sally said. When the waitress brought them a third beer, Sally raised her glass and tapped it against Jane's. "Here's to . . . oh shit, here's to another beer."

"So how did you wind up *here*, a city girl like you?" Sally asked before Jane could swallow.

"My dad was an outdoorsman, like Matt, and I always liked this country. It's beautiful, and I like all four seasons here. How 'bout you?"

"I grew up in a little town, much like Pine Rapids, over in Wisconsin. You know, with bars like this where everyone eats fried cheese balls and drinks beer from longneck bottles. I like small-town life," Sally said.

"There was one time when I wasn't so sure about this place," Jane said. "A couple years after we moved here—our boys were little, toddlers—and a bear came walking right up to our house, and Matt had to shoot it."

"John told me about that. Were you afraid?" Sally asked.

"God, yes!" Jane laughed, and Sally could see that the beer had lowered a few inhibitions. "But Matt just walked up, about ten feet from the bear, brought the rifle to his shoulder, and pulled the trigger. Do you have any idea how loud a high-powered rifle sounds when it's discharged *inside* your house? It sounded like a cannon went off." Jane took another sip of beer and added, "That bear was standing on its hind legs, leaning against the screen door in our kitchen, about to let itself in, when Matt told us all to plug our ears. The boys and I were huddled together behind him with our fingers in our ears when Matt pulled trigger. He shot the bear right in the chest. God, what a mess. The bear screamed and bled and spun around and shit all over before it wrecked the back porch and then died. What a scene." Jane looked at Sally and shook her head as she remembered the moment.

"I don't know if every man would have been able to do that," Sally said. "No more problems or visitors since then?"

"Nope," Jane said, then her face brightened with a different memory. "Well, that's not true. We had a bat get in the house last summer. Matt spent about twenty minutes trying to kill it, but all he did was break a couple lamps."

"Lemme guess," Sally interrupted. "He was swinging a hockey stick at the bat, right?

"Close; a tennis racket." Jane giggled.

"And he was wearing a fur hat too, right? In case a bat might want to bite his head, or lay eggs in his scalp, or some crazy thing like that?" Sally said.

"I was wearing the hat," Jane said with a laugh.

"OK, but Matt swung and he missed and broke some things, right?" Sally asked.

"Smashed the shit out of a lamp and some woodwork."

"How did you ever get the bat out of your house?"

"I just opened the door and it flew away," Jane said.

Sally's face softened. "Well there you have it!" she said. "Sometimes you have to *deal* with your problems, like bears in your kitchen. And other times, if you just open up, they'll just fly away."

Jane raised her glass and clinked it against Sally's.

"I guess you made it," Jane said.

"Whaddya mean?" Sally asked.

"*Brilliant*. You made it to *brilliant*! The beer worked. That was very insightful, what you just said about dealing with some problems and just letting others fly away. I'm not brilliant yet, I'm just dizzy. And I can't drive home like this. What are we gonna do?"

"I can't drive either. That last one sorta snuck up on me, too," Sally said. She reached into her purse, searching for her cell phone. "I don't think snuck is a word, yet. What's Matt's cell number?" she mumbled while preparing to use her phone. When Jane gave her Matt's number, she sent a text message:

< *We're at Buster's and we may have been overserved. Can you come and get us? Your wife is a stitch.*

—*Sally*>

Matt replied instantly:

<*Be there shortly. Having fun?*>

Sally replied,

<*Oh yeah*>

"OK, Matt's on his way to come and get us," Sally said.

"My nose is numb," Jane replied. "I haven't done anything like this in a *long* time."

"Matt's gonna think I'm a bad influence on you."

"Matt likes you," Jane mumbled.

"Do you have any idea how fortunate you are?" Sally asked. The sentence had rolled off her tongue almost as one word. "After what, forty years, Matt still has a crush on you. He thinks it's great that you're out goofing around and having fun with *me*. Every other man I know would be pissed off if he had to get up off the couch and come and get us." The third beer was slurring her speech a bit, too.

"Yeah, I see it too. And I love it," Jane said. She had a fine buzz going, and her side was sore from all the laughter. This time away from Matt, with a friend who made her feel good about herself, was just the right medicine, and so much fun.

"Hmm, I just got a text message from John," Sally said, and then she stared at her phone for a minute. "He says they made a potato gun and had a pizza. Then they watched a movie. Sounds like they're having fun. What's a potato gun?"

Jane shook her head and smiled. "It's a homemade cannon that uses hairspray as the propellant and actually shoots potatoes like bullets."

"Really? Why would they do that?" Sally said with puzzled look.

"It's a guy thing. Don't even try to understand."

"Sounds dangerous."

"Not really, but every time Matt and our boys made one, they played around with it until something got broken, mostly windows. Although Matt shot his new truck once and dented the door so badly that the window wouldn't open. That stuff used to drive me crazy. Sometimes I'd have the boys all ready for bed, and then Matt would start wrestling with them. Even at the time, Matt would say, 'Don't worry, I'm just gonna do this until *one* of the boys is crying.' Then he'd grin, and they'd chase around and play rough until somebody *was* crying. Then he'd turn them over to me again so I could spend a half hour helping them 'decompress,' as Matt used to say. Jeez, that used to bug me."

"But you're smiling?" Sally said.

"Those were good times, Sally. Matt would build forts with the boys— you know, put a couple blankets over a card table—and then they'd run around and shoot bad guys with plastic guns. Sometimes he'd spread a blanket out on the living room floor and they'd pretend it was a river raft, and there were crocodiles and hippos and sharks circling in the water around them. But pretending to be professional wrestlers was their favorite. They'd each assume the identity of some moronic wrestler and then throw each other around and jump on each other. It was so great to watch them play. We had a lot of fun."

Sally watched and waited for a moment while Jane stared into the past.

"I never thought those times would end," Jane said, still focused on a distant vision.

"Oh God," Sally broke the spell with a groan, obviously upset about something, and when Jane looked up she saw that Sally was looking at something behind her, over by the bar.

"What?" Jane asked.

"Two guys just came in the door and sat at the bar. They're looking at us now, and you can bet the farm they're gonna wander on over here and try to charm us into going home with them."

Jane looked over at the bar and said, "They're quite a bit younger than we are."

"Jesus, don't look!" Sally snapped.

"Oops." Jane giggled and covered her eyes.

"Yeah, well, it's getting late. We're the only two women in this bar, and I'm pretty sure they're even drunker than we are," Sally said.

"Nobody's tried to pick me up since Jimmy Carter was president," Jane said.

"Oh shit, they're getting up and coming this way," Sally said. "Don't say shit. Not a word. Just do what I do."

The two men found their way to Sally and Jane's table, and they pulled up a couple of chairs and sat down. "Hi girls," one of them said, while both of them studied the women at close range. The guy who'd spoken was about forty-five, and fairly hammered. The other guy was a bit younger, and a bit more drunk.

Before either of the men could say another word, Sally sprang into action. Her face was devoid of emotion, and she began to speak in sign language with her hands. Jane was fairly certain that Sally did not know how to sign, but she was doing a pretty convincing job of it.

The two men both stared at her, and every bit of confidence drained from their faces. Sally continued to look at the man who'd spoken to them for a few seconds while her fingers and hands fluttered. Then she turned to Jane and did the same thing. She was signing a message to Jane. Suddenly she stopped signing, and with her eyes she clearly asked Jane the question, "What do you think about that?"

Sally had thrown the ball to Jane, daring her to keep a straight face and run with it. Jane stared back at Sally for a moment, and then Sally jolted her into action with a soft kick to the shin. Jane made clumsy hand signals and struggled mightily to keep a straight face. She tried to imitate Sally, and others that she'd seen do this on TV and in the movies. When she was finished, she looked directly at the man who'd greeted them, and used her eyes to ask him if he understood.

The man stared at her, then looked at Sally, then at his friend. The look of bewilderment on his face was priceless. He looked like he'd just been asked to solve the math problem about two trains going in perpendicular directions at different speeds. Now he had no idea how to reply. He looked exhausted. His face was blank when he threw in the towel, like his team had just lost a heartbreaker on Monday Night Football. He stood up and walked away without so much as a "See you later" to Sally and Jane, and his buddy followed him.

The men hadn't reached their seats at the bar when Matt walked in the front door and waved to the Sally and Jane. Both women were giggling like eighth-grade girls a minute later when they tumbled into Matt's truck and buckled their seat belts. "What do you think you said to those guys?" Jane said.

"I was trying to use one finger at a time to spell out 'Fuck off!' You should have recognized *that*," Sally cackled. "That guy didn't know whether to shit or go blind! It works every time."

"You're brilliant. *Brilliant!*" Jane said, and the girls giggled as Matt pulled his truck onto the highway.

———

Jane was on a mission to get herself into bed when Matt opened the kitchen door and let her step past him and into the house. She'd dozed off in his truck, only a moment after they'd dropped Sally at her house. When they rolled to a stop at their home on Scotch Lake, she'd walked directly to the master bath, washed her face, brushed her teeth, and flopped into bed before Matt could turn out the lights in the rest of the house. She was lying on her back and snoring by the time Matt stood over her, watching her sleep and brushing his own teeth.

She was exhausted. She'd been tipsy for the first few minutes of the ride home, and then she'd run out of gas. Completely out. She looked weak, not peaceful, as Matt studied her. And he couldn't help but remember her sunken cheeks and gaunt face on the day she'd come back to him from her surgery.

When he finished in the bathroom and turned out the lights, he crawled under the sheets and lay beside her in the dark. It was their custom to hold hands before sleep came, so even though Jane was long gone, he reached over and took her hand in his.

In the dreamy, slow time before sleep carried him away, too, he stared at the cedar planks on the ceiling and let the random thoughts that always came before sleep drift by. He saw himself at the office, dealing with some vague crisis, then he was fishing over on French Creek, and then he was standing on Mo Glasnapp's front steps, kissing her goodnight and thinking how soft her lips were.

CHAPTER THIRTY-SEVEN

"Got a big day planned?" Matt asked Jane, as he poured coffee into her cup. Jane was seated in an overstuffed chair in the great room, with her feet propped up on an ottoman and wearing slippers and a bathrobe while she scanned a morning paper.

"No, not really. How 'bout you?" Jane replied.

"Long day, not a big day," Matt said, as he shuffled over and settled onto the couch with his coffee cup. He was wearing an old robe but no slippers, and before he took the first sip of his coffee he yawned and put his bare feet up on the coffee table in front of the couch.

They started most days like this, with coffee and small talk. They'd been doing it ever since the boys both went off to college, and as they got older they seemed to get up earlier in order to have more time to talk.

"Haven't seen much of Sally lately, since the night you were over-served," Matt said, as he scanned the sports page in the newspaper.

"She's pretty busy with John." Jane stared at the steam coming off her coffee cup for a moment, then added, "She told me he stayed overnight there a couple Fridays ago, so he could help her entertain a houseful of boys. Timmy had some buddies for a sleepover." She picked up a different section of the paper and without looking up, added, "S'pose he brought beer and cigarettes for the boys?"

"Lighten up there, honey. John's OK, and he's having fun. I think he's happy, and he likes Timmy."

"I suppose," Jane sighed. She closed the newspaper. "I know Sally sure likes him. She broke up with some other guy a while back."

"What other guy?" Matt asked.

"Oh, some guy she knew before John."

"Was she serious with the guy?" Matt asked, a bit more interested. "I never heard about another guy. Well, yeah, I guess I did, last summer. John actually admitted that he was jealous of some other guy."

"Yeah, that's the guy, and I think she was sort of serious, for a while, anyway, before she met John. Why?"

"I dunno, I just . . ." Matt paused. "You mean, two men?"

"Sure, it happens all the time." Jane looked over at him. "I was dating someone else when I met you. Andy was a nice guy, too." The words were given to him as if she was surprised he would ask such an obvious question.

"Yeah, I suppose," Matt said.

Jane picked up a supermarket flier and started flipping it. She was done thinking about Sally and John for now. "Do we have any hamburger left in the freezer?"

Matt was staring at his coffee again when he mumbled, "Uh, yeah, there's about five pounds left on the bottom shelf." But he wasn't thinking about frozen hamburger, or John, or Sally anymore. He was picturing Jane and the guy she'd been dating before him, on a date, laughing and talking.

Something was wrong. The image he'd stored in his mind all these years, of young Jane smiling and laughing and beckoning him, wasn't quite the same. Now she was laughing with someone else. A tiny fracture had appeared in the hard fabric of Matt's being, and like a pin-hole leak in a giant dam, the pressure behind it was immense. He looked at Jane and felt something funny in his chest, as if he'd had too much coffee and his heart was skipping.

"What?" Jane said when she met his glance. She could see a question in his eyes.

"Ah, nothing. I'm gonna go shower and get ready for work." Matt rose from the couch and walked toward their bedroom.

"OK, I'll shower when you're done," Jane called to him, and she turned back to the newspaper again.

Once he was in the shower, with hot water pouring over his head and back, Matt saw the same image of Jane on their first date. It was fixed in his mind and always would be, even though that first date, for both of them, was with someone else. Matt remembered that he said goodbye to the others—Jane and her roommate Linda, and his classmate Andy Hedstrom, out on Washington Avenue and went home by himself. And he remembered that he'd called Andy later that night and told him that he'd be glad to go out with Jane, but not her roommate.

He hadn't seen Andy for twenty years. He only thought of that date from time to time, if someone asked how he'd met Jane, and the memory of it always made him laugh. But not today.

In his truck, on the drive to the office, Matt turned on an oldies station and the first song he heard was "Running on Empty" by Jackson Browne. It had been sort of an anthem for the guys in his class when they were dental students because of the grueling academic pressure in both the classroom and the clinic. He loved the tune, and he always turned the volume up when it came on. But today it made his chest feel funny again when he thought of school, and Jane, and those good times. He wondered if Jane thought of someone else, not him, when she heard it.

The morning schedule was filled with regular patients who were coming in for routine fillings and bridges and root canals, and several emergencies were jammed in too. This would be a long and busy day.

Matt held his first patient's cheek in his left hand and introduced a needle just above the young man's lower left wisdom tooth with his right hand. "Feels kinda weird, doesn't it?" Matt said in a low, calm voice, almost whispering in the boy's ear.

"Uh-huh," the boy attempted to say.

"Yeah, don't talk for a minute, while I'm doing this." Matt made a point to let the boy hear a hint of laughter in his voice. When the tip of the needle was near the ramus of the boy's mandible, Matt pulled back gently on the plunger, and when no blood streamed back into the glass carpule of anesthetic he was certain that he hadn't placed the needle in a blood vessel. "You're gonna feel a little pressure now," Matt said, and he began to press on the syringe plunger with his thumb.

The boy raised his eyebrows and looked at Matt.

"Pressure?" Matt asked softly.

The boy gave a tiny nod.

"Pretty normal," Matt said. A minute later he eased the syringe out of the boy's mouth and asked, "How'd I do?"

"Good." The boy smiled and rubbed his left hand on his chin. "Didn't feel a thing, but it's getting numb already."

"The left side of your tongue, too?" Matt asked.

"Yup."

"Good, that means I got pretty close to the nerve, like I was trying to do. That's the one that provides feeling for your lip and tongue and teeth on the left side. You'll be really numb in about ten minutes and we'll get that wisdom tooth outta there."

"You sure I'll be numb enough?" The boy's smile was getting more crooked by the second.

"Yup. But all you need to do is tell me if something hurts, and I'll fix it." After a short wait, Matt said, "OK, open up." When his assistant turned on the suction pump, Matt brought a dental handpiece into the mouth and used the small drill to cut the boy's wisdom tooth in half. Then he brought an elevator—a short, straight instrument that looked like a screwdriver—to the mouth and used it to first pry one half of the tooth out, and then the other. But as he was twisting the elevator to lift the second half of the tooth out he heard a small snapping sound. "Did you hear that?" Matt said to the boy.

"Uh-huh."

"The distal root tip just broke off." Matt turned his attention to his assistant and said, "Gimme that little doo-hinky that we always use when this happens, will you, Tammy?"

When he had the pointed instrument he wanted, Matt adjusted the light on his headlamp and leaned close. He stared intently for a second and then brought the root-tip elevator slowly to the bleeding socket in the back of the boy's mouth. He found a solid purchase point and then added some pressure as he turned his hand. "There," he said, as he lifted the tiny root fragment out. "You wanna see it?" he asked the boy.

"Sure."

After that, Matt placed a suture, gave the boy postoperative instructions, and told him he was a great patient. Tammy led the boy back down the hallway toward the front desk, and Matt stepped into his private office and slumped into his chair. During the entire time he'd been with that kid, no matter what was happening in front of his eyes, or what anyone said, he'd been thinking about Jane, and that first date, and Andy Hedstrom.

Had Jane been in love with Andy? Had they been sexually active? Had Jane, his Jane, shared the intimate little things, and laughter, that young lovers share, with Andy before she met him? Did she still think of Andy sometimes in that way? Had she been thinking about him in that way for all these years, and simply hidden that from him? Was her connection to Andy still there? Was it ever there? His chest was funny again, and his breath came in shallow gulps.

"Doctor, we're all set out for a root canal on tooth number thirty in Operatory Two," Tammy said as she passed by his office.

"OK," Matt sighed.

But Tammy spun and reappeared in the door jamb of his office. "Are you all right?" she asked.

"Sure, I'm good."

Tammy cast a skeptical look at him. "You look like those GIs in the World War II documentaries. You know, the thousand-yard stare.'"

"Ah, I'm fine. I was just thinking about something else." Matt tried to smile, then he followed Tammy back to the clinic. But he wasn't fine.

During every complex procedure he performed that morning, no matter how intricate and involved, the little movie projector that played scenes for him while he was deer hunting played other scenes for him now. While his eyes were focused on one thing, maybe an X-ray or a tooth that he'd just prepared for a filling, a separate and unrelated vignette from his courtship with Jane played, too.

When he'd finished with his last patient of the morning, Matt splashed some water on his face and went back to his private office. He closed that door and sat at his desk for only a second before he turned on his cell phone and sent a text to Jane:

<Maybe the worst morning ever. I can't stop thinking about our conversation over coffee. Were you and Andy lovers before I came along? Do you still have feelings for him? I wonder if you chose me because . . . I don't know anymore, on the rebound?>

Jane's reply was almost instant:

<WHOA, WHOA, WHOA!! Slow down, Matt! Of course I don't have any feelings for Andy! Never did! You know that. I hardly knew him. We only went out a couple times and then I met YOU. You're the ONE! I'm in a meeting right now, can't talk. What's wrong?>

Jane's note was a small breath of fresh air, but the crushing sensation in his chest didn't go away. Matt sank back into his chair and sent his reply:

<I'm OK, just a little crazy, I guess. Can we talk tonight?>

Again, Jane's reply was instant:

<Of course. Relax, I love you>

Her text message was a reprieve, but a brief one. New thoughts of losing Jane, and Jane with someone else, began to swirl about in his brain. Every image that wandered through his mind involved the early years with Jane, and new concerns about what she'd been hiding from him all these years about her feelings, and actions, regarding Andy Hedstrom. Had she been torn between them? Did she still harbor feelings for him? Had they been lovers before, or after, Matt came into the picture? A new and terrible fear, of Jane in love with someone else, was suddenly as real as stone. Never mind the forty years, the lifetime of love and togetherness.

As the afternoon wore on it seemed that every comment he heard from patients or his own staff, or songs that played over the office radio, carried a thought that took him right back to the early days of his courtship with Jane.

When his workday finally ended, Matt hurried home and Jane was waiting for him at the door. "You scared me," she said, when her arms were around him. "What happened?" The house was warm and filled with smells of home. Jane had started a fire in the woodstove and there was a hint of wood smoke in the air, along with the wonderful scent of supper.

"We're having meat loaf? And you opened a bottle of wine?"

"It's your favorite," Jane replied. "And I came home early, just to get the house ready for you."

"Mmm . . ." Matt hummed in her ear, "nice."

"What happened today? Why all the craziness?"

"I don't know, honey. It was the strangest thing. This morning when you mentioned Andy, I just got the feeling that . . . I thought . . . I don't know." He held Jane close and kissed her cheek. "I kept seeing you and him together. You know; lovers. I saw you holding him, in that way. It made me feel terrible, like I was no better than Andy in your eyes. Maybe less than Andy."

"Really?" Jane's face wrinkled with surprise. "*Really?*"

"I don't get it either." Matt shook his head. "I kept feeling that I was losing you."

"Just because I mentioned *Andy?*" She said this as if it was the strangest thing she'd ever heard.

"I told you it was strange, but I just couldn't stop the feeling that . . ." Matt's words drifted off.

"But we only went out together a couple of times. I've never spoken of him like that, and I'm sure I don't even have any old photos of him. He never even met my parents." Jane shook her head. "I *never* had feelings for him. I think the only reason Andy liked me or wanted to be seen with me was because he thought I came from some money, and I had a car so I could drive him around. He never had any feelings for *me*, either."

"I know. I knew that at the time, too. But he *was* a college boy, and he'd have been willing to take advantage of things if you had feelings for him. I just kept picturing you holding him . . ."

"He wasn't clever. He didn't make me laugh." She kissed Matt on the lips. "He was just a nice guy who asked me out a couple times. There was never anything there."

"Hmph. Yeah, I *knew*," Matt said, with his lips close to Jane's ear, "on that first night I met you, that as soon as you had a chance to be with me, even for coffee, or a pizza, or anything else, that you'd choose me over Andy, or anyone else."

Matt could feel Jane's face bend into a smile. "And that's another one of those things I always liked about you: your confidence," she whispered.

Matt squeezed her tight, as if to reassure himself that she was still with him. Then he kissed her cheek and rocked slowly from side to side. He reached over to a small CD player on the kitchen countertop and hit the "play" button. A moment later Johnny Rivers was singing "Slow Dancing," and they moved together with the music.

"I can't do it, Matt," she said softly, as the song ended. She knew her lover's touch, and she knew what was on his mind.

"It's OK, just don't let me go," Matt said, and he held her close when Gordon Lightfoot started "Song for a Winter's Night."

Several more love songs, oldies that Matt had put together on a CD, played while they danced together in the kitchen, and when Sam Cooke finished "This Magic Moment" Jane whispered, "Thanks for not putting pressure. You know, for . . ."

"I love you, Jane." Matt shrugged, "What am I gonna do? It'll all be OK again someday." They circled the kitchen once more in silence and then Jane said, "Stay right there." She quickly opened the oven door, took the meat loaf out, and placed it on a cutting block to cool. "OK, where were we?" She stepped back into his arms and Mel Carter started "Hold Me, Thrill Me, Kiss Me."

When their slow orbit carried them past the silverware drawer, Jane opened it and removed a fork, but never let go of Matt. As they slowly circled the kitchen Jane began to pluck bites of meat loaf from the pan when they passed by. She'd hold a bite of meat loaf in front of Matt's mouth until he opened up, and then at the last second, when he moved toward it, she'd pop it into her own mouth and giggle. On the next pass by the meat loaf she'd give it to him, or maybe not. But every time she giggled. Then she put down the fork and did the same thing with a glass of wine. It was the kind of thing she'd always done, and her laughter hearkened back to those days when they'd first become lovers. Those were easy times. His world had been so small back then. All he ever thought about was loving Jane, finishing school, and getting on with their life together. That world was filled with limitless possibilities.

Jane held the wineglass close to Matt's lips, and as he expected, when he moved toward it, she naturally pulled it back. But in the process, she spilled most of the red wine on the front of his shirt. "Shit. Don't move," she said, and she snatched a towel off the kitchen countertop without letting go of Matt. She blotted the front of his shirt and then opened the top couple of buttons so she could dry his chest, too. "Yipes," she said, while blotting at the thick hair on his chest. "I think you're part Wookie," and she pulled at the hair on Matt's chest. "Or did you forget to take your sweater off?" She kissed his chest and then pressed her ear against his sternum. "I can hear your heartbeat," she said. Then she began to swirl his chest hair.

"Do you think I should shave my chest? I don't think all this body hair is 'in' nowadays," Matt asked.

"No, I think you'd plug up the septic system," Jane replied, and Matt had to let himself smile. "Besides—" Jane interrupted herself with a cough, then another, then she began to gag and make the sound of a cat trying to cough up a hairball. It was an old joke, she'd done it before, and Matt found it funny every time. As always, he laughed at the faces, and the noises she was making. Jane knew how to work the joke, and she kept on making the cat noise.

Finally, Matt stood straight and pulled her close so he could kiss her. She brought her lips toward his, but at the last second, she turned away once again and pretended to be trying to hack up one last hair. A moment later she pretended to pull a long hair from her mouth, and then she sighed, "There," before she kissed him.

"You think you're pretty funny, don't you?" Matt said, unable to stifle his own laughter.

"Why, yes, Chewbacca, as a matter of fact I do. Let's go sit on the couch and cover up. It's more comfortable there."

As they settled in together on the couch, Matt put the wine bottle on an end table beside him and tossed a warm fleece blanket over them. Then he put his arm around Jane and pulled her close.

"I love you, Jane. You're my best friend . . . best friend I ever had," Matt said.

"*My* best friend," Jane said. She wrapped her arms around him and pressed her face into his chest. "And that was really nice, what we just did. We haven't had a moment like that in a long time."

"Remember what it was like; back in our first apartment? Everything we did together was fun, and new," Matt said. "I remember waking up in the middle of the night and looking over at you. Sometimes I'd reach over to pull you close and we'd make love. All the passion came so easily. I thought it would never end."

"Good times," Jane nodded. "Remember the things we complained about: a professor or a final exam, or finding a parking place. It all seemed so important. I wish it could all be that simple again. Why does life have to get so complicated?"

A few minutes passed in silence. Each of them was floating along, thinking back on a different time. "You make me smile, after all these years," Matt said, then he asked, "How in the world were you still available when I came along?"

Jane held his hand and stared into the orange embers of the fireplace, remembering.

"You stood out in a crowd; a crowd of other college girls at a big school." He was just pondering an old question, not really searching for an answer anymore. "You were so pretty, and you had that great smile and sense of humor. You were usually the life of the party, too." Then he nudged her and added, "How *did* you manage to not have a steady boyfriend when I came along?"

Still, Jane made no answer. She was lost in her owns thoughts now. Matt knew her well, and he knew that she'd gone back in time too.

He'd seen all of her college photo albums, containing pictures of her with her friends; some guys, some women, most of them drunk, holding beer cans in a salute to the camera, and smiling. He knew very well how college boys' minds worked. He'd heard the names of all the boys she'd gone out with. Every one of them would have used his best moves to get Jane Monahan in bed. But he also knew she'd never had a steady boyfriend, never even taken a boy home to meet her parents. There must have been somebody. Matt moved his fingertips up and down along Jane's arm and watched the yellow flames flicker in the fireplace and remembered how he'd been so smitten by her. "I'd surely never met anyone like you; so beautiful and so much fun."

Jane sighed heavily, but kept silent. "But wow, honey, were you ever hard on guys," Matt mused.

"I knew what guys were after." Her voice had taken a cold edge, and she seemed unable to move her eyes away from something in the fire.

"I can't forget that poor guy at the Fraction on our first date. All he did was say hi, and you barked at him to 'Fuck off.' You know, that just didn't seem like something you'd do, but I saw you do it a few other times, too. Our friends noticed it more than once, also. Where did that come from?"

She stared, stone-faced, as if she was in a trance. She was reliving something. Matt could feel it. It was something powerful. "OK, so it wasn't Andy. Who was it? Who was your first lover?" Matt asked. He'd asked her before, usually teasing and hoping to make her blush. And she'd always given the same answer: "It was you."

But tonight, for the first time, Jane hesitated. And during that tiny hesitation Matt suddenly knew she was about to tell him something he didn't really want to know. He felt a weight, a heavy, strange weight, the same weight that had been there earlier in the day, jump on his chest again during that brief second before the words tumbled out of Jane's mouth.

"Mark Hansen," Jane said into the darkness.

There. She'd finally told him. Something, perhaps a melancholy brought on by the memory of a time and place they both knew was gone forever, had taken her to a distant place. And she'd returned with something that suddenly terrified him.

Matt had been solid, immovable through the ordeal of her cancer, his hip, his own fear of aging, and his fear of losing her to cancer. He'd been a dam, holding fast against immense pressure. But now, in the quiet darkness of his own home, a tiny pinhole opened up in the dam.

Jane had done a masterful job of keeping this thing, this person, a secret for *forty years*. But why? He must have been special. Jane must have been in love with him. She'd hidden him; lied about him, for a lifetime. And the way she'd just spoken his name told Matt there was much more to the story.

"Who?" Matt asked. "I never heard you say that name before." His heart felt like a fish flopping around in his chest, but he was fairly sure that Jane didn't notice the unsteadiness in his voice.

"He was older. A graduate instructor in biology lab when I was a freshman nursing student." Jane said. She felt rigid, distant. Her face was blank, her voice was sad, and still she stared into the fire.

"You never talked about him," Matt said. He hated this moment. Jane was reliving something that made him weak, but he had to ask.

"I hardly knew him," she said.

Matt struggled to hide the confusion and surprise and whatever it was that was tumbling around in his head. She wasn't joking or teasing, and there was emotion in her voice now. He couldn't tell what kind of emotion it was, but it was powerful, and Matt felt light-headed. "So tell me about it," he said.

"It was a college thing. It was a mistake."

"Did you love him?" Matt asked. The question made him sick as it passed over his lips. His Jane didn't make mistakes like that. There had to be more to the story.

"No," she answered, still staring into the fire.

He could see, feel, that Jane was reaching way back, and what she was remembering was more than a college mistake. This guy must have meant something to her. She must have been in love with him. Why else would she keep him a secret for a lifetime?

"Tell me," Matt whispered.

"We went out a couple times. Nothing special. I knew him from biology lab. He was kind of a celebrity for the young girls. A group of us went out for a beer after class several times. He paid some extra attention to me. I thought he was clever, and funny. I guess I sort of had a crush on him."

"So what happened?" Matt didn't want to hear any more, but he had to know the story. It was like coming upon an accident and not wanting to see everything but being unable to look away. His hands were shaking, but he tried to act as though he was only mildly interested.

"We wound up at his place one night after a couple drinks." Jane stopped. "He made it clear that if we went inside, we could have sex." It was clear that she didn't need to say any more.

"Did you *love* him?" Matt asked again.

"I suppose I wanted to think he was special. But no, I didn't love him."

Matt wished he'd heard more denial in her voice. "Then why . . ."

Jane still never looked away from the fire. "We sat there in his car for a long time. I just couldn't decide what to do."

"So, what happened?" Matt asked again. He knew there was more, much more, that Jane was leaving out.

"We went inside."

"That just doesn't sound like you; like something you'd do," Matt said.

"Well, it wasn't my finest moment. It was awkward and uncomfortable. I don't think I cried afterwards, but I think he knew it wasn't a good experience for me. I made him take me home right away so my roommates wouldn't see that I'd stayed overnight."

"That's it?" Matt asked after they'd both stared into the fire for a while. He'd never imagined that his Jane had been carrying this around for all these years. The person telling this story didn't seem like the person he'd always known.

"Pretty much," she said flatly.

"Did you see him again?"

"No, well, just in lab."

"That was it?"

Jane nodded yes.

Matt began struggling to assemble all the fragmented thoughts in his mind. He could actually feel himself tumbling, dropping like a stone, into the rabbit hole. And he feared that he might never find his way out. His lovely Jane had shared the truth, finally. It had happened more than forty years ago, several years before he met her. But as she told the story, it seemed to Matt as if it had all happened *today*. She'd said she never loved the guy, but she must have. Jane would never have done something like that if she didn't love him. And why else would she keep this secret for all these years? He'd heard it in her voice, hadn't he? She'd been stifling her emotions while she told the story. And the awful word picture she'd painted of herself with that guy. It was too much.

Later, while they lay together in bed, holding hands and waiting for sleep to come, Matt could find no peace. While they'd brushed their teeth and got ready for bed, Matt acted as though the story meant little to him. But when the lights were turned down, he stared at the ceiling and wondered about the things she'd told him. More than that, he wondered about the things she *hadn't* told him. He'd never met this other guy. Never heard his name. But now as all the images passed before his mind's eye, Matt created a face, a place, and a new disturbing image. When at last Jane let go of his hand and rolled away from him, he felt as if she'd left him, and taken someone else's hand. Sleep never came to Matt that night.

CHAPTER THIRTY-EIGHT

---•---

Clouds of steam fogged the bathroom mirror as Matt showered before work. He let the hot water cascade over him while he leaned against the wall of the shower stall and tried to think. But all he could think about, all he could see, was the awful vision of Jane with her first lover. He'd spent a sleepless night watching it over and over. She *must* have loved that guy, or she'd never have done that. And she'd done a masterful job of keeping it a secret. That just proved how much he must have meant to her. Matt dressed for work, sat on the porch and sipped a cup of coffee, and wished those thoughts would leave him.

Jane was wearing a bathrobe and slippers when she shuffled onto the porch with her own cup of coffee. "You're up early," she said, as she raised the cup to her lips and took a tentative sip, testing the temperature of the coffee. "Did you sleep OK?"

"Yeah, I slept all right," Matt lied. He glanced over at her and then brought his eyes back to his coffee.

"Got a big day lined up?" Jane asked. She had no idea that he hadn't slept, or that something was bothering him.

"Gonna work through the lunch hour, and then do some lab work. A short day in the clinic," Matt said. "But I'm going in a little early. Gotta get some other lab work finished up before I see my first patient." He stood up and walked to the kitchen, put his coffee cup in the sink, and went to the door. "I'll see you tonight," he called over his shoulder. For the first time he could remember, he chose not to kiss her goodbye. He sensed that if he stood too close to her now, he'd crack and reveal the anguish he couldn't shake. He had no reason to hurry away to the office; he was simply hoping that his mind's eye would stop replaying things if he could find a distraction.

No matter what procedure he did that morning at his office, he could not stop thinking about Jane. His mind pictured her, and her lover, while he extracted teeth, and placed dental implants, and placed fillings and crowns. About mid-morning, after Matt had dismissed one patient and was waiting for the next patient to get numb, he stepped into the small bathroom in his private office and closed the door behind himself. His heart was pounding. Something awful was building up inside him, and he tried to swallow it back. But when he looked at himself in the mirror his face twisted, and then little gasps leapt from his throat. He was glad that the ceiling fan was loud enough to muffle the noise of his heaving chest. And then the tears came. He brought his hands to his face and tried to hold things back, but it was no use. His Jane had loved someone else. She'd always loved him, but kept it a secret for all these years?

Matt took his glasses off, bent over the sink, and began to splash cold water on his face. Jesus, what was he thinking? Jane loved him. She'd loved him for a lifetime. They'd raised a family together and shared a great love. He made himself recall the passion and laughter of their young love; that was undeniable.

But those happy thoughts just would not hold. There were demons swarming, showing Matt the image of Jane with someone else. Thoughts and memories of Jane and him together were pushed away, far away into a void. And the demons were laughing at Matt, screaming at him. Jane was gone, she loved someone else, she always had. And the other guy was better than him—he was more handsome, more interesting, and a better lover. Jane had never stopped thinking of him, and he would have given her a better life than Matt had.

Matt stood straight and dried his face with a towel, then fought once again to drive the demons out of his head. That stuff was crazy.

Shortly before noon, as he was walking from one operatory to another, he heard a song on the office stereo that was from his college days. Then he remembered that the song would have been popular about two years before he met Jane, at roughly the time Jane and Mark Hansen must have been together. What if every time Jane heard it she thought of him? The tune entered his ear and then slugged him in the chest a millisecond later, while he was still in the hallway. And that was how the morning passed; every few minutes something else reminded him of what Jane had told him the night before.

"Are you all right, Doctor?" Tammy asked when the last patient was finished and the staff was cleaning up for the day. She'd stepped in front of Matt and blocked his route to his private office.

"Yeah." He smiled and tried to hide what he'd been unable to hide all day.

"You don't look very good. Are you OK? Is Jane OK?" Tammy asked.

"Everybody's fine. I just have a lot on my mind. Do I look *that* bad?"

"You weren't even *here* today," Tammy said. "Where were you? Your eyes weren't right. All day!"

"I didn't sleep much last night. I'll be fine tomorrow."

But Matt didn't know if he'd ever be fine again. He was lost, and he had to talk to someone. The office, with a busy schedule, in the daylight, should have been a safe harbor from the thing he kept seeing in the night. But he couldn't find his way to the calm waters.

"Is your hip still bothering you, Matt?" Donna Dilley asked, as the last patient was leaving.

"No, why?" Matt said, although he knew why she was asking.

"Your eyes don't look right," Donna said. "You look like you're in pain."

"Nah," Matt said, with a big, forced smile. "I feel great. Just a lot on my mind."

Donna cast a suspicious glance at him, then said, "Well it's a good thing you have the afternoon off. You go on home and take it easy. Get some rest."

"Thanks, Mom," Matt teased, to validate and then dismiss her observations about his appearance.

Once most of the staff had gone home for the day, he sat down at his desk and tried to do some paperwork, but John's comment about breaking Linda Pike's heart kept ringing in his ears. Jesus, he'd broken her heart? Really? He didn't want that to be true. But it *was* true. He'd seen it himself, shortly after it all happened, when they'd brushed past each other on campus and he'd seen it in her eyes. And he'd just walked away. He put his elbows on his desk and covered his face with his hands. "Shit."

His Jane had gone through her whole life with a broken heart, too, thinking about someone, and not him. It was all clear now. Finally.

Years ago, he'd read an article about "first lovers," and the author had claimed that a woman's first lover stays in her heart forever because the act of sex is different for men and women. He'd said that men, for the most part, are simply driven by lust, and by their genetic programming to spread their seed in as many places as possible. Women, however, attach much more emotion to sex, and they actually give something of their soul to their lover.

At the time he'd read that article, Matt assumed that the author was maybe just some conservative Christian who wanted to advance a message promoting abstinence. Fair enough, he'd thought, and interesting, but it had no importance in *his* life. But now those words were killing him. It was just one more passing thought that tossed a bit more fuel on the fire.

"Ah, God," Matt groaned. He had to talk to *somebody*, and John Velde sure wasn't the one. There had to be *someone* who could say something to make him snap out of this, and put an end to all the awful things racing through his head. Maybe Sally would have something to say, something from her life experience that might release him from the demons. She was a woman; perhaps a woman's perspective on all of this might clear away the things he was feeling. She was smart, experienced at life, and she'd become a good friend. Maybe he could start a conversation with her and lead it in a direction that would get her to open up and say something to make sense of what he was feeling.

Matt looked at his watch. The lunch-hour rush would be over by now. Sally might be able to take a few minutes to talk to him, so he stood up and decided to walk to the coffee shop. What would he say to her, he wondered, as he walked along the street and waved to other friends. He couldn't tell her *everything*; just enough to lead her into offering her opinion on something without her really knowing exactly what she was being asked to comment on.

Sally was behind the counter of her shop when Matt strode in, and she noticed him as he stepped through the door. "Hey," she waved, "nice to see you. Are you here for lunch?"

"Yeah, sure; a late lunch. Got a sandwich—whatever the daily special is—and a cup of coffee for me?" The noon rush was indeed long over, and only a few customers were still lingering.

"Sure, and it looks like your table is open, too." Sally grinned and pointed to the little table where she'd banished John and Matt many months before. "Have a seat and I'll bring it over in just a minute."

Matt picked up a newspaper and opened it to the sports page when he sat down, but his mind was busy with something much different than the early-season baseball scores. He'd have to come up with a simple, friendly topic of conversation that might offer a segue into how a middle-aged woman felt about the first time she'd had sex. This was going to be a challenge.

"Here you go," Sally said, when she put the sandwich and coffee in front of Matt. "How's your day going?"

"Pretty good," he lied. He pulled a chair out and said, "Can you join me for a few minutes?"

"Well . . ." Sally looked over her shoulder at the nearly empty coffee shop. "Sure, I think I can take a little break." When she sat down, she pointed at the sports page in front of Matt and asked, "Will you be coaching the boys again this summer?"

"I guess so."

"Well, good. Timmy is already talking about it. Some of those boys, Dave Norman and Mike Katzenmeyer, and even Bradley Hested, have become good friends with Timmy. They're at our place all the time."

"Good." Matt smiled, but he wanted to talk about something else. How was he going to move the conversation from Little League baseball to sex?

From behind the table where he was sitting with Sally, Matt heard the front door open, and then a familiar voice. "Hi, Sally!" It was DeeDee Katzenmeyer, and a young man was with her. DeeDee and her friend crossed the room quickly to Matt's table and greeted them. "We stopped in for a sandwich because we heard they're *so* good!" DeeDee exclaimed. Then, in her next breath, she said, "When I saw you sitting here, Dr. Kingston, I had to come over and tell you; you done such a nice job when I came to your office the other day. I didn't feel a thing."

"Well, you have beautiful teeth, and all I did was an exam," Matt said.

DeeDee turned to the young man with her and exclaimed, "No cavities!" The man grinned, but said nothing, and DeeDee failed to introduce him. "Yeah, but usually when I go to the dentist I get so scared that I just curl up in the fecal position," DeeDee said. "But you and your nurses were great. I'll be back!"

"Well, good! And thank you for the kind words," Matt said.

"Uh-huh." DeeDee smiled. "Well, see you later." She led her friend off to a table on the far side of the room.

"The fecal position?" Sally smiled and flicked her eyebrows.

"Dentists apparently scare the shit out of her," Matt said, shaking his head. But this might be his chance to lead the Sally in another direction. DeeDee and her friend had given him an opening, and it was time to go for it. "Who's the guy with her?" Matt asked.

"He works at the bank. Just got out of college. Seems like an all-right kid, but I don't think he's got much more going on upstairs than she does. Did you notice the way he was following her around like a puppy?"

"Well, they're young, and they've got plenty to think about. You remember what it was like when you were young?" Matt raised his eyebrows and smiled.

"Yeah," Sally sighed.

"Remember your first time?" Matt asked. *There*, he'd put it out there for her.

"Sex?" she asked with a grin.

"Yeah."

"Sure! He was the handsomest boy in school!" Sally tapped her hand over her heart and showed Matt something of a swoon. "It was nice. I still have a little thing for him. I see him at weddings and funerals, or I used to, anyway; I don't go back home anymore."

"So, it was good? And you still have a little pitter-pat in your heart for him?" Matt probed. This was *not* what he'd hoped to hear.

"Sure do." Sally grinned and made a show of fanning away the heat generated by the memory of their relationship. Far-off memories showed in her eyes for a second, then she shrugged and said, "He has a wife and kids, and probably grandchildren by now, but I still remember."

"Mmmm." Matt nodded and did his best to hide his disappointment with her answer.

Sally stood and said, "I gotta get back to work." DeeDee and her new friend were standing at the counter, looking at the menu on a chalkboard and waiting for Sally to take their order. "But before I go, when is the player draft?"

"Coupla weeks, I think. Just before school lets out for summer." Matt tried to look enthused about it, but he had no interest any longer. Everything seemed to have drained out of him in the past few days, and life seemed so heavy now.

"Great, we're looking forward to it!" Sally said.

"Yeah, we'll have fun. I'll let you know when I find out for sure." He'd been able to impart sufficient enthusiasm to the talk of baseball, but it was all for show. All he could think about was Sally grinning and fanning away the heat from the memory of her first lover.

———

Jane eased the door to Matt's man room open as twilight began to send long shadows across Scotch Lake. She had Matt's cell phone in her hand, and as she gave it to him she said, "Here. Roger Senesac just tried to call you. I'm sure he wants to know if you'll coach Timmy's team again this summer." She was about to close the door behind her when she took a second look at Matt and added, "You don't look very good. Are you OK?"

"Yeah. I'm just tired. I think I was dozing off there a minute ago." He'd taken a plate of leftover meat loaf into his room and held it on his lap while he ate dinner and watched a ball game. His eyes had indeed been at half mast when Jane brought his phone to him.

"OK. I'll be in the other room, reading. Come and sit with me after you return his call?" Jane said before she closed the door and left him.

"Sure." Matt hit the call button and held the phone up to his ear. He *had* been flirting with sleep for a few minutes there, before Jane brought his phone. The respite from a long run of bad daydreams had been good.

"Hey, Matt! You probably know why I'm calling: Are you willing to coach a nine-year-old team this summer?"

"Sure. I think Velde is actually looking forward to it this year. But I have to ask you, do we get the same players again this summer, or will there be another player draft?"

"Good news and bad news for you, Matt," Roger said. "Good news is that we redraft new teams every year. Bad news is that coaches all have to draft their own kids first, and just like last year, hell, like every year; the dads who are coaching all get together with a couple other dads who have boys that can play ball, and have them be assistants. So all the good players will be gone before you ever get a chance at 'em. Sorry, Matt. But you'll have Timmy and Dave Norman again."

"Great," Matt deadpanned.

"Look at it this way; at least the other coaches won't be out to break up that juggernaut that Velde assembled for you last year."

"Awesome. When is the draft?"

"Two weeks, in my room at the high school."

"I'll be there," Matt said, and he turned his phone off. He felt good for the first time all day. The talk of baseball, even terrible baseball, had taken his mind off everything else. He got up and went to the other room to sit on the couch, beside Jane. "Looks like we're gonna reassemble our All-Star team from last summer."

"Good," Jane said, and she put her hand on his thigh. "You wanna fool around?"

"Well, I suppose so," Matt groaned, as if he needed some convincing. "I was just gonna go over our team's batting order, but . . . OK then, you win," he acquiesced. Then he asked, "Really? You wanna fool around?"

"I can't explain it, Matt. It must be a hormone thing." Jane took Matt's hand in hers and led him to their bedroom.

An hour later Matt rolled onto his side, covered his eyes with his forearm, and sighed.

"What was *that*?" Jane asked. "What happened?"

"I don't know. I couldn't . . . it wouldn't . . . shit, I don't know."

"But you were doing just fine, and, what happened?"

"I dunno."

"Are you OK?"

"I thought I was."

"Oh, it's all right. They say it happens to all men sometimes."

"Never happened to me before."

"It's all right, honey." Jane reached over and pulled herself close to him. "You probably ate too much. Or maybe you didn't get enough sleep last night? Or maybe you have too much on your mind?"

"Or maybe I'm just a worthless old man."

"Don't say things like that. I love you!" Jane scolded.

"Even though I'm a worthless old man?"

"*Matt*! Don't do this. Everything was fine. Everything will be fine. We'll just get a good night's sleep and—"

"Everything will be fine?" Matt interrupted and finished the sentence.

"Yup," she said, then kissed his cheek. "I love you."

Sleep did come for Matt, but only after reliving yesterday's nightmare, and then today's.

CHAPTER THIRTY-NINE

Another day at the office came and went, but with even more angst and fear than ever. The same visions of Jane with the other guy were always nearby, and it felt like it had all happened only yesterday. And the new memory—failing at sex—rolled in on a *new* giant wave of angst. Making love was the thing that always opened the door for that connection with Jane. Now that was lost, too. And it was *he* who'd failed, not Jane.

"Doctor, you look terrible," Donna Dilley said to him just before lunch. "Should I make an appointment for you over at the clinic?"

"Nah, I'm fine," Matt scoffed.

"You look like the dogs had you under the porch," Donna said. "What's going on?"

"Nothing, just a couple late nights."

"Well, you go straight home and go to sleep after work today!"

"OK, Mom." Matt smiled.

But Matt didn't plan to go straight home. He had to talk to somebody. Maybe John Velde *could* help. Well, what could it hurt? What could John say that would make him feel any *worse*? When he left the office, he drove directly to Velde Taxidermy.

As Matt had hoped, John was still at his shop, and there were no other cars or trucks parked in front when he rolled to a stop. Matt let himself in the front door and walked through the display area and into John's workroom.

John was standing at the long workbench on the far side of the room, straightening tools and cleaning his work area. When he saw Matt, he called out, "Hi, buddy, what're you doing here?"

"Nice to see you, too," Matt said.

"Yeah, that didn't sound very nice, did it? But you never stop by at this time o' day, unless we're going fishing. Shit! Did we make plans to go fishing and I forgot?" John scowled.

"Nope, I just stopped by to shoot the shit. You done for the day?"

"Sure, I was just cleaning up."

All three of the work tables were covered with graphite fish, deer heads, ducks, and ruffed grouse, in various stages of completion. Matt weaved his way through the tables and went to the avocado refrigerator behind the rickety old kitchen table in the corner. He knew where he was going; he'd been there and done what he was about to do many times. Matt opened the fridge, checking for ice, and then peeked around the nearby shelves. "Where's the scotch?"

"Ah, shit. I hide it now. Got a coupla good-for-nothings that like to stop in here and waste my time; sit around and tell me stories about the big one that got away. They're pretty much deadbeats, like you. Anyway, they discovered the scotch one day, so now they come back looking for it every so often. Also, like you. If I didn't hide the stuff, they'd be in here every day and I'd never get any work done, and they'd drink all the expensive stuff."

"That's a fascinating story," Matt said glumly. "Where's the scotch?"

"Where we used to hide it."

Matt walked to one of the work tables, opened a drawer beneath the table top, and fished around behind a cluster of wooden hand tools. When he withdrew a green, half-empty bottle of J&B he turned an irritated glance at John and said, "This isn't what I left here."

"Yah . . . no . . ." John stumbled before he mumbled. "That stuff you left just doesn't keep. It's like the shit just evaporates."

Matt pursed his lips and scowled. "Don't be an asshole."

"Look farther back." John smiled.

Matt bent down and then stood up with a mostly full bottle of Aberlour in his hand. Then, from the single piece of plywood that functioned as a shelf above the laundry sink next to the refrigerator, Matt selected two Flintstones jelly glasses. He plopped an ice cube in each glass, then poured three fingers of scotch into each of them.

John was already seated at the wobbly, paint-stained kitchen table when Matt approached him with a scotch in each hand. "Still using the finest glassware, I see," Matt said.

"Please join me here in the employee lounge," John said, waving an open hand over the table. Matt eased himself into a wooden kitchen chair that was about the same vintage as the table, but quite a bit sturdier, and crossed his legs. "Tough day, buddy? You look like shit," John noted.

"Tough coupla days," Matt confessed.

"What happened? Damn, that's fine scotch." John smacked his lips and smiled.

Matt wanted to tell John about all the things that had been haunting him. He *had* to talk to *someone*. And sometimes it was possible to draw John into a grown-up conversation. But now, as he considered the words he might choose to start this story, he felt like an interpreter, trying to start a conversation with someone who had only a limited command of the language they were speaking. He wasn't sure how to proceed with John. He didn't mind revealing some sensitive feelings to John, because he'd done that plenty of times before. But no matter how he thought about telling the story, *this* wound was pretty personal, and he wasn't sure John would understand.

Matt took a small sip of his scotch and thought for a moment. "Do you ever think about old girlfriends, John? I mean old lovers?"

"Sure, I guess so." John shrugged. "Well, I'm not sure what you mean. Like when the monster gets hungry do I think old of girlfriends who were wild and nasty, and then do I wanna call them and get together and play hide-the-wiener again? Sure, I think about that."

Matt studied the ice cubes in his glass for a minute but said nothing.

"That's not what you meant, was it?" John asked.

Matt shook his head.

"You were asking me if I ever remember some girl and then think to myself, 'Oh, man, I shoulda never let her get away.' Right?"

Matt nodded. "Yeah, something like that. Do you?"

"No." John shook his head and smiled as if that thought had never, and would never, occur to him.

"You were married once," Matt said. "How 'bout her? Do you think of her?"

"Hell no. Especially not her," John scoffed.

"Really? How can that be?"

"Well, I was young, and it was in California, where all that mattered was how you looked. And after you're with somebody for a while, you both start to notice other people. And then pretty soon your wife is bangin' the high school baseball coach. And you both move on."

"Didn't that break your heart?" Matt asked.

"Nah, not really. She was a gorgeous woman, but the water was pretty shallow down there on her end of the pool; she was kinda dumb. We didn't have any money, so there was nothing to fight over. We just got a cheap divorce and went our own separate ways."

"Don't you feel sorta connected to her, emotionally?" Matt asked.

"Nope, not at all."

"I think that's really sad," Matt said.

"Yeah, kinda," John agreed. "But you know, I never met one woman the whole time in California who ever asked, or cared, about me in any way except how I looked, or how *she* looked when she showed up someplace with me on her arm."

Matt had no idea what to say.

John offered, "It made dating pretty easy. All you ever had to think about was yourself." He swirled his scotch, then added, "You know, that's a big part of the reason I came back to Minnesota. Everything out there was so phony." John paused. "Why are we talking about this, anyway?"

"Do you remember a while back, when you told me about staying up late and talking about your feelings, just so you could get some girl in the sack?" Matt asked.

"Yeah." John was grinning.

"Do you think you ever hurt any of them, hurt their feelings? You know, lied to them, tricked them and took something you could never give back? Do you ever feel bad about any of that?"

"No . . . I think they all got what they wanted, too." John shrugged. "OK, maybe, well, probably, I mighta hurt some feelings . . . Jesus, what are you getting at?"

He wanted to tell John all about the things that had happened with Jane over past few days, and then ask for John's take on it. And then he wanted John to tell him that Jane's short relationship with that guy meant nothing to anyone. And he'd hoped that John's words would make all the angst simply vanish.

Maybe listening to himself tell the story would provide the proper understanding, and allow all his heartache to vanish. Since John had such a far different life experience than his, he might even say something insightful. But now, as he looked at the grin on John's face, and remembered hundreds of other conversations with John, he began to lower his expectations. John Velde just wasn't the type of guy to take a long, introspective look at this story, and then offer up soothing advice. John was a solid friend, but this was a hard story to share with him. Maybe, as it had happened with Sally, John would make things worse.

"Hey!" John snapped his fingers and waved his hand in front of Matt's face. "Where are you, buddy? You've been sittin' there staring into space for about thirty seconds. You slip into a coma, or what?"

"Sorry," Matt said, and then something came to him. Maybe there was a way to broach the subject with John. "Do you remember Linda Pike?" Matt asked.

"Mmm, no. Should I?"

"About a year ago you came home from some sports show in Wisconsin, and you asked me if *I* remembered a girl named Linda Pike," Matt said. "Well, you couldn't remember her last name, but it was Pike."

"Oh, yeah. Real tall and pretty? You broke her heart? She's the one, right?"

"Yup."

"Sooo, that's what this is about?" John asked. "You're gonna tell me now? No, lemme guess. You had a love child and—"

"No," Matt interrupted. "Nothing like that. Sorry to disappoint you—"

"Well, good," John interrupted in turn, "'cuz I forgot to tell you, she died."

"What?" Matt gasped. "What happened? How would *you* know?"

"I told you that I met her *and* her husband at a sports show. Turns out he's a real outdoorsman. I've been doing alotta work for him, a couple deer heads and an elk—"

"What *happened* to her? I don't care about the guy's trophies."

"Brain cancer. Her husband just picked the stuff up yesterday, and he told me that she'd died about two months ago. Glioblastoma, 'zat sound right?"

"Uh-huh," Matt sighed. "That one can come on fast, and it's always fatal." He began to rub his forehead and try to get his mind around this news. Linda Pike's life was over. The thought troubled Matt. Had he really hurt her, broken her heart, like she said? Maybe he'd altered the course of her life. Had she ever told her husband? Had she been thinking of *him* for all these years? Should he have gone to her and told her how sorry he was? Would that have made anything better anyway? Now he'd never know. God, he wished he hadn't done what he'd done, and he could never undo it.

"You OK, buddy?" John asked. "Looks like maybe you were close to her?"

Matt shook his head slowly. "We were never close. She was a pretty girl—no, she was a doll. We went out a few times. You know, a movie and a pizza, and a goodnight kiss." Matt sipped his scotch and leaned back in his chair, one arm resting on the table. "She was a nice girl, too, really nice. But I didn't have any real feeling for her." Matt grew silent. "It's funny, though. You can tell . . . the little things . . . I remember looking at her, the way she held a drink in her hand, or the way she ate a slice of pizza, or the way she walked. I didn't want a future with her, I just wanted . . ."

"I understand," John said. "What you really wanted was . . .?" John raised his eyebrows.

"Yup," Matt replied, "I guess I just wanted to see what I had to do in order for her to give it up. Oh, she was a nice girl, a good person. But there was nothing there; I wasn't interested in her. I was twenty years old, maybe twenty-one, and all I thought about, or I should say that all I *cared* about, was the pretty face and the long hair and the long legs. I was in love with every pretty girl I saw. It was all about the chase, all about *me*. I was willing to overlook the fact that I felt no connection to Linda, or any pretty girl. I just wanted to see how far I could get."

"I know that feeling," John offered.

"I know, John, but I'm trying to get at something deeper."

"Keep going. But I prob'ly won't understand."

"Well, I guess I could see, by the look in her eyes and the way she spoke to me, that she felt a connection. Maybe she was kinda in love with me? Maybe she was beginning to think that I was the one? And I thought I might be able to use that in order to get, you know."

John broke in: "Wait a minute. I gotta get some ice and pour myself another drink. You want another bump too?"

"No thanks, I gotta drive home."

John opened the freezer part of the avocado refrigerator, got some ice, poured some more scotch over the ice, and then hurried back to his chair. "OK, you may continue."

"So, one day we met after class and had a beer at Stub and Herbs. It was a school night, we both had class the next day. Anyway, she came over to my place after the beer, and one thing led to another. I could kinda tell she was thinking about sex, but I could also tell that she wasn't so sure. I said all the right things, implied that I had deep feelings and that there was something really special between us." Matt sighed heavily and took another sip of scotch. "It was her first time." He paused.

John waited.

"It wasn't very good," Matt continued. "Well, I guess it was OK for me: I got her naked and had my way with her. That was all I wanted, a thrill. Like I said, I wasn't too concerned about her. She wasn't very good at it, and she said it kinda hurt, but I didn't think about that. I walked her home, had her back at her dorm before ten."

"So, you went out for a while after that, and then you broke up?" John asked.

"Never called her again. Saw her around campus a few times, and it was always bad, uncomfortable. The look on her face was really . . . she was hurt, and embarrassed, and probably angry."

"How come you never called her again?"

"Why would I? I'd had what I wanted: the sex, the thrill, the chase. She was like the wrapper that it came in, and I just threw her away. But I hurt her. I knew it at the time, too, and I was able to just ignore what I'd done." Matt finished his scotch and slumped back in his chair. "I wish I hadn't done that. If only I could have that to do over again."

"Bummer. Sorry I told you about her. I thought you'd get a kick outta that story. You know, a pretty girl who still thinks of you after so many years."

"I don't think like that. I feel bad."

"Well, you're not the first guy to do something like that. I may have done it a few times, too. And have you ever thought that maybe that girl simply got what she wanted, too? Maybe the chase, and the thrill, were what she was after, too? Maybe she was just curious about sex, and she chose you to help her answer her questions."

"Yeah, I wonder about that sometimes, and I've tried to convince myself that that's all it was for her, too. But I don't think so." Matt raised his glass and let the last ice cube slide into his mouth. "Hell, John, you saw her face. You talked to her, and that was forty years after it happened. You're the one who brought it back to me. What do *you* think?"

"Yeah, there *was* a lot going on there, in her eyes," John agreed. "You might be right on that one. But hell, what do I know?"

"I dunno."

"So why did you tell me all this?" John asked.

"It's been bothering me, off and on, ever since you mentioned her name last year. That's all," Matt lied. Just as he'd feared, sharing the story of Linda had only made him feel worse. He saw Jane's face, not Linda's, and now he was even more certain that Jane had harbored feelings for her first lover, too.

"Do you know what a contrapasso is?" Matt asked John.

"Yeah, isn't that the thing that Asian hookers do? You know, when they shove a string of beads in your five-hole one at a time and then yank 'em all out right at the end?"

Matt grimaced and let John see that he wasn't in the mood for this.

"I didn't say I *liked* it," John said, barely hiding his amusement.

"A contrapasso is a concept from a book called *Inferno*, by an author named Dante," Matt started. "Basically, what it says is that when we go to Hell we'll be punished in equal proportion to our sins on earth, and I've been thinking—"

"Yipes," John interrupted. "If that's true, I'm gonna be havin' a lot worse things than beads shoved up my ass for eternity!"

This little chat hadn't worked out the way he'd hoped, either. He couldn't tell the rest of the story to John. While he thought about things for a moment, his demons swooped in and showed him everything he'd been running from once more.

John snapped his fingers again, right in front of Matt's face. "Hey, you slipped into neutral again."

"Sorry."

"So that's *it*? You came over to tell me about a college girlfriend? That's all?"

"No, I just thought about her after I got here," Matt lied, and he tipped his head back and let the last ice cube in his drink slide onto his tongue. "Actually, I came over to tell you that the player draft for summer baseball is coming up," he lied again.

"I'll be there." John grinned.

"OK, then . . ." Matt sat his empty glass on the table and pretended that his next question was just an afterthought, "Hey, tell me about the Viagra."

"Whaddaya mean?"

"Tell me what happens."

"You've never tried it?"

Matt shook his head.

"So, no lead in your pencil, huh?" John's grin was gleeful.

"Don't be an asshole. I was asking about *your* pencil."

John leaned back and smiled. "OK, then, I'll tell you. You sure you never tried it?"

Matt shook his head again.

"Well, every time I take one of those pills, I expect to sprout a blue-veiner in about ten seconds. But it doesn't work that way. 'Bout twenty minutes later I get sorta flushed; hot and red all over. When everything is done, I have a headache and my nose is all stuffed up for a day."

"That's it?"

"Yeah, I think something good happens down there," John pointed under the table, "but I'm not sure. Remember I told you the little guy in my pants—I call him 'Emille the Destroyer'—sorta lost interest from time to time?"

"Yeah."

"Well, that was before I met Sally. Now I'm not so sure Emille needs any help. I think a big part of it all is in a guy's head, too. Know what I mean?"

"Unfortunately, I do. And the little guy in your pants has a name?" Matt's eyes narrowed as if he was searching for understanding.

"Miss Bureson gave it to him, back in fourth grade."

"I shoulda known," Matt said, as he stood up to leave. "I gotta go home now. Thanks for the scotch."

"Any time, old buddy; C'mon back tomorrow." Then, as Matt was about to step out the front door John called out, "I know lotsa secrets about fishing, too!"

Matt drove home, made a sandwich for supper, and ate by himself in his tiny man room. Despite the chuckle at the end of it all, his visit with John had made him feel worse. He tried to watch a ball game while he read a book.

When it was time for bed, he lay next to Jane and made small talk for a while. She didn't seem to have any idea about the things that were bothering him. Eventually he turned the light out, told her that he loved her, and held her hand until she drifted off to sleep. But for Matt, sleep came only after hours of listening to things that Jane had told him, and wondering about things she'd kept from him. As he relived their conversation when she'd told him about her first lover, he grew certain that she'd noticed how much it was bothering him, and she'd begun to leave things out in order to protect him from the rest of it. But now that his mind had created a face and a place for her story, his demons had something to keep showing him. Over and over. He saw Sally fanning the heat of her first lover away, too. And he remembered his terrible failure with Jane.

CHAPTER FORTY

The downward spiral began slowly. Familiar faces and voices were being pushed to the outer edge of Matt's world. Every morning when he woke from his fitful sleep, the first things that came to him were thoughts of Jane. He saw her as she was when they met, a lifetime earlier. He remembered the clothes she wore back then—shorts and T-shirts and sundresses—and the long, tan legs. Her hair was long, and she was always smiling and walking toward him.

He brushed his teeth and got dressed and drove to work with Jane right there in front of him, and he liked it. He fought to keep the image there. Then, somewhere along the way, the wheels would come off the wagon; some little thing would start an awful process in his head. Maybe he'd hear the words to a popular song that he'd once liked, or maybe the memory of a long-forgotten place or person or event would pop into his brain. The places and people and moments were always part of his time at the university. Some of the memories came from days before he met Jane. Some came from the time when they were new in love.

But all of the memories involved Jane, and they would quickly devolve into scenes that he'd never witnessed or been a part of. In every one, Jane was laughing and partying with someone else. She might be walking and holding hands with some guy, but in the same place where she once walked and held hands with *him*. Or she might be flirting with some guy at a keg party, or a bar where she'd also flirted with *him*. Sometimes she was with others at places that he'd never seen. At first, he knew that these little visions of the past were being created in his own mind. But as they continued, he wasn't so sure; maybe he'd finally come to see things as they really were? Then he'd begin to feel terrible because he just *knew* that when Jane thought of those places she recalled fond memories with someone else, not him.

442

The worst of it still came at night, though. He began to dread bed-time because he knew that when he closed his eyes, that was when the demons would show up in force and show Jane doing the thing she'd told him about.

A stiff drink before bed helped him find sleep, but then he'd wake a couple of hours later and the demons were always waiting for him. Most nights when that happened, he'd move to his man room and sit in his chair while he watched an old movie until exhaustion pushed the demons away.

He wanted to talk to Jane about it all, but he was locked in a terrible wrestling match with all the demons. He feared that she'd ridicule his weakness or continue to hide the rest of the truth from him anyway. He yearned to tell her how bad he felt, and that the awful visions never stopped. But the longer he put it off, the more he knew it would hurt to talk about it all again.

The one thing he could still do was to stop every time he passed close to her, and kiss her cheek or tell her she was beautiful, and that he loved her. He bought her flowers every few days, and wrote love notes to her. He held her hand whenever they walked together on the streets around Pine Rapids.

For the most part, Jane was all right with Matt's public displays of affection until one evening when a local band was playing at the city band shell down by the lake, and Matt kissed her cheek. "Matt, you gotta cut back on this stuff," she whispered.

"I love you," Matt said.

"I love you, too, but you're embarrassing me."

"Really?"

"Really." Jane squeezed his hand and said, "It's just too much."

He wasn't hurt by her comments, but he was surprised. "OK," he said, "but you're the prettiest girl in the park."

That night when they lay in bed, holding hands, Jane apologized. "I'm sorry about what I said at the park. If I hurt your feelings, I'm sorry."

"It's OK," Matt said. But it wasn't OK. He didn't think he could go on much longer. He was ready to turn the lights back on and plead for reassurance that she'd loved him and not someone else for all these years. The demons, as usual, were streaming in, and just as he was about to raise up on an elbow and start talking, he heard Jane snore. Just a little snore. Then another.

How could she drop off to sleep like that, Matt wondered. Either he was hiding things very well, and she had no idea about what he was feeling and seeing, or she was just hoping that by not talking about it the whole thing would just go away.

Either way, the things that came to him now when he closed his eyes were unbearable. Most nights, after an hour or two of struggling, he'd rise as quietly as he could, tiptoe out to the kitchen, and make a tall scotch for himself. Then he'd plop into the chair in his man room and wait for his brain to get numb.

As the weeks passed, Matt grew more and more sullen. He made no attempt to go fishing or join his friends for lunch during the week.

On the evening of the Little League player draft, all of the coaches, even John Velde, went out together for a beer. But Matt made up an excuse to come home and not join the fun. When the season started and the little postgame parties at the baseball field morphed into backyard gatherings or get-togethers at Buster's, Matt found a reason to miss every one of them.

"Are you all right?" Jane finally asked before he left for work one morning.

"Yeah, sure. Why do you ask?"

"Well, you just don't seem to have any interest in the things you always liked. You never see John or any of your friends anymore, and you've been drinking a lot."

"Ah, just a lot on my mind at work."

"No," Jane said, and she moved to block his exit. "It's more than that."

"Honest, it's just a bunch of things at work." Matt faked a smile, and he kissed her and tried to step around her once more, but again she moved into his path.

"Something is wrong. What is it?" Jane demanded. "I'm worried about you."

"It sucks to get old," Matt said.

"Your hip?" Jane asked.

"No, the hip is fine. But there are so many other things, little things. It just gets more difficult every day."

"Like what?" Jane asked.

"Like . . . I have to ask people to repeat themselves way too often. I can't hear like I used to. I need to go have my hearing checked, but I don't want to. I can't read anymore with my cheaters, and I need to bump up the magnification on my loupes at the office because my eyes are getting weaker. My hip is fine, but my knee clicks and pops all the time, so I probably need to have *that* replaced, too. My shoulder, the left one, hurts now too, and my hands ache at the end of the day. Just a lot of nagging little things that I know are never gonna get better."

It was all true, pretty much, he'd come up with it all quickly, and it was good enough to get Jane to step out of his way without any more questions.

"You're the youngest-looking sixty-three-year-old man I know. All that stuff can be fixed, honey," she said, and she gave him another kiss. "You need to find your smile again. Tomorrow is Saturday. Why don't you go fishing with John? You can try out his new boat. He calls you every couple days and asks you to go with him."

"Ah . . ." Matt searched for a good reason not to go fishing with John.

"Go! You should go with him. You always have a good time with John!" Jane prodded.

"I'll go with John some other time. I planned to take my canoe down to French Creek tomorrow. That's one of my happy places. Maybe that's where my smile is?" He turned to leave for work, but then turned back as if he'd forgotten something important, and he wrapped his arms around her. "I love you, Jane. I love you more now than ever, and I think you're even more beautiful now than you were when we met." He hugged her as if he was leaving for a month, instead of a day at the office. "I love you," he whispered. But when he stepped back it was as if he hadn't touched her.

"I love you, too." Jane smiled, but she seemed to be miles away already,

As he walked out the back door he was thankful that she'd bought the story about little aches and pains. He didn't want to talk anymore. Well, *part* of him wanted to rush back into the house and beg her to reassure him that he was her hero, and that she'd always loved him only, and not her first lover. But *she* had to offer those things without being asked. He couldn't ask about her first lover ever again; he'd look weak, and she'd just say the things she thought he needed to hear. What *was* the truth? Why had she kept that secret so long? And why did she seem so sad when she finally told him? And with that thought he was once again carried further down the rabbit hole by the same old ugly thoughts. After a lifetime of loving her, he was losing her.

———

Summer was slow in coming to the north. The sky and the breeze would hint at summer one day, and then the next day might be gray and frigid with snow flurries. On the first Saturday of June, the sun was shining, and autumn leaves from last fall, still strewn about the shore of Scotch Lake, rustled under Matt's wader boots as he dragged his canoe toward the lake-shore. Several feet of winter ice had turned slushy and then melted away a few weeks earlier. The water was still cold, for sure, and there was only a hint of new, green leaves in the hardwood forest yet. But the lake was open and the air was warm, and there just might be a Hendrickson hatch happening over on French Creek. He was excited to visit the hidden pool where so many happy memories had been born. Surely, a bit of joy from summers past still lingered there?

His canoe slid over the soft, new grass of early spring, then it scraped over a bit of sand on the beach, as he dragged it toward the lake. It seemed a bit heavier than it used to. But so did the rest of life. This thing with Jane—her cancer, and surgery, and now the distance between them—it was all so overwhelming. The hip seemed like a big deal at first. Now it was just fine again, but it was a harbinger of things to come. That terrible moment in the doctor's office when they'd first been told about Jane's cancer—that was bad. Really bad. But the night that Jane told him about her lover—that was when he'd lost his way. He'd never imagined that his *past* could change and that his Jane could be taken away.

Matt put several large pieces of firewood in the bow of the canoe in order to balance the weight, set his fly rod next to the pieces of oak, and shoved off for the trip to French Creek. He'd needed a jacket to cut the breeze when he first started out, but after paddling for a hundred yards or so he took it off. The lake was fairly calm, the water was clear, and he'd get a workout on the way.

This return to a happy place would be good for his soul, he thought, as each stroke of his canoe paddle drove him out onto the open water. This was a place where the world made sense, and he was safe. This place would drive the crazy thoughts from his head and help him find his way up out of the rabbit hole.

As Matt plunged his canoe paddle into the cold water of Scotch Lake, several strokes on one side, then several on the other side, he began to wonder what John was doing that afternoon. No doubt he was ramming around on some lake in the flashy purple Ranger fishing boat he'd bought from Ron Hested. John loved big boats and big fish and big lakes; he was almost certainly up on Rainy Lake, or maybe on Leech Lake, fishing for walleyes.

The gurgling sound of rushing water in the small rapids at the mouth of French Creek offered a pleasant greeting. Matt tied his canoe to the same tree he always did, and he set out for his favorite pool. Later in summer, when the forest canopy was green and lush, the trail leading to the pool would be dark and shrouded by thick green oak and maple leaves and cedar boughs. Today, the trail was bright and sunlit. The limbs of still-slumbering hardwoods looked naked against the bright blue sky, and the warm sunshine felt good on his back.

When he reached the little pool he'd been dreaming of, the bare limbs of the hardwoods were letting sunlight stream into what was supposed to be a dark and silent sanctuary. The deep greens and blues of a midsummer evening were still a few weeks away. Riffles at the head and tail of the pool sparkled in the sunlight, and a soft breeze whispered through trees that should have cloistered this place. The last remaining red oak leaves fluttered down through the bright sunlight, onto the surface of the creek, and were carried away by a gurgling current.

He preferred the dark and cloistered feel of the place in midsummer. But today the hint of better days was in the air, and that was so fine.

Matt sat down on a familiar rock at the head of the pool and looked around. There *were* a few Hendricksons, or *Ephemerella subvaria*, in the air. Hendricksons, medium-sized light gray mayflies, began their life cycle by hatching from streambeds in April and May. The Hendrickson hatches on French Creek were never heavy; they never filled the air in swarms, like the caddis hatches that came later in the season. But at least they made him feel welcome, like he'd come back to a happy place where he was always welcome.

Matt tied on a size 14 Hendrickson and made a few casts. Several trout rose to his fly, but only smacked it with a bump of their snout. When he was younger, he thought these fish were just missing his fly, but an old-timer, watching him from the bank while the same thing was happening many years before, had said, "They don't miss your fly, kid; they just don't want what you've got." He couldn't help but remember deep wrinkles and the gravelly voice of the old man, or the way he smiled when Matt changed flies and started catching fish. Matt reeled in, stowed his fly rod under his arm, and began poking through a weathered fly box in search of a fly designed to imitate a different stage in the Hendrickson life cycle.

A cloud passed in front of the sun while he was searching for a Hendrickson nymph, and a fish made a splashy rise by the riverbank. Naturally, Matt looked over there to see what had happened, and while he was watching, another snout appeared and snatched a fly from the surface. When he took a moment to look more closely at the surface of the water, and the air above the riffle at the head of the pool, he recognized what was happening. "Hmm . . . Baetis! There's Baetis hatch," he mumbled to himself. The mayflies in the air were tiny. Fishermen called them Baetis, or blue-winged olives, because of their color. There are many species of Baetis, but Matt never cared too much about precise taxonomy. He didn't know the exact Latin name for these particular blue-winged olives, but he'd tied dozens of flies to imitate the various stages of the Baetis life cycle, and the flies were all lined up like little soldiers in his fly box.

There were scattered fish rising all around him, but most of the bigger ones were lined up along the far bank, under some bushes that had grown out over the water. This was perfect, he thought, as he tied a tiny blue-green wisp of fur and feather onto his line. The fish he wanted to catch would require some skill. He crouched as he made a slow approach to the bank, and when he was close enough he waited until a hungry trout slurped a snack from the water's surface. Matt made a few careful false casts and then let his fly flutter to water. He'd put it exactly where he'd planned, and it looked like all the other Baetis flies on the water as it drifted. His fly had only moved about two feet downstream when a trout struck with a boil. Matt set the hook and felt a head shake at the other end.

This was medicine. Matt Kingston understood the way of *this* world. He'd done a difficult thing, and he'd done it well. He had a place here.

He caught fish for several hours. He caught them with different-size flies, and flies designed to imitate other flies that were about. He caught fish in the riffle above the pool, and the one below it. And when he was sated, he sat down on the bank with his boots in the water and poured himself a cup of coffee from the small thermos he carried in his backpack. His toes, even inside his waders and wader boots, were cold, but the hot coffee warmed the rest of him. He was happy, as happy as he could be these days.

He reached for the cell phone in his pocket, and with his elbows resting on his knees, he stared at the phone for a moment, and then made a call.

"What's wrong?" Mo said when she answered. "Is Jane all right?"

"It's nice to hear your voice, too," Matt said. "I just called to say hi."

"Oh, OK, good," Mo said. "I just thought . . ."

"I understand." Matt could feel a smile spreading across his face. He'd been texting back and forth with Mo for months, but he'd never called her until today. The texts had begun when Matt and Jane were at the Mayo Clinic, and then grown more frequent after. Mo sent photos and stories about her kids and her grandchildren, and her job. Matt replied with photos and anecdotes about John Velde, or Jane, or his frustrations at work. They wrote to each other about books they'd read, or movies they'd seen. Over the weeks and months, they'd opened up, or maybe picked up where they'd left off forty-some years earlier, and shared their feelings about God, and life, and work, and family. Occasionally one of them would ask the other if they remembered something that happened in school, or at a dance, or on a date, back in Sverdrup. They'd begun to joke about their "penpalmanship." They sent texts and emails back and forth every few days, and their conversations had grown more intimate as the weeks passed.

"I know . . ." Matt stammered, "I know we never actually talk. But today I guess I really wanted to hear a friendly voice. I hope you don't think I'm a creeper, calling you like this."

"Are you OK?" Mo asked. There had been noise and commotion in the background on Mo's end of the phone call when she first answered. It was quiet now.

"Yeah, I'm good. I'm just sitting by a little trout stream. What are *you* doing?"

"Cleaning the garage."

"So, I'm not interrupting anything?" Matt asked. "It's getting late on a Saturday afternoon. I thought maybe you'd be wearing a long black dress and some diamonds, getting ready to go out."

"Not hardly. I'm wearing rubber boots and using a garden hose to wash away spider webs and mouse turds from the dark recesses of the garage. It's like an archaeological dig in here; the closer I get to the back wall, the older the relics I come across. And John is away at a golf weekend with his buddies. I was about ready to quit for the day, anyway. I'm glad you called; you saved me."

"So it's OK to chat for a few minutes?" Matt asked.

"Don't be an idiot. Of course it's OK. What's up? I can hear something in your voice."

"Oh, I get a little *down* sometimes, since Jane got sick. But I'm having a good day today and I thought I'd call you. 'Zat make sense?"

"But she's OK? No cancer?"

"Yeah, that's what they tell us." Matt shuffled his boots around in the shallow water. He had no idea about the neighborhood where Mo lived, or what her home looked like. Nonetheless, he could see her at this moment, wearing old blue jeans and boots and sitting on a box in her garage, smiling as she spoke to him.

She was still his friend, maybe the only person who could understand what was troubling him, and he wanted to open up and tell her. He knew she'd listen, but the things he wanted to tell her about were pretty personal. Maybe too personal.

"What's wrong, Matt? The truth. I know you're not telling me something," Mo said.

"Well . . ." Matt sighed, and then shifted his boots in the shallow water by the stream bank.

"Are *you* OK?" Mo asked.

"Yeah, I'm fine. I'm just trying to decide where to start, or if I want to start at all," he said.

"You don't have to tell me anything. It's OK. But I'll always be here when you need a friend."

"Ah, Mo, you were my *best* friend for a while there, a long time ago, and strange as it seems, it feels like you're the only person I can talk to now. It's funny, isn't it, that our lives came back together again, now?"

"Things happen for a reason," Mo said. "My dad always said that people come into our lives for a season, a reason, or a lifetime."

Her words settled over him like a warm blanket, just like they had on the day of Alvie's funeral, and the day she'd talked to him and touched him, back at the little bar in Rochester when the nurse called to give him the good news about Jane's surgery. She'd always been that kind of friend.

"My Jane isn't the same person as before," Matt began. "I think her relationship with everyone *else* seems to be the same. But with *me*—it's like she's done with me, or afraid of me."

"Really?"

"Yeah, always before this when we had a problem, or a fight, or maybe we just needed to regroup, we had sex to bring us together."

"Make-up sex is always nice," Mo offered.

"Ooh . . ." Matt cringed, "it's *so* odd to talk to you about stuff like this. You're gonna think I'm a creeper."

Mo giggled. "Yeah, it does feel kinda strange."

"Well, anyway, I don't think it was the sex, as much as it was the close-ness, the touching, the laughter, the little things we said to each other, and the quiet moments that go along with sex. Those are the things that established a connection between us that was so good, and so special, and so powerful. Before this cancer came along, Jane used to sidle up next to me and stand close, or come and sit by me on the couch, and then . . ." Matt stopped and considered whether to say the words on the tip of his tongue, ". . . it was like a little switch got turned, and we both just, came together." Matt stopped again.

"Yeah, I know how that works," Mo said, to help him along.

"Back at the U, when we first met; we used to ride a city bus back to my apartment after class, and the instant we got in the door we looked like a couple hockey players fighting, each of us trying to pull the other one's shirt over their head."

Mo smiled, and covered her smile with her hand, even though Matt couldn't see her over the phone.

"Too much information?" Matt asked.

"No," Mo said, and Matt heard a little giggle in her voice again.

"So how do we maintain that great connection if the thing that brings it to us is lost?"

"What do you mean?"

"I mean that every time I kiss her, or stand close to her, or touch her, and try to turn that little switch on again, she turns away or gets angry, or pretends not to notice me. Or worse yet; maybe she actually *doesn't* notice me like she used to." There was a new intensity in Matt's voice that had not been there earlier.

"I feel bad for you," Mo said softly. "But you must remember that postmenopausal women sorta lose interest in sex anyway, that's normal.

I'm no different, Matt, I don't look forward to it like I once did. If I was told that I could never have sex with my husband again, I'd be OK with that. And then when you understand that Jane's still recovering from the cancer, and she's taking a powerful hormone blocker, I mean, that's enough to destroy her libido." From the other end of the phone call, Mo heard only silence. "You still there, Matt?"

"You think I'd hang up on you?" Matt said.

"Well, it just got pretty quiet out there, wherever you are," Mo said.

"This wasn't the conversation I had in mind when I called you. It's really strange, talking to *you* about all of this."

"I'm OK with it. Does it help?"

"There's a lot more," Matt said.

"Oh? OK . . . I'm here, if you want to tell me."

"It might be creepy for you."

"I doubt it. I'm your friend. I was once your best friend. You just said so."

"OK . . ." Matt started and then hesitated for a moment. "A few weeks ago Jane pretty much broke my heart. She told me about her first lover."

"Why would she do that?" Mo asked.

"Um, I asked her." Matt sighed. "I don't know if she understood what was gonna happen. We were sitting on the couch having a glass of wine, and I asked her. I just asked her about her first time, and she told me." Matt stopped and waited for Mo to say something, but when Mo kept silent, he went on. "We were just talking about college days and I guess she decided to tell me. Finally."

"So it was some guy she knew before you?"

"Yeah, a couple years before I came along."

"And that was it? He never showed up later and caused some sort of conflict for Jane?"

"Nope. She's never mentioned him."

"I don't get it, Matt. What's the big deal? Why all the angst and the broken heart?"

"I don't get it either, Mo. Jane and I have been solid; in love from the very first. We were both swept away back when we fell in love, and there's never been a day since then when we weren't in love. Like I said, I just don't get it either. Maybe it was the way she told the story; she seemed like there was some great emotion that went along with it, still. So, I can't help wondering if she's had feelings for him all this time. Maybe it's the fact that she kept it secret for so long. But now the worst part is that I've come up with this vision of how it all happened between Jane and this other guy, and I keep seeing it over and over again. It's a nightmare, all day long."

"Matt, I wish you could let this go, and—"

"There's a bit more," Matt interrupted. "I did some things. After I left Sverdrup, I had a few girlfriends and I took advantage of them. You know how boys will fake love to get sex, and girls will fake sex to get love?"

"I never heard it put that way before, but I understand. Actually, that was a pretty good sentence."

"Yeah, well, I took something from a few girls. I just used 'em and then walked away. I wasn't mean-spirited or anything like that, I just hurt some feelings. I didn't think about anyone but me. But then John told me that he'd met one of them about a year ago, and she told him that I broke her heart. I feel terrible about it."

"How in the world would this woman ever confide something like *that* to John Velde?" Mo asked.

"Long story. Just a chance meeting, and she found out that he knew me, and she just said something in passing. Just one of those things, I guess."

"OK, Matt, but so what? A lot of boys do that to girls. It's the thing that our mothers warn us about. It happens. You remember what you and I did—"

"She died a while back," Matt interrupted. "Now I'll never know, and I'll never be able to atone for it."

"All right Matt, I'm beginning to see things," Mo said. "I remember when we were together on the day of Jane's first surgery you talked of a contrapasso, a punishment for you. You still think like that, don't you?"

"Well, it's . . . yeah, I *do* think about that," Matt admitted.

"God doesn't work like that. Do you really think this is your contrapasso? Your punishment for what you did to some girls in college?"

"Seems like it."

"You don't think Jane just simply gave up a forty-year-old secret that she doesn't value anymore? A secret that means nothing to her?" Mo asked.

"Not sure what I think anymore, Mo. The future looks pretty shaky, and the past, the past that I always thought was rock solid, now seems to be gone away. And that past was so sweet. My Jane seems lost. I'm lost. Sometimes I just wish I was dead."

"I wish you wouldn't say that. You should talk to a doctor, and to Jane."

"I do talk to Jane, but I think she knows that what she told me really hurt, and now she's just trying keep the rest of it to herself and stick to her story about how it was just a one-time deal and it never mattered."

"I don't know what to tell you, Matt, but from where I sit I'd bet that's the truth."

"Can I still talk with *you* from time to time?" Matt asked.

"Sure you can, old friend. Any time."

"Thanks, Mo."

"Matt, does Jane know about you and me?" Mo asked.

"I've talked about you, and your brothers, and your dad, and my school days."

"That's not what I'm asking. Does she know about *us*?"

"Not really. Why?"

"Just curious."

"OK, Mo, now you tell me something about John, your husband. Have you two ever talked about stuff like this? Does *he* know about us?"

"We work together very well, John and me, and I respect him."

Matt waited for more. But that was all Mo had to say. It was an odd answer, Matt thought, and it was a bit of a conversation stopper. 'We work well together' and 'I respect him'? That didn't sound right. He'd opened up and told her everything. Then he'd given her a chance to talk about her love for her husband, just as he'd done about his wife. But Mo was not about to share anything. Now what should he say?

"Mo, I—"

"We're just different than you and Jane," Mo said, and Matt knew that was all she had to say about that.

So, Matt thought, what did *that* mean? Her answer about her husband made Matt feel bad. Was she in an unhappy marriage? Or was she just unwilling to go out on a limb and open up as he'd done? Ever since they'd reconnected, Matt had assumed that Mo saw the world about the same way he did, that her life experience was much the same as his, and that Mo was so happy and stable that she'd be the one for him to confide in. Maybe he'd told her too much?

He'd been staring at his feet and kicking little stones in the streambed for the entire conversation with Mo, and now it seemed like Mo had decided to stop things. He looked up, across the creek, and saw that evening shadows would soon stretch over the water. "Hey, Mo, I guess I should let you go. What do you have planned for tonight?"

"Gonna finish up in the garage and then curl up with a glass of wine and a good book. How 'bout you?"

"Mmm, tie some flies, watch a ball game . . . I dunno."

It was time for this conversation to be over, and Matt tried to end it. "Well, Mo, I'm sure you have more work to do, and I have a long paddle home, so—"

"There is no contrapasso, Matt. It doesn't work like that," Mo blurted.

"I'm just trying to find my way, Mo. Maybe I can leave the past in the past, and move on."

"That won't work either, Matt. The past is never in the past. It's what created us and made us who we are. It's always with us. The past is who we are."

"I don't think I want that to be true."

"Maybe the bad things you did are what made you a good man. Maybe Jane's thing with that other guy is what set her off in search of you. Maybe it was a good thing for you. Remember, things happen for a reason."

"That's a lot to think about, Mo."

"Well, think about it, old friend. Maybe we'll talk again?"

"Yup," Matt said, and the call was over.

CHAPTER FORTY-ONE

A hummingbird appeared at the birdfeeder just outside the window of the great room. Matt stared as he nursed his first cup of coffee. His brain was stuck in neutral, dealing simply with the rich smell of hot coffee while he looked out at the absolute calm on the glassy surface of Scotch Lake. For now, the woods and the lake were shrouded in gray overcast, as if something in the heavy morning air would not allow even a leaf to move. Only the far-off call of a loon broke the silence from time to time. A breeze would pick up in a while and stir the quiet lake, and the sun would eventually burn away the morning overcast. Then he'd go to work and do the best he could to get on with things.

Jane shuffled into the room a moment later. She wore a maroon terry-cloth bathrobe and pink slippers, and she was blowing on her coffee when she passed behind Matt and softly ran her hand through his hair. She sat down beside him on the couch and took his free hand in hers.

Several minutes passed, and then Jane reached over and touched the whisker stubble on his cheek.

"What are you thinking about?" Matt asked.

"The future . . . just wondering about the cancer, and if I'll ever get to see my grandchildren."

"Of course you will."

"What are *you* thinking about?" Jane asked.

"Mmm, nothing really . . . work, I guess," he lied. He was thinking of the thing that never left him alone. He wished that Jane would just figure it all out and then explain it away. "I gotta get ready for work," Matt said as he stood up. Then he stopped and looked down at her. "I love you more now than ever." He bent down and kissed her.

While Matt showered and dressed for another day at the office, he tried to prepare himself for the things he had to do at work, but only one thought played in his head, over and over again.

He was about to take his car keys off the kitchen countertop when Jane positioned herself in front of the kitchen door and blocked his exit. She wasn't about to let him go to work without a hug.

He smiled, as best he could, when he realized what she was doing. Then he walked into her embrace and held her close.

"I love you," Jane whispered.

"I love you, too." Matt moved his hands over her back for a moment, and then held her tight.

"Are you OK?" Jane whispered. She knew something was wrong. She'd seen it in his eyes earlier.

No answer came.

"Are you OK?" she said again. Then, as she held him, she felt something catch in his chest, and she heard him sniffle. He squeezed her, and she heard a small cry in his throat, then a louder one.

"Ah . . ." Matt felt his insides begin to implode. "Ah . . ." He tried to hold on. "Ah . . ." But a wretched cry that he couldn't hold back found its way up from his chest. Another moan rose up, then another, each one worse than the one before it, and then they came in a torrent. He sobbed and cried out in pain, over and over again. Jane hadn't seen him do anything like this since his father passed away, and she knew that all she could was hold him.

"This is all about me, isn't it?" she asked when the cries subsided.

"Yeah, I think so," Matt said into her ear.

"I'm gonna be OK. The cancer is gone. What's the matter?"

Matt made no reply.

"It's what I told you, isn't it? I never should have told you."

"It's gonna take a while for me to get my mind around it," Matt said, and the tears came again.

"It doesn't change anything, Matt. It happened two years before I met you. I chose *you*. I love *you*," Jane said, and she gently shook him.

This little scene in the kitchen was taking on the same feel as the night when she'd first told him. He knew Jane very well, and he felt a strong sense that she was still holding something back.

"Matt, is this just the old double standard thing? It was OK for *you* to have other girlfriends, but not me?"

"Yeah, maybe." Matt sighed and tried to push the feelings that grabbed at his throat back into his chest. "I wonder about that, too, but I don't think it's like that," he said slowly, as if he was trying to explain something to himself. "I suspected, no, I knew all along, I mean, you were twenty-two years old, and a senior in college when I met you, and knew you hadn't been just sitting around waiting for me to come along." Once again, he lowered his head and dissolved in his tears.

"Oh, honey." Jane reached an arm around him. "I *told* you; everything about that experience was awkward and uncomfortable. I never should have told you. I'm so sorry."

Matt sat still and tried to stifle the sobs in his chest for a minute. "Yeah, but Jane, something in that just doesn't ring true. That's just not *you*. The Jane Monahan I knew would never have done that . . . not like you told it. There has to be more to the story. *Were* you in love with him, or what?"

After a short hesitation, Jane shook her head and said, "No. Did *you* do things that made no sense when you were nineteen?" No reply was necessary, because she already knew about many of the senseless things he'd done. She waited for a second and then added, "I told you, no, I didn't love him. I don't know why I did it. It wasn't one of my finer moments; I was *nineteen*."

Jane stood firm with her arms around Matt. She'd never seen him like this. He was lost, broken. She waited for her Matt to reappear, because her Matt Kingston was indestructible. But the longer she studied his vacant countenance, the more she feared that something inside Matt was seriously injured. She slid closer and began to cry herself. "I'm so sorry, Matt. I never should have told you." Her words of apology made him feel weaker; she was apologizing for the truth as if he was a child who needed to be protected from it.

"I don't get it, either, Jane. I know it's irrational. I don't want to feel like this."

Jane put her hands on his arms and shook him gently while she spoke. "It was over forty years ago. I never think about him and I never had feelings for him. It was two years before I ever heard your name. Everything about it was bad." She shook him a bit harder, for emphasis, and said, "I chose *you*. I love *you*."

"I'm sorry, honey."

"You need to talk to somebody," Jane said.

"You mean, like a shrink?"

"Yes. I think you should call Ron Hested."

"Ron? Really?"

"Yes. Everyone says he's really good. And I know he likes you."

"I know, but . . . it's just . . . I'll be fine," Matt stammered.

"You're not fine. Call him! Today."

"But Ron . . ."

"Well, call someone else, then, but talk to somebody," Jane pleaded.

"We'll talk later." Matt walked out the door.

"I love you!" Jane called after him.

CHAPTER FORTY-TWO

——•——

"OK, Ed, we've gone over this before, but I'll explain everything again as we do this today," Matt said, as he wrapped a latex strap around the right arm of Father Ed Willet, the Catholic priest in Pine Rapids.

"Things have certainly changed in dentistry since I was a boy," Father Willet said. "I still remember the little spittoon, or that toilet bowl that my dentist had when I was a kid. It was right there so I could just spit whenever I wanted."

"Yeah, you won't find one of those anymore," Matt said, as he tightened the latex strap and tied it off. "You know, I'm old enough that I was taught how to do gold foils in school. You know, where the dentist uses a little hammer to pound pure gold into your tooth? That's quite a change from the computer-generated crowns and dental implants, like we're gonna do today."

"You know what the dentist says when he makes a mistake, don't you?" Father Willet asked.

"No, what?" Matt waited for the priest to deliver a punch line he'd heard a hundred times.

"Rinse!" The priest chuckled at his own joke.

"Good one," Matt said. "Are you ready to get going, Ed?"

"Yup."

"OK, it's pretty simple. I'm gonna draw some blood from your arm, and then put it in a centrifuge, a machine that will spin the blood until it separates into its various components." Matt introduced a needle into a vein in Father Willet's arm, and a line of red blood began to flow though the clear plastic hose and into a tube. "We're gonna use the part called platelet-rich fibrin; it looks like a booger, actually. Anyway, we'll mix that booger with some stuff we call bone putty and put it right back into that socket after we remove your tooth. That stuff we put back into the socket will generate the growth of new bone in a few months and then we'll

460

come back and put an implant in there to replace the broken tooth that brought you in here." Matt smiled at the priest and let the blood flow until he'd filled four test tubes. As he watched the blood flow steadily, he glanced up and made eye contact with the priest.

Matt smiled and Father Willet said, "Can't feel a thing! That's not like the old days, either!"

"Good," Matt replied. But watching the blood flow so easily also let a grim idea flow into Matt's head. The idea had come to him several other times, always at this very moment, but today, for the first time, it had weight. He withdrew the needle from Father Willet's arm and told him to hold a small piece of cotton over the tiny puncture wound for a couple of minutes.

"I'll be back in a couple minutes." Matt stood up and carried the four test tubes of blood back to his laboratory.

All the while that Matt ran the centrifuge, and then finished the procedure with Father Willet, he thought of that stream of blood flowing painlessly through the plastic tube.

When he was finished with Father Willet's bone-grafting procedure, he went directly to his private office and made a phone call. When a voice picked up on the other end of the line, he said, "This is Matt Kingston and I need to make an appointment to see Dr. Hested. As soon as possible."

———————

Matt was the only person in the waiting area as he filled out the questionnaire that Ron Hested's secretary had given him. Besides the usual stuff—contact information and medical history—there were three pages of questions that were obviously designed to give Ron a quick assessment of just how crazy the people in his waiting room were. When he was finished with the registration procedure, he returned the clipboard to one of the secretaries at the front desk and then took a seat in the waiting area. As he looked around, he was surprised at the number of children's books and toys.

He'd tried to resist Jane's plea that he get some help. But his demons never left him alone anymore, at least never for more than a few hours. He didn't sleep well, with or without alcohol, and was losing interest in all the things he used to enjoy. And now there was a new, darker thought that troubled him: The image of blood flowing steadily, painlessly out of Father Willet's arm never left him. He was ready to talk. Probably.

He wondered what this next hour would be like. He assumed that Ron would listen to him for a while, and then say a few things that were brilliant, and then all of the shit that was making him crazy would go away. Just like in the movies.

"You may go in to see the doctor now," the receptionist said, and Matt realized that he'd been staring at an old newspaper while he tried to imagine what was about to happen.

Ron was seated in one of the overstuffed chairs that Matt remembered from the day Ron had told him about his hip—his only other visit to this room. "Hi, Matt," Ron said, and he stood up and shook Matt's hand.

"Don't you have a couch for me to lie on?" Matt asked.

"Sorry, but no. Come in and have a seat. So, why are you here, Matt?"

"I think you already know, Ron. I'm struggling with something. And I didn't know if I should talk to you . . . you know, because we know each other so well. I thought maybe you wouldn't want to see me. So thanks for staying late today."

"No problem. When I heard that you'd called I told Amy to get you in here at the end of the day. I'll always make time for you. And I'll let you know if our previous relationship, our friendship, is a problem, after we get started. If I feel I should refer you to someone else, I will. But first I need to tell you about the questions you answered while you were in the waiting room."

"I'm crazy?" Matt tried to joke.

"Well, your answers indicate that you're dealing with moderate to severe depression, and severe anxiety," Ron replied, with no trace of humor. "I have to ask you if you're thinking of hurting yourself." He locked eyes with Matt and waited for a reply.

"Depression and anxiety? Severe?"

"Do you think about hurting yourself?" Ron asked once more.

"No," Matt lied. "Of course not."

"OK, Matt, obviously there's a lot going on in your head. So back up and tell me what's happened."

Matt had already said more than he'd thought he could, or would. But a moment earlier, when he'd heard himself lie about thoughts of taking his own life, he'd felt something shift inside. Maybe he should open up with Ron. But it was scary. It seemed as if he'd skied to the edge of a mountain and was looking down, between his skis, at all the danger in front of him down there. He had to decide, in the next few seconds, if he was ready to step off, or stuff everything back inside once again, keep that stiff upper lip, and back away from the edge.

It looked like a long fall down that mountain in front of him, and he was terrified to think how far he might tumble, or how it would feel. He knew if he took just one little step out there over the edge he'd be on his way, and unable to get back to the top. He decided to start talking, just a little; inch himself a bit closer to the edge, and then see if he really wanted to step off. He waited for the words to come, but they stuck in his throat.

"Can you tell me about it, Matt?" Ron asked.

"Yeah, I think so, but gimme just a minute." Matt knew he had to tell the story, but he didn't want to. "A few weeks ago . . ." Matt stopped and looked away. "Jesus, Ron, I don't wanna talk about this shit."

Ron waited with his legs crossed but said nothing.

Matt rubbed his forehead and thought for a moment before he went on. "Jane and I were just sitting on the couch. It was nice, real nice, and I thought that maybe things were about to get back like they used to be." Matt paused and blew his nose. "So, I asked her about her first time; sex, you know. I'd asked her a hundred times through the years and she always said it was me. It had become sort of a standing joke. Well, I knew she was pretty innocent, naïve, inexperienced, when we met?" Matt shrugged. "But I was pretty sure there had been somebody. We'd sorta joked about it forever, and she'd always just smiled and said it was me." Matt swallowed hard. "But that night . . . she told me. Everything. Well, now I really don't know if she told me everything."

Ron waited and watched while Matt stared at his lap and recalled the moment.

"But what she told me . . ." His chest began to heave. Then mournful cries came from deep inside, and he was swept away. All he could do was try to keep his cries quiet so the receptionist in the outer office didn't hear. Ron stood up and got the box of tissues off his desk and gave it to Matt. Then he watched Matt crumble and weep, and tumble down the mountain for several minutes.

Matt's face was still contorted when he cleared his throat, blew his nose, and then wiped his eyes dry. He began to tell Ron the story that Jane had shared with him, and he shook his head as he remembered. He was talking to himself as much as he was telling the story to Ron. When he was finished, he turned to Ron and said, "And you know what? It was pretty much what I'd always thought. That's the strange part. But it was a guy that I'd never heard of, not one of the guys that I'd heard her talk about from time to time, like everyone talks about someone they used to date. And I just knew that she'd never told me because she'd always harbored feelings for him and then married me because he wouldn't have her. It hit me like a hammer, right in the chest. At first, I tried to act like it was no big surprise, and it didn't bother me. It actually shouldn't have bothered me, because I knew better. But Jesus, after a couple hours of thinking about it, hearing her say the words over and over again in my head, I could hardly breathe, and I couldn't stop seeing it in my head. I still can't. I feel like she's been thinking of that other guy for all these years." He turned to Ron and his eyes begged for an explanation.

"Keep talking, Matt. Tell me more about the last thing that you said."

"You mean that I feel like she's been thinking of this other guy for all these years?"

"Yes, that."

"It's awful. Terrible." Matt closed his eyes. "And when I think about all this, and I see this vision—my Jane with this other guy—I feel as though she loves him, and not me, and it's always been that way, and when they had sex he was better than me, and when she closes her eyes at night she thinks of him, and she always has . . . like she had a connection him that was better than ours."

"Has she ever spoken of him in that way?"

"No."

"Has she ever spoken of him at all?"

"No."

"Has she ever done anything to cause you to suspect that she has feelings for that guy, or anyone else?"

"No."

"How is your sex life now?"

Matt drew in a long, deep breath. "Well, that's not so good. I guess the cancer and the surgery really changed the way she looks at herself. She says she doesn't feel very sexy. And then she's taking this hormone blocker as a precaution to prevent a recurrence of the cancer, and that's pretty much destroyed her libido." Matt shook his head and added, "But what are you gonna do . . ."

"Has any of this changed the way you feel toward Jane?" Ron asked.

"I love her more than ever, Ron. More every day. But I feel like I've lost her."

Matt's face twisted once more, and he struggled to keep going. "I love my Jane." His chin began to quiver but he didn't lose control. "We always hold hands when we get in bed, while we wait to go to sleep. We always have . . ." Matt had to stop and swallow; he was teetering on the edge again. "We just hold hands until one of us goes to sleep and turns away from the other. But now . . . I never go to sleep. And when Jane lets go of my hand I just want to cry. It feels like she's letting me go." His chest heaved again, and he tumbled still farther down the mountain.

"I need to be her *hero*," Matt said when he was able speak again. But when he said the word "hero" his eyes clamped shut and his throat clutched again. "I tried to live my whole life, just so she'd see me like that. I need to be the guy who rides in on a big white horse and saves her. I need to be that guy." He blew his nose and wept again while he wiped his own tears away and fought to stop crying. "When I close my eyes, I can see her as she was then; smiling, and tan, and wearing green shorts and a yellow T-shirt. She was so pretty." Matt had to stop and gather himself yet again. "I remember the way she looked at me, too. I could see it in her eyes, that she wanted to reach out and pull me close. And I remember the way she did just that. I can still see her, walking toward me on a warm summer afternoon, and I can see her smiling at me. Am I talking too much?"

"You're doing fine."

His breathing was steadier now, and the words began to come easier. Matt drew in a huge breath, and went on. "That first summer we were together? I remember lying in bed, under the covers, with the lights out, waiting for her to come to me." Matt smiled when he looked at his hands and relived the moment. "She would turn the lights out when she slipped out of her clothes, but she couldn't turn out the streetlights outside my window, so I could see plenty while she lifted the covers and came to me."

"That's nice, Matt. What a sweet memory," Ron said. "And it's about what I'd expect from you."

Matt nodded and wiped his eyes dry again. "And then I see her as she lay on that hospital bed, after surgery, too. God, Ron, I thought she was dead. And I see her scars, and I see the way she *doesn't* look at me anymore. We used to have this great connection, but now it feels like she doesn't even love me; like she doesn't care."

Ron waited for almost a minute to let Matt's words settle around them.

"Matt, I've known you and Jane for most of your lives, and I must tell you that from where I stand it appears that that's exactly the way she sees you—as her hero—and she always has."

"I always felt that way, too. But now, not so much," Matt said. "All I want is to have our connection back, but it keeps slipping further away, and I want to die when my demons come to me at night and show her to me with someone else, and they tell me that she had a connection with *him*, and that connection was deeper and better than *our* connection." Matt wiped his eyes and added, "I have the same nightmare every time I close my eyes."

"I'd like you to begin taking an antidepressant. It'll take away the lows. It won't affect your thinking at work, but it may have an effect on your sex life. It's called—"

"No," Matt interrupted. "I know how it works, Ron. It may take away the lows, but it'll take away the highs, too, and I won't do that. I don't want to miss the highs; I have to feel them. And I don't need anything that'll make me even *more* impotent."

"Oh, so there's a bit more to this," Ron said, seizing on Matt's last comment. "Tell me about the impotence."

"It was just once. A short time ago. Actually, it was our first try since all this other stuff happened."

"Keep going."

"Everything was fine at the beginning. And then it wasn't. That's never happened before. I was really embarrassed. Ashamed. It was like standing over a three-foot putt that I'd made a thousand times. But then I started thinking about it, and I couldn't do it. I'm not even a man anymore."

"All right, there's a lot going on here, Matt." Ron leaned back in his chair, closed the tablet of notes he'd been taking, then took a deep breath while he collected his thoughts. "Before I respond, or give you any sort of diagnosis, let me ask you: When did you begin to feel . . . troubled? When did all of this start?"

"When Jane told me about her first lover."

"That's what I thought you'd say." Ron pursed his lips and nodded. "But I've seen this coming for a long time, Matt. A long time before that."

"Why didn't you say something? Why didn't you tell me?"

"I tried, Matt. But you wouldn't hear it. You were so determined to keep that stiff upper lip and forge ahead. You always talked about being strong, and staying the course. I think this has its roots in her cancer, and before that."

"Oh?"

"I want you to think about your past few months, before the cancer and after it," Ron said. "You were healthy and strong your entire life, then you begin to struggle with this serious pain in your hip. I'm sure you know that long-term physical pain can leave a person weak, and open to serious psychological problems. So then you're told you need to replace a hip, which I know you viewed as an old man's problem. In addition to that, I know you really *are* dealing with aging. You're what, sixty-three now?"

"Yes."

"Things don't work as well as they used to, right? Your eyes, your ears?"

"Yes."

"And some things hurt that didn't used to hurt, right? Your hands, your feet, your knees?"

"Yes."

"And then there's this thing with the death and aging of some old friends. Also, Jane mentioned to me a while back that your family farm, the place where you grew up, had been bulldozed away. The happiest, safest place from your childhood has vanished?"

Matt nodded his agreement again.

"OK, so all this stuff is sort of churning, just off the radar, and suddenly your beautiful wife gets cancer, and has this dreadful surgery, and your relationship with Jane, the most precious thing in your life, changes. In addition to that, there is a very real fear that you could lose Jane; she might die. And then Vicky Velde, a friend from your childhood, dies." Ron made sure that Matt was looking into his eyes, and then he said, "You've had a few patients, longtime friends, pass away recently, too. Right?"

Matt nodded.

"And your boys have grown up and left you not so long ago, right?"

Matt nodded.

"So here it goes, Matt. Are you familiar with the idea of a perfect storm, like in the movie? You know, several large storms colliding to make a huge, devastating, once-in-a-lifetime storm?"

"Sure," Matt said. "Jane and I refer to our favorite fishing spot as the Flemish Cap, from the movie, *The Perfect Storm*."

"Do you see the winds of a perfect storm converging on you?"

"Never thought about it."

"Well, think about it. Any one of those things might be enough to break some men, but all of these things at the same time; *that's* a perfect storm, and you were in its path. You were like a fighter who'd taken a few good shots and was already woozy. All it took to send you into the maelstrom was this revelation from Jane, which wasn't actually much of a revelation."

"But it's so *real*, Ron, and so powerful. I can *see* it. I can see it all. I can hardly breathe when my demons come and show it all to me. And it seems like it happened yesterday, not forty years ago."

"OK, you have two things working there, Matt. One is that during a crisis, like this, time is compressed. There is no such thing as a long time ago for you; everything is *right now*, and you can't perceive things in their proper place in time. Something that happened forty years ago, and is of no consequence anymore, will seem *very* important, and be compressed into your *now*. To you, it did happen yesterday. Understand?"

"Sure do."

"The other thing is that your limbic system, the part of your brain that deals with the fight-or-flight response, takes over. The limbic system deals only in emotion: fear, anger, whatever. It's what causes you to take immediate and drastic action when you're threatened, in order to survive. All of these events began to circle around you at roughly the same time, and you kept a stiff upper lip, like you always do. But when Jane shared that one *last* thing with you, that was all you could bear. It was as if you were in a dark room, already afraid, and someone hollered BOO! You were instantly terrified. And at that point, powerful emotions will always overrule the things we know to be facts. What you understand intellectually is never as powerful as your emotions."

"OK, I think I understand all that, Ron. I think. But I don't feel any better. In fact, now that I've been talking about it all, I feel worse."

"Well, we had to *start* here, so let me go over this once again, Matt. Jane had no idea of the perfect storm swirling about you, so when you asked her a question, I think she simply gave up a forty-year-old secret that she thought no longer had any value. But you, well, you were already dealing with the very *real* possibility of losing her to cancer, and then suddenly the not-so-real, but very troubling fear of losing her to another lover. This fear, no matter how unrealistic, was the proverbial straw that broke the camel's back. The loving and powerful connection you'd always felt with Jane seemed lost; there was no safe ground for you, anywhere. Then, to add insult to injury, literally, you failed at sex. That's powerful bad medicine, Matt. A man's sexuality is a large part of how he sees himself, defines himself. Issues like this, involving sexuality, can cause psychological trauma—"

"Tell me about it," Matt interrupted.

"All right, I'm sure you're aware of that," Ron said. "And I think all of this was brought on by your fear of losing Jane. So, listen to me here." Ron stopped for emphasis. "Jane had already dealt with her cancer, and her losses. She'd moved on. But you hadn't, and when all this happened, well, as you like to say, it was down the rabbit hole for you. You said that Jane doesn't seem to care? Well, she doesn't understand. This is *your* problem, not hers. And you're a long way down there, Matt. It's gonna take *time* for you to find your way out. This isn't like a broken arm or leg, where we put a cast on it and then do nothing for a while. This won't heal by resting it. I want to continue to see you in here once a week for a while, and we'll talk. OK?"

Matt reflected for a moment. "That was good, what you just said. It makes sense. But why don't I feel better? Why are all those thoughts still in my head? Why do I still feel like I'm driving the crazy train all over?"

"I told you; this isn't like a broken arm or leg. This won't heal by resting it, or just taking a pill. You've been lugging that crazy train up a mountainside for weeks, no, months. You may be on the downslope now, but that crazy train is driving you, and it will be for a while."

"So how do I get off it?"

"You come in here and talk to me. More. A lot more," Ron said.

"What do I do in the meantime? I thought you were just gonna say something brilliant after I'd been in here for an hour, and then I'd be normal again."

"Sorry, Matt. This is a big deal. It's just going to take time. But you're married to the best person I know. Be with her as much as you can. And I never thought I would say this to someone who was dealing with anxiety and depression, but it would be good for you to spend some time with

Velde, too. I know he makes you laugh." Ron smiled and shook his head. "I can't believe I just told a patient to do *that*."

"Thanks, Ron, but I still feel crazy."

CHAPTER FORTY-THREE

---•---

Timmy, Dave Norman, Bradley Hested, and Mike Katzenmeyer all stood in front of the bakery display case at the Human Bean while they waited for Sally to finish their smoothies on a hot July morning. Business had slowed during the usual mid-morning lull, and only a handful of coffee drinkers were scattered about the coffee shop, reading newspapers and studying their smartphones.

"Let's go down to Catholic Park, by the beach, and try to catch some turtles after this," Timmy said.

"Aw, you just wanna see if the Compton twins are at the beach," Bradley teased in a not-so-quiet tone. "You got a boner for Heather!"

"Shut up!" Timmy hissed, and then he slugged Bradley's arm as he glanced across the counter to see if his grandma gave any sign that she'd heard Bradley.

"Ow," Bradley moaned, but he smiled fiendishly as he rubbed his arm.

"It's too hot to catch turtles. Let's just go swimming," Dave said, as if he hadn't heard any mention of girls.

"I think Whitney is better," Mike opined. "She can run faster."

"I like their older sister better," Bradley said, as he pulled his T-shirt down in a vain attempt to completely cover his belly. "She's gonna be in seventh grade next year, but she's already built like an eighth-grader. She's got boobs already, and—"

"Shut up!" Timmy blurted, and he reached over to cover Bradley's mouth. "My gramma is right over there."

The boys were giggling and scuffling when Sally appeared at the counter with four smoothies and a paper bag filled with pastries. "OK, quiet down, boys," she said. "And take this back by the fireplace and those two couches in the back so you can be away from the other customers. Just be quiet and don't make a mess." She thought for a moment and then added, "And when you're done with treats, let me know where you're going."

"Timmy wants to go and see if Heather is at the beach," Bradley said, as he picked up a smoothie for himself and the entire bag of pastries.

"Shut up!" Timmy hissed, shoving Bradley.

"Just stay back there and don't make too much noise," Sally said. The four boys moved as one, each of them trying to paw open the bag of confections in Bradley's hand as they moved toward the fireplace.

Sally was still watching the boys when a familiar voice brought her attention back to the counter. "Remember when life was that simple?" Jane asked.

"Oh, hi!" Sally said. "Yeah, I remember. And it doesn't sound like things have changed much. You should have heard the conversation here a minute ago: turtles, swimming, girls."

"That's childhood." Jane shrugged and changed the subject. "I'm going in to work late today, really late. I did some work from home this morning and I thought I'd treat myself to coffee with you before I go to my office. Got time to chat? I don't have anything important to discuss, I just thought I'd stop and see if you were waiting for someone to take a break with."

"Sure," Sally said. "It'll give me a chance to keep an eye on those boys, too." She turned to the coffee machine behind her, filled two large cups, and led Jane to a small table. "How are you feeling?" Her question was clearly directed at Jane's cancer, surgery, and recovery.

"Good. Really good," Jane replied.

"Are you gonna participate in that walk to raise money for breast cancer?" Sally asked. She pointed to a small poster someone had taped to the front door of her shop.

Jane pursed her lips and paused, then shook her head. "No, no I'm not." She thought for a moment and then said, "I think that's all good . . ."

"But?" Sally prompted.

"No buts . . ." Jane softened, "but I don't want to wear pink and label myself as a cancer survivor. I just want to move on. I was sick, and now I'm well, pretty much." She shrugged. "Does that sound bad?"

"No," Sally said. "I guess I never thought about it. But now that you put it like that, I don't feel like a chain-saw survivor, or a divorce survivor, just a person with some experience. So yeah, I guess you're about the same."

"Exactly." Jane raised her coffee in a salute. "Ready to get on with whatever comes next."

"Well, you sure look good," Sally said.

Jane sighed. "Oh, my body is changing, and I don't like it." She passed a helpless glance to Sally. "I have a lot of new wrinkles." She pointed to her face and tilted her head in despair. Then she raised one arm and used her other hand to point at her biceps muscle. "See that? My guns? Well, it used to be a gun, now I'm growing a bat wing." With that, Jane wiggled the small bit of flab that hung below her biceps. "Ugh! I think this hormone blocker is turning me into an old man; I'm getting a pot belly, too."

"No, you aren't! C'mon, Jane, you're beautiful . . . you should hear what people say about you."

Jane half-smiled. "The other day I was standing in front of the bathroom mirror, looking at myself and noting all these changes, when Matt stepped out of the shower. He was using a towel to dry himself, but he was looking at himself in the mirror, too. You know how men like to do that?"

"Mm-hmm." Sally smiled.

"Well, Matt was looking at himself for a bit longer than usual, about when he usually announced that he was still 'blue twisted steel.' But this time he sorta moaned, 'Jesus, we gotta put a five-watt bulb in here. I look like shit.'"

"Ah, he looks great, too."

Jane sighed. "We're changing. I don't know if it's just normal aging, or the cancer, or the drugs I'm taking. But I don't like it."

"You're healthy, and—" Sally was cut short by a loud and prolonged outburst of laughter from back by the fireplace. Then another. "That sounded like mischief. S'pose we should go see what it was all about?" she asked Jane.

"Oh yeah! It had a devious ring, didn't it?"

Both women rose from their table and walked slowly along an inside wall, hoping to approach the boys without being noticed. The area around the fireplace was now quiet; too quiet. When they stepped around the corner, Sally's mouth fell open.

Timmy, Dave, Bradley, and Mike had arranged themselves on a couch, on their backs, with their legs in the air, and they were all holding lit matches between their legs. At the instant Sally and Jane stepped close to them, Bradley farted and the match he was holding about an inch from the crotch of his blue jeans ignited in a plume of blue-yellow flame that flashed in a "poof" about the size of a basketball, and the boys exploded in laughter once more.

"What . . . what . . .?" Sally stammered.

"We're lightin' farts, Gramma!" Timmy squealed.

"What . . . where did you . . .?" Sally stumbled again.

Jane took over. "Boys, you can't do that in here. It's gross. If you're gonna do that, you go outside!" Jane didn't seem angry or embarrassed when she added, "On second thought, just go outside and leave the matches here. Just go outside and play."

As the boys filed past, giggling and shoving each other, Sally turned a stunned face to Jane. "Have you seen that before?"

"About a thousand times," Jane said, shaking her head to reveal her own lingering puzzlement at the phenomenon they'd just witnessed. "I don't get it either, but if you're gonna raise boys, you'd better understand: farts are funny." Jane shrugged, then smiled at Sally. "They just are."

"Your boys did that?" Sally asked, as they walked back toward the kitchen.

"Sure, and when they were done, they'd laugh about it some more. For years." Jane's smile widened. "When boys get together it's a certainty that one of them will fart, and then they'll all giggle about the sound, and the stink. They're likely to give it name, too. You know, like a blue dart, or a toad stool, or a freeper. If there are matches around, and no parents, they'll light one up, too."

"Where on earth would Timmy learn to do that?" Sally asked.

"Maybe the school bus, or the playground, or any boy in school who has an older brother."

Sally's eyes were squeezed nearly shut; she was still trying to comprehend what she'd seen. "My God, there was fire way out to Bradley's knees. I've never seen anything like that."

"It's a good thing John isn't here just now," Jane said. "Let's sit down and finish our coffee."

"Why is it good that John isn't here?" Sally asked, when they found their chairs again.

"Oh, he's got this whole shtick he does, I've heard him go over it with my boys. Several times. He just did it again when the boys were home for Christmas last year. He does it every time something like this happens. He thinks it's funny."

"So, tell me," Sally said.

"Well," Jane acquiesced, "he starts out with a stern warning."

"About what?"

"A warning for boys to keep their pants on when they do that," Jane said.

"Huh?"

"*Because* . . ." Jane went on, "two bad things can happen: suckback and bushfire." She waited to see signs of understanding in Sally's eyes, but there was not even a flicker of comprehension.

"C'mon, Sally," Jane urged, but Sally could only stare, and wait for the rest of the explanation.

"OK, I'll spell it out for you," Jane said. "Suckback is no big deal, 'cuz the flame goes, you know, right back up where it came from, and it goes out—no oxygen up there, you know." She shrugged, implying that common sense made no further discussion of suckback necessary.

Sally closed her eyes when she finally understood suckback.

"But a bushfire, well, that can be kinda bad," Jane continued. Her eyes glinted, but she was otherwise able to continue with an academic explanation of the health risks that accompanied fart ignition. "I'm guessing that bushfire won't be a possibility with these boys for a few more years—puberty, you know, but nonetheless—"

"Shut! Up!" Sally commanded with a burst of laughter, then she covered her face with her hands. Through her hands she said, "That's not funny." But she was laughing as she spoke. "Do *you* think that's funny? Lighting farts, I mean?"

"Well, I don't do it myself," Jane said, which created a word picture that Sally also found pretty funny. "But the boys think it is, and I wind up laughing too. Every time," she admitted. "And boys love to describe farts; the big boys do too. Details matter!"

Sally leaned forward, elbows on the table, and listened. Jane spoke with authority, as if she'd done graduate study in the male fascination with flatulence.

"Matt and John both love to tell about some kid on their basketball team who could clear out the gym. Honest to God, to this day Matt goes into hysterics every time John brings it up; he gets tears in his eyes from laughing. 'Course John always finishes the story by stating that the kid's farts sounded like . . ."—Jane used two fingers on each hand to makes air quotes—"like he was sitting in a bathtub, in an inch of water."

Sally was laughing, but she showed confusion when she turned her palms up and squinted. "I don't get it."

"Well, I don't either. But if you're going to raise a boy, you'd better understand that farts are funny. Now that I think of it, our secret adventure over at the mall in Duluth started out with a fart, too."

Sally covered her eyes. "And let's just keep that as our little secret."

"Sure. I don't know about Moose Knuckle or Camel Toe, or sign language for drunks, but I know about farts." Jane giggled.

"Ah," Sally sighed after a good laugh, "I'd better get back to work. I wish every day could start like this."

"Me too," Jane said, and she stood to leave. "See you at baseball in a couple days? It's the final game of the season . . . where did the summer go?"

"See you there," Sally said.

They hugged and went their separate ways. Smiling.

CHAPTER FORTY-FOUR

———•———

"Hi, you busy?" Matt said, as he eased the door open and stepped into Jane's office at the Pine Rapids clinic.

"What are you doing here?" Jane asked. She leaned back in her chair and stretched her back. "I thought you had another appointment with Ron this morning."

"I do; in about five minutes. I just thought that since I was driving the crazy train through the building I'd stop and say hi."

"Don't talk like that," Jane said. "You aren't crazy. But I'm glad you're talking to Ron. Do you feel any better?"

"No."

"Really?"

Matt shook his head no.

Jane stood and walked around the desk, then put her arms around Matt's neck. "I love you," she whispered.

"Good; I think you're stuck with me."

Jane rolled her eyes.

"You wanna go on a date tonight? Just you and me?" Matt asked. "We can get dressed up a little and go to a nice restaurant. Have a glass of wine?"

"We'll see." Jane glanced at her watch and added, "You'd better get going. You don't want to keep Ron waiting."

"OK, see you later, after work," Matt said, and he kissed her goodbye.

———•———

Ron Hested's secretary was waiting with a clipboard and several pages of questions to answer when Matt eased the door open and stepped into the waiting room. He answered the questions, returned them to the secretary, and then sat silently in the waiting area until he was told he could go into Ron's office. Ron was sitting in his overstuffed chair, waiting, with the papers Matt had just filled out, when Matt stepped into the peaceful little room where Ron talked with his patients.

"Hi, Matt."

"Am I still crazy?" Matt said as they shook hands and he took a seat.

"Yup."

"I figured," Matt confessed, and he let his chin drift toward his lap. "I still have a lot of bad days. Nights are worse."

"I'd say you rang the bell on both depression and anxiety," Ron said. "Nothing is any better?"

"No. Well, I did have time to think about the things you told me; the perfect storm, the compression of time, and the limbic system, and how under stress my emotions will always overrule the things I know, intellectually, to be true. I get that, and I guess there is some comfort in knowing about that. But then, when I close my eyes and see the things I see, it starts all over again." Matt shook his head and let the frustration show. "It never changes. Sometimes I sorta envy Vicky Velde; no more pain for her."

"Matt, are you thinking about hurting yourself?"

"C'mon, Ron. About half of those questions right there on the clipboard in your lap were about that. I already answered all of that, didn't I? I answered 'no' every time on that issue."

"Yes, but all the other answers you gave to other questions point to a problem with depression and anxiety. And then, what you just said. Tell me the truth."

"It was a grim thing to say; gallows humor. It sounded bad, but I'm not thinking about it," Matt lied.

"All right then. Good. Can you tell me what you *do* think about?"

"Nothing has changed, Ron. I see Jane, and she's in this guy's bedroom, and she's just about to . . ." Matt closed his eyes. "I don't want to spell it out. I *hate* it." He turned his head to the side, as if he could somehow look away and then not see Jane anymore. "Ron, remember last time we talked about this?" Matt started off with something else. "I told you that I needed to be Jane's hero?"

"Yes."

"Well, I think what I really meant was that I want all of Jane's special moments, all of the romantic stuff, for myself. You know, that great combination of love, and lust, and surrender, when you give everything to that other person? I want all of it. I don't want to feel like Jane gave that to someone else, because I want it for me. I don't care if that's selfish, either. Sorry, but it breaks my heart to think that I have to share that with someone else."

When Matt paused, Ron let him think for a while.

"I wonder if she gave that stuff, the special stuff, to someone else. Then she settled on me because I'm safe. You know, I was good to her, and she saw me as someone who'd be a steady companion." His face twisted as he listened to himself. "I don't want to be that guy. I don't want to be *safe*. I want to be the guy who makes her heart go pitter-pat. I want to be her hero, not the guy who fixes the toilet when it's plugged. Is that so bad, to love her like that? To want that?"

"You don't think that's how she really sees you?" Ron asked.

"No, I think she sees me as an old guy, who's kinda worthless."

"Matt . . ."

"I understand the things you talked about last time, Ron; the depression and anxiety, and the limbic system and the perfect storm. I get it, at least I think I do. But so what? Knowing about that stuff isn't making me feel any better."

"Have you talked about all of this with anyone else?"

"Well, I did try to talk to John Velde, but this isn't the kind of thing . . ."

"Yeah," Ron agreed, "maybe he's not the guy for this conversation."

"I tried to talk to Sally Durham, to try to get a woman's perspective, but it was so hard for me to share most of this stuff with her. And something she said made it even worse."

"How about Jane?" Ron asked.

"It's odd, Ron; the one person I've always been able to talk to, the one person I *need* to talk to, is the one person I can't talk to now. Oh, Jane will talk to me about all of this, but if I bring it up it just feels like I'm begging for reassurance that she loves me. And I feel like she's actually still holding something back. The story makes no sense; it's just not Jane. On the night she told me, I could hear it in her voice that there was more to the story. I think she's afraid she'll share another secret and make me even crazier, which of course makes me even crazier." Matt shook his head at the absurdity of what he'd just said. "The other thing with Jane . . ." Matt paused and thought for a moment. "Like I told you, I think this great connection that we've always had sorta had its roots in sex, and now that's pretty messed up. And as a result, it feels like our connection is, too, and it'll never get better. There's this distance between us that was never there before. Jane *wants* to help me, but it's gotten weird. Every time we start to talk about our relationship, we naturally wind up talking about old times, and then it seems to get even worse for me. I feel like just the mention of an old place where we hung out when we were in school, or an event from back then, or even an old song from college days, causes her to think about the *other* guy, not me, and then I wanna die. How do things get so fucked up?"

"There's no one else to talk to?" Ron asked.

"Well, I told you that I reconnected with my high school girlfriend a while back, and she's been a good friend."

Ron leaned forward immediately and made a point to let Matt see the concern on his face. "Bad idea, Matt."

"I know what you're thinking, Ron, but I told you, it's not like that. She was my best friend once. She's happily married and she lives far away, and—"

"You're playing with fire, Matt."

"Well, so be it, then." Matt's eyes hardened. "I'll play with fire. She's a friend I can talk to, the *one* friend I can talk to, and I'm not gonna cut her loose."

"Do you know how many men have sat right there, where you're sitting, and told me the same thing, and then a short time later confessed to an affair that actually did ruin their marriage and their life?"

Matt returned a defiant shrug.

"OK, you're a big boy, Matt," Ron said, but his tone made it clear that he had a problem with Matt's friendship with an old girlfriend. "Is there anything else you'd like to talk about today?"

"Do you know what contrapasso means?"

"Yes. It's from Dante's *Inferno*, and the idea behind a contrapasso is that when we die and go to Hell, our punishment will be in direct proportion to the sins we committed in life. Why do you ask?"

"Because I feel like that's what's going on here," Matt said.

"Whoa, Matt, this is a lot of talk about death and Hell. Are you sure—"

"This isn't about death and Hell," Matt interrupted. "Don't worry. I'm trying to get at something else."

"OK, what?"

"Well, when I was young, I was involved in a couple things like this thing with Jane. I guess I was like the guy in Jane's story. I didn't care about the girls, and how I might hurt them. I just wanted sex. And after I got it, I moved on to the next girl."

"That's a pretty common story, Matt."

"That doesn't make it OK, what I did, what guys do, you know. But yeah, I never gave it much thought, either. And then, a while back, I found out that one of those girls felt that I'd broken her heart."

"Oh?"

"So, I can't help thinking that there's some sort of payback for me in all of this. At first, I thought maybe Jane's cancer was my payback. But now I wonder if my punishment for those things I did is to find out that my Jane has been thinking of some other guy for all these years, the way that other girl was thinking of me."

"Matt . . ." Ron began, as if he wasn't sure what to say next, "I think you're looking for things to feel bad about. Do you think God would punish Jane for something you did, or punish anyone for something another person did, or use Jane to punish you?"

"It sorta feels like it," Matt replied. "Maybe not a punishment from God, but maybe I called down some bad karma."

"Well, we'll talk about that more at our next visit, but I want you to try to let go of that thought. It simply doesn't work like that. I think you're trying to make sense out of chaos; find order where none can be found. Can you do that? Can you try to find some peace in the idea that stuff just happens sometimes, and no one has any control over it?"

"Maybe," Matt said with a shrug. "But what am I gonna *do* about all of this? What are you gonna *do*? I can't go on like this."

"OK, Matt, let's think about that," Ron said after a quiet moment. "Have you ever heard of exposure therapy?"

"No."

"Well, when people are anxious or fearful of something, they tend to avoid the feared objects or activities, which can sometimes make the fear and anxiety worse. In such situations a psychologist might recommend a program of exposure therapy. In this form of therapy, we would expose you to the thing you fear the most. For example, if you were afraid of heights, we would begin by exposing you to gradually increasing heights until you were no longer afraid. Do you understand?"

"You want me to talk about Jane in the sack with that guy? Like that will make me feel better?" Matt said with a hard edge in his voice.

"Not exactly, Matt. But perhaps I would have you write everything down; the story Jane told you. The entire story. And then read it every day, twice a day, for several weeks, until it no longer causes the fear and anxiety."

Matt stared blankly for a moment, and then his eyes tightened. "You want me to put my worst nightmare in writing, and then read it every day? Maybe you'd like me to go find Jane's old boyfriend and then ask him how it was with my wife; have him tell me how much she liked it until I've heard it so many times that we get to be golf buddies?" Matt scowled.

"No, but as I said, I'd have you write the story and then read it several times every day for a while." Ron remained calm in spite of Matt's tone.

"But at the end of a couple weeks nothing will have changed. It'll make me crazier. That's the dumbest thing I ever heard."

"Sometimes it yields great results."

"How often? How many people have great results with that?"

"I don't know, exactly."

"Half of the time?" Matt asked.

"Yes, probably."

"And the other half get worse?"

"I wouldn't say—"

"It's just stupid, Ron." Matt looked away in disgust. "Look, Ron, this great love affair that I've lived out for my whole life is ending. I don't wanna write this awful shit down and then keep rereading it and reliving it until I don't care anymore." Matt stopped himself, then blurted, "I *am* getting to the point where I envy Vicky Velde."

"OK, hold it right there, Matt. A moment ago, you said all of this makes you want to die. You've referred to Vicky Velde twice now. *You're* holding something back."

"You mean my plans to end it all?" Matt said with a cold stare. Then, as if he were a serial killer, finally revealing his crimes, he gave it all up. "The thing that brought me in here last week was that while I was drawing blood for a dental procedure, I began to think about easing my own pain. I'd go out in my canoe on a hot summer day and start an IV, right here." He pointed to his left forearm. "It would be painless. I'd just lean back and let a summer breeze rock me to sleep. I'd bleed over the side so there wouldn't be a mess for anyone to find. That way, when I took off on my journey I'd be leaving from a happy place, too. I even thought about my lifeblood flowing into Scotch Lake, which has sorta been my lifeblood for all these years. How's that for some literary symbolism?" Matt turned a defiant look at Ron. "'Zat what you wanted to know?"

"That's not good, Matt."

"I don't think it's so bad."

"Matt, listen to yourself," Ron said. "I really think we should start you on an antidepressant."

"Not interested."

"Just for a while, maybe six months," Ron said. "It will help to even out these dark swings in your mood."

"Not interested, Ron. I told you before; those drugs may take away the dark moments, but they take away the bright ones, too, and I'm not gonna give those up. I'll just go ahead and feel everything, and I'll get through this. It's what I do. So you can quit asking about the drugs."

"Matt . . ."

"Save the lecture, Ron, I'm not taking any pills. But I'll tell you this much; for a while there, it did seem like such an easy way to escape. But it scared me, too. And it would destroy my Jane. You know I'd never do that."

Ron sat with his arms crossed and stared at Matt for a few seconds. Then he shrugged and said, "I believe you."

"Why would I lie?" Matt said.

"Everybody lies sometimes," Ron said. Then he added, "You know I could order a suicide watch, and have the police come and put you in a safe place for forty-eight hours?"

Matt stared defiantly and said, "Well, why don't you, then?"

Their friendship, along with the doctor/patient relationship, was at the breaking point as they glared at each other.

"Whoa, Matt. We need to step back here." Ron sighed. He put his notes down and readjusted his weight in his chair. Then he took a deep breath while he considered what he was about to say. "We've been friends for most of our lives. We don't need to do this. I never thought this visit today would get so heated. I'm really sorry, Matt, but I'm only trying to help you."

"I know you are, Ron. I'm sorry, too. What do we do now?"

"Well, I guess we keep going. I told you last week; this is going to take some time."

"Yeah, I said some things today, and I guess just hearing myself say the words sorta helped me understand where they came from. And I am sorry that I said those things."

As Matt stood up to leave, he let a smile come to his face, and he used it to banish the tension from a moment earlier. "When I get home, Jane is gonna ask me what you said today. I'm gonna tell her that you said I'm just a *little* bit crazy. Would that be about right?"

"Oh, you're way crazier than that," Ron said.

"Would you say *medium* crazy?"

Ron held one thumb up and gestured higher than medium.

"Shithouse rat crazy?" Matt joked as he moved to the door.

"Not quite." Ron made a point to shake Matt's hand, and while he had a firm grip, he added, "I like you, Matt. I always have. I'm glad you came to me. I know you'll get better, but it *is* gonna take some time. I want to see you every week, and remember, you can call me anytime."

"Fair enough, Ron."

CHAPTER FORTY-FIVE

—·—

Long shadows of tall pines were inching across Scotch Lake, away from the house and toward the far shore, when Matt arrived home. The kitchen was empty, with no signs of a meal being prepared, and he walked on through the house until he saw Jane sitting on the porch, reading. "Hi, honey," he said. He looked out over the lake and added, "Beautiful evening, huh?"

"Yeah, really nice." Jane looked up at the lake briefly, turned a page, and then looked back at her book. "How was your day?"

"Pretty good," Matt answered.

"What did Ron say? How did your visit go?"

"I really can't tell you about that," Matt said. "It's that doctor/patient confidentiality thing. You know."

Jane looked up and smiled at him.

"He did tell me that I'm still fairly crazy, though," Matt joked.

Jane smiled, lowered her glasses, and said, "I love you."

"I love you, too, honey," Matt said, then he plopped into one of the chairs on the porch and let his eyes wander out to the lake again. The surface of Scotch Lake was broken by a tiny breeze that barely rustled any leaves on the trees and made no sound as it drifted through the pine boughs just outside the porch. The lake held the light blue of the late afternoon sky, and the deep greens on the other side of the lake were turning gold in the setting sun.

Matt kicked his shoes off, leaned back in his chair, and stole a glance at Jane. She was still so attractive, he thought, even after all the years, and he let himself stare at her for a while. He liked the way it made him feel to just sit there and stare at his wife. She had some gray hair mixed in with the blonde now. She was wearing reading glasses, too, with large black frames, and that gave her an air of sophistication. Her eyes had some wrinkles at the corners. Her hands showed some age, too: her knuckles were a bit swollen—maybe from working in her garden, maybe just from a lifetime of work—and the tan skin on the backs of her hands wrinkled and bunched some when she turned a page.

He let his eyes move over her more, since she didn't seem to know he was staring. The long athletic legs had some cuts and scrapes, also from working in her garden, and there was a blue varicose vein beginning to show on her left calf. It looked like she'd recently put red nail polish on her toes, maybe just a few minutes before he came home. She was wearing a yellow T-shirt and khaki shorts; she must have changed clothes after work and then come out here to read and enjoy the end of the day before they went out for dinner.

The yellow T-shirt caused Matt to think back, way back, and remember another yellow T-shirt that she wore that first summer, almost forty years ago. He felt his face bend into a smile as he remembered the way that shirt looked, and the way it felt when he moved his hands over it, too. He saw Jane smiling and laughing with him as the movie projector in his head showed him vignettes from school days, and their first apartment. Then he thought of room 206 at the Ashley Hotel.

"So, where should we go for dinner?" Matt asked. "I think it would be smart to wait a while now, so the crowd dies down a bit, no matter where we go." He paused, then added, "I'm kinda looking forward to a big ol' burger at that new place by the lake in town. I heard the food was real good, and I think they have live music tonight."

Jane kept her face in her book for a minute, then closed the book and took an apologetic tone when she said, "I'm not very hungry." Her voice also carried the suggestion that she didn't feel well, as if she might need one more subtle reason not to go out for dinner.

"So, you don't wanna go out?"

"Well, it's so nice here, and I'm tired, too." She let out a sigh.

A wave of disappointment and frustration rolled over Matt. He wanted to go out with Jane, just as they once had. He wanted to laugh and flirt with her. He wanted to hold her hand in public and tell her how beautiful she was. But he knew the unmistakable signs: Jane didn't want to go anywhere, and she wasn't that excited to spend an evening like that with him.

"Can't we just stay home? Maybe watch a movie?" Jane asked.

"Sure." Matt wanted to roll his eyes and show Jane that he was disappointed. He'd been looking forward to a night out, maybe a return to the way things used to be, all day. Well, for months, actually. But if he made a childish show of his feelings he knew it would trigger an argument, and he didn't want that.

Two hours later, Matt was sitting on the couch, stretched out with his feet crossed and resting on the coffee table. In his left hand, propped on his stomach, was a lowball glass containing the remnants of a scotch that he'd made at the start of the movie that was winding down in front of him. His right arm was wrapped around Jane, who was resting her head on his chest. The movie was OK, but nothing special, and Matt was thinking about another scotch.

Jane's legs twitched suddenly, then her head popped up and she looked at Matt.

Her eyes were dull and a bit confused.

"What happened?" Matt asked, but he knew.

"I fell awake," she said, and Matt couldn't help but smile at her words. She knew it was a good line, too, but she was still struggling to drive away the remaining fog of her sleep.

Jane was looking at Matt in the flickering half-light of the TV screen. Her eyes were dull and her mouth still hung open when she reached a hand up to her chin. "Shit," she sighed as she wiped her hand over her chin, "I drooled on you." When she reached over and touched his chest she grimaced and smiled at the same time. "Nice . . ." she said, as she patted the large wet spot on the front of his gray sweatshirt. "*Very* nice. Sorry, honey."

Matt sat up, turned the movie off, and touched his chest. "Jeez, Jane, we're gonna need to start an IV drip to rehydrate you."

"I was really tired." Jane wiped her chin again, then she stood up slowly and said, "I gotta go to bed. I just can't stay up any longer." When Matt stood up, she kissed him, said, "Goodnight, honey," and turned away. She was finished brushing her teeth and the bedroom light was out before Matt could find a dry sweatshirt and toss the drool-soaked one in the laundry.

"G'night, Jane," Matt said from the bedroom doorway. No response came. "You awake?" Matt whispered a few seconds later. Jane answered with a tiny snore. A second later she did it again, then again. She'd slipped away and left him to deal with another evening by himself. "Nice . . . another good time," he said to himself as he walked to the kitchen. He plinked a handful of ice into his empty glass and covered the ice with a liberal dose of scotch.

He tiptoed out to the great room, and then to the porch. He walked to the far end of the screened porch, as far away from Jane as he could get. The only light on the porch came from the moon. A cool evening breeze rustled the pine trees on the north side of the house, and when Matt sat down on a wicker chair he covered himself with a blanket. Now what? He wished they could have gone out for dinner; just a chance to try and have a laugh, and hold hands like they used to. Why was it so hard to find their way back to where they'd been for so many years? He wanted to talk to someone, but who would care enough to listen to him? He knew one person who would care . . . he studied his cell phone for a few seconds and wondered if he should do it, or not.

He hit the text button on his phone and scrolled down until he came to Mo Glasnapp. "Huh, how 'bout that?" he said softly, when he realized that he'd entered her maiden name instead of her married name in his phone. Then he felt embarrassed, and maybe a bit guilty, when he saw that he'd sent her 243 text messages in the past six months. He'd probably sent at least that many emails, too, and he wondered how Jane would feel if she knew about that.

Nonetheless, he sent a text:

<Hey Mo. You still up?>

Mo answered immediately:

<Yup. Reading. You?>

<Can I call you?>

Again, Mo answered quickly:

<Sure but wait a few seconds. I'm gonna send you something>

When Matt's phone buzzed and alerted him that another text had arrived, he opened it and saw that Mo had sent him a photo of herself and her two brothers. They were standing together in a garden, surrounded by flowers, and Matt was taken aback at how good Mo looked. Her hair was longer than the last time he'd seen her, and she wore a radiant smile. She was stunning, and something in this little exchange told Matt that she'd sent the photo because she knew she looked good, too. Sure, her brothers were with her in the picture, and that might make anyone else who saw the photo think it was just a greeting from old friends. But Matt knew that Mo wanted him to see how nice she looked.

Matt hit the call button and listened while Mo's phone rang. Then he cupped his hand over his mouth and his cell phone to be sure that Jane wouldn't hear anything.

"Wow! You look like a movie star," Matt said when Mo answered her phone.

"I'm an old lady."

"Mo, c'mon now. You know you're a hottie," he teased.

Mo giggled. "Well, it *is* a pretty good photo."

"Where was it taken? Donnie and David are with you?"

"Donnie's house, yesterday. We had a little party. Is that why you're calling? Did John already tell you?"

"John? Tell me what?" Matt asked.

"So, you really don't know yet?"

"No. What happened?"

"Maybe John doesn't even know yet," Mo said. "Well then, *I* get to be the one to tell you. You know how so many high schools are beginning to create something like a Hall of Fame or a Ring of Honor or some such thing for alumni who did great and glorious things?"

"Yeah."

"Well, the school board in Sverdrup decided to do start one too, and they selected four people for their first group of inductees: my dad, some girl who won several state titles in track about twenty years ago, some guy who was a football star back in the leather-helmet days and then played for the Gophers, and John Velde. How 'bout that?"

"They overlooked *me*?" Matt asked, sarcastically.

"I heard the vote was close, but you just missed." Mo laughed.

"Well, that's nice. I mean it's nice for the ones who deserved to be honored. I s'pose there'll be a banquet and some sort of ceremony?" Matt asked.

"In the fall. I wish Dad could have been part of it." She sighed and then as an afterthought said, "Those days, school days, they were happy."

"Do you remember the dances in the gym, after ball games?" Matt asked.

"I remember you wouldn't dance with me."

"I was a worse dancer than I was a basketball player. It would have taken the last of my dignity."

"I remember riding around town in your rusty old red Ford after games, and then going to my house so we could go down to the basement and sit on the couch and watch some awful old black-and-white movie on that tiny little TV in the basement, until you had to go home at midnight."

What they did while they sat on the couch and watched old movies would have to go unspoken. There was no way to take this conversation any further without treading on some thin ice, and they both knew it.

"Those were happy times for me, too, Mo."

"Yeah," Mo agreed in a whisper. Then she let go of Sverdrup, and the old days, and spoke in a normal voice: "But hey, this isn't why you called. What's up with you?"

Over the past year his conversations with Mo had covered just about everything: their children, their jobs, old friends, current events, growing old, and their spouses. He'd even shared his darkest secret. But why *had* he called tonight? He didn't know either, so he decided to just go with the truth. "Um, I don't know. I just wanted to talk to a friend. No, I wanted to talk to *you*."

"What's wrong, Matt?"

"Well, nothing, actually. I was thinking of you and I just wanted to hear your voice. I shouldn't have called. I feel like a creeper now. Sorry."

"Ah, that's nice, Matt. Remember that James Taylor song, "You've got a friend"? Well, you can call me any time."

"It's late, and I should let you go."

"Don't forget to tell John about his big honor!" Mo said. "And get some sleep, you sound terrible."

"Good night, old friend."

CHAPTER FORTY-SIX

So, was this how it felt to be suicidal? Matt had never really given it much thought, but it seemed to him that a suicidal frame of mind required one to be enveloped in a deep, dark, silent frame of mind, unable or unwilling to speak, and moving like a zombie.

All he wanted was to be free from the thoughts that haunted him. The warm sun felt good on his shoulders. His feet were dangling in the lake while he sat on the wooden dock in front of his house, and a gentle breeze rustled the trees on the shore behind him. He'd made sure to let Jane see him carry a fishing rod down to the lake so she wouldn't come looking for several hours.

The canoe was ready again, with some firewood stacked in the bow seat to balance his weight, one paddle, and couple of cushions. The small camouflage backpack was there, next to him on the dock, too. Inside it, the needle and the rubber hose were ready. He'd been inserting the needle in other people's veins for years as part of a procedure for placing dental implants. It would be easy to start an IV for himself. And death would come softly. People who were bleeding to death often spoke of a chill. He'd just lie back in the canoe and let the sun warm him while his lifeblood poured into the lake.

He had to find some peace, and it would certainly come if he simply went on his journey. Wouldn't it? He just wasn't sure if he really wanted to do it. But *this*, this existence; this was no life. There was no joy here anymore. Surely his place in the cosmos would be revealed when he got to the other side of death? And there would be no more torment from his demons. Jane could move on, too. She seemed to be about finished with him anyway.

He didn't know if he had the courage or the desire to do it, but he knew that he needed to stand on the edge of it all, and see if he actually wanted to step off of this mountain, too. Everything was ready. Now he just wanted to sit here by himself and think about it.

There didn't seem to be much reason to go on; he'd already done every worthwhile thing he'd ever do. Most of the things in his life, the things he'd always thought of as successes, didn't seem so great anymore. And the one thing that he'd always known he could come back to when he was overwhelmed, well, that was gone now. He might as well just go on his journey. But *nothing* seemed clear today, even the things his demons usually showed him wouldn't stay there in front of him. He guessed he'd just paddle out, and see what it felt like when got there.

Way off in the distance he heard a motor emerge from the silence of the big lake. He couldn't see it yet; it was a mile or two away, just a soft hum. It was still far beyond the rocky point of land that stuck out into the lake, near the tree where he'd put his deer stand years ago.

The hum grew louder. It was coming closer, and Matt could tell it was from a big engine. "Great," he said to no one, "some asshole will be out there roddin' around when I want to be alone."

The motor noise droned on, and Matt knew it was coming his way instead of heading for the far side and one of the popular fishing spots there. He decided not to step into his canoe and push off for the middle of the lake until he saw who was driving the boat, and what their plans were.

The noise changed from a drone to a roar when the boat burst around the rocky point and turned toward Matt. A spray of white shot from both sides of a glittering purple bullet, and John Velde waved when he saw Matt sitting on the dock.

Matt didn't return the wave but couldn't resist the smile that snuck onto his face.

John turned the boat, still at full throttle, and raced directly toward the dock where Matt now waited. He knew exactly what John intended to do.

The motor screamed as John closed the gap between his boat and the dock, and Matt could see the childish gleam in his old friend's eyes as he steered the purple rocket closer and closer. John was three hundred feet away, then two hundred, and still grinning. Then, at about a hundred feet away, John leaned back, spun the steering wheel, and sent the boat into a power slide. A geyser of white foam and spray shot up from the hull and as it passed by Matt, far too close for safety, a tsunami of lake water washed over the dock and drenched Matt. It was a signature greeting from John. He did it every time he got the chance, and since he had this new kick-ass fishing boat, it was something that needed to be done.

Matt lowered his head and let the water splash over him. After the power slide was complete, John cut the throttle to idle and slowly cruised back toward the dock where Matt waited.

"Nice one," Matt said from his seated position.

"Thank you," John replied.

"What are you doing here?" Matt was trying to wipe his face dry with his soaking wet shirttails.

"We're goin' fishing," John ordered.

"I'm busy now. You shoulda called."

"I did. Your wife said you were just wandering around trying to find an excuse not to do something constructive."

"And you're here to help me not do something constructive?"

"Fuckin' A, Bubba! Get your shit and jump in. You gotta see this boat."

Matt sat on the dock and waited for John to ease closer.

"Get your ass in here!" John barked.

"I told you, I'm busy now."

When the boat was close enough for John to reach out and grab the dock, he tied his new prize to a dock cleat and got out. "Get your sorry ass up," John said, when he sat beside Matt. "I can see that you're waiting for me." Before Matt could hide the backpack, John snatched it up and looked inside. "What the hell is this stuff?" John asked. "Hey, it's the stuff you used when you made my dental implant. What are you doing, planning to make a house call to one of your neighbors on the lake?"

Busted, and in need of a good lie, Matt kept his cool. "I was gonna pound a few dents outta this old aluminum canoe, and I planned to use that rubber hose to protect the hull when I took the hammer to the dents." The lie was sufficient, but not his best effort. "I just grabbed that other stuff by mistake. I was in a hurry."

"Yeah, that old canoe has seen some rocks; you've got a few dents to pound out," John noted. "You should have a bigger hose." John turned an evil grin toward Matt and added, "I'm sure you've been told that before."

Matt tossed the backpack into the canoe and then tied the canoe to the dock. To his relief, the story about repairing the canoe had worked, and John had already lost interest in the backpack. "So what's the plan?" Matt asked. Standing on the edge of it all would have to wait for another day. But that was all right.

"We're going fishin'. But first, jump in there and I'll show you all the cool stuff on this boat."

After a quick tour of all the features, and a look at the sophisticated onboard electronics, Matt took his seat. John turned the ignition key and the motor jumped to life with a deep rumble. He put the motor in gear and slowly pulled away from the dock. When they were in deeper water, about a hundred feet offshore, he looked at Matt, smiled, and pushed the throttle all the way down. The purple boat leapt from the water even before the motor had reached its full roar.

"DO THE STREETLIGHTS IN TOWN GO DIM WHEN YOU PUT THE HAMMER DOWN?" Matt yelled over the engine noise.

"DON'T KNOW ABOUT THAT! BUT I SURE GET A BONER!" John yelled back.

Matt cringed; he understood the way sound carried over open water, and he knew that anyone within half a mile, maybe farther, could hear what John had just said.

"SPEAK UP! I DON'T THINK THEY HEARD YOU IN DULUTH!" Matt yelled. John tipped his head back and laughed as the boat screamed toward the open water.

Several other boats were already at the Flemish Cap when John and Matt arrived. John brought his boat to a stop, and he began to rig his fishing rod with a minnow. He said, "Hey, look at that. That guy over there has a fish on, and so does the guy in that green boat! Looks like it's gonna be a good day. You want a beer?"

"I usually wait until after noon," Matt replied, "but I would have a snort of coffee."

"Yeah, I guess that sounds better," John said. "I just figured, here we are on a big lake in a fine boat . . . it feels like a holiday. You know, like Christmas, with boats."

"Later, for sure. Let's catch some fish first." It was nice to be out here fishing, like old times, Matt thought.

"Remember in college, that opener when we were freshmen at the U?" John asked.

"Yeah, I do," Matt said. "You're referring to all the beer we drank, right? Not the fish we caught?"

"I don't remember any fish," John said.

"Do you remember *anything*?"

"I remember you were pretty funny, right up until you started puking." John laughed.

Matt sighed and kept his gaze out over the side of the boat as they trolled. "Why did it seem like a good idea to drink that much, and do all that crazy stuff?"

"College days . . ." John shrugged.

But then, what should have been a series of happy memories for Matt immediately morphed into a collage of all the things he'd been struggling with. When he began to recall his own good times, before Jane came into his life, those memories triggered only more questions about good times that Jane had had before he came along. No matter what he did to escape those thoughts, he kept sliding down, into a darker place. Now, just the mention of college days brought visions of bars and restaurants around the university campus. Jane was there in every one of the visions, laughing and flirting with someone else—someone she loved more than him. Someone she'd hidden all these years. Matt groaned softly, used his left hand to rub his forehead, and wondered if things would ever change.

"You OK, buddy?" John asked.

"Yeah," Matt replied with no conviction.

"Bullshit," John said, without looking over at Matt. "You look like hell, and you've looked like hell for a while. What's wrong?"

"I dunno. I think maybe I'm dealing with depression," Matt said. Then he wished he hadn't given John anything to work with.

"*Depression?* What the hell do you have to be depressed about?" John scoffed.

"I don't think it works like that."

"How *does* it work?"

"I don't know that, either." Matt tried to laugh. "Maybe my job, my office, makes me depressed." This explanation had just popped out of his mouth, but as soon as he said the words, he knew that it was pretty believable, and he wouldn't need to share any more than that.

"Oh shit, yeah. That would do it for me. I don't know how you do that awful job."

Good, Matt thought; John was on to something else. He was talking about how working in people's mouths was gross and disgusting, not like stuffing dead animals.

Matt waited an appropriate amount of time, then he changed the subject. "You know, sometimes lately you talk about Sally with genuine affection in your voice." Matt was teasing now. When John turned to look at him, Matt put his hand over his heart, batted his eyes, and made a dreamy, sappy face.

"Fuck you." John chuckled, then added, "It's time for a beer. Gimme one, will ya?" He extended his hand and waited for Matt to pass him a beer, and it was apparent that he had more to say. While he waited for the beer Matt was about to hand him, John reached into his coat pocket and produced his pipe and tobacco.

"Well, it *is* after nine," Matt said. He brought a beer out of the cooler, and he then noticed the pipe in John's hand.

"I felt something different, something special about Sally, right away," John started. He opened the beer and took a sip, then began to pack tobacco into the bowl of his pipe.

"You mean when she told you to shut the fuck up, and go sit in the corner?" Matt asked.

"Well, it mighta been just a little bit after that." John lit the butane lighter in his hand, and then held it over the bowl of his pipe while he huffed and puffed and drew in heavily to ignite the tobacco. "But when she sorta smiled and opened up a bit, I thought I could see so much more there, in her eyes. I liked the way she gave it right back to me, and I wanted more of her." John cast a sideways glance at Matt, and then began to expel large white puffs of tobacco smoke. "You must have felt something like that with Jane, didn't you?"

"Sure did. Don't think I could ever forget that first evening. I could see it in *her* eyes, too," Matt said. Talking about his love of Jane always felt good and pushed other things from his mind for a while. "I don't know that it was love at first sight, but I sensed something that drew me in right away. I think it was the way we made each other laugh." Matt stopped and picked up a whiff of John's pipe tobacco. "That tobacco actually smells pretty good, by the way. But it looks like you might hyperventilate; you're working *way* too hard to keep that thing lit."

"Smoking a pipe is an art," John said, his lips smacking vigorously between clouds of smoke.

"Chrissakes, suck a little harder—you've got fire belching out of the bowl between puffs. You're gonna burn your eyebrows off. Why don't you let up just a bit and pay attention to driving the boat?" Matt said.

"I can drink beer, smoke a pipe, drive a boat, fish, and screw, all at the same time," John said between puffs. It was the quintessential John Velde statement, and Matt, as always, marked it with a grin. Neither man spoke for a moment. John turned the boat to follow a drop-off on the lake bottom, and Matt poured himself more coffee.

John studied the sonar screen beside him and said, "You know something? I think that scar on Sally's face may have been a good thing for me."

"Oh?"

"Yeah, I think a lot of good men, better men than me, failed to notice her because of that scar. If it wasn't for that, somebody else would have swept her away long ago, and she'd never have found her way into my life." John was still staring at the sonar when he added, "Lucky me, huh?"

"Hmph," Matt said. "And maybe she needed a lifetime of pain and rejection in order to harden her enough to deal with you?"

John grinned and uttered "Good one!" between vicious puffs.

"Actually," Matt said, "that was nice, what you just said. You *do* have a heart beating in your chest—a soft one."

"Yeah, well, don't tell anybody. I have a reputation to protect."

"Do you think she knows about all your other girlfriends, and all your other successful relationships?"

"Yeah, I've told her about all that."

"All of it?" Matt teased.

"No, maybe not *all* of it." John turned to Matt, wearing a twisted grin.

"Do you think it bothers her? All those old girlfriends, I mean."

"No, why would it?" John asked.

"Just asking." Matt was hoping to see if John might share his feelings about Sally's other lovers, so he asked, "Did she have a lot of boyfriends?"

"Yeah, I suppose so. I don't know. Why would I care?"

"Well, you told me once that you were jealous," Matt said, still prying.

"Yeah, that was strange . . . and bad," John said. "You ever been jealous?"

"Uh-huh . . . I think maybe I was." The awful visions of Jane instantly threatened to billow up in Matt's head again.

"Really? When? Who?" John asked.

"Long time ago," Matt lied. He didn't know if what was torturing him these days was jealousy, or crazy insecurity, or actual demons. He certainly didn't want to admit anything or talk about any of it now, with John. "It was kid stuff."

"Ooh, fish on!" John said, as he lurched forward in his seat and raised the fishing rod to set the hook. "Shit, I missed him," he groaned. "Mark this spot on the GPS, will you? Maybe there's school of 'em right under us." Matt noticed that he'd dropped his pipe on the floor of the boat. A glowing ember of tobacco had fallen out onto the carpet inside the boat, and when Matt squashed it with his shoe it left a burn mark.

They trolled back over the spot for several minutes in silence, but there was no school of walleyes under the boat. John tapped the pipe against side of the boat and let the remaining embers fall into the lake.

"A while back . . ." John started, when he was certain that there were no fish under the boat, "back when I first took notice of Sally, and we started having dinner together a couple times a week . . . that was when I felt jealous." He took a long swig of beer and belched.

"Nice one."

"That was a *long* way from the rest of my life experience," John said, ignoring his own belch and Matt's compliment. "I'd been finding myself thinking about Sally when I was with other women, and when I was alone at work, and when I was alone at night, just waiting for sleep to come, too. I was missing her, and wishing she was around, so I could talk with her." He took another long swig of beer and belched again. "She makes me laugh; kinda like what you said about Jane. She makes me think, too, and she makes me like myself better. I had no idea she could make me feel bad, too." He cast a glance at Matt and raised his eyebrows to ask if Matt understood.

Matt smiled and rolled his index fingers several times, gesturing for him to keep talking.

"Well, then one night I took her out for a burger. We'd been going out for something to eat after baseball for a couple weeks." John grinned and shook his head. "We were just talking, like you do on a date. Then Sally got a phone call and said she had to go and take a minute and return the call. She got up and left our table, but she didn't come back and she didn't come back, and eventually the waitress came over and told me that my date was sitting with some other guy at a different table."

"That waitress you used to date?" Matt interrupted.

"Yup." John grinned. "She really enjoyed telling me that Sally had changed tables, too. But that's not really part of this story." He paused for emphasis, and to put his story back on track. "The thing is, I saw the other guy. He was a good-looking guy. And I'd noticed the look on Sally's face when she got up and left our table; there was a lot going on there. Then, all of a sudden, I felt terrible. I'd let myself really start to like someone, and then I was afraid for the first time in . . . ever." John shrugged. "I was afraid that some girl might choose the other guy, and not me." He shifted his weight in his boat seat and said, "Wait a minute, that didn't sound right. It wasn't about me . . . it wasn't that I was embarrassed or humiliated, it was that I really liked Sally, and if she chose someone else, she just wouldn't be with me, in that way. And it hurt. I *never* felt like that before. It actually made me feel sick."

"Yeah." Matt sighed and nodded his understanding.

"How would *you* know about that?" John scoffed.

"Now I need a beer," Matt said.

John finished his beer in one last gulp, then belched again and said, "Well, get me one, too, and why don't you catch a fish instead of just sitting there."

Matt set his fishing rod down and applied sunscreen to his face and hands, then opened his beer and turned to John. "So, what do you think *love* is?" he asked.

"What?" John was surprised at this question.

"The stock answer is that it's an *emotion*," Matt said, while he studied the top of his beer can. "But what is *that*? I mean, what is an emotion, really? Do you think love is simply a chemical that we make in our own brain; something that makes us feel . . . love?" He shrugged. "Or do you think maybe it's some cosmic thing that's tied to our humanity, and is designed to remain outside of our understanding?"

"I think we're gonna hafta go back and get more beer to figure that one out. Jesus, Matt. Where do you go to come up with shit like that?" John shook his head and added, "You know, summa the guys we grew up with didn't like to be around you 'cause you said shit like that. I always liked that about you, but I had no idea what you were talking about."

"Sure you did, you just liked to act like you didn't understand things, so the dumbasses you ran with would like you. But you were thinking," Matt replied, then he stared out over the water and remembered something. "Do you remember our last game, when we were seniors?"

"What sport?"

"Basketball."

"No," John answered, indifferent.

"I do . . ." Matt said, without looking away from the lake. "It was a tournament game and we were getting pounded by New Ulm. We were way behind with about three minutes to go, and all five guys on the floor were seniors."

"We weren't very good," John offered.

"Nope, we weren't," Matt agreed. "And that was when ol' Pigeon Tits threw in the towel. He started taking us out of the game one at a time, so our parents and the fans in the gym could applaud, and say goodbye, I guess."

"I do sorta remember that."

"Know what I remember about that?" Matt asked, then he answered his own question without waiting for John to reply. "I remember sitting there on the bench, next to you, and suddenly realizing that it was all over: the game, the season, my career. It was just over, and it was never gonna happen again. All the things I'd worked for, and dreamed of, were finished. And I'd never made it; never been a hero, never accomplished any of the things I'd dreamed of during countless hours of practice in my driveway, and at school. I was just a grinder; a face in the crowd." Matt thought for a moment. "And it was all over. My time in the game was over. As the seconds ticked away, I watched others play the game in my place. I wasn't even playing out the string; I was just watching from the sidelines while that part of my life vanished. I wondered what, if anything, was next for me." Matt sighed. "What were you thinking?"

"I had a six pack of beer in my car, and a date with one of the cheerleaders from Windom."

"No sense of regret at the finality of it all?"

"Sorry, buddy." John grinned. "I guess I was just ready to move on to the next thing."

"Hmph . . . that night; I felt lost," Matt said.

"Well, I guess you were wrong on that one," John said. "It wasn't long after that and things started to click for you . . . girls and school . . . and real life."

"Yeah, maybe you're right." Matt smiled. The thought that John had been sitting beside him that night, thinking about beer and girls and good times, while he'd lamented the loss of something that had, in fact, been a great time, began to strike him as funny. "So, how did it work out for you that night?" Matt asked with a smile, as he felt the disappointment of his high school days slide away.

"Ah, not so good, as I recall," John said, when he understood that Matt was asking about his date. "I put the full-court press on, but she broke it. And every time I 'took it to the hole,' so to speak, well, she was able to block the lane."

"You didn't score?"

"Fouled out. Too much grabbing." John's eyes narrowed as he smiled.

"You wanna know something I always admired about *you*?" Matt asked.

"Prob'ly a long list."

Matt smiled. "Not really. There was just one thing. When we were young, everything was so easy for you."

"Whaddya mean?"

"Well, for example, when we played basketball for old Pigeon Tits back in high school, you'd pull down a rebound and turn and dribble the ball through a crowd. You'd change hands and change directions. It looked like you were connected to the ball. And then you'd do some graceful thing when you got down to the other end of the floor and roll the ball gently into the basket. You were just *part* of it all." Matt turned his palms up and cocked his head before he continued. "But *me*, when I tried to do what you did . . . well, it seemed like the ball and I were the opposite poles of a magnet; we repelled each other. The ball just went away from me. I'd lose control of it and stumble, and kick the ball outta bounds, or shank the layup."

John placed a hand over his mouth to cover his smile. "I remember."

"But I *loved* it," Matt said. "The game, I mean; not kickin' the ball around. I wanted to master it, and feel the flow of things, like you. I just couldn't do it, though, no matter how hard I tried. But then, later on, I found that feeling when I met my Jane . . . and with other things. It felt like I found myself. Maybe that's what you were describing about Sally, a connection?" Matt looked at John and asked, "'Zat make any sense?"

"Sure . . . maybe. Shit, I don't know. We're gonna need more beer, though, if you keep talking. Do you really think about this shit all the time?"

"Unfortunately." Matt was now glad John had surprised him this day by showing up in the boat. And for the first time that he could ever remember, he found a bit of comfort in John's simple understanding of the complicated things in his life. They caught fish, drank a few beers, belched, and told more stories about school days as the afternoon drifted along.

"So what's the plan for the rest of the day?" Matt asked, when the sun began to drop toward the western horizon. "You wanna fry these fish up at my place? We haven't done that for a long time."

"Sure! That'd be great. Why don't you call Jane and tell her that we're gonna give it another half hour? I'll call Sally and have her meet us at your place for Gourmet Club? We haven't done that since . . . well, since before Jane got sick. When we get done fishin', we'll put the boat on the trailer and then drive to your house."

CHAPTER FORTY-SEVEN

J ust before five o'clock they eased up to the public boat ramp. "We had a good day. Thanks," Matt said to John. Six other boats were circling the public access area while they waited for their turn to use the ramp. A little old man and his wife had just loaded their boat on its trailer and were stowing their gear in the back of their old pickup truck.

"It's gonna be a while before we can trailer the boat and get over to your house," John said, showing some frustration. "C'mon, hurry up," he complained under his breath. "Other people are waiting."

"We're in no hurry," Matt reminded him. "The girls will be waiting when we get home. We'll clean the fish and have a nice dinner."

The old man and woman got in their truck and drove away, and before they were off the ramp another boat pulled up to it. One of the men in the boat jumped out and hurried up to the busy parking lot, where he started his truck and returned to the ramp with his trailer and backed it into the lake. His partner, still seated in the boat, drove the boat onto the trailer and the two men quickly secured the boat and drained it before they drove off the ramp to allow the next group to land their boat.

"Those guys are good fishermen," John said to Matt, and he pointed to the boat that was about to use the ramp next. "I know them. I do a lot of work for those two." Before Matt could ask their names, the guy in the boat waved at John.

John waved back.

"'Zat Doc Hested's boat?" the man hollered to John.

"It's mine now," John hollered back.

"It's a beauty. Did you guys catch any fish?"

"Two limits," John replied. The man gave John a thumbs-up before he turned and drove his boat onto the trailer that was now waiting.

When he drove his truck away to make room for the next boat to use the ramp, he waved at John.

"Those guys were lookin' at us for a while, scoping out my boat," John said to Matt while he waved at the man on the landing. "Damn, I look good driving this thing, don't I? Hell, everybody's looking. They all probably wish they were me, don't you think?"

"Just the ones who wish they had a smaller dick."

John ignored Matt's comment. "When it's our turn I'll get us up close to the ramp and you jump out and get my truck. Here's the keys."

Ten minutes later Matt backed John's truck and boat trailer to the water's edge and waited while John drove the boat onto the trailer and then secured it with the safety chain.

"Nice boat!" called a man who'd been working on another boat.

"Thanks," John said, and then he called to Matt, "OK!"

Matt drove the truck trailer and boat to an open place in the parking lot while they drained all the water from the live wells and the bilge and cleaned any weeds they could find from the trailer. Matt carried some fishing tackle and the fishing rods to John's truck, and when he opened the tailgate he was greeted with the smell of gasoline. "Jeez, your truck smells like gas," Matt called to John.

"Aw, I forgot. There's a small gas can in the back, for my lawnmower, and it leaks a little bit. Did it stink up the truck?"

"Pretty much."

"Well, put it in the boat for now. When I get home, I'll take it out. It's just easier to get that stink of gas out of an open boat than the inside of my truck."

Matt moved the gas can into the boat and tied the boat securely onto the trailer. "OK, let's head for home," he said.

John drove his truck down the winding road that led from the public access boat ramp on Scotch Lake to the highway. Rocks and ruts in the narrow road jostled both men and the boat they were pulling, no matter how slowly John drove. Tree branches from each side of the trail merged above them to make the rough road feel like a tunnel.

While John inched along, he groped his pocket until he found his pipe and tobacco and a lighter. When Matt saw that John was planning to light up once again he groaned and rolled his eyes.

John was bouncing along, trying to steer the truck down the bumpy little road with his left elbow, and using both hands to pack tobacco into the pipe and then light it. Soon enough, he was puffing wildly and a plume of smoke filled the cab of the truck. When Matt cast an unkind glance at him, John puffed even harder and returned a wicked grin. He knew he was aggravating his friend. Matt rolled down his window.

When they finally reached the highway, John switched his turn signal on and waited for traffic to clear before he could pull out onto the paved road for the twelve-mile drive back through Pine Rapids and over to the far side of the lake where Matt and Jane lived.

"Jeez!" Matt groaned, as he waved his hand to try to clear some smoke out of the truck. "Let's get out on the highway and get some fresh air moving through here." John was holding the lighter just above the bowl of his pipe and puffing furiously just to aggravate Matt. "That's some funny shit there," Matt groaned.

Through a fiendish grin, and between puffs, John said, "Fuck you."

"You've got way too much tobacco in there."

"Fuck you," John said again, between puffs.

"You can't suck and blow at the same time, John. The whole truck is fulla smoke and you've got flame shooting out the bowl of that pipe."

"You would know more about sucking and blowing than me." John resumed his frantic puffing. He waited for two more cars to pass, far longer than he needed to wait, just to irritate Matt. Finally, John pulled onto the road and when he accelerated to highway speed, fresh air raced into the cab and smoke swirled around and then out.

"That's better," Matt said. As the smoke swirled around, and then out, he coughed and waved both arms. He also grabbed at a few loose pieces of paper that the rushing wind began to toss around the inside of the truck.

"You pussy," John said, while he puffed and laughed. He knew he was puffing way too hard and fast, but he just liked the reaction he was getting from Matt. But when he said "pussy" into the pipe, a large, well-packed ember of glowing orange tobacco popped out of the bowl and the flaming fireball was instantly sucked into a jet stream vortex that carried it directly into Matt's left ear.

"OUCH! SHIT! FUCK! GODDAMMIT JOHN!" Matt yelped as he slapped at the side of his head. "THAT BALL OF FIRE IS IN MY EAR!"

Matt's fingers were black with soot, and his face was scrunched into a twisted beacon of hate. His eyes were hooded and reptilian when he turned to look at John. "You *moron*," Matt said, as he used his left hand to gently check his ear for damage. He turned the truck's rear-view mirror so he could see himself. "My ear is blistered!"

John was leaning away, far to his left, obviously in a reflex of self-preservation, touching his left shoulder against the driver's-side door. His window was open now, too. "Jesus," he laughed. "You actually had smoke coming out of your ears." He started puffing feverishly again, eyes bulging and cheeks drawing in with each puff.

"Gimme that fuckin' thing!" Matt growled, and he reached for the pipe in John's mouth.

John flinched, switched the pipe into his other hand, and held it out the window to keep it away from Matt.

"I'm gonna shove that thing up your ass!" Matt growled as he unbuckled his seat belt and lurched toward John.

"OK, OK, OK," John griped. "There . . . it's gone!" John threw the pipe into the air.

"You are a *fucking* moron," Matt reiterated, while he fell back into his seat and buckled his seat belt. He gingerly touched at his ear to check the rising blister. He expected some sort of an apology—even John Velde should be willing to say "I'm sorry" for what had just happened.

But none came. John was staring into the rear-view mirror when Matt finally looked over at him.

"You got anything to say to me, asshole?" Matt asked. "You know, like, 'Sorry to start your ear on fire'?"

"Did you see where the pipe landed?" John said.

"Just be thankful it's not in your ass right now."

"Ah, well . . ." John gave up on the pipe's final destiny with a shrug. "I didn't like pipe smokin' very much anyway." He grinned.

"Yeah, it almost got you killed." When Matt checked to see if John was laughing, he saw him looking into the rear-view mirror again and studying something behind them.

"I wonder if the pipe landed in the boat," John said. "Do you see some smoke?"

"No, but pull over and we'll have a look."

John lifted his foot from the gas pedal and steered the rig onto the shoulder of the road. "Damn, I think something's burning," he said, still peering into the rear-view mirror.

"Me too," Matt said.

The truck was still rolling, and both men had one hand on a door handle, ready to get out, when they heard the small gas can in the boat explode with a *poof.* The back half of John's boat was instantly covered in blue and yellow flames.

"FUCK!" John barked. "WHAT ARE WE GONNA DO?"

"IS THERE A FIRE EXTINGUISHER IN YOUR BOAT?" Matt yelled. "IT'S ON FIRE, TOO!"

The two men stared at each other for several seconds, each of them searching for a past experience to guide their next move. Neither of them had any idea what to do.

Matt spun his head around, watched the fire grow for a second, and when he finally hollered, his voice was panicked. "The paint and fiberglass is beginning to blister! You better start this rig and get outta here before the truck catches fire, too!"

"NOW WHAT?" John yelled as he stood on the accelerator and sped away. A plume of thin black smoke was slipping into the sky behind them.

"Turn around! Let's head back to the boat ramp. If we can get there quick, maybe we can just back the boat into the lake!" Matt looked over his shoulder and added, "BUT YOU BETTER STEP ON IT!"

"Maybe I should pull over and try to put the fire out!"

"With what? You gonna piss on *that?*" Matt pointed at the boat with his thumb.

They both turned around to see that the rising trail of smoke had turned much thicker and blacker. "FUCK!" John groaned, and he leaned forward, as if that would make the truck go faster.

His new boat looked like a rolling tire fire when he spun the steering wheel, crossed three lanes of traffic, and stood on the gas pedal. The public access road to Scotch Lake was maintained by the county highway department. It was intended to handle traffic moving at five to ten miles per hour, and they seemed to leave it rough intentionally to keep traffic moving slowly. The situation was getting grim even before they returned to the narrow road; yellow-blue flames were licking at the trees and the black smoke was growing thicker when John executed an impressive high-speed turn off the highway and then stood on the accelerator once more.

"FUCK! FUCK! FUCK!" John hissed. He was screaming through the woods at nearly fifty. Smoldering shoes, and fishing rods, and flotation vests were bouncing out of the boat as it slammed into each little obstacle along the narrow washboard trail. "I hope nobody's on the ramp when we get there!" he said, and he started to lay on the truck's horn.

Mercifully, two fishermen had just pulled away from the ramp when John and Matt roared into the parking area at the public access. John drove through a maze of other trucks and boat trailers in a maniacal rush to get his boat into the lake. Bewildered fishermen scattered safely away and then turned back to watch as John slammed his truck into reverse and backed the entire flaming rig into Scotch Lake as fast as he could.

The burning fiberglass was sending an ugly black cloud into the air when the boat's transom splashed into the lake, and John kept on backing up until most of the boat was under water, along with the rear end of his truck. Lake water lapped at the truck doors and flowed into the cab when Matt and John both scrambled out.

Both men stepped into water that was nearly waist deep, and they looked at their situation in disbelief. The carcass of a burned-out boat still sat on the trailer. John had backed far enough into the lake so that the water washed over the gunwales and extinguished the flames, but far too late to save the boat.

All the boat seats were burned black, along with the captain's console and the steering controls. The cover was completely burned off the outboard motor, and much of the boat's fiberglass was either slumped from the heat, or burned black. The smell of smoldering fiberglass, carpet, and rubber was thick, but not as thick as the black smoke above the pristine lake. Dozens of items—shirts, shoes, tubes of sunscreen, empty beer cans, and fishing tackle—drifted away from the boat, while pieces of smoldering metal and plastic hissed in the fresh water.

"What a fuckin' train wreck," John sighed.

"I think the truck is OK, but the boat's not so good," Matt said.

"Oh, no shit, Sherlock."

A minute passed, then another, while Matt and John splashed water on the black and steaming remnants of the boat carcass. Other fishermen scrambled over from the parking lot to see if they could help, and several boats pulled up to the landing to see what had happened, but all the excitement was over.

"I don't think we burned the tires off the trailer. Let's pull this thing outta the lake and onto that gravel parking lot over there," John said, when the fire appeared to be dead.

A dozen other fishermen, helpless onlookers, stood by and watched as John started the truck and slowly eased the hideous disaster out of the lake. When the boat was on the concrete ramp, John stepped out of the truck and looked back for a second. Then he closed his eyes, shook his head, and climbed back in behind the steering wheel. He drove what was left of the boat to the far end of the parking lot, onto a grassy meadow, as far away from the ramp and the other fishermen as he could get, and then he got out of the truck once more.

The truck, the trailer, and the ruined fiberglass boat hull were all dripping water on the ground while Matt and John walked silent circles around the entire rig and checked for damage. "Jesus, what a mess," John said finally.

"Even by *your* standards, this was a real shit show," Matt said. Then he walked over to a nearby oak tree and sat down in the shade.

After several more circles of the wreckage, John walked slowly to Matt and sat down on the ground beside him. John picked a blade of grass and put it in his mouth. "Ah, it's only money. I have a lot more money." He moved the blade of grass around with his tongue while he thought about things and watched the boat drip. "Money's only good for one thing, and that's to be spent. I can buy another boat. But all my tackle and my rods and reels . . . all of that's ruined too."

"Well," Matt offered, after a moment to think, "now you can buy all new stuff. That'll be fun."

"How's your ear?" John asked.

"OK."

"It coulda been way worse, I guess," John said. "The boat, I mean."

"How?"

John sighed, rueful. "I guess I don't think it coulda been any worse. That just seemed like a good thing to say."

Matt and John were still sitting and staring at the remnants of the fine purple boat when a little boy began walking toward them from the boat ramp, carrying two plastic bags from Walmart. The bags were full, and both men watched as the boy drew near.

"Here . . ." the kid said, as he held the bags out to John. "My dad and I found this stuff floating in the lake. I'm sorry your boat got burnt up."

"Thanks, buddy," John said, when he took the bags from the boy. Then he dumped the contents of the bags onto the ground and began to sort through the treasures that had been salvaged. "Let's see here . . ." he said to Matt, "a seat cushion, my sunglasses, a coupla fishing lures, some sunscreen . . ." He started to chuckle.

"What? What's so funny?" Matt asked.

"Look at this." John reached for the bottom of the bag and then held something up for Matt to see. "The kid saved my *pipe!*"

As they towed the charred wreckage of John's boat back to Matt's house, they began to chuckle and recall its final voyage. Clamped between his teeth, John held the equally charred remains of his pipe when he suggested that since the fish had been overcooked during their ride in the boat, maybe they should order a pizza for dinner.

While John talked, Matt wondered just how far he'd have taken things if John hadn't appeared. He was happy, sitting in the truck and laughing with John. It had been a while since he'd felt like this. Somewhere, mixed in there with thoughts of fish, John puffing on his pipe, and a burning boat, there was the image of the backpack and the rubber hose and the needle. And a sense that he'd stepped back from the edge of a cliff.

CHAPTER FORTY-EIGHT

—•—

Mercifully, Matt thought, summer was winding down. Or, at least, Little League baseball was over. Timmy and his Orange teammates were celebrating the season finale with Popsicles and some grab-ass while their parents exchanged goodbyes on the infield dirt.

In some ways, Matt supposed, it had been a good season. John Velde had stepped up and been a real coach, a good influence for the players. Bradley Hested, Mike Katzenmeyer, Timmy, and Dave Norman had all returned from last year's team, and they'd actually won a couple of games. Bradley showed some improvement. Timmy and Dave Norman had some individual success, and both of them looked like they might turn out to be ballplayers someday. Michelangelo Katzenmeyer had wielded his baseball glove/garbage-can lid with all the skill he'd shown in the past. By positioning himself close to Timmy or Dave Norman he'd been able to avoid any unnecessary entanglements with the ball all summer. But the best measure of his success in baseball was that he'd become friends with Timmy, Dave, and Bradley.

The Compton twins, however, had given up on the sport, and Matt missed them more than he would have expected. They played soccer and spent all their free time at their family's lake cabin. The rest of last year's Orange team wound up on different teams, or gave up on baseball, or moved away.

Tonight, Matt was glad to pick up the gear and bag it. Summer baseball with youngsters had become a chore for the first time in his life. The kids, the games, and the evenings at the park spent visiting with friends were just not fun anymore. But baseball *had* been at least a distraction from the gloom that had settled over him, and he supposed that was good.

All he really thought about nowadays was the way Jane had changed, and the things that his demons showed him. There was no joy in the things he used to love. He'd slipped away from it all several months ago, and he didn't think he'd ever go back the way he came.

He was stuffing the catcher's gear into a green canvas bag when one of the Orange players' fathers walked past and thanked him for coaching. "Yeah, you're welcome! We had a great season!" Matt said, with a fairly authentic-looking smile. But when he turned back to the catcher's gear his face was blank once again.

"Hey Matt, c'mere!" John called out from over by the Orange team's bench, where a group of parents had gathered. He waved his hand to summon Matt over to join the others.

Matt dragged the canvas bag across the infield dirt as if it weighed a thousand pounds. A small cloud of dust swirled behind him, and shadows from the pine trees surrounding the ball field were growing long. His hands hurt from the weight of the bag, and when he reached the bench he let go of the drawstring, so the bag fell to the ground at John's feet. "I gotta bag up the rest of the gear so I can drop it off at the middle school tomorrow," he told John.

"Hey, we're all going to Buster's for pizza. Sort of like our postseason banquet," John said, as Matt walked past him, toward Jane.

Matt ignored John, put his arms around Jane, and held her as if he'd been away for months. He whispered, "I love you, honey," before he kissed her cheek.

"I love you too," Jane said, with her arm around his shoulder. "Everyone is talking about going to Buster's for a little party to celebrate the end of the season. I think we should go."

"I don't wanna," Matt said.

Jane gave him a little shake. "C'mon, it'll be fun. You always liked to do this before. Now let's go; it'll be good for you."

"Yeah, get your sorry ass in your truck and let's go," John barked.

"OK," Matt said. "But first I gotta bag the rest of the gear. You guys go ahead and I'll join you in a couple minutes."

"I'll help you," John said.

"Nah," Matt said. "You guys go and get that big table by the deck. I'll be right behind you. Jane, you should ride along with John and Sally. I'll catch up."

The small crowd of Orange players and their parents shuffled off, en masse, toward a row of cars parked in the street. Matt began to pick up the twenty or so baseballs still littering the field. When he'd picked up the last ball and tossed it into the bag, he turned to see Ron Hested, all by himself and standing by the bench.

"Thanks for a good summer, coach," Ron said. He didn't look to be in any hurry to leave with the others.

Matt smiled. "Thanks, Ron."

"You missed quite a few visits at my office; you've been avoiding me." Ron lit a cigarette and waited for Matt's reply.

"Ah, just busy with work."

"Is that all? Really?" Ron pressed. "You're staying away on purpose, and I can see that you're still way off your game." Then he exhaled a plume of smoke.

"Are you psychoanalyzing me, Ron? Will there be a charge for this?" Matt tried to joke. Then he surrendered and gave up the act. He dropped the canvas bag full of baseballs, and sat down on the bench where his players had been sitting only a few minutes earlier. "You know I was sorta pissed off and frustrated when I left your office after that last visit. I'm still dealing with all the same stuff."

Ron sat down on the bench, beside Matt, and rested his elbows on his knees. "Your demons?"

"Still there."

"Every day?"

"Every fucking day." Matt sighed.

"I have to ask you again, has she ever been unfaithful?" Ron had asked the same question before. This was clearly an opportunity for Matt to open up and finally tell the truth, if he hadn't been all along.

"No. I've told you that before, Ron. We've always been solid, in love. We like each other. She's my best friend."

"And she's never given you reason to be jealous or suspicious that she has someone else?" Ron asked.

"Never."

"You don't do things like search through her phone records when she's not around her phone, or sneaky stuff like that?"

"Of course not."

"So, you trust her, and you don't worry that she has someone else?"

"No. I mean yes, I trust her. Completely."

"I don't get it," Ron said. He took a long drag on his cigarette. "And you. Have you been faithful?" Once again, he was offering a chance for Matt to come clean.

"Always, Ron." Matt tapped Ron with the back of his hand. "I've *told* you, I've never even been tempted. I do notice attractive women; not gonna lie about that. But I've never had a day, since the day I met her, that I haven't been in love with her. And all I've ever wanted is to be her hero."

"You mentioned an old girlfriend a while back, and I have to tell you, that makes me nervous. I'm afraid you'll make a pretty common mistake while you're . . ." Ron paused.

"Crazy?" Matt finished Ron's sentence.

"Yeah. That wasn't the word I was gonna use, but I guess it'll do. And you wouldn't be the first person to do that."

"I suppose so," Matt agreed. "But she's a friend, sometimes it seems like she's my *only* friend. She talks to me. About everything. There's no one else."

Ron sat for a moment, staring at the dirt in front of him. "You're *my* hero, Matt. *Don't* screw this up." He smiled sadly and looked at Matt.

"Huh?"

"This thing with you and Jane; do you know how rare this is? I just don't want you to screw it up." Ron tossed his cigarette on the ground and lit another. "Would you like to know how it feels to be unfaithful?"

Matt nodded yes, then shook his head no. "Are you about to tell me?"

"I was fooling around, on my first wife, and I got caught." Ron paused, reflecting. "The sex was fantastic; forbidden fruit, you know. If there *is* a good part, that's it."

"It's always fantastic."

"Good point," Ron said, and he pointed his cigarette at Matt.

"So, tell me what happened," Matt said.

"Well, her husband found out and then he called my wife. I was at a meeting in Chicago when she called to confront me." Ron stopped and remembered. "That flight back to Minneapolis, and then the drive back to Pine Rapids? Oh, God, it was terrible. I kept wondering, what was I thinking, why did I *do* that? I was so embarrassed and ashamed." He paused again. "I've been down that road more than once, you know?"

"I've heard."

"It was never the same between us again. I sorta ruined her life. Or, at least, I really hurt her. She didn't deserve it, and I couldn't fix it."

"Did you have feelings for the other woman . . . women?"

Ron shook his head immediately. "No, not really. It was just an adventure. Lust. Forbidden fruit. When it was over, I felt bad, terrible, but that didn't ever stop me. I've done it a few other times, and I've hurt others, too. That's why I admire you; you've had a lifetime of love with a beautiful woman."

"Yeah, well, why do I feel like I've lost it all, then? Why the demons?"

"You tell me, Matt." Ron pointed his cigarette at Matt once again. "I think, *maybe*, you know why."

Matt shuffled his feet around in the brown dirt by the bench they were seated on. "Everything was fine up until about a year ago. I thought it would go on forever." He felt himself standing on the edge of the mountain once again, about to tumble if he kept on talking. But he didn't care about falling down anymore. "Ever since the cancer . . ." He stopped and thought about how wanted to say it. "Up until then, nothing had changed for us. And I'm talking about being in love. Sex, too, I guess. There was always this great playfulness and laughter. You know, about a year ago she called me from the Ashley Hotel just before lunch one day. Said she was in room 206, and I should hurry over there because she was wearing her black lace and, well, I guess you know the rest." Matt smiled at Ron.

Ron tapped at his heart and said, "That's the kind of thing I was talking about, Matt."

"Well, you know, Ron, the sex was probably just about like what you described with your girlfriend. But it was with my Jane, and it was so sweet; the way we held each other, and teased each other. The look on her face. The little sounds she made." Matt's story had come easy, and he kept on: "It was always like a door. A door that I knew would swing open if I leaned on it, just a little bit, and it would open up and all the passion and laughter and touching would be there. And Jane always knew it would swing open the other way, too, whenever she wanted." Matt stared across the dusty infield. "Now it's like she never wants that door to swing open again, like she's done with all of that."

Ron nodded his understanding.

"It would be different if I didn't love her like I do. Makes me feel like there's no reason to go on. I mean, what's point, without her," Matt said. "Have you ever read *The Myth of Sisyphus*, by Albert Camus?"

"If you do what I do for a living you've heard of Sisyphus. Where are you going with this?" Ron asked.

"I'm telling you that Albert Camus wrote a book, or maybe an essay, about Sisyphus, the character in Greek mythology who was sentenced to spend eternity pushing a rock up a mountainside, and then watch it roll back down again."

"I'm familiar with the story."

"Then maybe you remember the first line in Camus's book? It goes something like this: There is but one truly philosophical question, and that is suicide."

"Matt—" Ron tried to interrupt.

"And Camus's *point* . . ." Matt raised his voice, "I think, is that we live our lives in search of order and understanding. And if there is only senseless repetition, with no joy or understanding, then why go on?"

"Matt—"

"*And* . . ." Matt raised his voice once more, "when I was with my Jane; in her arms? That was when I felt the closest to understanding my place in the cosmos. My love for her brought me the closest to that place I thought I was looking for."

"Matt—"

"But then I find out that I'm about like Sisyphus, doing this meaningless thing for my whole life. The more I learn, the more I realize how far I am from really understanding anything. And that's when things get absurd— when my need to understand the world around me crashes into the reality that every new thing I discover may just overturn all the knowledge that has given my life order. And then I'm required to learn a new truth . . . and get my heart broken." Matt shuffled his feet in the dust. "You know, when I'm standing in French Creek trying to fool a trout into taking my fly, I'm searching for some order in all of this; trying to find my place. *Damn*; sometimes I feel close. But that's the only place I feel it anymore."

"OK, Matt, now think about some of the things you've said to me recently. You're talking about Dante's *Inferno*, a trip through Hell, and your punishment; your contrapasso. And then Sisyphus's eternal punishment. You mentioned suicide. That's pretty dark stuff. I'd still like to start you on an antidepressant, Matt. I think this depression might be more of a problem than you realize."

"I told you before, Ron. No way. I need to feel all of this."

"You just mentioned suicide, and you've spoken of it before."

"It *was* on my mind for a while there, and I told you before that it would destroy my Jane. I only mentioned it now to let you know where my demons take me."

"OK," Ron sighed. "But I shouldn't have to come *here* to have this talk. Don't miss any more visits at my office."

"OK," Matt agreed. He looked at his watch and said, "I guess we should get going or we'll miss the party at Buster's."

"You're a good friend, Matt. You know I only want to help you. Just don't miss any more visits at my office."

"I won't." Matt shook Ron's hand and tried to lighten the tone of their conversation. "So, would you say that I've gotten *less* crazy? Jane will want to know."

"I'd say the talk of Dante and Sisyphus puts you right out there with the shithouse rats," Ron said, as he lit yet another cigarette. "No charge for that diagnosis. See you at Buster's in a couple minutes. Hurry up."

"Hey, I'm gonna charge *you* for this visit," Matt called to Ron when he was halfway to his car.

"Well, at least you didn't stick a needle in my head, too," Ron called back. "Hurry up."

———

Six Orange ball players were sitting in a booth near the large table by the window at Buster's when Matt finally arrived. The players were all laughing and talking at the same time while they drank sodas through plastic straws.

John, who was seated at one end of the table, between Ron Hested and a couple of younger men, waved at Matt and hollered, "Over here!" About a dozen parents and grandparents of Orange players were seated at the long, beer hall–style table, and there were beer bottles in front of everyone. The noise and music in the bar required those at the table to separate into several small groups and then lean close to each other to be heard above the din.

Matt made a point to kiss Jane as he passed by her, then he sat at the far end of the table, next to Ron. "We took the liberty of ordering a beer for you," Ron said.

"Good call. Thanks," Matt said. He had to raise his voice to ask, "Did you ever buy yourself a new boat?"

"Sure did. Got a twenty-foot Ranger with a—"

"What would you boys like to eat?" interrupted Lori, the waitress. Ron would have to wait before he could tell Matt how big the outboard motor was on his new boat.

Matt stood up and hollered, "Hey! Is pizza OK with everyone?" Those who turned to look at him nodded and shrugged, and he took it as universal approval, and permission for him to order the pizza. "All right," Matt said as he turned toward Lori, then he reached an arm around her neck and pulled her close so she could hear him. "Please make a large everything pizza for the boys seated over at that booth . . ."

Lori nodded her understanding.

". . . and then four large pizzas for this table. Bring four different kinds; surprise us with your choice." Then Matt pulled Lori so close that his lips were almost touching her ear, and he said, "But make one of them a Hawaiian Supreme, or whatever you call the one with pineapple on it, and set it down right over there in front of John. OK?" Matt smiled.

"Love to!" Lori beamed. "You want another beer, Doc?" she said to Matt.

"Keep 'em coming," Matt replied. The crowd, the music, the atmosphere of a celebration—it all felt good to him. He hadn't expected to feel this way, and he let himself begin to enjoy the party. He glanced at the other end of the table, where Sally and Jane and the other mothers and grandmothers were talking and laughing about something; the only conversation he could hear above the noise around him was the one on his end of the table. Then he twisted around in his chair to check on the ballplayers, who were all packed into a large booth, and using plastic straws like blow guns, shooting tiny bits of paper at each other.

"So how big was that new outboard?" Matt said to Ron, as Lori walked away. As Matt listened to Ron resume his description of the motor and all the other features on his new boat, he noticed that when Lori passed behind John Velde, she brushed her hand across his shoulders and then whispered something in his ear. He noticed John's grin, too, and the way he touched Lori's thigh while she paused beside him.

Lori returned with another round of beers every few minutes, and each time she passed by John she lingered for a moment to exchange a glance and pass along a subtle, nonverbal message. When she finally delivered the pizzas, John just smiled, knowing that the Hawaiian pizza had been placed in front of him on purpose. Then he made a show of carrying the Hawaiian pizza to the other end of the table and returning with a pepperoni pizza for his end of the table.

John's restrained behavior drew a round of applause from everyone at the table and added to the party atmosphere. Matt, along with everyone else, laughed when John raised his own beer in a toast to himself, when he reached for a slice of pizza.

An hour later, as the party was breaking up, Matt found his way to John's side and sat down next to him. "Hey, buddy; just one thing before I go," Matt said quietly.

"What?" John asked, still grinning from the party mood.

"Would you *lie* for me, if I asked you to?" Matt said.

"Sure," John replied, without hesitation. John understood from the tone of the question that Matt was checking to see if John would have his back, lie for him, if he was ever guilty of infidelity.

"Well, I won't lie for *you*," Matt said, frowning. "I won't *tattle*, but I won't lie, either. So don't ever put me in that position. Understand?"

"Sure," John said. His eyes returned a message of devious intent mixed with innocence and charming denial. Matt had seen it all before. Many times. But tonight, Matt didn't see charm and innocence, just bullshit and bad behavior.

CHAPTER FORTY-NINE

"There, have a look at *that*." Matt raised his patient's dental chair to an upright position and gave her a handheld mirror so she could examine her new smile. Then he leaned back in a satisfied posture and asked, "What do you think?"

Lila Belle Kofron held the mirror several inches from her face and studied things from every possible angle for nearly a minute, before she said, "Don't you think they should be a bit whiter?" Her shoulder-length silver hair was pulled back in a ponytail. Her blue jeans and pink sweater suggested the figure of someone many years younger, and the tan skin on her face and hands spoke of a life of leisure and affluence.

"I knew you were gonna ask me that," Matt said with a smile. He drew in a deep breath and said, "Lila Belle, you're a dentist's dream: a beautiful woman with a bunch of crappy old fillings and broken teeth, or at least that's what you were when we started this whole project. Now you're just a beautiful woman. But you're seventy-eight years old. If I make your teeth any whiter you're gonna look like a desperate woman who bought some piano keys in order look like a teenager. That never works. You look beautiful. I want you to tell everyone you know who your dentist is!"

A reluctant smile slowly came to the woman's face. "You're right," she said.

"Yes, I am. And that smile right there . . ." Matt pointed at her teeth, ". . . that's gorgeous, if I do say so myself. You look thirty years younger, and healthier, than you did before."

After a hug from Lila Belle, Matt went to his office and closed the door. The two-hour appointment with this woman had gone perfectly, and his day, his week, was over.

His job, his busy practice, had been the one thing that kept him relatively sane over the summer and the first few weeks of autumn. The office had been a relatively safe harbor, filled with enough distractions to keep his mind occupied with things other than Jane.

His visits with Ron Hested had helped some. The demons came around less often. Jane looked better, healthier, every week, and in about every way but one, she seemed back to normal. She laughed and joked with Matt in many of the ways she always had, but whenever he approached her, she seemed to recoil from his touch, and she never came to him.

In the weeks since baseball ended, and his visits with Ron Hested grew more regular, Matt had attempted to talk to Jane about things several times. But every time he brought up his feelings about their fading connection and the way he kept on seeing visions of her with her first lover, she seemed to clam up. For the first time that he could remember, Jane was hard to read. She seemed to think that she'd spoken of it enough, and Matt could just get over it. He wondered if she just couldn't see his anguish, or maybe she thought she'd covered everything in enough detail, and she had nothing more to add. Or maybe she knew that if she spoke of it any more, she'd only reveal something else, and it was safer to just try to move on.

Matt found himself staring out a window, watching the yellow leaves of autumn flutter by on a warm breeze, when his office phone rang. A moment later Tammy peeked in and said, "John Velde is on the phone. Are you still here?"

"Sure." He always liked to talk with John. Just the hint that John might say or do something a little unpredictable drew Matt away from the melancholy thoughts of Jane. "I'm supposed to meet him for lunch in a few minutes. You know that he got elected to our high school Hall of Fame? He asked me to introduce him, say something nice at a banquet tomorrow in our hometown."

"Something nice?" Tammy rolled her eyes. "Good thing he didn't ask me."

"He was a big deal back in high school."

Tammy made a face like she'd just stepped in something, and she backed away from the office door.

"Hey, John," Matt said when he picked up the phone.

"Are we still on for lunch? You done for the day?"

"Sure."

"Well, hurry up. I'm sitting at the coffee shop, waiting for you."

"Be right there." Matt hung up the phone and sprang to his feet before John could say anything more. The autumn sky was blue and the sun felt warm on his shoulders as he started on the short walk from his office to the coffee shop. He was looking forward to the Hall of Fame banquet.

Jane wouldn't be there. She'd made plans months earlier to go to New York with her sister for a girls' weekend to celebrate her sister's divorce. Initially, Matt had been disappointed that Jane wouldn't be there. But now, although he didn't want admit it, he was glad that he'd be going without her. He'd be more likely to find time to talk with Mo. That thought—the hope for a lengthy conversation with Mo—had been swimming around in his head for weeks. He knew it shouldn't make him so happy, but it did.

The noise of human voices and clanking dishes greeted Matt as he swung open the front door of the Human Bean. As always, he glanced first to the counter to see if Sally was there. And she was, smiling and waiting for the person at the front of a long line to order something for lunch. She noticed Matt, waved quickly, and turned her attention back to the line in front of her.

Matt's eyes moved to the dunce table, where John was waiting for him. As he weaved his way between tables to join him at his assigned seat, he noticed that John was looking at him and pointing to something across the dining area. The look on John's face said, 'How 'bout *that?*'

Matt kept walking but turned to search the crowd, and it didn't take long to find what John was pointing to. Snag was sitting at a small table, with a woman. His hair was washed and combed, and he was dressed like everyone else, almost, though some of the rough edges still needed work. Matt waved and called out, "Hi, Snag."

Snag returned the wave, and the woman turned and waved at Matt too.

"Wow, Snag has a girlfriend?" Matt asked John, when he sat down at their table.

"Here's a coffee for you. And I ordered a sammich for you too," John said, as Matt settled in. Then he answered Matt's question: "Yeah, he's been seeing her for a few weeks."

"I know her from somewhere. She works at the bank, right?"

"Yup."

"She's really quiet, I think," Matt said. "How did they meet?"

"Snag takes the money over to the bank from the Shorewood Furist, and one day they just started talking. All of a sudden he's got his hair cut and he's wearing nicer clothes."

"He got his teeth fixed, too. Oops, I just broke the law. I'm not supposed to tell you stuff like that about another patient. HIPAA, you know." Matt took another quick look over his shoulder. "He sure looks happy. That's great."

"I think he's porkin' her," John offered.

"I'm sure you meant that in a very loving way."

"I got a new boat," John announced. He'd moved on from Snag and his girlfriend.

"Oh?"

"Yeah, it's about like the other one, but it's red. A sparkly red metallic paint job, and a two-fifty Merc on the back. All kinds of storage space, too. You'll love it."

"Can't wait to see it."

"Do you have your opening remarks ready for tomorrow night?" John asked.

"Pretty much. It's gonna be hard to keep a straight face, though, when I'm trying to say nice things about you."

"Yeah, try to avoid the truth as much as possible. It's too bad Jane can't make it. I know she always *loves* to hear the stories about our high school days." He knew that Jane had heard them all a hundred times.

"This thing with her sister, this trip to New York—she had that planned before the trip to Sverdrup came up. But she was pretty broken up about missing your Hall of Fame speech."

"Here are your sandwiches, boys," said Sally, setting down their lunch plates. "We all set for the big day tomorrow?" She placed a hand on John's shoulder.

"Long ride in the car, but yeah, we'll have some fun tomorrow night," Matt said.

Sally said, "I can't wait to see where it all started," while her hand lingered on John's shoulder. "But I'd better get back to work now." As she walked away, she let her hand slide over the back of John's head and neck.

Matt watched Sally walk away, and a lightbulb clicked on in his head. "That right there!" Matt pointed. "The way she just walked away, that reminded me of Lori, the waitress out at Buster's."

John was sipping coffee, eyes fixed on the far rim of his cup when Matt spoke. He looked up quickly, over the top of his coffee, and his eyes told Matt everything.

"You went home with her that night, didn't you?" Matt said. The truth of it all clicked into place.

"Huh-uh. No."

"Aw, John, my bullshit detector is blaring, here." Matt grimaced. "I *know* what you did, you piece of shit!"

"I had to!" John leaned back and confessed, but with feigned remorse, as if it was funny. "She was asking for it." He gave no hint of contrition. It was as if Matt had caught him taking a few French fries off someone else's plate. Nothing more. Then John smiled. It was a smile that Matt had seen a million times. John was bragging about an amorous adventure, just as he'd done in high school. Clearly, John saw nothing wrong in what he'd done. Or at least he wanted Matt to believe there was nothing wrong in what he'd done. He seemed inclined to share more of the story, too.

"You asshole!" Matt groaned.

"She was asking for it," John said again, as if that somehow made things all right. It was a limp defense that oozed more bullshit, and John seemed to think *that* was funny, too. "She's a nice person," he added lamely.

"Not the point, dickweed. I think she's nice, too, but you're a shit-heel. What about Sally? You prick."

John made another run at false remorse by squinting his eyes closed and looking away, but Matt could see that he thought what he'd done was actually pretty cute.

"What the fuck is *wrong* with you?" Matt said. "This would break Sally's heart."

"*I'm* not gonna tell her."

Matt stared across the table at John, hoping to see some genuine remorse, then he said, "Jeez, you're an asshole."

John looked at his hands for a moment and tried to stop grinning.

"I told you, I'm not ever gonna lie for you," Matt said. "I should just go home, you low-life shitbag." He lifted a potato chip from his plate and then tossed it back. "You don't deserve friends like me, or Sally."

"It was just the one time," John said.

"I don't believe that, either."

"OK, it was twice." John grinned.

"What a complete *dick* you are."

"Yeah, I know," John sighed. "Sometimes when I do shit like this, it even makes *me* wonder about the way I was raised."

Over the years, John had done things like this many times. Then he'd say something like "I couldn't help it" or "It even makes *me* wonder about the way I was raised," and Matt would smile and look the other way. Today everything changed.

It used to be funny when John started a literal pissing contest with other boys back in the fourth grade, and then claimed that the teacher broke it up only because she wanted a look at his dong. It was funny when they'd started a garbage can on fire. And it was actually kind of funny when he insulted women in line ahead of him at Sally's coffee shop.

But John wasn't funny anymore. He'd crossed the line, and it left Matt with a weary, heavy feeling just to look at John and see the smirk on his face. He wanted to go home, and not finish his lunch.

"So, what are you going to *do*? I mean, with Sally?" Matt asked.

"Nothing," John said, with a shrug of his shoulders. "I mean, the thing with Lori; that was just unfinished business, I guess."

"Bullshit. It was a bad thing, and you know it."

"Yeah, well . . ." John was failing to come up with a better explanation, so he took off in another direction. "What time should we leave tomorrow morning?"

Matt wondered how John could have done what he'd done. He'd betrayed Sally's trust, and mocked the commitment that she'd made to him. He should have felt a connection with her, a bond that would keep him faithful. Happily faithful. John Velde had just gone over the top. He'd done one of those things that made Matt feel bad, bad enough to want to get free of John. But he couldn't. At least not until this weekend was over.

"Pick me up at nine." Matt shrugged, as if he didn't care if John picked him up at all. Then he began to shake his head in despair, and he sighed, "I dunno, John. I just don't get it. I s'pose Lori, the waitress, is cute, and sexy, and it's hard to say no to things like that."

"Not for you," John said.

"Women don't come up and offer it to me."

"Bullshit. I think you're just too dense to notice."

Matt shook his head and looked away. "I'm done with you."

As Matt slid his chair back, John began to realize that perhaps some irreversible damage had been done to his friendship with Matt. "Wait! Sit down again," John said.

"Why, do you have another shitty thing you wanna tell me about? Fuck you. I'm going home."

"Wait. Wait. Wait." John held his arm out toward Matt.

"What?" Matt scowled.

"I don't know why I do this shit. You tell me, what do *you* think? Really. Why *do* I do this shit?" John asked.

"You really wanna know what I think, John? Really?"

"That's why I asked."

"Well, you might just be a selfish prick who can't care about anyone else's feelings. A lot of people think that's the story, but not me. Well, check that; I do think it's kinda true. But more than that, I think you're afraid of *success*. Everything has always been so easy for you. You always got by on natural talent, and good looks, and bullshit. Success was just always *there* for you."

John looked at Matt with a question in his eyes, and waited for more.

"But there *always* comes the moment for you when you start to understand that in order to keep the success coming, you're gonna need to step it up and actually *try* to get to the next level. And that terrifies you, because you know it means you're gonna have to reach down inside yourself and come up with a little extra in order to keep it going, and that means you're gonna hafta think about somebody else. I think you're afraid there's nothing inside you, no real strength or character, so you just fuck everything up and act like you don't care." Matt picked a crumb off his plate and flicked it at John, as if it was a cigarette butt. "Now somebody finally comes along who thinks there's something good and strong in there, someone who just might need to lean on you someday and tap into your strength. But you're afraid she'll discover—no, maybe *you'll* discover—that there's nothing there, and you're not worth the bother, so you keep trying to fuck it up."

"'Zat what *you* think, too?" John asked.

"Are you asking me if I think you're worth all the bother? I don't know anymore, John." Matt looked away and shook his head. "I like being your friend. I always have. That's why the two of us are sitting here today, after all these years and all your bullshit. But I don't know anymore. You gotta do better than this, John. I never felt like this, but today? I'm thinking that I don't wanna know you anymore."

"You're the only person who's ever said stuff like that to me," John said.

"Yeah, well, maybe that's the problem. Or maybe you *are* just a selfish prick." Matt stood up and added, "I'm not gonna eat with you. Pick me up at nine. Or don't. I don't care anymore."

CHAPTER FIFTY

—·—

Heavy gray clouds rolled in over Pine Rapids before sunset. By the time Jane was headed home from work, the steady rain of a black October evening made their familiar driveway difficult to see. Her windshield wipers swept away a new shower of raindrops every few seconds, and the long driveway, lined with tall red pines, seemed like a dark tunnel. When Jane eased her car to a stop by the back steps of the house, she could hear the soft, muddy earth squish away from under her tires.

She took a bag of groceries in each arm, and then slumped over to keep the rain off her face when she walked up the back steps and into the kitchen. "Whew, it's wet out there, and getting cold!" she called to Matt as she set the grocery bags on the kitchen countertop.

"I love nights like this," Matt said, as he welcomed her home with a kiss. "The cool rain makes the woods smell so great." He peeked inside each of the grocery bags, then asked, "What's for dinner?"

"This isn't for tonight. I just picked up some things so we'll be ready in case there's an unscheduled Gourmet Club meeting next week," Jane said. "Are you all packed and ready for John's big weekend?"

"Yup. Are you ready for your trip to New York?" Matt leaned close and gave Jane another kiss on the cheek.

"I still have some packing to do. I don't have to leave for Minneapolis until later in the morning." She hung her coat by the back door. "Did you make a fire? I just got a whiff of wood smoke."

"Yup, and I straightened up a bit, too." Matt twisted a corkscrew into a bottle of wine. "A cool night, we're safe and warm in our home . . . what could be better? October is the best month. The hardwoods are so beautiful, and I'll be going out in search of Mr. Whitehorns again soon." The cork popped from the bottle, and Matt turned to Jane with a glass of wine in one hand. Here, would you like the first glass?"

"No," she said with a long face.

"Are you all right? You don't look so good."

"Yeah," she replied. "I'm fine."

"Well, you don't look like it. Are you getting sick? Jeez, you're leaving for New York tomorrow. You don't wanna miss the big weekend with your sister. You don't wanna get sick now."

"I'll be OK." She carried an armful of groceries to the refrigerator.

"Hey, look, if you're coming down with something, I'll call John right now and tell him I can't come over tonight."

"I'm OK," Jane insisted.

"I'll make some chicken soup for you. Sit down and relax. But first I'm gonna call John and tell him I can't come over. He just called, and wants to talk. But I didn't want to go over there anyway. I'll call and cancel."

"You were going over to John's?"

"Yeah, we had a—" Matt stopped himself; he didn't want to tell Jane what John had done. "We were gonna talk about my little speech for tomorrow night." That seemed like a decent recovery, and Matt went on. "But I'll call and tell him—"

"I'll be all right, Matt. Don't call him. You can go." Jane turned away and walked to the other side of the kitchen.

"You don't *look* like you're all right. You look like you have a sour stomach, or a throbbin' headache."

"I'm not sick." Jane's eyes were on the floor, then she looked up at Matt and confessed, "You made a fire, and cleaned up a bit, and opened some wine, and we're gonna be apart for a few days . . . I thought you were gonna want sex."

Matt slumped against the kitchen counter and stared at her. "Jesus, Jane." He sighed. "The look on your face. You were actually sick at just the *thought* of . . . me? All I did was make a fire and try to do something nice for you before the weekend. We won't see each other for a few days, and—" He stopped and sat at the kitchen table. "You know, it's bad enough that you make that face every time I touch you, or kiss you, or stand close to you, but Jesus . . . I make a *fire* and you get sick? It actually made you physically *ill* to think that . . . ." Matt stopped. "Aw, shit, I give up. I just made a fire for you. That was all."

"Matt—"

"Is it *that* bad? You *are* done with me, aren't you? Don't you feel *any-thing* anymore?"

"It's just different now, Matt," she began to explain. "We're older, and we're not making babies anymore, and that part of our lives is going away."

"Really? It's just simple biology? You're just done with it? Like that?" Matt snapped his fingers and felt his anger rising. "Where does that leave me? Do you remember me, the guy you used to love? The guy who aches for you to come back? Now that I've given you what you wanted, a little romance when we were young, a couple children that you see twice a year, and a comfortable home, you have no further use for me? Now that we're in the last part of our lives and I can just go sit over there in the corner and watch *Wheel of Fortune* until I die?"

"Oh, so this is all about sex." Jane's face turned hard.

"Well, *you* can reduce it to that; blame it on me, if that makes you feel better about tossing everything away. I thought it was about you getting sick, or faking sick, just to keep me away."

"That's not fair."

"It's the truth! Remember how it used to be? I could come up and stand behind you for a few seconds and you'd know . . . and I'd know . . . and there'd be this wonderful thing happening between us. We might be watching TV, or out in the yard, and if either of us came close to the other, there was this sorta *vibe* happening, and the other one would get it. I could reach over and touch you in the middle of the night, and you'd move close to me because you wanted it to happen. Now you make a face like you might throw up if I hug you in the kitchen."

Jane lowered her head and began to cry. "Don't you think I wish it could be like that again, too?"

"No, honey. No, I don't," Matt said. "As a matter of fact, I think you're pretty happy to put me on the shelf and live out the rest of your days like this . . . just a couple of old people sitting around and waiting to die." For the first time since well before Jane's sickness and surgery, Matt felt real anger, and he let it show. "I'm not ready for that yet."

"Well, there's not much I can do about it." Her voice trembled, and Matt knew that this conversation was about to end in a way that none other had. She was frustrated and angry, too. Her face was red, and her eyes were swollen with tears.

Over the years, they'd bickered about what radio station to listen to in the car, or where to go for dinner, or whose family they'd spend Christmas with; a hundred other things, some of them childish and frivolous, some of them fairly serious, but nothing like this. This was new, and it was bad. For the first time, it felt like their marriage was spinning out of control.

Matt reached out to her, but she stepped back from him. "You know, honey, I have all this other crazy shit going through my head all the time, and now it feels like you don't want me anymore," Matt said, and it felt like he was begging a stranger to understand.

Jane replied in a firm, stoic tone. "You know, the cancer and the surgery were bad enough, but this medication that I'm taking, this hormone blocker, it gives me those killer hot flashes. It makes it impossible to . . ." There was no anger, or frustration, only a sad confession. "I never feel romantic or sexy, and I can't just tap into those feelings like I used to before all of this. And when I see those expectations in your eyes, and I know what you want, I feel terrible. I just can't respond, but that pressure you put on me is terrible. Yes, it makes me sick."

"So why do you take the fucking medication? Why do you *take* that shit? The cancer is gone."

"Because I want to *live*, and that's what my *doctor* told me to do. She said that's what would give me the best chance to live!" Jane said. "Do you know more than she does?"

"They cut your cancer out, and it looks like they got some of your soul with it. I never thought you needed the medications they told you to take. I think they do that because they think a long life is a good life, but they have no idea about what they take from you." Matt shook his head and grimaced before he blurted, "Is this living?" He knew he should stop talking, because the things he was about to say would be hurtful to Jane, but all of *his* pain, all that had swelled inside him for the past year, was about to boil over. "You act like you're *happy* to be done with me. To be done with our life as it was, like you're just totally content to have me for a roommate, but nothing more. The closeness that we once had is just gone, and you seem to think that's fine. I know I shouldn't point this stuff out because it makes me sound like a selfish pig, but you seem to think the surgery and this drug will get you into your eighties, and there's something really good out there twenty years in the future, waiting for you. But you know, something *else* is fairly likely kill you, or me, in the meantime. And then your eighties won't matter so much. You're willing to trade now for later, and that's a bad trade."

Jane crossed her arms and issued a defiant challenge. "So, what would *you* do?"

"Well, if I had to take, or do, something that turned me into *you* . . ." Matt said, "I'd just as soon be dead. I'd go stick a needle in my arm and be done with it."

Matt knew instantly, before the words had left his lips, that his frustration and anger had made him blurt something he could never take back, and Jane imploded. She was angry, crushed, and confused. Her chin dropped to her chest and she began to cry.

"You'd rather that I was dead, if I can't have sex with you?" she sobbed.

"That's not what I said," Matt whispered as he reached for her.

"Get away!" Jane said, with an anger that she'd never directed at him before, and she flinched farther away from him.

"That's not what I said," Matt said again.

"Yes, it is! And you hurt me! You just don't understand. You'll never understand." Jane took a tissue from the kitchen countertop, blotted her eyes dry, and finished putting the groceries away as if Matt wasn't there. Then she turned and looked at him, and for the first time ever, Matt saw *nothing* in her eyes. She was more dead than when they'd wheeled her back to her hospital bed after surgery.

"You're right. I don't understand," Matt said. His frustration and anger had finally boiled over, so he decided to let it all go. "How *could* I understand what you've been through? I'll never know. But I know how it feels to lose you. I feel *that*. I felt it when I watched them wheel you into your hospital room after your surgery. I felt it on the day that doctor told us that you had cancer. I feel it every night when my demons come and show you to me, with someone else. I feel it every time you turn away from me now. I feel it every time I wonder if I'm still a man. One of us could just as well be dead . . . and set the other free. Or we could just go our separate ways!"

"I don't know what to say to you anymore," Jane said. "And I don't think I care." Then she turned, walked into their bedroom, and closed the door behind her.

For forty years, whenever they'd quarreled, their spats had ended with a hug and an understanding that things were back to normal between them. Tonight, they'd both said things, and heard things, they'd never dreamed of.

He'd never thought of leaving her. He'd never do it. He'd said the words in anger, because it seemed like hurting her would make him feel better. And when he told her that it didn't seem like she loved him anymore . . . she hadn't denied it and then reassured him that she'd always love him.

Matt walked to the bedroom door and called, "I can't go on like this, Jane."

Jane made no answer.

CHAPTER FIFTY-ONE

---·---

The day had begun on narrow roads that wound through pine forests. Now they were crossing an ocean of cornfields, and the steady thump-thump, thump-thump, thump-thump of a highway rolling by under their wheels had morphed into a monotonous lullaby. "Pretty quiet back there," John said. He glanced at Matt, who was slumped against the passenger-side door in the backseat of John's truck, watching field after field of corn and soybeans go by, and thinking about the awful things he and Jane had said to each other the night before.

"Just thinking," Matt said.

John was driving while Sally rode shotgun, and the three of them were only a few minutes from Sverdrup, where John would be inducted into the Sverdrup High School Athletic Hall of Fame that night.

"Turned into a nice day," Sally said. "It's too bad Jane couldn't join us."

"Yeah," Matt said halfheartedly.

"Do you think she's in New York yet?" Sally asked.

"She's not scheduled to arrive until eight o'clock tonight," Matt answered, without looking away from the farm fields passing by.

"Well, I'm sure looking forward to visiting Sverdrup. I've heard so much about this place where you boys grew up," Sally said.

"I'm pretty sure you'll be disappointed," John said.

Matt had been a silent passenger all morning. He'd pretended to sleep, with his head resting against the car door. Sally and John had been talking to each other for most of the four-hour trip, and they seemed to be enjoying an upbeat conversation. When John told Sally about some of his wild deeds back in the day, he actually appeared to be excited about the Hall of Fame thing, and the chance to show Sally around the little town where he grew up.

Matt had spent the morning remembering Jane's words, and the look on her face, and the fact that they'd spent the night in separate bedrooms and then parted without a goodbye earlier that morning. He felt terrible about the way they'd parted. Nothing like this had ever happened between them, and his insides were hollow.

"Are you nervous?" Sally asked John, and her question took Matt's mind off Jane briefly.

"Yeah, a little bit," John admitted, then he started to tell her another story about his school days.

Matt disengaged from their chat and returned to his thoughts of Jane. She'd told him that she no longer had any feelings for him, and he'd never seen such complete apathy in her eyes. Their failure to say goodbye had been an awful thing, and he'd expected some sort of message from her this morning. They'd had fights before, but every other time Jane had only been able to stay angry for a short time. Matt sent her a text message:

<I miss you, and I feel terrible. Are you OK?>

There was no reply.

The countryside grew more familiar as they drew near to Sverdrup. They passed the farm where a schoolmate had lived, and Matt sat up a bit, to watch it go by. The place still looked about the same as he remembered, and he wondered whatever happened to the kid who'd lived there. Then it flashed by and was behind him and gone.

An old one-room country schoolhouse with two separate outhouses, one for the boys and one for the girls, sped past on the other side of the road. The little ball field in back of the school was still there, too, and in pretty good shape. Matt had never been inside the school. In fact, he was pretty sure he'd never met anyone who'd been inside the school, but it had stood there for so long that it had become a part of his memory of home.

"You're about five miles from the center of the universe," John said to Sally, and he pointed to the right. "Matt grew up on a little farm down that road a coupla miles."

Matt sat up straighter and looked. He couldn't help it. But he looked away quickly, afraid of what he might see, or what he might not see.

"Hey! There's Donny and David!" John said when his truck pulled into the parking lot of the River View Inn, a drab, three-story motel that overlooked a muddy ditch called the Flambeau River. "Looks like *they're* staying here tonight too!"

Donny and David Glasnapp, and their wives, were standing in the parking lot beside a black Suburban, about to carry several suitcases from their car into their motel room. But when they recognized John Velde, the boys stopped in their tracks, pointed at him, and began to laugh.

"You guys look like shit!" John bellowed when he stepped out of his truck. A moment later, he had both of the Glasnapp brothers in a bear hug.

Maybe this ceremony tonight, whatever it turned out to be, would be all right, Matt thought. He stood beside the truck and studied the faces of three old friends. It made him feel somewhat better to witness this homecoming, but all the joy belonged to someone else, and he couldn't join in. The ugliness of Jane's words felt like a thousand-pound weight. "Hi, Donny, David." Matt waved and smiled. Then he walked over and greeted their wives, too.

Sally walked around the front of the truck and John motioned to her. "C'mere, Sally. I want you to meet Donny and David Glasnapp, my friends."

"Yes, it's nice to meet you," Sally said.

"Hey, Donny, what time are you guys gonna head over to the VFW? That's where this little ceremony is supposed to take place, right? Maybe after we clean up a bit we can get together for a little pre-party party?" John said.

"Sure thing, John. Just give us few minutes," Donny replied, and they all carried their bags up to their rooms on the third floor.

After check-in, a shower, and a quick change of clothes, Matt made a trip to the ice machine in the hall. He didn't like it that he was all alone tonight. The Glasnapp boys were here with their wives to celebrate Alvie's life, and John had someone to help him celebrate, too. But he was here by himself, and he couldn't stop thinking about the words Jane had spoken.

On the way back to his room, with a bucket of ice in his hand, Matt stopped in front of David's room, just a little way down the hall from his, and he was about to knock and ask if Mo was coming. It was the first thing he'd thought of when he saw David and Donny in the parking lot. But neither of them had mentioned her, so Matt assumed that he'd have seen her or her husband by now, if they were here. He decided to return to his room without inquiring about Mo. If he made a point to knock and ask why Mo wasn't here, he'd just reveal something that he didn't want to acknowledge, even to himself. Oh well, Matt thought, as he turned and walked toward his room. Something must have come up, and it must have been pretty important to keep Mo away.

He was seated on a cooler beside his bed, twisting the cork from a bottle of Aberlour, when he heard the door to his room squeak open. He'd left it ajar, so the others would know he was ready start the party whenever they were. "C'mon in," he said, while he poured some scotch into his plastic cup. Then he looked up to see who was pushing the door open.

It was Mo, and instantly Matt felt like a kid on Christmas morning.

"Hi, Matt," she said, almost in a whisper.

"Ah, Mo . . . it's you . . . I . . . c'mere!" He stammered and then stood up to greet her. She came to him and put her arms around him. "You look so nice," he said into her ear. "I was just gonna ask David if you were here, but I didn't want to look like a creeper."

"Is Jane here?" Mo asked.

"No, she's in New York, with her sister. How about your husband?"

"Nope. He stayed at home, said he had to work. He doesn't like to come here, he never has. I think he felt relieved at Dad's funeral, like he'd never have to come here again."

Matt did a poor job of hiding his pleasure with Mo's answer. "Where are you staying?"

"Right next door to *you*," Mo said. She squinted for a second and then chuckled at their exchange. "Now we *both* sound like a couple of creepers."

"Would you like a drink? All I have is scotch," Matt said.

"Scotch is good, but make it a weak one."

Matt gave the drink to Mo, tapped his plastic cup against hers, and they drank a silent toast to themselves. In the instant that followed their toast, they locked eyes and wondered: now what?

"'Zis where the party is?" David said, as he and Donny and their wives eased the door open and stepped into the room, with John and Sally on their heels.

Donny looked at his watch. "We have time for one drink before we should head over to the VFW so we can mingle for a while before this big ceremony." The others each filled a plastic cup with ice and some scotch. "Let's all raise a glass to old friends . . ." They clicked each other's cups, and Donny pointed his drink at Sally and said, "and to new friends." They tapped their drinks together again.

"And to Alvie Glasnapp and John Velde, Hall of Famers!" Sally replied.

"I'm a little worried about this thing tonight," John said after the toast. "What if I drove all the way down here and nobody shows up to see this thing?"

"You mean, like Willie Loman's funeral in *Death of a Salesman?*" Matt said. "I heard that was a concern for everyone on the selection committee. That's why they chose some other people to be inducted at the same time as you; people who had friends who *liked* them, and large families who lived nearby."

"Ooh, ouch." John held a hand over his heart and laughed.

CHAPTER FIFTY-TWO

W hoever had decorated the Sverdrup VFW hall had been reaching for elegance but come up short. Streamers, crepe paper, and colored balloons hung from light fixtures all around. Twenty-five round tables, all of them with some sort of sports-related centerpiece, and set with places for eight people, were covered with white tablecloths. A large buffet was set up on one side of the banquet room, and an ornate oak speaker's podium waited in the center of the room. Six-foot-tall black-and-white photographs of all the inductees, taken when they were doing glorious things for Sverdrup High, hung on the wall behind the podium. The tile floor, which was the original, circa-1950 floor, the folding tables that had spent most of their long lives stacked on top of each other, and the podium which had been donated in memory of a VFW member who no one remembered anymore, all showed their age. The faint odors of ancient cigarette smoke, floor wax, and the almond-scented candles on the tables, all combined with the well-worn facility and fixtures to accentuate a classic VFW hall ambiance, somewhere in between a senior prom and a Ducks Unlimited banquet.

The banquet hall had been prepared with two head tables. Matt, John, and Sally had been assigned to share a table with the five grown children of William Berg, the guy they'd been referring to as Leather Helmet for weeks. William Berg was long dead. He'd graduated from Sverdrup High in 1933 and then played on a couple of national championship football teams at the University of Minnesota before he returned to his family farm, just west of town. Judging from the picture of Leather Helmet hanging on the wall, he'd played all his games before the era of face masks. The photo was taken outside the old high school in Sverdrup, and it was an iconic photo from the Leather Helmet days. William Berg stood stiffly, wearing a bulky, soiled uniform. He held his helmet, which looked more like a baseball glove than a football helmet, by the chin strap, and it dangled at his side. His face was fleshy, and his wide nose had obviously been broken at least once.

The Glasnapps were seated at the other head table, about ten feet away, with the youngest inductee, Joyce Seirstad, and her husband. Joyce, an attractive woman in her forties, Matt guessed, had been a state champion four times: twice in the 400-meter run and twice in the 800-meter run. She'd also been a star volleyball and basketball player and then gone on to run track at the University of Minnesota.

The crowd began to gather shortly before seven o'clock, and the noise level in the banquet room rose steadily until the master of ceremonies, the Sverdrup High School principal, called things to order. After a greeting and an explanation of how this Hall of Fame had come about, and how the first group of inductees had been selected, a local minister delivered a blessing, and tables were sent, two at a time, to the buffet.

The event unfolded about the way Matt expected. Introductions were sincere, with a few humorous anecdotes, and the comments from the inductees were much the same. Leather Helmet's oldest son spoke on behalf of his father, and Donny Glasnapp accepted the honor for Alvie. At the end of his comments about his father, Donny took a moment to talk about John Velde, too. Donny told the crowd that later in life, Alvie had begun to refer to John as "Roy Hobbs," the fictional character in Bernard Malamud's novel, *The Natural*, because Roy Hobbs was "the best there ever was, and the best there ever will be."

In his introduction speech for John, Matt pointed out the fact that John still held most of Sverdrup High School's scoring records in every sport, and that he'd been selected All-State in football, basketball, and baseball in both his junior and senior years. He shared the story about the time their coach had called time-out in a basketball game and told Matt never to shoot the ball, just pass it to John. Matt kept his comments positive, and when he was finished, he whispered to John that proper decorum prohibited the sharing of the really good stuff. John whispered a thank-you in reply.

And then John stood up and stole the show. "I'd like to thank all of you for showing up tonight," he began. "It's been great fun to reconnect with so many old friends, and as I look out over the faces in this crowd, I see many more old friends that I'd love to visit with before this evening is over.

"And there's one special thank-you that I have to say tonight, to one special person. Alvie Glasnapp isn't here tonight, and I feel bad about that. Well, I guess Alvie is here in spirit, and I hope that for once I can make him smile. In fact, just out of curiosity, would everyone who played for Alvie, in one sport or another, please stand up?"

Over a hundred men stood up, some of them still young, others old enough that it was a chore to stand up. They all seemed proud to stand up for Alvie, and every one of them was smiling. "That's about what I thought," John said. "OK, now you may be seated, and I'm gonna tell a few stories.

"As some you in this room may remember, I was not known for my work ethic. It was easy for me, the sports, I mean. All I really did was play with my friends, and I think maybe that's what I'd like to celebrate tonight. We never won a state championship in any sport. We were never conference champions, either. Actually, I don't think we won half of our games, in any sport, but we sure had fun, and I think that's what I remember the most about my school days.

"Earlier tonight I met up with a few classmates and old friends. So many memories came back to me as we talked. It was so odd to see my friends now, almost fifty years after I last saw them. I was amazed at the way so many of them had changed. When I saw Joe Fogal," John pointed at Joe, "I was amazed. Joe was a childhood buddy of mine, kind of a dunce, actually, and today he's a pillar of this community. Well, at least, that's what he told me a few minutes ago." A wave of laughter moved through the crowd. Fogal covered his face and laughed along with everyone.

"I was sitting in study hall once, the big study hall up on third floor of the old building, and I was talking to Steve Saathe . . ." and John pointed at his classmate.

Saathe smiled, then covered his eyes and lowered his head in self defense when everyone turned to look at him.

"We decided it would be really funny if we lit a firecracker and tossed it out the window." A small wave of laughter moved about the room, and John added, "We never thought about the fact that the principal's office was directly below the study hall! When the principal came looking for the idiots who threw a firecracker out the window, we were shocked by his brilliance. We were not the sharpest tools in the shed!"

John told a few more self-deprecating stories about himself, including the time he scored a basket for the other team, and the time that some kid in study hall had given Ex-Lax gum to several of the football players and caused a "Code Brown" at practice. He never mentioned the honors he'd won in high school, only his friends.

As Matt watched John return to his seat, smiling and nodding to old acquaintances, he thought he saw something new and different in his friend. He wondered if John had finally let go of something, or perhaps taken hold of something? He glanced at John several times while the next speaker, Leather Helmet's grandson, began his speech.

Bill Berg's grandson was the final speech of the evening. He told a few stories about his grandfather and the life he'd led after his school days at Sverdrup. While the young man talked of the Depression and World War Two, and Sverdrup in the 1950s, Matt could no longer keep his mind away from the way he and Jane had parted. He hid his cell phone in his lap while he sent another text message to Jane:

<Are you there yet? I miss you.>

There was no reply. Matt stared at the table in front of him while Leather Helmet's grandson spoke; he was done listening. He wanted the banquet to be over, and he stole a glance at Mo every so often.

When all the acceptance speeches were finished, the master of ceremonies thanked everyone for coming and announced that everyone was welcome to stay and visit as long as they liked. Live music would be provided by a string quartet of students from the Sverdrup High orchestra.

Steve Saathe, Joe Fogal, their wives, and a few other old friends were telling stories about the good old days with John and Sally when someone asked about Snag and Darrell.

"They stayed at home," John said. "They get to hear me talk enough."

"Hey, whatever happened to Snag?" someone else asked.

"He lives in Pine Rapids and has a fur business with Darrell, just down the street from my shop," John replied.

"I'll never forget that day!" Joe Fogal said. He knew that everyone who was gathered around the table was thinking about the day Snag Velde stuck his shop teacher's head in a vice and then quit school. "I was standing right there," Fogal said, "right next to Snag! Mr. Wodnick was up in Snag's face about something they were doing, but that was nothing new. Anyway, when Snag finally snapped, it was like a dream. I just stood there and watched. I couldn't believe what was happening. There was a bit of a scuffle and then I heard Mr. Wodnick begin to whimper 'Ow ow ow' when Snag bent him over and cranked the vice in wood shop class on his head." The men at the table were all laughing as Fogal told the story.

"Were you there?" Sally asked John.

"No, I was in my social studies class."

"Well, here's the real kicker, so to speak," Fogal said, directing his words to Sally now. "When Snag had the vice cranked up good and tight, he stepped back from Mr. Wodnick and said 'Fuck you,' just before he kicked Wodnick in the ass. Then he walked out the door, got in his car, and drove away." Fogal paused and looked around. "That room, the wood shop, was the quietest room I've ever been in. Nothing even close, for about thirty seconds after Snag left. I went over and uncranked the vice on Mr. Wodnick's head, and we all stood still and watched him walk over to his little office. He was holding his smashed ears and crying. It was absolute silence in that room for a minute; nobody knew whether to shit or go blind. But then a couple of us started to giggle. Then that little Knutson kid ran away crying—from the stress of it all, I guess. Right after that everyone started laughing."

"Man, that story spread through our school like wildfire," Saathe said to Sally. "There was never a day like that one!"

"Hell, they should put Snag in this Hall of Fame, too," Fogal blurted.

Other old friends wandered close to John's table after the outburst of laughter over Snag Velde's story. Matt decided to stand up, get a refill of his scotch, and walk around the room. He was at the bar, putting a dollar in the tip jar, when he noticed that Mo had walked over and put a hand on John's shoulder.

"Stand up, John. I need a hug," Mo said. She had never liked John very much when they were young, but tonight seemed like a good time to put away grudges from so many years ago. "Your little speech was pretty good, John. It's nice to see you again," Mo said, when John embraced her.

"Really?" John asked, only half kidding.

"Well, I had to say *something*," Mo laughed. "I thought I'd see you at my dad's funeral."

"I know it, Mo, and I shoulda been there. I'm sorry, but your dad and me . . ."

"No need to go over all that again now," Mo said, and she changed the subject. "Your girl is really pretty, and nice. How did you meet her?"

"She told me to shut up and threatened to throw me out of her coffee shop," John beamed.

Mo laughed. "Some things never change," she said. You know, John, my dad had such high hopes for you. He really wanted great things for you."

"I wish I'd been different," John sighed.

"No you don't. You liked being you." Mo smiled and poked John's arm with her index finger.

"Yeah, you're right." John's smile widened and he added, "I like you, Mo. I always did. But we're never gonna get to know each other, are we?"

"I think we know each other pretty well, John," Mo said with her index finger still tapping John's arm. "Now you go home and live up to my dad's expectations; you have a good life."

"I will, Mo. You do the same," John said. "Goodbye, Mo, and thanks for the hug."

"Goodbye, John." Mo turned away from John and began searching the crowded room for Matt. When she found him, she walked directly to him.

"It's kind of like your dad's funeral," Matt said when she stood beside him.

"Yeah. A lot of the same faces," Mo said. "I never expected all this."

"You know, a couple years ago, if anyone had asked me, I'd have told them that I'd never be coming back here again," Matt said. "And now I've been here twice in the past two years."

"I think everything happens for a reason," Mo said. "Are you OK? I was peeking over there at you all night. You look . . . troubled."

"It shows? That much? I had a tough day yesterday." Matt moved his lips so close to Mo's ear that her hair tickled his lips. "You wanna go for a walk, just you and me?"

"Let's go." Mo took her coat from a rack by the door, and then she told David she was going outside with Matt. As they stepped out into the dark October evening, Matt couldn't help but wonder what Mo was thinking, or what she might say, or even where they'd go. But he liked being with her again, alone.

"Where should we go?" Matt asked.

"Does it matter?" Mo replied. They set off toward Sverdrup's downtown business district, which consisted of two rows of brick storefronts that had been built on Main Street and First Street nearly a hundred years earlier. No businesses were open at nine o'clock on a Saturday night, and except for a handful of parked cars, the streets were empty.

"So what made yesterday so bad that you couldn't enjoy tonight's little party?"

"Did I look *that* bad?"

"Pretty bad. Is Jane all right? The cancer?"

"Yeah," Matt said, but it was clear that there was much more on his mind.

"Are *you* all right; your health?"

"I'm all right," he said. "Well, it turns out that I'm a little crazy." He walked a few steps more, staring at his feet, before he added, "She told me she doesn't have any feelings for me anymore."

Mo's head spun as if it was on a swivel. "When? When did she say that?"

"Last night."

"What's going on? Is it all right for me to ask?"

"Mmm, I've told you everything. All those emails and text messages, and a couple phone calls; I think I already told you everything over the past year. It just never gets any better."

"So what happened last night?"

Matt grimaced. "I told her I'd rather be dead than wind up like her."

"Oh, Matt, no. Really?"

"Yeah, things were said. It wasn't good."

Mo reached over and took Matt's hand in hers.

They strolled back and forth all through the small business district of their hometown, and the tone of their conversation grew more comfortable. Eventually they wandered across each of the four small bridges that spanned the Flambeau River, and they strolled through two small city parks. They walked through alleys and streets where neither of them had ever walked before, and they sat on a park bench under a street lamp for a time.

"Hasn't changed much, our little town," Matt said as he looked at the silent streets.

"Seemed bigger and busier back then," Mo said. "Do you ever wish that you'd stayed here, or come back?"

"No, I knew I had to go."

"How did you know that?"

"I dunno, but I just knew." Matt shrugged. "And I was right."

"You wanna know how I knew? How I finally understood that you were never coming back?" Mo asked, but she didn't wait for an answer. "Your dad called me about the middle of October, when your dog died."

"Eddie. Eddie Munster. He was a mutt, and he looked just like Eddie Munster, from TV." Matt sighed, then he covered his mouth and waited for the rest of Mo's story.

"Yup, when Eddie died in the autumn of your first year away, you never came home to bury him. Your dad and I buried Eddie in that grove of cottonwoods, in that pasture down by the creek. We had a nice talk. Your dad told me you were just too busy with your studies, and I tried to believe him. But I knew you were gone; you'd let go of everything back here. You wouldn't even take the time to come home and bury your dog."

"A frat party," Matt said quietly. "A frat party, drinking beer with a bunch of morons. That was more important to me than Eddie." The sad memory made Matt look away from Mo. "You believe that?"

"Your dad was so nice to me," Mo said, and she allowed Matt to let go of a sad memory. "He told me how much you cared for me, and he made me promise him something."

"What?" Matt smiled faintly. "What did he make you promise?"

"I'll never tell. That was part of the promise."

"C'mon, tell me."

"Uh-uh. Can't do it! I made a promise. I guess it's like you just said; some things gotta stay a secret." She paused a beat. "But I will tell you something that surprised me all those years ago, after you were gone."

"OK, what was that?"

"When I heard you were going into dentistry," Mo said, and she shook her head, "it just didn't seem like a good fit for you."

"Really? Why?"

"It's hard to explain. I guess I thought you lacked the compassion for a career in health care." Mo stopped to rephrase. "That didn't come out right. I knew you had a tender heart, but I saw you as a coach, or a businessman, or a general in the army. And dentists always seemed kinda dorky. I never thought of you like that. Does that make sense?"

"Mm, I guess so." Matt thought for a moment about what Mo had just said. "It *is* kinda dorky," he admitted with a chuckle. "But I guess I was fascinated by the sciences. Every biology or chemistry or physics class I took seemed to offer a deeper look into the workings of the universe. I didn't know it at the time, but I think I was searching for an understanding of the cosmos." He shrugged. "I thought about medical school, but I knew that I never wanted to tell someone they were gonna die, and there was nothing I could do about that; it was going to happen if I chose medicine. But dentistry . . ."

"You actually thought about that kind of thing, back in college?"

"Yeah," Matt said, and Mo could hear sadness in his voice. "I didn't *ever* want to have that conversation with anyone. I know that thought shaped my actions, my plan."

"But you don't mind telling someone that they're gonna lose a tooth?" Mo joked.

"Nope." Matt chuckled. "I can fix *that*. I have some control over that."

"And you didn't want to coach because . . .?"

"Because I knew I'd have to deal with people like John Velde, and it was hard enough just to be friends with him," Matt chuckled.

Mo laughed. "I can still see my dad's face, grinding his teeth over stuff that John did. And that was good; what you just said about trying to understand the universe. I never thought about it in the way you said, but I guess that's what led me to a career in the health sciences too."

"I think a lot of people in the health sciences think like that. Maybe people in the arts, too," Matt said. "And I know that Albert Einstein spent his life searching for the Theory of Everything . . . the unified theory that tied *everything* together." They walked on in silence for a few steps and Matt said, "I only mentioned Einstein so you'd think I was smart. Just wanted to impress you, like when we were young."

"It worked, just like it did back then." Mo squeezed his hand. "You're my best friend, Matt."

Her words surprised Matt, and he glanced at her immediately.

"I know, it's a little weird, but we have something special, you and I," Mo said.

"Yeah." Matt nodded.

"I think Jane didn't mean what she said, about not having any feelings for you anymore. I think you just hurt her feelings, and you'd better straighten that out. That's on *you*, and you'd better fix it."

The park bench they'd been sitting on faced the small, quiet highway that separated Sverdrup's business district from the residential area. "Yup, you're right," Matt said. He was about to say something more when his phone buzzed, telling him he'd received a text message. "I better check this." He hoped it would be from Jane, telling him that she was safely in New York, and that she loved him. But it was from John Velde:

< Where are you? Are you with Mo?>

"It's John," Matt said to Mo, and he tapped out a quick reply:

< Walking, and yes.>

John's response was just as swift:

<I won't lie for you.>

<Don't be a prick.>

< The VFW is about empty. We're gonna take our private party back to the luxurious River View Motel. Sally and I will go back with the Glasnapp boys, but I'll leave my truck in the VFW parking lot for you. OK? Keys in the gas cap.>

< Thanks, but you're still a prick.>

<See you later?>

<We'll join you in a while.>

"They're going back to the motel, John and your brothers, but John left his truck at the VFW for us." Matt grinned.

"Just like high school days . . ." Mo laughed. "John taking the party with him, and you and I following after."

Finally, a pair of headlights eased into view and then rolled through a green light on the way out of town. Mo squeezed Matt's hand when the taillights disappeared. "Do you still think about that contrapasso business?"

"Yeah, some."

"That's crazy. Ooh, I'm sorry, that was bad, what I said." She laughed.

"Yeah, I'm paying some guy four hundred dollars an hour to tell me the same thing."

"Do you really think God would punish you like that?" Mo asked.

"Well, maybe not, but it sure seems that there are some cosmic forces at work here," Matt said, and the road was silent again.

"Does Jane know about your girlfriends, before you met her?"

"Yes, pretty much."

"And does she have a problem with all of that?"

"No."

"Then why should you have a problem with hers?"

"Well, I shouldn't," Matt started. "And if it was in my power to make a choice here, I would choose to not be crazy over this. But the thing is, I know my Jane, and I know that she'd never have done that unless she had powerful feelings for that guy. And that's OK, too . . . or at least it *should* be OK. But I guess *I* want those feelings. I want them to be for *me*, all of them. I want everything. It makes me sick to think about . . . you know, Jane and . . . Jeez, Mo, I can't be much more honest than that. She's hidden all of that from me for all these years, so I can only imagine what's been on her mind when she's alone with her thoughts."

"That's right, Matt; you can only imagine. You're the one who's thinking about it." Mo looked at the sidewalk for a moment and then asked, "Do you ever think about *me*?" The question surprised Matt, but he didn't take long to answer.

"Yeah." He nodded, and he understood the point she was making.

Mo squeezed his hand and pulled him into the crosswalk. "Let's keep walking. OK?"

The night was different on the other side of the road, as if someone or something was lurking there. Autumn leaves had shaken loose from most of the tall boulevard oaks. Every street in the old residential part of town looked like a mine shaft, and every street lamp on every dimly lit corner looked like it should have an exorcist standing next to it. Gnarled and barren trees cast crooked shadows on the sidewalks and front lawns of the small houses.

Off in the distance a car door slammed, then tires squealed. "That sounds like testosterone poisoning," Matt said.

"Some things never change," Mo said with a nudge.

"My car, that red Ford, couldn't spin the tires on glare ice."

"I was talking about the testosterone," Mo said.

The odds of someone hearing their conversation were pretty low. This sleepy little town was already buttoned up for the night. Nonetheless, it seemed important for them to keep their voices low and remain unseen. They walked on through neighborhoods where they'd played as children. Boulevard sidewalks were old, cracked and heaving in places. Small houses in the middle of most blocks were darkened by overgrown trees. Matt and Mo lowered their voices to nearly a whisper to protect the silence as they walked along. Then they'd emerge into the soft yellow light of a street lamp on each corner and raise their voices a bit.

Some of the houses were decorated for Halloween. Some were dark, and didn't appear to be lived in. More than a few houses offered a look inside, with curtains opened wide enough that a passerby on the street could see the people inside having popcorn and watching TV. Matt pointed out the house where there used to be a big yellow dog that chased his bicycle when he rode by. Mo stopped and stared at the house where her piano teacher lived, and then said she remembered the tune she played for her recital. They drew near to the city park across the street from the Catholic church, and Matt said, "Hey, I have to go check something out."

"What?" Mo asked.

"Well, look. The playground equipment hasn't changed since Velde and I used to play here. I carved my initials, and Gloria Prokes's, into one of those teeter-totters, and I gotta see if it's still there." Matt walked over and after a brief inspection of the teeter-totters he announced that all records of his love for Gloria Prokes were long gone.

"How old were you when you carved your initials there?" Mo asked.

"Ten?" Matt guessed.

"That was fifty-three years ago," Mo laughed. "They probably got new teeter-totters."

"I had to look. Know what else I remember? Velde used to jump off the teeter-totter when I was up in the air on the other end. He thought it was so funny to watch me come crashing back to earth."

"Whatever happened to Gloria?" Mo asked. "I remember her. She was older than you, black hair, dark eyes, real cute."

"Well, it turned out that she liked somebody else, not me, and she was pissed at me for carving her initials into that teeter-totter."

"Did it leave you scarred . . . dealing with the pain of unrequited love?" Mo teased.

"I took a few years off from women, until I met you," Matt joked, and he held a hand over his heart. "C'mon, let's keep walking, this place is too painful."

As they left the park behind, Mo pointed to an older stucco house and said, "Remember who lived there?"

"Sure do. Pigeon Tits!" Matt laughed, and the conversation returned to people and places from back in the day.

They walked, and talked, and pointed at homes that stirred forgotten memories until they turned a corner by the old high school. Mo stopped in her tracks. "It was right here," she said, and waited for Matt's response.

"I remember," Matt said. "My old red Ford, the one that couldn't spin the tires on glare ice, was parked right over there, on the other side of the street. And we were standing right here. And it was *so* cold."

Forty years had gone by, and once again they were standing on the spot where their friendship had begun; the sidewalk outside the old high school, a decaying redbrick dinosaur that had been replaced by a new school on the outskirts of town several years earlier. Back then, the boys on the basketball team parked their cars here, by the school entrance, while they were away at out-of-town basketball games. It was also the place where a caravan of school buses carrying players and students home from those basketball games would return afterwards, to drop everyone off. It had been a meeting place for high school kids back then, a place where they'd assemble briefly, then splinter off into small groups and couples. And it was the very place where a skinny sixteen-year-old Mo Glasnapp had stood and plotted and hoped for a chance to talk to a shy boy, after a Friday night basketball game.

"I remember the pep rally we had before the game. I thought I was hot stuff," Matt said. "And I remember running out onto the floor with my teammates when the band played our school song before the game, and the excitement, and the bright lights, and the smell of popcorn."

"Do you remember who won the game?" Mo asked.

"Nope. I don't even remember where the game was. But I do remember noticing *you* standing on the sidewalk after the bus ride home. You were with a bunch of older kids when I came out of the locker room, and I remember wondering why you were there."

"You had no idea I was waiting just for you, stalking you, did you?" Mo smiled.

"Nope. Even when everyone else had gone home, and you and I were the only two people left standing here in the cold. Even *then* I didn't understand. I just asked if you wanted a ride home because . . ." He shrugged. "Well, there we were, standing in the cold, and it was time to go home."

"I was trying to flirt. I *never* did things like that. I was so nervous, talking to you. Couldn't you see that?"

"Well, I still had emotional scars from that teeter-totter incident," Matt joked. "So I actually had no idea that you'd been waiting for *me*. But when I opened the passenger-side door for you, and then walked around to the driver's side and opened my door; there you were! You'd scooted all the way across that big ol' front seat, and you were sitting right where the driver's girlfriend would usually sit. *That* was when I figured things out."

"I never did anything like that, before or after that night!" she laughed.

"And I remember that you were sitting there with your hands folded in your lap with your head down, like you were waiting for bad news." Matt grinned.

"I think I *was*," Mo said. "I took a big chance, you know. I let an older boy, a handsome boy that I had a crush on, know exactly what I was thinking. That could have been bad. What if you'd laughed at me? It would have been worse than the teeter-totter incident."

"I loved it, Mo, I loved it." Matt's smile covered his entire face. "When I sat down and felt your leg touching mine, and felt you lean against me . . ." Matt stopped himself. "You know, I had a lot of great things happen here in this school, this little town, during my school days, but that moment, that ride home, that was the best of 'em. It was special, one of a kind."

"Me too," Mo said.

"But what if I hadn't offered you a ride home?" Matt asked.

Mo pointed down the darkened street and laughed. "It was only a three-block walk to my house."

"But it took me two hours to get you there," Matt chuckled. "And then your dad grounded you for riding around with me, an older boy."

"I should never have told you about that. He really did like you. I remember that you did eventually put your arm over my shoulder. And I remember that you acted like you were just trying to keep me warm."

"Yeah, well, you fell for it."

"I wanted to fall for it."

"Other than carving my initials in the teeter-totter, putting my arm around you that night was the most reckless sexual behavior I'd ever done, too," Matt said.

"I loved every second of it. I still remember the way it felt to sit beside you, and talk to you like that. I still get that wonderful feeling in my stomach when I think of that night," Mo whispered.

Matt began to nod, and then reached his arms out and pulled Mo close. He knew she was waiting, wondering, stirred by the moment, and she returned a firm embrace. "Me too, Mo," he said, when his cheek was pressed against hers. He whispered, "Where did all the years go? What happened?"

"Life. Life happened to us, Matt," she said.

They held each other but said nothing more until they released their embrace. Matt put an arm around her shoulder as they turned and walked away from the place where their friendship began. They walked slowly, without talking, for three blocks, until they came to the small, white frame house where Mo had been raised. "Do you know who lives here now?" Matt asked, when they were in front of the house.

"No. We sold it shortly after Dad died."

Matt walked to the front steps, sat down, and motioned for Mo to join him. When she hesitated, Matt said, "Looks to me like nobody's home. Besides, it's no crime to sit here. C'mon, take a chance."

Mo still balked. She stood on the boulevard sidewalk and stared.

"I don't think we're ever gonna be back this way again, Mo. C'mere and sit with me, like we used to," Matt said. His elbows were resting on his knees, as if he was there to watch the world go by, when Mo sat down beside him.

"Lotta memories here, Matt."

Matt reached over and held her hand. "We used to stand here when I kissed you goodnight, and hoped that your dad wasn't watching us."

"Mm-hmm," Mo purred. "That was nice. Did you know that I used to run up to the window in my room and watch you drive off, all the way across the bridge by the grocery store, and out of town, and then I'd lie there and think about you?"

"I thought about you, too, all the way home. And then I lay in my bed with the lights off and thought about you some more," Matt said. "Happy times."

"Do you remember Mr. Bojangles?" Mo asked, while she stared into the dark night. There; she'd finally asked him. It was the thing she'd wanted to ask about ever since her father's funeral. Ever since Matt went away.

Matt breathed in heavily. He wasn't sure just what he should say, or where this might take them. Then he breathed, "Of course."

"What do you remember?" Mo asked.

"You go first," Matt said.

Mo gave his hand a squeeze before she started. "It was a Friday night, after a basketball game, about a year after we started dating. It was a home game, and there was going to be a dance in the gym afterwards. Your parents were out of town for the weekend, and they'd given you strict orders not to have anyone come out to your farm while they weren't home."

"I remember that," Matt said.

"So naturally, after the game, we went to your house." Mo turned and grinned at Matt.

"I remember." Matt returned the grin.

Mo let go of Matt's hand and covered her face before she went on. "We'd actually talked, a little bit, about going all the way that night."

"I remember." Matt's grin was gone.

"So, we went to your house, and we made one of those pizzas that came in a yellow box, the ones where you made the crust first, and then you made your own toppings, and—"

"I remember," he interrupted. "We did that all the time, but that night I was nervous."

"Me too." Mo paused, then continued. "After the pizza we went into your bedroom, and you lay down on your bed. I stood there for a while, just looking at you, until you motioned for me to lay with you. Then I lay down with you."

Matt said nothing.

"You put your arm around me and just held me for a long time. We just lay there with all our clothes on, and didn't talk, or kiss, or anything. Finally, you kissed me and said, 'You wanted to go to the dance, didn't you?'"

Matt kept silent and let Mo share her memories.

"When I said yes, you got up off the bed and you said, 'I think the dance is about over.' Then you looked through some records beside your record player, until you found a little 45 rpm. You put it on the little record player in your bedroom and you said it was the only slow song you had. The song was Mr. Bojangles. Do you remember?"

Matt nodded.

"You stood there with your hand out, waiting for me to get up and dance with you, and we had our own dance. We just held each other and danced in your bedroom for a while. Then you took me home and we sat right here and talked for a while."

"That's pretty much the way I remember things," Matt said.

"But it was never the same for us after that. Why?" Mo asked.

"Ah, Mo, I hadn't thought about that night for so long." Matt frowned. "And then when I saw you at your dad's funeral, it all came back for me, too." He didn't want to say anything more.

"Talk to me, Matt, I thought I was your best friend."

The words "best friend" hung in the air for a second, and Matt remembered John Velde's manifesto about men having women friends.

"OK, I remember that night, too, Mo. I was all set to put the full-court press on. I wanted us to have sex, or I thought I did. I planned it all week, in my mind. But when we got there, to my room, and you lay down with me, I could tell that you weren't so sure, and I didn't really know how it was supposed to be done either. I was afraid, too." Matt wrung his hands while he chose his words. "But I thought I could probably, you know, play my cards just right, and . . ."

Mo took Matt's hand when she heard the hesitation in his voice.

"But then, after we lay there for a while . . . I knew it wasn't right. Well, I knew it wouldn't be right for you. You were too young. I knew that if I pushed, and you gave in, I was about to steal something from you that I could never give back. I knew I'd wreck the rest of your school days and put an end to your young years, and I couldn't do that. If we'd had sex that night it would have altered your life in a bad way, and I liked you too much to do that. I think maybe I loved you . . . as much as a seventeen-year-old is capable of love." Matt sighed, then said, "If we'd done it that night, we'd have both set out on a path, together, that we could never stay on, together. I wanted to do it, but I couldn't, Mo. And after that night, I sensed that we were about done; we'd never be together. It just wasn't meant to be. It was time for me to go, and you had to stay."

Mo softly rubbed a thumb over the back of his hand. "Really?"

"Really. I tried to hang on for a while, but then one night in the early spring we stood right here where we are now, and we talked for a long time. I told you that I loved you, and I wanted so much for you to say it back to me. But you wouldn't say it. I knew that night, that our romance, this thing that had been so great for a year, was over. I was ready for whatever was coming next, but you weren't. We were going to have to go our separate ways." Matt paused. "I kissed you goodnight, and while I was walking to my car I knew that I'd never be back."

Mo wiped a tear from each eye, then she squeezed his hand. "I did love you. I was just so young . . . I don't know why I didn't say it. And I wanted you to try a little harder that night, but I was afraid, too."

"*Now* you tell me," he joked, and his words hung in the cool night air for a few seconds before he added, "But Mo, there was no way that could have ended well. Ever since we reconnected, I've wondered about all the what ifs in this story. What if we'd done it and you got pregnant? What if we'd done it and then broken up a year or two later? What if we'd done it and stayed together until we got married, and then divorced. What if we'd done it and stayed together all this time. Would we be the people we are now? We just weren't ready for all that would have come our way."

"I've wondered those same things, Matt."

"The timing was just all wrong for us, Mo. And it was never going to be right."

Mo sniffled and wiped tears away.

"I feel sad, Mo. I feel sad that I couldn't share my life with you. My whole life. I think it would have been happy, good. But it wasn't meant to be. Even if I could change things, I wouldn't change one thing about the way my life has been. But I still feel bad. Did *you* ever think about that? Have you ever wondered?"

Mo sniffled again, and nodded. "Sure I did, but I moved on, too, and I'm happy. I love somebody else. I love my life, the one without you in it. But yeah, Matt, I still wonder about all of this. I wonder about all the what ifs, too. And I wish I could have shared my life with you, too. But . . ."

"Well, good. I wanted to hear you say that. I don't feel like such a creeper if you were thinkin' the same things."

"But it's good *this* way, too, Matt, the way it worked out. This way all of my memories of you are happy. We're still friends. We still have a con-

nection. You know that saying; that people come into our life for a season, a reason, or a lifetime. It looks like you and I got the lifetime deal."

"Yeah, it seems that way," he agreed. Mo's use of the word "connection" had tripped a little switch in his brain. There had been other girls,
women, in his life, but Mo was the only one, besides Jane, that he ever
felt any connection with.

"You *are* my best friend," Mo said. "And I think there's something more in
all of your craziness about Jane. I'm guessing that you know what it is, too."

"Yes, there is," Matt said. "I didn't realize it, didn't understand it, until
tonight." He drew in a huge breath and exhaled.

"So tell me; what is it?"

Matt reached an arm around Mo's shoulder and pulled her closer.
Then he leaned over and kissed her on the ear. "It's you."

"What do you mean.?"

"Think about it, Mo. Think about the Mr. Bojangles moment. You
must remember how it felt when we were young, and we stood right here
and kissed each other goodnight. I know you remember my hands on the
small of your back, and other places. I know you remember the kissing,
and the gentle laughter when we could be alone. The talk of the future,
and the touching."

"But we never—"

"Doesn't matter," Matt interrupted. "The connection was there. It still
is. And I think that's the thing that makes me crazy."

"I'm still trying to understand," Mo said.

"It's pretty simple, Mo. If Jane has those kinds of memories and feelings for some other guy, well, I feel terrible just talking about it. I know
it's the old double standard. I get that. But I can't help it, because I know
what I still feel for you, and how much those happy times mean to me. It
just makes me sick to think that Jane might have that, or worse yet, even
more passionate memories of someone else." He shook her gently, and
asked, "Do you understand?"

"What about the other girls you knew, after me and before Jane?"

"They were all pretty nice. But I didn't love any of them, and there
was never any connection. Sorry to say, but what I did with them was all
about me." Matt leaned close to Mo. "I'm just being honest here."

"OK, now it's my turn be honest, too," Mo replied. "You know that
stuff about Jane having a lifelong *thing* for some other guy after her first

time . . ." Mo made a face like she was looking into a bright light and shook her head again. "Ah, not so much."

"How would *you* know?" Matt asked.

"Well, it may happen that way for some girls. And maybe that's the way it was for the girl you told me about before, the one who died. But I doubt it. It's kinda sad, I understand, but you'll never know. So you need to let go of it." Mo sighed and rubbed Matt's hand. "And I *know* it's not like that for everybody."

"Well, look at what you just said about that night with Mr. Bojangles," Matt said. "And we didn't even—"

"We already had something, Matt. Something that *still* holds us together. I don't know if sex would have, *could* have, changed that. It doesn't always work like you're thinking. A little while ago you said that you could only imagine what Jane thinks about that other guy. Well, that's right, Matt. You can only *imagine*, because you have no idea what she really thinks. Here's what I think: I think *that* Jane . . . what was her last name back then?"

"Monahan."

"OK, *that* Jane Monahan, the one who was with that other guy? She wasn't the same Jane Monahan you met two years later. On that night she was still a kid, a work in progress. She was just trying to find out who she was. And you know, I think she was searching for you. Even then. You say you want everything, and I think maybe you don't understand that you *did* get everything. I think everything you did, and everything she did, before you met, was preparing you to find each other, so you'd know when you found the other half of yourself. And you need to know that a girl's first time doesn't always leave her warm and starry-eyed forever."

Matt slowly turned a puzzled face toward her and asked, "Are you talking about your first time too?"

Mo didn't look at him. She was staring at the quiet, dark street in front of them when she said, "I've never told *anybody*." She sat in silence for a few seconds, and Matt began to wonder if she'd changed her mind about telling her story.

"It's OK, you don't need to tell—" Matt said.

"Freshman year in college," Mo began. "He was a nice boy. I was curious. Happened in his dorm room."

Matt waited, and waited, for more. "That's it?"

"What you're really wanting to know, is whether or not I still have some feelings for him because he was my first, right? You're wondering if a random sex act could trigger a lifetime connection, right? You're wondering about all that because of this thing with Jane, right?"

"I guess so."

"Well, don't worry. I never think of him, and have no feelings for him, and the sex was just . . . nothing. When it was over I sorta felt like, 'so that's what it's like.' Except . . ." Mo didn't finish.

"Except for what?" Matt asked.

"Except that while it was happening, and for a long time afterwards, I wished it was you," Mo said.

It was not the story that Matt expected to hear, and both of them sat on the porch steps in silence for a minute. They were still holding hands, and Mo squeezed his gently.

"I met John a little while after that, and I loved him right away. We had a connection, too. I knew he was the one. Sex got to be fantastic, and we lived happily ever after."

Matt had no reply.

"I guess I shouldn't have told you all of that."

"No. It was nice," Matt said. "But, that part about me—"

"Don't say anything, Matt. The only reason I told you that is because, well, I guess in light of all you've shared with me, I wanted you to know. Maybe it's just my gift to you."

"Hurts and feels good at the same time," Matt said without looking at her.

"Tonight, earlier, when we first got to be alone, were you thinking about how it might feel to hold hands again?"

"Yup, I wondered; wondered about that for a long time. Tonight, when I walked into your motel room, I got butterflies in my stomach. And then, when you took my hand in yours a while ago, I got 'em again." Mo raised the back of his hand and held it against her cheek for a second. "And I really wanted to talk, like this."

Matt scooted as close to her as he could and put an arm around her shoulder. "That was perfect, Mo; what you just said. I felt the same way."

"We're gonna love each other for our whole lives, and never be together, aren't we?" Mo whispered.

"I guess so," Matt said. "But this thing with you and me, it just wasn't meant to happen."

"I know. I've always known," she said. "This is as close as we're ever going to be, isn't it? But it was good, really good, and I'm so glad that you were part of my life. If this is all we get, well, that's all right, I guess."

Matt nodded his agreement, and he let himself join Mo as they gently swayed from side to side for a moment. "Hurts more than feels good right now," he said quietly.

"So, what is it that you want, Matt? What do you want from Jane?" Mo asked.

"I want everything. I want to be her hero, her champion," he said, with a lump in his throat.

"OK, if you want everything from her, what are *you* willing to give?" Mo asked.

"Not sure I know what you mean."

"Are you willing to give everything? Are you willing to give me up; walk away from me again?" Mo asked. "You just told me a few minutes ago that when you left home all those years ago you just let go of me. Can you do it again?"

Matt nodded yes without hesitation.

Mo pulled him close and put her cheek against his. She was crying softly when she whispered, "I'd have been disappointed by any other answer. That's why I've always loved you, too, Matt."

"Do you understand what you feel right now?" Matt asked. "'Cuz I sure don't."

"No. But I know that we need to go our separate ways." Her voice was weak, but Matt understood the finality of her words. "If my husband or your wife could have seen us tonight, they'd be hurt. It could hurt both of our marriages."

"We were innocent," Matt said.

"I know, but what would anyone think? How can you ever explain . . ."

"Yeah, you're right," Matt admitted. "Maybe we can still write, from time to time?"

"I don't think so. What would be the point? I need to go back and be happy in my life; the one without you in it. You need to do the same. You need to go back and repair things with Jane. You need to go find your place, as you say."

"Yeah," Matt said sadly. "You're right."

"I like the way you call her 'my Jane,'" Mo said. "I noticed that way back at my dad's funeral. It's pretty telling. I think you two share something pretty special. Will you be OK when you get home? Do you think you understand things better now?"

"Yeah, but—"

"Then there's nothing left to say, is there, Matt, except goodbye."

Matt gave a sigh. "OK . . . but I'll always be part of your life, too."

More than four decades had passed since they'd stood on these same front steps. And now, just as then, they knew that they'd come to the end. A cool dark evening surrounded them tonight just as it had all those years ago, and it was time to leave again. This time forever.

They stood up slowly, and then turned to face each other.

"C'mere, Mo," Matt said, and he opened his arms. As she stepped into his embrace, he kissed her cheek and then held her close. She held him as if she never wanted to release him. Then she kissed his cheek, and stepped away.

They held hands, but said nothing as they turned and walked away from the old front steps. Their footsteps echoed softly as they walked along the dark streets and crossed through a veil of happy memories, back to their lives. They both knew they'd never return.

CHAPTER FIFTY-THREE

———◆———

The work tables at Velde Taxidermy were covered with tools and foam deer heads waiting to have fur and antlers fixed to them when Matt let himself in the front door on Thursday afternoon. An old radio on the far end of John's workbench was tuned to an oldies station, and John was fumbling with a large set of deer antlers.

Matt hadn't spoken to John since the previous weekend, and he'd been OK with that. Two days in the truck with John, and the evening at the Hall of Fame banquet, had been enough for a while. He was still upset with John over the thing with Lori, the waitress, too. But he had several hours to wait before Jane was due to return from New York, and he wanted to reach out to him before he went home for the day.

"Stinks in here," Matt said, to announce his arrival.

"What are you doing here?" John asked, after a curious glance at the clock above his workbench. "Get done with work early?"

"Yeah, a little bit. I just thought I'd stop by on the way home. Jane's s'posed to get home in a couple hours, and I had nothing better to do." Matt saw no reason to tell John that he'd had an ugly goodbye with Jane six days earlier, and only received two very curt text messages since she'd been away.

"Well, good. Grab a chair while I finish this," John said, without looking away from the deer antlers.

Matt took a tall chair from the table where John was working and sat down with his elbows on the table. "How did Sally like your hometown? I'll bet she was pretty impressed."

John was trying to stretch a deerskin cape around one of the foam deer heads. "I think she had a nice time, but one night in Sverdrup is about enough." He let the partially finished deer head rest on the table while he walked to another table and returned with some large pliers.

"I didn't realize that you held so many school records," Matt said.

"I didn't either." John returned to struggling with the deer head. "I had a chance to visit with Saathe and Fogal, and a bunch of old teammates. That was kinda fun. I hadn't been back there since graduation. I didn't recognize a lot of people, people that I should have known. I was kinda embarrassed a coupla times there. I had to look down at name tags, and then I couldn't hide my surprise when I realized who I was talking to."

"Yeah, that happens."

"Fogal's wife is hot, by the way. Did you notice the rack on her? Nice knockers! But Saathe's wife is a real TOG." John thought for a second, then added, "I said hello to Mrs. Pigeon Tits, too. She looks like Norman Bates's mother. Yipes!"

Mrs. Pigeon Tits did resemble a decaying mummy, and they'd both chuckled about her appearance on the night of the banquet. But now, John's careless reference to Steve Saathe's wife stung Matt. It hadn't been so long since John had flippantly spoken of his little fling with Lori, the waitress at Buster's, and the disappointment, or disillusion, or anger, or whatever it was that John had created in Matt's heart was still fresh. He'd tried to let it go during the return to Sverdrup, but now he felt the hard feelings begin to swell inside himself again.

The thing with Lori the waitress was bad enough, Matt thought, but now he was joking about women again. John should know better. He just didn't get it on so many levels. He should understand what had just happened to Jane. Her breast cancer had been the pivotal moment in her life, and Matt's. John should understand that Matt didn't need to hear him laugh and joke about nice knockers anymore. That was for high school boys. John should have outgrown that kind of thing a long time ago. But apparently, he never would.

At first Matt hid his hurt feelings. He was trying to let John's thoughtless words go. Again. He was willing to assume, for a moment anyway, they were just a slip of the tongue. But down deep he suspected, no, he knew, that John couldn't change that much in such a short time.

"TOG? What's a TOG?" Matt said, asking for the definition of another new term, and all the while asking himself why he never confronted John about this kind of thing.

"Tub...Of...Goo."

"She's really nice," Matt said, but he knew that John didn't care about that. "What did Sally have to say about the evening?" Matt asked, struggling for a reason to overlook John's shallow and insensitive words.

"She had fun, and a few laughs, but the thing she asked about the most . . ." John stopped and looked at Matt, ". . . was you and Mo. What the shit was going on there? I thought we were gonna hafta turn the garden hose on you to get you apart."

"Bull *shit*," Matt groaned.

"Well, I know your history, so I pretty much expected you to spend some time with her, but Sally noticed right off, something in your eyes, and Mo's. And then you disappeared for a couple hours."

"We just went for a long walk. We had a nice talk. But I think you were right about something."

"What was that? I'm not right very often, so clue me in here, buddy."

"I don't think men can have women friends, either," Matt said.

John's head spun to the side. "You porked her, didn't you? You started talking about your feelings, 'n then you porked her!"

"Sorry to disappoint you, John, but nobody got porked."

"Well, did she at least tune your meat whistle?" John asked.

That did it. Matt stood up to leave. "I gotta go, John. This is all way over your head."

"Hold on there, Matt. I'm just giving you a hard time."

"No," Matt said, as he walked toward the door. "You just hurt my feelings. Why did you have to say that stuff about 'nice knockers'? What's wrong with you? I came here to talk to a friend, and . . . I was gonna try to share something, but you're a fuckin' idiot. You got any idea how much it hurts me to think about what happened to my Jane? Any idea how it hurts me when some asshole starts talking about knockers and tits, like that's all there is to a woman, to my Jane? Any idea how shit like that might make my Jane feel if she heard you say shit like that?"

John stared at him.

"And Jesus, Snag, your own brother, after all the shit he's been through, he finally met a woman, a nice one as a matter of fact, a girl that seems to be making him happy, and all you can say is that you think he's porkin' her?" Matt shook his head in disgust. "And *I* laughed when you said it. That *really* makes me feel bad." Matt drew in a deep breath. "You gotta be better, John. You gotta figure out where to draw the line. You ever listen to yourself? When you talk about women, or your own lady friends, you always refer to them as some girl, or some chick, like they didn't even have a name, or any feelings. Goddamn, John, they're human beings, and they're all pretty nice to you. They have feelings, too. And you think it's funny, too, what you did with Lori, don't you?"

"Matt, c'mon . . ."

"I drove all the way home, to Sverdrup, and I said nice things about you. And I meant them. And that speech you gave, it sounded like you had a soul for a minute there. But then I come over here to talk to a friend, because something hurts inside me, and you wanna know if I porked Mo." Matt shook his head in frustration. "Well fuck you, John. I don't wanna know you anymore."

"Hold on, Matt."

"Fuck you! You don't deserve friends like me."

———

As Matt's truck rolled into the clearing in the trees surrounding his home, he saw that Jane's car was parked by the kitchen door and there were lights on inside. She'd come home several hours early! He turned off the ignition in his truck and sat in silence for a moment. Now what? Would she be packing her things and getting ready to leave him? Would she still be angry about the way they'd parted? She'd been away for five days and he'd received only two text messages from her. No calls. The texts were short and businesslike. She let him know she had arrived and she was OK, then four days later she said she was about to board a plane and she'd be home about seven o'clock on Thursday. The words "I love you" or "I miss you" never appeared. Her last words before she'd left had been, "I don't know what to say to you anymore."

As he trudged up the steps toward the kitchen door, he wondered how she'd greet him. Would she ignore him at first, and then pick up their argument right where they'd left it a week earlier? Would she pack a few more bags and move out? That wasn't very likely, but the last time he'd spoken to her she'd uttered the most painful words he'd ever heard. He had no idea what to expect.

She was waiting, standing in the kitchen, when the door swung open and he stepped inside.

"Hi, you're home early," Matt said, still uncertain what to expect from her. "Did you catch an earlier flight?"

"I missed you," she said, and she stepped around a suitcase and put her arms around him. She was still wearing her coat, and she buried her face between his neck and his shoulder.

"I missed you too, honey," Matt whispered while he stroked her hair and held her tight. This was what he'd hoped for, but he didn't understand the look on her face, or the intensity of her embrace. He kissed the top of her head, and stroked her hair.

"Don't you leave me!" she said without lifting her face away from his neck, and he could feel that she was crying.

"Huh?"

She lifted her face away and looked into his eyes. "I found your pack, the one with the needles and the tubes for drawing blood." And she waited for his response.

"I . . ."

"Are you planning to hurt yourself?" she asked.

There was no point in denying his thoughts; she already knew. Matt closed his eyes and put his cheek against hers.

"Don't you *do* it! Don't you even think about it!" Jane cried and held him close. "Don't you even *think* about it. What's wrong with you? Is it *that* bad?"

"Sometimes it's pretty bad."

"I feel terrible, Matt. I caused it all."

"No, I don't think that's true, but things sure got crazy. What are we gonna do, honey?" Matt asked, while he stroked her hair and kissed her cheek.

"I made a fire first thing when I got home. I picked up a couple bottles of wine on the way home, too. Give me a few minutes to put my stuff away. Then let's sit by the fire with a glass of wine, and talk."

Matt was waiting on the couch with soft music playing, and wine and a bag of potato chips, when she sat beside him. "It's nice to be home," she said, as she stuck her hand into the open bag of chips. "Jeez, you could have at least put 'em in a bowl."

"You shoulda called ahead if you wanted a formal dinner," Matt said, then he poured her a glass of wine. "How was New York?"

"Big buildings. Lotta rude people. We went to some great restaurants. Had a nice time, I guess."

"How was your sister?"

"She's doing OK; better all the time. It was nice for us to have some time together. How was Sverdrup?"

"Same as always. And John did a nice job with his award. I'll tell you about all that later." He leaned forward, put his elbows on his thighs, and assumed a posture that told her was ready to talk about other things.

"*Were* you thinking about hurting yourself?" Jane asked again, after a silent moment.

"Mmm . . . I guess I was wondering how to ease the pain. I don't know if I was ever that serious."

"It was *that* bad?"

"It was pretty bad."

"Is it getting worse?"

"I don't think so, but it's been like this for months. I just hide it from you. I tried to tell Ron, but I'm not sure he understands. He keeps asking me if I'm gonna do myself in, too."

"You think about that? Really?"

"I did for a while there. Not anymore. But I still struggle with the other stuff."

"Jesus, Matt. Every day?"

Matt nodded. "Most days. Sometimes a song comes on at work, and I'm reminded of you, when we young, back in school. But I don't see you with me. I see you with him, even though I don't know what he looks like. Sometimes I see you at a party, or a bar, and you're laughing and having fun. But sometimes I see you . . . you know." Matt shook his head and sighed, and he seemed to have lost hope that he could ever escape from those images. "Sometimes I have to leave a patient and go to my office so I can close the door and cry. I wanna beg you to tell me about it again and reassure me that I'm your hero, that you still love me. I feel like I need to win you back. Every day. But I can't. Especially now, after . . . after the cancer. It just makes me feel so bad I wanna die." Matt lowered his eyes and shook his head. "I can't believe how weak I am. I feel like you're protecting me from the truth now, because you know I'll get like this . . . so you just lie, or leave things out, to keep me safe. The time has come, Jane. Will you tell me how you felt about that guy? The truth, all the truth, this time, or I don't think I'm ever gonna be able to get on with things."

"Oh, honey, I've told you . . . I was nineteen and an older guy talked my clothes off me."

"The Jane I know wouldn't do that unless she was in love. There has to be more that you just don't want to tell me."

Jane sank back into the couch and stared into space for a moment, choosing her words carefully, before she went on. At last Matt felt like he was going to hear the truth, but now, that was just as frightening as all the things he'd been imagining for the past year.

"There is more, but it's not what you think. Not at all." Jane kept silent for so long that Matt thought she'd changed her mind and decided not to share the whole story.

"I thought he was clever, like you," Jane started slowly. "He was a guy with some standing, a grad student, and all the young girls in my class talked about how cute he was. I told you that before. Anyway, I suppose I was curious; I was young. He paid special attention to me, and I suppose I wanted to think he felt something for me. That first night, when he said we could have sex if I wanted to, I think I expected it to be a special, wonderful thing. But it wasn't. I knew I was just being used. It just seemed to be something for him to do. It *wasn't* special, and it *wasn't* good. As soon as it was over, he took me home, like he was dropping off some laundry. As I walked from his car and up the steps into my apartment, I felt bad. But I went back, several times, like a puppy after it's been scolded. I wanted it to be special, but I knew better. Then, after a couple more times, I told him I might be pregnant." Jane closed her eyes and turned away from Matt. "He acted like he'd heard it all before. Waved his hand and then told me to get an abortion. Then he opened up the drawer of his nightstand and showed me a bunch of rubbers. You know, like he kept 'em there for when all of his lady friends dropped by."

"Were you pregnant?" Matt asked.

Jane closed her eyes and shook her head no.

"Did you sit by the phone and wait for him to call, and feel bad when he didn't call?"

"No. But I felt like dirt. I knew I was nothing to him, just a girl who was there when he wanted a good time. The whole thing left me scarred about men. I knew I'd been had. From that point on, I was brusque, angry, mean-spirited with guys. Every time I heard some guy try a pickup line on me, I bristled. I was downright rude, *mean*, with guys from then on. I had my guard up so I'd never get myself in that position again. My father even noticed it. He took me aside once and told me not to be so gruff with men because there were plenty of nice ones out there. What father ever says *that* to his daughter?"

"Why did you lie about it all these years?"

"I didn't lie," Jane said.

"Well, you kinda did. And when you finally told me, I thought you'd kept all that secret because you were hiding something from me."

"I was! I couldn't tell you about *that*. I was so attracted to you, and we were in love so soon after we met; I was afraid that you'd think less of me. I could see the way you looked at me, and I didn't ever want that to change."

"So why *did* you tell me?"

"I suppose I didn't think it mattered anymore. I don't know. Maybe at last, I wanted to tell you about this bad thing I did all those years ago. But now I wish I'd never told you. It was nothing to me; it was bad. All bad."

"You don't think about him, and wish . . ."

"God no." Jane took Matt by the back of the neck again and shook him gently. "Matt, Matt. Listen to me. I love you. I mean, I love *you*. I don't love you *more* than him, because I never loved him, or cared about him. I just love *you*. Only! And forever." She shook him again. "And there was *never* a connection. Got that? I told you, I was nineteen. I wasn't a complete person yet." She stopped and thought for a moment. "Matt, I'll always have that memory of my first time, and you won't be in it. Sorry, but who cares? I have no special feelings, or fond memory of it." She sipped her wine, then swirled her glass slowly. "I know you, Matt. I know you have such a soft heart, and I know that now, after all this, you're always gonna wonder if I'm telling you the truth. I wish I could make you believe that." Jane sighed and stroked the side of Matt's face with the back of her hand. "I went out with maybe a dozen guys in college. There were a couple nerds in there, and a couple jocks, and they were all pretty nice guys. But I never had a boyfriend. I never even took a boy home to meet my parents. Nothing, until you came along. I didn't trust men, any men, until you. Think back, Matt. Do you remember our first date? We were standing next to each other at the bar and some guy walked up and asked me, nicely, if he could buy me a drink? I told him to fuck off! I barked at him. Remember?"

"I saw you do that several times," Matt said. "And I did wonder where the anger came from."

"Well, maybe now you understand."

"You never did that to me," Matt said.

"You were off-the-charts different, Matt. You were funny, and I could see in your eyes that you liked me. A lot. You were special. I knew you were the one. Think about this, too," Jane said. "If that incident hadn't happened like it did, it probably would have happened with somebody else, and maybe I'd have found myself in a relationship, and you and I would never have met. Maybe that incident is what let us find each other?"

Jane took Matt's hand in hers, kissed it, and held against her face while they listened to the fire crackle for a moment.

"Remember when we were new in love, and we spent all of our time together?" Matt said. "We made love several times a day. Every conversation we had over coffee or a burger in some little joint was the most important conversation of our lives, and every little chat we had over a little booth in some bar was *so* interesting and fascinating. We used to go for coffee and talk about the kind of car we'd buy if we ever had any money, or the house we'd build if we ever had any money. Then we'd go back to my place and make love again."

"Those were good times . . . the best," she said.

"I thought I'd lost all of that. You can't imagine."

"Oh, Matt, you know I'd never felt any of that or done any of those things we did together; the laughter and the long walks in the dark, and waking up together, and making breakfast in our underwear. I stopped hanging around with all my friends just so I could be with you. All the sexual stuff, Matt; you *knew*, you had to know, that was all new for me, and it never happened with someone else."

"Yup, I knew it never happened, but then it *did* happen. In my head. Maybe it *was* just my own imagination, or insecurity, or craziness. But the compression of time and all the psychobabble that Ron told me about— that made everything so real. Real as stone. It became the new truth, and that's why I wanted to just go on my journey; I couldn't bear the thought of you sharing those times with someone else. *That* was enough to die for." Matt smiled and shook his head. "I love you, Jane . . . more than I understood until all of this came along."

"You must know that I've loved you for my whole life, and no one else. You must know that, *don't* you?"

Matt nodded yes. "Just stay close to me, 'cuz I need you." Then he leaned back on the couch and put his feet up on the coffee table/cribbage board, and he took a sip of wine. "You know what you said about the things that we did before we met, and how maybe we out there searching for each other?"

"Yes."

"Mo said the same thing."

"You talked to Mo, about this?"

"Sure. Several times over the past year. She knew I was messed up, and she said some nice things. She was trying to help me."

"She was there, this weekend, too. Wasn't she? Tell me about that."

"The banquet? It was OK. There was a good crowd. John did a nice job with his speech. Sally got to meet some old friends. As you might guess, there was no shortage of colorful anecdotes about John."

"And you were with Mo?" Jane asked again.

Matt nodded. "Sure."

"Did her husband come with her?"

Matt shook his head.

"So, you were alone with her?" Jane asked.

"We had a nice talk, and we went for a long walk while the others rehashed the old stories."

"What did you talk about? Where did you walk?"

"We talked about you a lot, and we talked about the good old days, and we walked . . . well, you can only go so far in Sverdrup."

"How far did you go?" Jane asked.

"I set you up for that one." Matt grinned.

"The question stands," Jane said, without a smile.

"Are you asking me if I was unfaithful?" Matt asked. "Really?"

"I know you've been exchanging emails and text messages for a long time. I saw the way you looked at each other when I met her in the hospital. I know what kind of mood you were in last week; it didn't feel like we were very close."

"Jane, c'mon."

"Tell me," Jane said. "*You're* the one who had a connection with someone else?" She squeezed his hand.

"She was my best friend once, and she was good to me while you were sick, and I was crazy."

"Matt, this thing you have with her; it's an affair, an emotional affair, and it bothers me. I feel bad, jealous, I suppose. Especially after my surgery. I see the look in your eyes when you speak of her. It's exactly the thing that you fear about me, but in reverse. And in your case, it's real."

"I know." He began to nod slowly. "I know it now. I can see what you mean, and you're right."

"I am?" Jane questioned him with her eyes. "You don't want to argue about that?"

"Nope. You're right. And I'm sorry if I made you feel . . . uneasy? I sure didn't see it that way in the beginning, but I do now. When all this began, she was just a good friend who I reconnected with at a funeral, and then again when you and I were in the hospital. But Mo was my high school sweetheart. That had some weight. She was there with me back at the headwaters of my life, when everything was easy, and good. And then when I was crazy, she was a lifeline to a happy, safe time for me. And everything she said assured me that that part of my life was never going to change."

"So, last weekend . . .?" Jane asked.

"We walked, and we talked. We were innocent, then and now."

"OK, tell me about *then*," Jane said.

"Mo was the first girl I ever spoke to. She was my first kiss. She was sixteen."

"How innocent?"

Matt questioned her with his eyes.

"We both need to know the truth," Jane said.

"She was my first love. She was my best friend for a while there. We thought we'd always be together. We were . . ." Matt paused, "curious about sex."

"I thought you never—"

"We didn't. We never came close. I guess we knew it was right there for us if we wanted to. All the tender little things that young lovers share; we had *that*; cuddling on the couch, giggling, she wore my class ring and rode around town and sat right next to me in my rusty old car, and we talked about what our future together would be like. We never did anything to complicate that friendship, though.

"But we had a *connection*. You *are* right about that. And this thing between Mo and me; *that's* what made me crazy. I think I understand it all now."

"Well, I don't."

"OK, here's the heart and soul of it, Jane. I guess I assumed that if I had such good, and strong, feelings for Mo, and we never were lovers, well, I thought *you* must certainly have some powerful, hidden feelings for . . ."

"Ah, Matt, that's just not true. In fact, it couldn't be further from the truth."

"Yeah, but *I* didn't know that. All I knew about was how *I* felt. It seemed like you were leaving me, in about every possible way. I just want you to love me."

Jane moved closer and let her head rest on his chest.

"I'm sorry things got so complicated and crazy. I'm sorry for the things I put in your head." She sighed. "But tell me what else you talked about on your walk with Mo."

"Well, we had some unfinished business, I guess."

Jane held silent for a few seconds while she chose her words. "So what does *that* mean?"

"I think we broke up," Matt said. "Sounds crazy, doesn't it? But we walked all around through some old neighborhoods and wound up sitting on the front steps of the house where she grew up. It seemed like we'd made a complete circle. I was seventeen, maybe eighteen, when she made my heart go pitter-pat. We both lived with our parents, so we had no sense of real-world issues; not even little things like laundry and meals. All we ever had to think about was ourselves. We never had a quarrel. We never fought about money, or sex. We never shared a bathroom. Everything we did was easy. So yeah, I look back on those times and feel happy. But it wasn't real life. So, do I have feelings for her? Sure, I still remember the feelings that an eighteen-year-old boy had for his first girlfriend, and I like those feelings. She's not 'the one who got away,' she's not the path I didn't choose. She's the path I couldn't choose. It just wasn't meant to be. We finally sealed the deal, and broke up.

"And just to be clear; the path I *have* walked through life has been wonderful, and if I could do it all over again, I'd choose the same path, the one that led me here, to you, every time. That's the one that was meant to be, and my life would be so much less if I'd missed it. I love you. Only. How was *that* for an answer?"

"Very good, almost literary." Jane leaned over and kissed him. "Uh-oh. More wine, please." Jane giggled as she held up her empty wineglass. "I have a nice buzz going here, Matt." She leaned back and looked at the cedar planks in the ceiling. "Get the other wine bottle, will you?"

"Good to know," he said. "I'll be right back." When he returned with a second bottle of wine, he sat close to Jane and they both put their feet up on the coffee table/cribbage board, and leaned back.

They were both staring into space, with their wineglasses resting on their stomachs, when Jane said, "What are you thinking about?

"Mmm . . . I had a lot of time to think while you were away," he said. "I'm so sorry for the way I sounded on the night before you left . . . well, for what I said, actually. At first, I wanted to tell you that you just didn't understand what I was trying to say, like the fight was *your* fault. But I said exactly what was in my heart. And I'm so sorry. What a terrible thing to say. But I was really hurt, and I've been hurtin' for so long."

Jane reached over and stroked Matt's arm softly. "I had a lot of time to think too, over the past few days."

"Yeah?" Matt said.

"Some of what you said on the night before I left was true. I could try a little harder. I've been distant. And the sex; I still love it. It's always good. But it's so difficult for me to get in the mood anymore. You need to remember that all I thought about for a long time was staying alive long enough to see my grandchildren, and how uncomfortable I felt, and how terrible I look."

"Ah, Jane, you're still the prettiest—"

"Hold on," she interrupted. "You don't have say it. I know you love me still. I see the way you still look at me. And I know it's only been a year or so since I made that little adventure happen in room 206 at the Ashley Hotel. There's still a fire burning. All I have to do is try a little harder."

"We never used to have to try. It all just came so easy," Matt said. "I miss that."

Jane reached a foot over and rubbed it against his leg. "We're so lucky."

"Yeah, we have all of this, and we still have each other." Matt paused. "You know you're in love when you can't sleep at night, because reality is finally better than your dreams," he said, obviously quoting someone. "Know who said that?"

"No. Who?"

"Dr. Suess." He grinned, then said, "Nothing in my heart has ever changed, honey. I love you more than ever."

"It's been a great journey, so far, in spite of a few recent speed bumps,"

Jane said, then she rubbed foot a little higher on his leg. "You wanna fool around?"

"What if I fail?"

"Oh, I think there are a few things we can do to help with that."

———

Ninety minutes later Jane kicked the bedcovers to the side and lay spread-eagled, hoping to cool off. "I thought you were gonna have a heart attack there at the end."

"Me too, but it woulda been a good way to go," Matt said, as he lay beside her. "Well, I always get sorta carried away when you start calling to the loons."

"Me? You were making some noise too!"

Matt only laughed, pulled Jane close so they were spooning, and then drew the beaver-skin blanket over them both.

"They say it fades, Matt, the sex, I mean, and I think it has to."

"Fades to what?"

"They say it fades to something better. Something deeper, and richer. Do you remember a poet named Robert Browning?"

"Is he the guy who wrote, 'There once was a boy from Nantucket . . .'"

"No," Jane groaned. "He's the guy who wrote, 'Come, grow old with me; the best is yet to be.' What do you think about that?"

"Pretty stupid."

"I'm serious." Jane nudged Matt's ribs. "Do you think the best is yet to be? For us?"

"I dunno, but it's gonna hafta be pretty good if it's gonna be better than all we've had so far."

"We'll be OK, through this next part of our lives, whatever it is. We'll stay in love. Just don't leave me."

A cool rain tapped at their windows, and the woods outside were black. "This cabin, when I lie here with you and listen to the rain like this—I always feel safe, like nothing can bother me," Matt whispered in her ear. "What are *you* thinking about?"

"All of this. It's a lot to think about."

CHAPTER FIFTY-FOUR

The canoe wasn't exactly lurching forward with each stroke of the paddle, as it had when he was young, but Matt was moving the old Grumman smoothly back home across the glassy surface of Scotch Lake. The warm breezes of a sunny autumn Saturday had died away as twilight settled in and a big yellow October full moon began to peek over balsam spires on the east side of the lake.

The fishing on French Creek had been a little slow. He'd landed a couple of nice brook trout, though, all decked out in their spawning colors. Brook trout in the fall; that was some of God's finest artwork, Matt thought.

As the keel of the aging canoe sliced through the water, Matt made a point to look around him. Off in the distance he could see his home, with a line of smoke rising from the backyard fire pit. Jane must have made a campfire. Good, it was a perfect night for a fire. The deep greens and yellows of the woods that always came alive with the day's last rays of sunshine had given way to the deep blue, almost black, of the lake, and the softer blue of the evening sky.

A cold front was coming soon, so the weatherman said. The lake would be frozen over in a few weeks. Hard to believe on a night like this, but winter was coming. Soon he'd be taking Jane to the Flemish Cap. Driving on a thick sheet of ice again, and drilling holes through the ice in search of crappies, and a few laughs.

The thought of Scotch Lake freezing over with yet another change of the seasons, along with the sight of the full moon on the horizon, brought back a powerful image. As he shifted the paddle from one side of the canoe to the other, he looked far down the lakeshore to the place where his deer stand waited high in a tree. And he remembered the majestic old buck that he'd killed years earlier. Matt would never forget the way that dying buck had raced across a sheet of ice and sparkling fresh snow, framed by that same moon, and those same lofty balsams, in a desperate dash to outrun death. Now Matt wasn't so sure how he felt about taking another trophy.

A peal of laughter echoed across the lake, and Matt glanced back at the line of smoke coming from his backyard. He could see people moving around the circle of stones surrounding the fire pit, and then he heard more laughter. And he recognized John's voice.

Jane must have invited John and Sally over for a fire. He didn't really want to spend any time with John, but now he had no choice. He picked up the faint scent of wood smoke about a quarter mile from home.

John, Sally, and Jane were seated on the split log benches surrounding the fire pit when Matt emerged from the path that led from the house to the lakeshore. "We started without you," Sally said when she saw him.

"Yeah," Matt replied with a subdued nod. He wished that Jane had asked him first, before inviting John. He stood next to Jane and made a point to greet Sally, but not John. Then he sat down by the fire.

"No luck?" John asked. He was uncomfortable, too. He knew what was on Matt's mind.

"Coupla nice trout," Matt said.

"I wanted to surprise you; have a party. I thought we'd cook some brats over the fire, and then make some s'mores," Jane said. "I invited Ron Hested, and Snag and Darrell, too."

When Timmy's voice and then Dave Norman's laughter rose up from the lakeshore Jane added, "The boys are here, too, and I think Ron is bringing Bradley. I thought it would be nice to get together around a fire one more time before winter sets in."

"Yeah, sure. I figured," Matt said. His curt reply carried a message that was impossible for John to miss. Then Matt reached an open hand into the beer cooler beside the fire and splashed some cold water on his face before he took a beer for himself.

"I'm gonna walk up to the house and get all the fixin's for dinner," Jane said, as she stood up.

"I'll come with, and help you carry things," John offered.

When they were safely out of earshot, Sally walked over and sat beside Matt. "Did you and John bang heads over something?" she said softly.

"Whaddya mean?"

"I *know* you did. He came over to my place last night, and he was feeling bad. He said you were angry."

"'Zat all he said?"

"He said he was afraid that he'd lost your respect, and maybe your friendship."

"He was right."

"He told me that you were his only true friend back in school, and that you'd kept him from making some bad choices."

"Well, he made plenty of bad choices. So I'm not sure I had that much influence."

"You did." Sally tipped her head and waited for Matt's response.

"I'm done with John." Matt sighed.

"Don't do it," Sally said. "That thing that guys do when they get angry at each other; take some time away. Then come back and everything is forgotten. Women can't do that. They stay angry forever."

"How did you get to be an expert on male behavior?" Matt asked.

"I'm an expert on a lotta things. Like you." Sally smiled. "I just *am*. And I'm the kind of person John needs in his life. Like you."

Matt turned a half smile to Sally and asked, "Is there any more beer in that other cooler, by the fire?" He wondered if John had told Sally about his dalliance with Lori, the waitress.

"Matt . . . John likes you, needs you."

Matt shrugged. "John needs a kick in the ass."

"Beer's in the cooler under the picnic table," Sally said, and as Matt walked a few steps toward the cooler, she repeated, "He needs you, Matt."

Matt answered with only an ambivalent nod. He opened a beer and took a long pull, then returned to sit next to Sally, putting his arm around her. "Do you love him, Sally?"

"Yeah, I do."

"Well, then you're lucky, because you get to feel the butterflies again." Matt had moved away from John's need for an ass-kicking, and was on to something he obviously felt was more important.

"Huh?"

"Do you get butterflies in your stomach when you're with John?"

"Yeah. Why do you ask?"

"Just curious. You get to feel the butterflies in your stomach once more, like young lovers do. That's such a great thing. You just be sure to enjoy that, because some people *never* get to feel it, and others forget the feeling."

The sudden shift from John's bad behavior to the butterflies in young lovers' bellies caught Sally unprepared. She studied Matt for a moment and tried to find a reply.

"Pretty quiet down there!" called Ron Hested from the back steps of the house. Bradley was at his side, and when he saw the other boys playing by the lake, he ran to be with them. "I heard there was a party here tonight!" Ron said as he walked toward the fire pit. "Bradley said we might even light some farts!"

John and Jane were following Ron, each of them carrying one end of a cooler full of fixings for a meal to be cooked over the fire.

The screen door at the top of the porch steps swung open again, and Darrell stepped out too. An instant later it swung open again and Snag appeared, followed by the woman that Matt had seen Snag sitting with in the coffee shop a few weeks earlier.

Sally leaned over and whispered to Matt, "Party on."

When everyone reached the fire pit, Snag introduced the woman as Rene, his friend. Rene was plain, with dark hair pulled straight back. She was unremarkable in every way, except that she seemed to have a little thing going with Snag. She also carried a handbag, or a satchel, on a long leather strap over one shoulder. The handbag was made of beaver hide, and the fur was so rich that it still glistened in the fading light. Clipped to the strap on her satchel was a key ring that featured a small section of skunk tail. Sally and Matt quickly exchanged a silent glance, acknowledging that they'd both noticed the obvious gifts from Snag.

Tileen "Snag" Velde was sporting a new look, too. He'd shaved, washed, cut and combed his hair, and he was wearing clean clothes that fit him.

Jane made a point to scurry around the fire pit and greet him with a hug, then a kiss on the cheek. There were no blood or grease spots on his clothes for the first time in Jane's memory, and she told Snag that he looked like a movie star. Then she issued a welcoming hug to Rene, too. When the rest of the introductions were finished, Snag took a beer from the cooler for Rene, and one for himself. Then he sat next to Rene.

"How's the fur blanket business, boys?" Matt asked.

"Awesome," Darrell said.

"It's great," Snag agreed. "Rene designed a website for us, and things really took off."

"And how 'bout the mental health business, Ron?" Matt asked.

"Booming! Lots of crazy people here in Pine Rapids!" Ron answered with a thumbs-up.

And the party *was* on. Several conversations took off simultaneously back and forth across the campfire as everyone took turns using long, heavy wire forks to roast wieners or brats. As always, a wiener or a brat fell into the fire from time to time, followed by laughter and a bit of cussing.

As the partiers moved about the fire, talking and laughing, and asking each other for mustard or ketchup or one thing or another, John sat down beside Matt and made a point to catch Matt's eye. John raised his brows and passed a look of contrition, an apology, and an unspoken question: *Are we OK . . . you and me?*

Matt thought for a second, and he made certain that John saw his disappointment, and doubt. And then he gave it up and nodded. He could let it all go; he always had in the past, and he'd do it again. And who was he to judge John, anyway? John would always be his friend, but John would have to find his own way. He seemed to understand the pain that his insensitive words had caused Matt. The thing with Lori? Well, John would have to deal with that on his own. Matt hoped he would just keep his mouth shut and allow himself to be the one who felt bad about it. He was done trying to fix John. As the fireside equivalent of a handshake, he raised the longneck beer bottle in his hand. John raised his beer, too, and tapped the neck against Matt's bottle, and they shared a silent toast. No more would need to be said. Until the next time something needed to be said.

"Hey, where's Mike Katzenmeyer?" Snag asked when he noticed Timmy and Dave and Bradley sitting together. "I thought he was part of the group."

"He moved away," Bradley answered, with most of a hot dog in his mouth.

"Awww," Jane said. "He's such a nice boy."

"Yeah, DeeDee and Mike moved in with that young guy from the bank, and then he got transferred to Duluth," Sally said. "They just moved the other day. It's funny the way people come and go from our lives. Maybe they'll be back someday?"

"A season, a reason, or a lifetime," Matt said to himself.

"Huh?" John asked.

"Nothing," Matt said, but he let himself remember the way Mo said the words.

"Aw, shit!" came a muffled groan from Bradley Hested, and when everyone looked at him, a long yellow glob of mustard was slowly moving down the front of his green sweatshirt. Then another yellow glob oozed out the end of the hot dog bun he was holding and splattered on his blue jeans. "Shit!" he said again, and the other boys giggled.

"You don't see that very often," Ron said, and it was the adults' turn to laugh.

The moon, halfway up into the night sky, and the flames from the fire at their feet were the only lights in the backyard, when Jane opened the first bag of marshmallows and announced that it was time to make s'mores.

Wire coat hangers bent mostly straight, with two large marshmallows impaled on the end, were soon bobbing slowly above the flames. Everyone holding a coat hanger was searching for the ideal hot spot in the fire to put a golden-brown bark on their marshmallow. But at the same time, they were shifting and weaving to dodge excess heat and protect their eyes from wood smoke.

"Shit!" Jane said when her marshmallow burst into flames. "Gimme a graham cracker and some chocolate, John; it's sitting right there beside you."

"Double shit," Matt hissed, when both of his marshmallows sagged and then fell off his coat hanger. "Toss me a couple more marshmallows too, will ya, John?"

A few chuckles moved about the periphery of the campfire, but in only a moment everyone turned their interest back to their own marshmallow.

A quiet, reverent ritual took over the proceedings, as always happens around a fire. People wandered about the fire, eating, or searching for another graham cracker, or stirring the coals. "How's fourth grade going?" someone would ask. "How's that old truck running?" another voice would add. Then someone else would comment on the weather, or some local gossip. From the lake, only a stone's throw away, all that could be heard was the murmur of voices, and laughter.

Through the smoke and the shadows, Matt looked across the orange glow of the fire and studied the people in his life. John was teasing the little boys; joking about school, and girls. Sally and Jane were talking to

Rene; it sounded like they were mumbling about someone who worked at the bank with Rene. Snag and Darrell were explaining the beaver-blanket-making technigue to Ron. Every one of them had some awful baggage in their life. They'd come up against some big, terrible thing that they just had to get around, and they'd done it. They all had some heartache but were dealing with life as best they could. The little boys—they hadn't lost their innocence yet, but that would happen soon enough.

"OK, John, I need the Hershey bars and graham crackers too," Rene said triumphantly, when she brought two perfectly roasted marshmallows away from the fire.

Jane reached for Matt's hand and they both took note of the tenderness as Snag and Rene shared a perfect s'more. Neither of them had expected to see something like that from Snag. Ever.

"A season, a reason, or a lifetime . . ." Matt mumbled again.

"Hmm?" Jane said.

"Nothing."

The little campfire party was about to settle into story time when Snag announced that he and Rene had somewhere else to go. Matt leaned close to Jane and whispered, "He seems like he's in a hurry to get somewhere else."

"Well, duh. Did you see the way she was handling his wiener?" Jane whispered.

It was the old Jane, the one who'd met him in room 206 of the Ashley Hotel. The one who snapped herself in the forehead while trying to impersonate Elmer Fudd. Matt hadn't heard that voice in a while, and he loved the sound of it tonight.

The tire noise from Snag's truck was fading into the forest when Timmy, Dave, and Bradley announced that they were going up to the house to play video games. "No lighting farts!" Sally warned, and the boys giggled all the way to the house. "And we're gonna head for home in a little while, so don't make a mess in the house."

"It's nice to be here again, for a fire," Ron said, as he dropped two more logs into the fire pit and then sat beside Sally. "I haven't done this with you guys for years."

"Well, you had a couple wives who didn't like this kind of thing," Matt said.

"Yeah . . ." Ron said as he lit a cigarette, "I mighta made a couple hasty matrimonial decisions." He laughed and then added, "All it cost me was money . . . a *lotta* money."

"Where's Elaine?" John asked. "Why didn't you bring her tonight?"

"Well, that was a kind of a selfish decision on my part," Ron answered. "I wanted this campfire for just me. I wanted to visit with you all the way we used to. And that reminds me; have you seen Mr. Whitehorns yet this year?"

"Not yet," Matt said.

"My brother saw him on the side of the road last week!" Ron said. "Over by my place. Sure would be a shame if somebody killed that bruiser with a truck."

"Prob'ly wouldn't do the truck any good either," John said.

"My throat's kinda dry," Ron said, and he gestured toward the cooler. When John extended a cold beer, Ron made a face and said, "You all outta scotch, or what?"

"Picky, picky, picky . . ." John said, while he put some ice and then some Aberlour in a plastic cup.

"Much better," Ron said, after taking a sip. Then he turned to Sally and took the conversation in a different direction when he asked her if she was glad she'd made Pine Rapids her new home.

"I love it here," she replied.

"Tell me your story. How'd you wind up here? How's your first year or two been? How did you meet this guy?" Ron asked, and he pointed a thumb at John.

Aided by sporadic input from the others, Sally told her life story in about ten minutes; the chain-saw accident, an unwanted pregnancy, a divorce, college as a single mother, teaching high school English, the coffee shop. The fire at their feet sent a single line of smoke straight up into the sparkling heavens as Sally finished her story, and a full moon turned the placid blue lake to a sheet of glass.

"Yeah, but you forgot to tell me how you met *him*," Ron said, once again pointing at John with his thumb.

"He was being an ass in my shop, so I threatened to throw him out," Sally said.

"She told me to shut the fuck up," John said.

"You may need to repeat those instructions from time to time," Ron said.

"What a great night for a fire," Jane said as she stared into the flames. It was a fact, and there was unspoken agreement all around the fire. "But it's s'posed to get *cold* next week." Her words hung there above the quiet fire for a moment, like the others, until she connected them to another thought. "But that's OK. I'm looking forward to ice fishing this year. I missed all of last year." Everyone around the fire knew she was looking into the coals and seeing the worst year of her life. And then, without looking away from the fire, she connected one more thought. "Sometimes it gets too cold, though, and my hole freezes shut."

The lips on every face around the fire immediately curled into smiles. Matt leaned back and looked like he couldn't believe his ears. "Huh?"

"Yeah, I *hate* when that happens," John said.

"I hear about that same phenomenon during marital counseling," Ron added. He managed to keep a straight face, but the others had all dissolved in laughter.

"I didn't mean . . ." Jane tried to raise her voice above her friends', but it was too late, and she could only join in the hysterics. Minutes passed and the laughter died down several times, and billowed up again, like an old fire. "Oh God . . ." Jane said as she wiped tears of laughter from her face for the second time. Then abruptly she exclaimed, "Oh my goodness! Look at that! A mouse just wandered over here by the cooler and snatched some food scraps."

"God, I hate mice!" Sally said as she raised her feet up and then put them in John's lap.

"OK, that reminds me of something else!" Jane raised a hand to the back of Matt's neck while a sinister look came over her face.

"Jeez, honey, you've said enough already. Don't tell that story," Matt groaned.

"You shoulda seen this place when we first moved in. We had mice everywhere . . ." Jane began, ignoring Matt's protest.

"C'mon, honey; don't . . ." Matt moaned. "It's not funny." He put his face in his hands and sighed, "Sh-it."

"I like it already," Sally said.

Jane brushed Matt's objections away and went right on. "We bought this place from an old man who'd built it as a cabin, and then added on several times. It was kinda run down when we bought it, and it was full of mice."

"No it wasn't," Matt groaned.

"Honey," Jane chastised him, "we could lie in bed at night and *hear* them in the walls, scratching. We put out about fifty mouse traps, and sometimes at night we'd hear them . . . *snap* . . . *snap* . . . *snap*."

Matt rolled his eyes and poured a scotch for himself.

Jane leaned farther forward and grew animated as she continued. Her hands moved as she spoke, and the firelight made her eyes bigger. "So we were newly married, if you get my meaning." She paused for effect. "Anyway, it was late at night, and we were . . . well . . . we were having sex," she giggled.

Matt shook his head and stirred the fire.

"I'm listening," John said.

"So, we were . . ." Jane paused again.

"Going at it?" Sally offered.

"In baseball terms . . ." Matt offered, while he poked a stick in the fire, "I was having a big inning."

Ron Hested burst out laughing.

"So anyway, where was I?" Jane asked.

"Well, Matt was rounding third and heading for home," Ron said.

"Right!" Jane pointed at Ron for emphasis. "It was really good, I was on my back, and the end was near—"

"Something is happening in my pants," John interrupted.

"In the front, or the back?" Matt asked.

"Shut up and let her finish!" Sally barked, and she tossed an elbow at John.

This was classic Jane Monahan, and Matt was thrilled to see that a light had returned to her eyes. He'd seen a glimpse of it earlier when she'd joked about Rene handling Snag's wiener, then in her smile when she'd talked about her hole freezing shut, and now it was here again. He watched her wave her hands and raise her brows, and he remembered her making erotic gestures with a tube of toothpaste, and then snapping herself between the eyes with a towel. He saw her at the fishing contest, joking about sucking the chocolate off his nuts, and a thousand other times when she'd stolen the show.

"So anyway!" Jane's voice grew louder and she leaned farther forward. "It was getting good, *real* good. And then I felt something in my hair. I didn't know what it was. I thought maybe a piece of the old ceiling had fallen down, because things were, you know . . . *rockin'*. But the thing in my hair was kinda moving, so I reached a hand up to my head . . . and I had a MOUSE IN MY HAND!"

Sally covered her mouth.

"OH! I went wild—kicking and screaming and waving my arms . . ." Jane paused, to be sure she had everyone's attention before she deadpanned, "I mean *screaming*, and kicking my feet!" Jane stopped and made a point to be certain that everyone seated by the fire was listening, then she tossed a thumb in Matt's direction. "Boy, Matt sure thought *he* was doing something right for a minute there!"

After the initial wave of laughter, which also echoed up and down Scotch Lake, Ron got up and made himself another drink. He was still laughing when he returned to his seat and said, "I'm gonna stop on the way home later and pick up some cheese to put in Elaine's hair."

"On that note . . ." Sally stood up, arched her back, and stretched, "I think it's time for us to go home. Let's end the evening with a good laugh." She flipped an armload of paper plates and napkins into the fire, and added, "The boys will want to goof around for a while when we get back to my place, and I need to use the ladies' room, too. Let's go, John."

"I should use the bathroom too," Jane said. "I'll carry some stuff up to the house."

"Thanks for the nice time, Matt," Sally said, and she walked over and gave Matt a hug. "This was a fun evening." She whispered in his ear, "Let's do this more often."

"You guys stay put," John said to Matt and Ron. "I'll carry the cooler back up to the house." Then, before he picked up the cooler filled with campfire food, he extended his right hand to Matt. "We good?"

Matt took his friend's hand and nodded. "Yeah. We're good." It would do no good to threaten, or cajole, or preach to John. It never had. John would either figure out how to handle the love of someone else, or he wouldn't. "Thanks for coming tonight."

"G'night Ron," John said, as he picked up the cooler and turned toward the house.

Jane turned to follow the others. "I'll be back in a few minutes," she said. "Don't let the fire go out."

Sally, John, and Jane were talking with each other on the porch, about to disappear into the house, when Ron stood up and said, "I gotta toss a wiz too." He walked to the edge of the woods, perhaps thirty feet from the campfire, and unzipped his pants.

"Good idea, Ron. I'll join you," Matt said.

Standing together, just outside circle of firelight from the campfire, both of them assumed the unmistakable posture of a man peeing, and Ron asked, "How're you doing?"

"You mean my craziness, or my peeing?" Matt asked.

"Craziness," Ron said. "Your peeing sounds pretty good."

"It's OK, I guess. Less crazy all the time, I think."

"Still think about hurting yourself?"

"Mmm? No. I stood on the edge once, but I don't think I ever *really* wanted to do it."

"Your demons still come around?" Ron asked.

"Yeah, but not so much," Matt replied. He was glad to have a few minutes alone with Ron.

"Still think about your contrapasso; your punishment?"

"Mmm, a little bit," Matt admitted.

"It'll take a long time to come back from where you were. It always does. I told you, this isn't like a broken arm or leg. You can't just do nothing and expect it to heal," Ron said. As he zipped up and returned to his seat at the campfire he added, "I had a thought as I was watching Jane tell her story about the mouse just now."

"Yeah?" Matt said, following behind him.

"I was sitting on the other side of the fire from you two. I could see her face, and yours. I could see the way she was touching you. I could see the way she moved closer to you. I saw the look in her eyes, too, while she was talking. She loves that story. She loves it because it's about *you* as much as her. It's intimate. It has love, and sex, and laughter, and it's a charming story about both of you, *together*."

"Yeah, it's a good one," Matt agreed. "It always gets a pretty big laugh."

"She loves you. It's so nice to see that in her eyes when she speaks of you. You say you want to be her hero. Well, buddy, you *are* her hero. I've seen the two of you together for a couple *decades*, and I can't think of another couple who has a connection like you two." Then Ron used a gnarled oak branch to stir the coals and he dropped another log into the fire.

Matt found an oak branch of his own and poked at the glowing embers for few seconds. "OK, so I gotta ask *you* a question, Ron."

"Shoot."

"Do you remember when we were talking a while back, in your office, and I told you that I'd had a little trouble . . . in bed?"

"Yes."

"Do you remember that I used a golf analogy; that it felt like I was standing over a three-foot putt, and I lost my confidence?" Matt's voice rose in an unmistakable comic lilt as he spoke, and the corners of Ron's mouth began to curl into a smile when he recognized it.

"I do remember that," Ron said, a smile finally covering his entire face. "Why do you ask?"

"So, do you get a lot of that? I mean golf analogies. In your line of work?"

"You mean, as in your case, where your putter let you down, and you were unable to finish the hole?" Ron asked, his chuckle building as he spoke.

"Exactly!" Matt pointed emphatically at Ron.

"Well, golf is a game filled with euphemisms that work well in the treatment of sexual dysfunction. For example, it's considered bad form to tell your partner about other holes you've played; stuff like that. Again, why do you ask?"

"Well I just wanted to tell you that I made a long putt last night," Matt said. "Never any doubt. But I took a *lot* of strokes first."

Ron leaned back, lit a cigarette, and smiled at Matt. "You *are* starting to find your way back from the dark side, aren't you? What's changed?"

"Yeah, I think so, Ron. I'm not sure what's changed, though. This fear of losing my Jane; it's like an open wound. I don't think it will ever completely heal. But maybe that's not such a bad thing. I guess I'm learning that life, and love, just won't obey my expectations. And maybe that's OK too."

"Good one. Well said."

"It's hard to explain, but sex seems like a door. When she lets it swing open, somehow that's when I feel the closest to Jane. That's when our connection seems the strongest. And I don't think it's because of the sex; it's all the intimate little things that go along with it. Know what I mean?"

"Absolutely. And the funny thing is that men usually find that closeness *after* that door swings open. Women need to feel the connection *before* the door swings open," Ron said. Without another word, he extended his glass and shook it until the noise of the ice cubes clinking told Matt that he was out of scotch.

"Want another hit?" Matt asked. Ron nodded and held his thumb and index finger about an inch apart. As Matt poured three fingers' worth of Aberlour into Ron's glass, he went on. "You know how it feels when you're new in love? I just want to hold on to that."

"Thanks," Ron said, when Matt poured his refill. "New in love . . . I like that."

The night air was still warm and the single column of smoke still rose straight up. Only the popping noise of burning sap and pine knots disturbed the silence. Matt sniffed at the sleeve of his sweater to check how deeply the wood smoke had penetrated it.

"May I share something with you?" Ron started. "I was about the age you are now when I met Elaine. I was in an unhappy marriage." He took a long drag on his cigarette. "I knew Elaine from around the clinic; she worked over in administration. Anyway, we were talking one day. We were alone in a little conference room, and when we went to leave, we found ourselves standing close to each other, by the door." Ron looked over at Matt and grinned. "We kissed. It just happened, and it felt like thirty years had been wiped away. I was young, and happy, and strong again." Ron threw his cigarette into the fire. "We were 'new in love' . . . I know what you're talking about. I know how that feels."

"So how do you hold on to that?" Matt asked.

"That's the hard part," Ron sighed.

"Hey! Throw another log on that fire! I'm coming back down there!" Jane called out from the porch. Then, while she stepped as quickly as she dared through the dark shadows between the house and the fire pit, she said, "OK, boys; what am I missing?" When she sat down beside Matt she took his hand in hers.

"We were just talking about my craziness, and my demons, honey," Matt said.

Jane moved closer to Matt and nudged him until he put an arm around her. "And . . .?" she asked.

"Turns out Ron is crazy too," Matt said.

"No secret there, I guess." Ron sighed. "It's getting late, and I should go home soon. But I want to tell you how nice it was to sit around this fire with you tonight. Matt, you've enjoyed a lifetime of love and affection with the most attractive woman I know."

"I know it, Ron."

"Well then, I hope you can start believing it, my friend," Ron said. "Now I think it's time for me to wrap up this house call." Ron leaned back and kicked the charred end of his fire stick into the glowing embers.

"So, will there be a charge for this?" Matt asked.

"No, just have me over here to burn a marshmallow from time to time." He stretched his back and then added, "I gotta go home, but like I said before, I'm gonna stop and pick up some cheese to put in Elaine's hair before bed. That was a *fine* story, and you told it well, Jane. And thanks for the fire."

"Thanks for coming, and for talking with us," Jane said, before she kissed him on the cheek.

"Thanks, Ron," Matt said, and he shook Ron's hand. "I'll walk you up to your car."

"No, that's not necessary. You two enjoy the fire and beautiful night as long as you can. I'll find my way up the hill to my car. But tell me again, what kind of cheese do you think works best for that mouse in the hair thing?"

"It's not the cheese, it's the way you set the trap!" Jane announced.

"I'll call if I need instructions," Ron said. Before he turned away, he reminded them, "Think about all that we talked about tonight. You two stay in love."

Neither Matt nor Jane said a word until they heard Ron's car door shut, and then the engine noise from his car disappear into the forest.

The mercurial surface of Scotch Lake was blue-gray and shimmering against the night sky. Way out there in the middle of the glassy expanse, the yellow reflection of a harvest moon quivered gently. Matt threw several small logs into the fire and then stirred the coals.

"So, how do we get back to where we were?" Matt asked. He leaned close and squeezed her hand. "I love you, Jane. Always have, and always will."

"I don't think we get to go back. But I don't think we need to. Let's just keep going forward. I still love you, too. Always have . . . always will."

"You wanna go in for the night? It's getting kinda chilly," he asked.

"Yeah, OK, I'm tired, too. But this doesn't have to be our last fire. We can come out and make another fire after the seasons change. Just a small, defiant gesture to . . ."

"To who?" Matt asked.

"I guess I don't know." She giggled. "It just sounded like a good thing to say."

"OK, let's go in." Matt chuckled as he stirred the dying coals and covered them with some dirt.

They were both hunched over and shivering when Matt turned the hot water on in the shower. And they huddled together while they waited for steam clouds to fill the small bathroom and warm them before they let go of each other. It was impossible for them not to think back to that awful evening when Matt had helped her undress and then bathed her after her surgery. Each of them knew that the other was remembering the way Matt had eased her bandages off, and the tubes that drained her wounds, and her shattered face when she saw herself, and the way Matt had stepped into the shower with his clothes on. And the way they'd wept as one person. Tonight, as the hot water pulsed over them, they held each other again, and just holding each other was enough to make them happy.

———

Matt was dressed in a gray sweatshirt and boxer shorts when he stepped out of the bathroom and found Jane curled up and shivering in bed with the beaver blanket pulled up, almost over her head. "Get in here and warm me up!" she commanded.

"Better now?" Matt asked five minutes later, when her shivering stopped. They were spooning once again, and finally warm under the heavy blanket.

Jane nodded, and then brought her hand to her face. She sniffled and wiped a tear away, and tried to hide it from him.

"You're crying. What's the matter?" Matt asked.

She sniffled and wiped away another tear. "I always knew my parents would grow old and die, and I knew our children would grow up and move away. But I never thought there would be a time when things weren't like they used to be . . . for us. I thought we'd have that forever." She wiped her eyes once more and then brought his hand to her face and kissed it. "You're my best friend. Don't ever leave me."

"I still want to feel the butterflies in my stomach, Jane," he whispered.

"Me too."

Matt was staring at the ceiling ten minutes later, about to ask her what she was thinking again, when he heard the first of Jane's soft gurgles; she was out cold and beginning to snore. He waited until the snoring was regular and heavier. Then he moved away from her slowly, got out of bed, and shuffled out to the porch.

There was no breeze to stir the leaves or whisper through the pine needles tonight; only the occasional call of a loon, or an owl, and moon-shadows stretched across the backyard. Matt put his feet up on the little table in front of his chair and looked out over the lake. A few minutes earlier, Jane had said he was her best friend. Mo had said the same thing a week before. But there could be only one best friend, and although he wanted to deny it, he knew what he had to do. He brought Mo's contact information to the screen and held his thumb over the Delete button for a few seconds. He felt weak, and sad. "Goodbye, old friend," he whispered. Then he tapped the button and watched Mo Glasnapp, and his innocence, disappear.

He walked back to his bedroom and slid himself under the exquisite beaver blanket once more. The memory of Jane's crying lingered, though. He'd liked it, and that felt odd. He'd never thought that could be possible. But hearing her cry, and watching her face crumble in pain, had actually felt good tonight. She was frustrated, and hurt, and angry that age and illness kept on taking things from them, too. It was the first time he'd seen that pain in her eyes. Until tonight she'd seemed happy just to be alive, and she appeared to be willing to let go of so many other things just to stay alive. But on this night, she'd reached for him in a way that she never had before, as if *she* was the one who needed reassurance that he was still there. He liked that. No, he loved it. It was the thing he'd been longing for all along. She needed him. She loved him back, just as much as he loved her.

They'd spent a lifetime together. The successes and the failures of their lives together didn't seem to add up to very much one way or the other. What really mattered was that Jane had been there for it all. They'd laughed and cried as one. And mostly, they'd laughed.

"Come, grow old with me . . . the best is yet to be." Nah, that just wasn't true. The best of life, the great love and laughter and easy times were over. Robert Browning was wrong on that one, Matt thought. But if you were lucky, and you made it to the end, something else arrived with all the losses; the awareness of just how grand it had all been. And that awareness would linger, and shine, and maybe from time to time you could reach out and hold it . . . if only for a moment.

"I'm never gonna leave you," he whispered.

"Mmm, good. Don't drool on my head, either," she mumbled, and she inched closer to him.

His demons didn't have much to show him anymore. He knew they'd return every so often, forever, usually at his darkest, weakest moments, and show him a picture that he didn't want to see, and remind him that he could never really know about Jane's secrets. But that's the way it had to be. Love made everyone vulnerable. The greater the love, the more vulnerable lovers become.

He thought about his friends, too, the people who warmed themselves by his fire tonight. Sally took a chain saw in the face when she was two years old. She had a baby when she was sixteen. John caught his father trying to rape his sister and then threw baseball away. Snag stuck a teacher's head in a vice and then ran away and joined the navy. What about Rene, Snag's girl? Her journey through life may have been stormy too. He'd probably find out about that in the next few months.

His boys would have their trials, too. Maybe a broken heart? Maybe they already had? It wasn't the kind of thing that most young men would share with their father; he'd probably never know. He wished there was something he could tell them, warn them about. But they'd have to make their own way. He hoped he'd prepared them well enough.

He thought about Linda Pike, and wondered if he'd really broken her heart. He thought about standing on the front steps at Mo's house. He thought about the children, too: the Compton twins, and Michelangelo Katzenmeyer, and Timmy, and Dave Norman, and Bradley Hested. Before long, every one of them was likely to get involved with someone who'd break their heart. But that was just life. It was bound to happen to everyone, and to be honest, would we have it any other way?

Other thoughts came drifting by, like vapors on a summer breeze. There was no Sisyphus; that was Greek mythology. And Dante was full of shit; there would be no contrapasso. It was all just life, complicated and painful sometimes, simple and full of laughter sometimes.

He'd grown old, and that intimate connection that a young man shares with his lover was gone. Maybe it was just fading, but it would be gone someday. Someday soon. Those feelings couldn't return, not like they'd once been—urgent with passion and laughter—for they *had* grown old. And now it was time to start mourning that loss. But he'd been able to grow old with his Jane, and what a great life they'd shared. And they still had a few miles to go. Together.

Maybe all he'd really lost was his innocence? He could go on without that. Maybe it would have been better if he'd lost it long ago? He'd have to think about that. But he still had his Jane, and he'd never leave her.

Sleep stole into the room silently, and began to nudge all his thoughts away, into a shapeless gray corner. But just before everything went silent for the night, a last tiny wisp of a memory drifted by, and he saw his Jane, sitting across the table from him on that first night back at the Improper Fraction. She was smiling, laughing, and her eyes were inviting him into her life. Maybe they'd find their way back and be "new in love" again, and feel the butterflies? That thought made him smile, and he pulled her closer.

Maybe he'd catch a fish, too?

AFTERWORD

The beauty of the written word is that it allows the imagination of the reader to merge with the imagination of the writer. So, if you've just finished *Contrapasso*, and you liked it, I'm glad we connected.

If you're reading this in bed, about to turn out the lights and go to sleep, please wait a second. I have a few things I'd like to share with you.

This is a work of fiction. But I don't think any author can tell a long story like this one and not throw in some bits and pieces of real life. Sometimes as I'm writing, an anecdote from my life or the life of a friend, will call out from my memory and demand to be part of the story. Everyone is familiar with the kind of anecdotes I'm talking about. As they're being shared, over drinks, at a party, listeners all start to grin and inch a bit closer to the speaker while they wait for what they know will be a punch line. When an explosion of laughter marks the end of the story, inevitably, someone sighs, ". . . ah, you can't make that shit up."

Sometimes, maybe in the safety of darkness around a campfire, an old friend will share a grim piece of their personal past that leaves everyone around the fire staring, open mouthed, in pain or fear. You can't make that stuff up, either.

I once read that the difference between fiction and non-fiction is that fiction has to be believable. (Think about that for a minute). So, the trick for a writer is to move these bits and pieces of real life through time and space, change them as necessary (while keeping the heart and soul intact), and then weave them into the fiction of a totally different story. If you do it right, everything fits together seamlessly and no one (including the author) knows where the fiction ends and the real life begins.

When I need names for my characters I love to return to the headwaters of my life. I might take the name of a boy that I played sandlot baseball with, and then give it to a general, or a priest, or a criminal. Maybe a girl that I had a crush on in seventh grade will show up as a waitress or someone's grandmother. Borrowing these names is simply a nod to someone who made me smile back in the day.

My characters—the things they do and say? Well, now we're back to "making shit up" again. But as I tell their stories these characters become real, and sometimes they simply won't do or say things I want them to. They always know the story better than I do, so I allow them to take it where it must go. I'd heard other writers talk about this, but I never believed it. It's true, and it's fun getting to know the people I create. Well, most of the time.

Parts of this story were difficult to write. Really difficult. Other parts were a pleasure, more fun than I've had with any of my other stories.

In the writing of this story I had no profound insights to share. I simply hoped to tell a story that might allow readers to feel something, and to create characters they'd miss when the story ended.

If you enjoyed *Contrapasso*, please feel free to write a review. If you didn't like it, well, just keep your opinion to yourself.

OK, I'm smiling now. Thanks for reading. You may turn out the lights.

Nathan Jorgenson

www.NathanJorgenson.com